Praise for *The No...*

"Brilliant: hugely enjoyable,
you care about — exactly the ...
from sta...
**Conn Iggulden, author of *The War of the Roses*
series**

"A crowning achievement: meticulously researched, a
long-overdue insight into our Anglo-Saxon past."
Justin Hill, author of *Shieldwall*

"Edoardo Albert conjures up an extraordinarily vivid and
authentic picture of life in seventh-century Britain that
is hugely enjoyable. This is fabulous storytelling, with the
themes of greed, ambition, nobility, and the power of religion
woven together with consummate skill. It is the real Game of
Thrones — a fabulous story, beautifully told, that turns out to
be based on fact!"
**Andrew Norriss, author of *Aquila*
and creator of *The Brittas Empire***

"In Oswiu, the concluding installment in his Northumbrian
Thrones trilogy, Edoardo Albert takes readers back to
seventh-century England: a shadowy and turbulent era
when Britons and Anglo-Saxons, heathens and Christians,
contested for political and spiritual supremacy.
Albert writes with great passion; his love for this period of
history shines through at every stage. His research is worn
lightly, and yet his depiction of early medieval life has a
strong ring of truth.
Dynastic rivalries, shifting allegiances, and pagan mysticism
combine in this atmospheric novel, evoking a volatile world
in which life is uncertain, authority and respect are hard-
won, honour is all-important, and divine forces hold sway."
James Aitcheson, author of *The Sworn Sword*

OSWIU

King of Kings

The Northumbrian Thrones III

Edoardo Albert

LION FICTION

To David and Margaret,
for your support and your daughter.

Text copyright © 2016 Edoardo Albert
This edition copyright © 2016 Lion Hudson

The right of Edoardo Albert to be identified as the author of this
work has been asserted by him in accordance with the Copyright,
Designs and Patents Act 1988.

Published by Lion Fiction
an imprint of
Lion Hudson plc
Wilkinson House, Jordan Hill Road
Oxford OX2 8DR, England
www.lionhudson.com/fiction

ISBN 978 1 78264 118 6
e-ISBN 978 1 78264 119 3

First edition 2016

A catalogue record for this book is available from the British Library

Printed and bound in the UK, September 2016, LH26

Contents

Acknowledgments

Acknowledgments usually begin with the declaration that no book is written alone – and that is certainly true. However, I'm going to begin my acknowledgments with a different recognition: that no book is written for the writer alone, but for his readers. So I'd like to start by thanking you. Thank you for reading this book and (since it's the third in a trilogy) presumably two more of my books. Writers are just people making squiggles on paper without people to read what they've written, so I am immensely grateful to you all. I'd also like to give my particular thanks to everyone who has taken the time to write reviews on Amazon, Goodreads and social media, and all those who have recommended my books to friends and family; for a little-known writer with no literary cachet, these personal testimonials are more valuable than garnets and gold. Given the solitary nature of writing, I've also really appreciated the contact with readers who have taken the time to contact me through my website, or via Facebook and Twitter: your encouragement, criticism, and praise has been extremely valuable. In particular, my thanks go to Jared Detter (for your fascinating emails), Christina Fox (an Englishwoman abroad), Alison Skinner (hope there's not too much you disagree with here!), Holly Hocks and Val the Poet (Twitter encouragers), Tony O'Sullivan (northern correspondent), Anna Lacey (the medieval girl) and, last but certainly not least, Paul Langley (the epitome of the intelligent reader).

Something else that helps to alleviate the loneliness of the long-book writer is the companionship of fellow writers – mostly virtual, these days – scribbling in the same period and others that come afterwards (or, sometimes, before). I'm fortunate in the generosity and encouragement of my fellow authors, in particular Matthew Harffy, Justin Hill, James Aitcheson, Jill Dalladay, Teresa Tomlinson, LA Smith, and Henry Vyner-Brooks (when you've finished this book, take a look at their work). I would like to give my particular thanks to Justin Hill for reading all three of my novels (no, he's not a masochist) and Matthew Harffy for his generosity to an apparent competitor. That so many of them should read my work is wonderful; that they should enjoy it is even better.

Moving from the Early Medieval, I'm honoured to have had Conn Iggulden read *Oswiu* and even more pleased to learn that, when he mislaid the book, he spent a frantic day searching for it so that he could find out what happened next: I am forever grateful. Andrew Norriss writes for and of children with the discipline of a Waugh and the wit of a Wodehouse; his *Aquila* may be the most perfectly structured book I've ever read. Andrew and his wife Jane are simply the loveliest of people.

It was the people at Lion who first gave me a chance to write stories people would actually read: I hope I have repaid your trust. In particular, my thanks go to Tony Collins (now enjoying a very well-earned retirement) and Alison Hull, who together opened doors to me, and then a huge thank you to Jessica Tinker, as kind, generous, and smiley an editor as any writer could wish to work with. There seems to be a bit of a thing for names beginning with 'J' at Lion, so my thanks also to Jessica Scott for all her hard work chasing down rights and permissions (it's no easy task quoting actual Anglo-Saxon poems in a book about the Anglo-Saxons), and to Rachel Ashley-Pain who had the "painful" (sorry!) task of copyediting all 500 plus pages of this book (I didn't mean it to be this long, honest). A big thank you as well to all the sales team at Lion, and in particular Rhoda Hardie, for working so hard to overcome the reluctance of bookshops to stock books from publishers that aren't small parts of global corporations.

Professor Nick Higham of Manchester University (not to be confused with the other Professor Nick Higham, also of Manchester University) has forgotten more about Northumbria than I will ever know. I warmly recommend all his books on the subject – *The Anglo-Saxon World*, which he co-wrote with Martin Ryan, is probably the best introduction to the subject around – but I would like to make special mention of his latest work, *Ecgfrith: King of the Northumbrians*, which has almost made me think of writing volume four of *The Northumbrian Thrones*. That so eminent a scholar as Professor Higham should read my books (and like them, wonder of wonders!) is more than I could have hoped for.

Dr Alex Woolf complements Professor Higham, specializing in matters north of a border that had not yet been firmed up when the events of *Oswiu* were taking place. His book, *From Pictland to Alba*, sheds welcome light on the darkest period in Scottish history, when the Picts, and their language, mysteriously disappear, to be replaced by the Gaels. His learning is prodigious, as evidenced by the fact that no less than five languages (Gaelic, British, Pictish, English, and Norse) were spoken in Scotland at this time.

I am hugely grateful to Dr Woolf for taking the time to transliterate some of the harder-to-pronounce names in the book into modern English – as much for my sake as for the reader!

For something over thirty years I was a writer whom no one wanted to read (for the very good reason that most of my writing was rubbish). Indeed, my publication rate averaged out at one short story a decade (1980s, 90s, 00s) – not much to base a career upon. It's only in the last decade that things changed and that they did – and that I did not give up – is entirely due to the patience, encouragement, support, and help of my family. First, my parents, Victor and Paola Albert, immigrants from Sri Lanka and Italy respectively, who met and married here and encouraged me in every way possible while growing up, despite us having very little money (but so well did they look after us that I never noticed). And my mother has acted as an unpaid agent for my books, making sure bookshops and libraries throughout London stock them.

Speaking of parents, the relationship with in-laws is supposed to be fraught. Well, it isn't in my case. David and Margaret Whitbread have been unfailingly helpful and supportive, despite Margaret having had to cook more roast dinners for us than she ever anticipated (will we ever turn down a dinner invitation? No, we won't).

My brother, Steven, put up with me when we were young and helped me get as far as adulthood when it all looked a bit dodgy for a while. I was just about getting to the point of putting a lonely-hearts ad in *Time Out* (my first draft reduced a friend to such helpless laughter that he was, quite literally, rolling on the floor – I think it was the bit about tickling the belly of a wolf that finally did it for him) when I met the woman who would, in surprisingly short order, become my wife. Harry (her name is Harriet really, but she thinks the three syllables makes it sound as if I'm about to scold her), none of this would have been possible without you. And the boys. There's nothing more calculated to improve the productivity of a writer than to reduce his available writing time. So thank you, Theo, Matthew, and Isaac. All four of you – the time-taking team – make me write so much better than if I was shut up in a garret with a sheet of paper and no other demands on my time.

So, thank you. And, yes, I will relay the patio. Honestly.

Dramatis Personae

Names in *italics* are invented characters

House of Ida (the Idings), kingdom of Bernicia

Oswiu King of Bernicia and would-be king of Deira. Younger brother of Oswald, who ruled Northumbria before Oswiu; son of Æthelfrith and Acha.

Rhieienmelth Daughter of King Rhoedd of Rheged. First wife to Oswiu.

Ahlflæd Daughter of Oswiu and Rhieienmelth.

Ahlfrith Son of Oswiu and Rhieienmelth.

Eanflæd Daughter of Edwin and Æthelburh. Second wife to Oswiu.

Ecgfrith Son of Oswiu and Eanflæd.

Æbbe Sister to Oswald and Oswiu. Abbess of Coldingham.

Acha Mother to Oswald, Oswiu and Æbbe. Sister to Edwin, of the royal house of Yffi of Deira; married Æthelfrith, Oswald's father.

Æthelwin Warmaster to Oswiu.

Bran Oswald's raven.

Œthelwald Son of Oswald. After the death of his parents, brought up by Oswiu and Rhieienmelth.

Coifi Pagan priest to Edwin. In these stories, Coifi pledges himself to the Idings after Edwin's death.

Acca Scop to Edwin. After Edwin's death scop to Oswald and then Oswiu.

Romanus Priest to Eanflæd.

Garmund Brigand.

Characters in the previous books, but who are dead at the start of *Oswiu: King of Kings*

Oswald Lamnguin (the Whiteblade) High King of Britain and king of Northumbria, the combined kingdom of Bernicia and Deira, until his death at the hands of Penda of Mercia. Son of Æthelfrith and Acha. Story told in *Oswald: Return of the King.*

Eanfrith Half-brother to Oswald and Oswiu. Killed by Cadwallon of Gwynedd. His story is told in *Oswald: Return of the King.*

Æthelfrith Father to Oswald, Oswiu and Æbbe through Acha, princess of Deira, and to Eanfrith through Bebba. Became king of Bernicia in 592 and king of the joint kingdom of Bernicia and Deira, Northumbria, in 604. Killed in 616 at the Battle of the River Idle by the combined forces of Rædwald, king of the East Angles, and Edwin, exiled king of Deira.

House of Yffi (the Yffings), kingdom of Deira

Oswine King of Deira.

Hunwald Warmaster to Oswine.

Tondhere Retainer to Oswine.

Acha Sister to Edwin. See heading under House of Ida.

Æthelburh Mother of Eanflæd; Edwin's second wife. Fled with their children to Kent and then France after Edwin's death.

James Missionary sent to Edwin. He remained in Deira after Edwin's death.

Characters in the previous books, but who are dead at the start of *Oswiu: King of Kings*

Edwin King of Northumbria from 616 to 633 when he was killed in battle with Cadwallon of Gwynedd and Penda of Mercia. His story is told in *Edwin: High King of Britain.*

Osric Cousin to Edwin and father of Oswine. Claimed the throne of Deira following Edwin's death, but was killed by Cadwallon.

House of Icel (the Iclingas), kingdom of Mercia

Penda King of Mercia.

Cynewisse Wife to Penda.

Peada "the Red Hand" Eldest son of Penda and Cynewisse.

Wulfhere Son of Penda and Cynewisse.

Wihtrun Pagan priest to Penda.

Brandnoth Thegn of High Cross.

Coenred Innkeeper of High Cross.

Hutha Sentry

Characters in the previous books, but who are dead at the start of *Oswiu: King of Kings*

Eowa Brother to Penda; killed at the end of *Oswald: Return of the King*.

Cearl King of Mercia before Penda.

House of Cunedda, kingdom of Gwynedd

Cadwallon King of Gwynedd. Killed in battle against Oswald and Oswiu.

House of Coel ("Old King Cole"), kingdom of Rheged

Rhoedd King of Rheged.

Rhieienmelth Daughter of King Rhoedd; wife to Oswiu.

Monks of Lindisfarne

Aidan Abbot and bishop of Lindisfarne; friend to Oswald and Oswiu.

Finan Second abbot of Lindisfarne.

Utta Monk of Lindisfarne.

Glossary

Ætheling A prince or highly ranked noble who was throne-worthy; that is, a possible candidate for taking the throne.

Angles One of the three main peoples that migrated to Britain in the fifth to seventh centuries. The Angles settled in the east and north.

Bernicia Anglian kingdom centred on Bamburgh. With Deira, one of the two constituent kingdoms of Northumbria.

Britons Original inhabitants of Britain. Ruling families, and possibly much of the populace, displaced by incoming Anglo-Saxons between fifth and seventh centuries.

Dal Riada Sea-spanning Gaelic kingdom, linking Ulster and Argyll.

Deira Anglian kingdom centred on York. With Bernicia, one of the two constituent kingdoms of Northumbria.

Gododdin A tribe who lived in what is now the south-east of Scotland and the north-east of England, with strongholds at Edinburgh and Traprain Law.

Gwynedd Kingdom of the Britons in north-west Wales.

"Hwæt" The traditional way to begin a recitation or song. Can be translated as *listen, hear this.*

Jutes The Jutes settled in Kent and the Isle of Wight.

Loki Thunor's brother.

Mercia Kingdom of the Angles, covering the Midlands and beyond.

Picts The original inhabitants of what later became Scotland.

Rheged A kingdom of the Britons, roughly centred on Carlisle.

Saxons One of the three main peoples that migrated to Britain in the fifth to seventh centuries. The Saxons mainly settled along the Thames Valley and to its south and west.

Scop A bard and poet – the keeper of the collective memory of his people.

Seax A short sword/long knife, worn by all Anglo-Saxons (indeed, it gave the Saxons their name).

Spear The mark of a free Anglo-Saxon. Slaves were not allowed to carry weapons.

Strathclyde A kingdom of the Britons, with its chief stronghold upon Dumbarton Rock.

Thegn A nobleman – that is, a warrior.

Thunor Battle god of the Anglo-Saxons.

Witan The assembly of the chief men of a kingdom. An ætheling had to win the support of his witan in order to claim the throne.

Woden Chief god of the pagan Anglo-Saxons.

Wyrd Key Anglo-Saxon concept. Can be translated as *fate* or *destiny*.

The Kingdoms of Britain, c. 635

Iona

PICTS

MERCIA Kingdom ruled by the Anglo-Saxons

POWYS Kingdom ruled by the Britons

GODODDIN

Lindisfarne

Ad Gefrin

Bamburgh

Sea, swamp, or salt marsh

DAL RIADA

BERNICIA

Hadrian's Wall

NORTHUMBRIA

Monkwearmouth

Jarrow

Battle of Heavenfield

Carlisle

RHEGED

DEIRA

Isle of Man

York

ELMET

Isle of Anglesey

LINDSEY

GWYNEDD

Battle of Maserfield

Tamworth

Crowland

Oswestry

MERCIA

MIDDLE ANGLIA

EAST ANGLIA

POWYS

Oundle

HWICCE

Rendlesham

DYFED

Gloucester

ESSEX

Cirencester

London

Bath

Rochester

Canterbury

Glastonbury

WESSEX

Winchester

KENT

SUSSEX

DUMNONIA

Pronunciation Guide

How do you pronounce Æ and Œ?

In Old English, Æ (or "ash", to call the letter by its name) represented a vowel that sounded like a cross between "a" and "e". Try saying it like the "a" in "cat". As for Œ (the *ēðel* rune), say it as "oy".

A note on names

The names in this book are difficult to say. Two conquests – the slow-motion one of the Anglo-Saxons and then the lightning bolt of the Normans – have consigned most of the personal names in use during the seventh century to obscure history books.

Another factor in the loss of Anglo-Saxon names was the conviction among the Anglo-Saxons that a name was personal property and, as such, should be unique to the person and not handed out to later generations, even if related. A notable example of this is that while Cerdic founded the kingdom of the West Saxons, the most long-lasting of all the Anglo-Saxon kingdoms, none of his successor kings ever bore the name of their legendary forefather. As generations passed, and original names became harder to come by, the solution was to combine words in compound forms, so producing names like Godgifu (Gift of God) and Sigeberht (Victory Bright). But while names had to be unique, they also, particularly in the case of noble or royal families, had to indicate family relationship. This was done by alliteration and using the same stem. Thus Alfred the Great, the youngest of five brothers and one sister, was the only one whose name did not begin with Æthel. Presumably, once his parents had got through calling on Æthelbald, Æthelberht, Æthelred, Æthelstan and Æthelswith, they decided they could not face another Æthel in the hall (Æthel means "noble" – an appropriate name stem for an ætheling) and plumped for Ælfræd (which means "elf wisdom" or "counsel"). Although modern English is the direct descendant of Old English, the sound of the old language strikes the present-day hearer as akin to that of Danish – search on YouTube for readings of *Beowulf* in Old English to hear how it sounds.

To make matters more difficult, some names in this book come from Brittonic and Goidelic, the related languages that diversified from the original proto-Celtic, with Brittonic going on to produce Welsh, Cornish, Cumbric and Breton, and Goidelic giving us Gaelic, Scottish Gaelic and Manx.

To help readers (and the writer!), Dr Alex Woolf, senior lecturer in history at the University of St Andrews, has very kindly transcribed the most difficult names into modern English. Here they are:

Name	English equivalent
Oswiu	Oswíuh
Rhieienmelth	Hríenveld
Rhoedd	Hroyth
Rheged	Hreged
Lamnguin	Lav'ngwyn
Ahlflæd	Alch'flad ('ch' as in 'loch')
Eanflæd	Ay'anflad
Œthelwald	Oythelwold

Of the events in Edwin:
High King of Britain *and*
Oswald: Return of the King

Hounded through Britain by the man who had usurped him on the throne of Northumbria, Edwin takes refuge at the court of Rædwald, king of the East Angles. But the usurper, Æthelfrith, will not rest until Edwin is dead, and he attempts to suborn Rædwald into giving up his guest. But Rædwald withstands the pressure and, with Edwin beside him, catches Æthelfrith unawares and kills him in battle. With Æthelfrith dead, Edwin becomes king of Northumbria and, when Rædwald dies shortly afterwards, Edwin becomes the most powerful king in the land.

To strengthen his position, King Edwin contracts marriage with Æthelburh, the sister of the king of Kent. As part of the marriage agreement, Edwin, a pagan, agrees that Æthelburh, who is Christian, may continue to practise her religion and that she may bring a priest with her when she travels to Northumbria.

Faced with a series of signs and wonders, Edwin himself decides to adopt the new religion and puts the decision to the witan – the assembly of his leading men – to hear their voices on the matter. Coifi, Edwin's pagan priest, speaks at this meeting, decrying the gods of old, for they have turned their faces from him and he can no longer discern the workings of wyrd as he once was able to, and his words carry the day. The witan of Northumbria agrees to accept the new god – even though this is the god of the people their forefathers had defeated in carving out their kingdom.

As Edwin's power grows, opposition to him from the other kings mounts. The king of the West Saxons attempts to assassinate him.

Then Cadwallon, king of Gywnedd, enters into alliance with Penda of Mercia. They trick Edwin into riding after them and, at the Battle of Hatfield Chase, Edwin is defeated and killed.

When news of this reaches Æthelburh she takes her children and flees into exile, taking ship to her kin, first in Kent and then to her mother's people in France. James the Deacon remains to minister to the people of Northumbria, but Cadwallon ravages the kingdom, exacting revenge for the humiliations suffered by him and his people.

News of the High King's fall travels through the land and eventually reaches a small island off the west coast of Scotland, where a community of monks has established a monastery and where a young prince, in exile, has found peace for a while...

That prince is Oswald, son of Æthelfrith. With his mother Acha, his younger brother Oswiu, and his sister Æbbe, he had gone into exile when his father was killed by Edwin. While in exile, Oswald and all his family had converted to the new religion (although younger brother Oswiu found some of its sterner precepts hard to follow, having made a princess of the powerful Uì Neill clan pregnant), but the news of Edwin's death reaches Oswald just as he has resolved to lay down his sword and enter the monastery on Iona. But the abbot of Iona, Ségéne, has other plans for Oswald, seeing him as the instrument by which the new religion may be brought to the people of Northumbria.

Still determined to become a monk, Oswald delays returning to reclaim the throne when he learns that his older half-brother, Eanfrith, who took refuge among the Picts, has claimed the throne of Bernicia. But when Oswald hears that Eanfrith is dead, killed while attempting to negotiate with Cadwallon, he realizes he must return to save his people.

With Oswiu and a small party of warriors, and the blessing of Abbot Ségéne, Oswald lands in the kingdom of Rheged and is received by King Rhoedd. While gaining the king's permission to ride through his kingdom, Oswald and Oswiu see his daughter, Rhieienmelth, and King Rhoedd offers her in marriage to Oswald. Although struck by her beauty, Oswald refuses the match for himself, for he knows full well that should he succeed in gaining the throne of Northumbria, he will need to make an alliance, through marriage, with a more powerful kingdom. But while Oswald cannot marry Rhieienmelth, the princess would make a good wife for his brother, both for the political alliance it will bring and by providing a match for Oswiu.

So, with the marriage contracted, Oswald and Oswiu ride swiftly east, hoping to take Cadwallon by surprise. Although Cadwallon does receive news of their approach, he believes the brothers to be among the kings of the Old North, come to acclaim him as the new Arthur. So, seeing their approach, he does not form into a shieldwall but awaits their acclaim.

In the confused battle that follows, Cadwallon is killed and his army is destroyed. The king has returned.

Now king of Northumbria, Oswald sends to Ségéne for monks and priests to spread the new faith to his people. Ségéne sends him Aidan – an old friend – and other monks, who found a monastery upon Lindisfarne, within sight of the royal stronghold at Bamburgh.

With the kingdom now secure, Oswiu marries Rhieienmelth, and while it is a good marriage that quickly produces children, yet there is also, between Oswald and Rhieienmelth, considerable attraction that both are aware of, yet strive to avoid.

Alarmed at the death of Cadwallon, his ally, Penda of Mercia, launches an attack against Oswald. But Oswald gathers his allies and meets Penda with such overwhelming force that Penda is forced to surrender rather than risk battle. To secure peace, Penda offers his brother, Eowa, as hostage.

Eowa is, apparently, greatly angered that he has been used as a pawn in such a way, and slowly becomes a friend to Oswald – particularly as Oswiu is more often apart from his brother, guarding the northern marches of the kingdom.

Oswald contracts a marriage with the daughter of the king of the West Saxons. Cyniburh bears him a son, Œthelwald, but dies in childbirth. A grief-stricken king gives the baby to Rhieienmelth to raise, stoking the increasing jealousy of his brother.

Through alliances and campaigns, Oswald's power grows so great that he is able to impose a new king upon Mercia, forcing Penda from the throne and into exile and placing Eowa upon the throne. So, when Eowa sends a messenger to Oswald, calling for his help against Penda, who has besieged him at his stronghold at Maserfield, Oswald does not hesitate to ride to his relief.

However, Oswiu, in the north of the kingdom, learns that Eowa is calling his brother into a trap. With a small group of men, Oswiu rides south as fast as he can, hoping to intercept Oswald before the trap is sprung.

But he is too late.

Oswald is trapped between the armies of Eowa and Penda. But Penda first betrays his brother into Oswald's hands, so Eowa is killed. Only then, when Oswald's army has been diminished, does he attack. Oswald and all his men are killed.

After the battle, Penda dismembers Oswald, cutting off his head and arms to offer them in sacrifice before Woden's tree.

Oswiu arrives too late to save his brother. With Oswald dead, he is king. But without the charisma of his elder brother, will the witans of Bernicia and Deira accept him as king?

PART 1

Raid

Chapter 1

The column of riders rode through the water meadows that spread out from the broad river. Their spears glittered in the noon sun and their shields, slung over shoulder or held low and loose, glowed with colour. At the head of the column rode the standard bearer carrying the purple and gold flag of the House of Ida.

Just behind the standard bearer rode the king, Oswiu, king of Bernicia and king of Northumbria, upon a white horse, his cloak flowing behind, his shield, quartered and quartered again in the colours of the Idings, upon his shoulder.

The man riding beside the king pointed ahead, to the city on the river. "They will have had no word that their king comes."

Oswiu laughed. "That's why I made you my warmaster, Æthelwin: to tell me what I already know. But any thegn will know that in cruel and uncertain times like these, the king may arrive without warning."

"He might know that, but will his victualler?" The warmaster grimaced. "It has been a long ride and I am hungry and thirsty."

"It would have been longer if we had waited upon the boats."

"I know, my lord. That's why you had us ride." Æthelwin glanced ahead. A horn had sounded, distant but definite. The watch had seen the riders. "York has seen us."

"About time. If we had been a Mercian raiding party, we would almost have got to the walls before any were ready to meet us." The king grinned, but there was little humour in his smile. "I will have words with the thegn who has care of this city from us. Who is he?"

"He is named Hunwald, my lord. I know little of him."

"We will know more soon. I had little dealing with Deira when... when my brother was alive."

Æthelwin glanced at his king. It was but a season since King Oswald

had died, slain in the depths of winter by the treachery of a man taken
to their hearth. The traitor, at least, had died in the battle that had
claimed Oswald's life. Æthelwin knew, all the king's men knew, of the
great ride Oswiu had made, when he learned of the treachery, to reach
his brother. But the ride had come too late. Oswald and his men had
died. Oswiu lived, and now he ruled. But that rule was tenuous, and
though the men of Bernicia, sworn to the House of Ida of old, had
rallied to the new king, yet the men of Deira, followers of the House
of Yffi, held silence with their pledge and sent no embassy to give oath.
So now their king came to them, to York, the chief – only – town of
Deira, to claim their loyalty and to give gifts of gold and land.

Æthelwin shaded his eyes against the lowering, westering sun.
"They close the gates against us, lord."

"At this distance, not even the sharpest eye might see my standard
and know it," Oswiu grunted. "They will be glad enough to open
them when we get closer."

But they did not.

As the column of riders approached, now near enough York that
any man upon the walls might see the colours of the standard they
flew, yet the gates to the city remained closed.

Seeing the gates still shut, the column, without order, slowed
until the horses walked. Men, suddenly unsure, scanned wall and
tower, searching for any movement, but there was no sign. Outside
the city, where most of its dwellers preferred to live, in houses of
thatch and wood rather than the wraith-haunted stone and brick
buildings within the walls, some few children, ragged clothed and
dirt smeared, stared in silence at the riders, but made no move to
approach, until they were called inside their poor dwellings by
whisper and gesture.

Æthelwin, seeing this, turned to Oswiu. "They act as if we were
raiders, come to reive."

"They must know my standard – it is as the one my brother
bore." Oswiu shook his head. "I do not understand." He looked
ahead, to where the gates still stood closed. "Send a man on; let them
know who I am."

As the column slowed to a stately walk, a rider cantered ahead to the gates and, pulling his beast to a halt, made known who it was that came to the ancient city of York.

"Open the gates for Oswiu, king, Iding, of the House of Ida, brother of Oswald, king of Bernicia, king of Deira, king of Northumbria. Your king, my king. I say, open."

But the gates did not open, though the rider rode to them and beat upon the wood with the pommel of his sword. Then, when wood alone answered his summons, the rider rode back.

Oswiu held up his hand before the man could report. "I saw." He pulled his horse to a halt and sat staring at the gate and gate towers to the city. "Tell them, Æthelwin – tell this Hunwald, if it is he who holds the city against us – that we commend him for his caution in this time. It is indeed true that men use trickery and guile to achieve what arms might not, and a Mercian or other raider might indeed claim to be me. Tell him I will give gift for his care and his steadfastness, but now it is time to open the city to his king."

"If Hunwald should ask, what token should I give that you are as you say?"

"There must be some there, mayhap Hunwald himself, who had dealings with my brother. Any man who knew Oswald would know us for brothers."

Æthelwin made the courtesy and walked his horse on to the gates of the city.

"I am Æthelwin, warmaster to Oswiu, king, lord of the land of the mountain passes, master of the people of watersmeet. King Oswiu sends word to the thegn of Deira, commending his caution in these troubled times; he will give gift to mark such care. Now, let the gates be opened; let there be joy. Your king has come to you."

"Who is this king?"

The voice came from the gate tower. Æthelwin pulled his horse back, that he might better see who spoke, but the man stood in shadow and his face was dark.

"Who speaks? Who asks such a question?" asked the warmaster.

"If he is who you say he is, let him speak for himself."

"There is caution, and then there is stupidity." Æthelwin circled his animal. "Think you to gain some favour from such a display? We have ridden long and hard, and the king is hungry and thirsts. Do not keep him waiting any longer than you already have."

"I say again, if he is a king, let him speak for himself."

"I will."

Oswiu rode up beside Æthelwin, the column of his household retainers following behind.

"But tell me whom I speak with, for you can see us, but we cannot see you."

"That, at least, is easily rectified." A man stepped out of the gate tower and stood upon the rampart. A thegn – his dress and bearing and voice all told his status – a man of middle years, with fair hair and heavy shoulders. A fighting man, he stood at ease with his spear in hand, haft grounded upon stone, and he looked down upon the riders. "I am Hunwald. York master. Keeper of the river. And I have been charged to keep this city and this river for the king's returning."

"I am your king," said Oswiu. "I have returned."

"You are not my king," said Hunwald. "The witan of Deira has met and it has chosen. We will not have another Iding over us, but a man of our blood and our earth."

"But… but I am of your blood. My mother, Acha, she is of the House of Yffi, blood from your blood. And you had my brother Oswald to king."

Slowly, deliberately, Hunwald gathered phlegm in his mouth and then spat. The spit arced over the wall and landed, wetly, before the men outside his gates.

"You are not Oswald. Oswald died upon a far field, and you did not save him. Oswald's body was taken, and you did not claim it. Oswald's head sits on a stake in our enemy's land, and you have not brought it home. You are not Oswald. You are not our king."

Oswiu paled beneath this verbal attack. Heeling his horse, he rode up to the gate and struck it with his sword.

"I am your king," he shouted. "Open this gate or, so God help me, I will slaughter every last one of you and your children too."

But the man above him laughed.

"The witan has made a man more worthy king of Deira: Oswine, son of Osric, the Godfriend; he is our king."

"Where is he? Bring him out!"

"He is not here, but he left me charged to give over this city to no other king – and I will not."

Oswiu urged his horse towards Æthelwin and, in one fluid motion, grabbed the spear from his warmaster's hand and turned and hurled it up at where Hunwald stood upon the wall. The spear arched higher, its aim true, but just as it was about to strike home Hunwald stepped lightly aside and grabbed the haft of the spear as it flew past and, turning it, sent the spear arrowing back down, whence it came.

It was Æthelwin's speed and wit that saved the king. With the height from which it fell, even a good linden shield might have been pierced through by the spear, but he pushed Oswiu's horse aside with his own mount and deflected the spear into the ground, where it embedded itself in the earth, haft quivering.

"If you have not wit enough to know not to throw spears at a man so much higher than you, then you do not have wit enough to be our king," shouted Hunwald. Behind him and alongside him, men started appearing, for few things will bring men running quicker than to see the dismay of the great and the powerful.

For his part, Æthelwin sought to speak to the king, urging him to fall back, but such rage had fallen upon Oswiu that he could not speak, but rode once more against the gate, striking at the wood with his sword as if it were living flesh that he might rend and cut.

To such fury, the men above, safe upon the ramparts, responded first with incredulity and then, increasingly, with scorn. One after another after another raised voice in insult and jest.

Behind him, Æthelwin was all too aware of the disquiet of the men: to see their king insulted thus and, worse, to see his futile anger, was to weaken and endanger the bonds that held a warrior to his lord. They would all stand with Oswiu and die with him, but they would not long sit upon their horses and be insulted by his impotence. It was time to act. Urging his horse on, he rode to the king and grabbed his arm, trying to pull Oswiu away. But caught still in his fury, the king turned upon him, raising his sword arm to strike. Unready, and with shield and sword still slung, the warmaster might have died then, under his own lord's hand, if one of the men standing over the gate, raising insult to the physical, had not chosen that moment to throw a bucket full of cow manure over the battlements.

It landed upon Oswiu in a brown, stinking shower.

The king, shocked from his rage, stopped, his sword arm raised but now dripping. Æthelwin took the chance to free himself from the king's grasp and, grabbing the bridle of Oswiu's horse, pulled its head around and led it away from the city gates. As the two horses trotted away, the men over the gate, led by Hunwald, jeered, and a few of the bolder ones threw further handfuls of dung after them.

As they approached their waiting men, Oswiu wiped his forehead. He looked down and saw the dung covering his hand. For a moment he stared at his soiled hand, as the realization of what had happened, and the humiliation he had suffered in front of his men and the men of Deira, slowly grew. He glanced at his warmaster.

"That did not go as I might have wished," he said, speaking quietly.

"No," said Æthelwin. He too spoke quietly, his eyes fixed ahead, searching the faces of the waiting, watching men.

Oswiu glanced ahead and saw his men, and the way they broke eye contact with him, too embarrassed to share a gaze for more than an instant.

"Will they still follow me after that?" The king whispered the words.

Even quieter, Æthelwin replied, "I do not know."

Oswiu nodded. "Then I will have to do something." Heeling his horse, he sent it cantering towards the waiting men. Æthelwin, startled, followed.

The king, still a young man, pulled his horse up amid his household men, the retainers who shared his hall and ate his food, who travelled with him from one royal estate to another, the men who rode with him and fought with him: the men who would die for him.

Oswiu circled his horse, forcing them all to see him as he was: dung smeared, soiled and stinking. He made eye contact with man after man, holding each gaze past the comfort of his retainer, while they waited for him to speak. He wheeled his horse, round and again, and waited, waited, waited... Waited until every man was drawn in closer by his silence.

Then, Oswiu, king, spoke.

"Well, that was shit," he said. He wiped a finger across his forehead and smelled it. "Cow shit, in fact."

Æthelwin, tense with expectation, started. But the startlement, once loosened among the men, broke into first a snort, then a guffaw, until laughter, the first and best bond of men, spread among Oswiu's men as fire through tinder. Mirth took them and remade them whole, and Oswiu laughed no less than any of his men, but his laughter was open eyed and he looked as he laughed, and saw his men return to him.

"Other kings call fame and glory upon their household, but to you, to you all, I will give a name shared by no others in the long history of our people, and it will be a title known to us alone – a word bond broken only when the last of us is dead." Oswiu jerked his horse's head round, so they could all see him.

"I name you now my dung devils. What say you?"

"I say – " said one of the men, a smile broad upon his face, "I say we are now all your left hand, lord."

And, laughing, the men held their left hands in the air, and Oswiu rode his horse around them, striking his own, excrement smeared, hand against theirs.

"Let them keep their wraith-haunted city. We'll go back to our boats..." A groan rose among the men. "But not today," Oswiu continued smoothly. "I am as sick of cold and wet as any of you. We will find a thegn's hall, a man not so swift to turn his back on the favour of a king, and stay there for the night, then make sail north again tomorrow. What say you?"

The men acclaimed his words in shout and in gesture, clashing their spear hafts on shield rims, the wood ringing against metal or thudding on leather. Oswiu pulled his horse round to the warmaster.

"Do you know of any thegn's hall?" he asked Æthelwin under his breath. "Within distance?"

Æthelwin shook his head. "I know little of this land, or who rules it."

"Neither do I," said Oswiu. "Ask me where to find the best food and drink anywhere between the Simonside and Pentland hills and I could tell you, and two others beside, but here…"

"I too, lord."

Oswiu pointed east, following the river's meandering path. "That is rich land. If we ride through it, right enough we will soon find some thegn's hall. And we will keep the river in sight and watch for the boats."

"Yes, lord. I'll order the men."

But just as Æthelwin was about to urge his horse to the head of the column, Oswiu laid a hand on his forearm and leaned close to the warmaster.

"I did it, didn't I? I brought them round. I thought I'd lost them, but I brought them round."

Æthelwin patted the hand upon his arm. Oswiu seemed young to him, despite the king's thirty years, but then the warmaster did not know how many summers he had seen, nor how many winters. The frosting on his hair, and the creak of his bones and the leather of his muscles when he woke in the morning, blinking awareness and memory into whatever hall he woke to, told that he had seen many more years than his king. He had seen him grow from the young and headstrong brother who had taken rule of the northern marches when first Oswald claimed his kingdom, into… Æthelwin smiled, into the somewhat older and hardly less headstrong man who now ruled in his own name.

The warmaster took and grasped the hand on his arm, and his eyes were warm as he looked to the king. "Yes, lord. You brought them round." He chuckled. "The king of shit and his dung devils."

He shook his head. "Sometimes, I think your father must have been Loki, not Æthelfrith."

Oswiu beamed. "Ah, but my father was named Flesaur, the Twister: maybe he was Loki-sired and I be his grandson. Besides, I think my mother would have told me if a god had got me upon her."

"In my experience, women tell not these things if they be other than they ought."

"Not my mother," said Oswiu. "You know her, Æthelwin. Still think she might have accepted Loki into her bed rather than my father?"

Æthelwin considered but a bare moment. "No, not her, lord. No man would doubt her."

"Nor do I." Oswiu considered his warmaster for a moment. "Have you heard aught of my wife?"

Æthelwin paused, then answered carefully. "I have heard no ill spoken of Queen Rhieienmelth, lord."

"That is good. Good."

"Although it is passing strange that I have heard no whispers," said Æthelwin. "Only Queen Mildrith of the Middle Saxons was never doubted, and that because her donkey looked more womanly than she."

"That's what worries me," said Oswiu. "I am away often, and I know my queen's blood, yet never have I heard any word against her. Therefore, I fear the more." Oswiu made the horn sign, but surreptitiously, that the other men should not see. "I would not be the cuckold – not now, when I am king, and any child would be more throne-worthy than those I sired when I was yet only my brother's thegn."

"I am sure Rhieienmelth is faithful and loyal."

"Yes." Oswiu nodded. "Yes, I'm sure she is too." But as Æthelwin turned his horse away to marshal the men, he added, seemingly to himself alone, "But to whom?"

Chapter 2

"You did what?"

Oswine, known to the people of Deira as Godfriend for the light that shone from his eyes whenever he spoke of things holy and sacred, looked at Hunwald the thegn with ill-concealed horror. The Godfriend sat upon the judgement seat in the great hall of York, the hall that Edwin had had made, of carved, curved wood and a high pitched roof of wooden shingle. The hall stood among the tumbledown brick houses and buildings of York as the one living thing in a forest of the dead.

The thegn, for his part, paled, the red veins of his face, the tellers of many nights' feasting, standing out the more clearly as his skin grew whiter.

"Would you have had me open the gates and give him homage?"

"Oswiu is king, and you insulted him."

"He is a king, but there are many kings. The witan of Deira has given rule into your hands, and you have taken the throne – I heard you accept with these, my ears. Think you, if I had opened the gates to him, that he would have opened the gates to you?"

"But the insults…"

Hunwald laughed, although there was little humour in it. "I did not just insult him."

"What do you mean? What did you do?"

"When he rode away, Oswiu did not smell so sweet as when he arrived." Hunwald pointed at the night soil bucket. "He got that over his head."

The men standing beside the Godfriend gasped, then broke into laughter. But Oswine, for his part, shook his head.

"I would have peace with Oswiu, not war. We have enough, and more than enough, with Penda king to our south and demanding tribute. You would bring war to us from the north as well?"

"He came, and declared himself king." Hunwald shook his head. "I – I ask your pardon, lord, but when he spoke thus, I remembered you and the fair words you spoke when the witan declared for you, and my anger grew faster than my wit. Besides, I would not have done as I did if he had not thrown first. His spear would have split me if I had not caught it."

"He attacked you?"

"It was a fair throw. From horseback, and below – must have been thirty yards. But yes, Oswiu attacked first. Only then did I return his greetings, and in kind."

Oswine Godfriend nodded. His gaze turned inward as he thought on the matter.

"I will have to send word to Oswiu," he said.

"If you send soon, the word will reach Oswiu before he takes ship," said Hunwald.

The Godfriend looked up, startled. "When did all this happen?"

Hunwald looked surprised in turn. "Did you not know, lord? Oswiu and his men had barely ridden from sight when you arrived."

"Then he will still be nearby." Oswine Godfriend looked to his companions. "I will speak with him." But then he looked at Hunwald. "You had better stay here."

*

"Riders."

Æthelwin shook Oswiu from his nap. They'd given up the search for a hall after riding a few miles downriver and, with the prospect of rain blowing in from the west, made camp in a copse to wait for the boats.

"How many?" Oswiu asked.

Æthelwin pointed upriver. Oswiu looked through thin slit eyes, the better to see the men approaching. Fingers tapping the numbers on joint and knuckle, he counted.

"Twenty-five," he said.

"I made twenty-six," said Æthelwin.

"Even numbers." Oswiu looked at his warmaster. "So not raiders or brigands."

"They do not approach as for war."

"They don't always. Make the men ready."

"Horse or foot?"

Oswiu scanned the ground. They were camped on the river bank, with the only good ground being that on which the riders were approaching. Their own boats would be arriving soon, pulled upriver against the flow by sweating rowers. And no horse would break a shieldwall so long as it held fast.

"Foot," he said. "We'll stand with the river behind us; then they can't circle our position."

"The horses?"

"Tether them, put two men to guard." Oswiu pointed. "Put them there on that spit. Two men will hold it."

Æthelwin made the courtesy, then ran to order the men while Oswiu began to arm himself. The riding had been long that day, and his body had welcomed the chance to be rid of the weight of mail and jacket. Oswiu slipped his arms into his padded jacket, then lifted his mail, the links flowing over his fingers like metal water, and draped it over his shoulders, tying a belt, with his seax sheathed upon it and his sword, also sheathed but hanging down rather than across, round his waist. Then his gloves, thick, strong leather and, last, his helmet. But this he picked up and held rather than wearing it, his fingers hooked round the noseguard. Let the riders see him first. If it came to fighting, he would wear the helm, but Oswiu preferred to see his enemies face to face first.

Taking his spear, Oswiu strode to the centre of his line and stood awaiting the approaching riders.

*

"Halt."

Oswine Godfriend held up his hand and the column of riders behind him stopped. They were still some two hundred yards from where Oswiu waited, in loose but wary shieldwall, by the river. It was all too easy for such a meeting to dissolve into spear thrust and sword strike, and all through the nerves of a watching thegn rather than any wish for war on the part of the leaders of the two groups of men.

Oswine Godfriend desired no war. As such, he needed to go with care. Dismounting, he looked through his retainers. He wanted only the steadiest.

"Tondhere, bring my standard. The rest of you, wait upon us. Should you see weapons drawn, ride to us. Otherwise, wait." The Godfriend looked to Tondhere. "Are you ready?"

The thegn, a man who had grown up with him in the same hall, fostered by Oswine's father, nodded.

"Ready, lord."

"Hold my standard high. Make sure they see it." With his sword obviously sheathed, Oswine Godfriend walked towards the waiting shieldwall, Tondhere carrying the standard alongside and, when the breeze slackened, pulling the banner through the air so that its device, a white boar, streamed through the air. When they had halved the distance between the two groups of men, the Godfriend stopped and signalled for Tondhere to plant his banner.

"We wait," he said.

*

"That is the banner of Deira." Oswiu pointed to the white boar, streaming above the heads of the two standing men. "That is my banner."

"But they have it," said Æthelwin. "And they are flying it."

"I can see that." Oswiu planted his spear in the ground. If he should have to beat a quick retreat, a spear would only get in the way. "Let's go and see who is flying my flag. Æthelwin, with me. The rest of you...." Oswiu looked to where the two men were waiting. Beyond them, some fifty yards further back, waited the line of riders. If the meeting should come to blows, there was no doubt who could expect help first. "The rest of you come as well. Stop when we halve the distance. Then, if I draw sword, come as fast as your legs will run."

*

"They all approach."

Oswine Godfriend nodded. "I can see that."

"We are but two."

"I know."

"Shall I signal our men?"

The Godfriend measured the distance by eye, judging the time it would take men to run and men to ride.

"Wait," he said. "Wait."

*

"Put up my flag, Æthelwin. Let this upstart king know who he deals with."

The warmaster unfurled the purple and gold standard of the Idings and let it flow in the river wind.

Oswiu held up his hand. The men, loose and ready, waited silently beside him. Fingers itched upon sword hilts. Knuckles tightened on spear shafts.

*

"They do not look like men coming to talk." Tondhere looked to his lord. "We should go back."

Oswine Godfriend did not look to his retainer. His eyes remained upon the line of approaching men.

"If we go now, we will not have to run," Tondhere added. He looked to the Godfriend again. "But we will have to run if we wait much longer."

Oswine breathed out: a long, slow breath.

"They have stopped," he said.

"They are close."

"But not too close." Oswine Godfriend glanced at his old friend. "I would not have men say my first act as king of Deira was to run."

Tondhere grasped his king's arm. "They are coming closer."

*

The raven's shadow was huge. It glided down in front of Oswiu and landed upon the grass. The slaughter bird lowered its head and croaked, its sharp caw sawing through Oswiu's battle-ready senses.

"B-Bran?"

The raven turned its head one way and the other, its black eyes fixing upon the watching men.

"Bran?"

The raven struck at the grass at its feet, tearing at the earth with its heavy bill.

"He's digging a grave," Æthelwin whispered. All the men were watching the bird now, with the fixed attention of men fearing death and seeking tidings.

The raven croaked again, and ducked its head towards Oswiu and the watching Northumbrians. Some among them, it is true, made the sign against the evil eye, but more made the sign of the new god, Oswald's god, touching to head and heart and shoulders, and then, one by one, they began to kneel.

The raven gave a last, guttural croak and then it took flight. It circled above them once, and then flew away, heading south-west. Oswiu watched until the raven disappeared from sight.

"You always did have to look out for me," he said softly, then turned to where the two men still waited, under the standard of Deira. The wind had died with the bird's leaving, and the standard hung limp upon its pole.

"Let us go speak with this new king, Æthelwin," he said. He did not even have to give the order to his men to wait. Thought of battle had flown from everyone.

*

Seeing the two men step out from the battle line and approach, Oswine Godfriend let his breath go. Even after the raven had landed between them, and he felt the air change, he had remained tense. But now, seeing Oswiu and his warmaster approach, alone and with no more arms than he himself bore, he knew that he had not led his friend to death after all. The Godfriend knew that it was his own pride that had led him to stand, past all sense and retreat, as that battle line approached. Oswine resolved in his heart that never again would his pride leave his men in peril of their lives. Yes, he would fight, when fighting came, but it would be when battle led to victory, not when he sought only to save himself from ill fame.

*

Oswiu and Æthelwin approached to just outside spear's length, and stopped. Æthelwin planted the banner of the Idings in the damp earth, shaking out the purple and gold so all might see it, the gold of its cloth glowing in the late and slanting light, and then took one step further forward to announce his lord.

"Oswiu, Iding, king of Bernicia by right of his father, king of Deira by right of his mother, lord of Rheged, Master of the Islands, the gold giver and ring bestower, gives greetings to thee, and thanks thee for bringing to him the banner of Deira, his by right of birth and by right of his brother, Oswald, *Lamnguin*, the White Arm: king of Deira by the same right as Oswiu."

The Deiran standard bearer made to answer in kind, but before he could begin, the Godfriend silenced him, holding up his hand.

"I give you greeting, cousin. I am Oswine, whom men call Godfriend through no merit of mine, and we be cousins. I would have no bad blood between us and, to that end, when I heard tell of the ill way you were greeted when you came to York, I made to follow you, to ask your pardon, and to pledge friendship with you and with Bernicia." The Godfriend looked Oswiu full in the face, the men taking the measure of each other. "Do I have your pardon, cousin? Do I have your friendship?"

Oswiu looked long at the man before him. This Godfriend was tall – taller than he – and of a kind that seemed familiar. There was no obvious guile to his face and his eyes were steady under his gaze. This man might bend, but he would not easily break.

"You ask my pardon and my friendship, and call yourself cousin, although I have not known of you before this day. Yes, I suppose we are family – but then are not all men family, first through our father,

Adam, and then through our forefathers, who sailed the whale road to this land? As to pardon, yes, I would give it, and readily, but to the man who quits me of the dishonour done to me at York gate. And to friendship, yes, you shall have it, for as all will testify, I am generous and quick to give, gold and treasure and many white mares, to those kings who pledge themselves to me and give oath. I see you have brought the flag of this kingdom – it was refused to me before, and unrightly. Now, if you bring it to me and give your pledge, then I will give you friendship and the honour due to you, lord of Deira, oath bound to me."

Oswine Godfriend nodded his head slightly, as if he were giving assent, and Oswiu's face tightened with sudden surprise. But then the Godfriend spoke.

"I would that that might be so. But it cannot be. Once before, when Cadwallon ravaged our land, the witan came to me and asked me to take the throne, and I would not. Now, with our king dead and Penda raiding upon our borders, they have asked me again, and I have not refused. Oswine Godfriend, Yffing, is king of Deira, and so I will remain unless the witan acclaims another or death takes me."

Oswiu's eyes narrowed. "As you say. If not the first, it will be the second."

Tondhere, standing at his lord's side, stiffened at the words, his hand straying to sword hilt and resting upon it. Seeing the motion, Æthelwin mirrored it.

"Do you threaten me?" the Godfriend asked. His tone was mild, but his hand also now moved to where his sword hilt nestled against his hip.

Oswiu smiled thinly. So, there were limits to the Godfriend's goodness. "All men die. All kings die. Think you to be different?"

"We pay weregild for our father's crime. I am no different."

"You speak of our father, Adam." Oswiu, carefully, so all knew he did this with no threat, drew the seax from its sheath and held it up that all might see its handle: interlaced weavings of gold and garnet that picked out a cross in curving, crossing lines. "We pay weregild for his breaking of oath to his Lord. When King Edwin, my uncle, died, all Deira broke faith with the pledge he had made to our new god; all Deira abandoned their lord of heaven and spilled blood to stones and idols and the old gods. It was my brother Oswald who brought Deira back to its word and oath, taking no vengeance for its pledge-breaking. Now, will Deira prove faithless again?"

"No! No, even if I alone keep true, Deira will not break faith." The Godfriend held his hand to his heart. "This news, this hope, is dearer to me than heart's blood. I will not let it go."

"But who will keep it for you?" asked Oswiu. "Bishop Aidan dwells upon the Holy Island with his monks. What priest have you to perform the sacred mysteries, to bring God down from heaven?"

"There... there is one. James."

"James. Oh, James the Deacon. Yes, I know him. I saw him when first my brother brought a bishop from the Holy Isle. Bishop Corman sent him scuttling from the hall like a whipped dog, to skulk in some cave. Is there another?"

"N-no."

"One man for a kingdom as large as Deira. And him, I have heard tell, not even a priest, let alone a bishop. You do know you have as your deacon one of God's mules? He can work, but he can sire no priests for Deira. As a king makes a thegn, so a bishop makes priests."

The Godfriend nodded. "I see. And Aidan is the only bishop in these islands?"

"There may be one for the men of Kent. But Kent is far, and from what I hear its bishop is no more inclined to leave his church than you are to leave your kingdom."

"What would you ask to send me Aidan?"

"What would you give to receive Aidan?"

The Godfriend fell to silence, eyes turned inward, while Tondhere eased his hand away from sword hilt, as did Æthelwin.

Oswine looked up and sought Oswiu with his eyes.

"I would give aught I might, within the charge laid upon me that I guard this kingdom and keep it."

"Pledge to me, and I will give you leave to rule Deira beneath me, and send Aidan, and many monks, to open heaven's gate to you." Oswiu's lip twitched. "That God might give you better welcome than York gave me."

"I… I may not. Such charge was laid upon me by the witan: that I swear to no other king, nor give pledge to any other throne, that Deira be free of kings not of its earth and waters."

"But I am of its earth and waters! My mother…"

The Godfriend shook his head. "None here know you now. Some, at least, knew Oswald, for he was twelve when you left, but you were but a babe when your mother took you into exile. You grew among strange folk, far away, amid the Isles upon the World's Edge. I hear the wind over that restless sea in the sound of your words. You are not as we are. That is why the witan will not accept you, Oswiu, Iding, though you be flesh of Acha and nephew to Edwin."

"The witan does not always decide who will rule."

"Then you will have to fight. Would you win this kingdom, your mother's land of old, in blood?"

Oswiu stared at the Godfriend.

"I could have killed you," he said. "Just now you let us get too close. I could have cut you down before your men reached you. I do not think I will have to wait long before the throne comes to me."

"They would not have you, even were I dead."

Oswiu grinned thinly. "Think you so? I shall see."

For his part, the Godfriend nodded grimly. "War, then, between us?"

Oswiu laughed. "What said I of war? A king so foolish will not long sit upon the throne. All I have to do is wait." He looked to his warmaster. "Come, let us go. There is nothing to keep us here further."

With that, Oswiu and Æthelwin turned back to their men. As they approached the waiting line, Oswiu glanced back. He saw the Godfriend and his thegn still standing there, watching them, and in his stillness he suddenly saw the resemblance, and knew of whom Oswine Godfriend reminded him.

"He's like my brother," he said.

Chapter 3

Oswiu laboured up the steep steps to the gate. Below, on the thin spit of beach, the boats were being unloaded after their journey up the coast. Restless horses, too long confined on shifting platforms in the sea, were being persuaded not to run off. Oswiu's retainers, salt stained and damp despite the wax-rubbed cloaks they wore for the sea voyage, were busy slinging shields onto backs and removing swords and spears from the leather wrappings they used to keep them dry while at sea. The more careful among them – which meant the older men – also stopped to clean off the grease they'd smeared onto the iron before winding leather around their weapons. The younger ones, when they saw the red bloom of rust on the grey of sword or spear, would soon learn the value of such precautions.

For his part, Oswiu drew his cloak tighter around his shoulders. Climbing up towards the gate exposed him to the wind. The king looked over his right shoulder, to the north-east, whence the wind blew. There were clouds on the horizon and soon they would be over the Holy Island, Lindisfarne. Oswiu grimaced. He had hoped to send word to Aidan to come to him, but now he would have to wait for the weather to change. It was the season: the spring saw the wind change from day to day. This early in the season, there was little warmth to the sun, and the north-easterly still blew cold. It reached fingers in, past the fur at his collar, sending winter chills down Oswiu's back. The king grinned at the familiar touch. The north-easterly always blew cold, whatever the season. It was as familiar as the handle of his seax; he was home.

Oswiu looked up. He was almost at the gate, the single entrance to the great stronghold of his family. Bamburgh was set upon a great rock by the sea, commanding land and water and, so high did it stand, it seemed the very sky itself. Approaching the gate he hailed the door warden and the gate opened.

"A better greeting here than where last we sought entrance," he said to Æthelwin.

"We're not through the gate yet," said the warmaster.

"Please, say no more ill news."

Oswiu looked up. There was a woman standing in the gate.

"Mother." The king tried to smile, but the smile died as he saw the pain upon her face. Before, his mother had always smiled whenever she saw him, her face lighting up when he arrived upon Coll, the island where she had taken exile after the death of her husband. But that was before Oswald had died. Now, when Acha saw her younger son, he saw the pain of loss upon her face first, before any joy at his arrival.

"What has happened?" Acha stepped from the gate and took his arm.

"Nothing – no one dead." Oswiu looked down at the hand holding his arm, then into his mother's face. Some of the concern was dropping away, but still there was no joy in it. "Aren't you going to kiss me, Mother?"

"What – oh, of course. I am sorry, Oswiu. But you scared me when I heard what you said." Acha took his head in her hands and bent it down to her, that she might kiss her son upon his brow. Then, holding Oswiu, she looked again at the face of her youngest child.

"Whenever I see you, I am still surprised. My boy, so big, so tall…"

"So old."

"Thirty years is not so old."

"It is for a king, Mother. As you know." Oswiu gently removed the hands that still held his face. "Remembering my face again, Mother?"

"Yes. Yes. Do you blame me?"

"Do you remember his? Do you remember Oswald's?"

Acha paled. She shook her head. "No," she whispered.

"Neither do I." Oswiu paused, caught in thought, then looked at his mother. "I would have brought him home if I could."

"I know." Acha touched her son's arm. "I know."

"Penda took him. Coifi and Acca saw."

"I know, I know." His mother said the words with the same soothing, lullaby rhythm that he had heard when she rocked his own children to sleep, a rhythm that reached back into his childhood, and he looked gratefully at her pale smile, patting her hand with his own before making to move past her.

"But…"

Oswiu stopped.

"But what?"

"I should so wish to see his face again."

The king walked through the gate and into his stronghold, the keep of Bamburgh, and he felt its walls close in around him. The greetings of his people rang around him, but Oswiu barely heard them. There was still further to ascend, the gate being set halfway up the steep ascent of the rock, and he did not look back to see if his mother followed. He did not look up to see where he was going, but only to the rock at his feet.

So the first thing he saw was feet. Bare feet. Standing on the final step. He looked up, past the feet, his gaze travelling up over a coarse woollen robe, undyed and roughly cut, to reach a face, at once smiling and solemn, with no hair upon its brow but hanging long and loose from the crown and down onto the man's shoulders.

"Aidan!"

The man held out his arms as one greeting an old friend, for so they were. "Oswiu." But as Oswiu went to embrace him, Aidan suddenly blushed and stepped back. "B-but you're king now. I should kneel."

Oswiu laughed. "What, you? Kneel to me? Never, old friend, never." And over Aidan's blushed protests he embraced the man.

Then holding him at arm's length, Oswiu looked at his friend, the searching glance of a meeting after many months apart; months of ill tiding.

"I had thought to have to wait until after the wind turned to see you. How did you know to come?"

"There are so many to call, and so few doing the calling." Aidan smiled ruefully and, with a shock, Oswiu saw the lines of age, which before he thought lines of laughter, upon the monk bishop's face. "I can ill afford to spend time in feasting at a king's court."

"Even when the king is an old friend?"

Aidan smiled, and there was no rue in this smile. "Well, maybe then."

"Good. I will have need of your counsel as well as your friendship. Is the queen here? And my children?"

"Yes, they are here…" From across the courtyard came the sound of shouting and laughter. "No, they are coming."

Oswiu climbed the final steps and looked across the inner ward. A boy and girl were emerging from the great hall that stood against the far rampart, whooping and racing each other.

Aidan came and stood beside him, watching the race.

"Who do you think will win?" Oswiu asked the question of his old friend without taking eye from the race.

"Ahlflæd is the elder, but she is a girl and her dress is slowing her. See, already Ahlfrith is catching her. I think Ahlfrith will win."

"Think you so?" Oswiu grinned a sharp, quick smile at Aidan. "I know my girl."

And as Oswiu spoke, and Ahlfrith was on the point of overtaking his sister, Ahlflæd caught his heel with her foot, sending him rolling and tumbling to the ground, while she, more sedately now, completed the race and stopped, face shining, in front of her father.

But as Oswiu reached out to embrace her, Ahlflæd stepped back.

"I'm a big girl now," she said, and she made the courtesy, after the manner of women, spreading her skirt and bowing low. Then, courtesy made, Ahlflæd stood and jumped into her father's arms. "Daddy!"

Oswiu embraced his daughter, eyes bright with joy, then held her away from him. Ahlflæd, seeing his scrutiny, wriggled loose and twirled around, the rich fabrics of her dress flowing out from her.

"Do you think I look pretty?"

"Yes. Very."

"Do you think I'm prettier than Mummy? Granny says I am."

"Does she? Well, if Granny says so, it must be so."

Ahlflæd smiled, then made a face at the monk. "Uncle Aidan's always saying I pay too much mind to being pretty and I should think more about God, but I say it was God who made me pretty – I might not have been; look at Ahlfrith – so he can't mind."

Oswiu looked to Aidan. Yes, the monk was blushing.

"I–I do not say do not be pretty…" Aidan began, but it was too late. Ahlflæd twirled again, her hair flowing out in shining waves (being yet a child, she did not wear a headscarf).

But if Aidan was too embarrassed to act, Ahlflæd's brother was not.

"She cheated." Mud caking face and hands, Ahlfrith made to grab his sister.

Seeing the dirt with which he might cover her, Ahlflæd squealed and darted out of reach.

"She cheated," the boy repeated, tears of outrage making tracks down his cheeks. "I'd have beaten her if she hadn't tripped me up."

"I know, I know," said Oswiu, taking hold of his son's shoulders. "I could see how fast you have become."

Ahlfrith brightened. "I can beat anyone my age, and most of the older boys too."

Oswiu nodded solemnly. "I'm sure you can."

"But he can't beat me," said Ahlflæd, skipping into view from behind her father's back, then skipping back again when Ahlfrith lunged for her.

Oswiu pulled him up short, leaned close and whispered to his son. "Learn from this, son. Men, and women, play tricks, in life and war. Better you fall for them now, from your sister, than when you are older and are leading men in battle." Dropping his voice even further, Oswiu added, "I'm sure you'll beat her next time."

Ahlfrith nodded fiercely. "I won't run so close to her next time."

"Good, good." Oswiu let the boy go and turned back to his daughter. "Stop teasing your brother."

Ahlflæd stood straight. "Of course, Daddy."

"Don't try to pretend...What did you say?"

"I said, 'Of course, Daddy.'"

"That's what I thought you said." Oswiu looked suspiciously at his daughter. "I can't see your hands – are you crossing your fingers?"

"She is, she is!" Ahlfrith said, quivering with boyish outrage at this female stratagem.

"Ahlflæd..."

The girl held her hands in front. "I'll try, Daddy."

"You will?"

"Honest." Ahlflæd paused, then lowered her voice so only her father could hear. "Only, maybe you could tell Ahlfrith not to make it so easy for me."

"What did she say?" the boy demanded, suspicious.

But Oswiu held his hand up and shook his head. He bent down to his daughter. "Try, please."

"I will, Daddy." Ahlflæd's eyes were big and honest, but Oswiu still checked that he could see her hands.

"She's crossing her toes!" Ahlfrith pointed.

"Ahlflæd..." Oswiu sighed. "Where is your mother? Where is the queen?"

"Oh, she's looking after him."

"Who's him?"

"Him. You know. Our cousin." Ahlflæd put a slight lisp into her voice. "'My father was king and I will be king as well and tell you all what to do.' That cousin. Œthelwald."

"Mummy spends more time with him than she does with me," said Ahlfrith. "Not that I care, of course, 'cause I'm practising with the men most of the time," he added.

"Prince Œthelwald's father and mother are dead," said Aidan. "Your parents care for him as if he were their own."

"Yes," said Ahlflæd, "Mummy does."

Aidan glanced at Oswiu. "That is her generosity and kindness. Come, let us go find the queen. I am sure she is waiting for you."

"Good, good. But you – you have not told me how you come to be here. I had no chance to send messenger." Oswiu looked sidelong at his friend as they walked across the inner ward towards the great hall, scrutinizing him, but not too obviously. Although Aidan walked with his eyes fixed ahead, he coloured: his flesh felt the gaze upon it.

"I – I…Um, in prayer, in the early hours, when it is so dark a man might not see the fingers of his own hand and we send up the Great Work that God might send the day once more, I – I saw your need of me. So I came."

Oswiu paused at the bottom of the steps leading up to the great hall. "We are all here, then. Tonight, when the feast is done, we must take council. There is much to say and more to decide."

Chapter 4

"I – we – we have lost Deira."

The feast, the hasty, thrown-together feast to mark the king's return, was over. There had been no chance for the steward to find any choice items for the meal from the ships that pulled up upon the strand when wind and weather allowed. It had been a meal of mutton and mead, and bread and beer, with the steward forever bobbing his apologies before the king and his family at the high table, until in the end, as the beer flowed readily among the eating men, he had been driven from the hall by a volley of bones. The dogs, appreciating the game more than the steward, fell to gnawing the bones as the hall settled to a long evening of talk and riddles and stories and remembering.

But at the high table, the stools were drawn closer about Oswiu's seat, and cups were filled with beer or wine, and minds were turned to council.

"I say again, Deira is lost." Oswiu looked around the people gathered at table with him: his mother, Acha; his sister, Æbbe, prioress of the holy house at Coldingham; his wife, Rhieienmelth; Aidan, monk bishop of the Holy Island; and Æthelwin, his warmaster. Thegns and warriors, the men of his household and his most trusted battle leaders, sat at the near tables, ready to be called should he require them, but it was to his family that he turned most readily for counsel.

"You have heard the tale of York." Oswiu's gaze skated over Æthelwin, but the warmaster, inspecting his cup, gave not the slightest indication that the king might have missed out some of the details of the encounter. "I would hear what other news there is."

The other members of the council looked to each other, then gave way to Acha, Oswiu's mother. She looked up, her hands cradling a cup, but more to stop the slaves refilling it than to drink from it. A few strands of hair escaped the scarf she wore over her head, the hair as white as the cloth.

"You would have me speak? Very well. This is what I hear. The northern marches rest quiet. The Gododdin still render tribute, as they did when... as they did when your brother was alive. The painted people, it is rumoured, grow restless, chafing at your lordship, but their tribute too came, although it was a mean offering. Dal Riada remains faithful to its oath, but the king's mind is occupied with matters elsewhere, raising his arm against Strathclyde or sending ship against the Uí Néill, for the little good it does him: his army spent a full six months squatting outside Dumbarton Rock, and all they got for their efforts was the sweating sickness and the insults of the men of Strathclyde when at last they sailed away. As for the kingdom of Rheged, the queen will speak."

Acha looked to the woman sat upon the king's right hand. Rhieienmelth seemed to stiffen at Acha's words. The queen turned to her husband.

"Rheged is ever faithful to you, my lord."

Oswiu nodded. "Good, good."

"Is Rheged anything more than faithful?" The question came from Acha.

The queen looked askance, but only for a moment, then back to her husband, the king. With the slightest, most inconsequential of gestures, she laid her hand upon his. So commonplace was the contact that Oswiu bare realized it, but laid his other hand upon hers, as he had in the past.

"With the dangers that beset us, is anything more important than good faith?" asked Rhieienmelth. "Rheged is faithful, lord."

"With the dangers that beset us, is good faith enough?" Again the question was Acha's.

The queen, this time, did not cast her a glance, but took the king's hand in hers and leaned to him, as so often she had in the past bent to him, at feast and in council, that she might pass him word or jest.

"My father is old, lord, and the strength of his youth is lost to him. He sits in his hall, listening to the tale of his years, but few men stay at his side, for in his service now there is little gold and less glory. If it were not for your protection, the wolves and ravens would have fallen upon him and torn the throne from him. I would have my father live out his years and die in due time, and not be cut down upon the slaughter field like... like Oswald." The queen bent her gaze and looked down upon their hands, linked, and whispered, "He is my father, and he was good to me, after his way." Rhieienmelth looked up into the eyes of her husband. "Do not put him aside, as one of no more use to you, lord, but cleave to your oath and his pledge. This I beg of you."

Oswiu patted her hand. "Have no fear. I hold my oath."

"The queen is ever most solicitous for those placed in her care," Acha said.

For her part, Rhieienmelth made no reaction to Acha's remark, but looked down at her hands upon her lap, the cup of sharing set on the table before her that she might give to whomever thirsted: the picture of a queen.

"Our strongholds are secure." Æthelwin, warmaster, held by oath to his king's service but not, as the others at the high table, joined by blood or life friendship with the king, sat a little apart, and gave his report in like manner. "Bamburgh, as we can see, is supplied. I have received word from our other strongholds: Edinburgh also has supplies for siege, but not enough water; I sent word saying they must build and fill barrels sufficient for three months. Stirling is more ready even than here. Should Penda ride into Bernicia without warning, we should find ready refuge at any of these." The warmaster looked carefully around at the people listening. "If he comes in strength – and I do not think he will come in any other way – we do not have the men to meet him in battle. Not since our losses at Maserfield. I counsel that we retreat to one of these three places and wait. In our strongholds, we can wait longer than he outside."

"Have no men joined us?" asked Oswiu.

Æthelwin grimaced. "A bare handful, and them of the worst sort:

lordless men, exiles, seeking roof and hearth more than battle and service. Swords flock to Penda, I hear: young men seeking gold and glory always go to the last victor, never to the next."

Oswiu shook his head. "If we knew who would be the next victor, we would be wiser men than we are. So, Penda's ranks swell; ours stay the same?"

The rising tone revealed the question hidden in the statement, but Æthelwin reassured the king. "Your men remain true to you, lord. Any that might have gone, putting aside oath and honour, would have gone already."

"I have to speak." Aidan, monk bishop, spoke, and although his voice was quiet, all stooped to hear him. "It is of Oswald."

At the words, silence fell upon the listening people. Acha turned a face, suddenly pale, to the monk. Æbbe put palms together, eyes intent and shining. And the queen – the queen flushed, her pale white skin touched with beating blood.

And Aidan spoke, of a king's messenger, riding through the night and lost upon the road, whose horse was struck by an ælf arrow and taken sick. He spoke of how the horse was cured of its sickness and how the messenger, riding on, found shelter at an inn where lived a paralysed girl. Aidan told of how the girl was taken to where the horse was healed and, when she woke, the ties that bound the girl's limbs to her will were restored and she was made well.

Aidan finished his tale, and looked around at the people listening to his words.

"The place where the horse was cured and the paralytic healed was where Oswald's blood was shed. I have heard tell that people are coming from near and far to this place, and taking with them the dust from the ground, so that where Oswald fell is become a pit, ever dug deeper, and they mix the dust with water and give it to the sick and many are thereby made well. So I have heard; and others say that people take their sick, the blind and the lame, to this place that they might be healed." Aidan paused, suddenly, obviously, nervous.

"And they take them to another place, too. Near to where Oswald fell, some two miles or three, there is a tree, held sacred to Woden, and there I hear Penda took... took the head and arms and placed them, in sacrifice, before the tree."

Æbbe hid her face in her hands. Her shoulders shook in silent tears. The blood that had coloured the queen's face drained away; she became as pale as death. Oswiu, the king, gave no sign, for he had known some such fate must have befallen his brother.

But Acha gasped, with wonder and with awe, and all looked to her. And she looked to them all, and her eyes were lit with a sudden light.

"He still fights for us! Do you not see? Oswald, my son, he fights for us still; he has taken battle into the enemy's camp, set himself before the gods of our enemy and he defeats them. He fought for us on this middle-earth; now he fights for us in heaven!" And the old queen, exile and widow for most of her life, clasped her hands together and raised them, her gaze the brighter for the tears that shimmered upon her eyes.

"We must rescue him! We must bring him home, then he might fight at our side." Rhieienmelth spoke without thought, her gaze turned to Aidan, the bringer of this news, and she did not see the glance of her husband at her words.

"Could we?" asked Æbbe. "Now we know where he is – could we?"

"No," said Oswiu, his voice flat. "No, we couldn't." He looked around at the people of his council: apart from his warmaster, they had all known and loved Oswald – perhaps too much. "It would be madness. Self-slaughter. Maserfield is deep in Mercia, near its marches with Powys. It might be possible, just, to ride that deeply into Mercia without being caught and trapped into battle; to ride out again – that would be impossible."

"But if you are riding out again," said Acha, "then you would have Oswald with you, wouldn't you?"

"Yes..." said Oswiu slowly.

"If you have Oswald with you, then he will fight for you. Oswald always looked after you in this life; he will look after you from the Lord's great hall too, riding out with angels to guard you back home."

Oswiu shook his head. "Oswald couldn't save himself from Penda when he was alive. Do you think he will be able to save me when he is dead?"

Acha looked straight into her son's eyes. "Yes," she said.

Oswiu saw the light of certainty in his mother's face and it troubled him. But worse than the certainty was a terrible fragility, trembling behind the assent, the silence of nights of unanswered prayer, when only silence had met her heart's cry of "Why?"

"The rest of you, you don't think…?" The king looked around and saw, in wife and sister and mother, the sudden hope, the greater belief that he should do this thing, this mad self-slaughter. Even Aidan's face betrayed the belief that it be possible. Only the warmaster held from such madness, but he had no sway over people or kingdom. These others, though, held the strings of the kingdom in their grasp. He could not rule without them.

"Look, I would that it had been me that died, not my brother. I know you all wish it – I wish it too. But he is dead, and I live. Would you have me dead also, on a vain and foolish hope, in a raid that can but fail?"

"You will not fail," said Acha. "Oswald will protect you."

"B-but how do you know that?"

"I am his mother," she said simply. "He will not fail you."

Oswiu stared at them, feeling as a deer at bay before hunters. Only, these hunters hunted with love and longing and desperate hope, and he was as helpless before their arrows as the stag, ringed and trapped by baying hounds. "You'd have me die to save him – and he's already dead."

"You will not die. Oswald will protect you."

Oswiu stood up so suddenly that his seat rocked and all but fell. "Who would you have as king in my place when I am dead?" The king looked to his mother. "Oswald was ever with you in our exile, while I was little more than a baby: better than a husband, more than a son he was to you, and I blame you not for your love for him – I loved him too, Mother. But you –" and here Oswiu turned his gaze upon his wife – "I would have hoped my own wife would wish for my life rather than his."

Rhieienmelth made to speak, but Oswiu silenced her.

"No. No more. I go to think. To think what to do with a family that wish me dead."

The king went from the hall, and silence followed him.

*

Aidan found him upon the wall, standing in the shadow so he seemed as much stone as man. Oswiu was looking out to sea, to the east, whence the sun rose and the evening wind came. The king did not look around at the monk's approach, but he heard him.

Aidan waited.

Oswiu gave no sign.

To the north-east, the monk saw one or two lights flickering in the far distance. The Holy Island, beyond Budle Bay. The monks would be finishing the day's work, singing the Office and calling forgiveness and blessing down on the living.

"They do not wish you dead."

Oswiu turned to the monk. "So they would have me ride into Mercia for my good health, then."

"A – a mother's grief is like no other. Hold it not against her."

"I don't." Oswiu shook his head. "I really don't. You see, I understand it: given me, or Oswald, who were it best to live? My brother. See? I know that too. But God willed it otherwise."

"Sometimes – sometimes death can bring life. Think on the Lord's own thegns, great Peter himself, thrown down with despair at his Lord's death and then seeing him live again: life from death, and from that life, our life."

Oswiu shook his head. "That may be so for priests and monks, but not for warriors, not for kings. A dead king is food only for crows; he can feed his people no longer."

"That was true of the kings of old: in Woden's hall they give no thought to the living, but feast and fight and feast again. But that is not true of us. Our dead hold the living ever in their thought, as we hold the dead in ours. Your mother is right: Oswald fights for us still – he fights for you."

"You'd have me do it: throw life away in this mad attempt to reclaim my brother's remains?" Oswiu turned away and looked back to the grey sea.

"No, no," said Aidan. "You are king. It is for you to decide such matters."

"And if I leave him there, set before Woden's tree, then I lose the support of the Holy Island, I lose the support of my sister and my wife, I lose the support of my own mother."

"No. No, never." Aidan made to put his hand on Oswiu's shoulder, but the king shook it off.

"Tell them," Oswiu said. "Tell them I will go. I will ride into Mercia; I will claim my brother's body and bring it back." He glanced back at the monk. "Maybe then, if I live, they will think better of me."

Aidan saw the wind bleakness in the king's eyes, the winter touch that came upon warriors when they made the death bargain with their fortune, and he fought against it, in quick, silent prayer and in words.

"Lord, do not cast your life away in anger and bitterness. None of us will leave your side should you choose to stay; all of us will follow you in prayer should you decide to go. But... but there is one other thing..." Aidan looked questioningly at the king, then continued. "The warmaster, Æthelwin, sends word too: we have heard today, not all ride into Mercia – some go as pilgrims instead. I – I do not understand what he means, but as I was leaving the hall to come to you, he took my arm and told me this, insisting I say it to you. Do you know whereof he speaks?"

At the words, the winter cold seemed to leave the king's face, and then a slow smile, as welcome as spring, spread in its place.

"Yes," said Oswiu. "Yes, I think I do."

Chapter 5

The wagon creaked down the road. The oxen pulling it plodded along, heads swaying from side to side and, in response, the man driving them swayed too. His chin sank lower and lower onto his chest. The oxen, feeling the reins slacken, slowed, then stopped.

From the back of the wagon, a man stood from where he had been sitting watching the stones of the emperor's road slowly recede behind the wagon.

"We're never going..." He stopped, seeing the driver's drooping head, then poked him in the ribs. But unlike any other wagoner, this driver's first reaction on being woken was to reach to his waist.

"It's not there, Æthelwin," laughed Oswiu, for it was the king who rode in the back of the wagon, and the warmaster who drove it. "Remember, we stowed your sword in the back, under Coifi's pallet."

The warmaster shook his head, trying to force wakefulness back into his mind.

"It's these oxen," he said. "They put me to sleep."

"Not me," said Oswiu. He stretched out, breathing deeply, then looked around at the rich landscape stretching on either side of the road: copses and woods, fields laid out in strips or given over to pasture, the cattle pausing in their labour of eating to look at the wagon. "This is as I was in my youth; taking passage with some farmer, sometimes sleeping under hedges, just me and a few companions. Not the endless, ceaseless press of being king. You know, before we left, I was sitting with my bottom sticking out over the walls at Bamburgh, getting ready to let go, when a ceorl came up to ask me about a law case against his neighbour – and he wouldn't wait until I'd finished. So there I was, straining away – I must have eaten too much rich food – while having to decide whether his neighbour's cow had eaten his barley. That's being a king for you, Æthelwin: you can't even poo in peace. So this –" and Oswiu turned to take in the peaceful landscape – "is wonderful."

"All the same, I should not have fallen asleep. Though it appears quiet, yet we are in Mercia."

"But at least you've woken up," said Oswiu. "Unlike some others I could mention."

The warmaster peered into the wagon bed and saw two figures lying there in contented sleep.

"Are you quite sure these are the men to take with us? I would have brought one or two hardened warriors."

"One or a hundred. Where we are going, if we are caught, there will be no fighting our way out of it. No." Oswiu shook his head. "Everything relies on wit and stealth and luck. And something in my heart said these were the men to take: they were there when he died, they alone remain of those who were closest companions to him." The mouth of one of the men dropped open, and he began to snore, a great, rasping noise, enough to make the boards of the wagon shake. "Then again…" said Oswiu. He gave a short, sharp kick to the snorer.

"Wha…who?" The man sat up rubbing his eyes, saw the king standing over him, and groaned. "I was having a wonderful dream. The emperor himself had heard of my fame and invited me to his palace, and there I sang for him so sweetly that he stepped down from his throne to give me his favour (and a very thick gold armband) and just as he was about to embrace me –" the man looked up accusingly at Oswiu – "you woke me."

"You were snoring."

"There is music even in my sleeping."

Oswiu snorted. "The music of a pig, Acca."

"Indeed. Have you not heard it?" And the scop began to imitate a pig's snorting, but he put music and rhythm into the grunts, so that the listening men smiled in delight.

"If we live, Acca, I'll give you a thicker arm ring even than the emperor," said Oswiu.

"If we live, I will deserve it," the scop grumbled. "I can't believe what you said would have to be wrong with me."

"That's why I woke you." Oswiu pointed ahead. "There, see that line of trees, stretching west? That's the road we want – the old road of the emperors: Watling Street. Once we are on it, we will be deep in Mercian territory. There will be messengers, and king's men, and thegns riding and marching it, and all of them Penda's men. Before we go among them, I would know that we each know our roles." Oswiu turned to the other man, who still lay in the bed of the wagon. But his eyes were open, and they looked upwards into the sky, darting from cloud to bird to things only the man himself could see.

The man hunched himself up, squatting on the wagon bed and drawing around his thin shoulders the tattered raven-feather cloak that alone told of what he had once been: priest of the old gods, spirit walker and wyrd reader, fate spinner and rune reader. Coifi, abjured priest, almoner to Oswald, rocked upon his heels, hugging his knees and making clacking noises with his mouth.

Oswiu glanced at his warmaster, who grimaced in return. They had only been travelling for a day and Acca had spent most of the time complaining, while Coifi alternated between sudden, jerky movements and squatting on his heels, rocking backwards and forwards. They had sailed down the coast from Bamburgh and then up the River Trent to where it ran closest to the Foss Way. Leaving the boat to return north, the four men had quickly bought a wagon and oxen from a merchant who could scarce believe his luck at a deal struck so swiftly, and started along the old road of the emperors towards where it met Watling Street. There they would strike west, into the heart of Mercia, towards the tree upon which Oswald hung.

"We will go through it again," Oswiu said. "Now, who am I?" He looked at the two men in the wagon, neither of whom seemed inclined to answer his question. "Who am I?" he asked again, while giving the slightest glance to Æthelwin. The warmaster swivelled upon the driver's bench and flicked his ox whip – once, twice – over Acca and Coifi.

The whip had an instant effect on Acca. He sprang to his feet and, hands behind his back, recited in the sing-song voice of a young scop reciting the tale of his people while his master stands ready to correct any errors.

"You are a thegn of the kingdom of Lindsey, from Bardsey, and web in the eye struck you and took your sight. You go to seek healing where you have heard others have been healed, at Woden's tree. And you take us with you, companions in illness, each seeking cure."

"That's right," said Oswiu. Turning to Coifi, he asked, "And what is my name?"

The priest rocked his head. "Change a name, change a thing; new name, it's not the same thing."

"What's my name?" Oswiu repeated.

"Are you quite sure about bringing him?" Æthelwin whispered to the king.

"I was," said Oswiu. "Now…"

"You are named Nothelm." Coifi pointed at Æthelwin. "He is lame, from a fall." He pointed to Acca. "He is dumb."

"I can't believe I allowed myself to agree to that," the scop muttered.

"And I," said Coifi, "am mad." His eyes rolled back, until only the whites showed. "Will I serve?"

Oswiu laughed. "You will."

The priest's eyes rolled to normal, and he looked up, blinking like a young raven, at the king.

Oswiu looked to his warmaster. "There, I knew Oswald must have had reason to take Coifi as almoner. Not only does he see what others do not, but he makes others see him as he would."

The priest blinked again, his eyes huge and white against his raven-feather cloak.

"I make men hear as I would," Acca said, holding up his hand.

Oswiu sighed. "We have spoken on this. Your voice is too sweet, too known, for you to speak. Anyone, having once heard you in hall, will remember its sound, then wonder why the scop to Edwin and Oswald travels with a thegn of Lindsey." The king looked at the scop standing sulky faced in the wagon. "For such as I, without sweet voice, it is hard to understand how much we ask you to sacrifice by your silence, but think on this: what a tale you will have to tell when we return, and how many will wait upon hearing it."

The scop brightened, although only a little. "It will be a tale indeed. And, in this great silence, I suppose I can perfect the telling, hearing out the sound of the words and their rhythm in the great hall of my mind, working them and rounding them, till the time comes to unveil the song to the people."

"One final thing." Oswiu fingered the bandages that lay looped over his shoulders. "Remember, on the road, whenever we are in sight of people, I will wear these over my eyes. I spoke to Penda face to face. Some among his men might know what I look like. But they do not know you. You can pass without suspicion."

"Maybe we should say you have the pox," said the warmaster. "Then no one will bother us."

"And no one will give us shelter either," said Oswiu. "No, I will be blind. But, being blind, I can hear; there are inns upon the road where we can stay and learn of Penda's movements."

"If we want to get to an inn before dark, we had better get moving." Æthelwin nodded to the west. The sun hung three hand spans from the horizon. Time enough for them to travel six miles on foot, and maybe three with the wagon.

Oswiu looked to the line of trees that marched westwards. There were many gaps in their growing now, but the mind filled in what the eye did not see. The emperors of old must have planted them to shade their marching armies. Although time and wind had thinned the line, the line still stood. It was frost and water and many, many wheels that had rutted the road, but for the most part it too still survived, the local villagers charged with its maintenance against the king's passage and the swift riding of his messengers. That duty applied, Oswiu could see, as much here, in Mercia, as it did in Northumbria.

"There is a village and an inn at the crossroads where Foss Way and Watling Street meet," said Æthelwin as he flicked the reluctant oxen into slow motion. "We could rest there. There will be many travellers, and much news."

Oswiu measured the sun's progress against the slow creak of the wagon. "I would go further. But let us ask, when we get there, how much further to the next inn."

*

"Oh my, you'll never be getting there before nightfall – not with them oxen." The innkeeper stood at the door to his inn, stropping a large and gleaming cleaver in long, easy strokes upon a leather. "It be a good ten mile to the Fox and Hen. Beside –" and here he held up the cleaver and breathed upon the blade – "the beer there'll give your bellies the gripe."

"And yours won't?" asked Oswiu. He could not see the man, for he'd wound the bandages over his eyes, but he could picture him from his voice.

"Too right it won't," said the innkeeper. "Best beer in Mercia, if I says so myself, and like as not you'll say the same once you've tasted it."

"Then we will stay. If you have room?"

"Room? We can always fit another in, outside if not in. But you're lucky today; I'm not too busy. Should have seen it yesterday: could hardly move, what with all the king's men ordering this and commanding that."

"King's men? What were they doing here?"

"Don't rightly know. The king weren't with them, and they went off this morning in some fearful hurry. Wouldn't say what they wanted, nor would they give us a tale when asked, just sat and talked among themselves like they were too good for the rest of us. S'pose they were, really. Now, where would you be wanting to sleep: inside or out?" The innkeeper looked them over with an eye experienced in judging a man's wealth by his appearance. "Inside, like as not. Just as well, really. Looks like rain, I be thinking."

"Yes, inside, master innkeeper." Oswiu held out his hand. "Would you help me down."

The innkeeper looked around for somewhere to put the cleaver. Seeing nowhere obvious, he swung it through the air and left it, embedded and quivering, in the door post, before rushing over to the wagon, wiping his hands on his apron.

"Coenred I be called," said the innkeeper, taking Oswiu's hand, "only everyone calls me Red on account of my hair and my dragon. You just ask anyone around here after Coenred of the Red Dragon. They'll all vouch for me and my beer."

"And your dragon?" asked Oswiu.

"Oh, t'ain't a real dragon, master; just one I made myself when them down the road started up calling themselves the Fox and Hen. Painted it myself; I'm right proud of it too – what do you think, master?"

In answer, Oswiu pointed to the bandages covering his eyes.

"Oh, there I go again, putting my mouth in it before my feet are in the same village. I'm sorry, master."

"I'm sure a cup of your famous ale will put things right."

"You're right enough it will, master. Fact is, I've heard people say it cures all ills."

"Good beer does that, for a while." Oswiu took hold of the innkeeper's arm and allowed him to lead the way towards the door. "But I fear even your beer will not restore my sight."

"T'ain't often we sees a master like yourself out on the road in your, er…in your condition."

"It is not easy to travel when blind. But my men help me, and share my hope."

Coenred glanced back to the wagon, which was being slowly unloaded. "I'll get my boy to take care of your oxen. Hey, Behrtwald, Behrtwald, where are you, you lazy good for nothing? Behrt!"

A tousle-haired lad sprang out from where he had been watching proceedings from behind the stock fence that stopped the local animals, farmed and wild, coming into the inn's yard.

"Take care of the oxen, Behrt, and show the rest of the guests where to go. I'll take care of the master here." And holding Oswiu's arm, Coenred took him towards the inn.

"What hope be that, master? I'm sure if any hear of some way of healing the bad eyes, they'll be coming from miles around; like as not from as far as Bernicia!"

"As far as that?"

"Further! I'm not a man for travelling myself, but being an innkeeper I gets to hear all sorts of stories. But what hope be you seeking, master?"

Oswiu held his finger to his lips. "Mayhap I will tell you anon. After I've had chance to soothe my travel-dry mouth with your fine beer."

"Right enough, master, right enough. You don't want to be telling every Wulf, Behrt or Harry your business…"

As the innkeeper talked on, Oswiu sought to picture where he was going in his mind. While they were approaching, and when it was still safe to go unbandaged, Oswiu had looked with interest at the inn. It sat back from the crossroads, a large, sturdy timber hall, typical of the house of the chief man of a village, a ceorl, well known and respected in his neighbourhood, from whom a thegn would seek advice on pasturage and tillage, or the temper of the people.

Entering the inn, Oswiu smelled the smoke of the fire – though it was not a cold day, the hearth fire was kept burning – and heard the sudden silence of cut-off conversation as men left off their talking to see who joined them.

"I'll put you in the corner here," said Coenred, leading Oswiu, "and send your men over when they're finished with your things. You'll be wanting beer and bread, I take it?"

"To start." Oswiu's nose wrinkled. "Is that lamb?"

"Ah, they say blind men can smell a roast a mile or more off. Yes, lamb – fine, sweet lamb. It'll be ready afore you're all settled."

"Then some lamb afterwards."

"And here you go." Coenred eased Oswiu down upon a stool. "Right you are, master. Will there be anything else?"

"No, not for the present."

"Very well, master… Did I catch your name? Begging your

pardon, master. I know you might have told me, but like as not some other thing chased it right out again."

"I am Nothelm the Blind."

*

"Will you be joining us, master?"

Coenred stood, wiping his hands on his apron. Since they had arrived at the inn, the innkeeper had been rushing around, serving out cups of beer to the men sat on benches at either side of the long tables, then bustling over to the corner where he had settled Oswiu and his companions with their own cups of beer and thick slabs of bread, before bringing over the best cuts of lamb, dripping fat and trailing the most glorious scent. But with the immediate hunger and thirst of travel sated, the innkeeper moved on to the second, but by no means less important, part of his occupation: the making of fellowship among men strange to each other, who had fallen into each other's company for the night.

"You serve good lamb and better beer, master innkeeper," said Oswiu. "Is the company as fine?"

"I like to think it is, master. There's a saying in these here parts: as tall as one of the Dragon's tales. There's all sorts here, master, and more come up from the village on account of they heard of you and wants to hear your story."

"And how did they hear of me, master innkeeper? I would not have my news bruited around to every country lad and tinker."

"Ah, that'd be Behrt, master. Can't keep a thing to himself. Goes out blurting the news to everyone he meets – not like me." Coenred tapped the side of his nose.

"Of course. Well, since all wait upon us, we will join you shortly."

"That's grand, master, grand," said Coenred. But the innkeeper gave no indication of leaving them, and stood there, absently wiping his hands.

"Presently, master innkeeper."

"Ah. Right, right."

While Coenred bustled away to the men gathered around the fire Oswiu gathered his companions around him.

"Remember who we are," he whispered. "But use your ears, and learn what you can. We know Penda's men were here yesterday: find out what you can of the king's whereabouts and his plans." Oswiu turned to the scop. "Acca, it might be better if you were to go out and take the air – it will save you much temptation."

The scop, condemned to silence, made frantic "no" gestures, shaking his head and pawing at Oswiu's arm, but the king held up his hand.

"Take him out, Æthelwin, but return – I would have your ear among this crowd."

"And I?" asked Coifi, as Æthelwin led the resisting scop from the inn.

"The old gods still rule here in Mercia, Coifi. Look – see what you can of their plans – they will thwart us, if they might. And crossroads are ever said to be places where the gods walk, and watch. Go out with Acca, stay within, whatever you think best: but watch and listen, and tell me what you learn."

The old priest nodded his head and drew his raven-feather cloak around his shoulders. Then, when Æthelwin returned without Acca, Coifi began to rock gently upon his stool, his eyes rolling in time with his rocking, a low hum emerging from his lips.

"Hey, what's he doing?" The shout went up from the group of men gathered round the fire.

Oswiu stood, his hands raised blindly towards the voice.

"He means no harm." Then, in the gesture understood throughout the kingdoms, he pointed his finger at his temple and turned it. "He is a priest. Sometimes he sees the gods, sometimes he sees the Fair Folk, sometimes he sees his own dreams – if he screams, that's when he's seen his dreams."

"Come, join us." The same voice that had called out earlier asked Oswiu and Æthelwin's company. The voice was big; Oswiu judged the man possessing it to be bigger. The warmaster took Oswiu's arm and led him across the inn, shoving inquisitive dogs out of the way with knee and thigh, and helped him to a stool.

Despite the bandages wound tight around his head, Oswiu could feel the eyes upon him. The fire warmed his knees and he held his hands out to it.

"Tell us your tale, Nothelm the Blind, and we will tell you ours."

Oswiu turned his face to the speaker. "You know my name, though I gave it not to you, but I do not know yours."

"That was Red – best way of getting your news spread through the kingdom is to tell him it as a secret. But there's no harm in him, and only curiosity in me. I am Brandnoth, thegn of this village of High Cross and the land around, keeper of the crossroads and the royal roads in these parts, and, lately, nursemaid to little yelping æthelings too young to be taken from their mummy."

"It sounds, Brandnoth, as if you have tale enough to tell for the night."

"But these men all know my tales – they know them too well. You should hear them groan when I'm in my cups and I ask for the lyre – don't think I don't hear you! – so me thinks they'd thank me, and thank you, for asking your tale first. Then, if you wish, you can hear mine."

"Very well. My story is short to tell. Six months past, when the sun was running down the sky, the clouds went into my eyes and took my sight with them. I've been blind since that day – one who could once see the difference between oak leaf and beech leaf at a hundred paces.

"Then word came to me, from a traveller in my hall, that many cures and healings were happening in this kingdom, in its west, on the marches with Powys, where your king fought a great battle and cast down the High King. Word came of people and animals healed, who lay upon the ground where the High King fell, and others, going pilgrim to the tree where his head and arms are said to hang. The traveller averred he had seen some of these healings for himself, and heard of others from men he knew and trusted. So, taking these companions who likewise hope for healing, I set forth from Lindsey. Tell me, what hear you of this place, this Oswald's tree?" Oswiu turned his bandaged head, looking without seeing, but hearing the whispers and excited conversation.

"I hear many tales, as you have heard them: animals healed from the foaming sickness, men raised who could not walk, women with child who were once barren. I hear there are so many tales that the king himself goes to Oswald's tree, which was Woden's tree, to see the truth of these tales, and to make secure the head and arms, that they be not taken by thieves or sorcerers seeking their power."

"Ah," said the innkeeper. "That be why the king's men passed through yesterday in such haste. They were making to meet him upon the road."

"This… this is fine news. Know you how many days ahead the king is? Mayhap we might meet him upon the road."

Brandnoth shook his head, then laughed. "Your pardon: so keen are your questions, I forget you cannot see. Like as not King Penda goes by another way towards Shrewsbury, and then beyond, to the tree. Besides, it pays not a thegn of Mercia to tell a stranger the king's whereabouts, even if that man be blind."

"That is well and I understand. But mayhap you can tell me this. How be it that Penda cast down the High King when there is such power in Oswald?"

"Ha, you know not our king, or you would not ask! He is as clever and cunning as a raven, and as patient as a cat. I hear tell it was by plans long laid and deeper spun that he trapped the High King. Against such craft, even the greatest power might fail. Besides, we hear tell that the High King had given over the worship of the gods of our fathers and taken a new god, the god of the Britons: now he hangs upon the tree of the Lord of the Slain. I think that shows which gods we should cleave to."

"No doubt, no doubt," said Oswiu. "But if that be so, is it not most passing strange that these tales tell of the wonders done by his body and the very dirt where he fell?"

"Aye, that is truth. And that is, I think, why the king goes thence. If there is one thing I know of our king it is this: if there is power to be had, he will take it." Brandnoth fell silent for a while, but Oswiu heard the sound of drinking, and kept the peace of beer while the thegn finished his cup and, from the gurgling sound, had it refilled.

"Ha!" continued Brandnoth. "I remember Penda when he was

a boy, snot nosed and quick, always ordering his younger brother around. Back then, he was the son of the king's steward and a whore of the Britons: now, turns out, he's an Iclinga, and descended from Woden." Brandnoth slapped his hand upon the bench and then, from the slurping sound, refreshed himself of his cup.

"You said King Penda is travelling to Oswald's tree. I would get there before him, if I am able, that he may not take the relics into his keeping."

"These days, t'ain't safe for men to travel, save they go fast and on horse, or many and armed. I'll send men with you, far as Shrewsbury, to keep you safe on the road – I might even come myself. I would see these wonders with my eyes and not just my ears."

Oswiu stopped, startled at the offer, then held up his hands. "Such generosity! Such spirit! Now, wherever I go and when I go home, I will put an end to the lie."

Brandnoth sat back on his stool. "What lie?"

"That the men of Mercia are greedy and liars, ever eager for gold but ever ready to gain it through trickery, and most inclined to play those tricks on travellers. That's what I heard on the road through Lindsey; that's what I heard from travellers who came to my hall. Now I can say the lie for what it is."

"Who told this lie?"

Oswiu could tell, from the way the voice moved, that Brandnoth was standing up.

"Who told this lie?"

Oswiu turned his bandaged face up towards the man standing over him.

"Oh, everyone in Lindsey says so, and Elmet and the East Angles and the South Folk and the North Folk – didn't you know? I used to say it myself: as greedy as a man from Mercia – that was how the proverb ran. Now I can tell its untruth as we go along the road: wherever we stop, I will make sure to tell travellers and the people we meet the untruth of what we all say. What a merry journey we will make of it."

"I – I spoke in haste. I have duties to attend to that will not wait."

"Oh. Oh dear. Does that mean you won't be joining us on our journey, friend Brandnoth?"

"No. No, I cannot. I – I must leave. The roads are not so bad – I am sure you will be safe."

And the thegn made to leave the inn.

*

Deprived of his voice and the chance to sing to the people at the inn, Acca went to clear his head. But even so simple a pastime as walking was a frustration to Acca, for the villagers, sitting outside their houses to catch the last of the day's warmth or returning from their fields, passed greeting to Acca and all he could do was mime a dumb show of his lack of voice.

Passing between the whitewashed walls of the houses, smiling and nodding and holding his mouth and shaking his head, the scop soon began to feel like a leaf, bobbing upon the water. He would have passed out of the village altogether, but already the gateman had closed the gate and Acca, forced to silence, did not have voice to ask to be let out.

Not that it was much of a gate, nor was the fence around the village particularly formidable. In truth, it was more hedge than fence, with hawthorn and holly and hazel thickening the cut branches woven horizontally between regular poles. By no means all villages had fences and gates. Acca could not ask, but he presumed High Cross was fenced due to its position at the crossing of the old roads of the emperors: many strangers came this way, far more than to most villages, and not all of the visitors would be welcome.

Ahead, caught on thorn finger and hazel wand, Acca saw string and rag dangling from the hedge, twisting in the slight breeze that had sprung up with the evening. There had been others as he walked, but there were more here, and he suddenly saw them for what they were: offerings to whatever walked the crossways in the dark hours, when people sheltered indoors, and heard quiet hooves and quieter feet upon the roads, and knew that other, stranger folk walked upon their business.

The scop shivered. The shadows lengthened and the nearest

house, which before had seemed too close, now seemed too far. Of a sudden, Acca saw the folly of walking alone in a strange village as night drew down and, changing his way, he left the circuit of the village and went back towards the clustered houses. But first he had to pass the working huts, the low buildings that clustered like little mushrooms in groups on the outskirts of the village: threshing, carding, grinding and butchery were mostly done in these huts. Acca's nose twitched as he passed the first: the smell of mingled iron and offal told him that this, the outlying hut, was where animals were butchered.

A sound. A footfall. Acca looked around, and in the deep shadows under the hedge saw a deeper shadow, then two, and they moving. He stopped, opening his eyes wide to gather what light there was. Probably just village animals, a free-roaming pig or goat.

But then the first shadow reached the footpath he had taken, and took it also, becoming a crouching shape that might have been a man, cloaked and hooded, creeping towards him. Acca stood, throat working in terror: this had happened to him before, in dream and nightmare.

The second shadow followed the first, feeling its way along the path as if it were blind.

In dream, the shadows had no face. But they had knives. And Acca saw the dull gleam of blade blackened with grease to stop it catching the betraying light.

In dream, Acca stood, unable to move as the shadow figures weaved closer until they rose around him in a wall of darkness and their black blades found his throat.

This was not a dream. Acca told himself he could move. He did.

Running, not looking back, he escaped the dark mushroom huts and emerged among the paths weaving between houses and gardens. The night had come, and no one sat upon stools to wave to him. In his panic, he seemed to run through a village lost to life, each house a tomb, its inhabitants already slaughtered by the wights that pursued him.

Only the inn showed bright. Torches burned outside the Red

Dragon and Acca ran towards them. But, as he ran, he saw other shadows racing to cut him off.

Acca ran, not looking to left or right, for he knew if he looked and saw that which pursued him, his bowels would freeze and his legs give way.

With a final, heart-bursting effort, Acca escaped the trap that was closing upon him and, with the light of the inn throwing its welcome about him, he ran into the courtyard, daring for the first time to look back.

There he saw the shadows, standing, black blades pointing to him, and they seemed now more men than wights. Safe in the light, Acca gave them the sign of the horns, but at that the shadow men flowed closer and, holding back a shriek, Acca hurled himself at the door of the inn.

"Help, help!" he cried, as he burst into the Red Dragon. "Someone's trying to kill me."

Brandnoth, about to leave, stared at the scop. "I thought you were dumb?"

For the first and only time in his life, Acca stood with his mouth opening and closing but with no sound coming out of it. His eyes flicked to where Oswiu sat, frozen, and then to Æthelwin, whose hand had already moved to the seax at his waist, and then back to the big, burly thegn standing in front of him, beard bristling over his belly. Now, Acca really was struck dumb.

"It's a miracle!"

The cry went up from the corner, and all eyes turned to Coifi, squatting upon his haunches but with his arms raised.

"It's a miracle," Coifi repeated. "The blessings of the god, the blessings of the king, are upon us already, though we have just entered the kingdom. He can speak, who was dumb; he was saved, whom men would kill."

"Yes, yes," babbled Acca. "Miracle, I can speak, they were trying to kill me."

"Who?" demanded Brandnoth, drawing his sword and going to the door. Checking out into the night, he asked again. "Who?"

"I-I do not know," said Acca. "Mayhap they were men, mayhap wights. I was walking, taking the air, and they leapt upon me from the darkness. It was only fortune that saved me."

Brandnoth signalled some of his retainers over. "They were men, not wights, I'll wager," he said. "I'll not have thieves disturbing my land." He gestured for a couple of his men to stay at the inn, then made ready to lead the rest out with him. "They'll be strangers; the men of High Cross know not to raise hand against those staying at the Red Dragon." He glanced back at Oswiu. "I'll send word if I find the thieves, but like as not they've taken to their heels. And remember: tell all you meet that the men of Mercia are not greedy."

With that, Brandnoth led his men out of the inn.

When, a few minutes later, Coenred returned from the kitchens, carrying cups of ale, he looked around in puzzlement.

"Where is he?" he asked. "Where's Brandnoth?"

"He was called away," said Oswiu.

"That is strange," said the innkeeper. "I've never known him go afore, not when there were new people come, to hear his tales." He put down the cups. "Will you drink these in his stead, master?"

"Yes," said Oswiu. "Yes, I think we will."

*

They waited until the few other men staying at the inn that night lay snoring on floor or bench before gathering in the corner, in the dim red glow of the banked hearth fire, to talk on what had happened. Brandnoth had sent word that whoever had threatened Acca had gone — muddy tracks led to the fence and, outside, horses had been left tethered, but they were gone with their riders by the time Brandnoth and his men found the tracks. The thegn urged caution on their journey, but made no mention of his offer to send men with them or to accompany them in person.

"Thieves?" Oswiu asked in a low voice, as they sat close together.

Acca shook his head. "I do not think so."

Æthelwin snorted. "Wights do not leave tracks like men; nor do they tether horses to make their escape."

"Well, if they were men, they did not act like thieves," said Acca.

"Who knows where we go?" asked Æthelwin.

"My family," said Oswiu. "Aidan. I do not know of any others. Why do you ask?"

"This would be a fine chance for someone who wanted you dead to send men to make that happen: in Mercia, with only us to protect you."

"But only my family and Aidan know where we are going."

"Yes," said the warmaster. His face was red in the firelight as he turned it to the king. "Who of them would want you dead?"

Oswiu shook his head. "No," he hissed. "My mother and sister — we were exiles together."

"The priest, then. Aidan."

"He is my oldest friend."

"Friends turn; even old ones."

"Not him."

"Then that leaves the queen."

"B-but why would she want to kill me?"

"Who would be king in your place, lord?"

"Ahlfrith, my son. Or Œthelwald, Oswald's boy. Depending on which the witan chose. But they are too young."

"And close to the queen, I hear. A young king might listen well to his mother — or his aunt."

"No." Oswiu shook his head. "No, no. Not Rhieienmelth. I will not hear you speak of her in this way, Æthelwin."

The warmaster turned his face back to the fire. "I am your warmaster, lord. It falls to me to guard you from the enemy within as from the enemy without."

"Rhieienmelth is not my enemy!"

"As you say, lord. As you say."

Chapter 6

"Master, master, there ain't nothing like this ever happened afore at the Red Dragon."

Oswiu woke to absolute darkness and someone pulling his arm. One hand went at once to his waist, feeling for the seax, while the other grabbed out for the man holding him. But Oswiu did not need to unsheath his seax. As suddenly as it had begun, the pulling ceased, and another voice spoke.

"If you want to keep your throat uncut, you let go and step back."

The voice was low, clear and certain, and Oswiu knew it at once: Æthelwin. With the recognition came the realization of why everything was so dark: he slept with the bandages around his eyes.

Unseen by Oswiu, above him the innkeeper of the Red Dragon was slowly and very carefully straightening up, Æthelwin's seax blade tight against his throat.

"I-I meant no harm, master," Coenred said, as Æthelwin steered him backwards and away from Oswiu. "It-it's just, your oxen have been slaughtered and your wagon broken."

Oswiu sat up and held out his hand for someone to help Nothelm the Blind to his feet.

"Show us," he said.

Gabbling apologies, the innkeeper led Oswiu and his small party to the stockade where the oxen had been herded to spend the night, with the wagon, stripped of all valuables, left beside the stockade ready for an early start. The sun had not risen, but dawn was far enough advanced for it to be quickly apparent that the oxen were not lying on their sides from weariness. Long, red lines ran across the animals' throats – lines already beaded with the jewel bodies of clustering flies. As for the wagon, the spokes of its wheels had been broken, the splintered wood making the vehicle as immobile as a broken leg made a man.

"It seems someone does not want me to see again," said Oswiu.

"And to slow us down," said Æthelwin.

"Then we must needs speed up," said Oswiu. "Innkeeper, I would buy horses. I can ride, if someone leads. We have silver sufficient for four horses. Do you have horses to buy?"

Before Coenred had chance to answer, a call went up.

"Master Red! Master Red!"

The innkeeper looked to the sound, and saw Behrt running from the inn.

"What is it, Behrt?"

"The horses! The horses are gone, master."

"What? What you be talking about? Didn't I give you word to keep watch on them last night? You telling me the horses are gone, and you not? Where were you last night?"

The boy, already red faced from running pell mell from the inn, flushed deeper.

"Oh no, you weren't…" the innkeeper began.

"Master," said Behrt, holding up his hands placatingly, "I didn't mean to, only she were…"

He never got a chance to finish the sentence. The buffet knocked the words clean out of his mouth. Behrt took to his heels, with Coenred puffing and yelling after him, dodging between the houses and gardens of High Cross.

The innkeeper, no match for the spry heels of Behrt, soon returned, puffing and wheezing, to Oswiu and his men.

"I will send word to the thegn," Coenred said. "He'll know what to do – and mayhap he'll have some horses you can buy, though I haven't no longer. Oh, when I get my hands on Behrt…"

*

"I will do better than sell them to you. I will come with you."

In an effort to make up for the wagon and oxen, Coenred had plied Oswiu and his men with food and drink while waiting for the thegn to arrive. It had not taken Brandnoth long, for his hall was not far from the village.

The thegn, cup in hand, stood in the inn. "I and enough men to ensure your safety. Never let it be said, Nothelm the Blind, that the men of Mercia are greedy. We will take you to the king, for he goes where you go, and your road lies together. With him, you may travel in safety and I may relinquish my charge. But until then, I give pledge to see you safe and with no further loss. What say you, Nothelm the Blind?"

Oswiu cast around in thought for some way to refuse the thegn.

"The king travels with many men, does he?" he asked.

"Oh, many many men. Not to mention women, whelps, dogs, horses and enough whores to keep an army off the field for a month."

"We would not be a burden if we were to join his party?"

"Burden? He would likely never notice you."

"In that case, I will be happy, and grateful, to accept your offer, Brandnoth. And I will ever bruit abroad that the men of Mercia are the most generous of all the men of this land."

"Aye, right. That's as it should be." The thegn drained his cup. "Come, let's get going then."

*

The day was glorious. Oswiu could feel the warmth of the spring sun on his bandages and his hands, he could hear the songs of birds in wood and field, and he could smell the new growth as the sun stirred plant and tree into fresh life. But he could see none of it, and the blindness of his disguise wore heavily upon him.

At least the straightness of the old road made the riding easier. Brandnoth had given him an old and steady mare. She felt dependable and sturdy, and after the tedium of riding the ox wagon, the better pace the horse made was welcome. With the road so straight, his horse did not need leading. Instead, Æthelwin, Coifi and Acca took turns to ride, always a pair, with one on each side of him. Not that the mare showed any sign of wishing to leave the straight road.

Blind, Oswiu soon settled into the sound of the journey. The strike of metal on stone, the crunch of it on gravel, as the horseshoes struck sparks. He could not see the sparks, but he could smell them. Brandnoth rode his own land in his lord's kingdom – he had no need of stealth. There had been many times when Oswiu had ridden with his horse's hooves wrapped in cloth, to muffle the sound. Now, the troop of men – Brandnoth rode with ten retainers – and their horses made no effort at secrecy but rode loud upon the road, knowing that all would give way to the thegn.

For his part, Brandnoth was mostly content to ride at the column's head, taking and receiving greeting whenever they passed men and women and children working in the fields that lay to either side of the road. But after a morning's ride, Brandnoth drew his horse off the road, allowed his men to pass, then pulled in alongside Oswiu and his companions.

"What say we hear the fruit of this miracle?" he said, looking towards Acca. "Seeing as how yon scop has tongue in his head again, then he can give us song as we ride. What say you, Nothelm the Blind?"

"I say a song is poor payment for the generosity of the thegn of High Cross," said Oswiu.

"'Tis all the payment I seek," said Brandnoth.

"Then payment you will have." Oswiu looked round blindly.

"I am here, lord," said Acca, from his other side.

"You heard. Brandnoth seeks payment in song. Give it him."

"My pleasure," said Acca. He looked towards the thegn as he drew the lyre from where it hung over his shoulder. "And yours." The scop's fingers tuned and tightened the lyre as he rode, relying on his knees to hold the horse steady. The animal rode without demur, and Acca began to sing.

*

As they rode through the afternoon, Acca noticed that Coifi, his companion through many journeys and trials in the years since the death of King Edwin, was growing more nervous. The twitches and jerks that were normal to him were increasing; so much so that his horse, which had before been a placid animal more inclined to sneak snatched grabs at grass than to start, became skittish, dancing sideways upon its hooves and flaring out its nostrils as it breathed out its alarm. But Coifi went unaware of his animal's nervousness, head bobbing to left and right. Acca, who had seen this of old, knew his friend to be seeing, to be searching for the traces of wyrd in the movement of leaf and the flight of bird, in the play of wind and light and wood.

Charged with riding as guides to Oswiu, Acca had had no chance to speak alone with Coifi but, when Brandnoth dropped back to talk to Nothelm the Blind again, and with Æthelwin riding Oswiu's other flank, Acca took the chance to fall back with Coifi.

Acca leaned to the priest, touching his arm. At the touch, Coifi started, eyes rolling wildly as he sought to find who touched him. He was looking everywhere but at the man who rode beside him.

"Coifi, it was me," said Acca.

The priest's faced turned slowly towards the scop and, for the first time, Acca saw the man's age. Lines marked his face – the lines of suffering and exile, of loss and grief as much as years – but against the dusty black of his old raven-feather cloak, Coifi's hair was beginning to turn white.

"There are other touches than yours," said the priest, eyes still searching. "If only I can find whose fingers they belong to…" His gaze suddenly snapped back to Acca, focusing on him for the first time. "It is here," he said. "This place, this kingdom. In Mercia, they have not abjured the ways of their fathers. The old gods still walk here; I can smell them." Coifi looked around wildly. "Mayhap they can smell me."

"Don't you want to see them?"

"No!" In shock at how loudly he spoke, Coifi clapped his hands to his mouth. "No," he continued more quietly, eyes never still but always searching, "for if I see them, then they shall surely see me." Suddenly, he gripped Acca's arm. "They have no mercy. I abjured them, cast fire and spear into their holy place at Goodmanham. Think on what the terrible one would do to a faithless priest, should he see me."

"What can you do?" asked Acca. "You cannot run from the gods; the fate weavers spin your life."

"No, not before," said Coifi, "not before." His voice lowered to a whisper. "But now – now I think I can. The new god hides me, and the king, King Oswald, faces Woden's tree and fights with hand and eye before it, and the glory of his battle casts out healing. I think I can hide." The priest looked around fearfully. "But I had not known they would walk here, in Mercia, in the day as the night."

*

"We'll have to camp for the night." Brandnoth had ridden back along the column to tell Oswiu. "It's too far to the next inn, and though there be a village or two we might reach, I've stayed in both and each time it took me a month of flea cracking and nit picking to clear myself of the results. I'd not deliver you to such a blood feast, and particularly when you can't see 'em to crack 'em." The thegn made the nails-together gesture familiar to anyone who had slept in a louse-ridden bed, even though Oswiu could not see it. "Besides, I'd have a night under the stars in this season to clear the smoke of winter halls from my lungs."

"As you wish," said Oswiu. He sniffed as he had seen a blind man sniff before. "It is mild and smells fair."

"If it rains, I'll eat my hood," said Brandnoth.

*

"It won't taste good," said Oswiu, sitting with his own cloak thrown over his head to act as tent. "Wet wool never does. Besides, you'll need it to keep the rain off." The thegn had come to find him once the rain had set in with enough determination to prove it was not a passing shower, and had offered to carry out his promise.

"I said I'd eat my hood if it rained," said Brandnoth. "It has." He squatted next to Oswiu, water dripping from nose and ear and cloak. "We men of Mercia ever keep our words."

But Oswiu raised his hand as the thegn raised hood to mouth.

"You did not say when you'd eat it."

Brandnoth paused. "What?" he said, somewhat indistinctly, as his mouth was already full of wet wool.

"You did not say when you'd eat your hood," said Oswiu.

"Oh." Brandnoth's voice suddenly sounded clearer. "That's right. I didn't."

The rain continued through the early hours of the night, leaving the men beneath it sodden and tired, squatting in what patches of drier ground they could find beneath a tree or in a hastily made lean-to, but then cleared. Tatters of cloud streamed across the sky, but stars glittered between the clouds, and the men and animals settled into uncomfortable, damp sleep.

*

"Wake."

Oswiu woke to find a hand over his mouth and the word breathed into his ear.

"Æthelwin?" he whispered.

"Yes," said the warmaster. "There are men out there."

"Rouse Brandnoth," Oswiu whispered.

As the warmaster crept away, Oswiu lowered the bandages from his eyes. If they were to be attacked, he would see the faces of his attackers. In the east, the first hint of dawn was beginning to lighten the sky, but among the sleeping men, night still held dominion. Oswiu lay still, giving no sign that he was awake, but searching with eye and ear and nose for the signs that had roused his warmaster.

The first was the quiet.

In this season, the birds should sing the dawn, heralding it more loudly than Acca calling "*Hwæt!*" in hall, but they held silence.

The second was the stillness.

It was a stillness he'd felt before: the pregnant stillness of hiding in ambush, the waiting before blood was shed and lives were ended.

The third was the sound.

Rustle, and pause. Rustle, and longer pause. It could have been the dawn wind, ruffling leaves and grass. But dawn had not yet come, and its wind yet lingered below the horizon. These were the sounds of men moving closer, in stealth.

Moving with similar stealth, crawling over the ground so that he might not be seen by the eyes looking towards this camp, Oswiu roused Acca and Coifi.

In darkness and silence, hands reached for swords and drew blades from sheaths. Men moved, slowly rolling from back to chest, that they might the quicker spring to their feet.

Oswiu slid his seax from its sheath. Nothelm the Blind carried no sword, having given it to Æthelwin to bear on his behalf until healing came to his sight, but he had his knife. As he waited, breath misting in front of his face, Oswiu gave silent, quick thanks. It was good to see.

The attack came in a volley of screams.

Thinking the camp sleeping, the attacking men rose from their stealthy approach and attacked in noise.

Looking, listening, Oswiu saw dark shadows rising from the ground all around the camp and running at them, black blades held aloft.

But they were met, in turn, by shadows rising from the ground: men they thought to be sleeping, springing from the ground.

It was a brief but brutal battle. For his part, Oswiu held back. With only a seax as weapon, his part would be to finish off anyone who broke through the first line of defence. But, as it transpired, he had no need to wet his blade. The attackers, attacked, fled as quickly as they had come. Most escaped, running into the darkness, and Brandnoth, roaring like a bull, called his men back from blind, night-time pursuit.

"Hold, hold!" he yelled. And his men gave over their pursuit and fell back to camp. And many blades that had before glittered in the starlight were now black with blood.

"Torches! Light torches!"

Steel sparked on flint, flashing stars, and two, three, four torches were quickly lit.

Grabbing a torch, Brandnoth found the dead and the dying. None of his own men had been killed, and their wounds were minor, but in the torchlight he found three attackers, two already dead, and one dying.

Grabbing the man, Brandnoth hauled him up.

"Who sent you?"

The man coughed, spraying black.

"You're gut cut," said Brandnoth. "Tell me, and I'll make it quick."

"I-I don't know." The man coughed again.

The thegn held up the torch so he could see the man's face. The man met his gaze. Brandnoth nodded once, a single, sharp movement, then slid his seax in, through the man's armpit. The man stiffened convulsively, hands clawing for an instant, and then he relaxed.

Pulling the seax from the wound, Brandnoth cut off the brooch that held the man's cloak and walked over to where he had left Oswiu.

Oswiu saw him coming and remembered, just in time, to slip the bandages back over his eyes.

Brandnoth stopped. He rolled the brooch between fingers and thumb, examining it in the torchlight, then looked at Oswiu.

"This brooch came from a dead man, one of the men who attacked us," he said. "It looks to my eyes to be fashioned in the northern style: Deira, maybe Bernicia. And the man I took it from, he has the look of the northmen. So, Nothelm the Blind, thegn of Lindsey, tell me this: why should the men of the north want you dead?"

Chapter 7

"Make way for the king! Make way for the king!"

The proclamation, grown increasingly hoarse as the day neared its end, sounded down the road of the emperors.

Riding behind the proclaimer, Penda felt some satisfaction at the news he had heard, just recently, that people were starting to call these ways that the emperors of old had made royal roads.

Foss Way and Icknield Way, Ermine Street and Watling Street: the four royal roads. And all of them ran through lands he ruled or held sway in, although the heart of his kingdom lay west of the Foss Way.

Now he rode along Watling Street. Penda grimaced as the column came to yet another halt. "Rode" was not the right word. "Crawled" better described the progress of the last two days. At this rate, it would be another two days to the estate at Shrewsbury.

"What is it now, Idmaer?" Penda gestured his steward over. Idmaer, face flushed with anger, rode back down the column to the king.

"Some stupid shepherd with more sheep than sense," said the steward. "They're scattered all over now, and he's running around after them, scaring them the more."

They were riding west, so it was easy to see how long until the sun set: at the moment, it hung four hands' breadths above the horizon.

"Tell the shepherd to move his sheep or lose them. If we do not get moving soon, we shall have to make camp here; if we do, we shall eat mutton."

Idmaer made the courtesy and urged his horse back up the column, past the riders who went as vanguard and who now sat patiently, talking among themselves. Penda watched him go, noting those among his men, his wolves, who saw the steward's passing and those who did not. He had spent long days and weeks and months training his retainers to fight and act as a wolf pack: together, always together, in service of the pack leader. But he also wanted them like wolves in their alertness to danger and, its first presage, to difference.

The shepherd, giving up all attempt to keep his flock together, simply scattered them, hoping that way he would find more lost sheep than the royal party would leave him uneaten sheep, and Idmaer called the column into motion once more. The sun now stood three and a half hands' breadths from the horizon. Penda gentled his horse into a walk, using his knees to set it moving, and sat easy, enjoying the warmth of the spring sun on his face.

The last time he had been this way was winter, when he rode, huddled in cloak and fur against the cold, to the trap he had laid for Oswald. And his own brother.

Swaying upon the horse's back, Penda fell into memory. He had buried Eowa well, with riches and weapons fit for a king to present to Woden's door warden. They had laid him out, and left him, and left Penda with him, alone.

And he remembered…

There was no ghost. No shade of the man who had been his brother. Just white flesh and dead bones. And if Eowa heard, he gave no sign.

But whether his brother heard or not, Penda spoke, once and never again, in the silence of the grave.

"You did well, my brother. You kept silence, you kept faith, and you brought my enemy to me. Little thanks, you think, I gave you – only the sword, and your blood swallowed by the grass. But know you now, a throne is not shared: one man takes it, one man sits upon it, one man keeps it. So long as you lived, there was another who might claim the throne. Now, while my sons are young, there is no one. I sit secure. Mayhap, if the weavers had woven differently, it were me who lies listening, and you who speaks. But they cut your life; luck failed you, Eowa, in the end." Penda held up some dice. "Remember these? I was always the lucky one, you thought." Penda shook the dice in his hand and rolled them, sending the stones tumbling across the beaten earth floor of the burial chamber. "You were right."

The dice turned twin sixes upwards.

Penda, riding the royal road west, felt at his belt and took out the dice. He held them in his hand, turning one against the other, rolling them between his fingers. They were nearly as familiar to him as his sword, and more so than any woman, more even than his wife. Two pairs, identical in all ways save one. If he threw the pair he held in his right hand, he knew which numbers would roll. If he threw the pair in his left hand, then he did not.

Warriors might dedicate themselves to the Lord of Battles, or the thunder god, or Tiw One Hand, but Penda knew their great god, grasped before each battle, was luck. The fortune of the warrior.

He held luck in his hand. It had cost him a gold armband, the finest he had, and a horse, but it had been worth it…

The merchant sat, fat bellied, in the lee of his boat, pulled up on the strand. His slaves bustled around, laying out pots and salves and trinkets and jewels: the gleanings and leavings of the people of warmer climes, brought north and upriver, riding the tide of the Thames, past the pilings and ruins of the Roman bridge and city to the new town, the new London, made of wood and thatch rather than brick and tile. It was the biggest town the young Penda had ever seen: there must have been hundreds of people crammed into the houses that straggled along the river's shallow bank. He had made his way through the paths that threaded between the houses, slipping and cursing the mud and ordure, down to where the river ran, brown and sinuous and broad. The old city, the city of the emperors, still lowered at this wooden interloper upstream, but what really impressed Penda, as it impressed all who saw it, was the remains of the bridge. Though it was broken in two places now, many spans still remained, arches leaping from piling to piling, the river swirling impotently around them.

But it was not the boat that had brought Penda to London, but the market: boats, many boats, lay beached upon the shallow bank, pulled up just beyond the reach of the high tide. The river breathed broad with the tides, first sending brown fingers up well-worn channels, then overflowing them and washing out the rubbish the people of the town abandoned to the river's embrace, from the entrails of butchered animals, which the circling red kites waited upon, through the shavings of horn and the effluvium of tanneries. London, Penda thought as he made his way through it, was a stinking place.

On the river bank, the breeze cleared some of the smell of the town, but it was replaced by the scents of the goods on display: incense, perfumes, foods that Penda could not even name. He wandered among the merchants, fending off importunate hands pulling him to inspect wares laid out on display. But the fat merchant simply sat on his stool, fanning his face.

Penda stopped. Laid out beside the merchant upon the ground were gleaming trinkets and milk-white pearls; glazed jugs, gleaming red with the captured heat of their firing; bronze bowls filled with the sun.

"You like?" the merchant asked, squinting up at Penda.

"You speak my language?" Penda was surprised. The merchant clearly came from a distant, southern land. Elsewhere in the market, slaves – some bought for the purpose – did the selling.

The merchant stopped fanning and smiled broadly. "I speak good, no?"

"No," said Penda.

"No. But I speak more good than them." And the merchant pointed at his fellow traders.

"Yes."

The merchant nodded. "Few words. That is good. Better for me to understand. I speak good because I sell good. You want?" He spread his hands over the display beside him.

Penda shook his head and turned to go, his hand, as it often did, going without thought to rest upon his sword hilt.

"Wait." The merchant put hand to Penda's arm, pulling him back. "I have something for you. Something all men with swords want. You good with sword?"

"Yes," said Penda. His hand still rested upon the sword hilt. If the merchant touched him again without his leave, the hand would rest no longer.

"Yes, I tell. Come, come here." The merchant gestured Penda closer. "This too good for others to hear." When Penda leaned to him, the merchant looked around, making sure no one could overhear, then said, "You want luck."

"Luck?"

"Yes, luck. Fortuna. All men with swords want luck, no?"

"Y-yes."

The merchant's eyes gleamed. "I have luck. I sell it you. You buy, yes?"

"How can you sell me luck?" asked Penda.

The merchant reached into his robe, then thrust his hands, fat fingers closed, in front of Penda's face.

"Here is luck," said the merchant, and he opened his hands. In each palm nestled a pair of dice. He handed one pair to Penda. "Here is your luck," he said, and he pointed to the leather tarpaulin where his wares lay. "Throw."

Penda flicked his wrist. The dice bounced over the leather, then came to rest. Three and five.

"My luck," said the merchant, and he flicked the remaining pair of dice.

Six and six.

"Throw again."

Penda threw four and six. The merchant flicked his wrist.

Six and six.

"Throw again."

Two and one.

Then six and six. "My luck," said the merchant.

"How much?" asked Penda.

The merchant pointed at the gold arm ring, thick and richly worked, that wound around Penda's upper arm. Penda made to take it off, but the merchant held up his hand. "And horse," he said.

So it was that Penda started the journey home from London on foot. But after a day's march, his luck won him a horse. Over the years, his luck had won him much more. And, in the end, his luck had won him the throne.

Returning from the halls of memory, Penda rolled the familiar dice over his palm. His luck.

The great god.

Eowa had never understood. In the end, he had simply stopped playing dice with his brother. But the luck still remained with Penda. It had delivered Oswald to him – and Eowa. It had given him the throne, with none now left in Mercia – or any of the other kingdoms – to contest it.

Oh, he knew other kings would rise up. Penda smiled. He was looking forward to it. Let them rise: the richer the pickings when he rode against them, harvesting gold and glory.

Penda had realized that he, as king, was like a farmer. Of course, this thought he kept to his own counsels: the witan, that garrulous meeting of men more interested in recounting past glories and the list of their supposed ancestors – in most cases, as invented as his own – would not wish its lustre tarnished with the mud of the growers. But Penda had grown up among farmers, men scraping a living in the marcher lands between Mercia and Powys, and he knew how carefully they husbanded and how closely they reaped. As ruler of Mercia, he would let the other kingdoms grow, their kings waxing great in gold and treasure, and then he would reap them.

Mercia was different from the other kingdoms. It was the heartland – it was all land. Northumbria, Kent, the West Saxons and the East Saxons, the North Folk and the South Folk, Lindsey: they each, in their own way, turned their faces to sea, travelling by boat more readily and easily than by land. But Mercia sat at the heart of all these kingdoms: surrounded, but also in a position to strike, swiftly, to north and east and south. Only to the west would he stay his hand, for Gywnedd and Powys were bound to him in alliance, fruit of the blood that ran in him through his mother.

Penda kept this also to himself, but he was the great spider, sitting at the centre of the web of kingdoms that made up this land. Like a spider, he remained, still, waiting, until the moment a fly flew into his web. Then he would strike, as the spider wrapped the fly in its web more quickly than the eye could follow.

The dice clicked between his fingers. Penda smiled in his reverie. Not bad for the son of a whore. Though now, in the king lists his scop recited, his mother was a whore no more, but a princess of the Iclingas and he a descendant of Woden. Penda smiled again.

"Lord?"

Penda looked up, still smiling. Idmaer the steward, prepared for his king's wrath at the length of time this journey was taking, brightened at once.

"Lord, Brandnoth, thegn of High Cross, would speak with you."

"Bring him."

Idmaer pulled his horse's head away, but before he could heel him back down the column, Penda spoke.

"This journey takes too long, Idmaer."

"Yes. Yes, I know, lord."

"I will ride on with the queen and my children. I leave it to you to bring the rest."

"Yes, lord. I will."

"Tell the queen, and keep enough men to guard: there are rich pickings here, and I would not have them lost to some passing carrion crows."

"But you will need men to guard you, lord."

"We will ride to our hall in Shrewsbury, and fast. Catch up with us there."

Idmaer made the courtesy. "Yes, lord."

"Then send me Brandnoth. I will hear what he wishes…"

*

"Lord, I ask your favour and protection." Brandnoth rode beside the king.

Penda looked askance at the thegn. "We are bare out of your land and you ask me for protection?"

"Not for me, lord, but for four travellers I have taken under my protection. A thegn of Lindsey and his companions, and they travel to seek healing; they go in search of miracles at Maserfield and Woden's tree. They wish only to travel under your protection so far as they might, afore they continue to the field of slaughter which, men say, has become a field of healing."

"They seek healing from where Oswald fell?"

"Yes, lord, they do."

"I have heard of this – but you say the fame of this place has spread already to Lindsey? Bring them to me. I would speak with this thegn of Lindsey, for I travel to the tree and the field where I killed Oswald also, to see for myself if these tales be true."

While Brandnoth rode back to fetch the pilgrims to the king, Penda trotted his horse along the outside of the column to the queen's wagons.

"Cynewisse!" he called, slapping the palm of his hand against the waxed leather tarpaulin that guarded the queen as they made the slow journey from one royal estate to another.

There was a sudden flurry, and excited voices, from the wagon, before the flap was pulled back to reveal his wife and his queen, still hurriedly adjusting her scarf.

"My lord," she exclaimed. And in her surprise, there was a trace of the uncouth sound of her upbringing. Cynewisse was of no noble stock, let alone royal. She was the daughter of a man little more than a ceorl, with bare land and holding enough to rank as a thegn; but Kenward had taken the son of a whore, a boy barely old enough and scarce strong enough to hold a sword, as his retainer. And Kenward's daughter had not laughed at him when she saw Penda practising, apart from the other boys, with a stick for his sword, over and over and over again. Instead, she had brought him, unasked for, bread and beer from the kitchen, leaving it without a word for him to find when he turned from his relentless practice. Seeing the bread, still warm, and the cup of beer, Penda had known for the first time that he had a friend in this middle-earth, although he knew not who the friend was. He did not find out for a year or more – not until, finally, he laid trap and caught Kenward's daughter, and lifted her, grave and smiling at once, from the net he had strung for her.

"My lady," Penda said. "We ride ahead to Shrewsbury for this night, and onwards the day after. Make yourself ready, and what women you will have for the journey, and the children. They should come too."

Cynewisse smiled. "Too long we've gone at the pace of barley growing."

"Growing poorly at that," said Penda.

"I will be glad to ride with you, lord."

Penda nodded, then pulled his horse away. Cynewisse, suddenly urgent, turned back to her women, gathered in the wagon.

"Get the children ready, and my clothes and jewels. And, Edith, bring one of the slave girls, the fair one we bought at the last market: a ride such as this always sets the king's blood to fire."

As the queen's wagons boiled into activity, Penda made his way down the column, selecting the men he wanted to accompany him ahead. The rumour spread faster than he rode, sending ripples through the line of horsemen as the riders sat straighter to attract their king's attention. As he rode past, Penda tapped those men he wanted to accompany him. He did not need to look behind to know they rode on with their heads high, joshing their fellows left to the long, slow job of guarding the rest of the royal caravan.

Penda saw Brandnoth approaching, leading four riders, and he reined his horse to a stop, looking carefully at the men approaching.

"My lord." Brandnoth made the courtesy. "These are the men of whom I spoke, that I ask you to take under your protection for so long as you will, while they journey to Woden's tree."

Penda nodded.

"Who are you, and what do you seek?"

There was silence, a silence longer than a king was wont to keep, before the man in the centre, the man whose eyes Penda could not see for the bandages wrapped around his face, spoke.

"I – I am Nothelm the Blind, thegn of Bardney, and I ask the favour and protection of Penda the Great, king of Mercia, king of kings."

Penda pushed his horse closer to the group of men. "Where do you go, Nothelm the Blind, passing through my kingdom?"

The thegn held his hand up to his face.

"I go to seek sight, lord. The Ælf kin poured milk into my eyes. Where once I could tell a crow from a raven even on cliff top when I rode at the bottom, now I cannot tell whether it be day or night, for all looks white as fog to me. I sat in my hall, waiting to die, when I heard of the miracles wrought at this site in Mercia, where King Penda slew King Oswald: the very dirt where the old High King fell, when mixed with water, has brought healing to men with fever and with palsy, to women in childbirth and children with the sweating sickness, and horses too. Others, they say, have been healed where Oswald hangs, before Woden's tree. We go there, lord, if thou will, to seek healing, to seek sight. May we ride with thee, so far as our paths match?"

"Our paths will match all the way, Nothelm the Blind, for I go to Woden's tree as well. I would see for myself these wonders whereof you speak, and I would speak with those who have been healed, and learn by whose power these wonders are worked: whether it be by the power of the blood of him whom I slew, or through the blessing of the Lord of the Slain, to whose honour I gave Oswald's head and arms."

"For my part, I care little by whose power these wonders are worked, only that they work on me."

"You are not a king," said Penda. "It is a king's business to know by whose power such things come to pass in his kingdom." He pushed his horse closer to the blind man. "We ride for Shrewsbury, leaving the wagon train to follow, then on to Woden's tree on the morrow. Match our pace, and you will be under our protection. Fall behind, then ask the gods for theirs."

The blind thegn made the courtesy. "I thank you, lord."

"You have a priest with you?" Penda looked towards Coifi, sitting uncomfortably upon his horse, raven-feather cloak pulled tight around his thin shoulders.

"Yes, lord. A priest of the All-Father."

Penda nodded. "Have him speak with mine: his name is Wihtrun. He is ever miserable, bewailing men's falling from the ways of our fathers. It will be a mercy to me that he should have another to spread his gloom upon – and, like enough, they agree. Do you?" Penda spoke to Coifi.

The priest started, his eyes, rolling towards a glimpsed movement through the clouds, pulled back towards the man looking to him. Then Coifi's eyes flicked away, seeking Acca for some sign as to what question he had missed, but the scop, by the slightest motion of his eyes, told him that he could not say.

"Lord?" asked Coifi.

"Do you agree with my priest: that men fall from the ways of our fathers? That the gods are angered by this desertion?"

"The gods bestow favour and wrath where they will: I know not how men may call the one rather than the other."

Penda looked to Nothelm the Blind. "Not much use as a priest. At least mine says he can call down the gods' favour when I need it. Of course, their favour usually costs me dear in beasts and blood and gold." He pointed at the third and fourth members of the group. "And who else accompanies you?"

"My scop – that he might tell these wonders, should they come to pass – and my warmaster, chief among my retainers."

"Lord," said Brandnoth, his face flushed red with the news he was about to tell. "The scop has already been healed, for he had lost his voice and now can speak again."

"Really? Nothelm the Blind must tell me of this further." Penda looked ahead and saw the column of riders had formed and was waiting upon him. "When we get to Shrewsbury." He felt at his belt, rolled the familiar cubes between his fingers.

"Tell me, Nothelm the Blind: do you play dice?"

Chapter 8

The royal hall at Shrewsbury was large. Approaching it, as the sun sank into the west, Acca murmured in awe at the splendour of its carved door posts and the colour of its roof poles, intricately shaped in the form of serpents and beasts. In the late light, it caught into his memory the form of Ad Gefrin, the great hall of Edwin beneath Yeavering Bell, which Cadwallon of Gwynedd had consigned to the flames. But though he gasped, Acca spoke no other word. They were surrounded by the riders of Penda, his wolf pack, the men who accompanied him in the ceaseless round of his kingdom.

They had ridden hard and fast, making good pace over the royal road. Hearing the sound of hooves galloping, every wagon and walker upon the road before them had moved aside. On one occasion, Acca had seen a hapless wagoner scratching his head as he contemplated the wheel, cracked upon stone, that was the price of getting out of the king's way. But a wheel might be replaced. A king, in haste, might not wait upon a life, but ride it down.

Keeping Oswiu, swathed in his bandages, upon his horse and straight upon the road had taken all the concentration that the scop and his companions possessed. Of the two companions, Æthelwin had taken the greater part in the long ride, pushing his horse flank to flank with the king's. Coifi, no horseman, had his part in keeping up with them.

Acca had taken the chance to look at the riders that accompanied Penda. For the most part they were his retainers, but the queen rode with the king as well, with three of her women and a daughter and, near the head of the column, proud as a puffing frog, a boy that must be Penda's son.

In all, there were thirty riders upon the road. It would be a brave band of robbers that tried to stop such a heavily armed group of men; though woods marched in places alongside the road, heavy and silent and watchful, no one emerged from the green shadows to challenge the riders, and they arrived at the king's hall with the sun still a finger's breadth above the distant rising rim of hills.

The arrival was set amid the customary chaos and panic – on the part of the hall's wardens and stewards – and the demands and desires of the arriving riders.

In the hall, the new arrivals rattled as a dry nut within its shell: there were so few when the hall could hold so many. Oswiu and his companions sat apart, speaking quietly, sharing the bread, warm but tough, that had been pulled in haste from the store and heated rather than baked fresh, while slaves hurried around with jugs, filling cups with beer. Any steward surprised by the unexpected arrival of his king knew well to fill bellies with beer, and fast, before tempers frayed and the food was cooked.

But news of a king's arrival soon spreads.

Æthelwin nudged Oswiu. "Don't look, but someone has arrived."

In answer, Oswiu pointed at his bandages.

"Looks important," said the warmaster, as the new arrival, accompanied by the door warden, made his way across the hall to the high table, where Penda sat with the queen, his children and closest companions.

The man made the courtesy before the king. Normally, in hall, talk and boasts and singing would have drowned out the conversation between king and new arrival to anyone sitting as far from the high table as Oswiu and his companions, but with so few men present, the hall was uncommonly quiet.

"Edgar." Penda nodded to the man standing in front of him, but made no other move to welcome him.

"My lord, we had not thought to see you so soon."

Penda indicated the sparse meal laid out on the table. "So I see."

Edgar coloured. "If you would come to my hall, I would feast you as befits a king, lord."

"On another night. We spend but one night here, and then ride on."

"Then it is my fortune to have seen you."

"And mine to have seen you, Edgar." Penda made to return to his meal, but Edgar did not withdraw. Penda stopped, bread halfway to his mouth, then sighed and put the bread down again. "What do you want, Edgar?"

"I would speak with you, lord. The witan has tasked me with a message for the king."

"Then give the message and leave me to my supper."

Edgar looked questioningly at the king, then pointedly along the table to where the queen was sitting with the children.

"It's not that again, is it?" said Penda. "Cynewisse?"

"The witan believes the king's honour would be better served..." Edgar began, but Penda interrupted him.

"I will worry about my honour." Penda stared with thoughtful, calculating eyes at the man standing in front of him. "The witan. It was Herefrith and Odda who told you to speak to me on this."

"Lord, the witan speaks as one..."

"Spare me that, Edgar. I know with whose voices the witan speaks. Tell them, from me, that my answer has not changed and will not change: I will not put Cynewisse aside for another, more highly born. Tell them also, when they cavil, that this serves them. I would not grant any of them the advantage that would come from tying their family to me. Thus, they stand equal before their king: service to me shall bring reward; division and treachery shall bring downfall."

"But lord, it is the custom of our people. No son may be called ætheling who has not been born to a queen, yet you call your son Peada ætheling, though he were born when you were not yet king – and the queen certainly wasn't yet a queen."

"By my will Peada is ætheling, as Cynewisse is queen. Take this message to the witan, Edgar. It is my will that Cynewisse is queen, and my will that Peada is ætheling. Should the witan send to me again on such matters, then I will require of it reason that it goes against the will of the king. Do you understand?" Penda picked up his bread again. "Well, Edgar?"

The thegn, although he did not move, seemed to step backwards as all his weight shifted into retreat.

"Now, you may stay and share this meagre feast with us, or take my message and go and deliver it to those that need to hear it." The king stared at Edgar. "What will you do?"

"I-I will go, lord."

"Good."

The thegn made the courtesy and hurried from the hall.

Blind, Oswiu turned to his companions for their words.

"The queen sits as if she heard not a word of that," whispered Acca, "and by that, let's all know the favour in which the king holds her and her children."

"Would that all kings had wives and children worthy of such favour," said Æthelwin.

Before Oswiu could answer, he felt a hand upon his arm.

"The king calls for you," said Acca.

Taking Acca's arm, and letting him act as guide, Oswiu made his way across the hall to the high table.

"Lord." He made the courtesy.

There was a spread of laughter and, from his right, the king's voice, saying, "Hail then, King Cild."

"Your pardon, lord." Oswiu turned towards the king's voice, and made the courtesy again.

"When Brandnoth brought you to me for my protection, I asked whether you played dice, Nothelm the Blind. I would dice with you, but now I must ask how you say to play when you cannot see."

"If others will count, I may throw, lord," said Oswiu.

"Very well, Nothelm the Blind. We will play then."

"I will throw, and most willingly, lord. But to what stakes? I have little a king might want."

"We play for luck, for fortune's favour. Here. Take the dice. Throw."

Oswiu felt a hand – he did not know if it was the king's – push two dice into his grasp.

"What favour will fortune grant if I should win this contest?" asked Oswiu as he rolled the dice between his fingers. The cubes felt smooth and warm to his touch, more like things living than stone.

"My protection to Woden's tree and the field where I killed Oswald."

"And what favour will fortune take should I lose?"

"What have you to lose?" asked Penda. "Your sight has gone and you seek it back. Your lands are far from here and of no value to me. Your friends?"

"I would not lose them for the throw of dice."

"Your life then?"

"Nor so that, when I have come so far to seek these places."

"Your hand then. Your left hand. You'll still be able to eat."

"But after eating…"

"Indeed. That will be difficult." Penda looked searchingly at the bandaged man standing in front of him. There was something about him…

Oswiu's hand flicked, and the dice tumbled across the table, rattling over the wood, bouncing and tumbling while eager eyes – but not his – followed their progress.

The dice came to a rest.

"Six. And six."

A gasp, and hollow cheer, went up from the watching men. Further along the table, Acca saw the queen, Cynewisse, sitting with her women and the children. The queen, he saw, paid no mind to what the king was about to throw.

Then the scop knew.

"Double six."

A second roar, unfeigned and wholehearted, followed the king's score.

Acca sidled to Oswiu's side and, covered by the noise, whispered to him. "The dice are fixed."

"I know," said Oswiu.

But before Acca could ask anything more, Penda held up his hands for quiet. "Thought you had won, then, Nothelm the Blind?"

"I had hoped so."

"Luck's like that: sometimes she's a whore, spreading it everywhere; sometimes she's a virgin, and no one gets it. Throw again?"

In answer, Oswiu held out his hand.

"Better make it your left hand," said Penda. "That's the one that's going if you lose."

So Oswiu took the dice in his left hand. He rolled the cubes between his fingers, feeling them warm and smooth, while the cheering grew louder and less feigned. Though he was the stranger, yet every man present among the king's retainers had played, and lost, at dice with the king. They knew what it was like to play a man whom luck favoured.

Oswiu flicked his wrist. The dice tumbled over the table.

"Six and six!"

All work in the hall had ceased. Even the slaves were sidling closer, hoping that no one, amid the excitement, would see that they had stopped working to better see the game. Only the queen sat apart, and even she was looking with interest to the game.

"Such luck!" said Penda. "Will it rub off?"

He gathered the dice and tossed them.

"Yes!" The cheers were even louder.

Penda picked up the dice and held them up for all to see, turning them as a king might turn a sword or severed head on the battlefield.

Acca, watching, saw Penda clasp one hand with the other before passing the dice back to Oswiu.

"He's switched dice," he said to Æthelwin, not even needing to whisper amid the tumult. But the warmaster could do nothing other than watch.

Oswiu took the dice. For three days he had been without sight. Already, he sought through hearing, smell, and touch, to perceive a world he could no longer see.

The dice felt different. To any ordinary touch – to his own fingers a few days before – there would have been no difference. But now he could tell.

"Last throw," said Penda.

Oswiu put the dice to his lips and kissed them. His lips moved, but no one there could hear which god he invoked.

A flick.

The dice tumbled, bouncing, spinning, coming to rest…

"Six!" A quick, cut-off cheer.

"And five!" The cheer was long: the stranger's luck was good. But the king's luck was better.

Penda rubbed the dice between his fingers. His luck. His fortune.

"If you win, I take you to Woden's tree and Maserfield. If I win, I take your hand."

"Yes." Oswiu felt the air, tight at the back of his throat. Men still fought with one hand. But few would follow a maimed king.

Penda clicked the dice together, rattling them, as the watching men gathered tight in.

Blind, Oswiu waited for the rattle and bump of stone on wood, but still Penda clicked the dice together, clacking them as teeth on a cold, shivering night.

"Throw, will you!"

Penda threw. The dice hopped and dropped and skipped over the wood, the men turning to cheer as they tumbled, tumbled, fell and settled.

"Five and three…"

The cheers died to puzzled quiet. Men looked, one to the other, shaking their heads in disbelief. Never had they seen this before. The king had lost at dice. His luck, the luck that had taken him to the throne, had left him.

But the king, for his part, laughed. His laugh was loud and long, and there was no act to it.

"You win," Penda said, taking Oswiu's left hand. "You keep this, and I will take you where you wish to go." The king turned to his watching men. "And you – do you think this means the king's luck has gone? Take this chance to learn: the king's luck lies on the battlefield – where I leave my enemies bleeding – and in his bed – where I get my sons. Think on this king's luck: Oswald dead, and there, Peada alive, and the queen with child, and the others, my little pups, that I've given other women. What luck would you have your king have, men? This…" and he gestured to take in the hall and his family, "or this?" And he held up the dice.

The men acclaimed their king, while some took little Peada and carried him on their shoulders around the hall, the little boy pulling the hair of his human horse so hard that, by the end of the circuit, he had tufts of hair in both hands and the man was trying to pull him off.

"More, more," shouted Peada, refusing to dismount, and pulling out more hair as the man tried in vain to get him down.

In the end, and to the jeers of his peers, it took the queen, offering sweetmeat, to lure Peada from his mount. Penda held out his arms and Cynewisse carried the wriggling boy to his father.

"Why did you lose?" Cynewisse asked softly, as she passed the boy to Penda.

"They had come to trust more in the dice than me," said Penda, taking his son. He held the boy up for his men's acclaim. "But I am their luck."

Cynewisse bent closer and whispered into her husband's ear: "And mine."

Chapter 9

"Hold."

The door warden stepped in front of the group of men approaching the hall's great door. The only light came from the taper that burned in the sconce behind the warden, and the red embers of the hearth fire. Dim shadows lay sprawled on bench and floor, breathing night's rhythm, and the dogs lay beside them, twitching in dream.

"Where go you at this hour?"

"My master would take the air." Acca, holding Oswiu's arm and half supporting him, stepped into the taper's flickering light.

The warden looked at Oswiu, his face wrapped in bandages, and shook his head. "The king's word is that none should go forth without his leave in the night."

"We're not going forth. I'm taking my master for some air. He has the belly gripes." Acca gestured at Oswiu's pale face. "Would the king thank you for leaving him to void gut and bowel in his hall?"

The warden gestured at the shadows behind Acca. "What of these men?"

"These are my lord's retainers. Would you have us go out alone? We are strangers here."

The door warden paused, caught between command and courtesy.

"We do not ask for our swords to be returned," added Acca. "Does that not show we mean no harm?"

But as the door warden began to shake his head, Oswiu coughed and began to retch, liquid splashing onto the warden's legs. He skipped aside, then lifted the beam that barred the door, the great spar moving easily upon its pivot.

"Get him out," said the door warden, as Acca half helped, half carried the still wretching Oswiu from the hall, followed closely by Coifi and Æthelwin.

Acca, with Æthelwin taking the king's other arm, helped Oswiu down the steps from the hall. Behind them, the door closed, shutting out the hall light.

The night glittered. Mist pooled at feet and face.

"That way," said Æthelwin, pointing towards the further gate that closed the great enclosure surrounding Penda's hall. Beyond, fields pointed lines of shadow towards the low line of ruins that showed where once the road of the emperors had led: Wroxeter. In the dark, its ruins were darker still, shadow ports where wraiths dwelled and, in the night, prowled. Men did not live in such places any more, but built their halls and houses, made of living wood not cold stone, far from the old, crumbled walls.

But before they reached the gate, the men stopped. Æthelwin looked into a low, thatched hut, open mouthed to the night, and sunk into the earth.

"Clear," he said.

The little group disappeared into the dark.

"Æthelwin, take watch."

"Lord."

In the dark of the hut, Oswiu pulled the bandages from his face.

"It's good to get these off," he said. He looked around. "But I still can't see anything."

"I'm standing in something squishy," said Acca.

Coifi sniffed. "I think this might be where they slaughtered supper."

"I wish you hadn't said that," said Acca, squishing.

"Some light." Oswiu, with movements so practised he had no need of light, took flint and steel from his belt, and struck, once, twice, sparks, each as bright as stars, that caught the tinder and lit it.

"Eurgh," said Acca, looking down at what his feet had been squelching in.

"Stop!" said Coifi. "Don't move."

Acca froze, staring at the old priest. "What?" he said.

Coifi held up his hand. "Wait," he said. "Wait…"

"Yes?"

Coifi shook his head. "No. Nothing. Just wanted to keep you standing in sheep guts a while longer."

"What? You…"

As Acca stepped out of the entrails and approached the grinning priest, Oswiu held up his hand.

"Enough," he said. "We're here to decide what to do. Æthelwin?"

From his position at the door, the warmaster answered. "Take our horses, ride now to Woden's tree, find Oswald's remains and escape."

"Penda would find us gone. Do you not think he would send men after us? I would, in my kingdom. Do you think we can escape them and reach the tree first, Æthelwin?"

"If we go now, there is a good chance."

Oswiu shook his head. "I doubt the wisdom of this plan." The king turned to the scop. "Acca?"

"I leave such matters to you."

"Coifi? What do you see?"

The priest shook his head. "I know not what I see, lord. Before your brother returned, I saw victory for Osric when there was only death. Then I saw death for Eanfrith when it was too late to thwart it. My sight is vain and my counsel weak."

"You saw my brother's death."

Coifi stared at Oswiu. "Yes," he said.

"Do you see mine?"

Coifi fell silent. He looked at the young king through the shifting play of light and shadow. "Yes."

Oswiu nodded, slowly. "How do you see it?"

"B-before a great dark tree, hung with offerings to the gods."

"Sounds like where we're going."

"I-I have not seen that place with my eyes, lord. I do not know if it be where we go."

"There can't be that many trees hung with offerings to the gods." Closing his eyes, Oswiu thought aloud. "If we return now, I will have failed my brother and my mother. Mother said Oswald fights for us still. Mayhap he contends with the fate weavers too. Besides, we follow a different god now, and he is not tied by the weavers, as the old gods were."

Oswiu opened his eyes, and the flickering light caught in them. "It seems to me we live in times when all is changing, and what our fathers took as solid and secure we can no longer trust. Mayhap the fate weavers no longer hold the lives of men in their loom. Mayhap we are free, although the gods be not." Oswiu grinned, a fierce, wolf grin, his eyes going into shadow. "I threw the dice with Penda, and won. We shall throw the dice again: we ride with him to the tree. Then, when no cure comes to me, we shall venture to stay in its space, in hope of healing, waiting for the king to leave. When he has gone, then we can take my brother, and escape." Oswiu's grin grew broader. "I begin to enjoy this game of masks: though I speak to Penda face to face, he remembers me not from when I spoke to him before, standing at my brother's side." The king looked to his three companions. "Will you follow me, then? On this final throw? If Coifi sees truly, then I lead you to your death. I will not hold you to my side by pledge and oath, but only by love."

In answer, Coifi took the king's hand and kissed it, then knelt. Æthelwin likewise went down on his knee. Last of all, but not less willing, Acca put knee to ground.

Squelch.

"Oh, yuck."

*

Penda lay amid corpses – corpses piled so thick upon him that he could not move, though he alone was living among the stinking, bloody dead. His eyes, which alone he could move, searched wildly, looking, looking.

He knew it was there.

And it was.

The slaughter bird.

Picking its way over the mountain of the slain, setting its black feet on face and leg and arm, head turning this way and that as it searched for something living amid the unmoving dead.

Something like an eye.

It was a dream. Even in the dream, Penda knew it, but still the fear loosened his bowels and he felt the stinking release as he tried to fix his eyes, to stop them moving, when everything in him tried to turn his gaze towards the approaching, searching raven.

He looked. He could not help himself. He looked.

The bird stopped. It turned its head one way, away, and then, slowly, it turned its head back again. Its great, heavy butcher's beak clacked and its black eyes found his white, staring eyes, and the slaughter bird began to pick its way towards where he lay, buried among corpses, with only his single, staring eye free.

In some low, distant part of this dream world, Penda knew how it would all end: with him screaming to waking as the slaughter bird pecked his eye from his head.

But, this time, that was not how the dream ended.

A figure, cloaked and cowled, with a staff in his hand, appeared behind the raven. The man lived and moved, though Penda could not see his face for the shadows under his hood. And the raven stopped. The slaughter bird lowered its head and coughed, then took to wing, beating the air with long, slow beats. The hooded man, stepping on the bodies that lay beneath his feet, approached the mound where Penda lay buried.

As the figure approached, Penda began to hear, in the silence of this place of the dead, one crack and then another. Each time the hooded man took a step, it was accompanied by cracks. Then he realized what it was he heard. The breaking of dead men's bones, as the hooded man walked over their bodies.

The relief he had felt when the slaughter bird took wing drained from him. Now the fear returned, greater than before.

The hooded man came to the mound of bodies where Penda lay.

"You see not that which is before you." The hooded man stretched out his hand. "Let me help you."

He reached for Penda's eye.

*

Penda woke, screaming, reaching for his eye.

He looked around, sweating, but the face of the girl, eyes wide with terror, that he saw beside him told that he saw still.

"Lord?" She began to reach to him, but Penda pushed her off.

"Get away from me." He looked around wildly. "Cynewisse? Cynewisse?"

The queen had not needed his call; she had woken with his scream and already rushed to the king. Pulling the slave girl from the bed, she took Penda in her arms, cradling him, rocking him, as the shudders of waking were slowly spent.

"The dream," Cynewisse said. She did not have to ask. The king slept soundly, save only when the dream, always the same dream, took him.

But Penda shook his head. He pulled back from his wife.

"It was different. There was a man – I could not see his face. He told me I saw not that which is before me and he took my eye, and gave me his." Penda withdrew from dream memory, and looked at the queen. "But I see now. Yes, I see clearly now."

Chapter 10

"What hear you of these wonders?"

Coifi, riding in his usual daze of discomfort, started and almost fell from his horse. They had risen with the dawn and had been riding since sunrise – far too long for his aching thighs and rhythm-drowsed mind. The fording of the River Severn, which his animal had picked its way across with all the suspicion of a mother greeting a suitor for her daughter, had wet his feet and woken his mind, but the long ride since, along the decaying remains of the emperors' road, had lulled him to quiet.

Grabbing his horse's mane, he pulled himself upright, then looked to see who spoke to him.

It was Penda's priest.

Coifi had seen him the previous night, sat at the high table, alone and away from the queen and her women, and the other men: a man set apart. Even without the cloak – a wolf pelt with the jaw sat upon the man's head – Coifi would have known him as a priest: his eyes turned hither and thither, sometimes rolling like a newborn's, sometimes darting like a bird's. They were the eyes of a man searching, always searching, for the signs of wyrd. But though Coifi had seen him, he had not sought him out, despite Penda's wish. Now the man came to him.

"I have heard much, and seen also," said Coifi. "For one among us, the scop, was without voice, and now can speak – and will, without ceasing, if you give him chance. As to others, I have heard tell of a king's messenger whose horse was healed after being struck by an ælf arrow, and of a girl, paralysed, who can now walk. What tales have you heard?"

"Those, and this: a Briton, riding where King Oswald fell, saw the grass greener and more lush than anywhere else and, thinking it must have a great power on account of the blood spilled there, he gathered some of the earth in a cloth and took it with him. When, that night, he took shelter with some householders in a village, they invited him to join their feast and he hung the cloth, with the soil, upon a post in the house. But amid the feasting, the fire in the centre of the room grew too fierce, and sparks from it flew up into the ceiling and set the thatch there to fire, forcing everyone to flee the house. The fire consumed everything, save the post upon which the Briton had hung the earth from Maserfield, which remained whole and untouched by the flames." Wihtrun looked at Coifi. "I give you the story as it was given me. What think you of it? Whence comes this power?"

"I – I do not know," said Coifi. "Men say there was power in the High King – I have heard tell that there is a prophecy that his right hand will not know decay – and mayhap this power brings such wonders about."

"Oswald hangs before Woden's tree; his head and his arms. The king has taken his body, and his flag, and carries it with him."

"Oswald's body is here?" Coifi asked, startled.

Wihtrun looked askance at him. "Do you expect the king to set the body upon a horse? No. It is with the wagons."

"Yes. Yes, of course."

"Men must think it is Woden's power by which these wonders occur. Already, too many turn away from the ways of our fathers. Northumbria, Kent, the East Angles and the East Saxons: they turn their faces to this new god. All men know how Oswald defeated Cadwallon through the power of this new god, and many turned to him as a result. But now my king, Penda, has defeated him, surely they will see there is no victory, no power in this god? Yet still they come to where Oswald's blood flowed, to where he hangs, and seek miracles of him – as you do. You must join me in telling this: it is by the blessing of the Lord of the Slain that this dead man does such deeds."

"It would be better if such wonders were not, than that we try to make men believe they come through the Hanged One. He is not one to give favour to a horse – or to a Briton."

"My king knows this well. We go to see what truth there be

in these wonders. But he has told me that once we have seen for ourselves, then he will take Oswald's head and arms and burn them, and scatter the ashes in the sea, that his power be gone from this place forever and his memory be lost in the waves."

Coifi nodded, his throat suddenly tight. "That – that is well," he said. He felt, scrabbling at the corners of sight and mind, the first scratchings of sight, the wyrd sight that fell upon him sometimes, without warning or cause; and he fought against it. Not here, not now; gathering what shreds of pride he had left: not in front of another priest.

"If he has such great power, let him save his remains from the flames," said Wihtrun. He looked ahead as he spoke, his gaze exultant. "When men smell the sweet smell, they will know there is no power in this new god – this god who could not give victory to his favourite – and they will return to the old ways, the ways of our fathers; the ways that gave this land to us." He turned to look at Coifi, riding beside him. "That will be a fine day."

Coifi nodded, not trusting himself to speak. He felt the blood rushing through his head, and the closing in of sight; sweat, cold and sticky, pierced his skin, beading his forehead and pricking his back.

Wihtrun leaned over and grasped Coifi's arm.

"Make pledge to me. When we have burned Oswald, you will take news of his burning, and the blessing of Woden, and tell all you meet, in Mercia and Lindsey, in all the kingdoms of this land. Make pledge."

Coifi could not shake off the man's grip, nor the growing grip of the wyrd sight.

"I – I pledge," he said. And the wyrd sight broke upon him, in a single vision, and he saw a man, standing upon a field of blood, surrounded by the slain, making a cross upon his body and calling blessing upon the dead: he saw Oswald, at his ending. And as suddenly as it had come upon him, the wyrd sight left, leaving him limp but still upon the horse, and Wihtrun unknowing of what he had seen, for it was the sight of a moment, though it had seemed hours.

"I – I pledge to tell the power I find," Coifi whispered. Satisfied, Wihtrun let him go, and rode on, while Coifi sat, spent and pale, upon his horse, and wondered.

*

The column of riders made good pace. Although here, in the marches between Mercia and Powys, there were few villagers to keep and repair the emperors' road, yet most of it remained in good enough condition for horse and rider to proceed without fear of the unexpected hole that might pitch man from animal, or break a beast's leg. Penda rode near the column's head, with his son alongside him, bouncing upon a pony. Following in the middle of the column, Acca could still see the king and ætheling clearly, and he told Oswiu of what he saw: the boy, sitting proud beside his father, taking as his own the courtesy the advance riders made to the king on their return from scouting ahead, while the pony trotted hard to keep pace with the long-legged horse beside it. But when the little animal began to flag, Acca saw the ætheling turn at once to whip and kick, flailing with his heels and setting to the animal with leather to such effect that he drew wheals across the animal's haunches. This Acca did not tell the king, for the day by then had drawn up to its noon, and the king swayed upon his horse, blind and bandaged: without sight, he sank into the walking rhythm and the scop took note of his waking rest, and left him to it.

Then Acca saw Penda mark the boy's anger at his beast, and the cuff the king gave him, which made the boy all but fall from his mount. He saw the look the boy gave his father, the rage of it, and he saw well how Penda saw the boy's anger and laughed at it.

"Go ride with your mother."

The king's command carried, even down the column to where Acca rode, and the boy turned his pony away and sent it careering down the side of the column, pulling reins so hard that blood flecked the bridle foam.

Æthelwin, seeing the boy ride past, nodded to him and said to Acca, "Men say that none so threatens a throne but those born from it. Seems King Penda knows this well, and would halter the ætheling before he runs free."

Before Acca could reply, another rider made his way back along the column.

"The king would ride with Nothelm the Blind."

Acca nudged Oswiu to full waking. "Penda wants to ride with you."

But when Acca and Æthelwin made to accompany Oswiu, the messenger held up his hand.

"The king would ride with Nothelm the Blind alone."

Then, taking the reins of Oswiu's horse, the rider led him forward.

Acca looked the question to Æthelwin, but the warmaster shrugged. Here, in the middle of a column of Penda's men, there was nothing they could do but wait.

"Nothelm the Blind." Penda waited for Oswiu to settle his horse beside him, matching stride with the king. "As you have no sight, I would describe to you that which lies ahead, for we are approaching Woden's tree, where I gave the god the head and arms of Oswald, my enemy. Or would you rather we first went to where I slew him? Many wonders, they say, have been done there: mayhap your sight's return would be another of them."

Oswiu made the courtesy to the king. "I will go where you wish, lord."

"Yes," said Penda.

The king rode in silence for a while. Oswiu, blind behind his bandages, reached out with his other senses. He heard the crunch of hooves on gravel, the movement of harness, the call of birds, and the breath of their beasts. He smelled animals, and men, and the wind blowing fresh from the west into his face. But most of all he felt for the mood of the king beside him – and could not find it. He felt his skin prickle, and knew that he was watched, but knew well that he must give no sign of it.

"A king may not be blind."

Although he had waited upon Penda speaking, when he did again, he surprised Oswiu.

"No, lord."

"Mayhap a thegn may retain his hall without sight – as you have – but a king must see. He must be able to look men in the face – in the eye – to tell if they be true. What say you to that, Nothelm the Blind?"

"I say to that: would that I might see again."

"Indeed. Then I might see you face to face, I might look you in the eye and see if you be true, Nothelm the Blind."

"Do you wish me to remove these bandages now, lord, that you might see my eyes? I will, if that is your wish." And Oswiu reached a hand to his bandaged head.

"No. No. Keep your eyes hid. Come, I will be your eyes until sight is restored to you. We ride the old road of the emperors that runs through my kingdom: east to the narrow sea, and west through these marches and on into the kingdoms of the Britons. Ahead, though you do not see, the land rises: I see lines of hills, and their cloud blankets. There are woods at the base of the hills, though none near this road, and fields, though the land here is hard and clinging, sticking to foot and to hoof and to plough. A man may drag a crop from this land to feed his family, but the earth will take his sweat now and his bones soon. I have heard the soil of Lindsey is rich and generous."

"So men say, lord."

"If only you had sight to see, Nothelm the Blind, for there is a wonder ahead. We draw near to Woden's tree; already I can see the hills rise and the crown of green where the tree stands. But before we come to the tree, there is a hill of the old ones, called Caer Gogyrfan in their language, and it is set about with mighty walls and ditches. None live there now, for it is wraith haunted, but I have climbed to it and stood upon it, and they have whispered to me of their might, when all this land was theirs. Then – do you know what I said to them?"

By the change in sound, Oswiu knew that Penda had turned to him for answer.

"No, lord. What did you say to them?"

"I told them that this kingdom was mine now, and they were but wraiths, shadows of men, lingering among the living when they should be with the dead. And they left me."

The hooves of their animals crunched onwards, the sound deadening as gravel in places gave way to earth and mud, then crunched again.

"We pass in the shadow of Caer Gogyrfan now, Nothelm the Blind. In our tongue, it means the city of Gogyrfan. The Britons say Gogyrfan was a giant, the father of Guinevere, Arthur's queen and Arthur's bane. But then the Britons say many things of Arthur, and most of all they wait for him. And in waiting, they leave the land to us."

It seemed to Oswiu that the column of riders had fallen into something approaching silence. It might have been weariness from the long ride – he could feel the sun upon his face and, through his bandages, see its brightness in front of him as it swung low in the sky – but there seemed to him to be something more to the silence.

"Ah, they feel it. Ever when I pass here, a silence falls upon man and beast. In the shadow of Caer Gogyrfan, men hold their tongues and beasts pass uneasily. They watch. From the hill the ancient old ones watch, and curse the living their life."

"I-I feel of that too."

"They say the blind see more deeply than the sighted. Have you found that so, Nothelm the Blind?"

"I have not long been blind, lord. But it is true that without sight I hear and smell and feel what I did not before."

"Then it is almost a shame that your eyes should be restored to you."

"If such should happen, lord, I think I would not find it so."

"Nor would I, I suppose, if my sight were lost to me. But tell me, Nothelm the Blind, before your sight was lost, what did your eyes see? We have passed beyond the shadow of Caer Gogyrfan. There is still a little way to Woden's tree, and I would hear some tale of wonder from you ere we get there. Can you feel the road rising? We climb towards the hill of the tree."

"Yes, I can feel it."

"Then while we ascend to Woden's tree, where I offered Oswald to the Hooded God, tell me what you saw when you had sight. What wonders? Where did you travel? Did you ever see the Great Wall, the work of giants that runs from sea to sea? It is far north, of course. I expect you did not travel so far. Or York? That is closer. Men say its wall still stands."

"Men also say that Penda travelled much in those lands, when Cadwallon ravaged them and laid them waste. Why do you ask of me what you have seen with your own eyes?"

"One man may see what another might miss. And this journey has been long, and weary work. I but thought to share some words with one whose talk I knew only a little, rather than those whose tales I have heard, and heard again. But it is near done. Though you cannot see it, I see the grove atop the hill where grows Woden's tree. You gave to me to choose where first we should go: we go here. Maserfield is but a field, and even of the blood it swallowed there is no sign. But here there is trace, and more, of my victory. Mayhap it will bring you sight. Then, when I have seen what truth there is in these tales, I will take Oswald's head and arms and make of them a burnt offering to the gods, and have an end to these tales."

"But lord, I had thought to wait here a while if healing came not at once, and see if it would come later."

Penda laughed. "Think you truly I would leave you here when I had gone? No. We throw the dice and let them fall. Now, I would speak with my warmaster. Wait here for your companions, Nothelm the Blind. They will accompany you to Woden's tree."

Oswiu pulled gently on his horse's reins, bringing the animal to a halt. The riders flowed past until Acca, Coifi and Æthelwin caught up with him.

"He knows," Oswiu said, pitching his voice so only his companions might hear. "Penda knows who I am."

"You are sure of this, lord?" asked Æthelwin.

"Yes. He knows."

"Then why does he allow us to ride, unbound and alive, with him?"

"Mayhap he plays with me, as a cat with a mouse."

"I know," said Coifi. "We ride to Woden's tree. Penda would make a new offering to the god." The priest looked at his companions. He did not have to voice what the offering might be.

"That is what you saw, Coifi?" asked Oswiu.

"Yes, lord. I am sorry."

"The sorrow will be as much mine – should your sight come to pass. But think on this, friends: oft times, when a cat plays with a mouse, the mouse escapes. Besides –" and here the king smiled, so that his teeth showed sharp – "I am not a mouse."

And though they rode to death, there was no falsity in the king's smile: he smiled for the joy of it, and his smile spread among his companions.

"Think on this: ere this day's ending, we shall either stand in the Lord's hall, or have such a tale to tell that Acca will not cease from singing it all the days of his life – nor all the scops of days to come. This is better than the honey words of false counsellors or the pullings of women. So take heart and keep for me the watch I cannot yet. Penda takes us where we would go: there, my brother waits. So, tell me: what do you see?"

"We ride in mid column," said Æthelwin. "The king ahead. Behind, there are fifteen men, well mounted. Though they ride not close, there is no escape here without cover or attack."

"Acca?" asked Oswiu.

"I hear the hooves of the horses strike rhythm on the emperors' road; I have told tale to this rhythm and I will tell it again, should we live for me to tell it. I see the road rise, and to its right, upon the ridge, a green crown: the trees of a grove held over to the gods. The trees are thick there. Behind, not long have we passed another hill, ringed with ditch and bank; in passing it, I saw many a man make sign against the evil eye. Few of these would pass willingly onto its height."

"That was Caer Gogyrfan," said Oswiu. "Penda told me a giant raised its walls. Though his men might baulk before it, he would not, for he knows it of old and has faced down its fear. Coifi, what do you see?"

"I see your death, lord."

"Yes, yes. Apart from that. What do you see now?"

"I-I see us ride into shadows, lord." The old priest pulled the tattered old raven-feather cloak around his thin shoulders. "It is cold, and we ride to it, and I can see nothing in the shadows. But – but I hear…"

And as Coifi spoke, there came, over the crunch of hoof on gravel and the creak of harness and the weary conversation of men long riding, the unmistakable creaking call of the raven.

"Bran?" said Oswiu. He turned his head, searching for the sound. "Bran is here?"

The call came again. It was as yet distant, but it was coming closer.

"There," said Acca, pointing. And he saw true, for beating through the air, a great black raven approached, stiff winged and calling. The riders at the head of the column pointed its approach, then marked how it swooped low over them, calling, before rolling sideways and turning back to fly to the grove whence it had come.

"I have heard tell," said Coifi, "that a great raven stands watch upon Oswald, where he hangs before Woden's tree, and will not suffer beast nor bird to approach him."

"He knows we are coming," said Oswiu. "Bran has kept him for us; now he knows we are here."

At the head of the column, Penda called his priest to him.

"Wihtrun. Did you mark that bird, that raven?"

"Yes, lord," said the priest. He rode, as was required, a mare. A priest might not ride a stallion, nor bear spear, the mark of a free man, for he was bound to the service of the gods; he was no free man, but slave to the gods.

"What make you of it?"

"It is a mark of Woden's favour; come to greet you as you approach the tree set aside to him."

"But what of the tales of a raven that guards Oswald's remains? Have you heard tell of this?"

"I have, lord, and give thanks to the Lord of the Slain: for all the slaughter birds are his, tale bringers and messengers. To set such a one as guard upon our offering to him is a mark of his great favour."

"Oswald had such a bird. I saw it. It was with him the day he fell; some say it is this bird that guards him."

"What use is such a guard? Oswald is dead – why set a guard upon the dead? No, this raven belongs to the Raven God, the Lord of Battles, the Wolf Rider, the Frenzy Giver. He comes to greet you, gift giver."

"Then give him news, priest. Tell him I bring further gifts for the Lord of the Slain."

"I will tell him, lord." The priest paused. "What gifts do you bring, lord? We have left the wagons behind."

"Some gifts are easier to carry than others. Some gifts even bring themselves."

While Wihtrun the priest rode ahead, urging his horse up the path to the low hill crowned with Woden's grove, Oswiu and his companions rode in watchful silence.

The king, Penda, gave no sign of moving against them. But the day was drawing down – already the sun dipped behind the western hills. Shadows dripped from where they had hidden through the day, amid the leaves and branches of trees, and flowed out from wood and spinney and grove. The last streaks of light ran into the east, fleeing from the sun's setting.

"There will be chance in the night," said Æthelwin. "We might slip away then."

"Penda will not give us that chance," said Oswiu. "We must find, or make, another."

"Torches!"

The command went up from the head of the column, where Penda rode now with his warmaster, and the men pulled, from saddle or pack, brands wrapped in cloth, steeped in wax and fat. Steel rasped on flint, sparks flared, and the brands burned.

The approaching dusk was held at bay. Even full night would be driven back a little way before so many bright torches. Only Oswiu and his companions rode without torches: a patch of darkness in the centre of the bright, blazing column of riders that now began to make its way up the slope to the place of the god.

The path ran straight up the slope, for the way was not too steep for horse or man, but it was deeply rutted, for winter rains washed earth and even smaller stones away.

Coming out onto the wide ridge, Oswiu's companions saw the land fall away gently beyond, before rising in steps again into the west, towards more distant, dark hills. The sun had set behind the western hills now, but the king gave no command to set camp for the night, riding on towards the grove hallowed to the god.

The outer trees were rowan and oak, but most of all ash, sending branches curving up to the darkening sky. The trees were hung with offerings: shields, weather worn and bright and new; spears, dangling from branches like seed pods; tokens of cloth and carvings and rune-carved stones, set in branch curve and trunk hollow. Below, there had been but little wind, but here, on the ridge, it blew strong and steady, and the trees creaked and clacked with their burden of offerings. But these were minor sacrifices: made by those with little to give or smaller desire to return favour after favour was given. The richest offerings would lie at the heart of the grove, where Woden's tree grew.

As they neared the grove, Penda signed for silence, but in truth there was no need. Before such a place, men did not speak but trod warily, lest they draw the god's gaze to them.

Through that silence came the raven's call, creaking louder than any tree, and man and beast paused before it.

But Wihtrun called them on. For he waited now upon the boundary of the grove, standing beside his horse, the wolf cloak drawn around his shoulders, the beast's gaping mouth now set upon his forehead. Its eyes were black, though the torches burned.

Reaching the priest, Penda dismounted, and the other riders likewise, for it was not permitted that a man might ride in the presence of the god. Penda spoke briefly with his warmaster, who called some half of the men to him to wait outside the grove and guard the horses.

"We will not camp here," Penda assured his men. "This is no

place for night sleeping. After we have greeted the god, we will go down the hill and spend the night there – out of this wind." The king gestured to Oswiu and his companions. "Come. You will accompany us. After all, you have come far in search of healing; I would not have you wait another night."

As Penda stepped through the line of willow wands that marked the boundary of the sacred grove, Æthelwin looked to see if there would be chance to slip away into the dark beneath the trees, but Penda's men followed after as well as before, their torches scattering flickering light beneath the ceiling of whispering leaves.

Oswiu, walking in the blindness of his disguise, led by his companions, could not see the darkness that surrounded them, and that was for his blessing. For without sight, he felt his brother's presence and he knew that Oswald walked beside him.

"Wait." Penda held up his hand. They had emerged from the grove into the space that stood at its heart, a space with a single tree at its centre.

An ash tree, greater and taller than any of the others, its branches upcurved and weighed down with the offerings that ladened it: battle-won swords and shields, the sacrifice of herd and hearth. Oswiu smelled the blood iron of many offerings: ox and goat and horse. They hung upon the tree, some still fleshed, flanks crawling in the torchlight with the wriggling creatures that consumed the offering, others reduced to bone, gazing down upon them with shadow eyes.

Beside him, he heard Acca gasp, and Coifi's sharp breath.

The ground before the tree was spiked with stakes. On these hung the great offerings, the richest gifts to the Lord of the Slain: the slain themselves. Men they had known, whom they had sat next to in the great hall at Ad Gefrin and ridden beside on long and weary journeys, swapping tales and jokes and shared complaints against rain and wind and road.

And before the great tree, three stakes set apart from the rest. A hand and arm hung from each of the outer stakes, but on the centre stake there was a head.

"He's looking at us," whispered Acca.

For it was true. Oswald's head was set upon that stake, but it was turned outwards, so that it looked to all who came to the tree, rather than facing inwards to the tree itself.

"Wait here." Penda turned and looked back at his men, then, alone, advanced towards the tree. But his gaze was turned not to the tree, but to the man he had killed and set before the tree.

"Oswald."

Penda stopped in front of the stake where he had set the king's head. When he had put it there, he had left the head turned towards the tree, that the god might see the offering given him, but now Oswald had turned from the tree and looked outwards, and Penda would know how.

But first, he had a message for the king.

Penda bent closer to the head, holding his torch that he might see it more clearly. It was true. Save for the wound at the temple, the death wound that had pierced flesh and bone, the head was unmarked. He pushed his thumb against the cheek, and the skin gave way under his touch, then sprang back when he took the thumb away. The eyes were closed, but suddenly Penda was filled with a bowel fear that they might open and hold him in sight, fixed and unmoving.

"No," the king said. "No, Oswald. That won't work on me. When I'm done here, I'm going to burn you." Penda leaned closer to the head, whispered to it. "But before I do, I want you to know this: I killed you, and gave you to Woden, and your god could not protect you. Now I'm going to kill your brother too."

Penda turned around. He gestured to his men.

"Bring me Nothelm the Blind."

Two of Penda's men approached Oswiu. His companions backed towards him, hands inching towards sword hilt, but Oswiu, sensing their tension, laid hand to arm.

"No," he whispered. "Not yet. Wait for my sign, then come to me." Above him, with hearing made sharper by his blindness, he heard movement and feather rattle. Then, when Penda's men took his arms to guide him across the clearing, he heard the bough creak as a weight released it, and the rush of flight above the reach of the torches.

Oswiu followed the sound. He heard the bird land upon the tree in front of him and, though he could not see, he knew it waited upon Woden's tree.

Penda's men brought him to the king. Oswiu could feel the heat of the brands they carried, and he could feel the heat withdraw as, with unspoken gesture, Penda dismissed them.

He was alone with Penda now, set apart from the others at the far side of the space that hollowed out the hallowed ground, standing before the tree.

"Here he is," said Penda. "Oswald. Or part of him. The rest I keep with me, wrapped in the banner I took when I killed him. If there was power in him, I took it. There is no healing for you here, Nothelm the Blind."

But as Penda spoke, from the tree there came the rasping cough of the slaughter bird. Oswiu heard Penda start, and knew that the king looked up, aware that the raven was there but not able to see the bird.

"Bran says otherwise."

Penda glanced at the man beside him, then searched the tree again. "It is just a bird. It has no name."

"His name is Bran."

"My priest says he is Woden's bird."

"No. Bran belongs to no one, but he is faithful to one, and that is not your god."

"How know you this, Nothelm the Blind?"

"You know well I am not Nothelm the Blind, but Oswiu, Oswald's brother. How did you know me? You did not at the start."

"The god told me. In a dream last night. When did you know I knew?"

"Early this day, when I rode with you."

"Then you hid it well. You are brave, Oswald brother. I will kill you quickly. But as you came in blindness, I will give your eyes to the god."

"I have come a long way to see my brother. I would look on Oswald, while I may."

"Look then, Nothelm the Blind, and tell me what you see."

Oswiu reached for the bandages wound around his head. His fingers found their end, and he began unwinding them, round and round and round, until they lay loose, looped over his shoulders, and only one final piece of cloth covered his eyes. Then he lowered that.

Penda stood beside him, but he did not look to him.

Oswiu stared at his brother.

And in the torchlight, Oswald looked upon him.

Then, slowly, Oswiu bent to that face he knew better than any other, and he kissed Oswald on the brow.

"Ready, brother?" he whispered.

And he heard answer in his heart.

Oswiu turned his head. He looked upon Penda. And he smiled. "It's a miracle!" he cried.

He stood straight, turning half back towards the waiting men, and cried again, louder this time. "It's a miracle. I can see!"

Gasps of wonder spread among the watching men, and some began moving towards them, but Oswiu held up his hand. "Stop. Do not come closer. The power of the god still lies over me." And Oswiu lifted his arms up and darkness fell from the tree, clad in black feathers, and alighted upon his shoulder.

The raven, the slaughter bird. The black eyes of the Lord of the Slain.

Further gasps and cries came from the watching men. Those who had moved closer stepped back again, in fear and awe. Only Oswiu's own men edged closer, unseen by those watching the raven.

The raven dipped its head and turned its black eyes on Penda.

The king felt the cold sweat of remembered nightmares prick his skin. He could not take his eyes from the great black bird. The raven dipped its head again and cawed, its butcher's bill clacking.

"The power of the god calls to you, king of the Mercians."

Oswiu held his arm out and the raven began to walk down it, towards where Penda stood, transfixed and staring at the bird.

"He calls to you; he calls you to him."

From among the waiting men, Wihtrun called out to his king and his god, "The Lord of the Slain honours the king!"

But Penda did not hear the call. His eyes were fixed upon the bird. Oswiu held the raven out to him. It turned its head, one way then another, its black eyes upon him.

"Take it," whispered Oswiu. "The god would show you his favour."

Penda could hear the gasps and cries of his men. The slaughter bird had come down from Woden's tree. It stood poised to place the god's favour upon him. Though the bowel fear of dream held him, he must needs take the bird upon his arm and receive the god's favour – even though it stepped from the arm of the man he was about to kill.

A smile twitched Penda's face.

Then, after the Lord of the Slain had shown him his favour, he would give Woden a gift in turn: the man's life.

Penda held out his arm.

Bran stepped onto it, his claws digging into the king's flesh.

Another great gasp went up from the watching men.

The bird, its claws pricking, stepped up Penda's arm. The king, seeing its glitter-black eye, pulled his head back and the bird stopped, clinging onto his upper arm. The memory of his dream came to him, sudden and overwhelming; of the raven approaching, stepping over corpses to where he lay buried among the dead.

He must not blink.

Penda stared at the slaughter bird. It turned its head, looking upon him first with one then the other glitter-black eye.

He must not blink.

The raven stared at him.

Penda blinked.

In the moment of blindness, the raven struck. With its butcher's bill the slaughter bird plucked.

"My eye!" Penda fell back, his hands clutching his face. The raven, prize in beak, took wing into the darkness of the great tree.

As Penda knelt upon the ground, Oswiu pulled his brother's head from the stake where it was set, and started running across the grove. Acca and Coifi, having inched closer while Penda's men watched, pulled the arms from the nails that held them to the stakes, while Æthelwin, coming last, held sword against Penda's men. But with Wihtrun crying out to sky and tree that the god had shown his favour to their king, the Mercians hovered between worship and pursuit, unsure what to do. Penda staggered back to his feet, the blood tracks dark upon his face, but he could barely see.

"Back to the horses!" Oswiu cried.

He went first, crashing through the grove, while behind them came the confused sounds of men unsure of what had happened to their king.

Breaking from the grove, Oswiu saw Penda's riders gathered uncertainly around his warmaster.

"Attack!" Oswiu screamed. "The king's under attack."

Ambush was ever a fear for riders at night. Here, in this lonely place, with the cover provided by trees and darkness, the fear was magnified, and became real with the sounds emerging from the darkness under the trees.

Penda's men rushed to protect him. Such was the confusion, and their haste, that they left no one to guard the horses.

While Oswiu and Coifi gathered their own animals, Æthelwin and Acca set to the other animals, wielding seax and sword, cutting hamstrings and tethers, setting the beasts that they could not cripple to flight before running to their own mounts.

"Now, let's go!"

But as his companions urged their animals into motion, Oswiu turned his own to face the grove and Woden's tree. The first torches were beginning to emerge from the trees, but there were no horses left, and none of Penda's men carried bows. He did not look to them. Instead, Oswiu looked to the grove and the single tree that grew at its centre, Woden's tree.

He gave the fist against the god, and he laughed, for life and joy and relief, and he made to turn his horse away.

"Hold!"

The voice rang from the trees, and Oswiu knew it.

Penda stood there, supported by his men, his hand held to his ruined face.

"I will kill you!" Penda screamed.

And Oswiu laughed again.

"Like you killed my brother? You're more dead than he is." He pulled his horse's head around and set him racing down the hill, and he was followed by Penda's curses, but they held no power over him.

And above him, he heard the feather rattle and Bran's call. Oswiu looked up. There, against the stars, blotting them out as it flew, he thought he saw the raven.

"Thank you, Bran."

The slaughter bird coughed once, and again, its call receding. It was going.

"Farewell."

The raven made no answer.

Through the night and through the day that followed, Oswiu and his companions rode, the hooves of their beasts sparking on the emperors' road, outrunning the news of their deeds, going faster than the men Penda set in pursuit, until they came to the Red Dragon. There, Coenred the innkeeper met them with joy at Oswiu's sight, and with gladness sold them fresh animals, and with sorrow bade them farewell, all in the space of an hour, although he would have had them stay and tell their tales.

But they did not rest. They rode on to the River Soar and, riding along it, hailed a boat pulling downriver, and bought passage.

Then finally, sat on its benches, as the boat sailed into the broad channel of the Humber, they looked at each other, and the wonder of it all lit their faces.

"We did it," said Oswiu, taking each of his companions' hands in turn. "By God, we did it."

PART 2

Family

Chapter 1

"You did it. Thanks be to God, you did it." Acha held her son, planting his smiling features once more into her memory.

"Don't sound so surprised, Mother," Oswiu laughed. "You'll make me think it was even more desperate than I thought at the time."

"I prayed. I prayed so hard. Every day that you were away I knelt through all the hours of sun and most of darkness, asking God's blessing for you and calling Oswald to fight for you in heaven as he ever did on this middle-earth. And he did."

"It can't have been just you, Mother," said Oswiu. "Such a feat – to snatch my brother from beneath Penda's nose and to take his eye as well – must have taken the prayers of many, many people. Tell me –" and here Oswiu looked with sudden intent upon his mother – "who prayed for me?"

"Your sister, of course. Æbbe spent near as many hours in prayer as I, and this despite her cares in the monastery you have given to her. Aidan, naturally, and his monks, although they knew nothing of why they prayed with such urgency for you at this time. The children. While you were away, the brothers finished work upon the new church here in Bamburgh, and Bishop Aidan made it holy for the mass. Your children prayed there often for your return."

Oswiu nodded. "And my wife?"

Acha caught the sharpness of the words. "Not everyone is made for prayer, Oswiu. Rhieienmelth prayed for you too, in her own way."

"Where is she now? I had thought she would be here."

"Queen Rhieienmelth... chafes at being too long in one place. She grows restless. To ease her restlessness, she rode to the holy house at Coldingham with your sister, to attend to its business."

"It is not safe." Oswiu shook his head. "I gave order that she should remain here while I was away. What if I had failed, and Penda had come upon you, like the wolf pack when it senses the shepherd is away?"

"That is why she did not take the children."

Oswiu looked around, his glance taking in the great hall, already filling with people as news of the king's return began to filter out to the surrounding settlements. "Where are they? I would see them."

"Children grow more restless even than queens. I gave leave for them to visit Aidan: they took boat to Lindisfarne two days past." Acha smiled. "I think Aidan will be as glad to hear you have returned as they: Ahlflæd drives him to distraction."

"Send word to Aidan, Mother. Ask him to come with the children – I would take counsel from him."

"The boat sailed ere yours landed, my son. I knelt where I could see the sea, and though my eyes are old, they are patient. I saw your ship first."

Oswiu nodded. "Good. It must have been all the more difficult for Aidan, having to keep Ahlflæd and Œthelwald apart."

Acha pursed her lips. "No doubt it would have been. But Œthelwald is not with Ahlflæd and Ahlfrith. The queen took him with her when she went to Coldingham."

Oswiu stared at his mother. He made to ask why the queen did this, but Acha turned her eyes away; she looked to the sack that Oswiu had placed, reverently, upon the high table before speaking with his mother.

"Is he there?" she asked, her voice dropping to a whisper.

"Yes," said Oswiu, his own voice growing quiet as well.

Acha looked back to Oswiu. "Should...should I see him?"

Oswiu nodded. "Yes," he said. "But not here." He took the sack from the table, lifting it carefully. "Come with me."

Leading his mother, Oswiu took Acha from the great hall. Some of his retainers made to follow, but Oswiu waved them away. He walked across the ward to where the new building, without roof when he had left on his long, secret journey south, now stood complete. Candlelight streamed from the open windows, their shutters pushed back, as the wind had died away with the setting of the sun, and the evening was yet mild. Through the window came the high, clear sound of voices chanting the work of the monks: calling down blessings upon this middle-earth, that all might flourish. But this being a church in the first and greatest stronghold of the Idings, blessings were called down, first and foremost, upon the king.

Entering the church, Oswiu saw the three monks Aidan had left at Bamburgh to offer prayer kneeling before the altar. Hearing his entrance, the monks looked round from their chant and then, one by one, fell to silence. Standing, they made the courtesy to the king.

"Leave us," said Oswiu. "But first, close the shutters and then the door."

"Lord?" The first of the monks, a weather-beaten man of more than middle years, whose scars gave testimony to a life once lived more among swords and shields than prayer and chant, looked askance at the king.

"I – I would show my mother something. It would be best if this were done where no other eye can see."

The monk made the courtesy. "Very well, lord."

As he and his two companions made their way around the church, closing the shutters, Oswiu could feel the impatience radiating from his mother – but also the trepidation.

The monks closed the door behind them and the church became dark: only candles and tapers lit it now, throwing shifting shadows upon the rough walls.

"Wh-where should we do this?" Acha asked, her voice even more breathlike in the quiet of the church.

Oswiu looked around. The quiet was unnerving. He realized how very few places of silence there were for him, surrounded as he always was by people: retainers, servants, slaves, appellants. But the silence seemed to flow, in some way, from the sack he held in his hands. It was a sacred silence.

Oswiu looked to the altar. "There," he said.

They walked up the nave, their feet making scarcely a sound upon the reed matting, until they reached the sanctuary.

"Wait," said Oswiu. He went on, to the altar. The table of sacrifice was draped in rich cloth, gold woven into purple. Oswiu placed the sack upon the altar, and then carefully untied the rope binding it and folded back the material.

"Mother," Oswiu said. "He is here. He is waiting for you."

Oswiu heard the quiet steps approaching. Then Acha stood there beside him.

"Oswald," she said. "My son."

The old queen stood dry eyed before her son. But her face was pale and her hands trembled. Acha, in memory, took out all the images of Oswald that she had fixed in her mind against the day – against this day, when she would see him without life. She saw him, in her mind, as a baby born and bawling; as a boy, walking and running and always listening to tales; as a youth, when they fled into exile, taking charge of his younger brother and sister; and as a man, when he came to her and said that he would lay aside his sword and enter, as a monk, the holy island of Iona. She remembered all these and more, for each time he had left her, she had fixed his face in her mind anew, all against this day.

And now the day was here, and she was hollow with memories, and they were as nothing before the head of her boy, laid upon the altar.

"W-would you leave me with him?"

Her voice was scarce more than a whisper, but she could not have raised it higher, even if life itself demanded it.

As Oswiu made to go, he saw his mother smooth the hair from the death wound at his brother's temple. The sound his feet made on the rush matting as he walked down the nave was almost enough to mask the sound of his mother's sobbing. Almost, but not quite.

Closing the door to the church, Oswiu leaned against the wood, resting his forehead on the oak panel. It felt cool against his skin. He paused for a moment, gathering himself. It would not do for people to see him like this.

"Daddy!" The cry echoed across the courtyard, swiftly followed by the crier. Ahlflæd was running towards him, her dress held up above her knees, to the outrage of the lady squawking behind her. With the freedom of movement that allowed, she was easily outpacing her scarlet-faced brother.

Ahlflæd, from a good six-foot distance, launched herself at her father and made the jump with ease, such was the pace of her approach.

"You're back!"

"I'm back!"

"She cheated!" Ahlfrith plucked at his father's sleeve. "When the door warden told us you were back, she tripped me up just as I started running."

Freeing one arm, Oswiu ruffled his son's hair. "Next time, lad, trip her first."

Ahlflæd, poking her head over her father's arm, stuck her tongue out at her brother. "He's so slow; he'll never catch me."

"You…" Enraged, Ahlfrith made to leap at his sister, but Oswiu caught him up and pulled the two children together in a single embrace.

"I'm back," he said. And as the words sank in, he swung his children around, whirling in the courtyard of the great stronghold until they all sank in a dizzy, laughing heap onto the ground. As he lay in that heap, his children piled on top of him, with sky and rock and ramparts spinning around him, Oswiu repeated the simple, extraordinary truth.

"I'm back!"

*

"Why didn't you go with your mother?" Oswiu stood with his children upon the rampart of their stronghold. "Why didn't you go with the queen?"

Ahlflæd, of course, was the first to answer. She made a moue with her lips.

"She took him with her. I told Mummy that if she took him with her, I wouldn't come."

"But she has to look after your cousin," said Oswiu. "We – I – promised we would."

"He's horrid!" said Ahlfrith, clenching his fist. "If he wasn't so much smaller than me, I'd hit him." The boy looked up at his father hopefully. "Can I hit him, Daddy? Just a few times?"

"No, you can't," said Oswiu.

"Just once?"

"No."

The boy, still not dissuaded from retribution, pointed at his sister. "What about Ahlflæd then? She can beat him up."

"And definitely not Ahlflæd." Oswiu looked at his daughter, who was looking suspiciously innocent. "You haven't?"

"Only once. When he was really annoying."

"Ahlflæd." Oswiu shook his head, but he did so in part to try to hide the smile that threatened to break through his control. "I should send you to Coldingham and have my sister look after you."

"Not there!" said Ahlflæd, and for the first time Oswiu saw real concern in her expression. "That's the other reason I wanted to go to see Aidan. When I went to Coldingham, the sisters there spent the whole time telling me not to do this and not to do that. On Lindisfarne, the brothers – those who don't hide – just smile and tell Aidan, and all he does is go red and mutter stuff about being quiet and calm. But I can tell he doesn't really mean it, Daddy."

"Oh? And how can you tell that?"

"Well, he doesn't do any punishments. At Coldingham, I was smacked for singing too loudly, and then for singing too quietly, and for running around…"

"All very much deserved, I'm sure."

"No! Well, maybe the running around. We were playing hide and seek, and I didn't know the sisters had gone into the church – I thought it would be a good place to hide. It wasn't."

"She couldn't sit down all the rest of that day," said Ahlfrith.

Ahlflæd stuck her tongue out at her brother. "You'd never have found me if they hadn't been in there."

"Would too!"

"Wouldn't."

"Would."

As the assertions and denials circled around him, Oswiu looked north, to where Coldingham lay. Word of his safe arrival had been sent to the queen and Æbbe two days before. Today, they might arrive. So, after lunch, he had taken the children and come up onto the ramparts to look for riders.

He saw them. A column approaching, riding down the furrowed track that led north, the spear points of the guarding men glinting at the front, side and to the rear, while in the centre of the column rode the women.

"Your mother is coming."

The children stopped their squabbling and looked eagerly to where he was pointing. Oswiu turned into the courtyard and yelled a command.

"The queen approaches. Send an escort."

As men started clattering around below, Oswiu returned to watch. He had been long apart from Rhieienmelth and he felt the blood surge in his body. An image, unbidden, returned to his mind: of when he had first seen her, at the court of her father, in the castle at Carlisle. The kings of Rheged still held the stronghold of the emperors as their keep and it was within its stone walls, hung with cloths to keep the west winds out, that he had seen her, waiting upon her father. And his breath had caught then at her beauty. That beauty had scarce diminished in the years since. Now, Oswiu found himself leaning over the rampart, searching for the first sight of her dark, dark hair. But then he shook sense into himself. Riding a horse, within sight of anyone, the queen would not let her hair flow free, but would cover it with scarf and headdress. Only within hall, or with him, would she let it flow free.

"She's got him with her." Ahlflæd was pointing, and Oswiu squinted along the line of her finger.

Yes. There. The queen rode at the head of the column, with spear-carrying men flanking her and, beside her upon a pony, a figure to match the little animal: his nephew, Œthelwald.

"He'll be even worse now," groaned Ahlfrith. "He's always wanted to ride beside Mummy before, but she's never let him."

"Not till now," agreed Ahlflæd.

"Let us go down and greet your mother. And your cousin." Oswiu led his children down into the courtyard, which was seething with slaves and retainers. Now the queen's return was confirmed, everyone knew that tonight there would be a feast, and the steward was pulling his preparations to their highest pitch.

There was only one entrance to the stronghold: the gate, halfway down the rock, that looked out to sea. It would be yet a while before Rhieienmelth would appear. Oswiu stood at the door to the hall and signalled to his steward.

"Have my seat brought out. I will greet the queen here." Then, seeing his warmaster, Oswiu called him over. "Æthelwin! You shared in this great deed we did. Now come, share with me the queen's good pleasure."

The warmaster arrived with the judgement seat. The men put the richly painted wooden throne down upon the topmost step before the door to the hall, and withdrew. Oswiu sat down to wait for his wife. The children, after twin pleading glances, he gave leave to run around the inner ward until the spreading hush told that the queen climbed the steps from the gate.

"The queen returns, Æthelwin."

"Yes, lord. At last. She has not hurried."

Oswiu glanced up at the impassive face of the warmaster. "What do you mean?"

"A day's ride to Coldingham. A day's ride back."

"There are many reasons for delay upon the road, Æthelwin."

"Indeed, lord. Not least outlaws. There are many, I hear, in the hills and forests around Coldingham. Mayhap they delayed the queen."

"If there are so many there, you should take some men and clear them."

"With your leave, I would be glad to. Mayhap I will find news on the men who attacked us – their voices had the sound of those hills about them."

"Mayhap. Find Acca and Coifi, and bring them: they should be here to greet the queen."

The warmaster returned quickly. Scop and priest had both been in the hall, Acca preparing his voice for the coming feast by bathing it in rich red wine, Coifi attempting to see wyrd in the embers of the hearth fire.

Oswiu placed these companions of danger behind him and, hearing the spread of silence that indicated the queen's near approach, he called the children to him, and waited.

The queen appeared. Rhieienmelth, princess of Rheged and queen of Northumbria, as beautiful as he remembered. She approached, crossing the ward, a few stray hairs escaping and blowing free across the white of her headdress. Walking beside her was a small figure.

The queen stopped in front of the king and made the courtesy to him.

"My lord." Rhieienmelth raised her gaze. It was solemn, and Oswiu wondered on that, for ever before there had been, behind her eyes, some of the same fire that filled his daughter and drove her ladies to distraction.

"You gave me charge of your nephew, and I have kept him." She reached a hand out and touched the boy lightly upon the shoulder.

Œthelwald stepped forward and made the courtesy with all the elaboration of repeated practice.

"My lord." The boy looked up. The king began to smile. But then the boy saw his cousins standing either side of the king. Ahlfrith was scowling and Ahlflæd made the sign against the evil eye at him. Œthelwald looked back to Oswiu. "You have brought the king back?"

Oswiu leaned forward in the judgement seat, the better to see the tight, angry face before him.

"I am the king," he said mildly, "but yes, I brought..."

"She always calls him king," Œthelwald interrupted. "The queen calls my father king."

Oswiu looked to Rhieienmelth. She made no answer, but her skin, already pale, grew paler.

The boy looked to his cousins and smiled.

Later, that night, after feast and drinking, when he was finished, Oswiu swung his legs off the bed. He sat with his back to the queen. Rhieienmelth reached a hand to his shoulder, but he did not look to her.

"I loved him too," Oswiu said. Then the king stood and, wrapping his cloak around him, went out into the night.

Chapter 2

"They still won't accept me?"

When there were no tidings of war, Oswiu liked to spend some of the summer at the royal estate in Melrose. The weather was mild, few insects bothered them, and there was good hunting in the forests and hills. But the king's great hall there was protected only by a stockade and ditch; should rumour of war reach the household, then they would withdraw to the strongholds at Bamburgh or Edinburgh. The king had summoned his family and chief counsellors to Melrose, to hear the tidings brought back from Deira. Now, looking at Acca and Coifi, it was clear that the tidings were not good.

The scop shifted uneasily from one foot to the other, for once discomfited at being the centre of attention. Coifi too seemed uncomfortable, drawing his raven-feather cloak more tightly around his shoulders and sinking his head down within the collar of feathers.

"No, lord," said Acca.

A murmur went up from the assembled counsellors. The thegn next to Æthelwin leaned closer to the warmaster.

"Why did the king choose these men to bear his message and not the messengers of his household?"

It was true. All the kings of the land retained men trained in memory, swiftness and surety to act as messengers, both between kings and to all the thegns oath bound to the throne. But Oswiu had sent his scop and almoner to Deira. Travel-stained and weary, with Coifi's eyes beginning to roll in his head as he followed the play of light through the rise of hearth smoke, neither man presented an impressive figure. But the warmaster knew both from their expedition into Mercia.

"Be not guiled by how they appear," he told the questioning

thegn. "They went with me and the king into Mercia, and took Oswald's remains from in front of Penda's face. No man I know speaks more sweetly than Acca, and few indeed see further than Coifi. They were good men for the king to send, for they could also tell the story of our mission."

The thegn shrugged. "Doesn't seem to have worked then."

Sitting in the judgement seat, with his counsellors arrayed around him, the king sat in splendour. He wore a cloak of deep, rich colour, collared in white ermine, and bound at the shoulder by a clasp of gold and inlaid garnet. Upon his head he wore a gold circlet in the form of two dragons wound thickly around each other and with red garnets marking the glowing eyes of the beasts. Æthelwin had never before seen the king attired in such splendour.

"But you told them of what we did?" The king leaned forward in the judgement seat. "You told them how I brought Oswald forth from Mercia, from under the nose of our enemy. You told them that we have him here? And still they refused?"

Acca glanced uneasily at Coifi, but the old priest's eyes were rolling in an all too familiar way. As inconspicuously as possible, the scop reached out and pinched Coifi's arm. The old priest's eyes started back into focus, spinning around the hall and then settling upon the king.

"Yes, lord," said Acca. "We told the witan of Deira all that." He looked to Coifi. They had drawn lots on the long journey north to the royal estate at Melrose as to who would have to give the king the bad news. Acca had lost. "The witan of Deira gave us this message to take to Oswiu, king, and to the witan of Bernicia: Oswine Godfriend is our king. We want, and will have, no other."

Oswiu looked at Acca. "That is it? Nothing else?"

"Yes, lord. And no, there was nothing else."

Oswiu sat back in the judgement seat. His eyes scanned the ranks of his family and counsellors: his mother and sister had come from Coldingham; Aidan was there; Æthelwin, the warmaster; and many thegns, from those parts of his realm closest to Melrose. The queen too sat in the council, her seat beside the king, but his gaze passed over her and, among the slaves and retainers of the household, there were whispers of discord between king and queen.

The king addressed his counsellors.

"They are fools. Surely, Deira must realize that they make themselves into an apple, ripe and easy to pick when Penda chooses. As one, as Northumbria, we have the means to meet him, to beat him, but now, separated, he waits for us to fatten until he brings the butcher's block. Fools. My brother made them see this. Have they gone blind?"

Acca spoke up. "Lord, we put these arguments to the witan, but they made no odds. Still it would not listen."

Oswiu looked keenly at the scop. "You remember of that which we spoke ere you left? We knew for a surety that there would be no quick acceptance of our embassy, but with sweet tongue and sweeter promises, some must surely have been brought to my side?"

Acca shook his head. "Many an ear I whispered into, but it was as if my words were gall, not honey."

"Surely some thegn, keen for gold and glory, whispered that he might support me if I gave treasure enough?"

Acca shrugged. "No, lord. I could scarce believe it."

"You took the gold I gave you?" Oswiu leaned towards Acca and Coifi, a thread of suspicion working across his face. "It was a great treasure, and I bade you give it freely to any who might listen. Have you returned with it then?"

Acca, feeling the hall suddenly warm around him, shook his head. "No, lord."

"To whom did you give it?"

"There was one thegn, great in the king's council, who spoke with us when none were there to listen. He gave us to understand that he favoured the cause of the Idings and, harking to your command, we gave the gold over to him. But when we came to the witan, it was this thegn who proposed the message I gave you." Acca began to flush. "The thegn tricked us, lord."

"Who was this thegn who took my gold and gave ill counsel in return?"

"His name was Hunwald."

"Hunwald." The king's face grew pale, but it was the paleness of rage. "I know him. Why did you speak with him?"

Acca saw the king's anger but did not know the reason for it. "H-Hunwald is h-high in the king's council, lord," he stuttered.

"King?" Oswiu shook his head. "I spoke with him. Oswine is friend neither to God nor his people. Call him not king."

"Lord, your pardon. But this Hunwald stands first among the men around Oswine. There are whispers against him, for he is a grasping man, as we found, but Oswine will hear none of them, calling Hunwald as much father as friend. Some of those who spoke against him have died, although none by violence – yet they have died. In falling from horse, through fit and the sweating sickness, and one with a belly so swollen he cut himself open rather than endure the swelling longer. Now men hold their silence with Hunwald, but to us, while we were there, all acclaimed Oswine Godfriend for the gold he gives and the strength of his arm."

"Strength? What king has he ridden against? No news has reached me of battle or war."

"Not kings, but outlaws. Many bands of outlaws ravaged the land after Oswald's death, but the Godfriend, forswearing battle against the other kingdoms, has ridden against them, hunting the outlaws into marsh and mere, until the last hung from a tree."

Oswiu sat back in the judgement seat. He looked to his counsellors. "Have you aught to ask of Acca and Coifi?"

Æthelwin spoke first. "What news is there of Penda? Why has he not raided into Deira? It lies upon his border."

Acca smiled. This at least he could answer without fear.

"There have been messengers. We saw one when we spoke to the witan, although he spoke not; but he was of Mercia. Some say it is not only to his thegns that Oswine has given gold."

"He is paying Penda off?"

"That is what some men say. Others say further: that Penda keeps a son or daughter to betroth to a child of Oswine – when he has one. But the Godfriend has been wed five years or more and there is no child – and he will not put his wife aside and get another."

"Really?" The warmaster glanced at the king, then back to Acca. "That is… unusual."

"I told him that he may not."

The voice was Aidan's. Though he had been bishop now for near ten years, and ever the object of scrutiny, yet Aidan still coloured at the gaze of so many upon him.

"You told him?" Oswiu was staring at Aidan, with mouth all but hanging open.

"Yes. Oswine asked me if he might put aside his wife, as she had produced no child, and take another woman. I told him that he might not, for what God has joined together, no man may break apart."

"But… but how did you tell him this?"

"With words," said Aidan. "How else might I tell him?"

"No, I mean how could you give him such a ruling? You are here, in Bernicia; he is in Deira."

"He asked me to come to him, that the church in Deira might continue to flourish. I took ship down the coast, and met Oswine at a place called Hartlepool, where he was building a new monastery, to be ruled by a young cousin of his, a woman named Hild. She is of the line of Edwin, cousin to him, and new come to Deira, first from the kingdom of the Franks, where she was taken into the new life and received into holy orders, and then from Kent." Aidan smiled again, this time in memory. "A remarkable woman. She will be a worthy ruler of the holy house for men and women that the king is building there, upon the cliff top." Aidan looked at the king, and the smile of his recollection faded as he saw Oswiu's expression. "Has something I have said displeased you?"

"Displeased me?" The king's face, pale already, had grown paler. "Why should I be displeased that my oldest friend, the man I trusted more than any apart from my brother, should forsake that friendship and go to the land of my enemy and offer him friendship and counsel and… and knowledge of my plans. Some, indeed, might call such actions treachery, but could I call my oldest, oldest friend a traitor. Could I? Could I?" And as the king spoke, his voice grew louder and, finally standing, he flung the final questions at Aidan as whip shouts.

Aidan shook his head, and those near the bishop saw tears spring from his eyes, such was the violence of the king's emotion.

"No, no, no. I am no traitor, lord, but your friend, ever and always; aye, and servant too. But Oswine Godfriend sent word to me on the Holy Island, pleading for me to come – for the people of Deira, and he not least among them, thirsted for the holy mysteries so recently revealed to them and now hidden, for there were few among them able to minister to the people. I am bishop, lord. Abbot Ségéne, bishop of the Holy Island whence I came, gave these lands into my keeping. How could I hear Oswine's plea and not answer it?"

Oswiu, king, leaned forward, his hands upon the high table in front of him, and those near him saw the knuckles in his hands go white, so tightly did he clench them.

"He is my enemy, and the enemy of his people. The longer he rules, the wider grows the gap between the kingdoms my father first united, and the weaker we get. The longer he rules, the stronger waxes Penda. Already he has drawn Lindsey to him, and its king sends tribute to the hall at Tamworth and no longer to us at Ad Gefrin. The other kings, the kings of the East Angles and Elmet, of the North Folk and the South Folk, the East Saxons, the Middle Saxons and the West Saxons – all those kingdoms pledge-bound first to Edwin and then to my brother – they all now twist in the wind, wondering which way to turn and which king will prevail. The longer Oswine rules in Deira, paying off Penda with gold and honeyed words, the more they will turn to Mercia until, finally, Penda will march on us, with all the kings of this land behind him, and we will be utterly destroyed. The longer Oswine rules, the nearer I am to death. You ask how you could not answer Oswine's plea? That is how." Speaking softly now, each word weighted with anger, the king said further: "I command you, as your king, to have no more dealings with him or his people. Without priests and monks to offer the mysteries, he stands condemned before God. Let him burn."

Aidan blinked away the tears that threatened to blind him. "I-I cannot do that. His soul, and the souls of all his people, have been placed in my charge. They are my sheep; I cannot abandon them to the wolves."

"I will stop you."

Aidan shook his head, and the smile upon his face was the saddest smile ever seen by any man there. "How will you stop me, lord and oldest friend? If you bind me, I will escape. If you exile me, I will return. If you kill me, there will be another."

Oswiu stared at Aidan, and the council held the silence between them as tight as the silence when two armies first catch sight of each other.

"Get out," said the king. "Go. Before my patience does."

"Yes," said Aidan, "I will go. But I will not abandon you, my oldest friend."

"Go!"

The bishop went from the great hall.

Oswiu sat back upon the judgement seat, collapsing in upon himself as if the sinews binding muscle to bone were suddenly cut. The council spoke no word.

"Leave me."

The words were quiet but, in the silence of the hall, all heard them. One by one, the counsellors left the great hall until, at the last, the king sat there with only the queen left beside him, for Acha and Æbbe had gone after Aidan, to speak with him before he left.

Oswiu looked up from his silence and he saw Rhieienmelth waiting upon him. His smile, when it came, was a broken thing, the faintest ghost of that smile which had crossed his face when he first saw the princess of Rheged.

"You stay," he said. "But you can't help me." And he turned his face from the queen.

After a while, the king heard her steps, soft over the rush matting that covered the floor of the great hall, as she too left. But only sight, not hearing, could have told him of the silent tears that rolled down the queen's face, and the king's eyes were turned away.

Chapter 3

"My lady, may I speak with you?"

Acha looked up from the nodding doze that the motion of the wagon had induced in her. The royal household was heading south. After the council, the king had no stomach to stay longer in Melrose. The steward, having settled down for a month of relative calm, suddenly found that he had to arrange for the wagons and riders and horses and oxen to be made ready, and everything packed for the long, slow journey to Maelmin.

The warmaster rode beside Acha's wagon. She squinted up at Æthelwin, for the sun rode behind him in the sky and she could barely see him for its glare.

"Yes. Yes, of course," she said.

"It would be better where others might not hear," said Æthelwin, nodding to the wagon driver who, by the fixity of his gaze upon the plodding oxen, indicated all too clearly that he was listening to what the warmaster was saying. "If you will, I might drive this wagon for a while."

"No, no," said Acha. "I have been too long sitting. I would use my feet, before they drop off. So, if you will walk, then walk with me." Acha indicated to the wagon driver to stop, and he pulled the reluctant beasts to a halt. Shouts came from behind, but they ceased as soon as the following wagon saw Acha climb down from the driver's board and, grimacing, step over the ruts dug into the track and onto the sward, cropped by the flocks of sheep the shepherds moved up into the hills for the summer grazing.

The oxen, as unwilling to start again as they had been to stop, were being whipped and yelled at by the wagoner, but such was normal for the slow journey between the king's estates. The warmaster dismounted his horse and tethered it to Acha's wagon before following the king's mother.

Climbing a hillock that lay beside the path, Acha looked along the column. Some twenty wagons stretched into the distance, most pulled by oxen, although the lead couple of wagons had horses hitched to them. Before and after the wagons rode riders, spear tips glinting, thirty or so men ahead and a similar number forming the rearguard, while smaller groups picked out paths away from the main column, on either flank, acting as watch and guard. Children skipped among the riders, being told off to return to their mothers, but they no sooner retreated than they returned, playing games with horses and riders and the dogs that ran alongside the column. The queen's wagon was in the centre of the column, but the cloths that served, in bad weather, to protect the queen and her ladies were drawn, although the day was fine. There was, Acha knew, ill will between Oswiu and Rhieienmelth, but it was not of the sort that she had borne towards her own husband, Æthelfrith. At the very marriage feast, he had killed her father, making her brother Edwin flee into exile. In the years of their marriage, she blessed the fact that he had called upon her only rarely, preferring slaves to warm his bed and body at night. Such was not an uncommon fate for the daughters of royal families. A wry smile tugged at her lips. They were called "peace weavers", the human, fleshly binding to heal the wounds opened by wars between the thrones: in her experience, the peace weavers more often produced fresh warriors for battle than peace between the many royal houses of this land. But there had, once and for some years, been peace between her son and his wife; she resolved to speak with Rhieienmelth when the opportunity arose, to find what had caused this rift.

Shading her eyes, Acha looked for the royal standard and saw it, borne by the second rider of the column. There was no wind, and the summer sun was warm. The banner hung limply from its pole, but in the bright sunlight it still glowed purple and gold. The king rode behind his banner, but he rode alone. In the dark mood that had come upon him since the council, few wished to approach him save when required.

"The king is… preoccupied."

Acha looked round to see that Æthelwin, the warmaster, had joined her upon the hillock.

"Yes, you could say that," said Acha. She looked back to the column and the solitary rider near its head. "Or you could say that he broods because that which he desires will not come into his keeping."

"What does the king desire, my lady? You, as his mother, must know better than any other."

"He desires to escape the shadow of his brother, and to honour him. He wishes to outdo him, and to bless him. He wants... he wants all to love him as they did his brother."

The warmaster looked steadily at the upright woman standing beside him.

"Do you, my lady?"

Acha was silent for a long time, her gaze turned inwards. Then she turned to Æthelwin and her face was as blank as a mask.

"You wished to speak to me alone."

"Yes, my lady."

"Then speak. We are alone."

"There may be another way to win the witan of Deira to the king's side. I-I would not speak of this but for the fact that I have seen – all have seen – a division grow up between the king and the queen..."

*

Oswiu looked up. The flap to his tent was moving. He had said he did not want to be disturbed save in emergency. The journey had been tedious and interrupted by wagons losing wheels and horses going lame; they had not made half the distance hoped. As a result, they had camped by the side of the track, the harassed steward finding a space broad enough and level enough to take almost all of the wagons, while the lee of a hill – topped as so many were in this part of his kingdom by the tumbledown rock fortifications of the people who once lived here – provided some shelter from the wind. His tent pitched, the king had retired into it, telling the door warden, here reduced to tent guard, to put off any local people seeking judgement from the king in a dispute with neighbour or erstwhile friend. Hearing of the king's arrival in a district, the inhabitants would rush to him, all seeking to arrive first, that they might be first to put the case against neighbour to the king's judgement. Sometimes, it seemed to Oswiu, he did little else but hear how so-and-so's sheep had grazed so-and-so's barley, and then refused recompense. For an evening of freedom, he had told the door warden to drive such suitors away, but now, despite his command, the tent flap twitched.

"Yes, what is it?" he asked, not bothering to sit up from where he lay.

"Have you no other greeting for your mother?"

Oswiu sat up. "Mother. I greet you. What do you want?"

"Can I not want to spend time with my son?"

"You can." Oswiu waved to the stool beside his bed. "And you can ask me that which you desire at the same time."

"Do I do that so often?"

"Everyone does. It's what a king is for." He patted the stool. "Sit down."

Acha sat down upon the stool and smoothed her dress down over her knees. She did not meet Oswiu's eyes and, with a sudden surprise, he realized that she was nervous. He had not known his mother – daughter and wife and mother to kings – ever to be nervous before, and he wondered in his soul what matter might cause such hesitation.

"Speak," he said, feeling her nerves himself, for his voice cracked slightly as he spoke.

Acha glanced at her son, and as quickly her gaze skittered away. But then Oswiu saw her back straighten and her shoulders square: she had made her choice. She would speak.

"I have learned that there may be another way to win the witan of Deira to your side. But it will require sacrifice. Are you prepared to make a sacrifice?"

Oswiu looked at his mother. In his eyes, the bleak knowledge of his powerlessness to achieve what he wished flickered.

"Yes," he whispered.

"Deira rejects you because it does not know you. You were a child, only four, when we fled into exile, but your brother was already twelve, and known to many of the thegns of Deira, and beloved of them. Then, when we returned and your brother won the throne, he set you to watching the northern marches. Dal Riada, the Gododdin, the kingdom of Strathclyde and the king of the Picts know you, but not the men of Deira."

"But my father was king there, as well as my brother."

"Your father took the throne in blood and in treachery."

"He was a great king. All feared him."

"Yes," said Acha. "Yes, everyone did. And so they fear you, the Twister's son."

"But through you, Mother, I have more claim to the throne than Oswine."

"Yes, but Oswine is known to them, and beloved. You are unknown, and feared."

Oswiu shook his head. "Do you not think I know all this? You told me there is a way. What is this way?"

"Great is the reverence with which the men of Deira hold the memory of Edwin, their king."

"But his elder sons died, killed by Cadwallon and Penda, and tale came to us that his youngest son, Wuscfrea, died among the Franks when yet a boy. Edwin had no other sons."

"No. But he had a daughter." As she said these words, Acha looked carefully at her son. She saw him catch their meaning. "She is now of marriageable age, and lives with the kin of her mother in the kingdom of Kent. As with her mother, she is Christian, following the way of the Franks which the men of Kent follow too, and though many have proposed marriage, none have been accepted, for her family will take no pagan to husband; no, nor any petty king or thegn, for she is the daughter of the High King and, through her mother, descendant of Clovis, king of the Franks."

"I have a wife."

Acha's gaze did not leave her son. "Put her aside. Take Edwin's daughter for wife. Then, surely, the witan of Deira will hear your cause."

"I-I cannot." Oswiu's face closed upon itself and he turned away from her. "It is against God's wish. You heard what Aidan told Oswine when he asked to put aside his wife that he might produce a son."

"But what if Rhieienmelth wishes to lay aside her crown so that she may serve God more fully, in holy orders?"

"Does she?" asked Oswiu.

"She will," said Acha.

The king looked on his mother and saw there the woman who had faced down the king of Dal Riada when he would have thrown them from his hall. He thought of the fire of his wife, and it flowing over the implacability of his mother, and leaving not a mark in its passing, and he knew that her words held. But there was another thought, harder to shift, although on the surface more gentle. Oswiu shook his head. "Aidan will not hear of this."

"Love will open a door the law might close." Acha met her son's gaze. "Take your brother to Aidan. Oswald wished always to lay aside his sword and be a monk. Let this be so in death if not life."

The king stared at his mother in wonder.

"You would give him away? You would give Oswald to the Holy Island?"

"Yes," said Acha.

"Why?"

"To answer a question I was asked earlier."

Oswiu shook his head. "I-I…"

But before he could speak further, his mother put her hand on his. "Hush." She stood up, smoothing her skirt and adjusting her headdress.

Oswiu looked up at Acha. "You haven't told me her name."

"Her name is Eanflæd."

The king nodded. "Very well. Eanflæd"

But as Acha made to leave the tent, Oswiu stopped her once more. "How did you learn of this?"

Acha looked back to her son. "Æthelwin told me."

Chapter 4

The riders, strung out along the narrow path, sank deep into their cloaks against the cold wind blowing in from over the grey sea. As the path rose and fell, the sea itself came into view and disappeared again: grey and grim it seemed, in its present mood, foam flecked and sullen, like a man at the dog end of a feast, beer mad and searching for a fight. No boats would venture passage when the sea was in such temper and, at the column's head, Æthelwin permitted himself a brief nod that he had chosen to bring his charges to Coldingham by land rather than taking what had seemed the easier sea route. The warmaster, though, was more landsman than most of his fellows, and always happier sat upon a saddle than a rowing bench; the king had given him leave to choose the way, and he had chosen to ride. It had been a wet journey and a miserable one, for man and beast, but at least it was one they would all survive.

Æthelwin drew back his hood enough to see more clearly ahead. There, through the wind-torn gaps in the rain curtain, he saw the huddle of whitewashed huts, clustered around a central hall. To the landward side, a high earth rampart, dug by a king of the Gododdin, protected a hill upon the promontory from landward attack; the cliffs on its flanks prevented any attack from the sea. The local people called it Colud's Fort, although none now remembered the Colud who had had it built.

Riding closer, Æthelwin saw that the bank was faced with an equally deep ditch surmounted with holly and hawthorn, double rowed and twisted together to make a barrier impenetrable to any animal larger than a cat. It surrounded the buildings, with only a single gate allowing admission.

The horses, as miserable as their riders, plodded onwards, but the smell of habitation – of baking and ordure and sweat and thatch

– borne along by the tearing wind, pricked the animals' noses, and their ears, laid flat against the wind, stood and turned to where they were going. Habitation meant rest, and food, and warmth, for them as much as for their riders.

Pulling his animal's head round, Æthelwin headed back down the column, to the five wagons that creaked at the centre of the riders, the rain pouring off the waxed cloths raised over them. The wagoners sat streaming water from their hoods and cloaks, but the warmaster paid no attention to them. Instead, he rode around to the rear of the centre wagon and pulled at the leather flap. Tied against the wind, it hardly moved, but within someone realized that the fingers tugging it were of flesh rather than air, and pulled the flap open.

"Tell your mistress that we shall soon be arriving at her new home."

The face, looking out of the wagon gloom, nodded and disappeared within. The rider was on the point of turning back into the rain and wind once more when a second face appeared at the opening.

"Æthelwin. Is there an end to this rain? I would not first appear here out of the back of a wagon, but riding, as a queen."

The warmaster pulled his horse out from the protection of the wagon and looked ahead. The rain still blew in from the sea, and there was no sign of any break to cloud or sea, for there was no telling where they joined.

"No," said Æthelwin, pulling his relieved horse back into the shelter of the wagon. "There is no let up to the rain so far as I can see."

Rhieienmelth looked up at the warmaster. "I am, until I make oath to God, still queen, warmaster. Remember that."

Æthelwin looked down at the queen, and his eyes were flat. For a long, wind-torn moment there was silence between them. Then a slight, sardonic smile tugged at his lips, and he made an elaborate courtesy to Rhieienmelth.

"Of course, O queen."

Rhieienmelth looked again at the warmaster. The very blankness of his eyes suggested thought beyond any she had ascribed to him before.

"If that is all, O queen..." Æthelwin began to turn his horse away.

"Wait." Rhieienmelth called him back.

The warmaster turned a face so empty of expression to her it was as if the rain had washed his face away. "Yes, O queen?"

"You were with my husband through all his journey into Mercia. Tell me this. When he left, there was division between us, but one I hoped to heal by doing that which he bade: caring for his nephew until his return. But when he returned, his heart was turned against me, though I had discharged the burden he laid upon me." Rhieienmelth looked up at the warmaster. There seemed little hope of insight from this stone-faced man, but she would like as not have no other chance to speak with him. "Do you know why his heart turned against me?"

The warmaster stared down at her impassively.

"Was there, perhaps, someone else?"

At this question, Æthelwin did react, with the same sardonic smile that had greeted her reminding him that she was still queen.

"No, O queen. There was nobody else."

"Then why? I do not understand. I had not thought he would put me aside simply for a nobler queen."

The warmaster looked at her for a time, his face returning to the blankness of before. Then he began to speak.

"You are a woman. You have never stood in the shieldwall, half blind behind your shield, while the man in front of you tries to find a gap in the wall to strike. There, in the shieldwall, a man must use any weakness: if your enemy slips, strike quickly, before he recovers. If he wearies, weaken him with fresh attacks. If he turns, in fear or panic, slip your sword into his back. But even though your courage and strength still hold, if the men on either side of you fail, you will fall with them. To be a king is to stand always in a shieldwall, with your enemies ever around you, searching for weakness. To stay a king, a man must take every advantage he might; he must remove every weakness."

"You think I was a weakness to the king?" Rhieienmelth shook her head. "You must know a different man."

"I do not say you brought weakness. But an alliance with Kent, and further to the kingdom of the Franks, strengthens the king where he is weakest. Among the men of the old North, the king is known, and well respected, for his deeds and word. There is little advantage in alliance with Rheged."

"We were great once." The queen brushed a hand across her face. The wet upon it may well have been rain. "Great enough to push the Idings into the sea and reclaim all this land – as my grandfather would have done, if not for the cursed treachery of Morgant. May he rot in hell."

The warmaster nodded. "Treachery is ever the greatest threat to a kingdom." He looked, with blank eyes, at the queen. "Soon after we arrived in Mercia, we were attacked by robbers. In these uncertain days, there was no great surprise in that. But these were men of the North, of Northumbria, and they were a long way from home."

The queen looked up at the warmaster's hard face. "Surely the king did not think I sent those men?"

"The king knows not who sent them; he only knows someone did." The warmaster tugged his unwilling horse's head round into the full force of the rain. "We will arrive soon, O queen. Prepare yourself."

*

"Rhieienmelth."

The queen looked round. "Æbbe."

The two women stood looking at each other, each waiting for the other to speak. Outside the small hall, the wind had slackened and the rain eased, but still it sounded hard on the shutters, tight closed against the storm. In the gloom, lit by torches dancing in the stray draughts that blew through the shutters and beneath the door, both women seemed more like the great stones raised to old gods that stood upon plain and hill throughout this ancient land. From without there came the sounds of unloading and carrying and storing, as the wagons that had brought the queen and her women were relieved of their charge.

"You are welcome here, Rhieienmelth," Æbbe said eventually. "I will show you to your quarters."

But the queen held up her hand. "If you mean one of those huts, then I am afraid you are mistaken. I am yet queen, and a queen does not live in a hut."

The door of the hall was pulled back, and the dim, cloud light filled the space.

Rhieienmelth looked around. "But this will do."

And men began carrying in chests and hangings and bowls, while Rhieienmelth's women directed them.

"Wh-what are you doing?" asked Æbbe, taking her sister-in-law's arm. "This is my house. I rule here."

Rhieienmelth looked down at the hand upon her arm. Slowly, Æbbe released her. Rhieienmelth smiled, then took Æbbe's hands in her own. "Of course you rule here. You are mother of this house – and you shall stay mother of this house and all your little chicks, clucking around in their huts outside. But think on this: I, a queen, have stood aside and agreed to enter into this life so that the king might take a new wife. But if I do so, I will live here as a queen, not in one of those noisome little huts where your sisters live."

"B-but I live in one of those huts," said Æbbe.

"Of course you do," said Rhieienmelth. "You are good and kind and holy; naturally you share in the life of your sisters. However, I am not here to share your life, but to be out of the king's."

"You do know this was none of my doing," said Æbbe.

"I know, I know. You have always been gracious to me, Æbbe. But it was your mother who told me that the king wished to put me away; I think she may have done more than tell me his wish – I believe she put the wish into his heart."

"My mother would never do such a thing."

"No? Not to gain an advantage for her son – her last surviving son?"

Æbbe made no answer, for her eyes had turned inward, to memory.

"But I am sure I will do very well here," said Rhieienmelth. "I hear you have men under your rule as well? That is good. I will need some of them to run my hounds."

"You've brought your dogs?"

"Yes."

"Why?"

"Hunting, of course." Rhieienmelth looked round at a sudden, high-pitched cry, just in time to see her falcon flapping upon the wrist of the man carrying it. "Put Hebog there, by the fire. He will need to dry himself."

"Y-you can't," began Æbbe. "A falcon?"

"The dogs we'll leave outside. My men can find shelter with yours."

"Your men? How many have you brought?"

"A scop – he's new to me but his voice is sweet – my falconer and steward, my master of hounds…" Rhieienmelth put her finger to her lips, thinking. "Oh, and of course –" she turned to the door and gestured – "Prince Œthelwald."

A boy, who had been standing by the door watching the unloading, walked towards them. Seeing him, Æbbe felt the shift of memory, for he moved with the same ease as her older brother, Oswald. She looked to the woman beside her. "Your own children? Where are they?" At the question, she saw Rhieienmelth stiffen, but the queen did not look round.

"My daughter will spend half the year with her father and half with me; she begins with her father. As for my son, the king decided it was time he went to another court, to learn their ways and to make allies of foes."

"Where has the king sent Ahlfrith?"

"Somewhere he did not want to go." The young Œthelwald stood in front of the two women, one his aunt by blood, the other his aunt by marriage. "You should have seen him cry when he went. He only stopped when the king told him his sister could go with him. What a baby."

"He is not a baby," said Rhieienmelth sharply, but the prince merely smirked and, turning to Æbbe, made the courtesy.

"The king has also sent me where I would not have gone," said Œthelwald, "but I have come so I might learn more of my father. And I did not cry."

Æbbe held out her hands to the boy and took his shoulders. "You are the very image of him. For my part, I am glad your father has sent you here." She glanced briefly at Rhieienmelth. "Besides, it seems you will not have to endure the usual rigours of a holy house."

"I would not have come if all I was to do was pray. I am learning to fight. Here, see." And, stepping back, the boy drew a sword from the scabbard hanging from his belt. "The king gave me this before I left. He said it belonged once to my father." Œthelwald looked sharply at his aunt. "Is that so?"

Æbbe saw a finely worked sword with garnets inlaid upon its hilt, and running down the blade the intricate weave of its welding, marked in whirls and waves. She looked up at the boy and smiled.

"It is a sword fit for a king."

"That is good." Œthelwald began to sheathe the sword. "I will be a king one day. Like my father."

"Of course you will," said Æbbe.

The boy, who had struggled to get the tip of the blade smoothly into its scabbard, looked up at his aunt. "A proper king," he said. "Like my father. Not a king who holds his throne only through the strength of another, like…like…" Œthelwald cast around in thought, searching for such a king, then of a sudden his face brightened, and he looked to Rhieienmelth. "Like Rheged," he said. "Like your father."

The queen made no answer.

"The queen's father is a great king…" Æbbe began, but the young prince cut her off.

"Not according to the men. I've heard them in hall, laughing about him, saying how the only warriors who go to Rheged now are those who want to grow rust on their swords and fat on their bellies."

"He-he was a great king once," said Rhieienmelth.

"My father was always great," said Œthelwald.

"Yes. Yes, he was," said Æbbe. Glancing at Rhieienmelth, she saw the hurt in the queen's eyes, and as quickly looked away. "Come. You are right; of course you must have the hall." She took Rhieienmelth's arm and led her towards the bustling, arguing throng of women and servants. "It looks as if they need your guidance." Glancing back, to make sure Œthelwald was out of earshot, she whispered to the queen: "My brother's son may look like him, but he does not act like him. Still, it is hard, to have neither father nor mother."

"Yes," said Rhieienmelth. "That is what I remind myself when he speaks as he did just now."

"But what of your own son? You have not told me to which court the king has sent little Ahlfrith."

"One where I would not have had him go. But the king said, when the messenger came, offering to take Ahlfrith as foster son to this king, that he must needs go, for the peace and time it would buy the kingdom. So, he has gone." The queen turned a pale face to her sister-in-law. "I do not know if I shall see him again."

"But why? Taking a boy as foster son is a sacred bond – none would break it. You need not fear. Besides, it is time Ahlfrith learned the ways of other courts and different lands, for it will serve him well in due time. Where has he gone?"

"To Penda," said Rhieienmelth.

Chapter 5

The boy ran desperately across the courtyard of the great hall at Tamworth, dodging in and out between sheep pens and rooting pigs, round store huts and weaving sheds, while his pursuers, shouting and screaming what they were going to do when they caught him, drew closer. He'd led them a long chase, and what had started as little more than a game had turned dark; the easy pursuit his hunters had anticipated had turned into a lung-bursting run, and they had grown angry. Now, the cries that came from them were fainter – for the chasing boys were as breathless as he – but the threats they carried were greater. Before, he might have escaped with a few bruises; now, if they caught him, he would be lucky not to have an arm or rib broken.

Rounding the seething, reeking hut where the smith carried out minor repairs, the smoke from the ever-burning forge creeping out through the slats in the rough roof, Ahlfrith risked a glance back at his pursuers.

There were five of them: Peada, Penda's son, and four of his friends. All except Peada were bigger and older than him. Against Peada, Ahlfrith thought he might win; but not against the ætheling's friends as well.

The glance told him that they were not giving up the chase, although they had not managed to narrow the gap. The years he had spent racing his sister had made Ahlfrith quick. With the smithy shielding him from their view, he made use of that speed. Jagging to the side, he headed back towards the great hall. If he could get inside, then even Peada would have to let him go: everyone knew that Penda tolerated no fighting within its high walls.

"Get him!"

He heard the cry, but it sounded a little fainter. Ahlfrith glanced round to see Peada pointing after him. Looking ahead, he saw to whom Peada was gesturing. Some more of his friends were lounging by the training grounds, watching the king's men going through their exercises, but when they heard Peada's yell they looked round. It only took a glance for them to see what was asked: this was more fun than watching weapons drill. Yelling their joining of the chase, the boys angled towards him, cutting off Ahlfrith's escape.

Veering away, he still hoped to outdistance them and then turn back to the hall, but they were pushing him further and further away from it, out towards the high, rich tents, hung with banners, where the queen and her women made their daytime quarters, that they might make better use of the light.

Maybe, maybe, he could run round the tents and then back to the hall. But his lungs were burning and the muscles in his legs were turning liquid; he could not run much further at such a pace.

"Here! Come in here!"

Ahlfrith almost did not hear the call, his ears were so full of the sound of his own heart, but he saw the arm waving to him from the entrance to one of the tents, and he ran to it and dived inside.

"Ahlflæd," he gasped.

His sister put her finger to her lips.

"Shh," she said. "These are the queen's quarters; no men are allowed in here. Quick, hide." And she pushed her brother behind a bundle of sheepskins.

"Come out!"

The yell came from outside the tent.

"Come out, you little sneak, and fight me. Or are you too much of a coward – just like your daddy?"

Waiting outside, Peada saw the tent flap open. Despite his brave words, he took a step backwards. He had not expected the Northumbrian to come out and face him. But then he remembered the friends he had to back him up; one northern whelp couldn't hope to stand against them all, and he moved forward, raising his fists.

"My daddy is not a coward!"

It was a girl who had come out of the tent, fists bunched and face pale with fury.

"Your daddy and your brother too!" said Peada, turning towards his jeering accomplices. "See, he sends his sister out to do his fighting for him."

The turning away from Ahlflæd was a mistake. With all the speed of years racing her brother, Ahlflæd ran at Peada and, with his head only just turning back to her, fetched him such a blow on the chin that the boy fell backwards onto his bottom, landing with a squelch in a cow pat.

Stunned stupid, Peada looked vacantly up at Ahlflæd. "Wh-what…" he began. But he never got the chance to complete the question.

Ahlflæd jumped upon him, hitting his chest with all her weight, knocking the ætheling flat on his back and then, grabbing handfuls of hair in each hand, she began hitting the back of his head against the ground.

It was Peada's good fortune that the ground underneath him was soft and muddy. Blows that on rocky ground would have broken his skull merely dazed him, although they cut the invisible bonds of will linking his mind to his body. Try as he might, he could not command his muscles sufficiently to throw her from him.

All around, the boys who would have stood beside him and protected him from Ahlfrith stood and laughed, tears streaming down their faces, some having to hold on to others to stop themselves joining Peada upon the floor.

Although the ground was soft, if Ahlflæd had kept pounding Peada's head upon it for much longer his skull must surely have broken. But a hand reached down and grabbed the back of Ahlflæd's dress and lifted her, still striking and kicking, from the boy's prone body, then held her, thrashing in the air.

A single black eye stared at her.

Slowly, Ahlflæd stopped struggling.

"I came to find my wife and instead I find my son being beaten by a girl." The black eye looked down at the boy upon the ground.

Ahlflæd saw humiliation war with fear in Peada as he scrambled to his feet and stood, face downcast, looking at the ground.

"Look at me."

Slowly, reluctantly, Peada looked up. The black eye looked at him.

The watching ring of boys was absolutely silent, trying not to draw attention to itself, but it did not work.

"Go."

They ran, scurrying away in silence, hoping to be lost before the time for retribution came.

"D-dad…" Peada began, but his father held a finger to his lips.

"Shh," he said.

"But…"

"Shh." And Penda leaned towards his son. The boy struggled not to flinch from him.

"Did you know I had a sister?" Penda asked.

The boy shook his head.

"No, why should you? She died many years ago, and I have not spoken of her for nearly as long. Ymma was two years older than me, but I was a boy. When we were little, I would tease her and taunt her, but all she'd say was, 'You wait, boy; you wait.' One day, Ymma decided I had waited long enough. I was taunting her while she was doing her work – she was washing clothes in the stream and, I remember, her hands had turned blue from the cold of the water – and she stood up and wiped her hands on her apron. They were still blue though, I remember that. Then she looked at me, and said, 'Today is the day, Penda.' And she came at me. But she was a girl and I was a boy, and I'd grown fast the last year, so there wasn't much of a difference between us any more. I stood my ground." Penda laughed, a low, quiet laugh.

"Ymma gave me such a beating as I have not had from any man since." The king bent closer towards his son. "But, a year later, when I had grown, I beat her in return. It does not matter who you fight, son: boy, girl, man, wolf, wraith or dragon. It only matters that you win in the end. Remember that." But then he took Peada's head in his hand and twisted it so the boy looked, whether he would or not, at Ahlflæd, standing in still silence where Penda had put her. "But remember this as well: this girl is guest to me, and her brother is here as foster son. If you, or any of your friends, touch either of them again I will cut that hand off. Do you understand?"

Peada nodded. "Y-yes, Father."

"Good. Now run off."

As the boy made his getaway, Penda turned to see Ahlflæd inching her way back towards the queen's tents.

"But not you."

Ahlflæd stopped.

"I would see this girl who beats the son of the king."

She stood, still as stone, while Penda approached her, his face shadowed under his hood. The king slowly circled Ahlflæd as she remained standing, eyes staring straight ahead.

"Do I frighten you, Oswiu daughter?"

"N-no, lord," Ahlflæd said, her eyes fixed ahead.

"Then you are brave. Most men, grown warriors, fear me, and more since my... accident. My priest gave word that it was sign of Woden's favour: he sent his own raven to take my eye. Now, Woden marked, I have his blessing. Now, like him, I wander one eyed, and I wear a hood, like the Hooded One. That's what my priest says."

Penda leaned closer. Now Ahlflæd could feel his breath, warm against her cheek.

"But, it seems to me, Oswiu daughter, that too often the gifts of the gods are like this: hard to receive. I am a simple man: gold and glory are gifts enough for me. But my priest tells me Woden has blessed me. Ah, that we might only choose which blessings we receive from the gods."

Penda circled round, so he stood in front of Ahlflæd, forcing her to look at him.

"Hey. Hey, it's me you should be telling off, not her."

It was Ahlfrith. Emerging from the tent, the boy marched over towards the king and his sister. And if his heart was quaking with fear, he gave no sign of it, but came and stood beside Ahlflæd.

"It was me Peada was chasing. Ahlflæd saved me from him. So it's me you should be telling off."

Penda looked down at the boy, and though his eye was in shadow, his mouth lengthened into a smile.

"Oswiu is blessed with two such children as you. Would that my own son had your courage —" and here he looked at Ahlfrith — "or your brains —" and here he looked to Ahlflæd. "Tell me, Oswiu daughter, when do you return? You came with your brother, but he remains with me these next five years. When do you go back to your father's house?"

"At the month end, lord," said Ahlflæd.

"Good. In the time left, see what else you can teach my son. And when you return, give my greetings to your father. Tell him…" Penda's one black eye glittered, even though it was deep in the shadow of his hood. "Tell him I shall take payment for my eye when I will."

"Yes, lord."

"Very well. And, boy, should my son approach you again, tell me, not your sister. Peada shall learn to fight where I tell him, and nowhere else."

"Y-yes, lord."

"Good." Penda stood upright, for he had been stooping while talking to the children.

"Lord." The call came from the hall and Penda's attention snapped to it.

The children watched him stride across the courtyard.

"I wish you didn't have to go," Ahlfrith said to his sister.

"I wish you could come with me," said Ahlflæd, "but you must stay and be brave. Remember the mission Father gave us when he asked if we would come here: to be his eyes and ears, to learn whatever we can. I have to go back in a month, but you will be here for five years; think how much you can learn in that time."

"But five years is such a long time. I'll be grown up when I come back."

"I will come to see you. Every half year, someone from home will come to you. I will come with them. And then you can tell me what you've learned."

Ahlfrith shook his head. "I'm not as good at it as you are, Ahlflæd. All I've learned is that Peada hates me. You're the one who found out about Oswine Godfriend sending gold here, with that thegn of his… what's-his-name."

"Hunwald," said Ahlflæd quietly.

"And the promise he's given Penda, that he can ride unhindered through Deira whenever he wishes. Me, all I've done is try to avoid getting beaten up by the king's son and his friends."

"But you heard the king: Peada will have to leave you alone now. You'll be able to do what Daddy asked: find out stuff."

"That's all very well for you, but I'm no good at skulking round, listening in when people are talking. All I'm good at is fighting, and I couldn't even do that. You had to save me."

"Don't be stupid, Ahlfrith. One of the marks of a king is knowing when not to fight. You've already learned that lesson."

"Might not be a king at all, not now. By the time I get back, Daddy'll have a new queen. If she has a son, I bet he'll be king."

Ahlflæd shrugged. "Maybe. But even if he is, he'll need someone to rule with him: the kingdom's too big for just one king. You'll probably end up as king of Rheged or somewhere."

"Ew!" said Ahlfrith. "Who'd want to be king of Rheged?"

"I liked Grandad," said Ahlflæd. "He gave me lots of pretty things."

"That's because all the boys like you, even when they're old."

"I can't help being pretty – and a princess."

From the hall came the sharp blast of a horn: the call to eat.

"Race you!" said Ahlflæd, and she was off, hitching her dress up to her thighs, running across the courtyard.

"Hey! Not fair…" began Ahlfrith, but then he shrugged. After all, his sister never played fair. Instead, he set off after her and, this time, he very nearly caught her.

Chapter 6

"Your hair. Why you cut your hair like that?"

The question had hung unspoken for three days, but now, in a boat making its way up the east coast, it could wait no longer. Romanus, priest of God and man of the Franks, turned to the man sitting on the bench board beside him and asked the question that had remained unspoken since they first met.

For his part, the monk Utta was filling his lungs with the sea air and settling his too-long landlocked limbs into the familiar motion of boat on water. He had grown up on the islands of Dal Riada: his first memory was bobbing in his mother's arms and seeing a gull perched upon the lip of the curragh, grabbing for the fish in the bottom of the boat.

"Why do you shave your hair into a circle?" Utta returned question for question. Such had been the way with his teachers on Iona: question on question until he was driven to tearing the hair from his head in frustration. And then, sometimes, a glorious light would burst in his mind, showing all that he had been taught from a different angle, and suddenly everything would connect.

"It is sign of the Lord," said Romanus, pointing to his head, "in our body. He wear crown of thorns. We wear crown of hair, God's crown, not crown of man." He looked pointedly at Utta's shaven forehead and wind-streaming hair. "Why you not cut hair in crown?"

"We follow the example of the Blessed Colm Cille, who founded the holy house on Iona."

"I hear of this Colm Cille. He is barbarian?"

"No!" said Utta. "He could speak, read and write Latin."

"Ah, that is good. No barbarian. But you barbarian."

"*Non sum barbarus.* I speak Latin, and read and write Latin too."

"Ah, my friend, why didn't you tell me this before, rather than forcing me to speak that barbarous tongue which makes me sound as if I have rocks in my mouth?"

"It is the language of the kingdom where we sail, the tongue of the Angles, but it is not my native language either. Have you heard aught of my language, the speech of the islands?"

"There are so many tongues on this one island, I do not know if I have heard yours."

"There are many more islands than one here: I come from the other great land, the country of scholars and saints, which the emperors of old never conquered."

"Did the emperors ever try to conquer your land?"

"Well, no," admitted Utta.

Romanus nodded knowingly. "There are other lands also which the emperors did not conquer: desert and rock, of no account to man or beast."

"There are no deserts in my home land, although there are many rocks."

"You see? Of no account to man or beast."

Utta shook his head. "It is the land of Patrick and Colm Cille, of the seven saints of Derry and the holy ones of Dingle. It may be of no account to man or beast, but it is dear to God."

"Pah!" said Romanus. "Hedge priests and bog monks."

"What did you say?" Utta's white flesh began to flush red. His fingers began to clench.

From behind them, there came the sound of slow clapping.

The two men, sat knee to knee on the boat bench, turned to see a waxed cloth raised on wooden braces and held by ropes that made some small shelter from the wind and spray and, now, the first falling of another rain squall. Looking out from the shelter, her pale hands slowly clapping together, was a woman, with fur lining the cloak she had wrapped around her against the wind, the ermine as white as her hair, and a heavy gold brooch pinning the cloak shut.

"That went well," said the woman, her Latin as fluent as that of the two men. "I had thought to leave you to talk, that you men of

God might get to know each other, and already you are fighting like a pair of dogs fighting over a bitch."

"My lady!" said Romanus.

"Queen Æthelburh," said Utta, not so forward in his remonstrance – but then he had only met the queen a few days before, whereas the Frank had been her priest while she was in exile in the kingdom of the Franks, and had remained her priest when she returned from exile.

"So, I take it I am the bitch these two dogs are fighting over?" This second voice was light and young, as bright as water tumbling over stones, and its owner pushed forward beside Queen Æthelburh.

The queen slipped her daughter an exasperated glance. "Leave me to deal with this, Eanflæd," she said.

"Of course, Mother," the princess said mildly.

But just as the queen redirected her attention to the two priests, she piped up again. "Only, when I am married, you will return to Kent, but Romanus will stay, and Utta too. Mayhap I should speak to them now – while you can still correct me, of course."

Queen Æthelburh glowered at her daughter, but the look told that she could think of no suitable reply, so the girl came further forward, stepping over the rowing bench until she stood, swaying with the boat's movement, behind Romanus and Utta.

The two religious stared up at her. She smiled back at them.

"I like both your hair," Princess Eanflæd said. "Romanus's tonsure reminds me of the Lord's Passion – and of the sweet breads they made in the court of King Dagobert. And Utta's…"

But Eanflæd did not get the chance to tell them what Utta's tonsure reminded her of, for as she was about to speak, the ship's master hailed them.

"Ware," he cried, pointing to larboard.

There, from the west. Storm clouds, suddenly thick and dark, save when they flashed with internal lightning. And as the master pointed, and they all looked, the first thunder rolled over the boat.

Queen Æthelburh blanched when she saw the storm.

"Get to land," she yelled at the master, but he shook his head and pointed again. All trace of the land they had been following as they sailed north had vanished, swallowed into the storm cloud; to find safe harbour, they would have to sail through the storm, and already the sea was building up, the wind lashing the waves higher, the first rain stippling the water.

The master pushed Romanus and Utta back, out of the way and into the shelter, with the queen, the princess and their ladies, while he took over at the steering oar, calling orders to his oarsmen to furl the sail and then pull into the storm. The Frank and the Briton peered out from the shelter, with the two women looking between them, trying to see when the edge of the storm would strike. But when it came, it hit like a door slamming upon the boat.

In the sudden dark of the storm, Æthelburh turned a stricken face to her daughter and took her hand, although she could spare only one, as the other was needed to hold on to the side of the boat.

"I'm sorry," she said to Eanflæd. "This is my fault. I thought a sea passage would be safer."

"You had your adventure when you went north to marry," said Eanflæd. Lightning lit her face. "This is mine."

The queen tried to match her daughter's smile, but it was forced. Æthelburh was old now and she had seen too many of the people she loved die to think that her love, of itself, might shield against death. Only the lord of storms might save them and, releasing her daughter's hand, she turned to him now, telling her prayers upon her fingers and in the low breath of her heart.

The rain lashed into the boat. With visibility down to a square of rain-battered sea, the master had no choice but to hold the boat's head to the wind and listen for the deep drum roar of waves on rock, that they might tell him if he strayed too close to land. The sail rattled and flapped in the wind, moaning its wish to be free of restraint. The master fought against the wind, pulling the steering oar as an oarsman might, trying to keep the prow pointing into the wind.

But he was failing.

"Utta!" Eanflæd grabbed the monk's arm. He was a big man and she was slight, yet still she pulled him towards her. "You told me Bishop Aidan gave you tidings of this. Do what he bid you."

"Yes, yes," Utta muttered, reaching under his cloak to the pouch at his belt. "Here it is." He held up a small flask. "Bishop Aidan said to empty it on the waves when the storm came."

"I think it has come," said Eanflæd.

"Yes, yes." Utta made to go out from the shelter, but the heaving of the boat tipped him backwards.

"I'll help you." Eanflæd gave him one hand while grabbing the gunwale with the other.

Clutching the flask in his other hand, Utta made his way out from the stern shelter, with Eanflæd following.

Water broke over them, breathtaking in its chill, but she did not leave the monk's side.

Utta struggled with the seal, but his hands, numb and thick with cold, fumbled off the wax.

"I can't open it," he said.

"Hold it tight." Her fingers were smaller, the nails sharper, and though she could feel them little more than the monk could feel his, she could see what she was doing while he held the flask tight.

She peeled the wax off, and Utta pulled the stopper from the flask. The monk looked at her, and the girl nodded.

Crying a prayer that was torn from his lips before any sound of it could reach her ear, the monk leaned over the side of the boat and emptied the contents of the flask onto the water.

And the wind calmed.

The master, feeling the change, looked up and round. To the larboard the clouds ripped, and through the tears, the sun shone. At its touch, the waves eased, the foam-flecked crests settling back into long, easy ridges. The boat settled upon the surface. The squeal and squeak of flexing wood fell into the quiet talk of vessel to its master.

From within the dripping shelter, Eanflæd heard the voice of her mother, and mother now to the holy house at Lyminge, chanting in even low tones the Great Work of her house: the Divine Office.

The girl looked at the monk. Water dripped from his nose and ears. The monk looked at the girl. Her hair hung in rat's tails down her face.

"It worked," he said. He brushed the water from his nose.

"Yes," she said.

"My lady Eanflæd, it worked."

"Yes." Eanflæd brushed the rat's tails from her face. Then she turned and vomited over the side of the boat. Leaning over the side, heaving, she felt a hand upon her shoulder. Anger battled with nausea. She had gone so long. Now, when the storm was over, her body betrayed her, and in full view of all. She felt the touch on her shoulder as a reproach, and turned her face from it.

"You did well, daughter."

Eanflæd tried to nod, but it only made her body heave once more.

"I did not know of this flask given by Bishop Aidan," said Æthelburh. "He must be a holy man indeed, if God shows him such favour."

"He is, he is, my lady." The voice, and the enthusiasm, was Utta's.

"I look forward to meeting him, then." Queen Æthelburh put her hand on Eanflæd's shoulder. "Up, daughter."

Wiping her mouth clean as best she could, Eanflæd turned back inboard. She saw the rowers sitting in exhausted relief upon their benches, water still streaming from their forearms and hands, but with scarce enough strength to do more than mutter brief thanks to the god of sailors. The ship boys, two young lads who together couldn't have weighed much more than a good side of ham, were the only ones not stunned into immobility: they were still bailing frantically.

"Have you got any more of what was in that flask?" the master asked, as Utta and Eanflæd resumed their places. "I'll buy it from you, whatever you ask."

"I can sell you something better," said Utta. "And it won't cost you anything." And, while Eanflæd rested, the monk turned to telling the master of the mysteries. But before he could speak much on them, the queen pointed to where the land opened broad into a yawning estuary that seemed as wide as the sea.

"There," she said. "I know where we are." Æthelburh looked to the master. "That is Humbermouth?"

The master nodded.

"Take us into Humbermouth."

The master shook his head. Æthelburh might be a queen both spiritual and temporal, but here on this boat he was master, and he deferred to no one. "My orders are to take thee, and the lady princess, straight to the king at Bamburgh, not stopping nowhere on the way."

"Your first orders are to get us to him, alive and undrowned." The queen looked around at the exhausted men and the battered boat. "If another storm strikes, will we be able to ride it?"

"If we had more of what was in that flask, we could." The master looked to Utta, but the monk held the flask up and turned it upside down. No drop of oil fell from it. He turned back to the queen. "Then, no. But in all my days I ain't never seen a squall like that one."

Æthelburh indicated the battered ship. "With your boat in this condition, I do not think it would survive even a squall. Therefore, I tell you to sail into Humbermouth and make repair there, and let the crew rest." The queen looked away from the master, and up along the broad channel of water that carved through the land. "There is something I must do in the meantime."

*

Sitting in the prow of the river boat, the sun bright upon her face, Queen Æthelburh looked to her daughter. "This is madness," she said. But there was laughter in her voice, and there was laughter in Eanflæd's answer.

"Yes, it is, Mother."

"We should stay with the boat while it is repaired, and then set off to your new home as soon as it is ready."

"I know, Mother, we really should."

"What we shouldn't be doing is hiring a river boat to take us up the Ouse to York."

"No, that would be a silly thing to do, Mother. And you are never silly."

"No, never silly. But married, once…" The queen's voice trailed away as she stared ahead, as attentive as a hunting dog. "There," she said, pointing. "There. There it is. York." She turned to the young woman beside her. "Do you remember it at all?"

"A-a little. I think."

"I was younger than you when I came here for the first time. Bishop Paulinus brought me. Now I bring you." The queen paused, and when she began speaking again, there was a catch in her voice. "Do you remember your father?"

"Yes. Yes, I do."

The queen looked ahead. In the distance, the old walls, built by the emperors, reared up above the river.

"I can't remember his face any more," Æthelburh whispered.

They moored on the strand under the walls. The men climbed over the side of the boat and squelched in the soft river bank, laying wicker mats on the mud, that the two royal women might disembark. They had brought the two priests with them, and ten retainers, men who had done double duty on the journey up the coast by manning the oars, and who had served on the oars again during the long pull upstream from Humbermouth to York.

When all was ready, Romanus helped Queen Æthelburh from the boat, while Eanflæd, conscious of the many curious eyes watching from wharf and wall, accepted Utta's hand.

The queen looked to the two priests.

"Announce us, please. To the king, if he is here; to his reeve, if he is not."

As the priests made their way to the gates, Queen Æthelburh looked around. Her face was pale with the memory of a day, many years ago, when a rider had come galloping to York with news that her husband, King Edwin, was dead, and his killers were coming. She remembered the chaos and confusion as boats were loaded and what supplies could be found were rushed on board. She remembered looking for her son, little Wuscfrea, and finding him lost in the confusion. She had found him then, but lost him in exile, to the fever. Wuscfrea, Ethelhun and Ethelthryd. All gone now, save the eldest, Eanflæd, the young woman who stood beside her. Æthelburh sighed. Sometimes it was very hard to let her children go with God.

Eanflæd looked at her mother, and saw that she remembered. "You're thinking of them, aren't you? Wuscfrea, and Ethelhun and Ethelthryd, the twins."

"Wuscfrea loved talking to the boatmen here. They all loved him too – little otter, they called him, on account of how well he could swim." Tears sparkled on the queen's eyes, like water jewels.

Eanflæd took her mother's hand. "We could go back to the ship. The river is flowing fast; it would take us back much faster than we came."

But the queen patted her daughter's hand in turn, and blinked away the tears.

"Not all sad memories are cruel, nor is all pain bad. Coming here, I can see them again, Eanflæd. Over the years, their faces have grown dim, but now, here, where they lived, I see them." The queen smiled, and there was as much joy as sadness in her smile. "I see them as I see you."

Eanflæd nodded her understanding and left her mother to her memories, while she looked around with interest. Only London had greater, higher walls than those she saw in front of her, but those of the old capital were broken in more places, thrown down in the years of desperate defence that the Britons had mounted before the city fell. York's defences stood all but intact, the watchtowers still looking out over the rivers and marsh and water meadows that stretched out from the city.

This was the city, and the realm, that her husband-to-be hoped to win over by marrying her. Oh, of course that had not been mentioned during the marriage negotiations, but Eanflæd understood the reason for Oswiu's suit as well as anyone involved in the bargaining. She had been offered as proof of alliance, and bought with gold, and garnets, and land – much land. Her mother had told King Earconbert's men what to accept for her, and she had told well. Should Oswiu put her aside – and they knew well that he had put aside one woman and fathered a son on another – then all the gold, and garnets, and land was hers, to do with as she would. There would be more than enough land to endow a monastery, a holy house such as the one her mother led, as a place to retire to should such a thing come to pass. But she did not intend such a thing to come to pass. Eanflæd knew how to be a queen – her mother, a great queen, had told and shown her how. Now she meant to be one.

It was not long before Romanus and Utta returned. Seeing them approach, Eanflæd saw Utta beginning to rush towards them, his face eager with news, only to be called back by the Frank. Romanus had been priest to a queen for many years now. He knew the slow, stately walk that signalled the proper dignity due such a woman. Chastened, Utta fell in beside Romanus, and the two priests approached with the solemn diligence due their role as heralds to two queens: one who was, and one who would be.

Romanus stopped in front of the two women and bowed low in the Frankish manner. Utta, for his part, made the courtesy.

"We have announced you to York," Romanus said, his voice loud enough to ensure anyone attempting to overhear could do so without undue difficulty. "The king, Oswine Godfriend, is here in the city, but he is hunting."

"But Bishop Aidan is here!" Utta broke in, unable to maintain silence any longer.

Romanus dug an elbow into the monk's flank. Utta appeared not to notice, but Romanus winced, and rubbed his elbow.

"The king will return soon. Now, the king's reeve bids you welcome, and asks you to come within the city, to the king's great hall, where you may be made welcome until his return."

"We are blessed," said Utta. "I did not know Bishop Aidan would be here."

"Then we can thank him for the oil which calmed the sea," said Queen Æthelburh.

"We can thank him for our lives," said Eanflæd.

"Take us to your bishop, Utta," said Æthelburh. "And we shall all thank him."

They got the chance more quickly than they had thought. For

Aidan was waiting for them, at the city gates, standing alongside the door warden, the guards, a gaggle of excited children and gossiping fishwives, farmers and boatmen; such a crowd as was rarely seen save when the king arrived with all his court. But the king and his retainers were out on the hunt, so the people waiting with Aidan were the low born and the coarse; some few did not even carry spears, the mark of a free man, for they were slaves. All waited at the gate, leaving scant room around the bishop, but Aidan did not seem to mind. Instead, he waited with them, hearing the excited whisper pass through the crowd: Queen Æthelburh, wife of King Edwin, had returned to them, with her daughter. Some were already confidently proclaiming this as a marriage between Æthelburh's daughter and King Oswine, notwithstanding the fact that the king already had a wife. But all knew that a king might as easily put aside a wife as a farmer puts aside seed, particularly when that wife had made no children.

"You mark my words, it'll be like the old days, when good King Edwin ruled, and there was peace in the land and food on the table, and a woman could walk from one end of the country to the other, with babe in arms mind, and none would harm her for fear of the king's vengeance." So said one old fishwife to another, younger than her – too young to remember the legendary days her elder recalled.

"Don't know about that, but she is pretty, right enough," replied the younger. "Bet the king'll be eager to get some children on her."

Aidan, listening, tried not to. He put up a surreptitious hand to test his face. At least it was not flushed. Once, hearing such things would have sent him scarlet with embarrassment, but he was older now and, as bishop, had heard this, and worse, many, many times. Maybe he should bewail the loss of the gift of shame? Aidan laid the matter aside to think upon in the quiet watches of the night, when men slept and he lay awake, struggling with his conscience and his God.

Utta was leading the party, his eagerness pushing him on ahead of the other priest's measured stride, until he all but ran the final few steps to stand, then kneel, in front of Aidan. The bishop raised his brother to his feet, and kissed him, then turned to the party now standing before him.

Romanus nudged Utta to one side. In normal circumstances it was his job to announce the queen; even more so on this unusual day.

"Bishop Aidan of Lindisfarne, I present to you Queen Æthelburh, mother abbess of the holy house at Lyminge, wife to King Edwin of blessed memory, and her daughter, the Princess Eanflæd."

Aidan made the courtesy to mother and daughter. And then, despite Romanus's huffing and puffing, it was Utta's turn.

"Queen Æthelburh and Princess Eanflæd, this is Bishop Aidan, abbot of the Holy Island, the man who saved our lives."

Now Aidan really did blush, bright as cooked salmon, and all the more so when first queen, then princess, knelt to him and pressed their lips to the back of his hand. It did not help that he heard the fishwives, who had earlier been speculating about the princess marrying the king, laughing at his discomfort. Many a side was nudged to attract attention, and then fingers pointed at his red face.

As soon as he might, Aidan urged mother and daughter back to their feet.

"Please, I am not worthy of such honour. You are Yffings, of the House of Yffi and, by your marriage, joined to the Idings, rulers of Bernicia. My father was a fisherman. Do not do me such honour."

Æthelburh looked pointedly at Aidan. "The father of our Lord was a carpenter. Should I not pay him honour? And should I not honour the Lord through you, his servant?"

"Please, pay all honour to the Lord, but this, his servant, is a weak and foolish man – I would not have my head turned nor my chest puffed with honour, when I deserve none."

"If you will accept no other honour, accept this," broke in Eanflæd. "Our thanks, for the flask of oil you gave to Brother Utta; it calmed the storm when we were all but lost, and now we who had thought to be drowned are here."

Aidan waved his hand. "It was but a dream I had. There was no skill in it."

"Few men have the knowledge of dreams."

"This one does not," said Aidan. "The dream told what I had to do."

"Did a dream tell you of our visit?" asked Queen Æthelburh.

Aidan smiled, glad to admit his ignorance. "No, it did not."

"Then you should know that we may not wait long ere we continue on our journey. Do you know when the king will return?"

"I sent a messenger as soon as your priest told me of your arrival. King Oswine will, I am sure, return in all haste – most likely before day's end."

"That is well, for we may not wait longer. But –" and here the queen's voice lowered, so few apart from Aidan might hear her – "while he returns, there is another I would see…"

Aidan nodded. "Of course." He turned to the gathered crowd. "Make way for the queen! Make way for Queen Æthelburh!" Shoving and pushing against each other, the crowd nevertheless parted to make a passage for the queen. Going first, Bishop Aidan led the queen, her daughter, priests and retainers through the gates of York and into the city.

As they walked through its streets, Eanflæd marvelled at the size of the buildings that rose upon either side of her, and also lamented their decay, for few bore any sign of living, but rather slumped, as corpses upon a battlefield, in the pose of their last living. Men shunned the places built by the emperors of old, thinking them wraith haunted. But Eanflæd remembered the stories her mother had told her, when they were in exile and walked in cities as great or greater than this, but cities that still lived. Her mother had told her of this city of York, city of the emperors, and of how her father had grown up in its decaying splendour, and how he did not fear it, so that as a boy he wandered its ways and buildings, a child walking in the work of giants. Now they were going to where her father waited on them, and she looked at her mother, and saw the eagerness in her walk and the concentration in her eyes.

Aidan led them to the great church of York, the church of stone, the first such building made in the land since the emperor's legions had sailed back across the narrow sea. The building rose high before them, its wooden roof pointing to the sky. Bishop Aidan paused before its great wood door, and rapped upon the wood with his staff.

The door opened, and the sound of chant reached to them, standing without.

Aidan turned to the two women. "The king, Oswine Godfriend, has ordered that the monks here pray throughout the day for King Edwin."

The queen nodded her thanks at such news; she could not speak with words. Taking her hand, Aidan led her into the church.

It was gloomy within, the only light coming through the door and the row of small windows set high in the walls, but the darkness glowed with the richness of the hangings, woven gold, upon the walls, and the vessels upon the altar, and the torches burning in sconces. It was a light such as that which shines upon the world under a lid of cloud, when the sun, before it sinks out of sight, sends its light across the land to banish the gloom of the day with promise of the light of tomorrow. It was the hope light, and it shone in the queen's face as she followed Bishop Aidan into the church.

The chant continued, not catching or pausing despite the presence of the bishop, although the four monks watched the procession that went up the church towards the altar.

There, upon the altar, beside the Gospel book and the sacred vessels, was a rich, golden reliquary. Aidan went to the altar, and knelt before it. Then, standing, he opened the reliquary, but his body covered that which was within.

"Queen Æthelburh." The bishop spoke softly, without turning round, but the queen heard him well. She stepped up beside the bishop and looked, once again, after so many years, upon the face of her husband.

Aidan moved back, gently positioning himself so that he covered the queen from the sight of the others in the church.

"Yes," whispered Æthelburh, as she took in the face of her husband. "Of course. I remember now."

She leaned forward, and with infinite gentleness kissed the dry, withered lips.

"Watch over her. Watch over our daughter, our first born, little Eanflæd. I have grown old, husband – see, my hair is white now. It will not be long before I come to you. I hope I have done rightly, marrying her to an Iding. But as you did not hunt them when they were in exile, they did not hunt me when I was in exile. I think I have done what you would have wished, for you always wanted the two kingdoms, Deira and Bernicia, to be one, and by this match that may be so." Æthelburh looked back over her shoulder, into the nave, then back to her husband's remains. "I will show her to you, our little girl. She is grown now, grown beautiful and wise." Turning round, Æthelburh beckoned to her daughter. "Come, Eanflæd; come and see your father."

Eanflæd felt her mouth suddenly go dry. Pushing her hands together as if in prayer, but rather to stop them shaking, she went forward to join her mother. The queen was standing by the reliquary, smiling, although her cheeks were streaked with tears.

Eanflæd saw the leathery skin, stretched over skull, the loose hair and the dry lips tight on teeth; his eyes were closed, but now, seeing him, she remembered his eyes in life, the darkness of them and the intensity. She remembered her father standing over her, looking down at her and then lifting her, it seemed to the sky, and the face, that dead face, breaking into a smile as warm as a father's love. Eanflæd, once exiled princess, looked on the face of her father, and knew him.

Chapter 7

"We've got him!" Hunwald, thegn of Deira and hunting companion to Oswine Godfriend, turned to the king. "We've got him."

Oswine shook his head. "That boar will be well away by now. If the messenger hadn't called us back, I'm sure we would have got him, but he is long gone now."

"No, no, not the boar." Hunwald rode his horse closer to the king. The king's hunting companions milled around the two men, while the dogs cast upon the ground for a scent, making little forays off in all directions until the huntsmen called them back. It was the scene of a hunt in confusion. But this was through no stratagem of their quarry – a wild boar that had been terrorizing the villages around Skelton – but rather the result of the message, brought to the king, by the messenger who was now receding back towards York as quickly as he had come from the city.

"What do you mean?" asked Oswine Godfriend. The message had taken him by surprise; to think that Edwin's queen, Æthelburh herself, was now in York. It was as if Yffi himself, father of the Yffings, returned to see how his descendants fared.

Hunwald looked round, making sure none of the other companions were close enough to hear. "Our enemy has been delivered into our hands. Oswiu sends for a new wife, one to win the witan of Deira to his cause, and she comes here first. The gods…" Hunwald caught Oswine's sharp glance. "I mean, God has delivered her into our hands. You can make sure she never reaches him. You could even…" The thegn's eyes lit up with speculation. "Yes, why not? Lord, take her as wife for yourself. With Edwin's daughter by your side, you will have certain claim over the throne here and, mayhap, claim upon the throne in Bernicia too." Hunwald reached out and grasped Oswine's forearm. "Then, as king of Northumbria,

184

you may throw off the halter Penda has put upon you, for men will flock to you from all the kingdoms, eager for glory, and we will have such an army that Penda will flee before us, or fall to our swords. What do you say, lord?"

Oswine looked at the bright, feverish eyes of his thegn. They shone with the glory light, the glow he had seen in men's eyes in hall, when they recounted a tale of courage and strength such that all those present listened, in silent awe, and then, when the tale was over, raised such a cheer that the dead themselves might hear. He felt the glory lust tighten within him. That he might be free of the shame Penda heaped upon him, the constant demands for gold that left his chests empty and his warriors bare armed. It was true – the possibilities opened up before him. Keep Edwin's daughter from Oswiu, and soon all the thrones would know that the king of Bernicia was not able to bring his betrothed safely to his court. Then the ravens, the wandering æthelings who roamed the land searching for the pickings of weakness and the meat of the fallen, would turn their black gaze on Oswiu. They would converge upon Bernicia, as flies drawn to a carcass. Such constant attack would leave Oswiu unable to push his claim upon Deira. In the end, it might weaken him enough for Oswine Godfriend to challenge him in open battle.

Then Oswine's eyes too began to glow with the glory lust. With the men of Bernicia he could make alliance with the East Angles and the West Saxons, the North Folk and the South Folk, pulling tight the ring around Penda, threat to them all, until the noose choked him to death. That would end the shame of the gold wagons, the annual tribute that Penda extracted from Deira in exchange for the promise that he would not raise his hand against the kingdom. So far, Penda had kept that promise – but the demands for gold were becoming more frequent.

Yes, he could take this girl, stop her getting to Oswiu, keep her…

What was he going to do with her? He had a wife, and though she had produced no child, yet he would not put her aside, for her belly had swelled, once, twice, three times, only for the child to be lost ere it could be delivered. Besides, he had asked Bishop Aidan on this, and Brother James, when he went to visit the Roman at his hermitage near Catterick, and both had told the same: to God, marriage was an oath sworn, as man to lord, and thegn to king. To forswear it was to break faith, as if a man turned from his lord. It was to call down vengeance from heaven.

Oswine shook his head. He would have no part of that. Yet if he did not take the girl as wife himself, what was he to do with her?

"It would not be meet for me to take Edwin's daughter for my own wife, not while I yet have a wife. But what counsel have you, Hunwald? If we keep her, what should we do with her?"

"Lord, all know that sometimes kings put aside wives for another; there is no shame in that."

"No," said Oswine and, when Hunwald began to remonstrate further, he put up his hand. "I said no, friend. I know you have ever been loyal to me, and wish the best for the realm, but on this matter I will hear no more. But tell me, what think you if we keep Edwin's daughter, this Eanflæd? What may we do with her?"

Hunwald looked at the king. "What would any king do?" The thegn's brow began to furrow as he saw no nod of unspoken acknowledgment from Oswine. "You know. It is not what we would wish, of course. But the messenger told us she had come by boat into Humbermouth. The waters there are treacherous – many ships founder if their masters do not know the shift of shoal and sandbank. It would be very sad, but no blame could be attached to you, lord."

"Kill her?"

Hunwald looked around, making sure no one was near enough to hear. "Lord," he said, his voice dropping to a whisper as he drove his horse next to the king's, "please, speak softly. Such matters are best left unspoken, even among your own."

Oswine sat back upon his horse. He felt, around him, the swirl of things that might be. No. He felt the shift of who he might be. A great king, the High King, the king of kings, to whom all bowed. Had not the messenger said that the princess and her mother had come to York because their boat had only just ridden out one great storm? Who was to say it would not founder in another?

The princess and her mother.

Eanflæd, daughter of Edwin and cousin to him, and Æthelburh, queen to Edwin – the woman who had first brought to his people the news of life, the life he had himself entered when Paulinus had drawn the waters of the River Ouse over his head, once, twice, thrice, and pulled him forth as one new born. Shivering, crying, like a babe he had been; but the tears were of joy and the cold was the leaving of his old life.

This little thing Hunwald asked of him would leave the queen also dead. How would he answer to the door warden of the new life, when he asked of this? How would he answer for Eanflæd, or the priests that travelled with them, or even the ship's crew? How would he answer for any of them? That they were but small things in the way of his becoming the king of kings?

"No." Oswine looked to Hunwald. "I know you give this counsel in your love for me, but I will not take it. For it seems to me that a man comes into this middle-earth as a babe, but he might leave it as many things: as a wolf, ravening after the shepherd's sheep; as a fox, slipping into the coop; as a crow, feasting on the dead. But I would leave this world as a man, Hunwald, and to do as you have bid would be to change my skin: I would be a man no longer." The king grasped his counsellor's forearm. "You do understand?"

Hunwald looked long upon his king; he looked as one seeing clearly for the first time. Then he nodded.

"Yes, I understand," he said.

"Good." Oswine Godfriend released his hold upon his thegn and signalled to his huntsmen. "The boar will have to wait. We ride to York, to see the queen. Queen Æthelburh!"

And, taking his cry, the hunt turned back to the city.

"Æthelburh!" they cried. "Æthelburh!"

*

"I am a fool!"

Eanflæd looked up from where she knelt in prayer, to see her mother coming quickly down the church towards her.

"Mother?" she asked, getting to her feet.

Æthelburh took her arm and signalled to their men to follow.

"I am a fool, daughter," the queen said as she walked beside Eanflæd down the nave. "We should never have sent word to the king of our arrival; I could have come here as a pilgrim, without notice and unnoticed. Now, Oswine knows you are here, daughter. Like as not news has reached him of your betrothal. If we cannot get away from here before his return, Oswine will seek to stop it."

The queen spoke these final words as she was reaching to open the doors to the church. But the doors opened before she could touch them.

"Oswine will seek to stop what?"

Standing without the church was the king of Deira, Oswine Godfriend.

Queen Æthelburh stopped. She took in the man in front of her in one single, sweeping glance. Then she turned to her daughter.

"Eanflæd, I am a fool twice over, for I feared that King Oswine Godfriend would be a man without honour or truth; a man who might seek to stop you fulfilling the pledge of betrothal you entered into before God. But now –" and here the queen turned back to the man standing in front of them – "I see that my fears were baseless. This man, this king, would not stand between you and the marriage pledge you have given. Is that not true?" The queen looked upon the young man, and to him it seemed as if she saw all too clearly how close his soul struggle had been.

"Th-that is true, Queen Æthelburh. I will not make you break the pledges you have given, nor the oaths you have sworn, but rather will do all that I may to help you in your journey."

"Good, good." Queen Æthelburh smiled brightly. "In that case, you may feed us."

The queen took Oswine's arm as they walked from the church to the king's hall – the only wooden building standing amid the brick and stone of York – regaling him, as they went, with tales of Edwin, and a pointed retelling of her own journey north as a bride-to-be, when she was waylaid by King Cadwallon of Gwynedd, Edwin's sworn enemy. He too had let her go, although Cadwallon had taken the treasure that was meant to form part of the wedding settlement for himself.

Bishop Aidan walked with Eanflæd, but his tales were tales of woe: of his own haplessness with curragh and coracle, his gradual demotion, when he lived on the Holy Island of Iona, from working in the scriptorium, through preparing paints and colours, to, finally, the dirtiest, smelliest job on the island: curing and preparing animal skins to turn into vellum, for the writing and making of books. As he walked, the people who scurried after the king would run to him, and many would touch him or ask his blessing, so that every story was interrupted while Aidan laid his hands upon a man with sores all over his body, or a woman with a weeping wound; all the ills to which the people of middle-earth are prey.

As they approached the hall, the great building rising above the broken-down brick houses that surrounded it, the king looked back to Aidan.

"We missed you on the hunt, Bishop Aidan. Next time, you must come with us."

"To hunt, you need a horse, lord," said Aidan, "and I do not have one."

"But you do." Oswine stopped. "I gave you one."

"I do not have it any longer," said Aidan.

"It was a fine animal. Did it break a leg?"

"No, no. I am sure it lives yet. No, I gave it to a poor man who asked alms of me."

"What?" Oswine stared at the bishop. "You gave it away?"

"Yes," said Aidan. "Of course." He made to go on towards the hall, but the king stopped him.

"I gave you the finest animal I had, so that you could have use of it when travelling in my kingdom. If you wanted to give alms, I had many poorer horses, or other belongings, which you could have given to a beggar, rather than this horse that I chose especially for you."

Aidan shook his head. "Think on what you say, lord. Do you

really believe the son of a mare to be more valuable than the son of Adam to whom I gave it?" The bishop looked square at the king. "For that is what you are saying. But come, let us go in to eat, for we are keeping Queen Æthelburh and Princess Eanflæd waiting."

With that, the bishop continued on and, a moment later, the king followed. But Oswine was caught in thought, so that he offered only the shortest answers to the queen's questions as they went into the hall, and while Æthelburh and Eanflæd were shown to their places at the high table, Oswine Godfriend went to warm himself by the fire, for the hunt had been long and fruitless, and he had had no chance to warm himself since his return to York.

Holding his hands to the fire, Oswine slowly felt the warmth of it enter his fingers. And, in sudden memory, he saw again the hands of a woman, a young woman with a babe that slept in a sling at her breast, who stood outside her rude house in winter, washing the babe's swaddling clothes in water that clinked with ice. He remembered the sight of her hands, red raw, and pointing them out to his father as they rode past, returning from hunting to their hall.

"The poor get used to cold hands," his father had said, ruffling his hair. "They have to," he'd added, laughing. And Oswine, not wanting to seem foolish in the eyes of his father, had laughed too.

The king looked down at his own hands. They were warm now. The king unbuckled his sword and gave it into a servant's keeping. Then, Oswine Godfriend went to where Bishop Aidan sat at the high table and went down before him upon his knees.

"Bishop Aidan, I promise you this: never again will I question you over how much of mine you give away to God's children."

The hall fell into silence. Servants, seeing the king kneel, stopped in mid step. Thegns and retainers, engaged in games of dice, let them fall without seeing. Even the dogs stopped squabbling.

"You must not kneel to me, lord. Please." Aidan took the king's hands and raised him to his feet. "I know you to be a good man and a good king. Please, do not kneel to me."

But Oswine smiled at the bishop. "If not you, then who? The hardest part of being king is having no one to kneel to." Oswine clapped his hands. "Come, let us eat in honour of our visitors: Bishop Aidan, who visits us again, and, especially, in honour of Queen Æthelburh and Princess Eanflæd! You will tell your children and your children's children of this day, when the queen, Edwin wife, came back to us!"

There was great joy at that feast. Some among the king's servants remembered the queen, having served Edwin many years before, and they came before her, to ask her blessing and her memory, and Æthelburh gave both gladly. Others passed before Eanflæd, gazing in wonder at the young woman who had left them as a child. One came forward, a woman of middle years, who put her hand to Eanflæd's cheek and stroked it, as a mother strokes the cheek of a sleeping child. And Eanflæd, feeling that touch, started, and looked at her anew, and saw her with the years stripped away.

"Matilda! My nurse!" She looked to her mother for confirmation, and the queen nodded the truth of it. And, rising from the table, Eanflæd took the woman in her arms, returning some small part of the warmth she had been given as a child.

But as the feast continued in joy, Aidan fell into deeper and deeper silence. Amid such excitement, his quiet was not noticed, save only by Utta, who made his way to the bishop's side under the guise of bringing small beer to him – for Aidan would not drink wine or any rich drink, even at feast in a king's hall.

Bending down to fill Aidan's cup, Utta saw that his bishop's eyes were filled with tears, but he could see no cause.

"Father Abbot, why do you weep?" Utta asked, speaking in the language of the islands, which only he and Aidan, of the people at the feast, understood.

"I weep for the king. He is good and he is humble. Such a man will not survive long as king in this middle-earth."

Utta took his father abbot's hand. "We will pray for him," he said, "that he may live."

Aidan shook his head. "I do not think God will hear this prayer, although I cannot see when or where death will come to him."

"Then we will pray for him when he is dead," said Utta.

"Yes. Yes, you must." The bishop took his monk's hand. "And pray for me also, for my soul tells me I will not live long after."

"What are you talking of?" The queen looked over to Aidan, and the monk standing beside him.

"Of the goodness of the king," said Aidan.

"He has indeed been kind to us," said Eanflæd. She felt the king's gaze upon her and smiled to him. "If he were not already wed…"

"But he is," said the queen, "while the king of Bernicia is not."

"Not any more," said Eanflæd. "But he was married, was he not, Bishop Aidan?" She smiled at the bishop. "Do you know aught of this? How could he put aside his wife? She gave him two children, I believe. Surely, he must have sought guidance from you on this matter?"

Bishop Aidan blushed. "Yes, yes, he sought guidance," he mumbled.

"The king brought us the relic of his brother, Oswald," said Utta. "His head."

Eanflæd raised her eyebrows. "You have his head?"

"I-I knew Oswald of old," said Aidan. "He wished to enter the new life and become a monk on the Holy Isle. Now he has entered the new life of heaven, I thought to give his earthly remains the dearest wish of his heart, and to take them to Lindisfarne."

Eanflæd nodded. "As an old friend, of course you would want to grant his wish in death, even if you could not in life." The princess smiled brightly at the abbot. "Have you given thought to all the pilgrims who will come to the Holy Island seeking his blessing?"

"Pilgrims?"

"Surely you heard of the miracles worked from the very earth upon which the High King fell, and that took his life blood? We heard tell of them, even in Kent. And the messengers from my future husband told me of how he went, disguised as a blind pilgrim, into Mercia to bring his brother home. That sounds very brave, don't you think?"

"It was," agreed Aidan. "It must have been through Oswald's protection that he succeeded, for it was beyond the strength of mortal men to do as King Oswiu did."

"Then Oswald's protection and blessing must be great indeed. And you really haven't thought of all the pilgrims who will now come to the Holy Island, seeking his blessing?"

"No. No, I hadn't." Aidan looked at the princess. She looked blandly back at him. "Do you – do you think I accepted Oswald's relics for the riches the pilgrims might bring?"

"Oh, no. I'm sure it did not enter your mind," said Eanflæd.

"No. No, it didn't." Aidan began to flush, but this blush was not from the embarrassment that plagued him, but from anger. "You did not know him, princess. I did. Through all his life, Oswald had no rest, for always, always people wanted from him: strength, courage, hope most of all. Now, in death, I would give him that rest. We will not even tell of his presence with us, but pray always for the repose of his soul. Do you understand?"

The princess nodded, a small grave smile playing over her lips. "Yes, I understand. But I would ask one other question of you, if I may. What guidance did you give King Oswiu when he asked to put aside his wife? I ask because, after all, if he has done this once, he might do so again, and then I will be the wife he will be seeking to put aside."

"He told me the request came from the queen: she wished to lay aside the cares and temptations of this world and seek the new life in a holy house. Thus, the greater pledge, the oath we must make to the lord of all when we face him, took precedence over the smaller pledge that wife gives to husband when they wed."

"I see," said Eanflæd. "So one oath cancelled out the other."

"No, not cancelled." Aidan flushed again. "An oath may not be broken. B-but it may be subsumed in another. Queen Rhieienmelth goes to the new life with God, not to the same life with another man."

"So, if the day should come when my husband wishes to put me aside, he may only do so if I choose to enter one of the holy houses?"

Bishop Aidan flushed even redder. "I hope such a day will never come," he said. But he could not bring himself to look at the princess.

"As do I," said Eanflæd. She looked across the bishop to her mother, but Queen Æthelburh was speaking with the king. "As do I," Eanflæd repeated under her breath, and then, rising, she signalled to the servant who bore the great cup, the drinking horn, filled with the sweetest mead, to bring it to her. Taking the great cup, Eanflæd bore it to where the king, Oswine Godfriend, sat in his judgement seat. Making the courtesy with such grace that not a drop spilled from the cup, even though it was full to its brim, she held the cup to the king.

"May this cup ever be a sign and token of friendship between the two kingdoms, Bernicia and Deira, and a pledge of our good fellowship – for we are cousins, you and I, Oswine and Eanflæd."

The king, eyes shining, took the cup from her and raised it to his lips. "I take this cup right gladly from you, Eanflæd, Æthelburh daughter." The king raised it, but before he could bring the cup to his lips, the door warden hailed the feast.

"*Hwæt!* A messenger from King Penda."

And Eanflæd, her gaze still fixed upon the king, saw Oswine pale as the messenger was announced; she saw him put aside the great cup, still undrunk, handing it to the servant who stood beside him, while he turned his attention to the man who came and stood before the high table.

Normally, a messenger waited upon the king's command before presenting his message to the king, but this messenger expected Oswine to hear him immediately, and the king did as the messenger expected. Eanflæd looked round to see, and hear, what message this man brought, that it be so urgent.

"King Penda, the High King, sends greetings to his pledge king, Oswine, whom some name Godfriend. King Penda reminds him of his pledge, and tells him that the pledge is due."

Oswine Godfriend shook his head.

"No, there is some mistake. We sent our pledge, all our pledge, this six month past; it is not due again until winter has come and gone."

"King Penda, the High King, reminds his pledge king that he rules through his good pleasure and by his sufferance. It is not for him to say when the pledge is due." The messenger smiled, in calculated insult. "It is as if the sheep were to say to the shearer, 'My fleece is not woolly enough; wait for it yet to grow'; or the wheat to the reaper, 'We are not yet ripe: stay your scythe until we are taller.' It is for King Penda to say when the pledge is due – and he has sent me to tell thee it is due."

Oswine made to answer, but the messenger held up his hand and silenced the king.

"I have given my message; there is no more for me to say. I will withdraw and wait upon your answer, returning three day hence to hear it."

The messenger left the hall with silence walking beside him into the night. But the silence left with him; when he was gone, speech returned: quiet, furtive conversations, glances passed between men upon the benches, then thrown up to the high table where King Oswine, with the messenger's departure, had turned at once to Hunwald to ask his warmaster's counsel.

Standing forgotten in front of the king, Princess Eanflæd looked with new eyes upon the man in front of her.

"Lord."

She had not meant to speak, but the word escaped her. It cut through the whispers that surrounded the king, and came to his ear. And Oswine turned to Eanflæd.

"Yes?"

"Do you pay throne geld to Penda, the man who slew my father?"

Oswine glanced around, for the princess spoke clearly, although she had not raised her voice, and its pure tones carried the words over the low voices of his men, so that it took the question to the far corners of his hall. The king shook his head, signing her for quiet, but Eanflæd asked the question once more.

"Do you pay throne geld to Penda, the man who slew my father?"

And now she saw her mother stand too, and look upon the king for his answer.

Oswine glanced from daughter to mother and back again. "It's – it's not as simple as that…" Oswine glanced at Queen Æthelburh. "You understand…?"

But the queen held her hand out to her daughter.

"Come, it is time for us to leave. We may not stay here, in this hall, and feast with those who give gold to my husband's killer that they might rule in his stead."

The princess went towards her mother, the two women converging, while the king held out a silent hand to stay them, but no words escaped his lips. They cast no glance towards him, but together turned and walked towards the door. In the great stillness that had fallen upon the hall, not even their own retainers, nor their priests, moved, but stared in silent wonder at the queen and the princess.

But there was one who moved. Getting up from his seat by the king, Hunwald came and stood before the two women, so that they had, perforce, to stop.

"You're not going anywhere," he said, but under the queen's regard his voice tailed away, and Hunwald looked past them, to the king. "Are they, lord?"

"I remember you of old," said Queen Æthelburh, "when my husband ruled this land." And she began to advance upon the thegn. "I remember you of old, Hunwald; you were then snake tongued and gold greedy, looking always to stand beside those whose deeds were greater than yours, that you might steal some of their glory. In all these years, I see you have not changed. Now get out of my way, you witless, crawling thing, lest I crush you beneath my heel."

And though the man was a head taller and a ram heavier than the queen, he fell back before her, and the queen and the princess passed him by.

At the door, Queen Æthelburh stopped, and looked back to the king.

"I would think more of a king who keeps better counsel," she said. While her mother spoke, Eanflæd signed to their people, the two priests and the retainers, to follow, and the men hastily made their way towards the women. Then, together, they left the hall.

Outside, the twilight was fading, but there was still light enough to see.

"We must make haste," said the queen. "To the boat. On it, the river will carry us to safety." She glanced back at the hall, its door still closed, and looked to Eanflæd. "Humiliation is a bitter goad. Hunwald will come after us."

Eanflæd nodded. "Yes." She looked around. The door warden had gone within, to find the cause of their leaving, and his post was briefly unmanned. As the men retrieved their swords and spears, the princess saw the two great round iron handles upon the door.

"Quick." She motioned to one of her men and he, seeing what she meant, ran a spear through the handles

Just in time. The door heaved inward, but the spears locked it. Shouts rang out from within, and blows fell upon the wood, but it did not give.

The queen looked to her daughter. "If I fall behind, leave me."

Eanflæd gave a quick glance to her mother, shook her head, and signed the strongest of her retainers.

"Carry the queen," she said. And while the queen was hoisted protesting onto the man's back, Eanflæd gathered her skirt up and tied it off around her thighs. She caught Romanus' scandalized glance. "Don't look."

From within the hall, sound was rising. They would soon break open the door.

"Mother, show the way."

With the queen riding upon the man's back and pointing where to go, they ran through the darkening streets of the city. As night deepened, shadows bled from the ruined houses, pooling around their running feet so that they could no longer see where they stepped, and could only call God's mercy down that they not fall.

Romanus, running beside Eanflæd, stumbled and all but fell. Running once more, Eanflæd caught the pale flash of his legs: the priest had pulled his own robes up out of the way.

The way to the river was not long in the day. At night, with the Deirans chasing them, it seemed long indeed.

Turning past the ruined houses, the sound of the pursuit sometimes rose, sometimes fell, so that they could not tell whether the pursuers drew closer or not.

"That way!" The queen pointed through the dark shadows to where lamplight flickered briefly, moving upon the black waters of the Ouse.

But as they ran towards the strand, men streamed across in front of them, blocking the way. And though there was little light, for the moon had not yet risen, yet the starlight was itself sufficient to show the glitter of their swords.

"Put me down." Queen Æthelburh went out in front of her party. A moment later, Eanflæd joined her. "Go back," whispered the queen. "I brought this upon us. You may have chance to escape in the darkness."

"No." Eanflæd reached out and found her mother's hand in the dark. "We go together. Besides –" and now she squeezed the fingers she was holding – "I do not think ill will come to us: Daddy is here – he is with us."

"I gave you honour and respect, and this is how you pay me?"

The voice was hoarse and cracked, a half-broken husk of the voice that had filled the hall before. Standing out from the men behind him, advancing upon them with sword bright in hand, Oswine, whom some called Godfriend, could bare hold the sword steady for the fury that was in him. At his side, walking in time with the king, was Hunwald.

"Before ever I saw you, some had said I should retain you, keep you, kill you even. But, oh no, I had refused, thinking to follow my better soul."

The two men were closer now and as some of their retainers began to strike steel on flint and fire torches, their faces began to flicker in the light. Oswine's face was as pale as a corpse, drained of blood and cold, but Hunwald's was livid. Eanflæd felt fear gripe her bowels; both men had the death light in their eyes.

Eanflæd could see Hunwald whispering into the king's ear as they approached, always whispering.

"I thought that by holding my hand from you though you were delivered into my grasp, I was keeping my skin and staying a man; and so I was. But it is no part of a man, no part of a king, to be insulted in his own hall, in front of his own men, by those whom he had called into his hall as guests."

They were close now. The torchlight glittered upon the blades they held loosely in their hands. Eanflæd had spent many hours among men practising with sword and spear and shield. She knew well the ease with which such a grip could shift to killing thrust.

The king was ready to kill, and they were caught in the glare of his fury.

"Daddy." Eanflæd called on her father, although the word seemed barely to rise from her throat. At the same moment, she felt her mother squeeze her hand, and then the queen stepped forward, breathing her own call to her...

"Husband..."

Oswine raised his sword.

"Strike, strike, strike, lord! Strike!"

Eanflæd could hear the words, slithering like a snake from Hunwald.

The queen did not quail. The sword remained poised above her, quivering in the grip of the king's emotion, as Hunwald poured poison into his ear.

"Stop! What do you think you are doing? Stop!"

Aidan ran between king and queen, putting his body in the way of the sword.

"Get out of the way!" The king reached out to push Aidan aside, but the bishop pushed forward.

"Would you kill me, lord?"

"Move!" Oswine, in his fury, tried to pull Aidan out of the way, but the man, although slight in frame compared to the king, would not shift. Instead, he grasped the hilt of Oswine's sword and pushed the blade against his own chest.

"If there must be blood, it will be mine." Aidan pulled the blade towards himself, and now the king was pulling the sword away. "If you must kill, kill me."

"No, no." The king fell back, letting the sword go. It fell to the ground, where it rang upon the broken flagstones, setting sparks flying into the dark.

Hunwald, seeing the king fall back, raised his own sword as if to strike, but the monk turned his face to him and it was terrible, for in that moment the light of foresight filled Aidan, and he saw the end to which the thegn would come, and the pity of it filled him, and the waste, and for an unbearable moment Hunwald saw his own soul laid bare before him.

"Quick, quick." Aidan turned to Æthelburh and Eanflæd. "While there is time, to your boat."

Leading them, his staff tapping fast over stone to soft earth, Aidan pushed through the king's men. Without order from Oswine or his thegn, they stood irresolute, unsure of what to do, but certain only that they must lay no hand on this slight figure who was bringing the party to their boat.

"Get in, get in." Aidan handed the queen and Eanflæd into the boat as it bobbed upon the river, their men and the two priests quickly following.

"Come with us," said Eanflæd, as the painters were unhitched and the men shipped the oars, pushing the boat's head into the stream.

"No," said Aidan. "No, the king has need of me, lest his madness linger." Putting his foot to the stern of the boat, Aidan helped push it out into the middle of the river. Oars dipped and pulled, sending the boat surging downstream. The bishop raised his hand.

"Farewell," he called.

With all the men pulling, and the river in spate, it was the work of but a few minutes to leave the city behind, the few lights upon the quay lost as the river turned past stands of willow and alder. But York was still close, and the river not yet broad enough to offer safety from arrow shot – not now, with the moon rising. The men pulled on, settling into a fast stroke, while Æthelburh and Eanflæd kept watch for pursuit.

But as the Wharfe joined with the Ouse and there was still no sign of anyone following, the two women began to relax their vigil.

"Ease," called Eanflæd. "Ease the stroke."

The men, gasping, let the water support their oars for a while, as the river carried them along, on into the broad, dark mouth of the Humber.

Æthelburh took her daughter's hand.

"I am sorry," she said. "If I had known what would happen, I would not have taken you."

"If you had known what would happen, would you still have gone?" Eanflæd asked.

The queen let go of Eanflæd's hand. She linked her fingers in her lap, sitting with head slightly down, in the position so known to the sisters of the holy house at Lyminge. Now, though, Æthelburh was not praying, but casting her mind back, to a memory renewed and a face returned to her.

Æthelburh looked up at her daughter. "Yes," she said.

"As would I, Mother. As would I." Eanflæd looked back along the river flow, back to York. "For I saw my father again and I am glad."

Chapter 8

"There it is."

Eanflæd pointed past the prow of the boat to where a great rock rose from the sea, the waves white about its base, and high walls upon its crown. She looked back at her mother. "That is it, isn't it?"

But the queen, her sight dulled by the years, could see only the grey of sea and the grey of sky and the greys of the land merging into one. She shook her head. "I do not see it, daughter."

"Aye, that's Bamburgh, right enough," said Utta. He looked to the princess. "Your new home." He looked to the priest sitting shivering beside him. "Yours too."

Romanus scowled. "I mide hab down id wod be barbarid," he said. He'd caught a chill in the escape from York and now, two days later, it had matured into a proper head cold.

But Utta, taking no notice of the comment, poked Romanus in the ribs.

"There, see." He pointed north, to where the land curved into the sea. "The Holy Island. It's only a short trip by boat from Bamburgh. We go back and forwards all the time."

"Oh, dho," said Romanus, drawing his cloak tighter around his shoulders. He had never known a wind that cut so deeply as this one blowing over the grey sea.

"Don't worry, Romanus," said Eanflæd, laughing. "We won't be making any boat journeys for a while."

"Eber?" asked the priest, his head emerging from his hood.

"I can't say never – but not for a long time. After all, there is the matter of my marriage and wedding feast to keep us on dry land."

"Dood," said the priest. He pulled his head back inside his cloak.

"I can see it now," said Æthelburh. "It is the great stronghold of the Idings. But it is a cold and windy place, and my bones still remember the chill when the wind blows from the north-east – which it always seems to do. Your father's heart was in Deira, in York, and I am glad that is where he rests. But I would that you could have seen his palace at Ad Gefrin, in the shadow of Yeavering Bell, for never have I seen a hall more beautiful – but it is gone now. Cadwallon burned it." The queen shook her head. "Beauty is so hard earned and so easily lost." She looked at her daughter. "You would do well to remember that, Eanflæd. Your beauty will not last forever – not long past the children you must needs bear. Use it well, while it lasts. You know how to be a queen, for I have shown you and I have trained you; but to be a wife, that is a different matter, and one a widow and mother of a holy house is not best placed to teach."

Æthelburh looked appraisingly at her daughter. Although a scarf covered her head, some strands of hair had escaped, and they blew over Eanflæd's face. The sun was behind them, for they were sailing north, but even in shadow she could see the girl's beauty, and she knew her wit. "But I think you will do well. The king is still a young man, and by all I have heard tell of him, he will be well pleased when he first sees you. Yes, daughter, I think you will do well indeed."

*

"There it is."

It was, perhaps, chance that had brought Oswiu out upon the ramparts of Bamburgh at this hour. But standing on the rampart, he'd seen a boat, and a large one, square rigged, with many oars, beating up the coast. Could it be a raiding boat, carrying men hoping to find a lightly defended hall, there to reap a harvest of people to sell as slaves?

But then the wind turned, catching the banner that flew in the stern of the boat, and he saw the white horse, standard of the kings of Kent, and Oswiu knew from where the boat sailed, and who it brought.

"There it is." He'd said the words out loud, although there was none but him to hear them. But then it is not every day that a man sees his new wife for the first time – and he remembered well the reports of Eanflæd's beauty that Acca had brought back from his negotiations.

It had been a long time since he had put Rhieienmelth aside. For a while, there had been a slave girl, a dark-haired, dark-eyed little thing who scarce spoke a word. She had served well enough, but... His heart pricked him. He had tried to put the thoughts aside – he was a king, due his desires – but in the end, when Aidan had stopped for a day with him, he had called the priest aside and spoken to him alone as they walked in the rose light of the setting sun.

The answer, when it came, was not what he had thought.

"Put her aside." Aidan had turned to him, standing with his back to the lowering sun, and it had shone about him and through him, so that he seemed a man of flame, burning. "Put her aside, lest you burn."

"B-but if I have not her, or another, I burn." Oswiu had shaken his head. "You don't understand. You are a monk."

"I am a man as well. I understand." Aidan had stepped closer to his old friend and grasped his arms. Although the monk was shorter, yet he seemed tall then, for he spoke with an authority that was not his, yet spoke through him. "Put her aside."

But still Oswiu had shaken his head. This was not what he had wanted to hear. He had expected Aidan to quiet his misgivings, but instead he had given them voice.

"I am king," he had said. "She is a slave. She is mine to do with as I will."

And Aidan had let go of his arms. He had stepped back and the sun had cloaked him in fire.

"What is her name?"

And Oswiu had stumbled over the name, for though he knew it, his tongue could not say it.

"Name her."

"Eleri," Oswiu had whispered.

"That is God-given. She is God-given. Put her aside, old friend. If it will help, I will find a home for her in a holy house, that you may not be tempted."

"But I am king. Surely I may take what I wish?"

And Aidan had shaken his head. "That was the way with the kings of old: the law was their desire. But you are a king of the new way, Oswiu, and there is a higher law now than your desire. That law tells you to put aside this girl, and wait until you are wed."

"Wait? But for how long?"

"As long as it takes."

It had taken a half-year. It had felt longer. Oswiu had put the slave girl, Eleri, aside – she lived now in the holy house at Melrose – and there had only been one or two since. Well, three, but each for one or two nights only. Otherwise, he doused desire with battle training, working himself into a pig sweat as he trained with sword and shield and spear, or even, when the fire grew too intense, with water, wading into river or lake until the cold went over his waist and shrivelled all desire.

But now the wait was all but over.

"There it is."

Oswiu looked round. Æthelwin was pointing to the ship.

"Yes," said Oswiu. "There she is. Go and tell the steward to make ready my wedding feast."

"Lord." But the warmaster hesitated.

"Yes?"

"Lord, should I send messengers to your mother, that she may come here? For it was, I hear, through her that you heard tidings that King Edwin's daughter would wed."

"And she told me who gave her the news too, Æthelwin, never fear. I know that I may rely upon your counsel in matters other than war – and I do."

The warmaster made the courtesy. "Thank you, lord."

"As to sending word to my mother: do so. But I will not wait on her to wed."

Oswiu watched him as he made his way back down to the courtyard, sending servants and slaves scurrying off with orders and instructions as he went. Æthelwin was a most capable man. Most warmasters contented themselves with mustering and training the men of the shieldwall, drilling them to hold together, come what may. But Æthelwin looked further and deeper than the ordinary warmaster. He would befit further command. Maybe he should make him warden of one of the marches? Oswiu pursed his lips. It would wait. He turned back to see the boat much closer now. Looking, he could see the individual figures upon it. One of them was Eanflæd. He wondered which it was.

*

"Do you think he's watching?"

Eanflæd pointed up at the stronghold, squatting atop the great rock that thrust from the land's edge. She looked to her mother. "I can see people on the ramparts. Do you think he's one of them?"

Æthelburh peered up herself, then shook her head. "The eyes of youth. Mayhap he is."

"Should – should I wave?"

"No, certainly not. Give no sign."

"But he has waited long."

"Then he can wait a bit longer." Æthelburh sighed. "Be not so eager. Daughter, in this middle-earth we have few weapons, and men have many. Be sure to use yours well, that you may bind your husband to you the more tightly."

"But how may I do that?"

"Bind him with your body, your children and your wit. The body is first, and brings the children, but it fades first too. Wit grows as the body fails – and you bring alliance that will not fail."

Eanflæd looked at her mother, at the profile staring up at the rock, the grey sea moving beyond her. "Is that what you did?" she asked. For she remembered her mother's face, in York, in the church of St Peter.

"No." Æthelburh smiled ruefully at her daughter. "No, it was not what I did at all. Instead, I bound myself to him, in my heart. But God, in his goodness, did not punish me for my stupidity, but opened Edwin's heart to me, and to his own mercy."

"Is that not the best way to bind a husband then – by binding yourself to him as well?"

"It – it may be. But while none wholly understand the workings of men's minds and hearts, their loins are easier to know. This Oswiu, by what we hear, is still a young man, with a young man's desires. That will make him an easier subject to your heart."

"Young?" said Eanflæd, laughing. "He is thirty! That is old."

"Old?" The queen smiled. "Then I thank you for the blessing, Eanflæd, for I am years more than he, so I must be old indeed."

"Old and wise, Mother; old and wise. Would that the same may be said of me by my daughter some day."

The queen squeezed Eanflæd's hand. "I pray it shall be so."

Eanflæd pointed ahead. "We are near to land now. But I see nowhere to moor the boat."

"There is a beach on the far side of the rock that remains above the waves in all but the fiercest storms; we shall land there, and drive the boat up onto the sand. Then we climb." The queen shook her head in rueful memory. "It is a long climb and, in memory, every time I climbed it, the wind was blowing rain in from the north-east and I was wet and cold. But this is a lovely day." And she waved her hand to take in the grey sea, flecked blue in places where the sun broke through the clouds.

"Dhis id a lubbly day?" mumbled Romanus. He peered out from under his hood as the boat crested a wave, breaking the foam ridge and flinging it back down the length of the ship into the priest's face.

"Dho!" he cried. "Dhot again."

"Cheer up," said Utta, slapping Romanus on the back. "We're nearly there. The queen is right – this is a lovely day: barely any wind, no rain, just beautiful."

"Oh, dho," moaned Romanus, disappearing under his hood once more.

The queen, seeing Romanus take shelter again from wind and wet, smiled. He would get used to it. She had. But his hiding reminded her of something. Æthelburh reached for the pouch at her belt and brought out a cloth, thin worked in gold so that, as she held it up, the sun shone through it.

"I brought this for you," she said to Eanflæd. "When we land, fix it to your scarf, so that your face is covered. That way, the king shall be the first here to see your face."

"But I won't be able to see where I am going."

"You will. Here, look." Æthelburh held the cloth up to Eanflæd's face and she looked through it.

"I can see!" said Eanflæd.

"Yes, but no one can see you. Not until you wish them to."

So after the boat had landed beneath the great rock of Bamburgh, and the master and the men had pulled it up onto the strand and were busy unloading, Eanflæd pinned the veil to her scarf and looked out onto a golden world, while the queen fussed over her clothes, straightening here, pinning there, until…

"Yes." Æthelburh stood back. "You are ready." She stopped and looked more closely at her daughter. "*Are* you ready?"

"Yes." Eanflæd took a breath. "Yes, Mother. I am ready. Let us go to meet my husband."

*

"How do I look?"

Oswiu emerged from his chamber, servants fussing round him, adjusting belt and buckle and clasp, while one attempted to run a comb through his hair. The king held up his hands.

"Stop," he said. "Hands off."

The servants froze, hands poised. Oswiu glanced from side to side, checking for stillness, then, reassured, he looked to the person whose judgement in these matters he most trusted.

"Well?" he asked. "How do I look?"

"Hmm," said Ahlflæd, looking her father up and down, a finger pressed to her lip.

"No?" Oswiu looked down. "What's wrong?"

"I am not sure about the cloak," said Ahlflæd. "Or the belt. And that buckle – don't you have something better?"

Oswiu peered, cross-eyed, at the great golden buckle upon his shoulder, which held his cloak in place. Made of gold, inlaid with garnets swirling in dance, the buckle was heavier than a sword and worth more than some kingdoms.

"Better than this?" Oswiu asked. He looked aghast at his daughter. "Where could I get something better than this?"

Ahlflæd broke into laughter. "I was joking, Daddy," she said between giggles. "You look magnificent. Like a king."

"Just as well, since I am one."

Ahlflæd pointed at the poised servants. "Let them finish."

"All right, all right," said Oswiu. But he fixed them with a glare. "No prodding, mind."

While the servants adjusted belt and seax, buckle and brooch and arm ring, and even managed to run the comb, carved from whale ivory, through the king's hair, other servants hurried around the great hall, carrying tables and benches into place, kicking dogs out of the way and yelling at the excited children who crowded in, getting in everyone's way. The hall was alive with a cheerful, excited hubbub, and Oswiu noted it well. Many of the people had loved Rhieienmelth and spoken darkly when he had put her aside – for all knew the truth of it, though the king had had it proclaimed that she entered the holy house by God's calling – yet the news that the king was to marry Princess Eanflæd of Kent, daughter of King Edwin, had brought great excitement and some understanding of the decision the king had made. For it was through such an alliance that King Edwin had become High King, and many now whispered that the alliance, renewed, would bring such days to Bernicia once more.

"Acca!" Oswiu called to the scop, who was busy sweetening his voice in readiness for the demands of the feast with smooth, sun-filled wine, brought from warmer lands by one of the merchants who crossed the narrow sea and sailed up the coast, selling wine and garnets and gold, and buying furs and dogs. Always dogs, so that the boats could be heard, sailing back south again, by the barking of their cargo. Once Oswiu had asked a merchant about the dogs and been told that he sold every dog he could carry to the Franks and the Frisians and the peoples of the Low Lands, for they considered the dogs bred in Britain to be the best hunting dogs alive.

"Acca!" Oswiu called again, and the scop put aside his cup of wine.

"Lord?"

"Have you a new song for us? Or a riddle? I enjoyed the one you told…" Oswiu shook his head. No, that would not be a good idea. Acca had told a riddle at the feast for his wedding with Rhieienmelth – a riddle whose solution was a key, but whose clues were enough to make a bride blush (although, he remembered, Rhieienmelth had not blushed, but laughed as loud as any man in the hall). "No, not a riddle. A new song. Have you one? Remember, the princess is the daughter of Queen Æthelburh and, like as not, the queen brings her daughter to us: the queen is now mother of a holy house. Make the song something suitable."

"Yes, yes, of course, lord." Acca waited, smile fixed, until Oswiu turned away to answer a question from the steward. Then his smile broke, and he turned and gnawed his knuckles. "No, no, no," the scop muttered. "I had it ready, all worked out, and now he says no, he wants a new song, and one suitable for the mother of a holy house, and a princess." Acca groped for his cup and drained it. "Wine," he said, holding it out. What was he going to do? He looked around. "Wine, I said." A servant, rushing past, sloshed wine into the cup, then continued on his errand. "Well," said Acca, "I shall just have to compose a new song – a song fit for a king's marriage feast and the mother of a holy house – in an hour. It shall be my greatest feat." The scop pursed his lips. "Where's Coifi?"

Coifi was sitting in a corner, out of the bustle of preparation, his raven-feather cloak, now so old and worn that much of it looked like a bird in moult, pulled tight around his thin shoulders. Coming closer, Acca saw Coifi's eyes, darting round the hall, flicking from point to point, restless as a mouse. He knew that look of old. Although Coifi had abjured the gods he had once served as priest, yet still he sought, in the rise of smoke and the play of light, in leaf fall and water play, to see the workings of wyrd, the fates of men and thrones told in signs and, sometimes, vision.

The old priest's eyes snapped up to Acca, fixing upon him as he approached. Coifi rocked upon his heels.

"Ha!" he said. "Ha! You want my help."

"What gives you that idea?" Acca turned his back to the wall and leaned upon it, looking into the press of people preparing the hall. "I just thought I'd get out of the way. Like you."

Coifi rocked back, looking up at the scop. "You need a song," he said.

"Yes," said Acca.

"A new song," said Coifi.

"Yes," said Acca.

"And not a dirty riddle."

"No." Acca stared down into his cup. "That I could come up with before they finish climbing to the gate. It's got to be something fit for the mother of a holy house."

Coifi put his hands over his head. His rocking grew faster. He said nothing.

Acca shook his head. "Thank you," he said, and began to walk away.

"I dreamed."

Acca stopped. He looked round and saw Coifi's eyes, staring white through fingers spread over his face.

"You what?"

"I dreamed." Coifi spread his fingers wider. His eyes were very white, but this was not the white of one of his trances, when his eyes would roll to the back of his head and only the white would show. "I was watching the wind move. It was playing with a leaf, an oak leaf, and I followed it, into the holy house here, the house where they keep the king's arm."

"Oswald's arm?"

"Yes. The leaf went in there, and I followed. It blew to the altar and settled there, beneath the king's arm. I watched it settle. I watched until I slept. And then I dreamed." Coifi shivered, suddenly, violently, as a man does when the final struggle is upon him. "I will tell you the dream and you will make it a song for the mother of the holy house, and the princess, and the king. You will make it a song —" and here the old priest looked up at Acca with a great earnestness in his eyes – "that will be sung when this throne is dust and this stronghold has been thrown down."

"Yes, yes, yes," said Acca. He glanced towards the great doors of the hall. The commotion there suggested that they would soon be thrown open to welcome the king's new queen. "You tell me the dream; I'll decide whether it makes a song."

As the scop squatted down by the old priest, listening to a dream, the warmaster and the king's steward went to the doors of the great hall.

Ahlflæd turned to her father, who was sitting, waiting, in the great judgement seat of the Idings. "I wish Ahlfrith was here."

"Pardon?" Oswiu looked at his daughter.

Ahlflæd giggled. "I said, I wished my brother was here, but you are thinking on other matters, Daddy."

Oswiu smiled. "I too wish he was here. But Ahlfrith is doing well. The last report I had from him, and this not a week past, said that he was now friends with Penda's son, and that there was little love between Penda and Peada. That is good for me, for us, to know."

"I understand, Daddy, but I just wish he was here." Ahlflæd paused, looking carefully at her father. "I wish Mother was here as well."

The king's face stiffened. "You understand why I had to put your mother aside – at least some of it? If we are to stand against Penda, we need allies, strong allies, and Rheged has become weak; the wolves prowl its borders. With Kent, we start to put a net around Penda, surrounding him with kings allied to us. After Kent, the West Saxons and the East Angles; I believe they will come over to our side, for they all fear Penda. Then, when the net is complete, we pull it tight, leaving Penda struggling inside like a boar in a thicket. Do you understand?"

"Of course I understand, Daddy. And I know, when the time comes, it will fall to me to marry an ætheling from one of the kingdoms, to draw it tighter to us. But... but I still sometimes wish Mother was here."

Oswiu turned his face from his daughter and looked to the

door of the great hall. "So do I," he said, but the words were so soft Ahlflæd did not hear them.

The doors swung open.

Outside, the day was bright. The light silhouetted the figures standing in the doorway, leaving them nothing but shadows.

Slowly, one by one, the shadows came into the hall, becoming real and solid as they did so.

First, a priest, but one tonsured in a manner unfamiliar to the king, his hair a ring about his head. With him came a monk, well known to Oswiu: Utta. Then the retainers, the men sent by him and by Kent to guard the princess on her long journey north. As the journey was not yet over, and the princess not yet presented to the king, they alone of all men who sought entry to the king's hall were permitted to enter with their swords hanging from their belts.

Following the men were Eanflæd's women, the four ladies who had come on this journey and would stay with her: her hearth companions.

And then another woman.

She walked alone, with the bearing of a queen, but she wore the scarf of the mother of a holy house. At the sight of her, whispers rippled around the great hall, starting among the servants, many of whom had served King Edwin, then moving to the benches where the king's men sat, before moving up the hall to the high table and the judgement seat.

"Æthelburh, Æthelburh. Queen Æthelburh."

One of the servants ran to her and, falling to his knees, took the queen's hand and pressed it to his forehead. Another followed, and another, until the queen was surrounded by a group of weeping, exulting servants.

Naming them, the queen lifted them to their feet, one by one.

"Eadstan; Drythelm; Heiu; Botild; Cynferth." As she said their names, the servants rose and stood aside, eyes wet shining with tears, until at last Æthelburh was able to continue on through the hall.

As the old queen was speaking to the servants, Oswiu looked past her, to the final person in the procession, eager for a first sight of his new bride.

But he could not see Eanflæd's face. She was veiled, the golden cloth moving with every breath, but never moving enough to reveal the face behind it.

As the procession resumed, Eanflæd followed her mother up between the rows of benches, the men standing now, craning their heads to better see the new queen. Fresh whispers rippled round the hall, following on from the wonder of seeing Queen Æthelburh.

"What's she like?"

"Can't see her."

"Edwin's daughter."

The two priests leading the procession stopped in front of the high table, before the king's judgement seat. The small priest, the one with the circle of hair, bowed low, while Utta made the courtesy. Behind them, the men charged with bringing their precious charge to Oswiu's court slowly parted so that the women might pass through them.

"My lord." The small priest bowed again. "I am Romanus, a priest of God and a man of the Franks who has lived for many years on this side of the narrow sea, in the kingdom of Kent. As charged by King Earconbert, I have brought this, the most precious of his kingdom's gifts, to King Oswiu, lord of Bernicia, overking of Rheged and the lands of the north, that the two thrones may be forever joined, in friendship and in blood." The priest turned and bowed to the woman standing beside him. "And at her request, I have also brought one known to many here, for she would see again this land where she was queen: Æthelburh; mother now to the holy house in Lyminge."

Queen Æthelburh stepped forward.

The king rose from the judgement seat and, striding forward, he stepped up and over the high table, not caring that he knocked cup and bowl aside, and jumped down in front of Æthelburh.

"Welcome." The king spread his arms wide. "Welcome! For one who has come so far, for one who returns to where she once was

queen, it is only fit that I, the king, should come to meet you at the
end of your journey."

And the queen answered Oswiu's smile with one of her own.

"I have heard much of the generosity and cheer of this court and
its king. I see the tales are true."

"But you have brought me the greatest and most precious of
gifts, Queen Æthelburh. You have brought me the flesh of your
flesh. What greater gift is there than that?"

And all in the king's great hall turned to look at the veiled figure
who stood, silent, behind the queen.

Queen Æthelburh held out her hand. The veiled figure came
forward, and stood beside the queen.

"You are right, King Oswiu," said Queen Æthelburh. "There is no
greater gift I can give you than this, my daughter; of the royal houses
of Kent and Deira; granddaughter to the high king, Æthelbert of
Kent; daughter to the High King, Edwin; descendant of the kings
of the Franks."

Silence and awe fell upon the hall, for great indeed were the sires
from whom this new queen came.

Slowly, Queen Æthelburh lifted the veil from her daughter's face.
"Eanflæd."

Oswiu looked, for the first time, at the face of his queen. Her
eyes were downcast, but as she felt his gaze upon her, she raised her
eyes to his.

He moved his lips to try to speak, but no words emerged from
them.

Eanflæd looked into her betrothed's eyes. "W-will I do?" she
asked.

Oswiu tried again to speak, but still his mouth would form no
words. Instead, he nodded, and the movement served to release his
tongue.

"Y-yes," he said.

Eanflæd lowered her eyes again.

Oswiu swallowed. He looked to the steward, to call him to set
the feast. And while he did so, a quick, secret glance passed between

Eanflæd and her mother, a shared smile that the king's daughter, standing beside him, alone saw.

"I'm Ahlflæd," she said, stepping forward. "I'm the king's daughter. He has a son too, my brother, who'd be here today, only he is being fostered at the court of King Penda."

"Ahlflæd, what are you doing?" said Oswiu, reaching for his daughter. But she skipped out of his reach.

"No, no," said Eanflæd. "I have heard so much of your children. I would meet them." She turned to the girl. "So you are Ahlflæd."

"Yes," said the princess. She looked closely at the woman in front of her. "You are pretty; as beautiful as my mother."

"But not, I think, as pretty as you."

"No," said the girl. "No, not as pretty as me."

"Ahlflæd..." began Oswiu. But the queen put a hand on his arm. He looked at Æthelburh in surprise.

"When I married Edwin," said the queen, "he had two grown sons, who did not receive me well at first. Leave my daughter to speak to your daughter for a while, that there may be friendship between them, and let us speak while the steward prepares the feast and the priests prepare for the marriage."

Oswiu glanced at his daughter and wife-to-be, saw that they were speaking earnestly together, then nodded his agreement. As the steward directed servants around the hall, and the men ran the new arrivals at court through the gossip mill, Æthelburh quickly told the king of their journey north and, most particularly, of their visit to York and their reception by King Oswine Godfriend.

"Do not blame my daughter for this," the queen finished. "The fault was mine. I greatly desired to look on the face of my husband again, but I should not have taken Eanflæd with me when I travelled upriver to York. Now I have brought upset to your relations with Deira, and made it the more difficult for you to claim the throne there. But I say again, do not hold my daughter responsible for this, but me instead, and say, in light of this, whether you still wish the marriage to proceed."

Oswiu looked over at Eanflæd. Feeling his glance, she looked up from her conversation with Ahlflæd, and smiled.

"I will marry your daughter, Queen Æthelburh. I will marry her in gladness."

*

"*Hwæt!*"

Acca took his place by the great hearth fire. Round him, men settling into the final stages of feasting readied themselves for the last public act of the day: the wedding tale of the scop.

"Give us a riddle like before!"

That was the drunken yell that went up from many of the men in the hall. For while they had drunk much already, yet their heads were not so fuddled that they could not remember the last time they had feasted Oswiu in marriage and the riddle Acca had posed them then – a riddle many of the men still dragged from memory when they wanted to make a maid blush.

The scop, turning round the great hall, held his finger to his lips. And though most of the men were drunk, yet they saw Acca's gesture, and slowly obeyed it. Shouts and laughter and the thrum of conversation died away to the bare minimum of cups being refilled and the whisper of anticipation.

"You call for a riddle."

Shouts and cheers greeted Acca's words. But the scop waited again for quiet, and the catcalls died away.

The scop pointed to the high table.

"See you who sits there?"

Acca turned, taking in all the hall, locking every eye upon him.

"See you who sits there?"

Acca gestured once more to the high table.

"Our king – and two queens! Queen Æthelburh, beyond all hope, beyond all expectation, has returned to us, and you drunken louts want me to tell a dirty riddle. Shame on you! Shame, I say! The queen is mother to a holy house now, she is door warden to heaven's great hall – and you want me to sing a filthy song. Well, I won't." Acca turned through the silent hall, where not a man spoke, and few could hold his eye. "Well, not yet."

A great cheer went up, releasing the tension that the scop had carefully wrought.

Acca held his hand up for silence, and quickly the men gave it to him.

"But now, I will sing a new song, a riddle song, a song fit for our queens." The scop picked up his lyre and strummed the six strings, sending their golden sound through the hall.

"I will sing a dream, dreamed by Coifi." Plucking the strings, he played the start of an old, familiar lament: "Riddle me this."

> *"It was years ago, or so I remember,*
> *that I was torn from the trees' edge,*
> *ripped from my root.*
> *Strong enemies gripped me,*
> *made me a spectacle,*
> *swung their criminals from me;*
>
> *"I carried men on my crossbeam*
> *until I was fixed on a crag;*
> *many enemies set me there.*
> *I saw mankind's Lord walk boldly, quickly,*
> *eager to climb up.*
>
> *"There I could not, against the Creator's will,*
> *quiver or fall, though I saw quake the earth's surface.*
> *I was able to slaughter all the enemies,*
> *but I stood firm.*
>
> *"The young man, Heaven's King, cast off his clothes,*
> *strong and firm spirited;*
> *he stood on the gallows*
> *bravely, beheld by many,*
> *to break mankind free.*
> *I trembled as the man embraced me;*
> *I dared not topple to earth, fall to the ground;*
> *I had to stand fast.*

"As a cross I was raised, carrying the mighty king, heaven's lord.
I could not lean away.
They drove dark nails into me;
the dreadful cuts are still seen, open, malicious wounds;
I dared not harm one of them.
They insulted us both together;
I was all besmeared with blood from the man's side
once he sent forth his spirit."

Acca's voice died to silence. He looked around the hall. Not a man, or woman, or child, made a noise, nor moved. Even the dogs were quiet. He looked to the high table, and saw tears coursing down the king's face, and beading the eyes of the queens.

Slowly, Queen Æthelburh rose to her feet.

"That is a dream of the rood," she said. "The song of the great high tree that joined us, once more, with heaven."

"Yes," said Acca simply. He sought for more words, but there was nothing more to say.

The queen looked at old Coifi, and wide was the smile on her face, although the tears still brimmed her eyes.

"And you dreamed this dream, old friend?"

The priest rose from where he had been sitting, cloak wrapped around his shoulders, squatting close to the fire, that he might search its heart.

"I dreamed it, Queen Æthelburh."

"Then I am glad for you, and envy you too, that you saw such things, for few indeed have seen them."

The king rose from the judgement seat.

"I will have these words set down, inscribed in a great stone rood, that all may know them, and know the tree that we must climb to reach our great lord's hall."

Acca made the courtesy. "I thank you, lord. But would it be too much to ask that you might give reward in the more usual way too?"

Oswiu laughed and, taking a gold ring from his own arm, he sent it spinning through the air to the scop, who caught it with one hand, while taking up the lyre with the other.

"Now, you have the lyre; give us another song," said the king, "for the hour is yet early, and the time not come for me to go forth with my bride." Oswiu looked to the woman beside him. "But it will come soon."

And as the men put up a cheer, and Acca strummed his lyre and launched into the telling of a quite remarkably filthy riddle, the king reached over and took the hand of his new queen.

PART 3

Strife

Chapter 1

"Father."

Oswiu looked at the young man standing in front of him. "You used to call me Daddy before you went," he said.

"I was a boy then."

"Yes, you've grown." Oswiu put his hands on the young man's shoulders. "When you left, your head came to my shoulder."

"You've grown too, Father." Ahlfrith reached out and patted his father's stomach.

Oswiu laughed, and struck his fist to his belly. "All muscle," he said.

"If it is muscle, why did your fist bounce?" asked Ahlfrith.

"Ha, I hoped you'd come back with Penda's war plans, and instead you've returned with your sister's cheek." Oswiu gazed at the face in front of him. Ahlfrith had returned a man, with a beard fuzz on his cheeks and with a man's strength in his grasp. "Ah, but it is good to see you again." And he clasped his son in his arms.

They were standing by the old road of the emperors. Ahlfrith had ridden north with his men, the small group of retainers who had gathered around him during the latter part of the time he had spent at Penda's court. These were lordless men who had come, seeking a hall and an oath lord, and had attached themselves to the young ætheling, either through the raw recking of power – for a man who bound himself to an ætheling who went on to claim a throne might climb very high with him, whereas making pledge to an established king such as Penda was to take a place at the bottom of a ladder that had already grown very high – or through love and friendship, for in the dangers of the hunt and, even more so, in the dangers of war, a brave ætheling might bind many men to him through his courage and generosity. Ahlfrith, grown into his manhood, had taken leave of Penda and his court, and ridden north along the great road of the emperors, having sent word to his father that he was returning by this route. He had expected to meet Oswiu at one of his father's royal estates, but Oswiu, on receiving word of Ahlfrith's return, had ridden to meet him, setting camp and his tents by the Perch Inn.

"Is Ahlflæd with you?" Ahlfrith asked, looking round at the grouped men for sign of his sister.

"No. She waits for you at our hall in Hexham."

Ahlfrith shook his head. "That is for shame. I would have seen her." He grinned. "I have a message for her – from Peada."

"Penda's son?"

"No less."

"Why should he send message to Ahlflæd?"

"Why? For the wish he holds for her in his heart – and in other places, I should think. When Ahlflæd was yet young enough to visit me, Peada would always come to find her, bringing her gifts – which she spurned – and generally mooning around her like some young goose."

"What is the message he sends to her?" asked Oswiu.

"That enemy thrones may be united by marriage, and become each the stronger for it."

Oswiu blew the breath through his teeth, sounding as the wind through the trees.

"Peada asks marriage with Ahlflæd? Would his father stand for it?"

Ahlfrith shook his head. "No. But Peada chafes against Penda's bit, chewing and working it, seeking always more men and greater power – both of which the king is loath to give him. Peada recks himself a war leader, but his father gives him no leave to wage war, and he grows restless."

"Does he have support in the witan?"

"Little as yet." Ahlfrith smiled. "It would be as if I sought to take the throne from you, Father, still with only half a beard and little glory to my name."

"Nevertheless, we may make use of this when the time comes."

"Indeed." Ahlfrith's smile grew broader. "It is why, when we have met again after five years, I tell you this first of all, rather than asking after Mother, or Grandmother, and the rest of the family, that you may hear as well as see that I have grown."

Oswiu nodded, looking with even greater interest at the young man standing in front of him. "You have indeed grown." He laughed. "Maybe I should follow Penda's lead, and be wary of handing too much power to a son."

"You should – if I was like Peada. He has no patience, and less subtlety. There were rumours that Penda does not think him throne-worthy, and instead favours his younger son, Wulfhere. But this may be simply the opinion of bored men gossiping through winter nights. Wulfhere is still young." Ahlfrith paused and looked pointedly at his father. "Although he is older than your new son."

"Ah. So you have heard about Ecgfrith?"

"Yes. A son to the king of Bernicia by the daughter of Edwin: that is the sort of news to pass through all the kingdoms faster than a man might ride." Ahlfrith stopped. He looked carefully at his father. There were yet few signs of age upon him, other than the thickening of his girth and some lines upon his face. But looking closer, Ahlfrith saw the first few hairs frost touched by the passing years. Penda had more, but they were seldom seen, for near always he went about hooded, his single black eye peering out upon the world from the shadow beneath his hood.

"Where stand I, Father? Now you have got a son with the daughter of King Edwin. Is he more throne-worthy than I?"

"Ahlfrith." Oswiu reached out a hand to his son, putting it on his shoulder, but the boy – the young man – gave no sign that it was there.

"I would know your answer, Father."

"Ecgfrith is yet bare more than a babe. There is no question, should I die, who would be king after me."

"That may be true now, Father. But what of the years to come, when my brother is grown to manhood? What then?"

"God alone knows that, Ahlfrith. We know not even if he will live to manhood, let alone what sort of man he will be. Do not fill your head with such thoughts, when such things may never come to pass."

"You told me once, Father, that a king must be ready for whatever may come. I would be ready for what may come."

"I told you that?" Oswiu saw the memory in his son's face. "I see I did. And it is true. But it is not the whole truth. For now, I would be happy my son has returned to me, and returned to me a man. Will you not allow me this joy on our first meeting?" And the king held out his arms to his son.

Ahlfrith shook his head. "Father," he said. But he allowed himself to be embraced, and he smiled at the cheer the men – his own and his father's – put up as they watched, from a respectful distance, this first meeting after many years of king and ætheling. But as they embraced, he whispered to the king, "I would have answer, Father."

For his part, Oswiu, while he struck Ahlfrith's back – marvelling at the strength of muscle he felt beneath his hand – answered in whisper too. "But wait a little while, Ahlfrith, and I will give answer. For there will be land, and enough, for you to rule, and your brother too." Oswiu pulled back from the embrace and held his son again. "I can feel the strength in you. Now," the king smiled, "let me see it in earnest." Oswiu gestured to the men he had brought with him, watching and waiting by the tents set up around the inn. "Think you they are too many for a welcome party?"

Ahlfrith looked, with sudden keen interest, at the watching men his father had brought, his gaze then shifting to the horses, grazing within a hawthorn fence.

"They are ready for war," he said, turning back to his father. "Or… or a raid."

"Yes," said Oswiu. "Yes. I know you and your men have ridden far, but we will not be riding far from here, and I would have you join us – on your return, I would have you command us!"

"Where do we…" Ahlfrith stopped, as memory of where he was told him answer to his question before he could ask it. "Deira. Of course. I heard tell, at Penda's court, of the raids you make into

Deira, reaping a harvest of gold and silver from the thegns of King Oswine, until his messengers all but beg Penda to come to his aid."

"Yes, Deira," said Oswiu. "But we raid always, and only, the thegns who support the usurper on his throne, that they may come to know that their king has not the strength to protect them. Then, finally, they will give thought to my claim."

"I heard the messengers Oswine sends to Penda. Though they clothe their pleading with gold, pleading it is. But I do not think Penda would want Oswine to lose the throne – and for sure not to an Iding."

"In the end, Penda will have no say in the matter, for a king cannot be everywhere, and if Oswine has not the support of his thegns, he cannot long rule. Cut by cut, I am sawing away Oswine's support. In the end, it must fail."

"Judging by the poor tribute he sends to Penda, it has already weakened. And should he fall, then you will need someone to rule Deira in your name, won't you, Father? For as you said, a king cannot be everywhere."

"That is true. He would have to be someone the witan of Deira would accept – and I could trust."

"I can think of one not far from here," Ahlfrith smiled. "Tell me, whom do we raid? My men and I have spent too long hunting boar; it is time we hunted glory."

"Oswine has a kinsman, a cousin: Trumhere by name. He has a hall in the north of Deira, but I've had word that he goes to the strand market at Whitby, along with most of the thegns of Deira, for the winds have been kind, and brought many merchants north across the narrow sea. A few old retainers, too weary to attempt the ride, remain to guard his hall. He will return to find it ash."

"But if you have word of the whereabouts of Oswine, why do we not strike at him? This is a mean raid, with little glory."

"Mayhap little glory, but there will be some gold and it serves us well. You are young, and you still think war is as the scops sing. Know this, son: war is more often raids like this, where the foe is an old retainer, so crippled by age he can bare lift a sword, and witless servants, throwing turds then running away when you turn an eye upon them. No songs in it, little glory: but they serve. They serve to keep the men trained; they serve to get gold and to give it; they serve to wear away a king's fortune and give men licence to whisper on his luck." Oswiu gestured over towards his waiting men. "Æthelwin, my warmaster, has spent the summer raiding deep into Deira, and I with him when it were possible to do so. Now, you will join us, ere we return to our own lands."

Ahlfrith pointed towards the inn, its painted sign creaking as the wind blew it upon the bough that supported it. "I will join you, and right gladly, but I have heard from many a traveller of the beer they brew at the Perch Inn, and it has been a long and thirsty ride…"

Oswiu laughed, and clapped his son on the shoulder. "Of a surety we will drink first, drink to your return, and set off tomorrow – with light hearts but sore heads, I fancy."

*

The smoke told them where to go. Æthelwin, riding ahead, saw it first – a thin morning column, rising into the still dawn air. A fire set to warm away the night chill, but piled with wood not left long enough to dry. The warmaster, seeing it, held up his hand and the three men around him, alert to his gesture, pulled their horses to a silent stop.

"There," Æthelwin said, breath steaming from his mouth, and he pointed north-west, to where the trail, hoof marked from the passing of sheep going up from their winter pastures to the high moors, climbed up into the wold. The path wound into the trees and was soon lost to sight, but the smoke, rising from further into the wood, told its tale: the thegn's hall was set there, sheltered and hidden by the trees, but betrayed by the carelessness of its stewards. The warmaster selected one of his men, and sent him back along the trail to take word to the king – and the king's son. While the man rode off, Æthelwin led his remaining companions to the edge of the wold. Scraggly hawthorn and blackthorn marked its margins, the bushes trailing away down the slopes. The warmaster dismounted and hitched his horse to a may tree, making sure it was out of sight should any wandering servant be dispatched from the hall down the path. While Æthelwin awaited the king's arrival, he sent his two companions on to scout closer to the hall. They were yet to return when the king arrived with his son and the raiding party. Seeing the riders coming up the trail, Æthelwin swung out from his cover – he had climbed into the crook of a twisted crab apple, the better to see and be concealed – and went to meet them.

"Lord."

Oswiu reined back his horse and squinted down at the warmaster. "Æthelwin." The king winced as he spoke. The early morning ride had not eased his head.

Æthelwin pointed to where the smoke column rose from out of its nest of trees. The king looked to where the warmaster pointed, but the brightness of the morning sun, slanting in from the east, sent sparks across his eyes and arrows through his head.

"I have sent two men to scout," said Æthelwin. "They have not come back yet."

"Why wait?" Ahlfrith rode up beside them. "Even if this thegn were here with all his men, he could not stand against us."

Oswiu looked blearily at his son. The boy – the man – showed no sign of the night's drinking, and was as clear eyed in the morn as he had been when they met the day before. For his part, the king felt as if a dwarf was beating a hammer against his head, while another was attempting to scrape up his eyeballs and a third was digging over his tongue. Ah, youth. Ahlfrith was young, full of vigour and strength, while he was already more than thirty-five years old.

"Why wait, Father?" Ahlfrith repeated, looking at the king.

"We wait to give my head chance to stop ringing," said Oswiu.

Ahlfrith laughed. "You enjoyed the beer last night?"

"Last night, yes; today, no."

"Let me go on then, Father." Before Oswiu could answer, Ahlfrith held up his hand. "I'll take Æthelwin with me, to look after me."

Oswiu began again to shake his head, but this time the warmaster spoke. "I can take Ahlfrith to scout further; then wait upon you before we attack." Æthelwin looked up at the king. "Have you the head for this yet?"

"In truth, no." Even those few words felt as if they were splitting Oswiu's head apart. "Go, then, but wait on me before you do aught. Do you understand?"

Oswiu looked to his son as he made this reply, and it was received with the broadest of smiles.

"Of course I understand, Father," said Ahlfrith, and already he was beginning to wheel his horse round towards the path into the wold.

"Your sister is waiting for you," Oswiu called after his son. "She will be angry if you are reckless."

Ahlfrith half turned in his saddle to look back. "I won't be," he said.

Oswiu sat upon his horse, head throbbing, watching his son, with the warmaster and a few men, disappear among the trees.

He held out his hand.

"Give me more of that beer," he said. The keeper of the Perch Inn had filled their skins before they set out in the dark hour before dawn. Some said that only beer could heal what beer had wrought. Not having any other cure to hand – save time, and there was too little of that – he would try the beer.

*

"We should dismount here." The warmaster signalled to Ahlfrith, and the young man pulled his horse to a stop. Leaving two of the men to watch the horses, Ahlfrith and Æthelwin took the remaining four with them along the path, ears and eyes alert, but swords yet sheathed, although hands stood ready to draw them. Unless the enemy was in sight, it were better to make this sort of stealthy approach with blades sheathed, for naked metal might ring on armour or spark on stone. Deep into the wold now, the trees were higher but further spaced, with less cover growing between the trunks, and that mostly holly and yew.

Ahlfrith signalled Æthelwin to his side.

"Where are your men? They should have come back by now."

The warmaster nodded. "I will go ahead, off path." He pointed off to the left.

Ahlfrith nodded. "I'll go right."

"You should stay here."

Ahlfrith shook his head. "No. Leave two men here, to cover the path. I'll take one with me, you the other. Work your way towards the hall, staying under cover. Call like a tawny owl when you're in place: two calls, pause, then one. I'll answer the same way."

"I would wish you to return to the king," said Æthelwin.

"Miss everything for my father's hangover?" Ahlfrith grinned and shook his head. "I think not."

The ætheling gestured Æthelwin on and, shaking his head, the warmaster did as he was commanded, disappearing, so far as the cover allowed, off the path to the left. Ahlfrith, with one of the men following silently behind, made his own way into the wold.

There had been rain recently and the leaf litter, which lay thickly piled up in the lee of fallen trees and in unexpected hollows, barely crackled beneath his tread. More dangerous were the twigs, buried under the decaying oak leaves, that cracked as his weight came upon them. After the second such crack had caused him to stiffen in sudden alarm, listening and looking for reaction, Ahlfrith had stopped and taken off his shoes, tying them into his belt. Now, as he went, he felt the ground with his feet, moving twigs and branches out of the way with his toes, while he searched for the next cover. The retainer, Gadd, following behind, was an older warrior, disinclined to stoop too low or to scurry too fast but, to Ahlfrith's annoyance, he made not a sound, nor did he disturb so much as a leaf as he followed.

But while Gadd made no sound, the wold itself was filled with noise: birds, May-voiced, filled the wood with song, while the trees themselves all but creaked from the speed of their growing, sending up new branches to the light as they spread their fresh green leaves below the sky. The early chill was long gone, and plumes of sunlight spread out under the canopy, lighting the gloomy stands of holly and yew that skulked beneath the high branches of the oak.

Through the song, Ahlfrith heard movement, leaves shifting, scuffling over earth, and he held his hand out to Gadd, pointing whereaways the sound came. Gadd signed his hearing, and moved to circle round, but before he could get far, a pig emerged blinking from a thick stand of hazel, and stood, snout tracking right and left, as it looked for what it smelled.

A pig foraging in the wood meant they must be getting close to the thegn's hall. Ahlfrith signalled Gadd on, keeping a chain apart. As such, they were close enough to come to the aid of the other, if needed, but far enough apart for one to see what might be concealed from the other.

There. Through the trees. A clearing and a suggestion of a building. The hall. Gadd signalled that he had seen it too. Together, but still a chain apart, they began to worm their way through the final stands of holly and yew, into the thicker clumps of may thorn and blackthorn and hazel that grew along the edge of the wold.

As another thorn pricked through his cloak, Ahlfrith thought, fleetingly, that at least with holly the pricks did not go deep. If he should step, bare footed, upon a may thorn it would be the work of a man to keep from crying out. For a moment he thought of stopping to put on his shoes. Ahlfrith shook his head. He was a man, blooded in hunt and raid. If he stood on a thorn, he would bear the pain without a cry.

Crouching low, then moving into a crawl, Ahlfrith wormed his way on, through the cover of the thorn bushes, until the space opened up before him. He peered through the clumps of coarse grass and thistle that matted the sunward side of the thorn bushes and saw the clearing, cut from the wold, that held at its heart the hall of Oswine's thegn. The building itself stood at the centre of the clearing, high roofed but not so large – such a hall could hold no more than two score men, he thought. Around the hall were clustered a few small houses, round walled and low roofed. Outside one, willow frames were set for the drying and curing of meat, while a spinning wheel and many teasel heads stood outside another, alongside a pile of raw wool, ready for teasing out and spinning. It was what he had seen around many a hall, through Bernicia and during his time in Mercia.

But there was something here that he had not seen before. No people. No women sat outside the spinning house, gossiping while they pulled the teasel heads through the wool. There was no butcher skinning carcasses. There weren't even any dogs skulking around. There was no one at all.

Ahlfrith looked to his right. Gadd signed that he was circling further round to see if there was anybody concealed and waiting. Signalling for him to go ahead, Ahlfrith started creeping left, keeping within the scraggly hedge of thorn and hazel. While he went, he listened for the owl's screech that would tell him the warmaster had reached the edge of the clearing, but all he could hear was the chorus of birds singing.

But as he moved, the front of the hall came slowly into view. There were people there. Not many. Ahlfrith peered through the grass. Five. And two. Tied to the great pillars that supported the roof and, in this hall, were set outside the main body of the hall, under the eaves.

"Hey!"

The shout came to him, distinct but faint, over the clearing from the small group of people clustered at the front of the hall.

"Hey, I know you're out there. We've got your men. If you want them to live, come out."

Closer now, Ahlfrith could see that the people holding his father's men were wielding bows, while one held a spear; there wasn't a sword among them.

Farmers, servants, slaves, maybe, left to mind the hall while its lord was away. Though they had, by some chance, managed to capture the two men Æthelwin had sent out as scouts, they would be tasting fear right now, eyes searching left and right, not knowing how many others were out there in the wold, ready to emerge. The right thing, the sensible thing, would be to wait: to send word back to his father to bring up the rest of the men and ride them along the trail and into the clearing. Then, the spark of spear point and the rattle of harness, the sight of war shields hitched over shoulders, and swords ready to be unsheathed, would tell even the most faithful of servants and the bravest of slaves that this fight could not be won; better to let the men they had captured go, and hope in the mercy of the men waiting silently upon their horses. That would be the sensible thing to do.

Ahlfrith stood up.

He stepped out of the wold, holding his hands up, so all could see he was not carrying his sword, that it remained sheathed at his waist.

At the movement, the people at the hall started, some pointing wildly, while the two bowmen, who had arrows fletched, swung between pointing their arrows at him and keeping them trained upon the captives.

"They are my men," Ahlfrith said, starting to walk, still with his hands in clear sight, towards the hall. "I would that you do not harm them."

"Keep – keep back!"

The voice, Ahlfrith realized, was higher than he had first heard, and as he approached, he saw why. Standing out in front of the group was a boy of maybe twelve years, and the others, holding arrows and seaxes and the two men captive, were two more boys and, by the looks of them, two simpletons, older and bigger but with few wits.

Ahlfrith stopped. "Who are you?" he asked.

"M-my name is Drythelm," said the boy. "My lord left me to look after the hall and I will. Keep back." He pointed at the two bound men. "See, we've already taken your men. Come closer and I will kill them. I will."

"How old are you, Drythelm?"

"Old enough. Near old as you, like as not."

"You've done well, Drythelm. Your lord will have only praise for you when he hears of your bravery. But you have done enough. I have many men, awaiting my call. Too many for you, however brave you are. So go now. You have sent the women and girls into the wold already?" Ahlfrith searched for answer in the boy's face, and received it. "Good. Know we will not follow after you – we are not slaving. Go now, and leave us to our work."

"No!" Drythelm waved his seax. "You say you have more men – then show them to me. All I see is you, and these two we have captured. You tell me to go. Now it is my turn." He glanced back at his two companions, boys his own age, who held bows in arms that trembled at the tension the stringed arrows were putting on their young muscles. "If he doesn't go when I tell him, shoot his men, you hear? Put an arrow through their guts." Drythelm turned back to Ahlfrith. He was still a boy, quivering with the nerves of this confrontation, with fear and bravery and the overmastering wish to do right by the charge his lord had laid upon him. So focused was Drythelm on the young man in front of him that he did not see the slow, steady movement, working around the outside of the hall. But Ahlfrith, looking past the boy, saw the warmaster with Gadd and the other man making their stealthy way closer to the small group clustered at the front of the hall.

Ahlfrith held out his hands so that the boy could see them.

"See, I have not drawn sword. You are brave. Someday, the scops will sing songs about your deeds. Go now. While there is still time. Before I call my men. Go, Drythelm, go."

"He's not leaving," said Drythelm. "Do what I told you…" Half turning, he was in time to see the rush of movement, the thrust of shield and the swift slide of sword that sent one of the young bowmen tumbling from the hall and the other clutching his side. He was in time to see the warmaster, Æthelwin, plunge towards him. He was in time to raise his own seax to meet the charge – and to have it pushed aside with no more effort than a man pushes aside a thin branch that bars his way. He was in time to look down, with the eternal surprise of the young when seeing their death, to see the warmaster's sword run into his chest, and then out again.

Slowly, Drythelm stumbled round. He had his hands pressed to his chest, trying to hold in the blood, but it spurted out past his fingers. He looked up and saw Ahlfrith staring at him.

"You had more men," he whispered. And then he fell. He was a boy, with a boy's lean body. His fall made barely a sound.

Ahlfrith stared at him. Æthelwin didn't. He stepped over the corpse as if it was no more than a felled branch and, grasping the ætheling's shoulders, looked him over.

"You are not hurt?"

Ahlfrith glanced at the warmaster, shaking his head, then looked back past him to the dead boy. "You killed him," he said.

"Who?" asked Æthelwin, looking around, as if he did not know to whom Ahlfrith was referring.

"Him," said Ahlfrith, pointing.

Æthelwin looked round. "Oh, him. Yes. Of course." He looked back to the ætheling. "What would you have had me do?"

"You could have disarmed him."

The warmaster sniffed. "He'd taken two of my men captive. He was armed."

"He was a boy."

Æthelwin shook his head. "Boys don't take my men prisoner. Besides, you should be thanking me." The warmaster essayed a grin, which served mainly to make his face even grimmer than before, and pointed past Ahlfrith. "You'd have had some explaining to do if the king had arrived to find you being held captive by some boys and two simpletons."

Ahlfrith looked round to see his father emerging from the wold, with his retainers closely following. The column of men rode up to the hall, where ætheling and warmaster awaited them.

Oswiu reined his horse to a stop and looked down at them.

"What happened here?" he asked, his glance taking in the two bodies lying on the ground, and the three people held sullenly captive.

Ahlfrith looked up at his father. "I was foolish," he said, "and headstrong, and two boys died."

"Not our men?"

"No, not ours."

"Very well then." The king looked to his warmaster. "Strip the hall of anything of value, then fire it. We must leave –" he squinted south-east, over the trees, judging the sun's rise in the sky – "by another hand's span, or word may have time to travel too far."

As the warmaster turned away, directing some of the men into the hall while setting others on watch, the king slowly dismounted. He handed his horse off to one of the men with word to see to it, then came to stand by his son. Ahlfrith still stood by Drythelm's body. Oswiu did not look at the dead boy. Instead, he stared away, over the mantle of trees that closed this hall in a green embrace.

"Sometimes, war is as the scops sing: glorious battles, great warriors fighting each other. But just as often it's like this and no one sings about that."

"What can I do, Father?" Ahlfrith turned to look at his father and his eyes were full of tears.

"For him? Bury him, remember him, pray for him. For yourself?" The king turned to his son. He tapped a finger on his son's forehead. "Remember this too. And don't make the same mistake again." As he did so, Oswiu saw framed in the remorse of the young man before him the image of the boy he had sent off to be fostered in Penda's court, and he knew his son had truly come back to him.

So while the rest of the men ransacked the hall – and a mean haul it produced, little more than a reasonably rich brooch, two old and notched swords and some spearheads awaiting shafts – and then set flame to it, pushing burning tapers in under the thatch and between the timbers, Ahlfrith dug. Refusing help, he made a grave big enough to take the two dead boys: Drythelm and the other whose name he never knew. Then, as the fire took hold, he gave them over to the earth's silent embrace, covering them over, so that the dark soil veiled the sky from their blank, bland stares. This done, Ahlfrith pushed Drythelm's seax into the ground above his body and, for the other boy, he planted the lad's bow into the earth, so that those coming later might know where their boys were, and do them right.

And while Ahlfrith did this, his father watched. Then, when all was done, and the hall had been given over to the flames, and the boy and two simpletons who had been taken captive were tied to trees, that they might not too quickly give word of their leaving, the king mounted his horse, and his son and his warmaster and the men did likewise, and they rode from the clearing, in under the green tree light, away from the yellow flame flowers.

Chapter 2

He had not been easy to find. Of a truth, everyone in these parts had heard tell of him: the priest from afar, the man with the nut skin, who had come with Queen Æthelburh and Bishop Paulinus. Wherever they stopped and asked, of the men working the fields or the women sat spinning and weaving outside their homes, even of the children, peering out at them from the treetops or running alongside the horses yelling questions and asking favours, everyone had answered yes, of course they knew James the Deacon. But whenever they asked whereaways he was, some would say this way and others that, so that they circled round in a welter of confused directions, seemingly coming no closer to the man they sought.

But in the end, the circles tightened, pulling in around Catterick, and people in the hamlet there, when asked, had seen James, some said, on the week, and some two days before, and some on the eve before. And then one said he would take them to him, though of a truth he knew James welcomed no visits from men with swords, but only ministered to the simple folk of the region.

The man, still chattering of the small doings of his village and his people, brought them to a small river, willow lined and clear, but with a rocky shore rising up on the far side. And from this side, he hailed across the river, but to no answer. He hailed again, and then once more, looking sidelong at the men, armed and increasingly grim, sitting on the high horses above him.

Then, at last, there was answer, in movement. From a place concealed behind alder and scrub willow, a coracle appeared, bobbing upon the river as a duck upon the water, and poling it across was a man with nut-brown skin and hair cut to a crown about his head. He stopped the coracle in mid stream, letting it slowly spin round as he sat within it and looked at the riders lined up along the far bank. He waited for them to speak.

One of the men pushed his horse forward, so that its hocks splashed in the river shallows.

"We have come seeking James the Deacon."

The coracle, pulled by the current, turned its charge away and then, slowly, brought him back to face the riders again.

"Who is the 'we'?" asked the man in the boat. His words moved with a different, rising pitch, so while their sound was familiar their tune was not and they were hard to hear.

The rider pointed to the man on his right. "It is the king who seeks James the Deacon."

The coracle, still turning, turned the face of its occupant away and then brought him back.

"Which king?"

"Oswine, king of Deira, the Godfriend."

At that, the man's eyes widened. "Why does a friend of God come seeking me?"

"So you are James the Deacon?"

"Yes, yes, I am James. But I ask again: why does a friend of God seek me?"

But before the rider could answer, the man beside him held up his hand. "Peace, Hunwald. I will speak myself." The king dismounted and stood beside his horse. Then, not minding the cold of the water, he stepped forward into the river until it came to his knees. "I am Oswine, whom some call Godfriend, and if you would know why I seek you out, then speak with me."

Seeing the king walk into the river, James the Deacon poled the coracle rapidly towards him.

"Lord, lord, I had not meant you to come to me. Hold, hold, and I will come to you."

But even as James spoke, Oswine stepped out further to him, not knowing that the riverbed dropped away, and he fell, plunging into the water.

The deacon pulled him forth. Reaching from his boat, he pulled the king from the water and held his face to the air, while the king's men, scrambling from their horses, made a human chain to pull him back to land.

Dripping and coughing, Oswine looked to the deacon.

"Already you have saved me. I would ask you to save me again, by giving me your blessing."

"I will give you my blessing, but now, if you will come across with me, I will give you something of much greater worth: a fire and somewhere to dry your clothes." James pointed at the king's men. "But I cannot take them too. This is a little boat, and my home is smaller."

"I will come with you," said Oswine, "and they will wait here."

"Lord..." began Hunwald, but the king held up his hand.

"There is no danger here, Hunwald, other than in one too weighed down with finery and weapons to be able to swim. I will go with him. Besides, I would speak on these matters alone."

"You know what I think, lord."

"Yes, Hunwald, and I am of a mind with you. But I must know." The king turned to James and signalled him closer. "Come. If you will carry me across, I would find somewhere to dry these clothes and hear your counsel."

James poled the coracle to the bank and held it there, driving the pole into the soft river mud, while the king stepped carefully into it and sat down, still dripping. Then the deacon pushed the coracle from the bank and poled it carefully across the river, while the king's men watched in anxious silence from the far bank.

The deacon pushed a trailing branch of scrub willow aside and poled the coracle into a small pool, marked from the river flow by a half-submerged alder that grew into the water before turning upwards to the sky.

Stepping from the coracle as easily as the king dismounted his horse, James held out his hand and Oswine took it – and it was as well, for when he attempted to follow James ashore the coracle jumped back as a skittish horse might and, but for the deacon's grip, he would have fallen into the water again. But James held him and, with the grasp on his wrist, Oswine made the widening step to shore, while the coracle settled to bumping gently around its alder and willow harbour.

James led the king up a steep, rocky path, concealed by the birch and ferns that grew thickly on the river slope, to the lip of a small cave.

"My home," he said, gesturing for Oswine to enter.

Within, there was a fire, its smoke pooling in the ceiling and coiling there before creeping out of the cave mouth, and a small shelf carved patiently from the rock and set as far back from the entrance and the wind and rain as was possible. On the shelf was a book and, coming into the cave after the king, the deacon went past and made homage to the book, pressing it to his forehead and heart before returning it to its rocky niche.

"The book of goodness," James said, turning back to Oswine. "Bishop Paulinus left it for me when he took the queen and her children away. I wonder sometimes what became of them." The deacon looked piercingly at the king, but Oswine could make no answer, for the memory of Queen Æthelburh's visit still burned him.

"Here, warm yourself," James continued. "I will bring a cloak that you might dry your clothes."

Although there seemed nowhere in the small cave to hide anything away, yet James managed to retrieve an old and somewhat threadbare cloak from a dark niche that served as a store. Oswine pulled off his tunic and leggings, and gave them to James to dry before the fire, then wrapped the cloak round his shoulders.

"My men will fret if I am too long." The king looked up from where he sat upon the cave's one stool – a sawn short log – to where James stood, watching him.

"I have asked what I would of you. Now ask what you would of me."

Oswine turned his face away from the deacon. He looked into the fire, seeing the fire sprites dancing upon the logs.

"Oswiu is bleeding us," he said. "He rides into Deira, into my kingdom, and burns the halls of my thegns, taking whatever he finds. I thought at first it was an anger that would burn out, anger at... well, anger at something that happened. But the raids have not lessened in time but grown more frequent. Now summer does not pass without two or three of my thegns losing their halls to the red flower. Now, my thegns are no longer content to wait, as I counselled them, saying we must not raise hand in war against our neighbours and our kin, against fellow Christians. Now, my thegns whisper against me, saying it is no king who lets his kingdom burn. The truth is –" and here Oswine looked to James – "the truth is, I think that too. What sort of king will not fight for his throne? Therefore, I come to you to ask your counsel and your blessing. I would ride against Oswiu, that he may know he might not raid my kingdom without penalty and without fear. But I would know: may I do this before God and his church?"

"Why do you come to me to seek answer to this, when you have not sought me out before?"

"Aidan, Bishop Aidan, is my friend, and bishop of this land. But he is friend too, and for many years more, to Oswiu. It would be as if I asked a mother whether she would counsel me to take arms against her son. Besides, he is not here now, when I have need of this counsel, but away, and I know not when he will return to my kingdom."

"But he has left others to guide your kingdom in his absence. Why do you not seek counsel from them?"

"All say Hild is the most holy and learned of the masters of the holy houses in my kingdom; but I would not ask war of a woman. Therefore, I come to you – for you were here before the others, and you have endured longest, through the year of fear when Cadwallon and Penda ravaged the kingdom and killed my father, through to the present day." King Oswine turned to look full upon James the Deacon. "Tell me I may do this thing."

"You would cure war with war. You would stop raids by more raids. You would put out fires with more fires." James the Deacon turned from the king. "There is reason I have sought to stay far from the dealings of kings and the men with swords: to them every question is answered in blood. I will have no part in it."

The king rose to his feet, and his face was pulled with anger.

"Would you have me lose my throne?" he asked.

"A throne is but a little thing – a seat, like this." And James sat upon the stool. "It is where you put your bottom. But your soul – your soul is God's, and made by him, and it will not fail or break. But it may burn."

"That is why I seek your blessing and the armour of your prayers. I do not want to burn."

James the Deacon looked up at the young man standing in his cave home, and love leapt in his breast for the goodness of the king.

"If you would not burn, then put aside your throne and give away your riches, and you shall surely live."

But at his words, Oswine's face fell.

"If it were possible, I would do as you say, for I did not seek this throne. It was given to me, and what sort of ingrate would spurn a gift freely given?"

"A man might return a gift if it harms his soul."

Oswine shook his head. "God has given this cup to me, and none other; I will not put it aside. But I have a gift for you." The Godfriend squatted down upon his haunches, the old cloak wrapped around his shoulders, and looked into the nut-brown face of the deacon sat upon his log stool.

"What can you give me?" asked James. He gestured around the cave, his hand taking in fire and book and the place where he slept. "I have all I need."

Oswine reached out and put his hand on the deacon's shoulder. "You are blessed – I see that. But others might be blessed, through you, if you would but say yes. For, meeting you, I would give to you the church in York; I would make you master of all the holy houses in Deira. Then the word of hope you brought from so far away might be heard again, throughout my kingdom. If you will but say yes."

James stared at the young man looking earnestly at him. He searched the face, he looked deeply into his eyes, seeking sign of duplicity, but found none there. Then he turned his face away.

"You… you would give me so much?"

"Yes. Yes, I would," said Oswine.

"I will not deny that I have often prayed for this: for God to give me the chance to show that my coming here, to this far northern land, was more than a jest." James stood up and turned, so that he looked out through the opening of his cell, out to the trees and the hint of river and the distant strips of ploughed earth marked out by the fresh green of new crops.

"I remember… I remember all those years ago, when the pope sent word to our monastery that he sought men to go on mission. I was little more than a boy then, but with a child's faith, and I went at once to the abbot and said I would go. I remember the abbot taking my hand and leading me out of St Andrew's and onto the road, the Clivus Scauri – ha! I still remember its name – and pointing up to the Palatine and Caelian hills, at the Flavian Palace and the House of Tiberius. 'Here,' the abbot said, 'we live among the great works of the past. If you come, you will be part of building the great work of the future.'" James made a sound, halfway between a laugh and a snort. "Of course I came. But I have done little building, and that only when the king, Edwin, lived. Since he died, I have skulked in my cave, as fearful of coming out as a mouse when the cat waits outside. Now you offer me all that I could have wished, and more. You would make of me a bishop, a shepherd of souls. Then my coming here might be more than the ambitions of a boy. I might call men to life, and restore the church that Paulinus began. I might… matter."

The deacon laughed. It was a short bark of a laugh, as much the sound of a dog as a man. "I do not matter." The deacon glanced at the king, and making the sign of the cross muttered a phrase in Latin.

Not understanding what James had said, Oswine asked him, "Will you accept my offer? Will you be my bishop and minister to my people?"

James shook his head. "I will remain a deacon, and be James."

"Very well." The king shuffled off the old cloak and began putting on his still-damp clothes. When he was dressed, he turned to James.

Oswiu: King of Kings

"What did you say to me? Before you refused my offer."

"Oh, that. It was just a phrase in my language. It does not matter."

Oswine nodded. "If you should change your mind…"

"I will not."

"…send word to me." The king buckled his belt around his waist and settled his sword upon his hip, hand resting upon its hilt. He did not look at James as he spoke. "I go to war. If you will not give me your blessing, at least pray for me, that I not be lost."

At these words, James put his hand upon the king's arm. "I pray for you always," he said. "Always."

Chapter 3

The weather was not right for a funeral. Oswiu squinted up at the sun as it glowered down at them from a cloudless, bronze sky, like a great, unforgiving eye. Holding his horse on track with his legs, he took his helmet off with one hand and swept the other over his forehead, flicking away the sweat that was trickling down into his eyes. Some of the people who had gathered, from field and hamlet and hill, to see the great procession go past pointed at the king, and whispers passed among the watchers.

"The king weeps."

"See how he grieves."

But Oswiu, having wiped the sweat from brow and eyes, had put his great helmet back on and, with its burnished metal on his head, he could no longer hear the whispers of the crowd, nor see them other than as shadows, caught on the edges of sight.

Although the watchers had seen sweat rather than tears, there had been tears, and there would be again, for Oswiu knew, as did all but the most blessed of his subjects, that grief was subject to tides, ebbing and receding as the sea, sometimes washing in and covering all; then receding, only to sweep in again. For now, the king felt the thickness of his parched tongue and the wet of his hair sticking to his helmet, and his legs, stuck with sweat, inside his leggings; the grief tide had receded.

In its withdrawal, it left strange thoughts, popping unbidden into his mind.

In this heat, would the body keep until it could be buried? They had been one day on the road already, with no sign of this summer drought breaking, and there would be another before the funeral procession might ascend the long steps to the great keep at Bamburgh. The sisters at the holy house had, he was sure, done what they could to prepare and preserve the body until its burial, but in this heat it was surely only a matter of time before it became putrid and started to stink.

That was the thought that brought the tide of grief flooding back. She had always been so careful about how she smelled. Even in the desperate days of their early exile, she had always washed the mud and dirt of travel from her hands and arms, her face and feet. Then, when she had found a home, she had had the household slaves fill it with flowers and sweet-smelling plants when the machair was in bloom: thyme and heather.

Oswiu, king, wept for his mother.

The message had come three days past, the messenger finding him in the far north of his kingdom, at Stirling. He had at once taken ship, sailing with wind and every oar he and his men might wield down the River Forth and into the great firth, then around the coast to the holy house where his sister Æbbe ruled and his mother lived. The sun, in this blazing summer, had not relented as they went, but lay its hot breath down over the sea, suffocating the wind and forcing them to pull their way to Coldingham.

They had made the journey in two days, arriving as the sun set, and before the boat had even beached Oswiu had leapt from it and gone climbing and scrambling up the steep path to the holy house. The look-out had seen them coming, and monks waited, answering yes to his first shouted question as to whether she yet lived, but hurrying him on so that he knew the time left to her must be short…

There were tapers lit around the bed. They threw some light, but more came through the door from the last leavings of the setting sun. Seeing him standing as a shadow in the door, Æbbe rose from where she was sitting and came to him, taking his hand and leading him into the room while she spoke quietly of what had happened into his ear. Oswiu knew she spoke, and later the memory of her words came back to him, but for the moment the only sense given to him was sight: the sight of his mother lying upon the narrow bed.

Now, riding with her body back to where it would rest, he remembered what his sister had said. The fit had come upon Acha two days before, striking her down and leaving her insensible at first, so that Æbbe had feared she would never wake. But while the messengers rode and sailed in search of the king, Acha had woken. But though she moved her lips, no words came from them, only sounds, and it seemed that her body was stricken, for she could move only a hand and arm. As swiftly as messengers were sent for the king, so they were sent for Bishop Aidan and, being but a short boat journey down the coast, he had arrived first and given her the viaticum, the only food that might carry her across the great gulf between the living and the dead. Then Aidan had waited, sending continuous volleys of prayer to the hearer of all prayer.

Aidan was waiting still when Oswiu arrived, kneeling beside the bed, but the king did not see him – only the figure upon the bed. He went to her, knelt beside her, whispered her name, then spoke it and, at last, her eyes had opened and turned to him. Oswiu saw the recognition in her eyes as he leaned over her, for it seemed that she did not even have the strength to turn her head, and he saw her lips move as she tried to speak, but there were no intelligible words in the sounds she made. He laid his finger upon her lips, quietening her as he spoke himself, softly, continuously, while a stool was brought to him. But the king spurned the stool and remained kneeling beside Acha, with his sister upon her other side, and Aidan by the head of the bed, as night came down upon this middle-earth and his mother's breathing grew more laboured, each intake a greater struggle, until, in the deep dark of the night, the struggle ceased.

"I did not think she would die."

While the sisters prepared Acha's body for the journey south, readying it as much as possible for the fierce heat of this furnace summer, Oswiu spoke with his sister and Aidan, the three of them taking the cool of the dawn before the day.

The king made no move to brush the tears from his face. Nor did Æbbe, nor Aidan, as they told the tale of their grief to each other, and the long years of shared memory that none but they knew.

"I did not think she would ever die." Oswiu shook his head. "I am a fool. Death comes to all."

Now, with the bronze sun beating down upon him and the funeral procession winding along the track that ran towards Bamburgh, Oswiu shook his head again. His mother had been old, very old – she must have known seventy summers or more, for her hair, when the sisters unbound it as they laid her out, was as white as a lily – and it seemed that she would endure, unchanging, as the hills. But she had died, and now he took her to rest beside her son in the church at Bamburgh. A daughter of Deira, an Yffing, she would lie with the Idings in their great stronghold and, by her presence there and in God's great hall, help to keep it secure against all enemies, earthly and supernatural.

But they needs must hurry, lest the heat make it impossible to carry her further and a burial be forced upon them in this wild and open country, scoured by the wind. Oswiu turned his horse's head around and pulled it out of the procession, letting the solemn riders go past him as he waited for the ox-pulled wagon that bore his mother's body. The monks and sisters had done all they could to keep the sun from Acha, swiftly building a willow hurdle over the flat wooden bed of the carriage and covering it with whitewashed cloth. In homage to their mother, Æbbe had set off walking behind the wagon, followed by many of her sisters, but as the day shrank beneath the sun's weight, some had returned to the holy house, while Æbbe had sat upon the wagon, taking a place beside the driver, and leading the chanted prayer that flowed up from the procession.

Oswiu waited until the wagon came level with him, then turned his horse so that it paced in time with the oxen. Leaning over to his sister, the king asked the question that had grown in his mind through the day's heat.

"Will... will she keep?"

Æbbe did not have to ask further, for the same thought had grown in her mind too as the heat bore down upon them. But she could answer the king's fears.

"I went, just now, and then two hours before, into the wagon." Æbbe turned to look at her brother and there was wonder in her eyes. "There is no smell."

"Nothing?"

"Nothing. Or perhaps, though I wonder if this is memory, the scent, as if faint and borne from far away, of the machair in spring."

Oswiu nodded. "It would be. She loved the flowers of spring." The king smiled at his sister. "You have eased my mind."

Æbbe smiled in turn. "I am glad."

"There... there is one other matter I would ask you of."

Æbbe nodded. "Rhieienmelth?"

"Yes."

"She is well."

"That is not what I would know now."

"She asked me to ask your leave to attend the funeral. She wanted me to ask before we left, but I said I could not. Not then." Æbbe turned to look at her brother. "But now, I ask on her behalf. Rhieienmelth would have leave to join us, that she may stand with her children and make farewell to Mother. What say you?"

Oswiu shook his head. "No. I cannot have her there."

But from the wagon, his sister looked askance at him. "May you refuse her on this?"

"I am the king." Oswiu looked down at Æbbe. "Of course I can refuse her."

"But on this?" Æbbe persisted. "We go to pray our mother to God's great hall. The enemy, we know, will set many of his devils to stop such a one as our mother ascending to God's presence and taking her place in his hall – every prayer offered is protection for her."

"Rhieienmelth can send her prayers from your holy house – just not from Mother's funeral."

"Ah." Æbbe paused. "That is another reason I would have Rhieienmelth join us. Without me there, I fear that my house would not be very holy by the time I return – it is only with difficulty that I stop her turning it into a house of merrymaking and hunting when I am there."

"That is your task, not mine." The king made to pull his horse's head away so that he might again take his place near the front of the column. But Æbbe stopped him.

"Wait," she said. "There is one further reason for you to allow Rhieienmelth to attend the funeral."

Oswiu sighed and turned back to his sister.

"It was Mother who made me promise that Rhieienmelth be allowed to attend her funeral. Before you came, Mother made sign to me in great distress and I could not tell that which she wished, for she had no longer the power of speech. But I thought it must surely be some person she wished to see, so I spoke names, the names of children and grandchildren, of faithful servants and old friends, thinking it were one of these she wished to take leave from. But looking in her eyes, I saw there... fear. Not the hope of last meeting, but fear of condemnation, of a debt left unpaid and an oath unfulfilled. And, seeing that, I spoke more widely, thinking that maybe she sought to make good a promise and, in the end, I spoke of Rhieienmelth, and her eyes widened, and her mouth filled with sound, so I knew whom she sought." Æbbe turned her head away from her brother.

"Since you sent me Rhieienmelth, I have sought to govern her, to mould her to our ways, but in truth she has more moulded us to her ways. She is ever out upon the hunt with her hounds, or calling scops to sing for her, so that our hall, which was before a place of quiet and prayer, is now more often a place of laughter and... and scandal. My sisters no longer attend the hall, but remain in their own cells, and I myself only go to it when I must. For many months we had spoken barely a riddle's worth of words to each other, content to pass our lives separately, but with Mother's wish, I sought her out."

Æbbe's lips pressed together, squeezing the blood from them so they appeared a white line, like a healed scar, across her face. "She laughed at me. When I asked if she would come to speak to Mother, she laughed at me. 'Come to the woman who made me give up the crown and live here? Why should I come to her?' If it had been any other time, I would, I confess, have struck her. I asked her again, told her that this was Mother's wish, that she see her, and... and that Mother was dying." Æbbe looked up at her brother, and her eyes were bitter with memory. "She said, 'Good.' I left her then, before I disgraced my mother's dying by attacking one of my own sisters – however ungovernable – and returned to tell Mother that Rhieienmelth would not come. When she heard the news I – I thought she might die then, so great was her distress. But there was naught I could do save offer words of scant comfort, for I knew not why Mother wished to see Rhieienmelth with such urgent need." The abbess eyed her brother. "Do you know aught of this?"

But the king made no answer to her question. Instead, he stared with narrow eyes and narrow lips into the mid-distance.

"But later, in the dark hours of the night when I sat waiting with Mother and waiting for you, not knowing if she would live long enough for you to arrive, there came a sound from without. The sister I had left to keep watch and pray came in to speak with me: Rhieienmelth had come. Mother was sleeping, if such so close to death may be called sleep, and I went out to her. She was cloaked, with a hood over her head, as if she would not be seen acceding to the wish of a dying woman. 'I will see her,' she said to me. 'But alone.'"

"You didn't let her go in to Mother alone?" asked Oswiu.

"To see Rhieienmelth was Mother's only wish other than to see you. If Rhieienmelth would only see her alone, I had to give her leave. But I stood where I could watch."

"What did you see?"

"I saw her stand above our mother, looking down at her, and although Rhieienmelth's back was to me, I could see how tightly she held herself. She was as a man drawing a bow and then holding it until every muscle in his body trembles. Then, whether through some sign that Rhieienmelth gave or by some gift from God, I saw, by the movement of her head, that our mother woke and I heard, from the sounds she made, that she was trying to speak to Rhieienmelth. I would have gone in then, but Rhieienmelth turned to me and shook her head, and I stopped. As Rhieienmelth turned back, I saw Mother begin to raise her hand, as if she would touch Rhieienmelth, but she had not the strength to do so. Then Rhieienmelth went down on her knees beside Mother. I saw her speak with her, whispering into Mother's ear, but I could not hear what words she said.

"'Remember that I came,' she said to me when she came forth. I went in to Mother and her eyes were filled with tears. But whether they were tears of hope or despair I could not say, for the blight that struck down our mother seemed to take away not only the power of speech, but also the gift of expression, so her face was as blank as stone."

"Did you ask her? Surely she might have made some reply, if only with her eyes?"

Æbbe shook her head. "I should have done, but first I tried to settle her, and before I could try, Mother went to sleep again."

"So you do not know if Rhieienmelth brought comfort to Mother?"

"No, not for sure. But my hope is that she did, and the tears Mother shed were tears of relief, of forgiveness given and received, that she might better face the great judge."

"But you do not know?"

"No."

"Very well." The king rode in silence for a while beside the wagon that bore his mother's body for burial. "I would not see her, but if it is Mother's wish, then I suppose she must be there." Oswiu turned to his sister. "Send word to Rhieienmelth, but tell her that she is not to seek word with me, or the queen. Those are my terms. See that she agrees to them."

With those words, the king urged his horse into a canter alongside the slow-moving column, towards the banner that streamed at its head. When Oswiu had reached the head of the column, Æbbe turned and looked into the cool shadow space they had made over the wagon to take the body of Acha.

"Did you hear?" she said into the shadow.

"Yes," said Rhieienmelth, pulling the cloth back so that she might see the abbess. "I heard."

*

The clouds massed through the dawn and on into the morning, gathering in the west into great mountains. While the monks and priests chanted, and beat upon skin drums to chase away the devils who sought to drag the queen to their domain, the clouds began to flash from within, as lightning fought its sky wars. Then Oswiu and the queen came in solemn procession from the great hall, and all their thegns and ladies with them, and they went in a great circle around the inner ward of the ancient stronghold of the Idings until, at the door of the church, Bishop Aidan met them and they went within to bury the old queen, daughter of Ælle, wife of Æthelfrith, sister of Edwin, mother of Oswald and mother of Oswiu.

When Oswiu and Eanflæd entered the church it already seemed all but full. They were followed by their son Ecgfrith, their firstborn, old enough to walk, although unsteadily, between his halfbrother and half-sister, Ahlfrith and Ahlflæd. Many had sought the position of honour after the royal children, but such was the squabbling as to who should hold first place that the king, in frustrated desperation, had placed another first. Over Æthelwin's protests – for he repeated loud and often, for all to hear, that he had no wish for such honour – he chose the warmaster to follow after his children. Not a few among the assembled thegns, knowing full well that Æthelwin's blood was mixed with that of slave girls and vanquished kingdoms, threw daggers of contempt into the warmaster's back as he walked in front of them. But others among the people watching saw the strength of his bearing and whispered to those around them that the warmaster appeared more kingly than those, supposedly more noble than he, who followed behind. The dagger looks grew all the more pointed when many who had thought to enter the church with the king were denied entry.

"It's full," the monks, big burly men who were stationed at the doors to the church, told the thegns who pooled outside, trying to force their way in. But in the king's royal stronghold, none might bear arms save with the king's leave, and though some voices were raised in anger, they were soon stifled, and the offenders dragged away, while the sound of chant flowed from the church and settled upon the crowd. Nor were the waiting thegns made any happier when they saw a scraggly, decrepit man, wrapped in an increasingly patchy raven-feather cloak, and the king's scop, lips moving in silent rehearsal of a funeral lament, pulled through the press to enter the church.

But within, Acca and Coifi began to wonder if they might have been better off remaining outside, such was the sweaty heat rising from the mass of people who filled the church. The scop, wiping the sudden and immediate beading of sweat from his brow, took the chance of a break in the chant to whisper to his friend, "Do you want to go back outside?"

Coifi shook his head. Acca saw that despite being wrapped in his raven-feather cloak, the old priest was not sweating – a slight flush was all that indicated he felt any hotter than normal. The scop also saw Coifi's eyes begin to roll, turning over in their sockets so that they showed white, before locking back into place.

Acca had seen this before. It meant that Coifi was about to fall limp and unconscious, possibly after first thrashing around in a frenzy, only to wake later, clear eyed and babbling of what he had seen – and in Acca's memory this usually involved buildings burning and people dying.

So, quietly, smoothly and without anyone seeing, Acca unpinned the brooch that held the fold of his cloak as he liked it and pushed the pin into Coifi's scrawny shoulder.

It was just as well he did – it took near two phrases of the monks' chant before Coifi made any reaction at all, slowly turning to look with mild interest at what was sticking into his shoulder.

"Don't you dare," Acca hissed, as the priest's eyes began to glaze and roll upwards again. This time, he stuck the pin lower – somewhere no one watching would see, but where Coifi would certainly feel.

He did. Eyes that had been rolling back into his skull snapped forwards and glared at him.

"Why did you do that?" Coifi asked, surprise making his voice sharp. One or two of the people around them – high-ranking thegns who had managed to push aside others – looked askance at them, but most did not hear the old priest over the chant of the monks of Holy Island.

"To stop you falling over," Acca whispered. "And don't tell me you weren't going to. Besides, I want you to see someone."

Acca eased Coifi round a little, so that they stood with their backs against the wall.

"Look," he said, pointing with his eyes to where the sisters from Æbbe's holy house stood in a block, surrounded by the perspiring ranks of thegns wrapped in their finest clothes.

Coifi followed the scop's gaze. "What is she doing here?" he asked.

"What's more, she's here but Œthelwald is not," said Acca.

"Oh, I know that," whispered Coifi. He looked, with apparent innocence, at the scop. "You do not?"

"I... of course I do. You'd better tell me what you've heard – it's most likely wrong."

"I hear tell Œthelwald has sworn battle oath to his cousin Talorcan, king of the Picts, and gone to live among the men of the Old North."

"Talorcan? But he is the son of Eanfrith, half-brother to the king."

"Yes," Coifi nodded. "He is."

"Did the king allow it?"

"I do not hear that the king knew of it; not until Œthelwald had gone. But he has since sent word, pledging his loyalty to the king, but saying he seeks the knowledge of war his father gained from the men of the Old North. Of course, you know all this."

"Naturally," said Acca. "But I'm surprised you've heard it too."

"Oh, it's surprising what I hear. Men seem to think that when my eyes roll over my ears stop working."

"Yes, well." Acca nodded towards where they could see Rhieienmelth, standing among the sisters of the holy house. "What have your ears heard of her?"

"That she was the one who sent messengers to Talorcan saying that Œthelwald, son of Oswald, sought a battle lord to earn glory and honour and men ready to follow him."

"But she has a son of her own: Ahlfrith. Why would Rhieienmelth support Œthelwald over her own son?"

As Acca spoke, the chanting monks fell into silence. Coifi, hearing the silence, put a finger to his lips. Acca, almost beside himself with curiosity, had to wait while Aidan slowly rose from where he was kneeling, to begin anointing the body with oil and water.

As he did so, the monks of Lindisfarne began to chant once more, and Acca, leaning close to the old priest, hissed, "What have you heard?"

Coifi tapped a finger to his nose.

Acca looked as if he might burst.

And, seeing that, Coifi smiled, but relented.

"I hear men say that Rhieienmelth's children take the part of their father, holding the whispers men make about her conduct in the holy house against her. I hear that Ahlfrith himself went to her, and said that if she continued then he would have no more to do with her. Of course, Rhieienmelth said that the hunting and the merrymaking would end, but… well, you must have heard. Is there a wandering scop in the land who has not found welcome in her hall?"

Acca stared at the old priest, his eyes wide, and such was his surprise at this news that he barely heard the words Bishop Aidan spoke – words of blessing and guidance – as he gave the old queen into the keeping of her lord, the lord of all, with the constant plea that he would forgive where she had failed, but reward her faithfulness.

Then, as the words ended, and the body was slowly lowered into the ground, the heavens opened. The thunder was so great, the lightning so bright, that most of those in the church, and all those without, cried out in terror and distress. The dogs, skulking around the edges of the great press of people, sent up a volley of barking and howling, which, as the second crash came, fell away to whimpers and silence.

After that, the rain. Such was the violence of the storm that those people without the church were forced to run to shelter. Those nearest the king's great hall streamed inside, shaking off the rain within, alongside the dogs. Others hid in the storehouses and workshops and sheds that were dotted around within the inner ward, while an unfortunate few had to find shelter alongside the pigs in their sties.

They buried Acha while the rain came down, giving her into the earth's embrace. Oswiu stood for a long minute on the edge of the grave, looking down at the shrouded figure within. He held in his hand the first clod of earth to seal her return to the earth, but he did not release it.

In the end, Aidan came to him and spoke quietly to the king, so quietly that none but Oswiu could hear his words. Then, slowly, gently, Aidan took the king's hand and held it over the grave, parting the fingers. Grain by grain, the earth trickled down onto the king's mother. Then, still holding Oswiu by his hand, Aidan led him from the church and into the cleansing, cooling rain, and thence to his great hall, for the great feast of farewell. And, one by one, the other members of Oswiu's family followed. All, it seemed, except one.

"Ecgfrith!"

Eanflæd looked around for her little boy. She couldn't see him in the great hall, but even though the rain had stopped, it was thick with people. Ecgfrith was four now, and fast with it, forever running off after the king's warriors or hiding in the stables. To keep him from mischief, the queen had set a young girl to follow him and to rescue him when his boldness grew greater than his sense. She had once stopped him trying to clamber over the ramparts so that he could climb down to a boat he had seen moored below. Eanflæd looked around for her.

"Ah, Inga. Where is Ecgfrith?"

The girl looked at the queen blankly. "I thought you were looking after him – the church was too full for me to get inside, and I saw Ecgfrith was with you when you came out."

"But I told him to come and find you when we got back in the hall."

"I… he didn't come to me. I've not seen him."

The queen looked around, a sudden clutch of fear gripping her.

"Ecgfrith," she called out. "Ecgfrith!"

"I'm sure he'll be all right," said Inga. "He's probably gone with his brother or one of the men."

Eanflæd grabbed the girl's hand. "Look for him. Call my women and set them to looking for him too. He is too bold..."

Inga, fear tugging at her face too now, set off, weaving through the throng of men in the hall, casting looks in all directions.

Eanflæd told herself not to worry. She scolded her heart as it began to beat faster, but nevertheless, she too began to press her way through the crowd, heading to the door.

"Have you seen my son?" she asked the door warden, taking his arm.

"Why, I have, right enough," said the warden. "He went out not a few minutes past with one of the sisters from the holy house."

The queen breathed out her relief. If Ecgfrith was with one of the sisters, he must be all right. But she would still know where he was.

"Whither were they going?"

"I don't rightly know, your majesty," said the warden. "I didn't think to ask. But last I saw, they were headed that away." And he pointed across the wide courtyard, towards the upper gate.

The queen set off across the courtyard, looking left and right as she went for some sign of the boy. All the people of the nearest hamlets and villages, and many from those of two or three days' journey away, had come to the stronghold of the Idings to bid farewell to the old queen and, afterwards, to partake in the feast of farewell. Long tables had been set up around the courtyard and, the storm having passed, the pantry servants were already beginning to ferry out food from the kitchens – additional, temporary ovens had been built to bake enough bread – while the children played chase and hop step. Many among the assembled villagers hailed Eanflæd as she passed, for she was well known among the common people, and even better loved.

Some among the folk had seen Ecgfrith pass, not long before, and they pointed the queen on, towards the upper gate.

Why would anyone, even a sister of the holy house, be taking Ecgfrith out of the castle when the feast of farewell was about to begin?

Eanflæd gathered her skirts up and rushed onwards, towards the gate.

"Stop!"

She sent her voice across the courtyard, over the throng of people assembling at the long tables, past the scurrying servants, to the door warden, pulling back the great gate.

And he heard her.

Squeezing past the last knot of people, squabbling over who would sit where, Eanflæd saw the upper gate, half open, the door warden standing beside it and, beside him, Ecgfrith, hand in hand with one of the sisters of the holy house.

"Ecgfrith!" The queen ran to him and picked him up. "Where were you going? It's time for the feast."

"Let go, Mummy." Ecgfrith struggled in her arms. "I want to see the ships."

"What ships?"

"The ships on the beach. She said she'd take me." The boy pointed at the sister, who was now standing beside the door warden looking, with level, even gaze, at the queen.

Eanflæd nodded to the sister. "It was kind of you to take him, but he must come – the feast will begin soon."

"Let me go, Mummy." Ecgfrith began to kick out. "I want to see the ships."

The boy, although only four, was strong, and his sharp kicks dug into Eanflæd's ribs. She put him down and turned to the sister.

"Would you tell Ecgfrith it's time to come back. He can come with you later, after the feast has started, if you would take him then."

The sister, her eyes cool and level, did not take her gaze from Eanflæd, but spoke to the boy. "It is time to go back, little one."

"But you promised!" Ecgfrith's face began to crumple into tears at this further evidence of adult unfaithfulness.

"Thank you," said Eanflæd, and she took hold of the boy's hand. Without adult support, he began, disconsolately, to follow her. But before returning to the great hall, the queen turned back to the sister of the holy house. "I will look out for you later. What is your name, sister?"

"My name is Rhieienmelth."

Eanflæd stopped. The answer had come when she had already turned back towards the great hall. She gestured towards the nearest party of people, calling towards her a woman, a villager she knew from a case that had come before the king and which she had heard in his absence.

"Will you take Ecgfrith back to the hall for me, please, and give him into the keeping of my women there. Careful, he's fast – he'll try to get away."

Eanflæd watched the woman head towards the hall keeping careful hold of Ecgfrith's hand. Then she turned round.

Rhieienmelth was still standing by the door, but it was closed now and the warden had returned to his post.

The two women looked at each other.

"If you ever come near my son again I will have you thrown from the highest rock I can find into a pack of starving dogs." Eanflæd spoke the words calmly and softly. Only someone standing close might have heard what she said, and there was no one to hand.

"Eanflæd the Wise. That's what they call you. Not wise enough to know I simply wanted to meet my – well, shall we call him my nephew?"

"My husband, the king, told me you sent men to kill him. I didn't know whether to believe him before."

The icy calm with which the old queen had faced the new one up until now suddenly gave way a little, for Rhieienmelth's voice cracked in her questioning reply.

"What men? I did not send any men to kill him."

Eanflæd turned her head away in disgust. "A liar too. It was as well my husband put you aside." And she turned to make her way back to the hall.

But Rhieienmelth grasped her arm. Eanflæd looked down at the fingers, then slowly turned back and regarded the previous queen. Eanflæd saw that Rhieienmelth's previous calm had gone: great emotions worked beneath the surface, sending waves of feeling across the woman's face.

"I did not send any men to hurt or kill my husband." Despite the emotions Eanflæd could see warring within, Rhieienmelth mastered herself to speak clearly. "Why should he think I sent them?"

"The men who attacked him and his party when they were in Mercia – they were Northumbrians, paid to find and kill the king."

"I did not do such a thing. I would not have done." Rhieienmelth looked back at the new queen, and Eanflæd saw how she regained control over her emotions.

Eanflæd turned to go.

"One more thing."

Eanflæd looked round.

Rhieienmelth gave a strange smile, one caught halfway between fear and spite. "If I did not send those men to kill the king, who did? Think on that, Eanflæd the Wise."

Eanflæd gave a single, sharp nod, then headed back to the great hall, entering it to find the final preparations for the feast being made. Seeing the king standing and talking with Aidan, she made her way over to him.

Oswiu, seeing her approach, looked significantly towards the great cup, carved from the curved horn of a great bull and bound around with gold, that it would be Eanflæd's duty to pass to the most notable of the king's thegns and warriors. But Eanflæd shook her head, the slightest motion, and, with her eyes, told the king she wished to speak with him. Aidan, seeing the sign, understood and stepped aside.

"What is it?" Oswiu asked. "The feast is all but ready."

"Rhieienmelth is here."

"Ah." The hand came off Eanflæd's shoulder. "You've seen her. I did not think you knew her."

"I did not. But I sought Ecgfrith and could not find him until I went from the hall and saw a sister I knew not taking him by the hand."

"Rhieienmelth?"

"Yes."

"But…" The king slowly straightened and his face hardened. "Was she going to hurt Ecgfrith?"

"I…" Eanflæd looked back, searching her memory of the woman she had spoken to for some subtle sign of lying or dissembling. "No," she said, deciding. "No, I do not think so. Or she is a better liar than I think."

"Oh, she can lie. When we tricked the Gododdin into letting us into their fortress on Edinburgh rock, it was Rhieienmelth who did most of the talking."

"But she had you with her then; for her, I think, it would have been as much game as untruth."

Oswiu nodded. "I think you are right. She was alive then as children are when they play."

"If I am right, then we must think on this: she says she did not send those men who attacked you in Mercia. If not her, then who? Who else knew where you were going?"

"No one else. Only my mother and sister – and Aidan." Oswiu glanced at the bishop, talking to one of his monks, and shook his head. "No. It is impossible."

"Could he have told another, one of his monks perhaps, so that rumour of where you were going spread?"

"Trying to get anything out of Aidan these days is like trying to prise open a clam without boiling it first – more likely to notch your knife than open the shell. But I will speak to him."

Behind them a man coughed for attention and Oswiu turned to see the steward. "All is ready, lord," he said.

"Very well."

While the steward went to martial the servers, Oswiu turned back to the queen. "Take the cup around. As you do so, I will speak with Aidan."

The bishop, hearing the announcement of the feasting cup, had stopped his conversation with his monks – and with Romanus, the queen's priest, Oswiu noticed. The little Frank was not looking happy. Despite being surrounded by priests and monks who let their hair grow long down the back of their necks, Romanus had retained his distinctive tonsure. And there were rumours that there might come a season when Romanus and the queen celebrated Easter and the Lord's rising on a different day from the king and his priests. But until the matter arose, Oswiu was content to put it aside. He had once asked Aidan to explain to him how Easter might arrive one year when there was still snow on the ground and yet on another it would wait until the willows were in leaf and the oaks beginning to break bud. The explanation had taken from the sun's zenith to its setting and at its end he understood no more than he had at the start, although he could add to his ignorance a pain across his head that had begun behind his eyes and spread across his forehead to both ears. No. He was well content to leave such matters to the priests, so long as he and the queen both ended the fast and began the feast together.

"Aidan."

The bishop made the courtesy to the king. "Lord."

Oswiu looked at his old friend and saw how the lines of his smile were now ever present around his eyes and how his hair was streaked with white.

"While we wait for the queen to take the cup to my thegns, I would speak with you. It is long since we spoke, the two of us."

"I am always happy to speak with my king."

"Then why does it take the death of my mother to bring you to me? I can see the Holy Island from here, yet I have not seen you this last year, old friend."

"I know. But you are not always in Bamburgh, and when you have been I have not." Aidan shook his head. "I fear the lot of a bishop is to travel near as much as a king."

"If you did not go to Deira you could spend more time with your people here, in Bernicia."

Aidan pursed his lips. "I… you know it were best we not speak of this. Until they have a bishop of their own, I must needs see to their care, lest I go before God and he should ask me how so many of the sheep he gave to my charge I lost to the wolves of the enemy."

"If you were not my oldest friend…"

"But I am." Aidan smiled, and in that instant Oswiu saw again the shy, uncertain monk of Iona. "And you are mine. Now, what would you speak on? Other than the memories of days gone by, when we could each do as we would wish."

"Two matters. First, a question. Did you say aught, to anyone, of my journey into Mercia to bring back my brother?"

"No," said Aidan. "Of course not."

"You are sure? No word, not even to one of your monks?"

"I am sure. I am no man for war, but even I know that to speak of that was to put your life in even greater danger than it was already. I spoke of it to no one. Why do you ask?"

"Because someone did speak, and I do not know who."

"Could… could it have been your mother? I know she would do you no harm, but she was so certain that you were under Oswald's protection that mayhap she might have said something?"

Oswiu shrugged. "If it were her, we cannot ask."

"Not until we stand beside her again." Aidan smiled, but the smile turned into a cough – a deep, wracking fit that bent him over, so that the king had to give his hand for Aidan to hold on to.

"How long have you been ill?" Oswiu asked, when at last the coughing fit subsided.

"Oh, I am not ill. It is but a cough that comes and then goes. You said you have two matters to speak on? For I also would speak with you, now, before the feast begins." Both men glanced at the hall, seeing how the queen progressed around it, passing the cup to the king's great thegns and, in her passing, leaving calm and quiet. But there were still many men for her to greet, so there was yet time for talk.

"For my part," said Oswiu, "I would tell you of how I have done the work of a priest." He saw the look of surprise on Aidan's face and laughed at it. "Is it so strange?"

"It is, perhaps, not what I expected, although I know your belief is strong."

Oswiu's smile broadened. "Not just my belief; my wit too. You see him, over there?" The king gestured towards the high table and the men standing grouped at the end of it. "The one richly dressed, with fair hair and moustache but no beard, whom the others wait upon? He is Sigeberht, king of the East Saxons – and through my words, he wishes baptism." Oswiu's smile grew even broader at the mingled surprise and joy on Aidan's face. "Yes, my words – who would have thought it?"

"Ah, but with God all things are possible!" Aidan laughed too. "That is good news – the best news. How comes he here and what did you say to him?"

"Sigeberht came, as do all the kings of the small kingdoms that wait in nervous, waiting rings around Mercia, to seek alliance and pledge of help against Penda. And, for my part, I will pledge that help, for I seek to draw tight a ring of oaths around Penda: to hold the kings of the East Saxons and the East Angles, the West Saxons and the Middle Saxons, and the men of Kent in alliance against Penda, that he might not know where to strike, for fear that another will attack his kingdom when he is not there to guard it."

"Yes, yes," said Aidan. "That is what I hear from kings as they play their games. Instead, tell me of what truly matters – how you brought the king of the East Saxons to want the new life."

"Now, that is a different matter." Oswiu put his arm around his friend's shoulder and turned with him away from the noise of the hall. "You see, I was clever, very clever. When I agreed to our alliance, he wanted to make sacrifice in thanks to his god, for he had brought his god with him, from the land of the East Saxons. So I asked to see this god, and he showed me a log, cunningly worked, of Tiw. It was fine indeed, and must have taken the carver many months to cut, but this was where I was clever, Aidan. I asked him, 'Is this your god Tiw?' Sigeberht of the East Saxons looked at me as if I were mad. 'Yes, of course,' he said. 'But,' I said, 'what will happen to Tiw when you are dead and can no longer guard and ward him?' He was still looking at me as if I were mad. 'My son will honour him then, and his son after him.'

"'But what would happen,' I said, 'if there were no one to guard and honour Tiw? What would happen then? After all, he is made of wood.' Then I pointed at my hall. 'This is wood too, and no greater hall is there. But I have seen halls greater than this reduced to charcoal and cinders. Wood burns, my friend, and it rots. Gods are not made of wood.'

"Then the king of the East Saxons looked at me as if he feared my madness might spread and, under his cloak, I saw him make the sign against the evil eye. 'What are gods made of, then?' Sigeberht asked. 'In my kingdom, in the grove sacred to my ancestor, Woden, the god is a tree and there are other shrines, to Thunor, where the god is a great stone, raised high.'

"I shook my head then. 'Trees can be cut down; stone ground down. But this –' and I pointed at the carving of Tiw – 'this *is* your god. And he can be burned and turned to ash.'

"At that, I saw the king of the East Saxons look within, as a man before battle looks within to see if he has the courage to make his stand in the shieldwall. Then he told me he would think on this, and we would speak again."

"And?" asked Aidan, as agog as a child hearing a story. "Did you?"

"Yes, we did. The next day, the king of the East Saxons came to me and asked this question. 'If not of wood and stone, what then are gods made of?' I told him that God is not made by man but made man, and all the heavens and this middle-earth too. I told him that so great a god cannot be seen by human eye. For who can see all the sea and land and sky? And God made the sea and land and sky. I told him that God is a king greater than any other, a lawgiver and just judge, who gives to each according to his deeds, in this world and the next. This is how I answered the question of the king of the East Saxons, old friend. Tell me, did I answer well?"

"Better than I would have." Aidan glanced round at where the king of the East Saxons stood with his companions. "And you have brought him to the new life. Thus, you will have his thanks, in this world and the next." The bishop smiled. "You are indeed doing my work for me."

"Well, it were better I be allied to a king who lives and rules in hope than one whose only hope is to be taken by Woden's daughters." Oswiu leaned closer to his bishop. "I would tell you something, Aidan, for you will tell me if this is madness. I begin to hope that I may end my days not as my brother and uncle did, hewn upon the field of slaughter, but with my children around me. What say you? Is this some fever dream?"

"No, no." The bishop turned eyes, bright with hope, on the king. "It is a true dream – one sent by God I should think."

Oswiu nodded. "Do you think so? I thought myself mad, for what king dies in bed? But if you say…"

"I do. And I would say more, for there is something I wished to speak of with you before the feast begins, and it answers to this secret desire."

Oswiu looked back over the hall, and saw the queen was nearing the end of her duties. "Tell quick, for the feast begins soon."

"I ask you to put aside your warring with Oswine Godfriend." Aidan saw the immediate hardening of the face that had, before these words, been turned to him with friendship, and he fell upon his knees. "On my knees, I beg you to stop."

The thrum of conversation in the hall suddenly stopped. Eyes turned to where king stood aside with bishop, and the bishop was on his knees.

Oswiu felt all those eyes upon him.

"Get up," he hissed at Aidan. "Get up. Everyone is watching."

But Aidan did not rise. And, looking down, Oswiu saw that there were tears in the bishop's eyes.

"Please, I beseech you, stop fighting against a brother Christian."

"Get up." Oswiu risked a sidelong glance. Almost all movement had stopped as well. "Get up," he hissed. He looked again at the hall and saw Eanflæd, saw her fierce gaze as she sought to tell him something through sight alone. Then, slowly, the queen went down on her knees and made the Lord's sign over her body while her eyes held his and, suddenly, he understood.

The king knelt down beside the bishop. He bowed his head briefly, and when he looked up again, he saw that all in the hall were following his lead.

"Let us give thanks for the food and drink we are about to receive, and for the life of the best of queens, my mother, Acha, queen of

Bernicia, queen of Deira." But as Oswiu spoke of the best of queens, his gaze turned to his wife and Eanflæd understood well his thanks, for he saw the flush on her cheeks. "Bishop?"

Faced with such a request, Aidan had no choice but to offer prayers of thanks and praise. While Oswiu waited, on his knees, for him to finish, he slowly mastered his anger so that when, the prayers over, the steward summoned them all to feast, he stood up beside Aidan with no sign of the fury he had felt earlier.

And amid the bustle of men taking their places on bench and seat, Oswiu leaned to the bishop and whispered, "I will never call brother any man who allies with the man who killed my brother. Do not ask this of me again, old friend."

When Aidan made to answer, the king held a finger to his lips and, whispering even lower, said, "Besides, I hope that soon I may be able to call the king of Mercia Christian, and son."

Aidan looked, startled, at the king. "What do you mean? Penda?"

"Not Penda, but his son."

"Surely not."

But Oswiu looked along the high table to where his son Ahlfrith stood, ready to take his place beside his sister Ahlflæd.

"Watch them. I have tasked Ahlfrith with asking his sister if she be willing. It should be clear enough when he does."

It was.

The cry, when it came, soared over the hubbub of talk and laughter and song as far as one of the great, yellow beaked gulls soared over the stronghold of the Idings on its rock by the sea.

"No!"

Oswiu looked to Aidan. "She will agree…"

"No, no, no, no, no!"

"…in the end."

Chapter 4

The riders trotted south, their animals' hooves sounding loud on the stones of the road. The emperors of old had built the road, laying it straight across the country as if they sliced land with a knife, and now messengers from the throne required all the villages and hamlets that lay near the road to put aside three days a year to work on the king's road, maintaining and repairing it so that his messengers might travel quickly from one corner of his kingdom to another. As they rode south, the riders appreciated the more the value of this road, for this was a landlocked kingdom they passed through, unlike the sea-washed one they came from, and though its rivers were broad and, for the most part, navigable, yet the old roads brought all its distant parts together.

The road south from York had been well looked after and, when they reached the Foss Way and entered the kingdom of the Mercians, they found the highway broad and firm, with the bridges so obviously in good repair that they had not needed to send a rider ahead to test them. The same was true on this final stretch, along Watling Street, as they rode east into the heart of Mercia. From the many strips of ridged and furrowed soil that ran alongside the road – and the stands and copses of trees that interspersed the fields, with their edges marked by the straight, rising stems of coppiced stools of hazel and hornbeam – the riders could tell that this was rich land; sight of the men, women and children working the fields or shepherding animals made clear that it fed many people.

There were five riders. They rode with one hand upon the bridle, and the lead rider carried a banner that proclaimed them king's messengers. The people working the fields stopped their work to watch as the men rode by, moving fast, then spoke among themselves for a while, wondering whence these messengers came and whither they went, before an old head said to the others that this was all the business of kings and no concern of theirs, and told them off for wasting the good daylight in idle talk. Such rebukes drew, as always, ribald replies and much pointing out that if old grey hair was so keen to put hand to plough, he was welcome to do so himself and give those who had been sweating through the day's heat a rest. But after talk and laughter, once the riders had disappeared down the road, the farmers turned back to their work and the serious matters of the day: the prospects for rain and the state of the crops.

The riders, for their part, paid little mind to the watching farmers; they were as much a part of the landscape as barley and grass, and only of interest when the time came to collect food renders. Then they would endure the usual round of excuses about there having been too much rain that season, or too little; the frost had come late and blighted the crop or it had not come at all and the crop never hardened. Marauding goats, truffling pigs, floods, droughts, giants and dwarves – they'd heard all the excuses. In the middle of the small group of riders, Hunwald, thegn and warmaster to Oswine Godfriend, reflected that these farmers of Mercia were no different from those in Deira. They were, no doubt, just as reluctant to give up the crop of their labours as the men, women and children who farmed the land around his own hall.

That Hunwald gave thought to the farmers working the land showed how uneventful his mission had been so far. But then the lead rider, the one carrying the streaming banner of Deira with its charging boar, pulled up, his horse tossing its head and snorting at the abruptness of the halt after so smooth a ride.

"Riders," he said, circling the horse and pointing ahead.

Hunwald shaded his eyes – the sun was high and bright – and squinted, to better see into the distance.

There. Emerging from the haze that shimmered over the further reaches of the road. Hunwald tried to count off the spear tips, but with the riders approaching in straight column, it was impossible to make an accurate count. All he could be sure of was that there were many more spears approaching than he had with him. But then, he was in Mercia as a messenger, not a raider, and as such should be given safe passage to the king. The only fear was that the men approaching might be a thief band, bent on quick plunder and swift retreat into the marsh meres to the east. However, lordless men rarely dared enter a land ruled by a strong king – and there was no doubting that Penda was a strong king. Besides, the riders approached in good order with none of the ill discipline that characterized bandits.

"We will wait beside the road," said Hunwald to his men, "that they may pass if their business lies elsewhere, or stop if their business is with us."

They stopped.

The riders – there were twenty – formed in line along the road, their horses shifting and stamping, striking sparks on stone. The leader turned his horse and rode towards Hunwald and his companions. He held his spear high but, Hunwald noted, he held it loose: a grip that could, in an instant, lower the spear for the charge or pull back the double-tipped weapon for throwing. Hunwald glanced at his own spear with its single leaf-shaped blade. When he got back he would have the armourers make some spears like the man in front of him carried, that he might try them out himself.

"Who are you, strangers, who ride through Mercia without the king's leave?"

The man spoke roughly, but Hunwald did not answer in kind.

"If we had known we needed the king's leave to ride the king's road, then we would have sought it, for I mean no offence against the king."

"In Mercia, you need the king's leave to do anything." The man danced his horse sideways, the animal showing his mastery of the skill. "Even to fart."

Some among the men lined up along the road laughed at their leader's jest and one let loose an accompanying blast.

"So don't expect to do anything here without the king's leave." The rider dipped his spear, so its point was directed at Hunwald. "What is your name?"

"My name is Hunwald. I am a messenger, from King Oswine

Godfriend to King Penda. If you would not hinder the king's message, then let me pass."

"This Oswine: if he is such a friend to God, tell me why he has sired no sons yet, Hunwald." The rider pushed his horse closer, with the spear still held level, pointed at Hunwald.

"I am the king's messenger. I have told you my name. You have not told me your name, nor your business with me."

"Guess. Guess right, and I'll let you take your message to the king. Get it wrong, and I think we'll have us some sport. What do you say, men?" The rider half turned back to his men, raising their cheer. But in his turning, Hunwald saw the richness of his harness and the gold of the buckle that held his cloak; he noted the garnets worked into the hilt of the man's sword and the burnish of his helmet. He saw the bluster and bravado of a boy new come into manhood and unsure yet of his place among men. And he knew who the rider was.

"Peada. Son of Penda. Ætheling of Mercia."

The rider turned back and his face fell into the scowl of a disappointed child. "You guessed…"

"Even in Deira, we have heard many tales of the Red Hand."

"Do you know why they gave me that name?"

"The tale is that in a duel, when both you and your enemy's swords had broken, you ripped open his stomach with your hands and strangled him with his own entrails. That's the story – now that I may, I ask if it is true."

Peada glanced back to his line of men. "He asks: is it true?"

Their cheer told the answer.

"Then I would ask so strong a warrior to let me pass with my message for the king."

Peada Red Hand looked at Hunwald with eyes that, in the blood shotting them, told of a night spent in the cups. He had not let his hand drop: the spear still pointed, without tremor or lowering, at the messenger.

"My father has, at last, given me some of my right. Tell your king, when you go back to him, that I am the king of the Middle Angles. Tell your king to mind his thegns and his young men: my father did not give me leave to raid into Deira, but if I am attacked, that is a different matter. Better still," Peada Red Hand grinned, "don't tell your king." He pulled his horse's head round, back towards the road. "Come, men. We have a land to rule, beer to drink and women to find."

The Red Hand's riders cheered, while some among them made clear what they intended to do with the women they found. Peada looked back to Hunwald.

"When you see my father, tell him this: this land is mine now. Let him remember that. Let him remember that well."

*

"He says the Middle Angles are his now."

Hunwald stood before the cloaked figure of the king of Mercia, sat upon his judgement seat in the great hall at Tamworth. Although many torches burned in the hall, Hunwald could see little of the king's face, for his hood cast shadow upon his face. Men said that the king was one-eyed and far seeing, as like Woden as any mortal man might be. Indeed, some began to whisper that the king was the god himself, walking among men.

The hooded figure on the judgement seat merely nodded. Hunwald waited. He had given his message; he had passed on to the king his son's message.

"I will give my answer on the morrow."

Penda, king of Mercia, watched as the messenger returned to his men, sat about a table further down the hall.

So. Oswine asked for aid from his tribute lord against "the cruel and rapacious king that most sorely afflicts him, raiding his thegns and waging unjust war against him".

Oswiu.

At the name, Penda's hand went, without thinking, to his face, to where his eye had been before the raven plucked it out.

Penda had watched Oswiu's son grow into a man; watched him grow alongside his own eldest son and outmatch him in every way, save the simple strength of arm and thew.

If Woden had blessed him through the taking of the eye, then why had he not spread that blessing to his seed too? Instead, he had a brute and a fool as his eldest son, while Oswiu's boy had the wit of his father. At least Wulfhere, his second son, showed sign of wit – but he was yet a boy and there were many dangers left still in his growing.

"Wihtrun?" He looked around for his priest and saw him, sat on his own, as was his wont, by the fire. "Wihtrun."

The priest, hearing his king's call, looked up from the fire lines. He had been watching the flames move over log and ember with squinted eyes, searching for some trace of the patterns of wyrd. But he had seen nothing.

"Lord."

Penda beckoned him over. "What god did I offend in siring Peada? Was it Frige? For I know that if you mate a dog with wit to a bitch with wit, then the pups will have wit too. Yet I have wit, and so also Cynewisse, yet the first fruit of our mating is… is Peada. What god did I offend, Wihtrun, in my rutting, to produce such a whelp?"

"Wulfhere, from what I have seen and from what I hear tell, has his father's wit."

"Wulfhere is a child. Peada is grown, and lest he turn on me I have given him somewhere to rule. I thought the land of the Middle Angles would provide little chance for even one as he to cause trouble, yet now I receive message from Oswine, calling on me for aid and arms against Bernicia. So I have, through an excess of wit and cunning, put my fool of a son right in the path of war. He will be pleased." Penda slowly stood up. "Read the runes for me, Wihtrun. What say wyrd and the fate weavers? Should I go to war now, at last, with Oswiu? I have waited long."

The king watched his priest withdraw towards the fire. Men, seeing him come, pulled away, and those that did not see were nudged back when others saw Wihtrun squat by the flames and begin to run his hand over them, the yellow tongues running over his fingers. From deep in his throat, Wihtrun set a hum, low and continuous, so that it seemed he never drew breath but exhaled one continuous stream of sound.

Penda looked around his hall. The messengers from Deira sat in a quiet, wondering group, eyes flicking to the richness of the hangings and the tattered banners that told tale of battles won and kings brought down. His own men were largely away now, sent out from the king's great hall at Tamworth to gather and bring the food renders and to give justice, in the king's name, to the countless petty disputes that divided farmers and neighbours.

"Cynewisse." He called for his wife and, as always, she heard. Whatever she might be doing, Cynewisse always had one ear tuned to her husband, ready to answer his call should it come. She came now, and stood before him.

Penda held out his hand to her. "Come," he said. And taking her hand he led her to the room that, alone in the great hall, he had to himself and whomever he wished to share it with.

Penda sat upon the bed and lowered the hood from his head.

Cynewisse smiled slowly and began to untie her belt.

Penda felt his loins tighten. But that was not why he had called his wife aside. "No," he said. He patted the bed. "Sit down. I would have your counsel first, where none other might hear us."

"Lord?"

"What think you of our son?"

The queen made no answer for a while. Then she shrugged. "If I were a man, I should say I would want Peada beside me in the shieldwall but never over me, upon the throne."

"Will he stand aside for Wulfhere?"

"No. He is proud, and though he will not say, he knows he has not the wit of many others. This fires the anger that is within him. He will stand aside for no man."

"That is what I thought." Penda glanced at his wife. "Did you do aught to offend Frige when you brought him to birth? You made the sacrifices?"

"I did everything, lord." Cynewisse smoothed her hands down over the lap of her dress. "He was my first. Would I do other?"

"No, I did not think so. But I do not understand how you and I may have produced a son such as he. Do you?"

"He-he is your son, lord. There is no other."

"I can see he is my son, in his flesh. But I do not see how he is my son in his wit."

"Mayhap, now you have given him the Middle Angles to rule, he will learn. It... were hard for him to have such a father."

Penda looked with some surprise at his wife. "How so?"

"He wished, always, to be as you – and yet there was no matching you."

"How could there be, when he was a child and I a man?"

"A man might see that – but a child?"

Penda nodded slowly. "Yes. I see."

"But it is as well you have sent him away. Peada seldom thinks on that which is not set before him and, away from here, he will not have his brother before him."

"You saw that too?" Penda asked.

"Yes." Cynewisse sat with her hands upon her lap and her head bowed. "I was beginning to fear for Wulfhere." She looked to her husband. "But with Peada and his men gone, he will be safe."

Penda smiled, but it was a bleak smile. "As safe as man or boy may be in this middle-earth."

"Do not say that, lord." Cynewisse looked down at her hands again. "I have lost too many."

"I as well." Penda put his hand on hers and the queen looked to her husband with gratitude. Then Penda stood up and began to unloose his belt. "Come, I will give you another."

The queen began to smile.

*

He was a bird, a great black slaughter bird, flying over the earth. Beneath him, the ground ran wet with months of rain so that rivers flowed over their banks, and streams became rivers. Through the wind hiss, he heard the cries and clashes, the screams and shatter of battle. Without thought, he turned his wings and, riding the moving air, he slid down towards the battle. Others of his kind had heard it too and were there already, circling in great gyres, waiting for the roars and shouts to give way to the sobs and moans and long, sighing silence of the dead.

He joined them, circling, seeing the armies beneath, but already the dead more than outnumbered the living, and as he watched, the last few fell, and those that brought them down were themselves, in their triumph, swept away as the bank collapsed beneath them and the river pulled them into its silence.

The victors floated downstream. The vanquished, just as dead, lay broken and pierced upon the ground, mixing the mud into a dull red paste.

The slaughter birds began to circle down and he among them. The ravens, slow stepping, moved among the dead, their heavy, sharp beaks turning one way then another as they looked for the bright morsel, the first easy fruit of their battle spoils. The eyes. They always went for the eyes first.

Stepping between the corpses he saw a great pile of bodies, with banners trailing in the mud about them, as if here a group of men had fought and died, making their last defence against death. Trying to protect one among them.

There. Half buried in the heap of bodies. Marked by the richness of his armour and the fury of his foes. That was the one these others had been trying to save. The slaughter bird tilted its head and fixed the corpse with its bright, black eyes. He saw a single eye stare back at him. The bird saw the eye blink.

He was buried. He was buried with bodies, among bodies, so that he was not able to move arm, nor leg, nor even finger. All that he might move was his eye. His one, his single eye. And with that one eye he stared at the raven. He looked at the slaughter bird as it tilted its head, first one way then the other. He saw it dip its head towards him, and call its coughing, rasping call. He saw it step over the face of the man before it, its claws finding ready purchase in flesh slack in new come death.

He was in dream again, and knew it, and could not escape. The bird stepped closer.

He knew he must not move his eye. He must not look aside, nor blink, nor give any sign of life, for the slaughter bird liked best to pluck the last life from the dying. And he was not dying. Though he was trapped, pinned beneath the dead, he felt no wounds. Only the weight of the dead.

The slaughter bird stopped.

It ducked its head and called again, turning to look behind.

He looked to where the bird looked, and he saw a man, moving through the battlefield – the only man upon it. A man cloaked and hooded. His face was shadowed, but in his hand he carried a tall staff, and as the hooded man moved through the field of slaughter, he prodded the dead with his staff.

The raven called again and the hooded man turned towards it, making his way between the bodies, but now walking with urgency. The hooded man stopped in front of the mound of the dead, and the slaughter bird ducked its head and pointed with its beak. The man bent down and looked to where the bird pointed, to where you lay, trapped among the dead.

He pushed his staff in among the dead, until it pressed against your face, wood on cheek.

But you made no sound, nor did you move.

And the hooded man began to roll the dead off you, sending them rolling down the slope, one by one, so that you felt the weight on you gradually lessen. First, you could move a finger and then a hand, then one arm, then both arms, and finally a leg, as the bodies were rolled off you.

The weight gone, you felt the rain falling, wet upon your head, and you stared up at the man standing over you, with the raven, the slaughter bird, perched upon his shoulder.

You spoke then, asking his name. But the man shook his head against the name you gave him and, slowly, he pulled back his hood so that the blood light shone upon his face and you knew him, you knew him…

*

Penda woke, panting, sweating. "Oswald."

Cynewisse, alert as ever to her husband's needs, woke with him. "What is it?" she asked, putting her arms around Penda.

But the king shook her off.

"Find Wihtrun. Bring him to me."

For once, Cynewisse hesitated, wondering whether she should leave Penda when she could see the fear sweat breaking through his skin.

"Now," Penda snapped.

Wrapping a cloak around her, Cynewisse slipped from the king's chamber. There would be slaves waiting outside whom she could send to find the priest while she summoned her own women to dress her. While the king, in such mood, brooked no delay in his wishes being carried out, it was not meet that any more men than absolutely necessary should see the queen in such disarray.

While the queen went to do his will, Penda sat upon the edge of his bed. He was, he realized, shaking. He looked down, from the memory distance into which he was staring, to see his hands trembling.

Oswald.

"Why won't you stay dead?"

He had watched Oswald die. He had hung him before Woden's tree. Yet such was the fame of his powers to heal and protect that the very earth where he had fallen was being dug away, so that now there was a pit some five feet deep at Maserfield. Penda had forbidden the taking of relics from the battlefield, even posting a guard, but it made no difference. In the dark of night, when there was no moon, the locals would creep upon the battlefield, past the sleeping guards, and scoop more earth into bags and cups, to be mixed with water and drunk for the griping disorders, or mixed into a poultice for the sweats or boils and tumours.

"Lord."

Penda looked round and saw Wihtrun waiting at the door. He nodded leave to enter and the priest came in.

"I asked you to read the runes of war with Oswiu. What tale did they tell?"

The priest rubbed his hands together.

"The – the runes were not clear, lord. I could not tell what they said."

"Dreams tell sometimes of the working of wyrd, do they not? Hear mine then, and tell me what it means."

The king told the priest his dream. At the last, still staring into thought, Penda said, "I have dreamed a dream like this before, many times. But then, always, I was lying among the dead, trapped by their weight, as the slaughter bird picked his way over the bodies towards where I lay trying not to blink, lest the bird see my movement and pluck my eye out. But in dream I always blink, and the raven sees me and pulls my eye from my head. This time, though, there was another moving through the bodies, a figure cloaked and hooded. I thought it must surely be the Lord of the Slain come to claim me. Then, indeed, he pulled the bodies away that I might look up and see his face. But when I looked, I saw not the face of the Battle God, but the face of my enemy: the face of Oswald.

"What means this, priest? Tell me now, if you would be my priest longer."

"It means..." Wihtrun, who had before been hunched over, his hands twisting together, began to stand upright, stretching high, and his hands spread wide while a great understanding came over his face. "It means, lord, that the Lord of the Slain has taken the offering you made him, the offering of a slain king, and accepted it. For all know that Oswald followed the new god, leaving the ways of our fathers, and did only what the priests of the new god told him. Would Oswald come to you, in dream, in the guise of the Lord of the Slain? No. I tell you truly, the Wanderer wears many faces, those of enemies and friends, the better that enemies be deceived and defeated. Yes, I tell you truly, lord. Woden has shown you favour once more; he has come to you in dream and promised you victory in battle – for among all the dead, you lived. Is that not sign of victory?"

"A poor victory, if I alone live."

"The Father of Victory pays no mind to the fallen, save to send his daughters to gather them to his great hall. He turns his eye to the living, and each day sends his ravens to gather the tale of this middle-earth from men's minds and from their dreams. The One-Eyed has marked you as his own. Now, in taking the face of the champion of the new god, the All-Father appoints to you a new task: to win the people of this land back to the ways of their fathers and to heap up the corpses of the followers of this new god as a great offering to the Lord of Battles."

Penda nodded slowly. "So, you say that is what the god asks of me. Tell the Lord of Battles this, priest: I will fight his wars on this middle-earth, but he must look to his own warriors to fight the war in heaven. Men follow kings who win. Gods do the same. Let him give me victory in middle-earth and the Slaughter God will have victory in heaven. Tell him that, priest. Tell him that."

"He knows," said Wihtrun. "He knows."

"Very well." Penda stood up. A winter light filled his eye, although the season was summer, and a winter smile spread over his face. "War it is. But while I make ready, I would have you do something first, Wihtrun. Take message to the king of the Bernicians, telling him that unless he ceases forthwith all attacks, raids and forays against the thegns and halls of Deira, and pledges homage to me, then I will take up arms against him and lay waste his land and slaughter his people." Penda's smile broadened. "He will, of course, refuse. But in delivering the message, you will find where Oswiu is. Also, seek out the old priest. Speak to Coifi. See if he wishes to protect the ways of our fathers and renew the pathways to the gods. Should that wish be in his heart, then offer him what he would – gold or women or fame, whatever you priests wish for – that he might send word to us of Oswiu, and his whereabouts and his strength. Do you understand?"

"Yes, lord." The priest's face shone. "I thank you, for my heart has burned at our falling away from the paths of our fathers. Now, the old ways will return and we will be secure in this land, until the serpent rises and the wolf breaks its fetters."

"Go and make ready. I would have you leave before the sun reaches its height. But send to me the messenger from Deira. I will send my reply to his king."

As Wihtrun went to make ready and find Hunwald, Penda set to dressing, calling in his slaves to garb him.

Hunwald found the king dressed, a cloak edged with gold thread hanging from his shoulders, clasped in place by a brooch of such weight and richness that it must surely be enough to buy some of the poorer thrones.

Penda turned to him, and Hunwald made the courtesy.

"Lord, I have come at your summons."

"I have answer for your lord, Hunwald, thegn of Deira. But first I would speak with you." Penda looked to the chief of his slaves. The man nodded: they had searched Hunwald before bringing him through to the king's chamber. A king that would not face Penda in open battle might seek victory by other means.

Satisfied, Penda signalled his slaves to leave.

"You are Oswine's warmaster?" asked Penda.

"Yes, lord," said Hunwald.

"None knows a king better than his warmaster. So, Hunwald, tell me of Oswine, whom some name Godfriend. What manner of king is he? For he asks me to go to war on his behalf. Yet I have heard no tales of his wars, and little rumour of his battles. What say you of him?"

"He…" Hunwald paused. "King Oswine, all say, is a good man, a generous ring giver. He gives to the people too, for he seeks to follow the lead of his priest, Aidan, who gave the fine horse the king made over to him to a poor man asking alms. Therefore, the people of Deira love him dearly and proclaim their devotion to him, although in truth their love does not mean they give the renders due the king with any more eagerness than those given to a king less loved and more feared – indeed, I think, the opposite."

"So, men love him. But, you say, they do not fear him?"

"The king was fierce against the robbers and bandits who plagued the kingdom after…" Hunwald glanced at the watching king. "…after you killed Oswald."

"Any king will slay robbers and bandits. Do his neighbours fear him?"

Hunwald looked at Penda. "Do you?"

Penda shook his head. "He is sworn to me. But the other kings: has he ridden against them?"

"No. He is content to rid his kingdom of evil, but though I have often asked, he will not ride against other kings – not even Oswiu, though he makes war on us."

"Why will he not ride against Oswiu?"

"It is the doing of that priest. He tells Oswine he must not make war against another Christian king, and thus people name him Godfriend. But Oswiu does not listen to the priest, and makes war on the Godfriend, although they both follow the new god."

"And you? Do you follow the new god?"

"I? I follow the god of my king – as do we all in Deira."

"So, if the king were to return to the ways of his fathers, you would do so too?"

"Oswine will not return to the old ways."

"I did not ask of Oswine. I asked whether, if the king were to return to the old ways, you would do so."

Hunwald gave a tight, thin smile. "I would, of course, do as my king does."

"Is it true that the Godfriend has no children?"

"Yes, that is true."

"And this despite his taking wife?"

"Yes. The Godfriend married five years past, but the queen has not even quickened in that time."

"If this is how his god treats his friends, I would not wish to be his enemy."

"I have told him to put aside his wife and take another, but he will not." Hunwald shrugged. "The priest forbids it."

"Has he got any children on slaves?"

Hunwald shook his head, an incredulous expression upon his face. "He does not take slaves to bed."

"Really?" If any of his thegns or his wife had been in the chamber, they would have seen something they had not seen before: Penda, surprised.

"Yes, it is true. Even when I offered him the choicest girl, a little dark-eyed, dark-haired thing, he refused to take her. I said he must needs get a child on some woman, even if it be not the queen, that there be a son in some way throne-worthy. But he would not."

"He is not one of those men who prefers boys?"

"No, I think not. He desired the girl I brought for him, but then he forced his eyes away from her and would not look upon her again." Hunwald allowed some of his bafflement to appear on his face, testing it against Penda's reaction.

But the king gave no sign that he had seen. Instead, he remained quiet in thought for a while. Then he looked to Hunwald again.

"Without a son to the king, who else is throne-worthy in Deira?" Penda asked.

"Should the king die, then it would be for the witan to decide. Without the kingdom, there are many who might claim the throne. One, we know: Oswiu, king of Bernicia. But then there is the son of Oswald. Œthelwald was fostered by Talorcan, the king of the Picts, but I hear that he has lately returned to Bernicia and seeks men to follow him and gold to give them. And Oswiu has a son now, with the daughter of King Edwin. Ecgfrith is a child yet, but he will be most throne-worthy when he is older."

"I know of all these. I do not ask who might claim the throne from without Deira, but from within. Is there one in the kingdom whom the witan would hail king?"

"There... there is none by blood. Should the king die, then the witan must needs turn to someone they know and trust; someone they know to be fierce in war and generous in peace, loyal to friends and bringing death to foes."

"Is there such a man in Deira known to the witan?"

Hunwald paused. He looked at the king and saw his keen gaze. "That is not for me to say, lord."

"No. I suppose it is not." Penda nodded. "Well, no doubt we shall not have to ask the witan such a question, for I have an answer for your king, Oswine Godfriend. Say to him I have sent messenger to the king of Bernicia, telling him to cease all raids and forays against the thegns of Deira, and demanding he pledge himself to me. The king of Bernicia will refuse. Then I will wage war against him, and Oswine with me. Tell the Godfriend to raise his men. He will be going to war."

Hunwald made the courtesy. "I thank you, lord."

Penda gave the smallest of acknowledging nods. Hunwald withdrew, leaving the king alone in his chamber. The chief slave checked quickly that his master was all right, then waited outside.

The king stood staring into space. To wage war against Bernicia was no small matter. He would have to raise men, and call on allies and subject kings. But the main matter concerning him as he thought on war was his son.

"How am I going to keep Peada out of this?"

Chapter 5

"We must withdraw."

Æthelwin turned to his king. They were both hidden by the gorse thicket they had wormed into as the moon set, leaving their swords and anything that might strike spark or make noise behind, dug lightly into the soil under a tall finger of stone, taking only their seaxes, rolled in cloth. Oswiu gave a small nod to show he had heard. But when the warmaster began to worm backwards, Oswiu stopped him.

"I would see more," he whispered.

Penda's army was camped at the foot of the dark hill, on either side of the track. The emperors of old had built no roads here, north of the Wall, but there were many tracks that led from the Wall into the north before finally petering out in the mountains of the Picts. The army had crossed the rivers, the Tyne and the Wear, by the fords over their upper reaches and then ridden up to the Great Wall, with heralds going before, blowing horns and beating drums to announce their arrival. The news had been sent to Oswiu at Stirling: Penda of Mercia marched into Bernicia, reiving and burning as he came, and alongside him rode the Godfriend.

Hearing the tidings, Oswiu had come south with all haste, but already Penda and Oswine had reached the Simonside Hills. Along the way, they had set torches to the king's halls, even those far from their line of march, sending troops of men off to burn as the main army headed north.

But now, looking down on the encampment from their hiding place, Oswiu saw this host was composed of more than just the men of Mercia and Deira. Counting the fires spread out on either side of the north way, and the tents clustered around them, and the shadowed mass of horses, told a tale of numbers beyond anything Oswiu had seen before.

"How many think you?" he asked the warmaster.

But Æthelwin made no answer to this question. From the darkness within the gorse where they were hiding, he looked for sign of movement on the slope below them; he listened for it. Such a host had men and enough to post many sentries. If he were in command, he would set regular patrols around the encampment to flush out spies, as beaters flushed wild boar from marsh and copse. But he saw no movement upon the side of the hill; only the light of camp fires – more camp fires than he had ever seen before – and the shadows of men moving near their fires. Perhaps, having so great an army, led Penda and the Godfriend to believe none would attack. Indeed, they were right in their belief: so great a host was surely beyond attack. But even with so many, the host was not yet complete.

From the south came first the rumour of horses approaching, their hooves sounding dull on the hard-packed, dry summer earth, then the sight of the riders, spear tips glinting in the starlight and catching the yellow of the firelights and scattering them into the night.

"More," whispered Oswiu, and the whisper was as much one of awe as of caution. That a king might be able to gather so many men – he had never thought it possible. With the troop now arriving in the camp, there must be…

"More than five hundred." He glanced at his warmaster. "Have you ever seen such an army?"

"No." Æthelwin shook his head in a single, sharp motion. "Never so many as this."

"This is more than Mercia and Deira. Can you see which banners fly?"

"No. There is no wind. The banners hang limp."

"I must know who rides with Penda." Oswiu looked down from the shelter of the gorse and saw the commotion in the camp as the riders dismounted and sought food and drink, while their horses were unsaddled and led to the paddock the army had set up for the animals. "With so many arriving, they will not notice."

Æthelwin looked at the king, the surmise of what Oswiu intended dawning in his eyes.

"No, lord. It is foolishness – madness."

Oswiu looked to his warmaster and smiled. "More foolish than riding into Mercia? Madder than going in disguise to fetch my brother home?"

"Maybe not so mad as that." And, despite himself, Æthelwin felt a smile creep across his own face. He already knew the king would not be dissuaded.

"Positively sensible, I'd say." Oswiu began to worm his way forward, out from the shelter of the gorse. "Coming?" he asked, looking back.

The warmaster sighed, then followed.

With the king leading, they crawled downhill, sliding from shadow to shadow. They found the first sentry by all but falling onto him. The man sat with his back against a rock, head turned uphill but with his eyes closed. His breathing, regular and even, and then shifting into a snuffling snore, told the story: the sentry slept.

Æthelwin slid his seax from its sheath. He would make this a sleep from which the sentry never woke.

But Oswiu, seeing the seax in his warmaster's hand, shook his head, making sign with his hand so that Æthelwin could see: leave him.

The warmaster answered by gesture, asking why. But the king made the sign that said the answer would come later, before pointing Æthelwin on, down the hill and through this ring of sentries, to the camp. Easing the seax back into its sheath, the warmaster followed the king as he wormed his way down the hill to where the first of the camp fires burned.

Then the king stood up.

Æthelwin, seeing him, all but cried out, but the discipline of years stayed his tongue. Swallowing sound, Æthelwin crawled towards the king, while his back prickled, expecting any moment a spear to pin him to the ground. But the king saw Æthelwin first and reached down to him and hauled him to his feet.

"With so many men in camp, they will not know who we are," Oswiu whispered into the warmaster's ear. "We can learn much, and quickly, then leave our mark."

"Mark?" But Æthelwin had no chance to seek answer to his question, for already the king had gone ahead, moving between the tents, leaving a trailing hand to pull out the limp banners hanging from the poles impaled in the ground so that he might read them quickly.

With Æthelwin following, Oswiu made his way towards the centre of the camp. For the most part he kept to the shadows, but more than once he was hailed by men sitting around a fire. Then Oswiu answered railery with railery, joke with joke, and question with question, not pausing, that he might not be drawn further into the talk of men far from home and camped in the realm of their enemy.

Ahead, where the tents were pitched closest, a voice rose, pitched to anger, carrying easily over the quiet talk and occasional laugh that formed the night talk of the camp.

"When were you going to tell me?"

The question came to them, and Oswiu and Æthelwin made their way towards it through the tents, stepping from shadow to shadow.

They stopped and saw ahead, where three fires burned brightly in front of the largest tents in the camp, a travel-stained man standing with helmet in one hand and his other upon the pommel of his sword, facing Penda. Although the firelight shone upon the king of Mercia, yet his face remained in shadow beneath his hood.

"Peada."

The two watching men looked to each other. So this troop of horsemen, hard riding through the night, had been led by the king's son.

"I am the lord of the Middle Angles," said Peada. He held up his hand, the one that had rested upon his sword. "The Red Hand holds your land. Yet you ride through my land when you know I am far away, summoning all your vassals and thegns, even him…" And here, Peada pointed at the man who had emerged from a tent, amid the raised voices, to stand near at hand to the king of Mercia. "Him. Deira. But you send no word to me, oh no. Tell me, Father, when were you going to tell me? When you'd given my land to Wulfhere?"

"Wulfhere is a boy."

"I am not. Why did you not summon me? I can only think it was to keep from me the spoils you think to gain from this war."

"No. I intended for you a gift – a gift you greatly desire."

"What is there that you can give me, Father?"

"What your heart desires." Penda stared at his son. "Ahlflæd."

From where they watched they could see the Red Hand stiffen at those words, as a hunting dog stiffens when it first catches scent. But they too grew tense at Ahlflæd's name, straining their ears to hear every word spoken.

"Ahlflæd." Peada breathed the name out. He stared at the hooded man, clothed in shadow, standing before him. "I will take her for myself."

Penda stood, cloaked in silence, staring at his son. Then he nodded abruptly. "Very well," he said. "Ride with us. This time, I will go to war with my son."

But here Oswine stepped forward. "Lord, you said to me that it would be us alone that marched against Oswiu. Already, I see the banners of kings who have long been enemies of Bernicia flying among us – the king of Gwynedd, the banner of Elmet – and their men wreak great damage upon the people of this kingdom. Now you allow your son to ride with us – and all have heard tell of him."

Peada turned to the Godfriend, and even from afar it was possible to see his knuckles pale as his fingers tightened upon the pommel of his sword.

"What have you heard tell of me?" Peada asked of Oswine. "Think well on your answer before you make it, friend."

The Godfriend stood, hand also upon the pommel of his sword, but as yet his fingers rested lightly upon the weapon.

"That you are cruel and brutal."

Peada stood waiting, as if he expected more, but Oswine spoke no further, and at last Peada made answer.

"I am the Red Hand, red with the blood of my enemies. You think this an insult?"

"I think it the truth," said the Godfriend.

"Then I am content with what men say of me. You would have

Oswiu pay for the hurt he has caused you? The Red Hand will leave this land red."

"I would not have others pay for Oswiu's fault."

Before the Red Hand could answer, Penda spoke. "It is always others who pay for the fault of a king."

"But I ask that you – we – do not despoil this land, but march through it as quickly as we may and then, should Oswiu not come to battle, we return whence we came, with all knowing that Oswiu cannot protect them against the wrath of the High King."

Penda turned towards the Godfriend, and from the shadow beneath his hood his eye glittered in the firelight.

"You asked my aid as your tribute king, Oswine Godfriend. Know this, then: when I go to war, it is not by half-measures. We will burn as we march, turning this land to waste, and those we do not take as slaves we will lay out in the fields, that their blood may feed the harvest when a new king sits upon the throne of Bernicia – a king whom I have chosen."

Oswine made to answer, but Penda held up his hand. "I would speak with my son. Tomorrow, I will give your men the honour of the vanguard – and the riches that come from taking whatever they might find."

Oswiu had heard enough. He pointed where he would have the warmaster go: the paddock where the horses and oxen were picketed. But as the warmaster started towards the enclosure, his foot caught on a tent rope and he fell into the side of a tent. From within the tent, there came a muffled shout as the man who had been sleeping was woken by someone falling on him. From without, there came a shout.

"Hey, you. Who are you?"

Oswiu looked up to see the Red Hand staring at them. His eyes flicked beyond Peada. The king, Penda, was not looking in his direction, but had turned aside to speak with Oswine.

"Who are you?" Peada repeated, picking up a brand from the fire and holding it towards where Oswiu stood over the stricken warmaster.

"Too much…" Oswiu replied. He tried to pitch his voice so that it would carry to the Red Hand, but die away before it reached his father. "He's had too much." In the cover of the tent shadow, he kicked Æthelwin, and the warmaster, picking up the cue, responded with a deep, heartfelt groan. The sort of groan a man makes before his insides rush out.

"Get him away before he's sick," said Peada. "I've spent all day and most of the night riding – I don't want to sleep with the smell of vomit in my nostrils."

"Yes, lord," said Oswiu, keeping his voice low while bending down so that it seemed he was hauling Æthelwin to his feet. Still groaning, the warmaster stood swaying beside him, then when still Peada had not turned away, Æthelwin retched, hunching over as if he was about to throw up.

"Get him out of here," said Peada, turning away in disgust as the warmaster heaved once more. With one arm round Æthelwin's shoulder, Oswiu pushed the warmaster away from the kings towards the paddock. As they went, Æthelwin began to sober, first regaining the power of speech – "Whash… wash in that beer?" he said, still playing the part of the drunken soldier – then walking more steadily, so that by the time they came to the paddock, it seemed two sober men, restless in camp, walked abroad for conversation and to await the dawn.

Then: "Who are you?"

The questioner was the guard who manned the makeshift gate of the paddock. The gate itself was but a bundle of hazel and hornbeam wands, gathered together and laid in the X-shaped ends of the rough paddock. The shepherds who passed this way twice each year – in spring driving their flocks up into the hills for the summer pasture and in autumn bringing them back down – had made the folds that lined the track as it ran beneath the hills. Now, for a night, kings' horses used the fold as a paddock. But they would be gone on the morrow, leaving the fold for when the shepherds came down from the hills again.

"Who are you?" The sentry repeated the question, walking towards the two approaching men.

"Come on. You know me," said Oswiu, as they got nearer. "You don't have to ask."

"Is that you, Eanred?" asked the sentry, peering through the night at the two approaching men.

"No, not Eanred," said Oswiu, and as he spoke, he slid his seax from its sheath, "but the king of this land you ride through and despoil."

The sentry, making sense of words and sight, began to open his mouth to give alarm while his hand went to his sword hilt. But Æthelwin, leaping forward, put one hand over the sentry's mouth while the other held his head, and Oswiu, stepping into an embrace that smothered the man's arms, slid the point of the blade up under his ribs and into his heart.

They held the man as he shivered into death, holding his dying tight and quiet. Then, when he was still, they laid him down in a shadow pool, so that it would take daylight to reveal him.

"Only one sentry?" Æthelwin whispered.

"Reckon on others," said Oswiu. "We must be quick."

"Kill or scatter?" asked Æthelwin.

"Scatter," said Oswiu. He pointed. "And that one we take."

He was pointing to a white horse tethered slightly apart from the others, its coat so bright that even at night it gleamed in the starlight.

"Penda's?"

"Surely," said Oswiu.

"I will take the black." Æthelwin pointed to another horse, nearly as fine, tethered near the white. The other horses and the oxen, not being so valuable, had been left to wander freely within the paddock, cropping the starlit grass. They lifted the gate out of the way. Now, as the two men approached the tethered horses, the others looked up from their grazing, and the slow, quiet grinding of teeth on grass stopped.

"You have it?" Oswiu whispered, as they began unhitching the horses.

"Yes."

"I'll take these outside."

Æthelwin nodded and began to approach the huddling mass of horses, while the king walked the white horse and black horse out of the paddock.

Holding the animals, Oswiu waited, peering into the night for sign of his warmaster. There. He was among the horses now. They were shifting, becoming uneasy. Then Oswiu saw the warmaster unwrap the thin bundle he carried at his belt, peeling off the waxed leather and taking out the skin – the wolf skin.

The smell of wolf gradually spread among the horses, those nearest reacting first, their panic transmitting faster than the smell. Æthelwin threw his head back and howled. It was the same sound as echoed round the hills.

The horses stampeded. Even the oxen, finally realizing something was happening, began to move, crushing forwards in an overwhelming mass and breaking through the flimsy fence.

Æthelwin ran too, towards Oswiu, sat now upon the white horse and struggling to keep it and the black under control. Jumping up onto its back, Æthelwin urged the horse after Oswiu. The two men drove their horses up the hill as the camp exploded into activity behind them, men bursting from tents and chasing after the scattering horses and oxen, or belabouring the wagoners from their wagons to fetch their lumbering beasts.

There was only one challenge as they rode back uphill. The sentry they had left asleep upon the hillside called out to them, standing, with sword drawn, across the path.

But Oswiu pointed his seax towards the man.

"You live, who should be dead, for I held this knife to your throat while you slept. Stand aside and live, or I will kill you now."

And the sentry, seeing the two terrible riders, stepped aside and let them past, and lived.

From the hilltop, king and warmaster looked down upon the camp they had stirred. The first dawn light showed it seething now, as an anthill seethes when poked with a stick. Men on foot tried to grab panicky horses, while enraged oxen simply pushed aside whatever was in their way.

"That will slow them down," said Æthelwin.

"But it will not stop him," said Oswiu. He looked to his warmaster. "Can we meet him in battle?"

"We can always meet him in battle," said Æthelwin. "It is the riding away afterwards that I fear."

Oswiu nodded. "So think I. We will withdraw into our stronghold. Let Penda come. He will beat against the rock at Bamburgh with no more success than the sea."

"This delay will give us longer to gather supplies."

"And there is something else." Oswiu turned to his warmaster. "He has given us the wedge by which we may split his kingdom."

"Lord?" asked Æthelwin.

"Ahlflæd."

Chapter 6

The messenger stood under the flag of truce. He had come up towards the gate of the stronghold in the night and taken his stand there while he waited for the stars to wheel around the heavens and the sun to rise and reveal him. He stood at the edge of bowshot, waiting, while the dew rose and wet his feet, and the sea whispered under its cover of mist.

The dawn revealed him.

"Wait," the sentries called to him, while they sent word up from the gate, and he waited, eyes searching the sand falls and the waving of the marram grass for the workings of wyrd. Wihtrun, priest and messenger, waited.

From where he stood, he could see little of Penda's army. Most of the men were camped to the landward side of Bamburgh, their tents dotting the broad pasture that surrounded the stronghold. There had been a village there before: houses, sheds and stores, sheltering in the lee of the great rock. But they were all gone. Torn down, the timber piled up in great stacks beneath the rock. And more wood was added to these stacks each day, as men returned with the spoils of their raiding – new slaves carrying the wood that had once made their homes and adding it to the stacks before the stronghold before being herded down to the beach and the waiting slavers.

The slaves had earned them much gold and silver, but there had been precious little else to show for the weeks they had spent beneath the rock. During the new moon, after two weeks, Penda had allowed a group of young men, eager for glory and bored with waiting, to try the climb. They were brave men. The only sound they made when they fell was the breaking of bone and flesh on rock.

A week later, they had tried to force the gate. But the path to it was so narrow that only two men might stand next to each other, while the defenders sent arrows and rocks and slingshot down upon them from the battlements. They barely even made it to the gate, and those that did were cut down before they could bring more than one or two axe blows upon it.

But during all that time, troops of men rode off into the surrounding countryside to return with lines of slaves carrying their demolished homes on their backs, to build higher the great wood stacks.

Now Wihtrun came, in the king's name, to speak with Oswiu.

"Closer."

The call came from the ramparts. Wihtrun looked up and saw there a man he recognized: the king's warmaster.

"Closer."

Wihtrun pulled the flag of truce from the sand and, shaking some life back into his feet, approached the gate.

"What have you to say?"

Wihtrun looked up. "What I have to say is for the king to hear."

The warmaster stared down at him in silence, then disappeared from sight. Wihtrun waited. Turning, he looked out to sea. The Farne Islands rose sheer from the sea, their white-streaked cliffs rising some fifty feet from the wave froth at their feet. The priest squinted. As befitted his calling, he was far sighted. There, on the nearest island, Inner Farne, was that a man? He slit his eyes so that he might see more sharply. There. That was no rock. That had to be a man.

Staring at the distant figure, Wihtrun became convinced that the man was looking at him too. He made the sign against the evil eye, for the eyes that he felt looking at him were not earthly eyes. Under his breath, Wihtrun began to mutter a charm against the working of magic.

Behind him, the gate creaked and he turned round to see it open, sufficient for a man to enter, and an arm beckoning him to come. With a single glance – the man upon the island was still staring at him, he was sure of that – Wihtrun went in and the gate closed.

Æthelwin, the warmaster, stood in front of him, with two other men at his side, swords sheathed but ready at hand.

"If you would speak with the king, then I must search you."

In answer, Wihtrun held his arms out wide. The two men each took an arm, pinning the limbs tight, while Æthelwin searched the priest.

"Who lives on the island?" Wihtrun asked as he was being searched.

"Only birds," said Æthelwin. He stepped back, satisfied the man was not carrying any weapon. "Why do you ask?"

"No reason," said Wihtrun. "Save I thought I saw, while I waited, a man upon the nearest island."

"Inner Farne. No, no one lives there. But I hear that sometimes one of the monks from the Holy Island goes there to fight devils and see God."

"There is one there now," said Wihtrun.

"Well, we will leave him to his fighting; you shall see the king, to speak of yours. But first…" Æthelwin gestured to one of the men, who lifted a long strip of cloth. "Do not think you will take word of what you see back to Penda."

Wihtrun would have protested, but already the cloth was being wrapped around his head, and the words were sealed in his mouth.

Led by the hand, he was taken upwards into the stronghold. Deprived of sight, he listened, and smelled, and felt. The sounds of metal striking metal, the smell of bread, the swirl of wind, caught behind walls. He was being led across the great open space atop the rock, surrounded by the high walls that edged the stronghold. Then he felt the outrush of familiar smells – tallow and beer and smoke and fat and sweat – that he had smelled in every hall he had entered through the years of his life. The sounds too were familiar: conversation, dying to silence as those speaking saw who entered, the swish of feet on rushes, the crack of the logs on a fire.

He was led on through the hall, his passing marked by jibes and muttered insults and promises of long and painful deaths.

The hand that had been leading him stopped him.

"You would speak with the king. Speak." It was the warmaster's voice.

Wihtrun turned his head towards the sound. "I would see the king, to know I speak with him."

"He is before you. Tell your message."

"Unless I see him, I will not know my message has been delivered. I would needs tell my king so."

"Let him see me, Æthelwin."

The warmaster unwound the cloth.

The priest blinked his eyes open. The king sat before him. Wihtrun remembered him. He remembered him well. He glanced around. He had been brought into the king's chamber. The king himself sat on the judgement seat. The seat, carved and engraved with flowing beasts and knots, was painted in rich reds and blues and golds. Standing beside the king was a woman – from her clothes and her bearing, the queen. Upon the king's other hand was his son Ahlfrith, whom Wihtrun knew well from his time of fostering at Penda's court, and his daughter Ahlflæd, whom the priest also knew from when she had visited her brother in Mercia. And, squatting on his heels in the corner of the room, rocking backwards and forwards, was the old priest, Coifi. The old priest's eyes were rolling upwards, but Wihtrun saw the sharp, sudden glance they paid him. The priest remembered…

This was not the first time Wihtrun had been sent as messenger to the king of Bernicia. He had gone earlier in the year, with Penda's demands that Oswiu cease his attacks on Deira and give tribute to the High King. Both of these demands Oswiu had refused, as they had known and expected he would. But while Wihtrun waited for the reply to come from the king, he had sought the old priest, finding him walking alone by stream and under wood.

Wihtrun had made the courtesy to the old man and Coifi had stared at him. For once, his eyes did not flick to the scatter of light on the stream or the twitch of water across rock, but remained upon the man, clad in wolf cloak, who stood before him.

"Is it so long that anyone made the courtesy to you that you should stare at me?" Wihtrun asked.

Still Coifi made no answer, but rather drew his raven-feather cloak tight around his thin shoulders, although the wind was mild and the day warm.

"In Mercia, where the king still follows the gods of our fathers, I, priest of Woden, am given the respect and honour due to a priest."

"Honour?" Coifi's eyes darted away, then came back to the man standing in front of him. "What is honour?"

"Honour is a place at the king's right hand; it is the casting of runes before he sets forth for war; it is the gifts of war, given to the gods. Honour is to serve the gods, the gods of our fathers. Honour is to hold to the old ways when others abandon them. This is honour."

Coifi turned, his eyes following the movement of a leaf upon the stream. "I like to watch the water in Clashope Burn."

"I prefer to watch the smoke of the offerings I make to the gods."

The old priest crouched down by the stream. His finger moved over the water, so near the surface it seemed it must surely touch it, yet never breaking the liquid's thin skin.

"When I was a priest, I sent many, many offerings to the gods."

Wihtrun crouched down next to the old priest.

"Woden has blessed the High King; he has marked him, he has visited him in dreams. He calls him to bring our people back to the ways of our fathers; the All-Father calls us back to him. Coifi, Woden calls you back to him. Will you not answer?"

The finger that had hovered above the water slipped into the stream. The water divided around it, then flowed together again.

"Wyrd flows," said Coifi. "It flows around us and through us and over us." He lifted his finger from the stream and watched the drops of water fall back whence they came. "Would you have me make a dam?"

"I would have your help. I would have the old gods honoured, as they were in our fathers' day. I would have the ways we brought with us over the whale road continue. I would smell the smoke of sacrifice rise from the sacred groves. I would have all things renewed, Coifi."

At that last sentence, the old priest looked sharply at the man squatting beside him.

"As would I," Coifi said.

"Then remember, should I call on you again, that you too wish all renewed, and that the king, the High King, would have it so as well. Remember, and all the honour due to you will be restored, and much more besides." Wihtrun stood up.

Coifi looked up at him. "I – I will remember…"

The memory of their previous meeting played out in an instant in Wihtrun's mind. Coifi's sharp glance told him the old priest remembered too. But now he pulled his gaze back to the king.

Oswiu looked at him. "Give the message you were sent to give."

"The message is this: the High King, Penda, king of Mercia, lord of the Magonsæte and the Tomsæte, will grant you mercy and the continued rule of this kingdom, should you pay him homage as High King and render him such tribute as is fitting for so great a king."

Oswiu looked in silence at Wihtrun. The priest waited, feeling his skin begin to colour under the scrutiny. But still the king said nothing.

Finally, Oswiu spoke. "No more?"

Wihtrun shook his head, puzzled at what he heard. "Lord?"

"I said: is there no more to your message? You said no less when you came to me before, and now you come again with the same message and think me to make a different answer. Why? I am on this rock; you are below. You may not come against me here. So why should I give a different answer to before?"

Now it was the messenger's turn to stare at the king.

"Have you not seen what we have lain before your stronghold? The timbers and roofs and thatch of every house from many miles around. Whole woods we have made your people fell and carry here. There has scarce been a drop of rain this past month. Should the High King deign to set fire to this pyre, it will send up such a flame that you will be burned from your stronghold, flushed out like a boar from the marshes. But the High King is merciful. Render him the homage that is his due and he will forgive your offence and turn his face from your insult. For you have caused the High King much hurt over the years. But he will forgo the vengeance that is his right if you will but swear to him and render him some small tribute in token of your pledge."

Oswiu looked at the messenger. "What is this small tribute that the king of Mercia asks?"

"That you stop all attacks upon his friend Oswine, called the Godfriend, king of Deira, and on Oswine's thegns and realm and people."

"I have seen from my walls the banner of Deira flying among the ancient enemies of my people and I wonder: are not the men of Deira ashamed to camp alongside those who killed their king? But no matter. That is for Deira to decide. Is there any other tribute the king of Mercia asks of me?"

"As pledge and token of your good faith, and as promise of future peace between his kingdom and yours, he will marry his son Peada to your daughter Ahlflæd." As he gave this final condition, Wihtrun looked to the young woman standing beside the king, and he saw the look of mingled disgust and horror that passed over her face before she regained control.

"Anything else?" asked Oswiu.

"No," said Wihtrun. "That is all the High King asks of you."

"Very well." The king paused, as if absorbed in thought. While Oswiu's gaze turned inwards, Wihtrun glanced at Coifi. The old priest still rocked upon his heels, but at Wihtrun's glance their gazes met, and it seemed to Wihtrun that Coifi gave answer to his unspoken question. But with so many eyes upon him he could not long look at Coifi, and he turned his gaze back to the king.

"Give the king of Mercia this answer. He shall have nothing from me: not treasure, nor pledge, nor daughter. And tell him this also: if he lingers here, he will lose the other eye from his head. Now go."

Before Wihtrun could make any answer, the warmaster pulled the cloth up over his eyes and, more roughly, led him back the way he had come, sending him forth from the gate, still blindfolded, by means of a foot pushed into the small of his back that sent him tumbling down the path. If it were not for the sand that had blown up in dunes around the stronghold, he might well have cracked his skull in the fall. As it was, Wihtrun lay winded and unmoving for some minutes where finally he came to rest.

Sitting up, the priest opened his eyes. His vision, blurred at first, slowly cleared. He was looking out over the long line of waves to the islands crouched low over the sea. And there, on the nearest island, he saw him again. The distant figure, standing on the edge of the low cliff, silhouetted against the sky. Surely, from that distance, the watching man could not see him? But he was certain that the man was looking at him.

Making again the sign against the evil eye, Wihtrun scrambled to his feet.

Time to give the king his answer.

*

"Burn it."

Penda turned and looked at the great rock, with walls rising from the edge of its plateau, walls of stone but topped with wood. The rock, all but sheer, rose from the level coastal plain and his army swirled around its base as impotently as a wave. But Penda had, in the weeks he had been camped here, stood upon the beach and watched stones that had seemed immovable gradually washed away, as first the withdrawing waves sucked the sand from beneath them, then rocked them, forwards and backwards, until finally they were pulled free. Now he would do the same to this stronghold that Oswiu thought so impregnable.

Penda gave the signal. From the waiting lines of men, torchbearers ran forward, throwing their brands into the wax-soaked tinder stuffed into the bottom of the pyre. From the ramparts high above, arrows rained down to little effect. There were too many men, too few archers, to stop the fire taking hold. The defenders had had no more success when they had tried to stop Penda building the pyre in the first place: Penda had merely pushed the local people into the job of laying the timber in place while his own men remained safely out of bowshot.

Indeed, the best defence had come from the man who was

camped alongside him, and whose pleas had persuaded Penda to go to war: Oswine.

Two nights before, the Godfriend had come to him in his tent…

"Oswine." Penda sat up.

To the Godfriend's eyes it had seemed the Mercian was sleeping, but Penda merely lay in silence, searching the darkness above his head for answer to the problem of bringing Oswiu down from his stronghold and into battle. Away from the talk of men, in dark silence, Penda thought, and pondered, and did not sleep.

"High King." Oswine made the courtesy. The Godfriend stood at the entrance to the tent with his warmaster, Hunwald, beside him.

"I have never known a man come to seek me at such an hour, lest he wished to ask something of me, or there be bad news from some quarter. For what reason do you come to me, king of Deira?"

Oswine looked at the High King sitting upon the piled skins that made his bed. Penda had a way of pausing before he said "king", which made it clear he was king by Penda's sufferance.

"I have no war with the people of Bernicia. Yet you break their homes and spoil their crops, so that even when we leave, hunger will stalk this land. I would ask you to leave off the war you wage against the people here."

Penda shook his head. "They are like weeds, these peasants. Cut one down and three will sprout in his place. If they were mine, I would husband them. However, they are not mine, but his. Let him come down and protect them. But then, what need has Oswiu to protect them when you seek to do so on his behalf?"

"I don't seek to protect them, but to help us. To win this kingdom, it were better we made its people love us than hate us: to see that we shall protect them and ease their burdens, not use them as dogs and then throw them from the hall."

"I am not here to win this kingdom," said Penda. "I am here to destroy it."

At these words, Oswine stared at the High King as if seeing him for the first time. "I will have no part of this."

"You already have."

"A man may push another under the river, but let him up before he has drowned."

"Then that man is a fool. Are you a fool, Godfriend?"

Oswine continued to stare at the High King, a vein pulsing at his temple.

"A fool?" he said at last. "Only a fool would wait so long to ask what is done in his name. Yes, I am a fool, but one no longer." Oswine turned to go. "Come, Hunwald," he said. "I will be a fool no more." The Godfriend walked from the tent. But before his warmaster followed, Hunwald looked to Penda. And though he spoke no word, by his face he told the story: this was no doing of his. Then he followed his king.

The men of Deira had ridden from the camp the next day.

Now, as a hundred fires bloomed in the base of the great pyre, Penda looked to his son.

"With Deira gone, there will be the more for us."

Peada, the Red Hand, was looking at the conflagration taking hold in the base of the bone-dry pyre. Fire burned in his eyes too and he was breathing in short gasps; by the sound of him, his father might have expected him to be tupping some slave girl rather than watching a fire take hold. And such was the young man's fascination with the fire that Penda had to repeat the comment to get him to hear.

"What?" Peada Red Hand turned uncertain, wandering eyes to his father. But even as he spoke, he looked back to the flames.

"Is it not time you went?"

Peada looked round again, his eyes stupid with fire lust, and only slowly did they clear.

"Oh, yes," he said.

"Then you can claim the prize I promised you."

"Ahlflæd." The Red Hand's eyes glazed again, but with a different lust. Then, snapping back into life, he set off, summoning the men he'd picked to join him. Penda watched him go, heading round the rock to where the rest of his men were waiting.

"Wihtrun, go with him."

The priest, who had been standing, as was his wont, near the king, nodded and set off after Peada. He did not need to ask why Penda sent him after his son: he knew the High King expected him to observe and report.

With the fire rising, all the attention of the defenders would be on putting out fires in their defences. Already, tall streams of sparks and embers were flying upwards and, caught by the west wind they'd been waiting for, were being blown onto the wooden top level of the walls and over them, into the stronghold, there to set flame to the tinder-dry thatch and wattle-and-daub walls. When the defenders were completely taken up with fighting fires, then Peada would launch his attack on the gate, breaking it down with axes and storming into the stronghold, while sending some of the more agile men to scale the walls.

*

"What do the gods say?" The Red Hand turned to the priest standing beside him. "Will we have victory today?"

Wihtrun started at the question. He had been staring up at the stronghold. The path to the gate wound up the side of the rock, the gate itself being halfway up. But it was the halo of flames and smoke, rising above the rock, that had taken his eyes and his attention.

"What did you say?" the priest asked, dragging his sight away.

"Do the gods say we will have victory today?" Peada repeated.

"Yes," said Wihtrun. "Yes, of course."

The Red Hand looked at him, his already narrow eyes narrowing further. "I did not see you cast the runes."

"There are other ways of telling the will of the gods," said Wihtrun. "Ways of which you have no knowledge."

"You're sure?"

"Yes. I'm sure." Wihtrun put all the reassurance he could into his answer and, satisfied, the Red Hand grunted and turned back to staring at the fire glow. With Peada's gaze turned away, the priest relaxed. In truth, he had cast no runes for this day, nor sought guidance of the gods, for the High King had not asked for such tidings. Even if he had, Wihtrun knew well enough that when men waited to attack, the assurance of victory was what they needed to hear rather than doubts as to the meaning of thrown runes. Even if the runes had told, without doubt, of defeat, he would not have told Peada that – not now, when their course was set.

Looking up, he saw the yellow flare of new fires breaking out along the length of the ramparts above them. The defenders would be desperately trying to put out each fire before a new blaze had the chance to take hold, running from one to another with thick cloths to smother and slopping buckets of water to throw. There would barely be a man left on watch.

The Red Hand agreed. He gestured sharply to the men spread out around him to start moving. They rose from where they had been hiding in among the tussocks of marram grass and red fescue, and began scrambling upwards, converging on the gate.

But as the men climbed, Peada waited.

"Aren't we going with them?" Wihtrun asked.

The Red Hand turned a wolf smile on him. "Of course. But I want my sword to drink blood, not hammer on wood. Let them breach the gate, then I will be through it. Besides, I must needs see the others have received my command."

"What others?"

Peada pointed south with his gaze, down to the further end of the rock. "There," he said. "They have. They are climbing."

Turning, Wihtrun saw a small party of men scrambling up the side of the rock.

"If we cannot break the gate, at least we will hold their attention. Those are allies of my father, Britons from Gwynedd. They climb like goats. If we can but stop the defenders dropping rocks on them, they will get over the wall and in." The Red Hand looked back to the gate. Already the foremost men had got there and, under cover of shields held aloft, were beginning to rain axe blows against the wood. From the ramparts above, only a few arrows flew, striking hedgehog spikes into the shields but getting through to wound only one or two men.

"But I think we will break the gate," Peada said, and he turned his wolf grin again to the priest. "And then you will see why men call me Red Hand."

"I have heard tales…" said Wihtrun.

"Tales are not the same as seeing with your own eyes." Peada glanced back to the gate. Already, the wood was beginning to splinter and crack under the weight of the unceasing rhythm of axe blows, for his retainers had formed a roof over the axe men, their round shields overlapping like the feathers of a duck.

"Come, let us go up," said the Red Hand. "The door will break soon; I would not miss its opening." Without waiting, Peada started up the path towards the gate.

Wihtrun made to follow him, but as he put foot to path, he felt the weightless touch of sight. Someone was watching him. He stopped, with his foot barely touching the path, and turned, with all the care of a fox, to see whence the watching came. The priest scanned the narrow beach, but it was bare. The fishing boats that would have lain on it before, awaiting the tide to carry them out to the rich fishing waters around the Farne Islands, were all gone, their hulls piled up on the far side of Bamburgh rock and feeding the flames.

His gaze went out to sea, skimming over the waves advancing on the land, but only ducks, grey and black, broke up the green and grey, bobbing atop the waves. Following the lure of the horizon, Wihtrun's gaze was drawn outwards, over the sea, to the islands.

There. On the nearest island, on Inner Farne. There was a man there, standing upon the island's cliffs, birds wheeling around him in a great choir, while the man looked upon the land and the doings of men there.

Wihtrun, with trembling hands, made to sketch the sign against the evil eye, but before he could complete the sign, his hands fell to shaking uncontrollably such that they could make no sign of warding at all. But if hands might not protect against the magic worked from afar, words might suffice. The priest began to pronounce a charm, a powerful protection against the workings of witches and the glamours of the ælf folk.

But the words turned to ash in his mouth. Wihtrun felt his tongue become so dry that it could no longer speak. He tried to call a warning to Peada, the Red Hand, but no sound came from his mouth. Using all his strength, Wihtrun turned his head, slowly, slowly, away from the sea.

The priest began to scramble upwards. In his urgency, he grabbed handfuls of marram grass, unmindful of the cuts the sharp blades of the grass made on his fingers. As he went, he felt the gaze of the man upon the island beating upon his back, but he would not turn and look at him. Wihtrun feared that if he did, he would never look away again.

But he was nearly there. He could see Peada waiting with the best of his men, ready for the call that the gate was down and the stronghold was lying open. Scrambling up the last few feet, the priest saw that the defenders were few indeed, for barely more than two score arrows stuck into the raised shields of the warriors defending the axe men, and only a handful of men had fallen. Even the fallen, at least those who still lived, urged their comrades on, yelling for each splintering axe cut.

Making his way to Peada, Wihtrun laid hold of his shoulder. "Lord, there is magic being worked against us, great magic," he said.

Peada looked down at the hand upon his shoulder.

"You are the Red Hand now, Wihtrun," he said.

And it was true. The marram grass had cut the priest's hand open so that it made the blood mark upon Peada.

"Lord, you must hear: magic is raised against us. A great wizard stands upon the island and works a spell against us."

Peada turned his head towards the Farne Islands and, squinting for far vision, looked whither the priest had told him.

"I see only wave and rock," he said. "Tell me what you see, and where."

"Lord, I dare not. The wizard is beyond my strength. Should I turn my eyes upon him once more, I would not turn them back to you."

"What magic does he work?"

"Lord, I know not, but I am sure it is to your ruin, and the ruin of your father."

The Red Hand looked down at his bloodstained shoulder. "So far as I can see, the only ruin he has made is of your hands – we are all but through the door. Once in the stronghold, let him work what magic he will. The day is ours."

And as he spoke, a great splintering crash came from the gate.

"It's down! It's down!"

The cry went up from the men gathered round it, a great roar, and Peada turned a flashing, wolf grin on the priest standing beside him.

"Let the mage work his magic – my sword will cut through any glamour. Come, Wihtrun. See the work iron and steel make of magic." Peada ran, with his warriors around him, to the broken gate.

"The king's daughter is mine – the rest are yours for the taking!"

And still with his men around him, the Red Hand pushed through the ruined gate.

Bamburgh, the ancient seat of the Idings that had withstood every siege, had broken. The enemy was through the gate and, amid screams and cries, he was ascending to the main body of the fortress. Soon the fight would dissolve into desperate knots of scattered men, standing and falling in defence of women and children, while the fires that had stopped any help coming to the gate gained hold and raged unchecked.

Standing at the gate, Wihtrun still did not dare to look round at the island. But behind his back he made a fist against the mage who had so overmastered him, and yelled obscenities into the rising wind, that the westering winds that had carried the flames up and over the stronghold would carry them over the sea to the mage.

The wind...

The wind, which had blown steadily from the west for the past week, was now blowing upon his back. He could feel its cold touch upon his neck, sending fingers of dread down his spine. For without his noticing, it had changed direction. It was blowing from the east now, and it was strengthening.

Wihtrun peered in through the gate. The way led upwards, on a narrow path, up to the height where the stronghold stood, and men struggled and fought upon it, the last line of defenders stopping the onrush of Peada and his men into the open killing spaces of the inner ward. The way lay all but open. The magic would fail.

But still he could not turn and look out to sea, to the man standing on the island, raising the storm.

Chapter 7

Aidan watched the flames rising in a great halo over the rock at Bamburgh. Around him, the birds of sea and wave flocked in screeching alarm: fulmars, guillemots, shags and terns. Rising from the wave ridges, slick dark heads turned also to land: the seals were watching too.

The abbot of the Holy Island had been on Inner Farne since shortly after Pentecost and he had been there alone.

Solitude was not possible for abbot and bishop: always, there were the needs of his monks, the disputes of his people – seldom would two farmers, arguing over straying cattle or wandering sheep, settle for any judgement other than that of the abbot – and the calls of kings and thegns. Of them all, kings were the least able to wait, demanding his presence and his counsel and his prayers.

Aidan had given his counsel and his presence and his prayers, and given them willingly and without stinting, for years; first to Oswald, then to Oswiu; to the Godfriend, king of Deira; to the other kings new come to the new life. It seemed that though he was abbot of the Holy Island, he spent his whole life upon road or water. Amid such constant movement, there was barely time to give thought to God, to seek him in the quiet of prayer. And slowly, over the years, Aidan had felt a gap form, and then widen, so that where he had once but to still his mind and fix his gaze upon some sign of God for him to be aware of his presence, as subtle and all encompassing as the air of a still, quiet day, now, when he sought God, he found only absence. The same absence a man might find when, returning to his home from a day's labour in the fields, he enters upon the back of a greeting only to find no one there but the pot upon the fire and the tablets for weaving scattered on the floor by an upturned stool. Then fear would strike the man, clutching at throat and gut and bowel, and he would run out, looking and searching and calling, fearful lest raiders had come while he was in the fields and taken his family.

Such fear an abbot might not own. Yet Aidan felt it. No matter how he struggled and persuaded and cajoled, he could not bring peace and an end to the fighting between Bernicia and Deira. As bishop, their care lay on his soul. As God's presence slowly left him, he knew his failure the more bitterly.

But what man could not accomplish, God might.

Bishop Aidan, after Pentecost, had called together the monks of Lindisfarne. They met in the church, the only building on the island large enough to take all the members of the community, and there he had told them that he must seek solitude for a time, the better to know and understand God's will. Great had been the upset this had caused, and greater yet when Aidan proposed that he should go forth unknown and unmarked, to wander a while by God's grace and under his favour where he might lead. That they might be without their abbot and their bishop for a while, the monks were prepared to countenance. That he should go they knew not where, so that they would be unable to seek him out should need demand, this they were not able to accept.

So, Aidan made a promise. They were to sail him to one of the Farne Islands and leave him there. Without a boat, he might not leave. Without a boat, none could come to him. But should the necessity arise, the monks of the Holy Island would know where he was and be able to seek either guidance or send a boat to fetch him.

Leaving the community under the care of one of the brethren, a most able monk named Finan, the monks set sail with Aidan to the islands, bobbing across the sea in a leather-skinned curragh that brought to mind the boats of his youth that sailed between the islands of the west.

Aidan had given no thought as to which of the many islands of the Farnes should be his hermitage, so he let the monks taking him to his retreat make the way.

They landed him upon Inner Farne. Despite their pleas, he would let none of them land with him, for he would be alone there from the beginning, trusting to God for food and shelter and water. But he should have known his monks better. As they pulled away from the small cove where they had left him, Aidan climbed the short path up the cliff onto the main body of the island, only to see that his monks had already been there. They had made for him a small hut, roofed with turves, set in the shelter of one of the little dips on the rocky surface of the island. By the hut they had made a small paddock and in that paddock, bleating eagerly to be let out, were two goats: milk. Lain out by the hut were fish traps and fishing lines with bone hooks. They had built him an oven too, and stacked firewood beside it — wood that must have been brought from Lindisfarne, for there were no trees upon this island for the making of firewood.

Seeing the care they had for him, Aidan ran back to the cliff top, that he might call after his brethren — although whether he meant to offer them thanks or send imprecations after them for striving to make his short exile the more comfortable he did not know. But getting to the cliff, he could do neither, for the cough took him, wracking his body and leaving him, when finally it was spent, bent over and panting. To clear his throat and mouth, Aidan spat, and the froth that fell over the sea campion at his feet was pink.

That wracking cough had been troubling him more frequently in the months before he had come to this small island. But as Aidan settled into solitude, the attacks lessened. He might still find himself doubled over and spitting pink froth, but it happened now once or twice a week rather than every day.

The days themselves had taken their rhythm from his duties as a monk. He woke when it was yet dark — and the sun rose early at this time of year — and sang the office of the night, his lone voice weaving between the many voices of the sea. Then, as the sun rose, he walked the bounds of the island, pacing prayer into stone and grass. As the sun rose, he sang the office of the dawn, wherever he happened to be on the island, the Latin psalms rising with the new light. Then he took what breakfast he might, depending on whether the day was one of fast, a day in ordinary time, or a day of feast. The rest of the time he spent in prayer and work; prayer, that his soul might live; work, that his body might endure.

The birds of the island soon came to know him. When the great rafts of puffins came in June Aidan had to take care, lest he, all unaware, step into one of their burrows and break either ankle or egg. But the birds themselves welcomed his presence, and often he would return to his hut to find an offering of the little fish they ate laid at his door. When the skuas came, great savage-beaked birds circling in great gyres above the island while they waited for a fluffy-feathered chick to wander from the nest, Aidan patrolled the island, waving the birds off with arm and curse. Then, when the puffins were gone, he had sat by the sea and watched the grey heads of the seals pop from the water and look, with their big dark eyes, at the strange creature who now lived where they would, later in the year, drag themselves up to give birth to pups.

Through all this time, and despite the prayers and psalms he offered every day and most of the night, Aidan felt no sense of God's presence: there was only void.

At first, he sought to fill that void with prayer. But the void received every prayer and yet changed not: it was as if he sought to fill the space between the stars with his thoughts. Then, thinking there must needs be some hidden knot in his soul, some sin and stain of which he was unaware, Aidan set to disciplining his flesh. He stood to his shoulders in the sea, until all feeling was gone from his body and only the movement of his eyes told him he was still alive. He fasted, going without food for many days and drink until his tongue was so thick he could only croak the office of prayer.

But still there was no presence in the void that lay at the centre of his heart.

The monks from his community respected his solitude. Every week, Finan would send a boat from the Holy Island and it would stop, bobbing upon the waves, some fifty yards from the shore, while the monks aboard hailed their abbot and asked after his health. Reassured, they would return and report to their brethren that the abbot was well – and determined to abide a while longer on his island. Aidan asked them for no news of the world beyond the island

and they gave him none, although there were times when he sensed they would have spoken had he but asked.

Then came the day when a second sun rose behind the rock of the Idings.

From Inner Farne, the rock of the Idings rose where sea met land, with but a thin spit of beach before it when the tide fell. The rock was crowned with a wall, a stone rampart that ran around the top of the rock surmounted with wood. Only in one place did the wall break, where it ran steeply down the side of the rock to the gate halfway up. From the island, Aidan could trace the line of the wall around the rock, but it was too far for him to see any man, either upon the ramparts or upon the narrow beach. A little further north, the beach was wider, and merchants would sometimes pull their boats up onto the sand to sell their wares to eager buyers from the fortress. Watching from his island, Aidan could see the boats on the beach and the people milling about them, although from so far the people were tiny to his eyes.

But when the merchants should have come, no boat came.

And Aidan thought he saw companies of men circling the rock, as the pack circles the boar at bay.

Though he would not know the doings of the world, Aidan determined that when next Finan sent the boat to ask after his health, he would ask what had happened at Bamburgh.

But before the boat came, the second sun rose. It rose in yellow and orange, making a crown of fire over the rock. Standing, staring at the stronghold, Aidan thought in horror how great the fire must be to send flames so high.

This must be the hand of a king, raised against the Idings.

From where he watched, Aidan saw new flames rising from wooden wall and roof. The season had been dry: wood would burn with a single spark.

The wind carried the smoke to him across the sea. As yet it was just smoke; there was none of the sweet tang that told of burning human flesh.

Aidan raised his arms, and without taking his eyes from the rock, he began to pray. The words came to his mind without thought. He spoke them. He sang them. He shouted them into the wind.

And as he prayed, he became aware that there was another, standing beneath the rock of the Idings, who was aware he prayed and who strove against the answering of those prayers. But Aidan paid no mind to him, praying all the more, until beads of sweat sprang from his forehead and his raised arms trembled with the effort of holding them aloft.

Then the coughing came. From the depths of his lungs, from his guts and his heart, the coughs wracked through Aidan's body, doubling him over though he strove to hold his arms aloft, then pitching him to his knees as the daylight swam before his eyes and dissolved into grey.

Slowly, slowly it stopped, and Aidan came to himself, staring down at a patch of grass a hand from his face. He was on his knees, and the strength was gone from him, drained utterly, so that he thought he might never be able to rise.

His prayer had failed.

The absence he had felt had become a denial. God had left him – because of some great sin or fault on his part he did not doubt – and in leaving him, he had turned his ear from his prayer.

The stronghold would burn.

The king was going to die.

A final cough convulsed Aidan and, in its ending, he fetched up a thick and bloody paste. It spattered over the grass under his face. The wind, catching the leaves heavy with his lungs' heavings, bent them over, towards the distant rock.

Towards the rock?

Aidan sat back on his haunches. He did not have the strength to stand. Around him, flowing over the sea campion like the tide streaming in over sand, the wind blew; it blew from the east. Already, in the few moments he had taken to sit back, he could feel the wind strengthen, and now he felt it grow stronger, so that the hair that grew long down the back of his head whipped over his face. He saw the first riders of the wind race across the wave tops towards the shore, skimming the white froth from them and pushing the waves up the beach. He saw the wind spread the marram grass that grew up around the rock, making great channels through it. He saw the wind reach up and round, over the rock, and he saw it push against the yellow fingers of flame that were threatening to clasp the stronghold in their grip. He saw the wind push open the flame hand and uncurl its fingers; he saw the wind turn back the fire.

And Aidan, on his knees, with his lungs red raw and not strength enough to rise to his feet, sent up a prayer of praise and thanksgiving – for his prayer had been heard.

But as he sent up his prayer, he heard distant shouts from across the sea, of men fighting, hand to hand. The enemy was in the stronghold.

*

"Get Ecgfrith safe!"

Oswiu pulled his wife aside, under the shelter of the east wall. All along the west wall, fires rose: some the great tongues of flame that came from the pyre Penda had raised at the base of the rock, others from new fires that were starting to take hold along the length of the wall. Men ran from one to another, smothering sparks beneath cloaks and tunics, sometimes stamping on them or even falling upon them. But so many were the sparks and embers falling down in the castle that for every one that was extinguished another five fell. Already, the roof of the hall was smouldering in three different places – with Oswiu unable to spare anyone from the walls it would surely burn. Many of the storehouses and huts scattered through the inner ward atop the rock were already smouldering and one or two were in flames. Only the church remained untouched, the sparks falling from it as if they were rain falling off the back of a duck.

"Find somewhere safe – stay there with him."

But Eanflæd, holding the boy's hand tight in her own, looked around and saw nowhere safe.

"We will stay with you."

Oswiu made to tell her to go, but before he could, Ahlfrith ran to him across the courtyard. His sword was in his hand and the dark stain on it told that it had tasted blood.

"The gate is down!" he cried.

Oswiu grabbed his son's arm. "Who holds the path?"

"Æthelwin, but there are many. He cannot hold long."

"Then we shall hold it for him." Oswiu drew his sword from its sheath. The swirling pattern on its blade caught the firelight, and the garnets on its pommel glowed red. Such a sword knew well when it was going to drink, and drink its fill.

"To me! Idings, to me!"

With his son beside him, Oswiu ran across the courtyard to the corner that led down to the gate. Eanflæd, hearing well what Ahlfrith had said, held back. Fear griped her bowels, but she put it aside. Now, she must think, and clearly, that the child might live.

It was said that none had ever taken Bamburgh rock, and she prayed, swift and hard, that that might be so. But for now, she pulled Ecgfrith after her. She must know what was happening before she could decide what to do.

The boy pulled against her, struggling to free his hand and follow his father.

"Mummy, I want to fight," Ecgfrith cried, tears of frustration coursing down his cheeks. But she pulled him on, towards the steps up to the east wall.

"Come, we can see what's happening from up there."

Still protesting, but pleased that he might see the battle, Ecgfrith followed his mother up the steps onto the battlements. Here, on the east wall, there was no one, for the fire had not reached so far and all its sentries had been summoned, first to fight the fire and then to meet the invaders at the gate.

Eanflæd, still holding the boy's hand, led him along the walkway. To her right, the wooden palisade that was embedded in the stone wall below it rose to head height. Every ten feet, a break in the palisade allowed for a sentry to see – and fire – down the almost sheer face of rock below. But there was no danger on that seaward side, so Eanflæd hurried past the arrow ports with barely a glance; she had to get a sight of what was happening at the gate.

At the north-east corner of the fortress, the wall ran steeply downhill to the gate. Reaching the point where it plunged downwards, Eanflæd stopped. Despite herself, she gasped, her hand going to her mouth. For she could see, as it were from above, the desperate struggle in the narrow passage up to the main body of the castle. The men were joined in a shouting, struggling, squirming mass, squeezed in between the confining walls. In such a fight, skill or courage or strength counted less than fortune, for all skill was reduced to a fatal slip on a bloodstained cobble. In amidst the struggling men, she searched for sight of Oswiu.

"Where's Daddy?" Ecgfrith pulled her hand. "Where is he, Mummy?"

Eanflæd looked down at her son. In that instant, she saw for the first time the shadow face of her husband in his. But before she could answer, Ecgfrith pointed excitedly.

"I can see him! There he is, Mummy! There he is!"

She followed his finger and saw... Yes. Near the centre of the ragged line holding back Penda's men. Ecgfrith had recognized him from the crest that ridged his helmet. Surrounded by his closest followers, Oswiu stood at the centre of the line, holding his shield against the tide of men pushing up the hill while he hacked and thrust with his sword into whatever gap appeared. By their shields and helmets, Eanflæd could tell that Ahlfrith and Æthelwin stood near him, the son by his father's side, the warmaster holding the line fast against the wall, that none of the attackers should be able to outflank them.

But while Æthelwin held one wing, there was no one of his strength to hold the other. And as she watched, Eanflæd saw the right flank of the line, the side nearest to her, begin to crumble as the outward man stumbled, slipped and fell. It was a fall he tried desperately to scramble away from, but the Mercians were on him before he could get to his feet. Even from where they watched, Eanflæd heard the man's cry as sword and seax ripped apart his stomach.

The queen looked on in horror, for the man leading the Mercians was standing back from the line and, seeing the opening, made for it himself, with his sword companions around him. The banner flying over his men was not Penda's flag but a red hand, and she realized that these men were the hearth warriors of Penda's son, the Red Hand.

"Mummy!" Ecgfrith pulled his mother's hand. "We must go and help Daddy." The boy drew his wooden sword from its scabbard.

From where they stood, high above the fight, Eanflæd called down into the inner ward. There were men there, fighting fires, who had not yet realized what was happening near the gate. But with the great noise of the fire, and the wind, her voice did not carry down to them.

The wind.

Eanflæd looked to the east, and through the gaps between the palisades felt the wind, harsh and cold upon her face. The wind had changed direction. It was blowing from the east. She glanced quickly at the west wall and saw the fingers of fire falling away from the walls. Without the wind to drive it up and over the stronghold, the fire was falling back. She could call all the men from fighting fires to push back the invaders at the gate.

"Quick," she said to Ecgfrith. "Down to the courtyard. We must call the men to Daddy's help."

They turned back to the nearest steps.

"Where are you going?"

The swordsman, his blade pointing at them, smiled while behind him more men scrambled, breathless but whole, over the palisade.

Penda's allies, the Britons of Gwynedd, had made the climb. They were in the castle.

*

Ahlflæd felt the change in the wind too. She was in the courtyard, directing men and women to fresh fire falls, smothering those that fell by stamping them out or, if the flames had caught, falling on them, so that the fire was extinguished by her thick red cloak.

But the wind's change, swirling in cold eddies around the courtyard, meant that the streaming trails of sparks that had been spraying all over the tinder-dry buildings of the courtyard faltered and then stopped. Looking up, she saw the fire trails arch backwards, away from the castle. Thence she heard, faintly, cries of surprise and shock, as if fire rained down where it was not expected. But there were other cries, and closer, that she had not harkened to before. The princess turned her head, searching for their origin, and saw a blood-smeared, wild-eyed man stumbling up from the passage down to the gate, waving for aid.

Ahlflæd ran to him, but he fell. Reaching the warrior, she turned him over, but saw at once the cause for his falling – and that he would not rise again. Here, at the start of the defile down to the gate, the sounds came clearer to her: shouts, cries, metal striking metal.

The Mercians had broken through the gate. They were in the castle.

Ahlflæd grabbed the nearest man, an old servant still stamping out a sputtering fire.

"Get every man to the gate," she told him. "The enemy is in."

The old man turned horrified, smoke-teared eyes towards the passage, as if expecting to see a wave of men waving swords erupting from there at any moment.

"Go!" Ahlflæd screamed at him, pushing the old man towards where others still fought fires, then she herself turned and ran towards the passage.

"To me!" she screamed as loudly as she could. "To me, Idings! To the gate!"

Reaching the neck of the passage, Ahlflæd stopped and looked down the steep path. Where it widened, halfway down, men were struggling, and her quick, sharp eyes fast saw the crests of her father and her brother, standing shoulder to shoulder, holding the centre of the line. But she saw also the gap open on the right, as a man fell and the enemy began to push through, seeking to turn the flank of Oswiu's shieldwall. Should they do so, then it would not matter that the wind had turned and the flames were being pushed back. The king would fall and the kingdom with him.

That banner. There, flying behind the Mercians. The Red Hand. Peada's banner. He was here?

The princess looked back to the widening gap in the Idings' shieldwall. The Mercians, the men fighting under the Red Hand, were pushing back the edge of the line, using their shields as rams to force the gap wider. And in that gap appeared a man she knew all too well.

Peada. Ahlflæd knew him from his armour and his helmet, for he had proudly displayed them to her the last time she had gone to Mercia. She knew him from the way he stood, and moved, head tracking to and fro like a pig snuffling for husks. She knew him from the depth of her contempt.

And she knew what she had to do to stop him.

Ahlflæd glanced back across the courtyard. Men were starting towards her, but they would have to cross the wide expanse of the inner ward to get to her before they started down to the gate. There was no time to wait.

Gathering her skirts up round her knees, Ahlflæd ran up the stairs and onto the top of the wall. She was on the west side of the passage to the gate. Peada could see her easily on top of the walkway. She ran along it, jumping from step to step as the wall snaked downwards along the line of the cliff.

"Peada!"

She was screaming at the top of her voice and waving her arms, doing all that she might to attract the attention of the Red Hand.

And he heard her. As the hole in Oswiu's line widened, and Peada emerged with his hearth troops around him, he heard her. He turned and looked, and saw Ahlflæd standing on the edge of the walkway, shouting down to him. And he was not the only one who heard her. Even in the shieldwall, surrounded by the cries and shouts of his men, Oswiu heard his daughter's voice, and he pulled back a little, and Ahlfrith with him.

The struggle had lasted many minutes already. And as was the way with such fights, it had its rhythms: pauses, while both sides took breath; resurgences, when they pushed anew. With Oswiu pulling back from the line, the Mercians facing him took the chance to breathe too, to tighten their line, to rest for a moment before the renewed push and the sweat-stung staring through the small, shifting gaps between the shields for an opening: an unprotected face, an exposed knee, a foot searching too far forwards for grip.

"Peada!" Ahlflæd called the Red Hand's name again, but with the sudden slackening in the fight, it was not just Peada who looked to the princess standing upon the wall – all did.

"Peada, if you want me, stop."

And Ahlflæd stepped to the edge of the walkway. Here, the wall rose high above the passage it protected, rising some forty feet above the stone.

"Stop, or you will never have me, Peada." She put one foot out into space. "Never!"

"Wait!"

"Stop!"

The calls were in two voices: the voice of the Red Hand and the voice of her father. But she knew Oswiu would seek to stop her, and she paid him no heed. Instead, balancing before the fall, she looked to Peada and saw he held his hands up, as if he would catch her.

"Pull back, and you will have me, I swear. Stay, and watch me die."

Peada, his hands still raised, looked up at Ahlflæd. He saw her: the fierce, wild girl who had outraced her brother and outfought him, the young woman with golden hair who had turned her face from his every attempt to impress and woo her. He saw her and he wanted her. His father had promised Ahlflæd to him, but he suddenly realized that this girl was not Penda's to give. She was her own, and he wanted Ahlflæd to give herself to him. He wanted that more than glory and gold and the renown of men. He wanted her so he might live.

In that pause, as Peada stood caught between different lives, through the sudden silence that had fallen upon the battlefield there came the distant sound of cries, and screams, and hoarse, enraged shouting. The men standing with Peada, and the Red Hand himself, were tuned to those voices and accents: they were the sound of the men of their home. And they were calling out in panic and fear.

Something had happened to the main army – something terrible, for this was the sound of an army in rout.

The men behind Peada, those who had been eagerly crowding into the castle, hungry for gold and glory and the pick of the women, began to shift and look over their shoulders. Anxious voices asked downwards, to the men left to guard the shattered gate, what was happening, but they could give no news. Only that the stream of reinforcements coming to join the assault on the gate had suddenly ceased, leaving them alone in the castle, fearful of what had come to pass.

"Something's happened." Peada's warmaster spoke to him as the Red Hand remained caught in indecision. "Outside the castle." The warmaster looked round fearfully at the narrow passageway they had fought so hard to enter. "We could be trapped."

Peada stared up at Ahlflæd. She still stood, poised before the fall. The wind was blowing her hair, and he realized she must have lost her headscarf, for her hair blew freely in a way he had not seen since she was a girl. He would have answered her, but his throat was too thick with feeling to speak.

"Lord, we have the queen!"

The shout broke across them all. Heads snapped to the other wall, there to see Queen Eanflæd and Ecgfrith the young ætheling standing before the swords of a small group of men upon the walkway.

"No!"

In the space when others stopped, unsure what to do, Oswiu acted.

"Get your sister," he told Ahlfrith. He himself broke from the line and ran to the stairs.

The man holding Eanflæd saw the king climbing the stairs towards him. He saw the blood light on the man's blade and knew it for a sword that would cut through his shield of leather and lime as if it were not there.

"Lord?" he called, seeking guidance as to what to do.

But Peada was looking back to where Ahlflæd stood on the brink of the fall. She had seen the queen brought, struggling, along the walkway, and had thought to push Peada into withdrawal before the queen's captors could bring her to the struggle. Now they had, she had to push him harder.

"Peada, you will have me! Only let my family live."

But as she spoke, she leaned forward. Now, only the grasp she had on a post kept her from falling – let that go and she would fall.

"Swear it!" The call came up from below. From Peada. "Swear it!"

"I..." The words stuck in her throat, but she forced them out. "I swear it."

Peada raised his hand and grasped her pledge, then turned to his warmaster. "Let's get out of here while we can."

"What about them?" The warmaster pointed up at the men holding Queen Eanflæd captive. Men were starting to flood onto the passageway from the main body of the castle.

"They're Britons," said Peada. "Leave them."

"Fall back! Fall back!" The warmaster gave the order and started pulling the men back. The Red Hand took one final look at Ahlflæd. Her brother had hold of her now, and was pulling her back onto the walkway.

But he had her promise.

Peada started back down the hill to the broken gate.

Oswiu came up onto the walkway. If the men holding his wife and his son had had any sense, they would have fought him from the top of the stairs, but already they were beginning to back away. Frightened eyes looked past him, to where the Mercians were beginning to pull back.

But swords still pointed at Eanflæd and Ecgfrith, and a knife was still held to the queen's throat. And frightened men might do from fear what they would not from courage.

The king straightened from his crouched fighting stance. He sheathed his sword.

"Daddy, what are you doing? Kill them!" Ecgfrith struggled against the man holding him, trying to get free.

Oswiu held up his hands.

"I don't want to kill anyone." He looked into the frightened eyes of the man holding the queen. "Do you understand? I will not kill you. Only let her and the boy go."

"If – if we let them go, what's to stop you killing us?" The man's eyes were darting this way and that, searching for some escape.

"If you harm them, I swear you will be begging me for death long before you die." Oswiu pointed at the palisade. "But go the way you came, and you will live."

The man glanced back at his comrades huddled behind him, and spoke sharply in his tongue. Immediately, some of them swung over the palisades, grasping the ropes they had hung down the walls.

"You will all follow," said Oswiu. "But let them go."

Seeing the first disappear over the walls, the others could not wait for them to reach the bottom but began immediately to follow, until only the two were left who held queen and ætheling hostage.

The man holding Ecgfrith could not stop himself: he looked over the palisade to see if there was space on the rope for him to follow and, in looking, he loosened his hold on the boy. Ecgfrith at once slipped free and ran towards his father. The other man, the one holding Eanflæd, heard the curse at his shoulder and saw an arm reaching forward to grab the escaping boy. But Eanflæd, seeing her son escaping, pushed his pursuer.

The man was on the edge of the walkway. The push was enough to send his foot over the edge. Wailing – even his scream had a musical edge – he fell.

Oswiu gathered the boy in his arms, then swiftly pushed him to the rear. He held up his hands again, open, without weapons.

"Don't be like him," he said, as the man holding the queen backed against the palisade, his knife paling the skin of her throat where it pressed. Oswiu pointed. "The rope. It's there. Take it. Go."

The man looked around desperately. He was cut off on the other side too, for Æthelwin, with more men, had come on that side.

"Swear it," he said.

"I swear," said Oswiu.

The man pushed Eanflæd so that she stumbled forward, teetering upon the edge. Grabbing the rope, he swung over the wall and started climbing down. Oswiu leapt to Eanflæd, grasping her arm and hauling her back before she could fall off. The queen clutched hold of him, her arms tight.

"I thought I was going to fall," she said.

"So did I," said Oswiu.

"Lord?" Æthelwin stood by the wall. He held a knife to the rope. From the way it quivered, there were still men climbing down it.

"I swore," said Oswiu.

"I didn't," said Æthelwin.

Oswiu nodded.

The warmaster began to saw through the rope.

"No!" said Eanflæd. "You gave your word."

"He tried to push you to your death."

The warmaster paused, his knife held over the fraying rope.

"You mustn't," said Eanflæd.

But before Oswiu could render a decision, the final strands of rope broke.

The screams ended in the sound of flesh and bone striking rock. Then there came the moans.

"God decided for us," said Oswiu. He stepped back from the queen's arms. There was still much to do. He looked to Æthelwin. "Send someone to finish them off."

The warmaster issued swift orders, while Oswiu looked to his queen. "I must go to see what has happened."

Eanflæd gathered herself. "I would see also," she said. Her voice trembled but a little. She held her hand out and Ecgfrith took it, but only for a moment. He ran to the wall and started to jump, trying to see over.

"Did you kill him, Daddy? Did you, did you?"

Laughing, Æthelwin lifted the boy and held him so he could see.

"He's still moving," Ecgfrith complained.

"Not for long," said the warmaster.

"Come," said Oswiu. With Eanflæd following, the king made his way down the stairs and across the courtyard. Only a few isolated fires still smouldered, rendering a storehouse and a workshop to ashes, but no longer were streams of sparks and embers falling on the castle.

They climbed the stairs to the west wall. Many of the timbers along the wall were scorched and some bore the charcoal of proper burning, but none now were in flames. Nor did the flames rise up over the wall as they had before. Climbing up the stairs, they felt the wind blowing hard and steady past them: an east wind. Reaching the walkway at the top, the king and queen looked down to where Penda had made what he had intended to be the castle's pyre, and beyond, to his camp.

The camp was in chaos.

The change in wind direction had sent long trails of flames over the men gathered to watch the fire, scattering them. Then, leaping over the dry grass and setting fire sprites sprinting across the plain, the flames had reached out to Penda's camp. The Mercians had placed their tents and wagons far enough away from the rock that no ordinary fire could have reached them. But this was no ordinary fire, and the wind that blew it neither relented nor deviated, but pushed the flames onwards to the leather and waxed tents, and the wooden wagons.

Such materials were food to the fire. It fastened its fingers on the first tents and pulled them apart. The smell of burning wax and burnt leather filled the air. Seeing their camp and, more to the point, all the plunder and treasure they had won through the season of war under threat, the Mercians had abandoned the siege and streamed back to their tents and wagons, pulling clear what they could and leaving the rest to burn.

From the wall, Oswiu and Eanflæd looked down at the chaos and confusion as men strove desperately to drive panicking horses and oxen to safety while carrying their own goods out of the fire's way.

Oswiu pointed to where a man sat astride a horse, some way apart from the destruction. Beside him, another horseman flew the wolf banner of the Iclingas.

"Penda."

Although it was too far for man to hear, even if the day had been as still as a moonless night, yet the horseman looked up at the castle's walls when Oswiu pointed to him. He looked up a long time, before drawing his hood over his head, turning his horse and riding away, the banner bearer following.

The siege of Bamburgh was broken.

Oswiu looked to his wife. "We live, who should be dead – or taken."

"Through God's grace, for he sent this wind to blow the fire back in Penda's face, and by the courage of your daughter." Eanflæd looked into the distance, after the withdrawing wolf banner. "I think he will return."

"Yes," said Oswiu. "Yes, he will." The king stared after the receding banner. While he looked, Æthelwin joined them upon the wall.

"Where is Ecgfrith?" the queen asked him.

"He is safe," said Æthelwin. "He wanted to go and help finish off the man who held you hostage."

"You didn't let him go, did you?"

"No. There will be stragglers outside the stronghold, and desperate men may attempt desperate acts. But I told him he could watch from the wall. I left three men to guard him." The warmaster smiled grimly. "He will make a fierce king."

"I would not have my son rejoice in the death of another."

"Even one who would have killed his mother?" asked Æthelwin.

"Even so. Send for him."

"Eanflæd." Oswiu turned from watching after the departing siege army. "To be a king is hard. Time he started learning the lessons of kingship."

"Are you telling me one of the lessons of kingship is watching men die?"

Oswiu looked at his queen. "Sometimes," he said.

Eanflæd looked away. "Mayhap it were better if he does not become king," she said.

"Mayhap," said Oswiu. "But he will never have the chance if such a day as this happens again." He turned to his warmaster. "I take it we do not have the strength to stand in open battle against Penda?"

Æthelwin nodded. He pointed to the withdrawing army. "He has three men, at least, for every one of ours."

"Then we must find another way to stop him attacking us." Oswiu looked into the courtyard. Some people were beginning to clear up, while others sat in exhausted silence, faces turned in relief to the sky. From the church, which alone had escaped the fire, chants of thanksgiving went up. And over by the entrance to the passageway down to the gate, the king saw his son and daughter. "They saved us, Ahlfrith and Ahlflæd, but particularly Ahlflæd. And now I must repay her by marrying her to Peada."

"You can't," broke in the queen. "You know she despises him."

"He is Penda's son. Marrying Ahlflæd to him will detach him from his father." The queen made to interrupt, but Oswiu held up his hand. "Besides, I will insist that he forsake the old gods and become a Christian before he marries Ahlflæd. That way, Aidan can teach him how to behave."

Eanflæd looked to the distant figures of Oswiu's children. "She will not be happy."

"She swore it. Before many witnesses."

"And she saved us by doing so."

"I know." Oswiu's face was suddenly stricken. "I know. But I can see no other way."

The king fell silent.

"Lord," said Æthelwin. "You said there was more that we must do."

"Yes." Oswiu shook his head. "We must make it harder for Penda to reach us." He looked to warmaster and queen. "We must put another king on the throne in Deira. One who will not allow Penda to ride across his land or – if he is not strong enough to face him in battle – will harass him as he goes, as the Brigantes did to Cadwallon's army, when first we took the throne."

"But Oswine withdrew from the field," said Eanflæd.

Oswiu turned on her. "That does not matter. He led Penda to

us, he joined in the reiving of our lands and people. Enough. I have waited too long for the witan of Deira to see sense. Now I will make a new king in the land of waters. Let Oswine fight. We saw his army. He has not the men to stand against me."

"Bishop Aidan will say it is wrong that two Christian kings should fight one against the other," said the queen.

"Then let Aidan stop him marching with Penda!"

"I know he has tried." Eanflæd nodded. "Very well. But who would you have as king in his place? It is clear the witan of Deira does not trust you. And if it does not trust you, then it will not accept your son, Ahlfrith, as king either."

"That is true," said Oswiu.

"It must be someone you trust completely, lord," said Æthelwin. "But one who has less connection by blood to you than your son. Someone whom you know will hold the land on your behalf and stop Penda riding across it." The warmaster paused. "Perhaps... Œthelwald. As Oswald's son, the witan may accept him where it will not accept your son. He is old enough now and, I hear, learned much during his time with Talorcan, king of the Picts."

But Oswiu shook his head. "I have seen little of the boy – though he is now a man – these past few years."

"And he is close to Rhieienmelth," added Eanflæd. "I – I am not sure that she would counsel him to our good."

"No." The king smiled. "But there is an answer – one I should have seen before." He turned to the warmaster. "Æthelwin, you tell me I should make king a man I trust completely; one who is not related to me but who will defend the land against Penda?"

"Yes, lord. Do you know such a man?"

The king's smile broadened. "I do. You."

Æthelwin stood in silence, as if struck by the lockjaw. But the queen said, "Of course," and the king's smile grew even broader.

"You, Æthelwin. I will make you king of Deira."

"Me." The warmaster finally breathed. "But lord, I am not of royal blood..."

"It's amazing what a scop can find in a man's background should he look. You will be royal, or royal enough, old friend." Oswiu clapped his warmaster on the back. "And at last I will be able to reward you as you deserve for your faithful service."

The warmaster smiled then, but it was a strangely strained smile.

*

On the island of his solitude, Aidan saw the flames blown back. He knelt upon the cliff top amid the sorrel and campion and grass, while about him wheeled the birds of the sea, the gannets and fulmars and guillemots and skuas, giving cry to his silent thanks.

He held his hands up to heaven, to the God who had heard his prayer and delivered the king from his foes. And he began to sing.

But as the words came from his mouth and joined with the unceasing praise of sea and wind and the wild birds, Aidan felt a claw, a dark, scaled claw, reach deep into his chest, squeezing the air from his lungs, and he clutched at his throat, searching for the breath that would not come, and the song died in his mouth and he fell forward upon his face.

The monks found him there. Finan had sent the boat early, for the news of the breaking of the siege had come quickly to the Holy Island, and Finan sent the monks to bear the glad tidings to Aidan. But when the bishop made no answer to their hailing, the monks had come ashore and searched for him. They found Aidan where he had fallen. He yet lived, but try as they might they could not wake him. So they carried him down the steep path to the cove and put him aboard their boat. Then, cradling their abbot's head, they took him back to the Holy Island.

Chapter 8

"Where is the king?"

Hunwald, the sweat and dust of the ride staining his face, threw the question at the door warden. But the warden did not point within – rather to the city of ruins.

"The king prays," said the warden. "At the stone church."

Hunwald stifled a curse. The news would not wait, and now he had to make his way through the wraith-haunted streets of the city of the emperors. Steeling himself, Hunwald set off into the city. It was strange: he could stand in the shieldwall without fear while all around him men mewled for their mothers, but set him to walk alone at dusk through the works of the men of old, and his bowels turned to water and he found himself starting at every sound and movement. Surely he would meet the king, returning to his hall, without needing to go all the way to the church?

But he did not meet the king.

The shadows grew and his pace quickened. He tried to keep his eyes ahead, not skittering into the yawning dark of door and window, but with each movement he looked, eyes jumping from side to side. For many creatures lived among the ruins of the men of old, bats in particular, and as the day waned, they woke and took wing.

At last, although Hunwald suspected that the time had not been long, he saw light ahead, pin bright in the gathering gloom: a torch, set outside the church. Its flames flickered over the fresh stone of the church. For among the stone buildings of this city of the men of old, only one was new built, its stone gleaming and white. Edwin had begun it, Oswald had continued it, but Oswine had completed it.

It was dark, though, as Hunwald approached the church of St Peter, and the light shone from the windows into the dark world outside. The warmaster was glad for that light, for it pushed the fear shadows back among the slouching, broken buildings that surrounded the new church.

There was a guard standing outside, and hearing Hunwald's quiet approach, he emerged, blinking, from the torchlight, trying to see into the shadows. Holding his spear out in front of him, the man called out, "Who is there?"

"It's Hunwald, you idiot." The warmaster stepped into the light. Seeing him, the guard relaxed.

"Where is the king?"

"He's in the church," said the guard. "He's been there all day." As the warmaster went to go past him, the guard asked the question that had been preying on his mind for the last two hours: "Do you think he'll stay much longer? Only, I'm starving."

"No," said Hunwald, opening the door. "No, he won't be much longer."

The king was kneeling before the altar.

Some of his bodyguards knelt too, but others stood at the back of the church. Their whispered conversations ended when they saw the warmaster, but the monks who lined the church did not falter in their chant, for they were praying the office of the setting of the sun, when they commended the dark world to a new rising.

Hunwald strode down the nave of the church. The king must surely have heard his approach, but Oswine did not look round.

The warmaster put his hand on the Godfriend's shoulder and bent down to him. "He is coming for you," Hunwald whispered.

"Oswiu?"

"Yes."

The king closed his eyes briefly. "Very well," he said. He turned his gaze back to the altar and the mysteries upon it. "I will be with you in a little while."

But it was night by the time King Oswine emerged from the church. Hunwald was waiting for him outside, although the warmaster remained within the circle of light cast by the torches.

It was a warm night, but the king wrapped his cloak around his shoulders. "Mayhap you were right, old friend. I should have stayed with Penda, for my withdrawal from the siege has brought me no friendship with Oswiu. But I thought, then, of what James the Deacon had told me, of the shame that two Christian kings should fight each other, and I saw the devastation being wrought in my name through Bernicia, and I would not have it so. But now, I suppose, Oswiu brings devastation to my realm?"

"He does, lord. He burns as he goes, driving thegns and ceorls alike from their homes and their land." The warmaster stared at his king. "What will you do, lord?"

"What will I do, Hunwald?" The king returned the warmaster's stare. "I sought to avoid war. But a king, when he is struck on one cheek, may not turn the other, for the cheek he turns is not his own, but the cheeks of his people, of his thegns and warriors, of his priests and ceorls and slaves, from the highest down to the lowest. If Oswiu will not grant me peace, then I will give him war." The king started towards his hall, with Hunwald struggling to keep pace beside him. "Tell me, how many men has he, where is he heading, and how long before he comes to our walls?"

Hunwald gave answer as they hurried back to the king's hall, so that by the time they came to its wooden walls, Oswine knew well the straits his kingdom was in. He stopped outside the hall, under the eaves of its roof.

"So, you say that we do not have enough men to face Oswiu in battle?"

"No, lord, we do not. Not unless you can summon another hundred or more to your side before he gets here."

The Godfriend paused, looking in thought up at the night sky. "I cannot. I have not the men. But there is another who can, and with ease."

"Penda?" asked Hunwald.

"Yes."

"But surely he will not give us aid – not since we left the siege."

"Penda must surely thirst for revenge. For already the news of how the flames ate his camp has spread far, and the scops make tales of it." Oswine turned to his warmaster. "Go to him, Hunwald. Go fast. Tell him that the chance to defeat Oswiu has come, and come more quickly than he could have hoped. For coming into our realm, he is far from the sure defences of that great rock, and with some of Penda's men – mayhap with the High King himself if he will come – we can defeat him in the open where we could not upon the rock." Oswine grasped his warmaster's shoulders. "But you must be quick, Hunwald, and you must tell Penda to hurry, whether he comes himself or sends men."

"Very well," said Hunwald. "I will go at first light."

"If the need is as urgent as you say, old friend, it were better you go now." Oswine looked towards the eastern horizon. "The moon will rise soon. There will be light, and enough, for riding."

"I – I will go," said Hunwald. "But where will I find Penda at this season? He spent June and July in war, so the year is out of kilter."

"But ask. There will be people who know. Now, you must go. I will gather all our men here, but our aim must be to meet the Iding on the open field and defeat him there. But for that I must have more men – the men you must bring back, Hunwald. You understand?" The king held his warmaster in his gaze.

"Yes," said Hunwald. "I understand." He made the courtesy. "I will go."

*

"I must go." Aidan sat up on his narrow bed.

The monk who had been keeping watch over him started and fell off his stool. For the abbot had barely stirred since they had brought him back. The monks had lifted his head and parted his lips to trickle water down his throat; when he had stirred and the veils that covered his mind had thinned, they had spooned food into his mouth. But in the weeks since he had been brought back from his island hermitage the abbot had not spoken a word. So it was no great surprise that the monk set to ward him had found his head beginning to nod. And though he caught himself the first time, and the second, yet the day was warm and somnolent, the thrum of bees filled the air, and the third time his chin went down it did not bounce back again, but rested upon his chest.

So when the abbot sat up and announced that he must go, the sleeping monk jerked awake, forgetting in the instant that he was sitting upon a stool and, tipping over, he let out a cry.

The cry had the virtue of bringing others, and quickly, to see what caused it, and first among them was Finan, abbot while Aidan had lived in solitude on his island, and abbot still while Aidan remained unspeaking.

With Finan leading the rush, the monks tumbled into the room to find Aidan sitting up, and the monk on watch crouching by him, offering the abbot water to drink.

"What happened?" asked Finan. "Who cried out?"

The monk, blushing, began to answer, but Aidan put his hand over his.

"It was a bird," he said.

Finan looked puzzled. "I have lived all my life by sea and on island, and never in that time have I heard a bird make call like that."

"It was a strange bird," said Aidan. He began to struggle from the bed. "Help me up."

Finan and others rushed to him, and in the confusion one monk was knocked from his feet and another fell upon the abbot's bed.

Aidan, grabbing hold of Finan, pulled himself up.

"There," he said, "that's bett..." But before he could finish the word, a fit of coughing took him, so that Finan had to hold him, lest he fall. And when the fit had passed, Aidan wiped his arm across his mouth, and the mark the saliva froth left on his habit was pink. Finan saw the stain too, and turned shocked eyes on his abbot.

"You must sit down... rest," he said. "Sometimes, I have heard, rest and good air can heal consumption."

Aidan shook his head. "You know as well as I that only God can heal consumption. But I must go. I must see the king."

"The king? King Oswiu? But he is gone. The siege is ended and he left soon after."

"Where has he gone?"

"I did not think to ask. Perhaps to Ad Gefrin."

"Then you must take me there." Aidan paused, wheezing for breath. When breath had returned he looked to Finan. "I think we had best be quick."

Chapter 9

"Oswine asks men of me?"

Penda sat upon his judgement seat. The seat was set by the side of the road, for Hunwald had found the king journeying between the royal estates at Tamworth and Lichfield and, as was the way with such journeys, a wagon had broken its axle and blocked the road. While the wagoners lifted the wagon up on blocks, amid much swearing and blame, the local people had come seeping from field and hut and hall, bringing with them suits and arguments and judgements, all for the king's attention. So, while he waited for the wagon to be repaired, Penda sat upon his judgement seat by the side of the road as a succession of farmers and peasants and slaves came before him to ask for the king's justice.

There Hunwald had found him, after two nights' and two days' hard riding, asking after the king at every hamlet, inn and hall he passed along the way. In Bernicia, it would not have been possible to find the king so quickly, save with the greatest fortune, for there were few roads there and to travel quickly men went by boat. But Mercia, the land of the marches, was criss-crossed with roads and paths and trails: some made, of gravel and flagstone, by the emperors of old; others trodden into the ground by the feet of men long forgotten, but who had found the driest and best paths across the country.

Penda regarded Hunwald from the shadow under his hood.

"You say Oswine asks men of me?"

Hunwald made the courtesy. He had already done so, but now he did it again. "Yes, lord. He even dares ask that you might come yourself – for Oswiu is sprung from his holt and, together, you might catch this slippery otter that escaped you before."

Though Penda had but one eye, Hunwald felt as if the High King were looking into his soul. But he made no effort to conceal his soul from the High King's scrutiny, for he would that Penda knew he spoke the truth.

The High King stood up. "Come, walk with me," he said.

With Hunwald by his side, he left the milling mass of suppliants and suitors, and started up the road, the gravel grinding rough beneath their feet.

Penda stopped. They were far enough now from other people that none might hear what they said. "I would send men, and gladly, to a king who would stand beside me in battle... and in siege." The High King turned his single eye upon Hunwald. "Is there such a king in Deira?"

Hunwald paused. He too looked to see that none might hear them.

"There are... whispers. The witan has seen the halls of many of its thegns burn. Many marched with you, lord, into Bernicia, thinking to find there glory and gold. They returned with nothing. Mayhap the mind of the witan turns to a new king in Deira."

"And is there a man in Deira who would stand beside me in battle and in siege? To such a man I would gladly give my support, should the current king meet some misfortune."

"Could the High King support a king who is of noble blood but not himself royal?"

"Oh, I think you'll find that the king is always of royal blood, whoever his parents were."

"Then I can say there is such a man in Deira."

Penda looked at Hunwald with his one eye.

"Then I fear you must disappoint your king. Penda will send no men in his defence. If he is God's friend, then let God defend him, for I will not."

*

"He's not coming."

Hunwald, after three more days upon the saddle, had found King Oswine camped with his men at the foot of Wilfar's Hill, ten miles north-west of the village of Catterick. Riding into the camp,

Hunwald had made rough count of the men the Godfriend had under his command: no more than fifty. Oswiu was marching south with twice, possibly thrice, that number, and the rumour of his coming, and the burning and looting that accompanied it, filled the countryside, for all knew that Oswiu came to take vengeance, and none expected quarter from him.

"What do you mean, he's not coming?" said Oswine. Hunwald had been led to the king as he took sight from the top of Wilfar's Hill, searching the horizon for the signs of Oswiu's approach. As Hunwald had climbed the hill, he had found those signs all too easy to see: columns of smoke rose into the still August day. No rain had fallen through the summer and the sky was bronze with foreboding. There would be a great burning before this summer ended.

"Penda will not come, nor will he send any men."

"But Oswiu is here, in the open. He is ours for the defeating. He just needs to send me some men."

"He will not. I tried, lord. I made every argument I could; I offered him all the spoils of victory, but he would not have them. He said that he would not come to the aid of a man who had abandoned him."

Oswine shook his head. "I – I did not abandon him. But I could not stand and see the land and its people despoiled."

"I do not think any words of man will change his mind, lord."

Oswine the Godfriend passed his hand over his face. He was looking north, looking at the smoke of Oswiu's coming.

"That it should come to this." Oswine shook his head, and Hunwald saw that there were tears streaming down his face. "Men call me the Godfriend and when I first learned of what God had done for us – done for me – I thought it true. The more so when, though I had desired it not, I was set upon the throne. I wished to be God's good friend, that his word be heard throughout my kingdom and men come to the new life that I had found. But now I think that God's friendship is not as that of men or kings. It brings neither gold, nor glory, nor the promise of victory. All it brings is... hope."

The king turned his face to his warmaster. He shed no more tears now, but their tracks still marked his skin. "I will not lead my men to death. Give order, Hunwald. Disband the army. Tell them to return to their halls and their women and their children. For my part, I will go to your hall at Gilling, for it is not so far away. There, if God grants me time, I shall give thought to what we may do next: whether we should wait until Oswiu's anger is spent, then rise against him; or whether I should do as Sigeberht, king of the East Angles did and step down from the throne and seek an eternal crown."

Hunwald stared at the king as one staring at a thing unknown. He opened his mouth, but no words came forth and, seeing him, Oswine knew mirth for the first time in many days, and laughed.

"Is what I say so strange, old friend? I fear it may be – but we live in days when all we thought fixed and secure has become as leaves, blown from the tree. These musings are but a fit of mine. Take no mind of them, friend. But give the order, that my men may live."

Hunwald shook his head. "Lord, it is not meet that you should flee before the foe. Even were you – were we – to die, it were better than… than this!"

"Ah, the glory and honour of men. It is what we strive for. The songs of the scops, the regard of men." Oswine squatted down and dragged his hand through the dry earth. Standing, he opened his fingers. "Dust. Dust and ashes. The dream of boys, playing with practice swords." He wiped his hand over his tunic, drawing a dust smear down the cloth. "Send the men home, Hunwald. I will take Tondhere, for he knows the ways round here, and make for Gilling. We will meet there, if God wills."

Hunwald watched the king make his way down the hill. "Yes, we will meet there," he said.

Chapter 10

"Hurry, brothers. Please hurry."

The brothers, four monks each holding an end of the hurdles upon which their abbot lay, were too breathless to answer. The sun had burned down on them on the journey from Lindisfarne, blinding them in the morning and cooking their backs through the long afternoon heat. When Aidan had insisted that, despite his weakness, he must go to the king, Finan had first tried him upon a horse, the calmest, most sure-footed beast they could borrow from the farmers who worked the land across the strait on the mainland, for the monastery kept no horses of its own. But though Aidan had been helped upon the beast, after only a few steps the coughing fit had come upon him again, and he had all but fallen from the horse. It was only the swiftness of one of the younger monks that had caught him. Seeing that the abbot could not ride, Finan had the monks make a hurdle of two ash poles and woven hazel and willow wands. Onto this he lay cloth and straw, so that the ride might not be a corporal penance, and asked whom among the monks of Holy Island would be willing to bear their abbot to the king at Ad Gefrin.

All had cried, "Aye!"

And Finan saw Aidan, at that cry, turn his face away, that his brethren would not see the tears that started in his eyes.

Though all had said "Aye", not all were able to make such a journey in haste. Finan chose eight of the strongest and youngest, gave them food and drink for the journey, then took his place holding one of the poles as they lifted Aidan from the ground.

Aidan turned to Finan. He shook his head. "I say unto thee, When thou wast young, thou girdest thyself, and walkedst whither thou wouldest: but when thou shalt be old, thou shalt stretch forth thy hands, and another shall gird thee, and carry thee whither thou wouldest not." He smiled and put his hand on Finan's arm. "Not that you are old. But you must stay and feed the sheep. I will not say my sheep, for they belong to another, but still they need a watchdog. Watch them well, Finan, and bid me farewell."

Finan bowed his head and pressed his lips to the back of Aidan's hand. "You have been as a father to me," he said.

"And I could not have wished for a better son," said Aidan. He laughed, but the laugh became a cough, and for a moment he was overcome. But he regained mastery of himself and smiled at Finan. "No woman would have had me to husband, I fear, but I have had sons such that any woman would be proud to call her own." Aidan looked round at the gathered monks of his community. "Help me stand, Finan," he whispered.

With Finan holding his arm, Aidan stood in front of his many sons.

"I leave you in the care of Finan. Be with him as you have with me: ever attentive and kind. I ask you to forgive me where I have failed you, to overlook any offence I have given and to cleave, always, to the example of the Blessed One, Colm Cille, for then you will surely know you tread the right path."

Aidan looked around at the sea of faces staring at him. Many, most, wept openly. There were so many of them now, and he had come to this land with so few. Back then, all his monks had spoken, among themselves, the song language of the islands of his birth. Now, most of those entering the community spoke the drumbeat language of the Angles. He had found it crude and uncouth once, particularly when he had struggled to learn it from Oswald, but now he heard its own particular music. Not so sweet a music as his own tongue, that was true, but a music nonetheless. He would leave that music to flow into the hearts of the men of this land and bring them to the new life that called to them.

"Pray for me. I will pray for you. Always." As he spoke, Aidan prayed that he might be spared another coughing fit, at least until he was away from the sight of his community.

One by one, they came to him seeking his benediction and his blessing, and he gave it, with a word to one, a gesture to another, sometimes a smile, or a finger to wipe away a tear. When he had made farewell to all, Aidan sat upon the hurdle. The monks taking him to Ad Gefrin lifted their burden – and it was light, for the disease had consumed much of Aidan's flesh, leaving him as light as a child – and started on the long walk to the king's palace in the shadow of Yeavering Bell, the hill of the goats. Aidan watched the waving monks until they merged with land and sea and sky. Then, spent, he lay back upon the hurdle and looked up into the bronze sky.

The journey to Ad Gefrin had taken three days. The monks sweated carrying him, Aidan sweated beneath the sun. He felt himself sweating his body away. Waking once from a fever sleep, he held his hand up and saw the sun through it, so thin had his flesh become. But at each stop he forced himself to eat and drink, though he had no wish to do either. For Aidan knew he must live to deliver his message lest the king die, and die indeed, for this were death in the spirit.

"Hurry, dear brothers."

Now, at last, the golden hall lay before them. Its great posts, carved and painted, pointed to the sky, and in the great paddock that lay riverward were many cattle and sheep. Aidan, sitting up as the monks approached, saw the offering and knew this for the render of the hills, given by the Brigantes. But if the render were here, the king must be too. The sun was behind him now, so he had no need to shade his eyes, but his sight was growing watery and dim. Aidan turned to one of the monks carrying him.

"Are there wagons there? Many wagons? I cannot see."

"Yes, abbot. Many wagons."

Aidan, breathing a great sigh, lay back upon the hurdle. "I am in time," he said softly. And sleep took him.

"Aidan."

The monk opened his eyes. It was day still, but there was no sun glaring into his eyes from a bronze sky, so he knew he lay inside the great hall of Ad Gefrin, the palace of the kings.

There was a face above his, and for a moment he could not

recognize it, for the features swam into memory and he saw, as if it were again true, the face of his mother as she had nursed him when he was a child.

There was a hand on his and he looked to it. But his memory was wrong, for he saw that his was the hand that was aged, while the one upon him was young.

"Aidan."

The voice told him whose hand held his.

"Eanflæd." Aidan closed his eyes for a moment, such was the relief. "It is not too late. I must speak with the king."

But the queen shook her head. "The king is not here. He rode south, five days past."

"Where…" Aidan began to cough, his torso wracked. "Where does he ride?"

Eanflæd sat back. She turned her face from the abbot, and Aidan knew then where the king had gone.

"Deira," she said. "He has ridden into Deira."

Aidan fell back. "Then I am too late," he said.

But the queen looked to Aidan again. "It may be that is not so, for I can send a messenger, well horsed and swift. What message do you wish to send him?"

"Tell him… Tell him that he goes in danger of his soul. Tell him not to do that which the tempter lays before him. Tell him to forbear."

Chapter 11

It was dusk and the sentry was nervous. At this time, when the shadows lengthened and time stood balanced between day and night, the eyes played tricks on the mind. Behind him, he could hear the sounds of camp: the low note of conversation, the shifting of horses, the crackle of fires. But in front, all he could see was shadows. He could swear that something moved in those shadows, shifting in the wood that reached a long finger towards the king's camp. Most likely a badger or a fox, as wary of him as he was of it, but nonetheless the sentry got to his feet. Cursing the twilight under his breath, for it was easier to see in the night when the stars were out than in this half-light, he shifted his head left and right, trying to see into shadows that grew with each passing moment.

There. There was something there.

He raised his spear.

"Hold!" he cried. He wished his voice firm and bold, but it cracked like a breaking twig.

What he saw did not hold, but came on, and on, growing bigger and bigger...

"Hold!" His voice was pitching higher, as it had been before it had broken this last year. He looked around for someone close to call, and seeing no one on hand, thought on whether he should fall back into camp and the help of older, more experienced men. But then whatever was coming, be it wight or ælf or ghost, might enter the camp unhindered, and he would have failed in his duty. So he held his spear out in front of him and hardened his voice.

"Hold!" he cried a third time, and this time it was the voice of a man.

And the figure, coming from shadow into the glimmer of firelight, diminished and became a man. A man holding his hands out, so that the sentry might see he bore no weapons. A man who stopped and spoke.

"I have word for your king."

The sentry heard the words and knew their speaker to come from this land that they marched through and not the land of high passes that was his home.

"Who are you, that would speak with the king?"

"I am Hunwald, warmaster of this land your king rides through."

The sentry nodded, trying to keep the excitement from his face. That such a man should give himself up, and to him. This would surely merit the king's notice, and mayhap even his favour...

*

The king looked up. Although there were no clouds the stars were dim. The heat pressed down upon the world even as it slept, and it slept uneasily. There was sound in the camp – motion that told of something happening. He glanced to his warmaster.

"Æthelwin."

"I will see, lord."

Ahlfrith looked after the warmaster. He sniffed. "I hope it is something of interest. So far we have done nothing but chase shadows."

"At least it is dry," said Oswiu. "When we campaigned against that clan of the Picts who raided our northern marches, we spent three months riding shin deep through mud and rain with never a sign of them. This is better."

"To be sure, but it has been dry for so long, I would be glad of some rain."

Oswiu made to answer but then fell silent, for the warmaster was returning and he was not alone. A man came with Æthelwin, prodded at spear point, his hands bound behind him. A man Oswiu knew.

The king slowly got to his feet.

"You."

The man went to make the courtesy, but at his movement the

men guarding him pitched him forward so that he fell, face first, into the dust at the king's feet.

Oswiu stared down at Hunwald.

"For the man who captured this nithing, gold. But for the nithing, payment in kind." He looked up at the curious men who'd followed the sentry as he prodded Hunwald forward through the camp. "Piss on him before he dies."

"Lord." Æthelwin stepped forward. "He was not captured – he came to us."

Oswiu looked down once more at the man lying at his feet and now there was surprise in his face as well as anger.

"Why did you come to me, when you knew I would kill you?"

Hunwald struggled onto his knees. He made to stand up, but one of the guards pushed him down again. In the firelight, Oswiu could see the fresh bruises on Hunwald's face. The king was not the only one who remembered what had happened outside the walls of York.

"You wish to know why I come to you?" Hunwald looked up at Oswiu. "Then let me stand and speak as a man. Or slay me as I kneel, but then you will never know why I walked, and walked freely, into your camp."

Oswiu stared down at the man. He nodded, once.

"Stand."

Hunwald got to his feet.

The king looked him in the face. Hunwald met his gaze and did not flinch.

"Speak," said Oswiu.

Hunwald cleared his throat. One glance at the waiting, watching, silent men betrayed his nerves, but then he looked back to the king.

"I came to you, lord, because thrice now my lord has fled from you: when you raided into Deira, and he would not meet you; when we besieged you at Bamburgh; and now, again." Hunwald looked round at the circle of men, then brought his gaze back to the king. "Oswine has fled. He ordered me to disband his army. He will not meet you in battle, lord." The warmaster of Deira summoned spit from his dry throat and spat upon the dust. "My king is a coward. Better you kill me than I serve him longer."

Oswiu regarded the man. "You say Oswine has fled. What proof have you?" He glanced at his own warmaster. "Think you this a trick, Æthelwin?"

Æthelwin nodded. "So I think, lord. He must mean to draw us into a trap."

"It is no trick, lord. The army is broken. I can show you the camp where we waited for you, under Wilfar's Hill. It is empty now."

"Any army may move camp," said Oswiu.

"I – I can take you to the king."

"Oh yes, with all his army about him. Do you think I am fool enough to walk into such a trap?"

"No! No, he is alone, save for one man. Oswine bade the army split up, that the men might have better chance of evading you. He himself went with just one warrior."

"Where did he go?"

"To Gilling." Hunwald straightened. He stared at the king. "To my hall."

"So," said Oswiu. "You would betray your king under your own roof."

"He is king no more! He put aside the throne when he ran from the field. Oswine is no longer throne-worthy."

Oswiu laughed, though there was no humour in the sound. "That is what I have tried so long to tell the witan of Deira. It has not listened to me. Why should it listen to you?"

"It would have to listen – if the king was king no longer." Hunwald looked to king and warmaster and ætheling. "Oswine has but the one man with him. I swear it. Would I have come into this camp unless there were reason? This is my reason. Oswine is no friend of Deira. Let him die."

"You would deliver your king into my hands?" asked Oswiu.

"I would. I will take you to where he is. There you may make a new king in Deira. One whom you trust. One that the witan will accept."

Oswiu looked to his warmaster and his son. "We will speak on this." He gestured at Hunwald. "Take him away and keep him safe. But should he make any move to escape, kill him."

While the guards hustled Hunwald away, the king gestured his warmaster and Ahlfrith to him. Seeing Acca, the scop, the king called him over as well.

"It may be a trap. But it is also a chance we may not overlook."

"If Hunwald speaks true, and Oswine has only one man with him, then it will not need many men to bring him back to you, Father," said Ahlfrith. "Let me take a score of men and ride to Gilling, and bring you back a great prize."

Oswiu looked to the warmaster. "What say you, Æthelwin?"

The warmaster shook his head. "I should say not. For Oswine it were a risk worth taking, to lose his warmaster but gain the son of the king as hostage. A brave and loyal warmaster might suggest such an idea himself. Ahlfrith should not go."

"Did you see falsehood in what the man said?" Oswiu asked his counsellors.

"No," said Ahlfrith.

After a moment's consideration, Æthelwin shook his head.

"He spoke truly," said Acca. He looked round the other men. "Though I would wish Coifi were with us, that he might see the truth of the man."

"I would have brought him too, if we went more slowly," said Oswiu. "Without him, I think we must see if Hunwald speaks the truth."

"But if the whole army goes," said Ahlfrith, "then it runs the risk of falling into a trap laid for it."

"That is true," said Æthelwin. "But one warmaster sacrificed for another would be no great loss, and the chance of taking the king is too great to pass up." Æthelwin looked to king and ætheling and scop. "Ahlfrith was right. A score of men, riding fast to Gilling, could take the king with ease if he has but a single guard. Ahlfrith's only error was who should go: it should be me. Then if it be a trap and I be lost, Oswine gains no great advantage, for he too will lose his warmaster."

"I would not lose mine," said Oswiu.

"Nor do I intend to be lost. But I must be the one to go."

Ahlfrith made to speak, but the king held up his hand for silence. "No, son."

"But, Father…"

Oswiu shook his head. "I know what you will say, but Æthelwin is right. He must go and bring me back a king."

The warmaster made the courtesy. "I have one question, lord," Æthelwin said. "Oswine waged war against you and allied with your enemies. You say to bring him back to you. But if I find him alone, would it not be better to kill him?"

But before Oswiu could answer, Acca spoke. "There is no glory in killing a man alone, even if he be a king. No scop will ever sing of such a deed. No, but they will make gossip and riddles of it, such that all the kingdoms shall hear of it and account it an inglorious deed. Would you have the king held up to such talk?"

Æthelwin shrugged. "I care little for the prattle of scops or the chatter of women. It were better for us that Oswine die than that he live."

"Acca is right." Ahlfrith turned to his father. "Such an act would live long after we are dead. It would stain our memory and haunt our children and be repaid in blood through the generations. To kill Oswine when he has lain down his sword would mean feud, blood feud, between his family and ours. You say you are the true king in Deira, Father, and such you are. But do not baptize your throne with blood, lest the blood debt be paid by our children and our children's children."

"You counsel mercy to a man thrice traitor." Oswiu turned away and looked to where Hunwald stood captive. "But I will think on this. Æthelwin, choose the men you will take. The night is bright with moonlight. I would set my hounds running before the day comes."

While the warmaster gathered his troop, Oswiu sat and thought.

Ever and again, his mind circled back to Aidan. He saw the abbot, his old friend, pleading peace with him, asking him to raise no hand against the Godfriend. But Aidan had not been in Bamburgh when its walls burned and the gate was broken. He had not stood on the battlements and seen the flag of Deira drawn up next to the wolf banner of the Iclingas. He had not wife nor children, but Oswiu had, and the memory of Eanflæd and Ecgfrith, held at knifepoint, pushed into his mind.

He closed his eyes and slept.

And dreamed.

He saw a king pulled from a monastery. He saw a man, soaked in sweat, coughing blood in a great hall, then turn and look at him with haunted eyes. He saw his mother, as she took his face in her hands, as she had done on every leave-taking. But now she looked as if she saw him not. He saw his brother, as if from far off, and he tried to get to Oswald but, looking down, he saw that the feet he thought bore him towards his brother were walking away from him.

"Lord."

Oswiu jerked awake, gasping.

Æthelwin stood over him. "I am ready."

The king stood up, shaking the dreams from his mind. They made no sense.

The warmaster leaned towards the king, speaking softly so that none of the men nearby might hear. "Do you wish me to bring Oswine back to you?"

"Yes," said Oswiu. "Yes, I do."

"Very well." Æthelwin stepped back, his face expressionless.

Oswiu knew well that blank face. It meant the warmaster disagreed with his decision. Oswiu stepped forward to embrace Æthelwin. But as the man stood stiffly within his embrace, Oswiu whispered, "I didn't say to bring him all."

The warmaster gave the slightest of nods to show that he had heard. "And Hunwald?"

"There is a warmaster I trust to take the throne of Deira, but he is not Hunwald."

"Lord."

"A king may call another king brother. Go, brother. Make Deira yours."

Æthelwin stepped back from the king's embrace, made the courtesy and turned to where his men waited with Hunwald, bound, in their midst. Mounting his horse, the warmaster saluted Oswiu, and then turned and rode away into the night.

Chapter 12

"It is... it is too hot in here." Aidan, lying sweat-soaked upon his bed in the great hall at Ad Gefrin, turned his head to a figure passing by.

"Please," he asked. "Help me to go outside."

The man paused. Though the hall was stifling in this summer without end, yet he pulled his raven-feather cloak tighter around his thin shoulders. He did not look at the figure upon the bed, but searched, through the dark corners of the hall and in the play of dust through the pillars of light cutting through the gloom, for some sign as to what he should do. It was chance that brought him by Aidan's bed when, for some short time, he lay there unattended. Normally, one of his monks sat always by him, cooling his face with a wet cloth and fanning air over him with his robe. But he had seen the monk scuttle from the hall, gripping his belly with the look of a man whose bowels are about to explode. The noises that came shortly afterwards from outside the hall told they had. Then, dancing through the blades of light that pierced the darkness of the hall, he had seen a sprite and followed where it led, clambering over benches (as well that there were so few men in the hall, or he would have kicked over many a cup in his pursuit of the sprite) and tripping over sleeping dogs, until he came to the corner where Aidan lay.

The abbot, seeing the figure stop but not turn, looked to where Coifi was staring, head bobbing as he tried to follow the motion of the sprite. Holding out his hand, palm open, Aidan whispered in his own tongue, and the sprite darted and swooped to him, and sat there, wings opening and closing.

Coifi stared at it. What was before a sprite was now a butterfly.

Aidan, with great effort, pushed himself up so he rested on one elbow and brought the butterfly towards his face. He breathed on it. "Go before me, little one." The butterfly spread its wings to his breath, then took flight again.

Coifi, neck snapping, turned to watch, and as it flew in and out of the rays of light towards the door, it seemed to him to be sometimes butterfly and sometimes sprite. It flew out of the great doors to the hall. The old priest's gaze snapped back to the abbot. Aidan lay upon his bed, but his face was turned towards Coifi.

"You saw it?" asked Coifi. "You saw it?"

Aidan smiled. "I had not thought to see you here, for I thought you to have gone with the king, and I am glad. For the reign of three kings you have been their shadow, the tale of their past – men say you were less easily separated from them than the pearl from its shell." The abbot began a smile, but he could not finish it, for the coughing fits came upon him again, wracking his body. But this time they did not last too long, and he regained himself, though new sweat beaded his forehead.

"Why did you stay?" Aidan asked, when he could speak again.

Coifi squatted down on his haunches beside the bed. "Acca went with Oswiu, but I grow too old to chase after kings," he said. "The sprite they do not see; I do not see that which they pursue."

"That is because no man may see it, for it exists only in their minds and on the lips of the scops: glory."

"Mind, they chase gold too, and that I can see. But gold has never come towards me, though I served the gods well when I was their priest and even now, when I am a priest no more, I still serve."

"That is because God does not pay in gold, which a man may also give, but in that which no man may give, be he High King or the least slave."

Coifi rolled his head. There, he'd seen something. But he hauled his gaze back to the man lying upon the bed.

"What does your god pay with, that no man may give?"

"Life," said Aidan.

"Life…" Coifi began to rock backwards and forwards on his haunches, while making strange squaffling noises, and only after Aidan saw him wipe tears from his eyes did he realize that the old priest was laughing.

"Life," said Coifi. "And you, lying here, with one leg in this world and the other already among the shadows. When the other priest came, the one from far, and I did as the king wanted, and abjured the gods and put fire and spear into the sacred grove, I too went under the water and took the salt and oil, for he said it would give me new life. But it seems to me I have had little but my old life, ever chasing the tail of understanding, yet feeling it always dissolve in my hands before I grasp it." Coifi turned eyes rheumed with thought and age upon the monk. "I do not understand."

Aidan held out his hand and the old priest took it.

"Oft, I do not understand either. I do not understand why I was made bishop, who was barely able to prepare the skins for tanning on the Holy Island. I do not understand why the worthy perish and the evil thrive. I do not understand why men hearken so easily to the evil promptings of their heart and turn away from good counsel – and hope. Come, if you will help me. We have been inside, in the dark, too long. Let us go out into the light."

Aidan struggled to sit, and held out his arm. Coifi took it and helped him from the bed. Together, with Coifi half holding, half supporting Aidan, they went out from the hall into the light and warmth of the day.

"I – I will sit here," said Aidan. He put his back to one of the great pillars of the hall and, with Coifi helping him, slid down to the floor. He looked out, from under the eaves of the hall, to the hills rising smoothly from the valley floor. "It is good to feel the breeze again." Aidan looked up at Coifi. "Will you sit with me? I would hear tales of the old days, when Edwin was king, and the queen's mother reigned beside him."

So Coifi squatted down next to the abbot and, rocking upon his heels, told him tales of Edwin and his sons, and when the monk who was meant to be caring for Aidan returned from his ablutions – for such had been the explosion from his bowels that he had had to go to wash in the river – the abbot told him to rest, for he was well looked after for the moment.

But when Coifi paused, mouth dry from the telling, Aidan put a hand on his arm. "Would you go and call the queen, and her guard. There are riders coming." He pointed with a glance down the valley, and Coifi saw them too. A score of men, their spear tips held aloft and glittering in the sun, their armour bright and flashing in the light.

While Coifi went in search of Queen Eanflæd, Aidan's monk, hearing the news, came to him and would have moved him within the hall. But the abbot refused.

"I would see who comes to call," he said.

*

The queen waited, standing in the open doorway of the great hall. Her guard stood, for the most part, discreetly aside; but there were men ready and armed should the riders raise arms against her. But by their approach, Eanflæd expected no trouble. There were a score of them: enough to serve as escort for a thegn or ætheling, but not so many as could attack a hall and expect to succeed. And the riders came riding behind a banner. No band of reivers, bent on plunder, would ride in such a manner. But such was the stillness of the day and the lankness of the air that she could not see the banner, for despite the steady trot at which the riders approached, the banner did not unfurl, but hung limply from its pole.

There was, however, something familiar about that banner, about the colours she could glimpse as it shifted and sought to unfurl, only for the lack of wind to collapse it once more.

As the riders approached the fence to the compound, and the gate, they sped up a little, enough to tug the banner loose. And Eanflæd saw that they rode under the colours of purple and gold – the colours of Bernicia.

Eanflæd looked to her priest, Romanus the Frank, who stood beside her. "Who is it?" she asked.

But Romanus shrugged. "I do not know. Perhaps..." He looked round and saw, for the first time, Aidan sitting with his back propped up by the pillar. "Perhaps he will know."

The queen, seeing Aidan there, gasped. "Aidan, you should not be here. You are ill; you must rest."

But the monk slowly shook his head. "There will be time, and enough, to rest soon, my lady. For now, I will wait to see who calls on us this hot summer day when all hide from the sun rather than ride through it."

"See you the banner?" asked Eanflæd. "It is ours, the flag of this throne, but that is not the king, nor his son, so who flies it?"

"There is another who may, by right, fly the flag of the Idings," said Aidan.

Eanflæd turned back to the riders. They were at the gate now, telling their business to the gate warden.

"Œthelwald."

*

The riders pulled up their horses in front of the great hall and almost as one man dismounted. The leader of them, who wore a thin circle of gold around his head, stepped forward and stopped before where the queen stood at the top of the short stairs up to the hall. He looked up at her and made the courtesy.

"Well met, at long, long last, Aunt Eanflæd," he said. "Since you greet me alone, I take it my uncle is not here?"

"Ætheling Œthelwald. Brother son, I give you greeting, and make you welcome in the king's hall and in the king's name."

"And I give you greeting too, queen and aunt and cousin. We would needs marry to be more closely related." Œthelwald came up the steps and stood before Eanflæd. "I would have met you before."

"Before?" asked the queen.

"Before you married my uncle!" The ætheling smiled and his smile was broad and white. "But I have a gift for my uncle – one that since he is not here I must give to you. For since he will not ride with his nephew, so that I may earn the glory and gold due to me, I have ridden with Talorcan, king of the Picts – and cousin to me also – ridden on the marches with Strathclyde and Dal Riada and Rheged. And there I met and killed a band of thieves and bandits who had been raiding and despoiling all the farms and villages for miles around. I killed all save one, their leader. For he had a strange tale to tell; a tale that I thought the king should hear. But I bring this bandit here, ready to sing, and the king is not present to listen. What say you I should do?"

Eanflæd looked at the man standing before her. He was, she realized, younger than she had first thought – and, of course, he must be, for he was younger than Ahlfrith and Ahlflæd, her husband's children with Rhieienmelth. But he had, it seemed, the vigour of his youth, and its confidence.

"If this man has tale to tell, then let him tell it to me. If it be something the king should hear, then I shall tell the king."

"Indeed? The king must trust you indeed if he would leave to you the charge of his great hall. But then I have heard that men call you Eanflæd the Wise, and come to you for judgement as they do to my uncle." Œthelwald smiled. "No wonder my uncle put aside Rhieienmelth for you: they say no man ever went to her for judgement in dispute, although I have ever found her patient and kind. Still, I hear that you have outmatched Rhieienmelth in other areas too – the king greatly loves his new, young son." The ætheling stopped and looked round. "Is he here? I would see my cousin Ecgfrith."

Before the queen could say anything, a little body squirmed between the guards and came to stand next to her. "I'm Ecgfrith and I'm going to be king. Who are you?"

Œthelwald crouched so he could look Ecgfrith in the face. "My name is Œthelwald," he said. He leaned closer to the boy. "And I'm going to be king too."

"Mummy." Ecgfrith grabbed his mother's hand. "He says he's going to be king. He can't be, can he?"

Œthelwald held up his hands, laughing. "Little prince, little prince, fear not. There are other thrones and other realms and many kings. You can be king and I can be king, and then we can play the game of kings together. What do you say to that?"

"Oh, yes," said Ecgfrith, clapping his hands. "I'd like that. Wouldn't you, Mummy?" He looked up at the queen.

"Yes, I'd like that," said Eanflæd.

"Really?" Œthelwald stood straight again. "I am glad. It is a great game and I have been amusing myself in preparing for the playing. Such is how I came by this prize that it seems I must give you." The ætheling gestured, and his men thrust a captive forward. He fell on his knees before the queen. The man was bound, and there were the signs of hard usage on him, but from his face and manner, Eanflæd could see that he had been used no harder than he had used others.

"I spared you that you might sing to the king." Œthelwald gave a sign to his men and one of them pulled the captive to his feet. "Since the king is not here, you will sing to the queen. And you had better sing as tunefully to her as you sang to me, or you shall not live to see the sun set."

The man shifted on his feet, his eyes flicking to the ætheling and the men around him. He tried to speak, but his voice failed.

Œthelwald glanced at the queen, then looked to the captive again. "Sing. Tell the queen what you told me. Tell her now."

The man tried again, but his voice cracked and no words emerged.

"I find," said Eanflæd, "that gentleness may bring forth what harshness hides." She looked to one of the household slaves. "Bring this man something to drink." The queen turned to the ætheling. "Can you not see his lips are so dry that he cannot speak?"

"He had to drink yesterday," said Œthelwald.

"And you have ridden hard and long since then, and in this heat too. It is a wonder he can stand."

The slave returned before Œthelwald had chance to give answer. Looking to the queen, the slave received her permission and held the cup to the captive's lips. The man, his eyes turned to Eanflæd in gratitude, drank swiftly but in the small, quick sips that told he had before been long without water and knew it best not to drink, as the body demanded, in one long draught, but to take a little water at a time.

The cup drained, the slave looked to the queen with a question in his eyes.

"Yes, give him to drink more," said the queen. She stopped the slave as he went to refill the cup. "Ale will smooth his throat and leave him able to speak – or sing, as the ætheling says. So bring ale, and a cup of mead." The queen looked to Œthelwald's men, hot, dusty and no doubt thirsty after their ride. "Mayhap your men might like to drink too? There is beer, and ale, and mead, and wine within. Go in, leaving only ill will outside, and drink your fill." She looked to Œthelwald, whose face had soured at the invitation, but who could not gainsay it. "My guards will watch this man while yours take their rest."

Œthelwald made an exaggerated courtesy to the queen. "I thank you for your great kindness. Men through all the northlands speak of the wisdom and kindness of Eanflæd, calling you Deep Minded and Summer Kind; now I see they speak truly. But, for myself, I will spurn drink to ease the great dryness of my throat that I may hear my bird sing."

"For my part," said Eanflæd, "I am glad that you are able to struggle through that great dryness – are you sure you would not wish my servants to bring you ale or wine to drink, that you might speak more freely?" The queen smiled sweetly at the ætheling with no glimpse of the iron hidden behind the honey, although Œthelwald knew it was there.

Acknowledging his besting in this particular field of battle, Œthelwald stepped back to allow his men into the hall, waiting while they left swords and spears outside the door – as was custom – before going in. For her part, Eanflæd by small gesture and quiet word ordered that enough of her own guard remain ready and armed, but out of sight on the far side of the hall, to deal with any trouble that might come from this unknown band of warriors.

"Œthelwald."

The voice was weak, but it carried between the creak of wood and the sound of conversation to the ætheling's ear. Œthelwald turned and saw a man in a monk's rough habit, sitting with his back against one of the pillars of the hall, with another squatting beside him wrapped, despite the heat, in a raven-feather cloak.

"Aidan." The ætheling smiled to see him and there was no guile in this smile. "And Coifi." Œthelwald went to them, but as he neared Aidan, the smile left his face. "You are not well?" He crouched down next to the monk and took his hand. "So hot."

Aidan lifted his other hand and touched Œthelwald's cheek. "There is so much of your father in you," he said. "Do not fight it."

The ætheling shook his head. "Mayhap you see it, but it seems others do not. Else why would my uncle keep me from this kingdom and send me, always, among the north men, far away?"

"The king sees it," said Aidan. "He sees it too well."

Œthelwald looked away. "Does he fear me so much?" A smile touched his lips. "Good."

But now it was Aidan who shook his head. "It is not fear, but longing. He still misses Oswald."

"As do I." Œthelwald stood up. "It was good to see you, Aidan, and you, Coifi."

The old priest rocked back on his heels and looked up at the ætheling. In the end, Œthelwald looked away, back to where the queen waited for him, now that all his men were safely in the hall. "I have a bird to make sing."

But before he could go, Aidan called to him again. "Wait." The monk beckoned Œthelwald back and held his hand up so that the ætheling had to squat down beside him.

"I will pray for you always, in this life and the next." Aidan traced a finger down the side of Œthelwald's face. "So like your father."

The ætheling stood once more, but as he turned to go back to the queen, Aidan spoke again. "In the end, Œthelwald, you will hold true."

The ætheling stopped. He did not turn round. Then he saw that Eanflæd was speaking with the captive.

"Wait," he called. "Wait for me."

Hurrying over, Œthelwald looked to queen and captive. "What did he say?"

"That his name is Garmund."

"Has he said anything else?"

"Other than to thank me for that which he had to drink, no."

"Good." Œthelwald turned to the captive. "Tell the queen what you told me."

Garmund made the courtesy to Eanflæd. "You would not think

it now, but I was not always like this, an outlaw and a brigand. I was a thegn once. But by the jealousy of another, I was traduced before the king, and he outlawed me, who had only ever been loyal to him. I had my vengeance on the man who betrayed me – his screams as I made him watch his children die still ring sweetly in my ear – but such killing meant that I could never return to my land and my home. So I became what you see before you. But since men knew I had once been more, some took to coming to me to do that which they could not. I avenged insults, removed rivals, smoothed the way for those seeking favour with the king. And while the kings changed, I remained, offering my services to those who sought me.

"Then one found me with a commission most strange. I was to follow a small party, not more than four, and as they made their way through Mercia, I was to attack them, but in such a way that only my own men be killed, though I might wound some of those I attacked. Then, when I had lost two or three men, I was to withdraw. It was no hard task to find men to lose, and the trail was easy to follow, for the man who gave me gold laid marks, cut in trees and by the path, to know which way they had gone.

"So I did as he had said, although when I found him, there were more than four of them, for they had joined with others. However, I had men, and more than enough, to lose. I did what he had bid me, and withdrew when enough blood had flowed. Returning the next day, I found the rest of what he had promised me, buried beneath the ashes of the fire."

Garmund looked at the queen. "The king who outlawed me was Oswald. This was my land. And I knew the man who came to find me in the wild lands, and who paid for the lives of my men, although he sought to conceal his face from me. Would you like to know who it was?"

"Yes," said Eanflæd. "Yes, I would."

"Æthelwin. The king's warmaster."

"Æthelwin. You are sure?"

"Yes. I am sure."

The queen stared at the outlaw. "Know this, and know it well.

Your testimony will not win your lands back. It will not win favour with the king, or with me. You will be judged and sentenced as an outlaw, as one who set his sword against the king – and that is a crime that shall be met by death. Do you still hold to what you have told me?"

Garmund shrugged. "I am going to die anyway. Why tell me that which I know? But you did not know what I have told you. I was a faithful thegn and true. By telling you this I may die as one."

"Very well." The queen gestured for her guards to take Garmund away. "Give him to eat and drink, but be sure he does not escape." Then, with Garmund gone, she turned to Œthelwald. "That is what he told you?"

"Yes. When I ran his gang down, I was going to hang them all, there and then, but he told me he had news that the king must hear. When I made to hang him anyway, he told me the story. Does he speak truly?"

"Very few people in our kingdom know of the attack upon the king when he travelled into Mercia. That Garmund does know suggests he speaks the truth. But why should Æthelwin hire men to attack them?"

"Oh, that is not so hard to understand, Eanflæd the Wise. To win favour for himself. To cast suspicion on another. No, it is really not so hard to understand."

But still Eanflæd shook her head. "Yet I have sat at table with him; I have given him the cup to drink after battle. Æthelwin seeks ever the king's greatness."

"And so his own." Œthelwald spat. "How else could such a man, with the blood of farmers and peasants, rise so high but by the king's favour? But so tight is he in the king's counsel, I would wager he might try to climb even higher – even to claiming a throne."

"You do not think he would kill the king?" asked Eanflæd, still seeking to understand that which she had heard.

"No. But my uncle may soon have a throne in his gift to give. And who better to give it to than his most faithful and loyal servant?" Œthelwald grimaced. "Certainly my uncle would rather give it to a servant than someone of his own blood – for the throne of Deira taken by an Iding he sees as a threat to him. But a warmaster, raised by his favour, will seem no such threat to my uncle. So Æthelwin will be a king while I continue to ride the marches, playing hide and seek with bands of outlaws. Such is the way with kings."

"But not with queens." Eanflæd held her hand out to the young ætheling. "I will remember what you have done."

Œthelwald looked at the hand held to him, but he did not take it.

"Rhieienmelth was as a mother to me. I will not take the hand of the woman who took her place. But know this, Eanflæd whom men call the Wise: now I have met you, I will put aside the despite I have long nurtured for you in my heart, for I can see that men speak truly when they speak of you. Wise, and subtle indeed, knowing well how to sow confusion in the hearts of those who would oppose you. For me, it were best that I go, lest this honey grow too sweet. But you are beautiful indeed, queen to my uncle. Do not forget me." And suddenly Œthelwald took the queen's hand and pressed it to his lips.

Before Eanflæd could say anything, Œthelwald let go her hand and, leaping to the door to the hall, called his men to follow.

They were well trained. Only a little grumbling attended such a call, and within a few minutes they were all out of the hall again and astride their horses. At their head sat the ætheling. He made an elaborate courtesy to the queen.

"I give you Garmund as a present for my uncle – may he learn from him whom he may trust, and whom he may not. I go to ride the marches until I am called." Œthelwald signalled his men forward, and then turned and waved.

"Farewell," he called.

Under the purple and gold banner of the Idings, the ætheling, son of King Oswald, rode away.

Eanflæd the Wise remained standing without the hall watching, until he and his men disappeared into the shifting haze of the summer's heat.

"Mummy, Mummy, can I go down to the river to swim?" asked Ecgfrith, tugging her arm. "It's too hot."

But the queen, still looking to where she had last seen Œthelwald and his men, slowly shook her head.

"No," she said. "No, you had better not." The queen turned to her guard. "Bring me a messenger. I must send word to the king."

"Hold."

Eanflæd heard the call, weak but insistent. From where he sat outside the hall, Aidan gestured to her and she went to him, with Ecgfrith trailing behind.

"You heard what this Garmund had to say?" the queen asked Aidan. "The king must know of this."

"Yes, he must," said Aidan. "But such a message would best be given in person."

Eanflæd looked past the monk and out of the valley. She looked down at Aidan. "You are right. I will go to the king when I receive word of where to find him. But... Æthelwin. Why should he do such a thing?"

Aidan shook his head. "The tempter is subtle and twists men to their ruin by dangling the good in front of them." His eyes narrowed. "And he has laid his snares for one greater than Æthelwin. It is our task, O queen, to free him from those snares."

Chapter 13

"It is too hot to sleep." Oswine the Godfriend sat up, only to see Tondhere, his guard and companion, already awake. He looked at him in the dim light of the few torches that still burned. "I will go outside. It will be cooler there, at least until the sun rises."

Tondhere stood up as the king rose, but Oswine held up his hand. "You do not have to come with me. We are safe here, in Hunwald's hall."

"I would come with you, lord, if I may. For the heat has kept me from sleep also, and I would take some air with you."

Oswine nodded, not wishing to wake any of the slaves and servants who lay about the hall, wherever they might best find some shred of breeze to cool their sleeping. Picking their way through the dark shapes, it seemed only the dogs stirred at their passing, raising heavy heads and staring up at the two men, then letting weary muzzles fall back onto outstretched paws.

The door warden, sitting at his post, head nodding as he battled sleep, roused at their approach.

"We go to take some air," Oswine said quietly.

Stifling a yawn, the warden unbarred the door and pulled it open. The night air greeted them. It was cool and carried the scents of this hot summer: ripening wheat and barley, the dust thrown up by the day's hot wind, the faint taste of smoke. Even without the burnings of Oswiu and his army, there would have been smoke in such a tinder-dry season: sparks from metal horseshoe on stone, a dry lightning strike, embers left untended – each of these might start a fire. But now, men burned their way through Deira.

Oswine stepped out from under the eaves of Hunwald's hall and looked up at the sky. Although the night was clear and cloudless, the stars seemed veiled and indistinct, as if the finest of nets had been hung over the sky. Try as he might, he could not see the Milky Way. The king walked further away from the hall, with Tondhere following, letting his night sight develop. But when he stopped again, with the hall but a distant shadow against further shadows, he still could not see that which he was looking for. Oswine turned to his guard.

"My mother told me that when the world was young and there were as yet no stars in the sky, a young boy was sent by his stepmother to climb a tree, for there was a hive in its topmost branches. But the boy, being wise, thought that the bees would sting him for taking their honey. So, before he climbed, he went in secret to his stepmother's cow, the one that she never allowed him to drink from, and filled a bucket with sweet milk. Then, putting the handle of the bucket around his neck, he began to climb the tree. He climbed and he climbed, yet the hive at the top of the tree seemed to get no nearer, even though he had been climbing all day. For though he did not know it, his stepmother had set him to climb the tree that holds up the sky. Looking down, he saw the world far below, and his stepmother looking no bigger than an ant and waving a stick at him, shouting that she would beat him if he did not bring the honey from the tree. So, despite his fear, the boy kept climbing, higher and higher, until the day ended and the night came. But there were no stars and the boy could not see his hand, even when he held it in front of his face. Holding the tree, the boy clung on. Then, in the quiet above the world, he heard a hum: the sound of bees, sleeping in their hive. They were close, very close. So, feeling his way, he crept closer. But as he got closer, he could hear the hum getting louder and angrier, for the bees could hear him, and they would not have anyone steal their honey. Then the boy reached for the pail, telling the bees that he had brought them sweet milk to drink in return for their honey. But in reaching for the pail of milk, he slipped and fell, and the milk spilled from the bucket. As it fell from the tree that held up the sky, it made the Milky Way that we see to this day."

Tondhere waited. But the king said no more.

"What happened to the boy?" Tondhere said eventually.

"He died," said Oswine.

"And the stepmother?"

"Went without honey."

"Oh," said Tondhere. He stared up at the sky too, trying to make out the Milky Way. "I don't like that story."

Oswine laughed. "Nor me. My mother said I cried when she told it to me." He breathed the cool night air. "It is good to be outside, even if we can't see the Milky Way." He turned to Tondhere. "Do you think me mad, or a coward, for disbanding the army and sending them home?"

Addressed with such a question, Tondhere was glad that the night concealed his expression.

"I – I know you had true reason, lord, for what you did."

"Yes. Yes, I did. I would not, as that boy did, be made to climb a tree without end for a prize beyond reach. There would have been no victor in the battle we would have faced, only different defeats. Therefore, it were better not to climb the tree at all." Oswine laughed again. "My mother always said I would understand the story when the time came. It seems she was right."

But Tondhere did not hear the king's answer. Alert to every sound in the night, he heard the crack, as of a branch breaking when some unwary foot steps upon it. He turned, searching for the source of the sound, trying to pierce the dark that lay over the world and see into its shadows.

There, just west, beyond the hedge and fence that marked Hunwald's hall from the farmland surrounding it, were the small humps of the houses of Gilling. No lights sparked from them, nor any movement, for there was as yet no hint of dawn in the eastern sky and the people slept as best they could against the weariness of the long heat of the day to come.

But then, turning towards the hall, Tondhere saw shadows moving towards them.

"Lord," he whispered, taking Oswine's arm. "Look."

Oswine, seeing, whispered to Tondhere, "It is most likely the door warden, come to see if all is well. But…" He pointed towards a nearby shadow. There, trees and bushes tangled together so that two men hiding might never be found on a night so dark.

As they began to make a silent way towards the trees, a voice hailed them from the darkness.

"Lord."

A familiar voice.

"Lord, it is I, Hunwald."

Oswine straightened from his crouch and turned towards his warmaster. Tondhere followed, but since the hail was not meant for him, he looked beyond the approaching shadow of the warmaster and saw there many more shadows, spreading quietly to right and left, and he heard the faint hiss of metal sliding from oiled wood, and he leapt for his lord, seeking to get his hand over the king's mouth before he could reply and give away their position.

"Hunwald, over here."

Too late.

The shadow, hearing Oswine's call, straightened its path towards them. Tondhere, looking beyond, saw the other shadows each align towards them, and approach. Slipping his sword from its sheath, Tondhere stepped to the king.

"Lord, this is not right. Hunwald brings too many men with him."

Oswine, seeing the shadows closing in around them, called again.

"Hunwald?"

"It is I, lord."

And out of the darkness, the warmaster emerged. But he was not alone. At his shoulder stood another.

"Æthelwin." Oswine looked to his own warmaster. "I do not suppose you have brought Æthelwin here as prisoner?"

"You shall be the prisoner taken here," said Hunwald, drawing his sword.

From all around there came the sound of metal sliding over wood. Tondhere, standing with his back to his lord, saw that they were surrounded. He scanned around, counting. A score or more of men. Against two. And with Hunwald among the attackers, there would be no help coming from the men of his hall. They were alone.

"So, you would betray me, old friend?"

"You are no friend to Deira," said Hunwald.

"I am its king. And you are pledged to me, Hunwald." The king stood with his hand upon his sword, but he had not yet drawn it. "There is still time. Mayhap not to save me, not when you have brought so many to take one man, but to save your soul. There is time for that."

"I will have saved Deira, by ridding it of a coward king."

Oswine stood still. For the moment, Hunwald and Æthelwin were advancing no further, but he could hear the slow, stealthy movement of the men encircling them. There was no escape.

"Lord," whispered Tondhere, his back to his king and his eyes looking behind, while his sword slowly tracked from right to left, "I will attack. Come behind me. In the dark, you may escape."

"No," said Oswine. "No, I would have no more men die for my sake, in body or in soul." He looked to Hunwald and the silent figure of Æthelwin beside him. "Spare Tondhere. He has no part in this."

"No!" said Tondhere. "I would not live at your expense."

"Oh, do not worry," said Æthelwin. "You won't." He looked to the warmaster standing beside him in the dark. "Finish this, Hunwald, and prove your loyalty – prove that you are throne-worthy."

"So they promised you a throne, did they?" Oswine laughed. "For such little things we sell ourselves – and I no less than you. I would give you the throne myself, Hunwald, if it would save you. But I fear that it will condemn you instead."

"You are the one condemned!" Hunwald rushed forward, sword raised, ready to bring it down in the killing cut that ran from where the neck met the shoulder crosswise across the body.

But Oswine the Godfriend did not raise his sword to meet the charge. He looked steadily at the onrushing thegn and there was no fear in his eyes at death's approach. There was no hatred either; only pity.

And before those eyes, Hunwald's charge faltered.

He stood before the king, his sword raised, but unable to bring it down. "Fight me," Hunwald screamed. "Fight me!"

But the king slowly shook his head. "I will not fight a friend, Hunwald." He spread his arms. "If you will, do what you came to do."

"Take your sword," said Hunwald. "Fight me." Across his face, emotions warred. "Please…"

But Oswine stepped towards his warmaster and embraced him. The sword dropped from Hunwald's hand.

"You will live," Oswine said. "You will…"

But he had no chance to finish what he had to say.

"You won't," said Æthelwin.

The blade pierced Oswine, emerging from his chest, and Hunwald saw the king look down at it. There was no surprise in his eyes as he saw his own death. He looked up, one final time, at his warmaster, then fell.

"No!" Tondhere leapt towards Æthelwin screaming, but before he had moved more than a few feet three blades cut him down.

Hunwald stared at the two bodies lying at his feet. He heard Æthelwin approaching and he did not have to look to know that the warmaster's sword was raised.

"Finish it," Hunwald said.

Chapter 14

The horsemen rode into the king's camp. They rode under the flag of the Idings, though they passed through Deira, and the sentries on watch knew well their faces and their mission, and let them through the picket to ride in haste to where the king waited.

Hearing the hooves, then seeing them, Oswiu rose from where he had been playing dice with his son and Acca. Ahlfrith and the scop rose to their feet too, waiting while the dust- and sweat-stained rider hauled his horse to a halt and dismounted.

Æthelwin, warmaster of Bernicia, made the courtesy to his king.

"Well?" said Oswiu.

The warmaster grinned. "There shall be a new king in Deira."

Oswiu closed his eyes briefly. Then he looked to his warmaster. "You have done well, Æthelwin. I will not forget this."

The warmaster bowed his head. "Thank you, lord."

"Hunwald?"

"He will not be the next king of Deira."

Oswiu looked to the troop of riders dismounting, scanning down their line.

"Any casualties?"

"No." For the first time, Æthelwin looked somewhat disconcerted. "He did not fight."

"Who? Who did not fight?"

"Oswine. The Godfriend. He would not draw sword."

Oswiu nodded slowly but, hearing this, Ahlfrith stepped forward. "Are you saying you killed the king in cold blood?"

Warmaster looked at ætheling. "What would you have had me do? Leave him to raise an army against us again?"

"You could have brought him before the king alive." Ahlfrith shook his head. "This is murder." He turned to his father. "You want the rule of Deira? They will never accept you now."

"They wouldn't accept me before!" said Oswiu. "Now they will fear me, and take as king a man they will have reason to fear: Æthelwin."

"Æthelwin." Ahlfrith stared at his father. "You would make him king in Deira? His mother was a slave!"

"He is loyal to me."

"So am I!"

Father and son, king and ætheling, faced each other, and the camp, hearing them, fell into the listening silence that always came upon men when there was open discord in the ruling family.

"I have ever served you, Father, faithfully and well. And now, when you would make a king in Deira, you turn to one who is not even of our blood. Tell me, where have I failed you to earn such despite? For fail you I must have done to be treated in such manner."

But Oswiu shook his head. "No, no, you have not failed me. Indeed, you have served me too well, for I cannot be without you, even to place you on a throne. Not yet. Not while your brother is still a child and can take little part in ruling the kingdom. But you must also know that the witan of Deira would never accept a son of mine as king. That is why I have chosen Æthelwin to be king, for they will accept him."

Ahlfrith stared at his father, then shook his head. "I would not take a throne earned by murder, for it will surely be tainted by Oswine's death, and blood feud shall follow he who takes the throne." He turned to the warmaster. "You earned this throne by treachery. Know that treachery will follow you wherever you go."

Æthelwin merely smiled at that. "Let it," he said. "I know how to sniff out traitors. And how to deal with them."

"Very well," said Oswiu. "Send out messengers. Summon the witan of Deira, that it may help choose a new king. And Acca…" The king turned to the scop. "Take some men and carry the good news to the queen. And make a song of this."

Acca made the courtesy. "I will take word to the queen," he said. "But there is no song in it," he added softly, as he turned away from the king.

Aidan saw him coming. He had seen him even before he came into sight, but the short line of riders appearing and disappearing as the path to Ad Gefrin wound over the dips and ridges of the land told him by sight what he had already learned in his heart.

He signed to the monk who was caring for him – signed because his breath was so short he could speak at nothing more than a whisper – and when the monk leaned to him to hear, Aidan asked him to fetch the queen.

"And Coifi," he added. The old priest would be happy to see his friend.

Aidan closed his eyes to wait. In this hot summer, he had asked to be left outside, sitting against the hall with sight of land and sky, rather than being brought within where all he could see was walls. There was no danger of him getting cold. Even were the nights not so warm, his own body burned.

"I'm sweating out my sins." That's what he had told the monks who tended him, bathing his brow and applying cold compresses to his wrists and ankles. He hoped it was true. The weight of his wrongdoing hung over him, as much in what he had failed to do as in what he had actually done. When his mind was at its clearest – for sometimes, when the fever grew more intense, he lapsed into a waking dream – he had called a priest to him and, over many hours, told out the extent of his failings, calling down God's mercy on him, that the Ransomer might know the full extent of the ransom he must pay.

Now, he waited. He heard steps approaching, then stopping beside him. The queen. Others followed, more hesitant, setting off in one direction then taking another. Coifi.

"It is Acca," he whispered.

In the quiet of waiting, they heard him.

Through the quiet, he could hear the hooves, drumming over the dry earth. If there was not rain soon, there would be famine next year, for the crops were failing in the fields, withering under the relentless weight of the sun.

The riders were coming close. Aidan began the long struggle to open and focus his eyes.

As he succeeded in seeing, the riders drew up outside the hall. Seeing, as it were, for the first time, he saw the foam flecking the beasts' flanks, for they had ridden long and hard under a cruel sun. Saliva dripped from bits, but not enough – the animals were parched with thirst, their eyes rolling as the knowledge of the nearness of water coursed through them. Their riders were almost as thirsty, with lips dry and cracked, and eyes red with the kicked up dust of their riding.

Once, Acca would have swung from his horse as lithely as a boy and come striding to those watching with all the spirit of a man who has just won three duels on the cloak. But now, older, with his hair near as much grey as gold, he eased himself from the saddle. On foot, Acca held to his saddle for a moment, as he made sure he could stand. Only then did he let go and make the courtesy to the queen.

That at least was done, Aidan saw, with all the flamboyance of old. Acca had an audience and he was going to play to it.

"O queen, I come bearing tidings from his majesty, our king."

But, unfortunately for Acca, Eanflæd was not inclined to let him drag out the message giving.

"Yes, yes. Tell me, what news? Is he well? Has he found Oswine? I see no signs of battle on the men with you."

Acca, unable to refrain, sighed. News, properly told, required preparation, teasing, riddling and revealing. It seemed, though, the queen did not want it properly told, but simply related. For that, any fool messenger with ample memory and no wit would have sufficed. But no, the king had chosen the scop, and now he had to give the message like an ordinary messenger. However, Acca knew that such were the indignities that attended his calling.

"Yes, the king is well. Yes, he found Oswine. You see no sign of battle because there was none. Oswine disbanded his army and fled from us."

Eanflæd relaxed with the first relief. Her husband lived. But there was the other fear that had been gnawing at her heart, and now it surged anew.

"You say there was no battle. Has the king taken Oswine hostage then?"

"No." Acca shook his head and this time there was no artifice to his sigh. "Oswine was betrayed to us by his warmaster. Æthelwin rode to where the Godfriend was to be found and killed him there."

He did not think he had the strength left to him, yet Aidan, hearing his fear made word, groaned, and all heard his pain. The queen, for her part, did not hear, for hearing the news her face had blanched.

"He murdered him," she whispered.

And though Acca would have denied it, he could not.

"The – the king asks you to join him, and swiftly. He has summoned the witan of Deira to hear whom he wishes to be their king."

"And who does he intend to put on the throne?"

Acca paused. This was news indeed, and it seemed wrong to waste it, but the queen stepped forward in her eagerness to hear, and even Coifi had given over looking after the shifting of sunbeams and the play of wind to wait upon his answer.

"The warmaster. Æthelwin."

Acca had thought the news would bring surprise – the son of a slave made into a king was, after all, worthy of surprise – but he had not expected to see horror. However, that was what he saw on the face of the queen, and on that of the monk, while Coifi spat in the dust, and the watching and listening guards and slaves looked to each other and whispered, with much shaking of heads.

Aidan signed to the queen and she bent down to him.

"You must go to him," said Aidan. "Take Garmund. Take guards too. If Æthelwin has had word of what we know, it may be that he will try to stop you reaching the king."

Eanflæd took the monk's hand. It burned within hers.

"It will be difficult to convince him, for he has trusted Æthelwin through many years and many campaigns. If you could speak too, it would help."

But Aidan shook his head. "There is only one journey I will make from here, and it is to stand before a different, greater king. But remember this: Æthelwin is the lesser part. We fight, together, for the king's soul, that the stain of this murder not dye it black."

Eanflæd nodded. "Yes. We will fight for him."

Aidan smiled. "If not us, his wife and his oldest friend, who else? Now, my child, you must go in all haste. I will wait for you here…"

Even as the queen rose and took her leave, she knew the monk's final words to be a kind leaving. She would not see him more in this middle-earth.

The preparations were all but made, for the queen had known that she must seek her husband to give him the news of his warmaster's treachery. Eanflæd left before afternoon had drifted down to evening. Before her leaving, she had gone to bid farewell to Aidan but, finding him sleeping, she spoke not. Kneeling beside him, she pressed her lips to his hand and then went, without word, to the waiting horses. On such an urgent errand, the queen was determined to ride rather than take the slow-moving ox wagons that usually carried her from one royal estate to another.

Aidan woke after her leaving. The evening was drawing in. The sun had settled behind the long ridges of the Cheviots, and the hills cast their shadows over the land. He watched the night draw down over the land. He watched the stars come out. He watched, finally, the Milky Way lay its cloak of light over the sky.

He would not see day again.

Aidan knew this. He knew it as he had known that Acca rode to them.

The tempter had caught the king in his snare.

Here, lying against the wall of the king's hall, unable to move and barely able to speak, he must strive to set him free.

The soft breath beside him told that the monk watching him slept. That was as well.

There had been a story, his mother had told him, of how the Milky Way was the river by which men's prayers ascended to heaven. She said that if you looked, you could see them leaping upwards, as salmon leapt a waterfall, sometimes falling back but always trying again. As a boy, he had looked but not seen.

Now, as a man, he looked and finally saw.

He had a prayer to send up the river of prayers to the high heaven.

He prayed it now, his lips moving, but no ears of man might have heard what he said.

"Lord, I ask that you take my life as blood payment for the king's crime. Lay it not against him, but let him live."

Aidan looked up, searching for sight of his prayer ascending the river of stars. But his sight was fading and the stars were growing dim.

"Please, let him live," the monk said.

And then the stars went out.

Chapter 15

The witan had assembled. For the first time since the death of Oswald, the witan of Deira had come together with an Iding present.

They were crammed into the hall of the thegn of Ripon; he was a thegn of little fame, and his hall was the match to his name: narrow and mean. The thegns were squeezed upon the benches within, and though the doors were propped open and slaves had been set to waving sheaves of bulrushes to create a breeze, yet heat hung over the tightly packed thegns, and the smell of their sweat filled the hall.

Oswiu stood. All eyes in the hall turned towards him. All except those of the man sat beside him. Æthelwin looked at the assembled thegns as a king, assessing them, measuring them, weighing their worth in his mind.

Oswiu looked around the hall. Some faces he had known as they arrived, memory of them dredged from when Oswald ruled in Deira and he had ridden alongside some of these thegns in battle and on patrol. Those, reminded of the time they had marched alongside Oswiu, had thawed a little, and gifts of gold had melted them further, along with hints, to be spread among their peers, that Oswiu had no wish to claim the throne of Deira for himself, but would bring before the witan a man acceptable to them.

But others had turned their faces from him when he greeted them, and had spoken against him to their fellows. For many now knew of the manner of Oswine's dying and those who did not were soon told. Some had muttered against Oswiu, but none had turned their hand against him. They were waiting for the relatives of the Godfriend to come – but they had not come. Oswiu had sent further messengers to summon to the witan the branch of the Yffings to which Oswine Godfriend had belonged, but the messengers had returned unanswered: either the halls they had sought were empty, or the men they had delivered their summons to would not give answer to the call.

Oswiu nodded to Acca.

"*Hwæt!*" The scop, his voice trained in calling to attention a hall full of drinking, talking, boasting men, had no difficulty in summoning those watching to silence.

"Men of Deira." Oswiu spoke, and they looked upon him, but most of the eyes looking to him were hooded and more of the faces veiled.

"Men of Deira, you have heard tell that I killed your king by treachery. You have heard that he was murdered, when he sent you home to live. Men of Deira, you have heard that God's friend was killed by the devil's deed.

"Men of Deira, you have heard true."

Every eye turned to Oswiu, and where they were hooded before, and the faces blank, now they were filled with surprise. Whispers filled the hall, flittering between the benches and spreading to the men standing without. And, sitting beside him, Oswiu felt another gaze turn upon him in surprise.

"One of your own gave your king into my hands – Hunwald, the king's warmaster. One of your own betrayed him."

The whispers grew, but more men nodded, for rumour of Hunwald's part in Oswine's death had already spread far and wide.

"But one of my own betrayed my wish that Oswine be taken captive, and killed him."

Beside him, Oswiu sensed the warmaster staring up at him, but he did not take his eyes from the witan.

"One of my own is traitor to me as Hunwald was traitor to Oswine."

They were with him now, as they had never been before.

"I have nurtured a viper in my house and he has bitten you and he has bitten me. Men of Deira, I ask your forgiveness and I bid you take vengeance, for you and for me. For a traitor to his lord does not deserve to live."

Oswiu let the knife hiding under his sleeve slip down into his hand. With a single, smooth movement, he brought the point against his warmaster's neck.

The men of Deira rose to their feet as one. Shouts and cries and calls rang through the hall. Blood vengeance, a vengeance they had thought denied them, woke in red mist.

And Æthelwin stared up, as helpless as a spring lamb, at his king. "Lord," he asked, "why?"

For answer, Oswiu pointed to the hall door. There, the men gathered were slowly parted, and in the gap appeared Eanflæd the queen and, with her, Garmund.

"How many others did you cast down, warmaster? I gave over my queen, the mother of my children, because of your lies."

Æthelwin put his hand to the blade. He began to push it in.

But Oswiu pulled the knife free, its edge cutting red slices along the warmaster's fingers.

"You die by my will, not yours," he said.

The warmaster slowly stood. Blood dripped from his hand. Around the high table, men were gathering, looping rope to make a noose.

"My only betrayal was that I sought to serve you where you could not help yourself. Rhieienmelth was no queen for you. But you could not see that. So I made you see it." The first hand reached for the warmaster, but he shook it off. "I did for you what you would not do for yourself."

More hands reached for him, and this time there were too many for Æthelwin to shake off. They pulled him from his feet and laid him out on the floor, binding his hands and his feet, looping the noose around his neck.

They threw the rope over one of the beams holding up the ceiling. They pulled the warmaster to his feet, then they drew him into the air. Æthelwin stared at Oswiu when first the rope tightened round his throat, but the men surrounding him rained blows upon him, jerking him this way and that, taking vengeance for their king, and the warmaster spun away. But his dying was long, and he turned back to the king many times before the end.

Even after Æthelwin was dead, the men of Deira continued to strike and spit upon the body.

"Cut him down," said Oswiu, eventually. "Cut him down!" he shouted, when they continued to rain blows upon the warmaster.

The men of his own army, faces still shocked and appalled at what had happened, cut Æthelwin down.

"Take him outside and bury him," Oswiu said. "Bury him well, for he was long my friend."

As the men carried Æthelwin out, Oswiu turned to the death-sated faces of the witan. "Men of Deira, I would give you a king. A king that you may trust, for I know you will not trust one of my family. A king that I may trust, for I have been too trusting. Would you have such a king?"

The witan was still too blood full to cry out, but many men nodded, and some cried "Aye", and none gainsaid the king's words.

"I too. An ætheling, most throne-worthy. A man who has proven his truth to me when I gave him no chance to do so. A man of your blood, men of Deira." Oswiu turned towards the door, where the queen stood with Garmund beside her. But now another stood there with her.

"Œthelwald, Oswald son."

And the men of Deira acclaimed him.

When Œthelwald came in and passed among his people, speaking to some, shaking hands with others, Oswiu slipped through the excited crowd of thegns to the queen.

"You did right, going to fetch Œthelwald before coming to me," he said.

Eanflæd nodded, but her mind was elsewhere. "Pray we have not an end like Æthelwin," she said.

Oswiu's face hardened. "He betrayed me," he said.

The queen looked up at him. "He did that which your heart most darkly desired," she said.

"I did not desire to put away my queen…"

Eanflæd looked to him, and the king fell silent.

"I meant the murder of Oswine."

"It is not murder to kill a king who has taken up arms against you," said Oswiu.

"But what of killing a king who has lain down his arms? Is that not murder? Will the blood price not stalk us, and stalk our line, until it is paid?"

Oswiu looked away. "There be few Yffings left. There are not enough to pursue a blood feud."

"Nevertheless, let us stop it now." The queen came and stood once more in front of her husband. "I will make a holy house near to where Oswine died, and endow it and the monks therein to pray perpetually for the soul of the Godfriend, that it may rest. I have spoken already with some people here, and they have told me of a kinsman of Oswine, a good man and holy, who has been ordained a priest. He would be the abbot of this holy house, and by making him so, you would heal the blood feud now, before it begins."

Oswiu nodded. "Yes. Let it be so. Now, I must go and speak with Œthelwald. We have much to settle."

Eanflæd the Wise watched her husband go back into the hall. And as he went, she said under her breath what she had said already: "I will make a holy house near to where Oswine died, and endow it and the monks therein to pray perpetually for the soul of the Godfriend.

"And for yours, my husband. And for yours."

PART 4

Reckoning

Chapter 1

"They're here, Mummy! They're here!"

An excited Ecgfrith ran to find the queen, and tugged her, although she protested unavailingly that she was in the middle of weaving, to his vantage point.

"There, look!"

He pointed and the queen saw. Rowing across the great river, the Tyne, the ferry boats were bringing riders. The men had dismounted and were standing by their horses, calming them through the river crossing, while excited fishermen, seeing the prospect for silver, rowed their own boats towards the southern bank to offer rides across the river for the riders who still waited on the southern shore.

The riders had come north on the road of the emperors. Once, when the emperors still ruled this land, the Tyne had been crossed by a bridge, but the bridge had fallen many years back, and while some of the starlings still stood in the river, the bridge itself was reduced to broken-down towers and trailing timbers. Ferrymen now carried travellers across a river they had once walked over, dry shod. One boat was usually enough, but a crowd of impatient riders swirled around the pier on the south bank of the river, waiting to be taken over.

"Go and tell your father," said Eanflæd. "He'll need to know."

"And Ahlflæd? Should I run and tell her, Mummy? She'll want to know, won't she?"

The queen thought for a moment, then shook her head. "Ahlflæd will know soon enough. Leave her in peace for the time left her."

While Ecgfrith ran off to find the king, Eanflæd walked out from the hall to a rise that looked down to the river. From there she could see better. The first ferry had all but crossed the river. There was a banner flying from the boat, but as the river wind blew it, the shape shifted before her eyes, refusing to resolve into a shape she could make out. But then the wind settled and held the banner out for her: the sign of the Red Hand.

Peada had come to claim his bride.

*

"So, we are agreed." Oswiu looked over the table to where Peada sat holding a cup of wine in his hand while he looked round the king's hall. "The bride price shall be seven white mares, a hundredweight of silver…"

"Yes, yes," said the Red Hand. "What we said."

"I will have Utta write it down."

Peada looked at Oswiu, surprised. "Can't you remember it?"

"Of course I can remember what we have agreed. But by writing it down, should there come a day when memories do not agree, we can look to see what is in the book."

The Red Hand suddenly focused on Oswiu. "And who will read what is written down? Your priest?"

"You will have priests of your own to read what is written. You remember that?"

"Yes, of course. Ahlflæd will bring her priest. And I will go under the water. I will take the salt." The Red Hand smiled. "I will abjure the gods of my father."

Oswiu nodded, slowly. "That is no small thing you have agreed to. Think on it well before you say again yes."

"My father has made me the king of the Middle Angles, but I rule them only in his name. I would rule in my own name, with no grasping hand reaching to me for the gold I have taken in battle and tribute. Let all know that I follow this new god, and then all will see that the land of the Middle Angles is mine, whatever my father might say." The Red Hand leaned over the table towards Oswiu. "If he wants the throne back, let him try to take it. Then we shall see who is the greater man."

The king, seeing that Peada's cup was near empty, signalled to a slave to fill it again.

"It is no small thing for a father to meet a son upon the field of slaughter – and such a meeting would bring grief to a mother," said Oswiu.

Peada, his wine cup full again, proceeded to drain most of it. "My mother takes always my father's part. What do you expect? She is the daughter of a ceorl. Look hard enough and you can see the earth under her nails. But I, I am a descendant of Icel and of Woden."

"I have heard other tales of your father's descent."

The Red Hand stared at Oswiu with suddenly narrowed eyes. "They are lies," he said. "I come by true line from Icel, and he through five generations from Wihtlæg, Woden son."

Oswiu smiled and, reaching across the table, filled the Red Hand's cup himself. "Then we are cousins," he said. "For we Idings are descendants from Woden too."

Peada raised his cup. "Your health, cousin."

Raising his cup, Oswiu returned the toast. "As cousin, you will of course want the marriage terms for your wife to be right as well," he said.

Peada, working his way through this new cup of wine, grunted his agreement. Oswiu, glancing at the line of empty jars along the back of the hall, wondered just how much the Red Hand could drink. So far, all that he could see was a redness in the man's eyes and a slight slur to some of his speech. But he still picked up each cup unerringly and drank without spilling any wine.

Oswiu continued. "The gold and silver Ahlflæd shall bring with her when she comes to you will be hers to use."

Peada grunted his agreement. "I have gold enough – I don't need that which a woman brings me."

"Ahlflæd shall have a priest to serve her – one selected by Abbot Finan. And even if a bishop be found for the Middle Angles, the priest serving my daughter shall not answer to him but to Abbot Finan."

The Red Hand waved his hand. Oswiu noted that there was to the movement, at long last, some of the imprecision that takes limbs when they are steeped in wine.

"These priests – I do not think it matters which god they serve. They are all more concerned with how close they sit to the king at the high table than anything else."

"Really? I could hardly ever persuade Aidan to sit at the high table with me," said Oswiu.

Peada's eyes suddenly focused on the king, and in that instant Oswiu knew what it must be like to stand opposite the Red Hand in the shieldwall. It would take a brave man not to flinch.

"Then, by his reluctance, did you not bring this Aidan to a place of even higher honour than before?"

"You did not know him," said Oswiu. "He sought no such honour."

But Peada shook his head. "All men seek advantage, whether it be in battle or bed." He leered at the king. "Let us finish this, that I may the quicker take my wife to bed."

Oswiu nodded. He could not help but glance to the door of the hall. His daughter waited without, to hear whether marriage terms were settled; whether this man before him would be her husband. He had seen her when he went into the hall, her face white and set, like that of a man about to go into battle for the first time, setting his courage against that which was to come. And he remembered Ahlflæd as a girl, forever racing her brother across the courtyard and alongside the wagons as the royal household made its slow way from one estate to another. Forever racing and forever winning, her tongue stuck out in triumph as her panting, angry brother followed her to the finish, then skipping out of the way as he tried to pull her down. He remembered her, a woman, standing on the wall at Bamburgh and calling all eyes upon her as she challenged the men fighting beneath her to stop. There were few like his daughter. She was as a horse from the morning of the world.

Oswiu looked across the table at the man before him. Could he really marry his daughter to the Red Hand?

He got up.

Peada looked up at him, eyes finally bleary with wine. "Where… where are you going?" he asked.

Oswiu pointed at the drained cups on the table. "What goes in must come out," he said.

Peada nodded, then held his cup out to a slave. "It's empty."

While the servant refilled the cup, Oswiu hurried to the door.

"Let him through, door warden," Peada yelled after Oswiu, "or your king will piss his trousers."

As the door warden stood aside, attempting to hide a grin, Oswiu grabbed him. "Where is my daughter? Where is Princess Ahlflæd?"

The warden, startled from the joke, pointed north, to where the Wall ran across the ridgetops as they slid down towards the sea twelve miles to the east. "She took the path to the Wall, lord."

"How long hence? You did not let her go forth alone, did you?"

"Not long, lord. Soon after you went into the hall to speak with the Red Hand. I would have sent men with her, but she would have none – the Princess Ahlflæd is a difficult one to shift, lord. I – I could have come in and told you. But I thought you would not wish to be disturbed while you spoke with the Red Hand. Did I do wrong?"

"Yes, but I have no blame for you. She is the least biddable child I have known, ever fixed upon doing her will. She would not change from it, not if all the people of this middle-earth bid her. You could only have stopped her by laying hands on her, and that you may not do." Oswiu glanced back into the hall.

"Go in to the Red Hand. Tell him Oswiu, the king, must needs remain without a while longer, and when he asks why, let him know, without saying, that it is the wine that has told upon me, and that which was within has come out by the way it went in. He will be pleased with that. Then see that he is given to drink, to his fill and more. I will return as soon as I may."

While the door warden went in with his message, Oswiu looked for sign of his daughter. He saw her, picking her way through grass and gorse and rock towards the Wall. The king shook his head. Even this close to a royal hall, it was still not wise for a woman to walk alone.

"Ahlflæd." He called to her, and again. "Ahlflæd!"

She gave no sign of hearing, but began, by the steps cut into it, to climb upon the Wall. In some few places along its length, the Wall had broken, worn down by wind and frost and rain, or else by attacks from the people north of the Wall, when the emperor's soldiers still manned it; but for most of its length it cut straight and intact across the land, as unyielding as a blood oath.

Oswiu saw his daughter standing upon it now, her back turned to him, looking to the north. The king did not call to her again. If she had not heard him the first time, he did not want to risk her hearing him the second time and making off along the broad path atop the Wall. Should Ahlflæd decide she would not speak with her father, it would be an easy matter for her to outpace him along the Wall.

Climbing the steps onto the walkway, the king at once felt the wind's lash. Steadying himself, he marvelled at the ease with which Ahlflæd faced the wind, as if it were no more than a breeze.

"Ahlflæd."

Now she heard him. She turned to her father. Her face was white and pale, like wind ice.

"I love the wind," she said. "One day, such a wind will rise that it will blow all before it and leave everything scoured and clean, like the new tide."

"I would speak with you," said Oswiu.

"Speak, then," said Ahlflæd. "I will hear."

"It is very windy here."

"The wind will bring your words to me."

"Or blow them away."

Ahlflæd smiled. "Mayhap. But then, if that be so, they were never destined for my ear."

"I have made the terms. He agreed to all that I asked: you may have a priest, and gold, and ladies to serve. Is there aught else you wish?"

Ahlflæd made no answer, but stared into the wind.

Oswiu nodded and drew his cloak around his shoulders. He turned and looked south, down to the river, and east, towards the sea.

"Though it be my right, as father and as king, to find fit husband for you, Ahlflæd, yet I would tell you this: if it be not in your heart to marry Peada, then I will send him forth without you. For you are too precious for me to sell for my advantage and for the kingdom's. Tell me but nay, and the Red Hand will not be joined to yours."

Then Ahlflæd turned her face to her father. "Standing in the shieldwall, waiting for battle, were you to hear me say to you, 'Tell me but nay and you may stand aside,' would you? I know that you would not. It is the part of women in this middle-earth to weave together kingdoms in our bodies and on our beds, to requite war with desire, to make peace with the children we breed. That is our part, and I gave my word; I pledged myself to Peada. I would not have the world know me faithless, Father. If he has made terms, then I will go with him and be his bride, and keep his hand from being raised against you." Ahlflæd turned back into the wind. Its cold fingers rubbed the tears from her eyes. "But it is hard."

Oswiu stepped to his daughter and put his hand on her arm. "Know this: I will always receive you. Should there be cause for you someday to leave him, I will take you and I will keep you, even if all the armies of this land pursue you. Do you understand?"

Ahlflæd laid her hand upon her father's. "Do not worry, Father. If you can stand in the shieldwall, I can marry."

Oswiu looked into his daughter's face. "I hope I have not failed you."

Ahlflæd laughed, the sound as sudden and unexpected as thunder on a clear day. "How could you have failed me, when you have sought to bring about that which I gave oath to do? But tell me, Father: how did you bring Peada here? I am glad you did, for I feared that I would have to go to Mercia to marry him, having only my women with me."

"Peada came here because he does this without his father's knowledge or his consent. In marrying you, and in baptism, the Red Hand has pledged not to raise his hand against me – and that will strike deep into his father's guts." Oswiu joined his laughter to his daughter's. "I would give much gold to be present when Penda hears that his son is wed to you and allied to me. But Penda has raised his son high and made him strong: he is king to the Middle Angles now, and it would be a grave matter should Penda seek to bring his son to heel; such a war would tear Mercia apart. So, I judge, with this marriage we will have bought peace between us and him, for I do not think Penda would risk war with me while leaving his great halls unguarded, their bellies lying bare ready to be ripped open by the Red Hand. No, with you wed to the Red Hand, Penda will not go to war with us."

"Then marriage to Peada will be worthwhile," said Ahlflæd.

"Thank you, my daughter. I will return to the hall and finish the terms." Oswiu turned to face the wind himself. "This will help. I made Peada think I went forth because the drink was too much for me. Let the wind blow just a while longer and I will look pale enough to pass as a man who has been throwing up."

"Better you do as Aidan did, and stand in the sea in November."

"As well it is not November!"

"As well you are not Aidan." Ahlflæd kissed her father. "I will marry Peada, Father, for you and for the kingdom."

"I know. But, you know, I would have married your mother even were she not a princess of Rheged. Æthelwin poisoned my mind against her, and then I had need of the alliance with Kent, else I would not have put her aside. But she was, for the most part, a good wife to me."

"And you?"

Oswiu looked the question to Ahlflæd.

"Were you a good husband to her?"

The king gazed into memory. "Yes, I think so. For the most part."

"Well, that is good to hear."

Oswiu looked to his daughter, unsure whether she spoke true or forked, but she looked blandly back at him and gave no answer.

Finally she said, "It were best you go back, Father, and make my marriage come about. If it were done, it were best done quickly. I will be here, speaking with the wind."

*

The Red Hand was baptized in the River Tyne. Abbot Finan had some of his monks dig into the bank, making a low shelf where he could sit up to his waist in water without being pulled downstream by the current. Then, with other monks roped together, standing as pillars out into the stream, Abbot Finan invited Peada, dressed in a white cloth, to step down into the river.

His men were gathered on the river's edge. Oswiu, as sponsor, sat upon the judgement seat, itself brought down to the river for this day, and watched as the Red Hand stepped into the Tyne. His face tightened as the cold water bit, but Oswiu was impressed that he did not, even by so small a sign as a grimace, give sign of the water's chill. The monks, of course, were used to it, using sea and river to numb the flesh and contest its mastery over the body.

Finan began to intone the words of baptism, the Latin phrases sounding clear over the water, while he put his hand to Peada's forehead. Then – and it always came as a surprise to Oswiu, although he knew well what was to happen – Finan pushed Peada, setting hand to his forehead and driving him down, down, down under the water, and holding him there. He held him under water long enough for some of Peada's men to stir and lay hands upon sword hilt.

Abbot Finan kept Peada under water for longer the second time. This time, some of his men stepped forward, while others began to slide their swords from their sheaths. But when the Red Hand came to the surface again, gasping but without hurt, they stepped back and slid swords back into sheaths.

Finan kept Peada under the water longest the third time.

Watching from the judgement seat, Oswiu began to lean forward to see what was going on. Through the water, he saw Peada's face staring up at him, eyes open and wide. It seemed he pushed against the abbot's hand, and though the Red Hand was a big man, with the strength that accompanied such a size, yet all the Mercian's strength seemed of no account. Try as he might, Peada could not push Finan's arm away and rise to the surface.

Then, finally, when Peada's men were poised to draw sword and leap into the river, Finan pulled the Red Hand from the water.

Peada stood up, the river streaming from face and hair and body, coughing and gasping and, for a moment, unable to speak.

Then, when breath had returned to his body, he turned upon the abbot and said, "What was that all about?"

"You are clean now," said Finan.

"I know I'm clean – you didn't have to drown me to clean me."

The abbot looked calmly at the man before him. "I think I did."

The Red Hand slapped his hand onto the surface of the water, sending spray flying. "It is done." He looked to his men. "Those of you who want to follow me, get in. But you'd better hold your breath!"

Most of the men, faithful to their lord, followed him into the river, although it was notable how none of them were held under water for as long as Peada had been.

As his men followed him, dripping, back up to the hall, Peada asked the abbot, "You can marry us now?"

The abbot shook his head. "There is the baptism feast. You have been washed clean in Christ's blood, Peada, son of Penda. Now is the time to rejoice, to refrain from the flesh and to turn your eyes towards the eternal kingdom that awaits you."

"I've been washed clean in the Tyne. It was cold and you nearly drowned me. I've done all that was asked of me. I want my wife. I want her now." Peada stared ahead, to where Ahlflæd walked with her father. "I have waited long enough. I will not wait longer."

Finan looked to the grim-faced man staring hungrily ahead of him. "I will see what the king says."

*

The marriage feast had been long. Whenever one of the men called out to the high table that the groom should take his bride, Ahlflæd had called for a further song, or a new riddle, or for the horn to be refilled that she might, for this day taking the place of Queen Eanflæd, pass among the men and offer the horn to each one to drink his fill. By the end, Acca was reduced to signing to the steward that he had no more riddles to sing and then, in desperation, slashing a finger across his throat to show that his voice was going. More men slept than sang, and at the high table Peada, the Red Hand, rose to his feet and, though he swayed, he stood. Ahlflæd looked at the men around her, most with their heads laying upon the table. She looked at her own father, swaying in his seat, his eyes turned to her in bleary half smile, half sympathy. She looked to Eanflæd, the queen, who nodded to her. It was time. There was no more value in delay.

Ahlflæd held her hand out to the Red Hand.

Peada took it.

Those men still awake sent up a cheer.

Ahlflæd looked at her husband, at his eyes heavy with desire, at the hand that grabbed hers, and though she would have spoken, no words came to her.

"Are… are you ready?" It was Peada who spoke, and his voice was gentle, but Ahlflæd did not hear it.

"Yes," she said, turning away towards the chamber that awaited their nuptials. "Let's be finished with it."

So she did not see the blank, animal hurt that passed over Peada's face, as dumb and unspoken as a donkey belaboured by its master.

In the bed chamber, when they were alone and Ahlflæd stood before Peada, she turned her gaze away while he disrobed. Nor did she look to him as he uncovered her. Only then, when for a long time she stood before him without him touching her, did she look to him, and she saw him staring.

Peada had drunk many, many cups of wine and mead. His jaw hung slack, and his eyes were wide. It was wonder that he felt, and awe, at the knowledge that that which he needed was there, standing before him, and had come to him freely and of her own will.

But Ahlflæd, thinking him to stare witlessly, said, "Know you not what to do? I would this to be quick done with."

Peada felt the wonder wither and in its place he felt the old red anger flare. As he stepped towards the woman who had become his wife and his queen he said, "Oh, I know what to do with you."

Chapter 2

Wihtrun, priest of Woden, spirit walker among the dead, held the squirming, struggling goat down with his knee while he tried to open the animal's throat to his knife. The animal, already panicked by the iron tang of blood that hung about the sacred grove, had begun to kick the moment Wihtrun had pulled it past the series of painted and carved poles that marked out that which belonged to the gods from the realm of men. It had taken all his strength, and cost him a number of bruises and scratches from the animal's sharp little hooves, to wrestle it to the ground, but still it would not lie still.

The sweat pricked Wihtrun's face, and his eyes as well, as he strained to pull the animal's head back. The goat, feeling its throat being exposed, bleated its fear, but in doing so it relaxed its struggles just enough for Wihtrun to pin it down firmly and, with a swift, single draw, pull his knife across its throat.

The throat blood, the hot life blood, spurted from the goat's neck, spraying over the sky stone, the dark, pitted lump of rock that had fallen from the upper heavens in the days of Wihtrun's father as a gift from the gods to the men of this middle-earth. Wihtrun's father had told him how, when it first came to middle-earth, it had been hot with sun fire, the whole rock glowing from within as if a great candle burned inside it. Only slowly had the candle dimmed and then gone out, but in the days of its burning, many sacrifices had been made upon the sky stone, the thrown blood sizzling upon the stone, some disappearing into its crevices, the rest twisting upon its surface as oil upon water. Many were the questions Wihtrun's father had asked the sky stone in the days of its burning, and as many were answered, for it made clear the ways of wyrd and the weavings of the fate singers. But as the sky stone cooled, its answers grew more opaque, becoming as dense as the rock itself, embedded on a shallow rise above the river. Now, in Wihtrun's days, the sky stone spoke rarely. But when it did speak, it told of great matters: of the fall of kingdoms and the death of kings; of battles beneath the earth and war in heaven.

Wihtrun had come to the grove as the afternoon drew down towards evening, leading the goat by its halter. He had left the king's hall behind, further upriver, hidden by stands of willow and alder. For the priest would have words with the gods, and in particular with the Lord of Hosts, the Gallows' God, and he would have the words alone.

In the shadow dark of twilight, as the night crawled over the day, the blood of the goat splashed darkly onto the stone. Colour had been sucked from the world. Only darkness remained.

The animal jerked towards its death, then lay still. Wihtrun, aching from its kicks and butts, slowly got to his feet and, pulling his wolf cloak tighter around his shoulders, lay the wolf's head over his own. He was an animal with two heads now, man and wolf, and both smelled of the blood trickling down the stone.

Wihtrun, crouching, circled around the sky stone, eyes searching over the pitted surface as the night shadows grew, pooling out from the pits where shadow lingered through the day, spreading over the whole stone. He traced the movement of the dark with his finger, seeing how it felt its way towards the animal's blood.

The sacrifice was accepted.

Wihtrun howled.

The wolf upon his head howled too, its empty eyes staring up at the night, its jaw snapping open.

Then silence.

The gods listened.

Wihtrun spoke. "Tell me. Tell me what I must do. Men turn away from the ways of our fathers. They turn from you. If you would have the sweet smell of sacrifice, if you would have the songs of scops and the praise of kings, then tell me what to do. The king's own son, the Red Hand, turns from you and gives leave to the priests of this new god to pass among his people, pulling them under the water and turning them from the ways of our fathers. Even the High King lets these priests speak to his people, and some turn from you. Would you not have the fire bringing the rich fat to your tables? Would you not hear the scops sing your praises and tell your deeds? Have you turned your face from us? Why? What have we done?" Wihtrun's voice trailed away.

"What have we done?" he said again. And the night, in its silence, gave him answer.

Wihtrun fell to his knees in front of the sky stone. He sat back upon his haunches and the starlight glittered upon his cheeks, shining from the tears that trailed down them.

Then, from behind the sky stone – or mayhap it stepped from the stone itself – a figure emerged, hooded and dark, with staff in hand and shadow face.

"L-lord?" Wihtrun stuttered. "Is it you?"

But the hooded figure gave no answer.

Wihtrun made obeisance, hiding his eyes lest they see that which mortal men should not see.

"Lord, I will bring your people back to your ways. I will hold them to the ways of our fathers. Give us only your aid upon the field of slaughter and we shall send you up such an offering of the slain that has not been known since the days of Icel himself. Then men will turn from this new god and send up the fat meat in sacrifice, and the sweet smoke shall fill your halls. Lord, scatter our enemies, strike down the god that would take men's hearts from you, that they may know it is you who sends favour and victory in this middle-earth. Lord, help me. Lord. Lord?"

Wihtrun turned his head to listen, but he could hear no sound. He looked at the dark earth, not daring to turn his head, but he heard nothing more. Then, finally, when the rain long promised began to fall, he turned his head and looked towards the sky stone. There was no one there. Wihtrun went to where he had seen the hooded figure. He bent down and felt the damp ground with his fingers. There were marks there, the marks of feet, but he could not remember if he had already stepped this way when he had first come to the sacred grove. But he searched further over the ground and, by touch, found further marks that seemed to head along the river towards the hall.

"My king," he whispered. "Beware."

*

Penda woke. He stared up at the wooden beams above him. Of all the men who slept within his hall, he alone had a chamber to himself, separated by wooden screens and hangings from the hall itself. The rest of the men slept where they might, upon floor or bench or cloak. Only when a man had done great service did the king grant him rights to land and a hall of his own, on pain that he come when summoned. Then a man might take a wife and make children of his own. But in the king's hall, the king could take wife and make children. Penda had made many such, some with Cynewisse, others with slave girls. But they all slept now. Penda made his way from his chamber, leaving a girl asleep there, into the hall. No one stirred. Even the dogs did not twitch in their sleep.

Then Penda heard the silence.

There was none of the soft hiss of breath that came from many men sleeping. The hall was silent, and it was the silence of death.

Penda bent down to the nearest man and touched him. But at his touch, the man rolled from the bench and lay upon the floor, his throat, and the great wound there, exposed.

Then Penda saw the dark stains upon floor and table and wall, and knew them for what they were, and he knew why there was no sound of breath in his hall.

But there was another sound. The sound of the door to the hall. The sound of it opening.

Penda looked towards the door and saw a figure there, hooded and cloaked. The figure stood with its back to the hall, for it was opening the door. Then, without backward look, the figure went out from the hall.

The figure stood outside the door. It did not turn to him as he approached, but it knew he came. Oh yes, it knew he was there.

Of their own will – or by the will of the hooded figure – Penda's legs stopped, and he stood upon the threshold of his hall, neither within nor without.

The hooded figure pointed, and to Penda's eyes it was as if his hall stood upon a high mountain, for it seemed all the realms of this middle-earth were laid out before him.

Then the hooded figure turned to him and, though he would not see, yet Penda could not turn his gaze away.

Reaching up, the hooded figure slowly drew back the hood that covered his head. The face that regarded him was his own.

The single eye stared at him.

Then the figure held out his hand. "I will have your eye," he said, and the voice was Penda's own.

And Penda felt his own hands rise to his face; he felt his own fingers push in behind eyelid and under socket and he began to scream...

The scream woke him. Penda, the High King, woke soaked in sweat but in his own bed, and the girl beside him stirred in her sleep and reached for him, but he pushed her away. He stared up at the ceiling. Through the horror of the dream, he remembered the sight of all the realms of this middle-earth laid out before him, as if in promise. And Penda, waking, dreamed.

*

Penda rolled the dice between his fingers. He felt them warm under his touch, for the dice were like living things. Holding them between thumb and fingers, he moved them round his hand, clicking them together.

The men before him could hear the clicking, but they did not know where it came from. As they stumbled over their embassy, it seemed as if every time the dice clicked, one or other of them would fall over their words or forget the next part of the message they had rehearsed.

For their part, the two men, thegns of the East Saxons, shifted under the king's dark stare. Riding to Mercia, they had heard tales of how no man could long endure the king's regard. They had scoffed at the tales, told in whispers at the inns where they stopped along the way, but now, standing in front of Penda, they learned in the discomfort of their hearts and the unease of their minds that it was true.

"So, you would kill your king." Penda stared at the two shifting, uncomfortable thegns. For an hour or more the two men had circled round the idea, telling the High King of their troubles with Sigeberht, king of the East Saxons, of how the whispers against him in the witan grew, but in that time they had not said that which was in their hearts.

But Penda had seen what they desired and spoke it, an idea terrible and proud. "You would kill your king, because he forgives his enemies and overlooks those who insult him." Penda, in one sentence, said what they had taken half the morning to speak. "A strange king, indeed, who accepts insults and does not kill his foes. But then, does Sigeberht not simply do that which he is enjoined to do by his new god – and yours? For if your king has left the ways of our fathers and adopted the new religion, then surely you have too?" Penda regarded the two thegns with his single eye. But what made them even more uncomfortable was the sense that he looked on them with both eyes, even though one was gone. "Well?"

The two thegns, brothers, shifted under that unwinking gaze. They exchanged glances, and the elder, Swithhelm, spoke.

"It is true, we have gone into the water and taken the salt. But that which the king does is madness. One thegn, an evil, low character, raided the king's estate at Bradwell – where he has made a holy house – and took from there his cattle and also the gold and silver plate Sigeberht would have given to the monks of the holy house when he came again to Bradwell. But when the king rode after this thegn, and brought him into the field, the thegn sued for peace, saying he had raided in error, thinking the estate belonged to another. We were there, we knew this thegn lied – and so did the king. Yet Sigeberht forgave him, and embraced him, and let him go. This he does with all who wrong him, until all men laugh at us, saying the East Saxons, having a fool for a king, must be fools themselves. But when we speak to the king, telling him he must strike down his enemies, he tells us that if a man strike him on one cheek then he should offer that man the other to strike as well." Swithhelm shook his head. "This is madness, lord – a madness of which the king will not be dissuaded."

The thegn looked to his brother, who nodded for him to continue. "But if the king will not be dissuaded, then he must be removed. Will you aid us in that, lord?"

"And who shall take Sigeberht's place on the throne, should he be... removed?" asked Penda.

"I will," said Swithhelm. "And if, in striking, I am struck down, then my brother Swithfrith will rule."

"To whom will you, as king of the East Saxons, offer allegiance?"

The two thegns made the courtesy to Penda. "To the High King."

"Very well." Penda sat back upon his judgement seat. "You may tell the witan of the East Saxons that you have my support. Go back, and do what you intend – and do it swiftly. For once you have struck down Sigeberht, then I will strike the throne that neighbours you, else Anna, king of the East Angles, would march against you."

The thegns made the courtesy again. Penda held out his arm, a thick gold ring upon it. It was a ring of great cunning, made of strands of gold woven together to make running hares and hounds, and mustering the hares a hooded figure. Such was its beauty that any other king would have made sure that all might see the ring upon his forearm, but Penda kept it hidden. Only now, holding out his arm, did the sleeve slip back and the ring appear.

The two thegns approached the judgement seat and each put a hand to the ring.

Penda looked from one man to the other. He said nothing.

Then, throat cracking, first Swithhelm and then his brother swore oaths, binding themselves to that which they had declared – the killing of the king – and allegiance to Penda.

*

"Tell me, priest, the meaning of a dream."

Penda rode with Wihtrun around the bounds of his estate at Repton. He had called the priest to him in the hall but, seeing the jostle of people seeking the king's justice, he had taken the priest outside. Some of the petitioners had followed, trailing behind king and priest at a respectful distance, but others had remained in the hall, waiting by the judgement seat for the king's return. Wihtrun, waiting on the reason for the summons, had walked with Penda across the compound to the stables. There, taking horse, the king had ordered a horse made ready for the priest as well, and the two men had ridden through the gate and begun to circle the long fence and ditch that marked out the king's compound from the village beyond.

"For that is the task appointed to a priest: to see the workings of wyrd and make its ways clear to the king."

Wihtrun pushed his horse closer to the king's, so he could better hear Penda's words. The wind had risen, and tattered clouds ran above the two riders, bearing tale of the hills that had torn the rain from their grasp, but the wind also grabbed at the king's words, pulling them out of the priest's hearing.

"If you tell me your dream, lord, I will interpret it," said Wihtrun.

So Penda, the king, told the priest of how he woke, in dream, in his hall with all the men about him dead; of how the hooded man had called him from his hall and shown him all the kingdoms of the land laid out before him and then asked of him his eye. Penda told the priest of how he had given it.

The dream told, Penda drew back his hood so that he rode bare-headed. The wind ran through his hair, and Wihtrun saw that the age frost lay now upon his lord.

The king pulled up his horse and looked out over the land.

"All this I rule," said Penda. "And beyond the bounds of my realm, other kings bow to me, for I am the king of kings, and they are beholden to me, save those who still think alliance with the Bernician the surer safeguard to their throne. And I have been content with that. But now, it seems to me this dream promised me something more: all the lands of this middle-earth were laid out before me as a table is laid out at feast. At the price of my eye." Penda turned his black eye upon Wihtrun. "Riddle me this, priest. How may a blind man rule even the smallest kingdom, let alone all the lands of middle-earth? The price to pay makes the gift beyond receiving. Is this one of the Deceiver's wiles: to give with the one hand while taking with the other? It is what I think. But you are priest, and tasked with telling the meaning of the gods. So tell me the meaning of this."

Wihtrun nodded. "Very well, lord. I will give it thought and give answer when Woden has made his will clear to me."

"Oh, no," said Penda. "I will have answer now, or never. If Woden wishes me to act, then let him tell me clearly or not at all. If you cannot tell me the meaning of this dream ere we return to the hall, then the dream shall be as those other night phantoms: something to be dismissed by the sun's rising. Do you understand?"

"Yes, lord." Wihtrun looked back to the distant hall. "When shall we return?"

"You wish to know how long you have?" Penda pointed to a hillock, some two miles further, that commanded far views of the surrounding land. "We will ride there, for I would take a view of the land hereabouts, and then return. If Woden's words are so twisted that you may not tease out their meaning in that time, then I would have none of them." Penda glanced at Wihtrun and his black eye glittered. "Mayhap this new god speaks the more clearly to his people; mayhap he would speak clearly to me as well, for I am weary of the hints of the hooded one. If he would speak to me, let him speak plainly, as one king to another, not in dream riddles."

"Do kings always speak plainly to each other?" asked Wihtrun, greatly daring, but so shaken by his lord's hint that he might abjure the old gods that he spoke what was in his heart. "Such has not been my experience."

Penda laughed. "Truly, it has not been mine either. Kings speak unto kings with all the truth of a farmer telling his harvest to my gatherers. But are the gods no more than men who know not death?

I would that Woden be greater than that. So, tell me his meaning, priest. I have given you time and enough to search it out."

With that, Penda urged his horse into a canter towards the distant hillock, the animal's hooves beating a muffled rhythm upon the earth. Wihtrun, no great horseman, followed as he might, but in truth his mind was ever upon the king's dream, turning it in search of its truth.

Penda drove his sweating animal up the side of the hillock, then pulled it to rest at its rounded top. A barrow, long and ridged, rose from the top of the hillock. Its mouth, dark and open, was turned to the east. Penda dismounted and walked to its entrance. The barrow breathed out darkness.

"Lord, stay!"

Turning, Penda saw Wihtrun dismounting from his horse and rushing towards him.

"Lord, this barrow is wraith haunted! Do not enter it."

Penda nodded and stepped back. "Such it seemed to me. But there is little danger in coming here on a clear day, for I would not cede, even to a wraith, such a prospect of my kingdom." The king swept his hand around, taking in all the wide prospect laid out before them from atop this hillock. "From here, even a single rider may not hide from the clear-sighted. I wonder: is this how our middle-earth appears to the gods from their high hall?"

Wihtrun made to answer, but Penda signalled for silence. "It matters not. Tell me, Wihtrun, have you answer yet?"

The priest shook his head. "Lord, you said I would have until we returned to the hall to think on it."

"There is no need." Penda looked out over his realm. "I have seen that which Woden asks for myself." The king turned to the priest. "The Receiver of Sacrifice asks sacrifice of me, that much is clear. But a blind king is no king. That also is clear. In taking my eye, in dream, Woden tells me that he will give all the lands of middle-earth to me in return for that which I most value. The Wealthy One would have my most precious treasure in sacrifice."

Wihtrun nodded. "Yes, lord. I think you must be right. But what is your most precious treasure? You have many rich jewels, and gold, and buckles and arm rings most cunningly wrought."

Penda shook his head. "No, it is not that sort of treasure that Woden asks of me."

Wihtrun pointed to the king's side. "A man may not be king without a sword – and that is the sword you took from Edwin. I have heard tell there is no finer blade in all the kingdoms. Is it that?"

Penda put his hand upon the pommel of the sword, but he did not draw it. "This sword sings when it drinks blood. I have heard its music. But no, this is not my greatest treasure."

Wihtrun blanched. "Surely, lord, Woden does not ask your son of you in sacrifice?"

Penda gave a harsh laugh. "I would hardly call Peada my greatest treasure. Such a sacrifice is no sacrifice at all."

"I – I did not mean the Red Hand, but Wulfhere," said Wihtrun.

Penda nodded. "He would be a sacrifice, it is true. But Woden does not ask blood of me, for I have given the Lord of the Slain lives and to his fill in my battles. No, the God of Victory asks my dearest possession of me: he asks my fortune." And Penda held out his hand.

Wihtrun looked at the hand, then back to the king. "Dice?"

Penda closed his fingers over the dice. "My fortune," he said. "Woden is subtle and full of guile. These I would give to no man – no, not if he offered me all the treasure of this world. But now the War Father asks that which I would not give." Penda looked to his priest. "Should I give him that which he asks?"

Wihtrun looked upon his king and saw him holding fortune in his hand as gift to men and to the gods, and he fell upon his knees before him.

"Lord, I had not known you before. I thought it but the mark of your favour. I beg your pardon."

Penda looked down at the priest scrabbling on the ground in front of him. Wihtrun was pulling his nails through the dry earth atop the mound, digging it up and throwing the dust over his face and hair. The king, for his part, had not the faintest idea what the priest was speaking of, but he looked down and gave no sign of his lack of understanding. He waited for Wihtrun to speak further.

"Lord, you are right: strike me down for my blindness." Wihtrun leaned back upon his haunches and ripped his tunic open so that his thin, pale chest was exposed. "For you were ever before me and I did not see you; I sought answer to my prayers and you were ever beside me. It is only just that you strike down so blind a servant. But if, in your mercy, you should let me live, I would ever serve you now that I know you have heard and answered my prayers." Wihtrun stared up at the king and his eyes were shining. "My lord and my god."

And Penda understood.

He began to reach out his hand to raise up the priest and tell him his mistake, but then he stopped. If one as close to him as Wihtrun, a man who had seen him bleed and sicken and heal, believed him to be Woden, then how many others, who knew only the tales of Penda, the One Eye, might believe such a thing? And men who believed their king a god would be a mighty army indeed – for had not the emperors of old been worshipped as gods and their armies had brought the whole world under their dominion? Such a belief, widely spread, would be valuable to him, more valuable than any treasure. More valuable, perhaps, even than his fortune.

Mayhap that which the god proposed to give in exchange for his fortune was worth it after all.

"That you should come among us…" Wihtrun looked up at Penda, his eyes shining with the brimming tears of hope realized beyond hope. "That you should come among us to restore the old ways among men who have fallen away from them; that is beyond any hope, any prayer I offered you, lord."

Penda put his hand on Wihtrun's head. "I would that you not speak of this," he said.

The priest bowed his head. "I will speak of it to no one," Wihtrun said.

*

413

"Would you have me bring you someone?"

The voice was familiar, the question less so. Cynewisse, so sensitive to her husband's desires, did not normally have to ask if he wanted to slake the desires of the body. Penda seldom chose, now, to slake those desires on his queen, for the marks of childbearing lay heavy upon her, and the first frosts of ageing had touched her hair. It had been four years since Cynewisse last gave birth to a child, and that, a girl, had lived only a short time. There was still chance that she might produce another child, so sometimes the king would have her stay with him in his chamber, but that chance lessened with each passing month.

"No." Penda gestured to the queen. "Stay with me."

He saw how her face brightened at his command. But he desired something other from her than the chance for another son.

Cynewisse came to him and began to unfasten the buckle that held her dress. But Penda put his hand over hers.

"I would speak with you here, where we may not be heard."

The queen stopped, her hand still upon the buckle, but her eyes upon her husband, quick with understanding. "There are strange rumours," she said. Cynewisse looked at her husband questioningly, for she saw the knowledge in his eyes. "You know of these?"

"Yes, I know." Penda smiled. "If you would have the whole world know something, then tell it as secret to a priest." The king's smile grew broader. "It has taken only half a day for my secret to be told round my hall. In a week, the whole kingdom will know; in a month, every kingdom."

Cynewisse stared at Penda with eyes that, to the king's surprise, were suddenly questioning. "Is it true?"

Penda thought to answer, then seeing the doubt still upon his wife's face made answer into question. "What think you? You, who have known me longest."

"I? I think you are king, High King." Cynewisse looked at Penda through narrowed eyes. "The father of my sons. But does not every royal house claim descent from the All-Father? Then should I wonder that men might think you the Lord of the Slain, walking among the living? For me, it is no great surprise."

Penda looked at his wife. She returned his gaze.

Even she believed the truth of it.

"Very well. But it is of other matters I would speak with you."

Cynewisse nodded and Penda saw at once that she understood.

"Peada?"

Penda nodded. "Word came to me, this day only. He has married the daughter of Oswiu and taken oath to the god of the Northumbrians. Already, he has returned to his halls amid the Middle Angles, and is gathering men to him, giving the gold that his father-in-law gave to him." The High King looked to his wife, and the mother of his son. "Think you he will rise against me?"

Cynewisse closed her eyes. A shudder ran through her body. "That I should see such a day." She opened her eyes and looked to her husband. "Will you kill him?"

Penda looked, with interest, at his wife. That even she thought he might kill his son told well the fear he held over his people. And how much more, now that men suspected he might gather the slain to his hall? But Cynewisse at least could be trusted to hold tight to her tongue.

"No," he said. "No, I will not kill him. A wolf does not kill its own pups, nor does a raven cast its young from the nest. But if he takes up arms against me… Ah, that is a different question. And that is the question I ask of you. Do you think Peada will rise against me?"

At Penda's first answer, the tension that held the queen in its quivering grip relaxed, and great was the relief that showed upon her face. Then, at his question, she took thought, searching through memory for answer.

Slowly, the queen shook her head. "He will not rise against you. Peada hates you, but he fears you more. He hopes, in his heart, that you will strike against him, that he might face you, but he fears that also and he knows his fear to be greater than his hope, and hates you the more for it."

Penda nodded. "So think I also. But in this at least Peada has shown wit: his wife. Ahlflæd I remember well, from when her brother was foster son with us. She was a fierce girl then, and a wild one, but she had great spirit and courage. It is no wonder that Peada was drawn to her – I would have given her to him if I could. But now he has bought her himself. Think you Peada has wit enough to make such a match?"

"Not on his own."

"I think likewise. But now that match is made, there is one in his bed who might counsel him to do what he would not do otherwise."

"I too saw much of Ahlflæd when she was younger," said Cynewisse. "Such a girl will not learn to bend a man with wiles, but will tell him to his face what she desires. But Peada has never been one to bend to the will of another." The queen looked to her husband as she said this.

Penda sighed. "It is the lot of the father to bend the son to his will, to break him as a horse is broken to bridle and to whip."

"You have never wielded whip against Wulfhere, nor sought to bridle him."

"He has not needed it! You must see this also: Wulfhere has wit and courage. Peada has no wit, and his courage is the courage of the bully, and most of it comes from beer. He ever reeked of drink before battle, even the smallest skirmish against some band of brigands."

"It was not the battle he feared, but your eye upon him," said Cynewisse.

"If not my eye, then whose? But if he will not strike against me, will he stand with me?"

"No. He would never stand with you, not unless you went to him and begged him. Then he would stand with you, and gladly, against all the thrones of this middle-earth and against the powers of heaven, and against all giants and monsters and fell creatures. If you would ask him, then he would stand with you, lord."

Penda smiled. "I know it well. But a father shall not ask aught of his son – and particularly not when I have other, and better, sons."

"Wulfhere is too young to lead the wolves," said Cynewisse.

"But he is not too young to hunt with them," said Penda. "And already they love him, as they never loved Peada, for he always turned the hunt to his own glory, where Wulfhere is content to let the hunt bring glory to all the pack – and thus the men love him the more."

"Peada knows that," said Cynewisse. "He knows that too well."

"If he would outdo his brother then he must outmatch him."

"That is what he seeks to do, I think."

"He shall have chance," Penda said. "I see clearly whose face lies behind this and who seeks to suborn my son from me. Ever he has sought to surround me with enemies, to east and south, that I might not turn the full weight of my arms upon him. He thinks himself secure now he has made Peada into a hedge between us, and one that I may only cross at risk of going to war with my own son. His strategy has been laid clear to me: like a master of hounds, seeking to bring down a boar, he has filled the boar's valley with traps and blocked the escape with his hounds. But the boar has wiles of its own, and such a strategy is only as strong as the least of the traps he has laid. And now the boar will test his strength against the traps, and his tusks against the hounds, and his wit against the master of hounds. Then we shall see who is the trapper and who is trapped."

Penda stood up. "Oswiu has tried to take from me that which is nearest to me. He took my eye and he has suborned my son. Now I shall take everything from him." He looked to Cynewisse. "Everything."

*

Penda rode through the silver night. He rode alone, for he rode to meet the god. The door warden had risen as he came to the door but, seeing the hooded one, the door warden had fallen back before him and, all but gibbering with fear, had pulled the door open and even more swiftly closed it behind him. Penda left his men asleep in the hall and a girl upon his bed. Only Cynewisse had woken at his rising, standing from where she lay outside the chamber, but he had silenced her with a gesture of quiet, and she had stood aside, waiting upon her lord's will.

The moon lit his way. It lay a silver path over the land, marking the way to the grove where Wihtrun made sacrifices to the gods, and farmers hung gifts for harvest, and wives made offerings for birth and health and life.

The ring of posts tied with the small offerings of poor men marked the line where the middle-earth ended and the high heaven of the gods began. When they crossed the boundary, men might walk over grass and earth and under trees, as in the middle-earth, yet they walked then under a different sky and beneath a different sun.

Reaching the boundary markers, Penda pulled his horse to a halt. The night was very still.

Dismounting, Penda stood beside the beast. Despite the ride, the horse remained unmoving, neither tossing its head nor shifting upon its hooves. Penda ran his hand down the animal's flank. In this stillness, he felt for the horse's breath, and its heart, lest he find all the world had stopped beneath the moon. But his fingers told that the horse yet breathed and its heart still beat. The world lived, and he in it.

Penda put a hand to his belt and felt for the pouch. Within its smooth leather, he felt the two stones of his fortune.

He had come to lay his fortune on the altar of the god.

For a moment without time, Penda stood poised outside the grove. He looked at the pole nearest to him. The moon lit the offerings tied to the pole: corn dollies, dollies of barley and rye and grass, the mean offerings of poor folk asking more children of the gods, that they might have the hands to plough and till and harvest, to mend and weave and make.

Poor offerings? He had two stones.

Woken from his stillness, Penda stepped forward and crossed the boundary between this middle-earth and the high heaven of the gods. Taking the pouch from his belt, Penda took out the dice.

The altar, a dark wood table, stood before the tree of the world, the ash that held the heavens from the middle-earth and whose roots held the underworld from the light. Although the altar stood clear in the moonlight, yet it stood dark. The smell of it told why: the throat clutch of blood spilled in sacrifice. The wood was stained with darkness, beyond even the silver touch of the full moon to lighten.

Penda went to the altar.

Standing before it, he looked about him. This high heaven of the gods looked no different to his eyes than the middle-earth of men.

Penda tossed the dice upon the altar. The stones rattled upon the hard wood.

The night breathed in.

The dice rolled to a stop.

"There, you have it. My fortune. I give it to you."

The world exhaled.

Penda felt the mist rising about his feet, reaching up to his ankles and shins, its grey fingers winding upwards.

Penda stepped forward. He looked down at the dice. Seeing the throw, he nodded, then turned and walked from the sacred grove, from the high heaven of the gods, into the middle-earth of a still, quiet night. He mounted his horse and urged it back towards his hall.

The sacrifice was made and accepted.

Behind him, upon the altar, two eyes stared up at the black sky.

Chapter 3

"The High King would speak with you."

The messenger stood before Œthelwald, the king of Deira, in his hall at Beverley. The king, for his part, looked warily at the messenger, and just as warily at the thegns and counsellors who stood around him. Only the warriors who had followed him from the lands of the north, where he had ridden with Talorcan, were friends of old. The thegns of Deira were still mostly unknown to him – and he to them.

But then Œthelwald, son of Oswald, had not been king in Deira long. And while the witan had acclaimed him king, there had been some who whispered against his imposition and some who held silent but fingered their swords – and these Œthelwald was the more wary of.

"The High King would speak with me…" Œthelwald rose from his judgement seat. Let the men who doubted his throne-worthiness hear this. "Why does Penda, king of the Mercians, wish to speak to me?" Œthelwald asked.

"The High King would give you greetings… and counsel. For there are many who seek the ear of a king new come to the throne, but some among them will speak with honey tongues that have been dipped in bitter poison. The High King would not have you hear lies spoken of him by those who have causes in their heart above that of Deira. Therefore, he would meet you, one king speaking to another, so that you may know the truth of him, and learn the falsehood of others."

Œthelwald nodded. He looked round the ring of counsellors. Some of them inclined their heads at the messenger's words, others gave no expression to the thoughts of their hearts, while one or two shook their heads at what he had said. But there was no counsel from any of them. So Œthelwald turned back to the messenger. He was, Œthelwald saw, unusually young to be entrusted with such a message, a man who had barely left boyhood. Still, he carried himself well, with the dignity due a messenger from the High King.

"In this realm there are many who will speak cold words of the king of the Mercians, for he has treated Deira harshly. For my part, I have reason enough to treat ill the king of the Mercians – reason you know full well: he killed my father. Some will say that this invitation be no honest parley but a ruse, for we have heard strange tales of the king of the Mercians. What say you, messenger of the king?"

"I say the High King speaks to all men according to their worth: to he who is true, he speaks truth, but he who is without truth he answers in wiles such that no man might escape them." The messenger regarded Œthelwald full and frankly. "It is true, he killed your father. Penda is willing to pay the blood price for the killing, to end the enmity between our houses, for he is a man of rare generosity, a king over kings. Are you a man of truth, King of Deira? If so, you have nothing to fear from the High King."

At the news that Penda was willing to pay Œthelwald the blood price for his father, many whispers went through the hall. Such payment would be great indeed, and Œthelwald was no less aware of this than any of his thegns. But first he must answer the messenger. Œthelwald waited for the whispering to die down, then gave answer, but he uttered it as much for the benefit of the men in the hall.

"You will find I speak truly, messenger. But like your king, I too answer like with like: honesty with truth, lies with anger, treachery with vengeance. Still, it is true, I am but new come to the throne and I must needs lack the wit that has sustained the High King upon his throne these many years." Œthelwald turned to his gathered thegns. "What say you, men of Deira? As men of experience, what answer shall I give?"

Slowly, the thegns gave their counsel, some saying that it was an honour for the High King to speak to one new come to a throne, others urging caution, for it might be that Penda would impose a different king on Deira, one of his own choosing.

"Say you aught to this?" Œthelwald asked the messenger.

"I say, if the High King's word and the High King's pledge be not sufficient for the men of Deira and their king, then they scarcely merit to be called men and he is too craven to be king."

Many words were raised against such an insult, and some of the men put hand to belt, only to remember that in the king's hall no sword might be unsheathed without permission of the king.

But Œthelwald held up his hand for quiet.

"Rash words for one among so many. Tell me, though, where does the High King propose we meet? In his kingdom or in mine?"

"As a mark of his great favour, the High King proposes to meet you where the two kingdoms meet: upon the Humber."

Œthelwald laughed. "That is a strange place to meet and, I fancy, a cold and wet one. I suppose he wishes me to cross the river and speak to him upon its southern bank, in Mercia?"

"No, you misunderstand, my lord. The High King has great regard for you. Where he would require other kings to come into his realm, he will come to you and meet you where neither king may call himself master, upon the river itself – for none but the Humber is master over its waters."

"But how does Penda propose to do this?"

"Each shall take boat and meet upon one of the islands of the Humber, at slack water. Thus does the High King show his great courtesy."

"That is high courtesy indeed." Œthelwald rose. "I will give answer tomorrow." He made to dismiss the messenger, but the young man held up his hand that he might speak once more.

"Before you give answer, lord, think on this. The messenger the High King sent to you, the man who stands before you, is Wulfhere, his own son."

At the news, whispers and gasps of wonder passed around the hall. All knew of the Red Hand, Penda's eldest son, but many had heard tell of his second son, newly come to manhood. That Penda should send Wulfhere as messenger to the court of Deira was a tale to keep the fireside talking through many a long winter's night.

"That is a great and signal honour, Wulfhere, Penda son," said

Œthelwald. "We will remember it well when we think on our answer." Œthelwald restrained his desire to look for the reaction of the men of the witan – he did not need to, for he could hear it well enough. Men who had just lately come to think that their new king might be worth dealing with were rapidly raising their estimation of him.

The thanks for this were due to Penda. Oswiu, having made Œthelwald king, had left as rapidly as he had come, leaving no men and little in the way of advice beyond his parting words: "Choose your warmaster well and your enemies better." Œthelwald had taken as warmaster one of Talorcan's men, a Pict from the far north, whose body and face bore the marks of his tribe's other name, the painted people. As for enemies, while Œthelwald sought to firm his grip upon the kingdom, he had decided to make war only upon those who attacked him. Peace he would meet with peace, and even war might be met with a better offer, so long as it would buy off the attackers until he was strong enough to meet them upon the field of slaughter. For now, Œthelwald knew he needed to gather men to his banner. Without the glory of battles won, the only other way to attract young men keen to hear their names sung by the scops was with the open hand of the ring giver. So Œthelwald gave rings to all he might – even a good throw in the hunt might earn a ring for a surprised but pleased warrior staying in hall while he sought service for his sword. Faced with such generosity, the first new men were beginning to bind themselves to him by oath and pledge. The news that the High King himself was willing to meet him, and on neutral ground, would soon spread, and more men would hasten to his court, eager to give their swords to a king whom the High King favoured.

"We will speak on the morrow, Wulfhere, Penda son," said Œthelwald. "Now I will take counsel on what the king of the Mercians proposes."

After Wulfhere had made the courtesy and retired, Œthelwald worked his way past the talking groups of men to the door and went out. The Humber lay only a few miles south. If Penda had sent Wulfhere while he was staying at one of his northern halls, they might meet in two or three days. But before he could decide, Œthelwald determined to ask counsel of one he could trust.

A great barking told him where to look. Setting off from the hall, across the compound, he greeted those who gave him good afternoon without being waylaid into conversation. The dogs kept up their barking, the cheerful, musical note that told of food being given.

The king found the hounds milling around the huntsman. But it was not the huntsman he sought. Beside the huntsman, handing out scraps to favoured animals, was Rhieienmelth.

Looking up, Rhieienmelth saw Œthelwald looking at her. For a moment, she saw the face of his father, and memory stabbed its bitter pin into her side. But all her memories were bitter to her, and she barely gave sign of its striking.

The king – Rhieienmelth still caught herself thinking of Œthelwald as a boy – gestured to her and she made her way through the swirling mass of dogs towards him.

"The dogs are hungry, for they hunted well this morning," she said. "We took a red deer, a stag with twelve tines. You should have come with us."

Œthelwald nodded. "I would have wished to. But a messenger came and I had to hear his embassy."

"The messenger from Penda?"

"Yes. You heard?"

"How not? All the hall was alive with the news. I doubt there has been such excitement since... Well, since I came to visit you."

Œthelwald smiled. "Probably not. Though much of the wonder was that you could come at all."

"It was not so difficult. Æbbe, my abbess and my warder, grew weary of me, I think." Rhieienmelth laughed. "Her sisters complained that my dogs drowned out their prayers – though it seems to me that dogs send their praise to heaven too. I think it was a great relief to her when Bishop Finan asked her to return to Ebchester, her first house. Apparently, the brethren there had lapsed from their earlier purity. When you sent word of what had happened and of how you had come to the throne, the abbess that Æbbe left in her place was quite happy for me to travel south to see my heart's son and give him my courtesy."

"I am glad this was so. Both for the joy of seeing the one who was as a mother to me and for the chance to ask counsel of one who will give me answer with no thought for advantage."

Rhieienmelth looked sidelong at Œthelwald. "Are you sure you can trust me that far? Few indeed can give counsel without any thought to their own advantage and I have had little enough of advantage to me these past years…" Her voice trailed away, but Œthelwald had no need to ask what she left unsaid.

Œthelwald took her hands in his own. "I am sure," he said.

But Rhieienmelth took her hands from his. "I less so," she said. She wiped the back of her hand across her eyes. "It is windy here. Now, what would you ask me?"

Œthelwald told her that which Wulfhere had told him: that Penda wished to meet him upon one of the islands in the Humber.

"Would you tell me go?" he asked.

"So long as I go too," said Rhieienmelth. She looked at the young man in front of her. "I am too long in Æbbe's holy house. Such a trip gives me reason to delay my return further. Besides —" and here she smiled grimly — "I would see the man who cast down your father."

"Wulfhere said his father will pay the blood price," said Œthelwald.

"Will he?" Rhieienmelth turned away. "What price would suffice?"

Œthelwald looked to the woman who had been queen.

"We will see what price he offers."

*

The island had grown where the rivers Ouse and Trent met. It had slowly risen from the brown water — so slowly at first that, as the tide flowed in, the island disappeared beneath the water again. But the fishermen and ferrymen who lived by the rivers had watched the island grow. They had seen the first birds, birds with long beaks and longer legs, curlews and sandpipers, pacing the sand and mud. They had seen it grow higher, so that the sand in its centre was no longer dark but, drying out, became as yellow as the flowers of trefoil that began to flower upon the island.

The river folk did not give the island a name, for it had appeared as something given up by the rivers, and they waited upon the rivers to name it. But then the kings came, and by their presence named the island Two King Island.

The day when the kings came to the island, Œthelwald stood upon the northern bank of the Humber. The flag of Deira flew beside him. Holding his hand up against the glare of the sun, Œthelwald peered across the wide river to the further bank. There, where the ferrymen pulled their boats up upon the southern shore, he could see a party of men standing. By the glint of sun on spear tip and helmet, he could see they were warriors. He squinted his eyes. Though his hand shaded his eyes from the sun, it did nothing to stop the glare reflecting from the river. But then the wind pulled the banner out and he saw, even across the width of the river, the black wolf of Mercia.

"He's here." Œthelwald turned to the woman standing beside him. "I did not think he would come himself."

Rhieienmelth made no answer but shaded her eyes that she might better see. Her heart was clutching at the back of her throat. The old pain, the pain that she had thought dead, was pulling at her again.

Œthelwald saw the paleness of her face and knew it for what it was.

"I don't remember him," he said. "I wish there was a memory of him somewhere in my thought, but there is not. But you remember him."

"Yes," said Rhieienmelth. "I remember…"

The ferryman pulled his boat to the bank and Œthelwald, Rhieienmelth and their party got in, sitting upon the boards that held the boat open against the river's push. The ferryman started by pulling almost directly upstream, into the current. For it was not yet low tide, and the flow of water was still strongly out to sea. Once he had pulled past the island and up into the mouth of the Ouse, the ferryman spun the boat round and, using the current, let the river take the boat towards the island. Watching, past the oarsmen, Œthelwald saw the island approach. It was fringed on the downriver side with marram grass and vetch, but on this upriver side the island shelved almost imperceptibly from the water. Feeling the water becoming shallower under their oars, the oarsmen pulled harder, sending the boat further up onto the sand until it stopped fast.

Œthelwald looked to his standard bearer, one of his old retainers from his days among the Picts, and nodded. The standard bearer clambered out of the boat. His feet splashed into the water, still ankle deep, that surrounded the boat, before making his way to the dry sand. The other men followed, taking up position on the shore. Œthelwald looked to the far shore of the island. There, another party of men were disembarking from a ferry boat under the banner of the black wolf. He turned to Rhieienmelth.

"Are you sure you would come?"

Rhieienmelth stared past him to the wolf banner flying on the opposite shore of the island. "I am sure," she said.

Following behind their banners, both parties of men made their way to the centre of the island. There, a few bushes of gorse and some scrubby willow formed a small break against the wind. The Mercian flag bearer planted the pole of his banner in the soft sand behind the willows, and the men with him formed into a line behind. Seeing what they did, Œthelwald indicated for his own banner bearer to do the same.

Then, from among the Mercians, a single man stepped forward. He was hooded and his face could not be seen, for the sun was at his back. Œthelwald, seeing him, thought of the tales that were starting to be told near the fire after the flames were banked. Some said that Woden, the Lord of the Slain, walked middle-earth in the guise of the king of the Mercians.

"Would you meet him alone?" Rhieienmelth asked. "I have heard tales of the magic the High King wields. With none beside you, Penda might place a glamour upon you."

Œthelwald shook his head. "If Penda would meet me without a second, then what sort of king would I be if I did not do likewise?" He glanced at Rhieienmelth. "My father would have met him alone."

"I know," said Rhieienmelth. "And we lost him."

Œthelwald smiled at her. "You can hardly lose me here, in clear sight, when I will be but fifty yards away." He glanced back and saw that Penda had neither slowed nor stopped his slow, steady approach. "I must go, or he will think me fearful. Besides –" and Œthelwald's smile grew broader – "what honour the High King pays, by coming forward to meet me."

With that, Œthelwald set off, striding briskly forward to make up for his later start, that the two kings might meet midway between their men.

The ground, new risen from the river, was soft beneath Œthelwald's feet. Drifts of marram grass and vetch spread along the troughs between the banked sand, shot through with the white heads of campion. Birds, sandpipers and dunlins, walked stiff legged over the wet mud where the island joined the river, darting off in new directions for every four or five paces that Œthelwald took.

The king of Deira realized that he was looking at birds and plants to avoid looking at the figure he was approaching. Pulling his gaze back to the front, Œthelwald looked at the hooded figure coming towards him. With the sun in the south, the man's face was shadowed. The cloak he wore was dark and plain, without even a rich border, although a gold clasp gleamed at his shoulder. Many said that Penda was a true ring giver, pouring out the riches of his treasury upon his men and keeping little for himself; from what Œthelwald could see, this was a time when what many men said was true. The hooded man walked with a staff in his hand, but Œthelwald could glimpse the pommel of a sword beneath the folds of his cloak: Penda had not come unarmed. But then neither had he. Œthelwald felt the weight of his own sword, as familiar to him as the weight of his legs.

They were nearing each other. Thirty yards, now twenty-five, twenty...

Should he stop and hail Penda, Œthelwald wondered? But as the High King continued to advance in silence, so did he.

Fifteen yards, ten, five…

Penda stopped and raised his hand.

Œthelwald did likewise.

"Greetings." Penda raised his hands to his hood and slowly drew it down from his head.

Œthelwald looked upon the man who had killed his father. He said no word.

Penda looked at Œthelwald. "You are like your father," he said.

Still Œthelwald could say no word.

"He was a great king. There has been no other like to him since."

Œthelwald felt his throat working with emotion he had not known he felt. His breath came thick and his tongue tasted iron. Without thought, his hand began to crawl towards sword hilt.

"You would strike down the man who killed him, extract the blood price in blood." Penda's black eye did not move from Œthelwald's face, although surely he must have seen the hand creeping to sword.

"I am here to pay that blood price." Penda spread his arms wide, leaving his chest open and unprotected. "If you would strike me down, when I have come to you, then do so."

Œthelwald, still without thought, drew the sword from its sheath and pointed it at Penda.

From behind the High King came startled cries and shouts of alarm but, hearing them, Penda snapped his head round and shouted, "Stay back!" before turning to face Œthelwald once more.

"Here I am," he said. "The man who killed your father. Kill me, if only blood will pay for blood." Penda stepped forward, so that now Œthelwald was within range: a single thrust would push the blade into the High King's chest.

The black eye met, and held, Œthelwald's gaze.

"You have heard tales of me: tales of treachery, tales of deceit. Tell me, do such tales match he who stands before you, offering blood for blood, life for life?"

A single thrust.

A father avenged.

The sword tip wavered.

"No," Œthelwald whispered.

He dropped his hand. The tip of the sword buried itself in the soft sand. Œthelwald looked down at the ground.

Penda pulled his cloak back over his shoulders, then turned and gestured to his men. At the signal, two men started forwards, carrying a chest between them.

"The blood price must still be paid." Penda signed for the men to put the chest down. "Would you see what I will pay?"

Œthelwald glanced back at his waiting men. Seeing the look, Penda asked, "You would have counsel as to the worth of what I give? Call to you any who can answer such a question."

Œthelwald gestured his men closer.

"No further," Penda said quietly.

Œthelwald held up his hand. "Warmaster, to me," he called. "Warmaster... and Rhieienmelth."

As he called for the woman who had once been queen to come to him, Œthelwald heard the quiet hiss of inbreath. Penda was surprised.

The surprise relieved him. Would the Far Seer have been surprised that Rhieienmelth accompanied him? Those dark-night tales he had heard must be just that: dark-night tales, told to make the listening maid huddle closer to the teller.

Rhieienmelth and the warmaster approached. Penda had already made his way to where the two men waited with the chest. While Œthelwald quickly explained what they were about to see, he noticed that Penda had sent one of the two men who had carried the chest back to the line of Mercians: thus there would be two armed men upon each side – and Rhieienmelth.

Penda stood behind the chest as the three of them approached, with his warrior to one side. They had laid the lid of the chest open and, coming closer, they could see golden light pooling within. But Rhieienmelth merely glanced at the treasure therein. As she came closer, she looked upon Penda.

For his part, the king of the Mercians had drawn his hood back over his head, so his face was once more in shadow. As Œthelwald came to the chest, Penda stood back from it.

The new king of Deira looked down into a chest of gold: arm rings, finger rings, gold hacked from the hilts of broken swords, pins, clasps, buckles, and coins. Running over everything else, a river of golden coins. Bending down, Œthelwald scooped up a handful of the coins and let them trickle through his fingers. With such a treasure he could bind many, many men to his service: enough men that none of the thegns of Deira would dare raise arms against him. His throne would be secure.

The coins ran away, until one only remained. Œthelwald held it up to his gaze. There was a picture upon it – the picture of a man.

Œthelwald looked past the coin to where Penda stood watching him.

"Whose face is this upon the coin?" he asked.

"Earconbert, once king of Kent."

Œthelwald turned the coin. Upon its reverse was the figure of an animal, cunningly worked into the gold so that it stood out from the surface.

"That is a lion," said Penda. "I have heard tell that among all the beasts it is the king."

Œthelwald let the coin drop back into the chest. "I have seen no lions in this land," he said.

"Mayhap they have them in Kent or among the Britons." Penda turned his gaze upon Rhieienmelth. "The lady here might tell us."

Rhieienmelth regarded the king of the Mercians. "We have many such coins among us," she said. "But there was only one king to match this king among the animals."

"Yes," said Penda. "I agree." He looked back to Œthelwald. "It is no wonder that the king who came after him is not his match." Penda's black eye glittered in the shadow. "A lesser king than your father might use even a relation as defence against an enemy." The black eye turned back to Rhieienmelth. "A lesser king might put aside a wife to take another for the advantage she might bring."

Penda reached up and drew his hood back from his head. "A greater king would keep the faithful wife of his youth, and meet those who hate him face to face. The greatness of a king is not a matter of blood, but of action." Penda looked to the man and woman before him, one a king, the other once a queen, and said, "I would have peace with you, Œthelwald, son of my enemy. More, I would ask you to think on this: would a king who murdered to gain your throne not be likely to put you aside, as he put aside his queen, when he has a son of his own that he would put upon the throne of Deira? Think further: which king would you pledge your throne to? One who came to you, who offered his blood for your father's, who can give you gold running over to win the oaths of many warriors; or one who summons you to wait upon him and gives not gold nor men nor mastery?" Penda, king of the Mercians, looked upon Œthelwald, king of Deira. "Think on this, Œthelwald, Oswald son."

Œthelwald nodded. He glanced at Rhieienmelth, but she was staring at Penda and did not see his look.

"We will speak on this," he said.

But before he could step back, Rhieienmelth said, "No." She turned to look at Œthelwald. "I have looked upon the face of the man who killed Oswald. I have looked upon his face and seen that he speaks the truth. Your uncle uses you in the games he plays to keep his throne, but once he has used you, he will discard you. I should know." Rhieienmelth turned back to Penda. "Once I thought that, should I ever meet you, I would fall upon you myself, woman that I am, and by the strength of my arm try to exact the blood price of my king. But now I am content to take the price you offer and, if my nephew will hear the advice of a woman, he will accept the price and pledge himself to you."

Œthelwald looked to his memory hoard. He remembered the grace of Eanflæd the Wise; he remembered the scorn of his cousins, Ahlfrith and Ahlflæd; he remembered the kindness of the woman beside him, as much mother as the woman who had brought him to birth and died doing so; but most of all he remembered the king, Oswiu, placing him before the witan of Deira as their king.

He was king by the will of his uncle, and his uncle could as easily take the throne from him. But not if he had the support of the king of the Mercians. Then, too, with the threat of the High King standing behind his throne, the thegns of Deira would look on him, not as a king imposed upon them from Bernicia, but as a man who ruled in his own name, son of Oswald and grandson of Acha, offspring of the House of Yffi as well as the House of Ida.

Œthelwald, king of Deira, closed the door upon his memory hoard and looked with new eyes upon the king before him.

"Penda, king of the Mercians, lord of the Tomsæte, master of the Magonsæte, High King of Britain: I pledge myself to you."

Chapter 4

"My father sends for me."

Ahlflæd heard the words, but she did not answer them. She lay upon her side, turned away from her husband, pretending sleep. The Red Hand had finished with her for the night surely.

But Peada desired speech.

He lay also on his side, turned away from his wife. He was spent, but the sleep that usually came afterwards would not come.

Peada rolled over onto his back and looked up at the roof beams. The dim red light of the banked fire in the hall shone upon them, but the roof beyond them lay in darkness. He could hear rain running down the thatch.

"The messenger came today. You were not in the hall, so you did not hear him. He said my father wants me to come to him, with all my men." Peada glanced sideways. Ahlflæd lay unmoving, giving no indication that she heard, but he was sure she did not sleep. She usually didn't, not after he had finished with her. Peada clenched the satisfaction of that to himself and wrapped it tight around the pain.

"I have heard that my father, these days, oft times sends Wulfhere as his messenger when treating with a king." Ahlflæd still did not move. Peada let his head roll back, so that he looked again into the red darkness over them. "He did not send Wulfhere to me. Am I less a king than these others? I hear he even sent Wulfhere to speak with the king of Deira, whose father he had killed. Yet, to me, brother and son and king, he sends some young pup whose chin has never known a hair. I would have wished to see my brother. It has been a long time."

Still Ahlflæd gave no answer. But she listened, he knew she listened, and so he continued to speak. For how rarely did she listen to his words, but rather turned her head and, eyes blank, withdrew from him into the sanctuary of her mind?

Sometimes he looked at her, stealing glances when she was turned inward and unaware of him. Sometimes he saw a smile, quick as a swallow, flash across her face. Then he remembered the girl, racing her brother across one of his father's compounds, and winning, always winning, before turning on her panting, angry rival and skipping out of his way as he attempted to catch her and push her down. Then, without realizing it, his own hand would reach to her. But a touch from him was always enough to jolt Ahlflæd from memory and bring her to the present. And, each time, when the disappointment of finding where she was flashed again across her face, the Red Hand felt the red hand deep within him clutching his guts, squeezing there. Sometimes he saw her face relax, and a peace, like the dawn quiet, flow across it. Then, always, he spoke, or touched her; if he might not know peace, then neither would she.

But, this night, he did not need to wake her, although she pretended to sleep.

"Mayhap my father fears that if he sent Wulfhere I would not send him back. But I am not such a man that kills his brother – I leave that to my father. Or did Wulfhere himself refuse to come, fearing me? In that, he is right – but so should any king who crosses me be afraid. I would not kill him. I am not a monster who kills his brother."

The Red Hand looked again at his wife and queen. Never once had he seen her look at him without his calling her gaze to him – never, not since the day they had married. Instead, she spent her time with the women she had brought with her from her own kingdom, and the priest who had come with her to the land of the Middle Angles where Peada now ruled. Ruled by sufferance of his father. The messenger had seen fit to remind Peada of that.

"My father is gathering all the kings of this land to him. That is what the messenger told me. There is a new king among the East Saxons now. Sigeberht, who was their king, is dead. He died in his own blood, a knife sticking in his side." Peada looked at Ahlflæd.

Even the regular breathing that had moved her flank up and down had ceased. She listened now as a mouse within its hole listens for the cat waiting without. "I have seen men die like that. They drown in their blood." He reached out and touched her shoulder. He saw the skin move beneath his finger. "The new king is sworn to my father. Wihtrun will be happy, for the new king has put aside your new god and returned to the ways of our fathers. They sacrifice to Woden again in the fields and woods of the East Saxons."

"He's your god too."

The voice, the answer, was as unexpected as his father's messenger. Ahlflæd did not roll over so that she might look upon her husband, but she spoke. "He is your god and he will not be mocked."

"I have not mocked him. I gave my pledge that I would put aside the gods of my fathers and cleave to this new god, and I have not broken my pledge."

Peada waited for Ahlflæd to speak again, but she held silence, not moving.

"He has put down the king of the East Angles too, placing his own man upon the throne, and driven the king of the West Saxons from his land. You must see that which my father does."

Peada waited for an answer that did not come, so in the silence he spoke the answer himself.

"All those kings that your father thought to tie to himself by alliance, making a net about my father, he has destroyed: they are either dead, or driven into exile. All that your father sought to build up, my father has brought down." Peada looked at the back that lay unmoving beside him. "Have you no care for that? I know you to have no care for me or my people, but do you not have care for your own father?"

"I – I have care for him." Ahlflæd's back moved, her ribs expanding and contracting as she breathed convulsively. "I have care for him, or I would not be here."

Again, like a blow upon a bruise, Peada felt the words inside him.

"Then if you have care for your father, think on these words from the messenger. My father is drawing all the kings of this land, with all their armies, to him. There is but one kingdom they will march against, and but one king they will bring down. Would you have me answer my father's call?"

"You will do as you wish. For my part, I will send every prayer and sacrifice to my god, that he defend my father, and that he cast down all his enemies."

"I am not his enemy."

"My father stood as father to you when you entered the new life. Would you turn upon him now, when all hands are raised against him?"

"When all hands are raised against him, it is harder to stand back from the march."

Ahlflæd rolled over and looked upon her husband. She had hoped that the revulsion she felt for him would lessen with time, but it had not. Rather, it had solidified, becoming a solid block of despite, ice about her heart. Safe within its coldness, she could allow him to use her when he desired and it had no more effect upon her than the rain or snow. Sometimes she saw the pain in his eyes, a dumb pain, like that of an animal ill used, and a fierce joy sprang up in her at the sight, for she knew that he could never hurt her so deeply as she hurt him. And with her marriage, she held the Red Hand from her father – held his men back from marching into Bernicia. But now, from what he had told her, Penda was preparing the final campaign against her father. The siege of Bamburgh had failed, but with so many men marching behind the banner of the black wolf, even such a stronghold would surely fall. Any men that she could keep from the campaign would be of help to her father.

"If you would hold your hand back from my father, I would be grateful," Ahlflæd said. And she reached out and touched her hand to Peada's shoulder. She saw the flare of his hope, and she felt her contempt for it in her heart, but she forced a smile to her lips. "I would be grateful indeed."

"When all kings march behind my father's flag, I cannot simply refuse his call. What would you have me do?"

"A call may be answered but too late. There are reasons, and enough, for men not to arrive where they are meant to arrive: roads, rivers, sickness, weather. Each of these may stop you doing that which you told your father you would do. With all these other kings marshalled to his side, he will have no chance to seek after you, but will be grateful enough that you make no attack upon his rear."

But Peada was barely listening to what she said. He reached for her and she did not flinch from his touch.

"I would send word to my father of what you have told me."

"Send it," murmured the Red Hand, "send it."

When he had finished, and slept beside her, Ahlflæd lay upon her back and looked up into the dark, and to her eyes the dark had no ending.

Chapter 5

Ecgfrith ran towards his mother, waving a sword.

"See, see!" he called. "It's a proper sword; not wood like the last one."

Eanflæd sat down. The hall was spinning. When she had seen Ecgfrith standing at the door, looking around and calling for her, she had stood up to call him over, but that had been a mistake. She shook her head, trying to clear it.

Ecgfrith held the sword out to her. "See this edge," he said. "I bet it could cut through anything." He turned to one of his mother's women and reached for the cloth she was weaving. "Give me that," he said. Eanflæd tried to tell him to stop, but the words brought up bile and she gagged. While she sought to swallow back the bile, Ecgfrith took the cloth and, raising it, let it fall upon the edge of the sword… where it sat, unmoving and uncut.

Eanflæd took the cloth from the sword and handed it back to her woman. "Gytha spent many days weaving this. She would not wish it used to demonstrate the sharpness of a sword."

But Ecgfrith was looking with disgust at the sword that, a moment before, he had been waving around in high excitement. "It wouldn't even cut a cloth," he said. "Wældhelm told me this was a special sword; that it would cut through anything."

"I don't think he had cloth in mind."

"Then I'll try something else." Ecgfrith looked around wildly, then his gaze alighted on one of the dogs, asleep under a table, and with a determined light in his eyes he began to advance towards it.

"No!" said Eanflæd getting to her feet.

But that proved a greater mistake. The vomit that she had swallowed down surged back up her throat and it was only by the swiftness of one of her women, passing her a bucket, that she did not throw up on the floor of the hall.

"Mummy, are you sick?" asked Ecgfrith, in his concern forgetting his mission to prove the sharpness of his sword.

Eanflæd heaved again, then waited, breathing deeply, to see if that was all. It was. She wiped a cloth over her mouth. Now, her stomach voided, the room felt still. But she knew that it would start spinning again.

"Are you sick, Mummy?" Ecgfrith asked again.

Eanflæd managed a weak smile. "No, I am not sick. But, God willing, you will have a brother or sister before Christmas."

"I hope it's a brother," said Ecgfrith. "Girls are no fun." He ran off to demonstrate his new weapon to a fresh audience.

"You should rest."

Eanflæd turned to see the king looking at her. She shook her head. "Lying down just makes me feel worse." The queen smiled. "Besides, for now I feel better."

Oswiu nodded. "Then, if you are able, I would have you join us and give your counsel. There is much to speak on."

"The messenger from Ahlflæd? Was the news not good?"

"No," said Oswiu. "It was not good."

*

"Penda is raising all the kings of this land against me – against us."

Oswiu, king of Bernicia, stood outside the hall of his estate at Maelmin. The hall was newly built and the smoke from the fire had yet to steep the thatch and wood slate and find its way to the air without, so the air within was thick and hard to breathe.

Oswiu looked to his wife. "Shall we walk?"

She cast him a grateful glance. "That would help," she said. Walking in the cool air might serve to fight back the nausea that was rising again in her stomach.

"Come," he said, looking to the others present: Ahlfrith, son and warmaster, Coifi and Acca, and Romanus, priest to the queen. "Let us walk."

With the queen between them, they stepped down from the hall. The wind blew from the west, round Coldside Hill, but in the valley bottom they were spared the worst of it. Outside the fence that marked the king's compound from the usual straggle of fields petered out into the gorse and heather that trailed down from the hilltops. The king pulled his cloak around his shoulders. The wind was brisk.

"Are you warm enough?" he asked Eanflæd.

"This wind is good for me," she said, her cheeks reddening under its lash. "It clears my head and steadies my stomach."

"Good, good." Oswiu indicated the line of willows and alder to the east of the hall that stretched from north to south. "Let us walk down to the river. There we may talk without fear of others hearing what we have to say." He glanced back at the hall. "Unlike there."

"A secret told in hall is no secret at all," said Acca. Everyone looked at him. "It's an old saying," the scop added.

"To which has been added a new saying: a secret told to Acca shall be sung in every hall in the land," said Coifi.

Acca spluttered his indignation, but his protests were covered by the laughter of the others.

"Take no offence," said Oswiu. "If I did not know you to be true, I would not have called for your counsel. Come."

With the king leading, they made their way along the paths that fringed the fields, down to the River Till. There Oswiu stopped, standing on the riverside between banks of sedge. Bending down, he scooped up a handful of pebbles and began to throw them, one by one, into the river.

"Penda has killed Anna, the king of the East Angles, our friend and ally, and placed his own man, Æthelhere, upon the throne. Our friend Sigeberht, king of the East Saxons, was murdered, cut down by two thegns, men tied to him in blood. But the ties of blood mean nothing to the king of the Mercians. He suborned those wretched men, promising them the throne, and they struck that bargain, not knowing that its true cost shall be their souls. But, while they live, they will trouble us, for they are tied to Penda by this deed of treachery and, doubly treacherous, they have expelled God's priests from their kingdom and are sacrificing to the gods of old."

Oswiu paused, weighing the pebbles remaining in his hand, before tossing what was left into the river.

"Cenwalh has fled his kingdom. There will be no aid from the West Saxons. At least Earconbert remains king of Kent." Oswiu turned to look at his wife. "I do not think you need fear for him. The Kentmen are tied by blood and marriage to the Franks, and I do not think Penda wishes to call down their wrath. But for his part, Earconbert does not wish to attract Penda's glance: he will not come to our aid. So that leaves, to the south, only Œthelwald. We can at least count on him; but the men of Deira have not the strength they once had." Oswiu shook his head. "And what strength they had left we sapped in the campaign against Oswine.

"As for the men of the Old North, Talorcan, king of the Picts, will send only what aid he can spare, and that will be little indeed, for Penda has raised his old alliances against us. Gwynedd and Powys and those kingdoms of the Britons that my father put down: they seek revenge on the father's son. And Rheged…" Oswiu grimaced. "There will be no aid from Rheged. Not since…" He glanced at his wife and then looked away. "Well, they will not help us. Some men might come from Dal Riada, but with Rheged hostile and the men of the Rock ever looking for advantage, there will not be many."

The king looked at his counsellors. "I fear we stand alone before the storm."

At first, only the river made answer, whispering its reply through the trailing tips of the willows that hung down into the stream. But then the queen spoke.

"You learned this from Ahlflæd?"

"Yes. She sent word. Penda sent a messenger to his son, telling this and calling him to come to him."

"Think you not that this might be a ruse? Penda is subtle – surely he might guess that messages sent to his son will be relayed to you."

"I think he knows that well – and wants me to know. Besides, I have sent messengers myself to check on this news. Not all have returned, but those that have confirm it. I sought to catch Penda in a net of alliances, but he has burst the net, cutting down those who found friendship with me and putting in their place men beholden to himself. It seems to me that this time he seeks also to force men back to the old ways, to worship of the old gods, for those kings he has placed upon thrones have turned their backs upon the new life and gone back to the ways of before." Oswiu shook his head. "This I do not understand. Never before has Penda sought to do this." Oswiu looked to his counsellors. "There is some new devilry at play here, although I cannot discern what it is."

"What of your daughter's husband?" asked Romanus, the priest. "The Red Hand."

"Ahlflæd sends word that the son will not heed the father's call."

At that, Eanflæd looked sharply at her husband. "I fear Ahlflæd buys peace for us at the cost of great suffering for herself."

"What would you have me do? Bring her home and have the Red Hand raised against us too? That is the burden of women, the peace weavers: to be pierced to buy peace. It is what my mother faced."

Now Ahlfrith, Ahlflæd's brother, spoke. "My sister knew well what she faced when she went to the Red Hand. Her courage won us the day when it seemed that Bamburgh would fall. Now it strips the enemy of the Red Hand – and I saw him as he grew. Peada has not the subtlety of his father, but the name he has for brutality is well given. For my part, I am glad not to have to face him on the field of slaughter, and I give thanks to my sister for winning us that battle."

"I too," said the queen. "But I wish there was another way."

"Don't you think I wish that too?" said Oswiu. "She is my daughter." He stopped and turned away for a moment, breathing hard. With his back to his counsellors, he asked, "What counsel have you for me? My heart tells me that, in the end, I must fight, but my wit tells me I would be a fool to contend against such odds. What say you all?"

"If a woman may speak of that which best concerns men, it seems to me that many kings gathered beneath one banner shall be as uncomfortable as many women cooking the same meal. The longer we delay them, the more likely there shall be some falling out between the kings Penda has gathered. The longer we give these fears and doubts to grow, the more dangerous they will become."

Oswiu nodded. His eyes looked out over the river, but his mind thought of the high paths and trackless places of his kingdom; places where many men might pass unseen to those who did not know the land.

"Men do well to call you wise, my queen. Have my other counsellors aught to say?"

"I would speak, Father," said Ahlfrith. He looked to the others around him; by sign they bade him tell what he would.

"If time be our strategy, then here is another way to buy it: send a messenger to Penda, a man of standing, to meet the king. The messenger shall tell Penda he has authority to treat with him, and he shall offer him great reward, in gold and silver, that Penda might stay his march and keep his armies from our land."

"Pay Penda off?"

"If he will be bought. I think it more likely that such a messenger will but gain us time – but if time be our strategy, then we should seek whatever means we can to gain it."

Oswiu turned from the river back to his counsellors. "How much should we offer?"

"I should say much." Ahlfrith looked to his fellow counsellors for confirmation. "I would give all that I had, Father."

But Oswiu shook his head. "Not all. We shall offer Penda much, but keep as much back, for we may have need of it later." He looked around his ring of counsellors. "It might be as well to find somewhere to keep our treasure safe, for I foresee that we shall have need to travel swiftly in the weeks and months ahead, and nothing slows a man more than the desire to make sure his wealth is safe."

"Bury it?" asked Ahlfrith.

"That would be best," said Oswiu. "Somewhere safe, where we may find it again." He looked to his son. "I give you this task, Ahlfrith. What we do not give to the messenger to take to Penda, we bury, against the day we have need of it."

"But who shall be the messenger?" asked Ahlfrith. "I would go, but…"

Oswiu held up his hand. "There is no need to say further. I would not give my right hand as hostage to Penda. Once, I would have sent Æthelwin…" Oswiu paused. "But now I do not know who to send."

"I will go."

The words were quiet. The speaker, as he spoke them, saw the wind part the curtain of sedge and, as the sedge parted, he saw the glitter light atop the water, playing with the joy of new creation. Then a swallow, skimming low, jinked over the river's surface before flying past the line of people who had all turned to look, with open eyes and open mouths, at Coifi.

Brought back to them by the swallow, Coifi looked at the faces of surprise.

"Is it so strange? If Penda should slay me, would that be any loss to you? I am old now, and weary – and I have always hated riding as much as the animals have hated me. If you need swift movement and fast riding, I would surely be but a hindrance." The old priest snorted with laughter. "The greater the need for swiftness, the more surely shall I see some mark of the working of wyrd, and turn aside to follow it, when all are urging me on. Besides, if it be true that Penda seeks now to restore the worship of the old gods, he will like enough treat with me where he would not treat with others. So I say send me, with what treasure you would give, and I will seek to stay Penda's marching and prune some of his support." Coifi smiled, although this smile was sad. "I fell from my old ways through love of that which the warriors wear as mark of the king's favour and their glory: surely I might prise a few away from the enemy's army with some of the baubles I once sought."

Oswiu came forward to stand in front of the old priest.

"In truth, I wondered once why my brother saw fit to retain your service after Edwin died. Already, I have seen some of what my brother saw in you, but now I see it clearly: you are a good and faithful servant."

"Wait." Romanus the priest held up his hand. "If this priest of the old gods will go as a messenger to a pagan king, then I should go as well, that the new life be brought again before Penda."

But Oswiu shook his head. "If Diuma could not bring Penda into the new life, then I doubt that you might. Nor would I lose you now, when the queen is with child, for we will have need of you when her time comes, to call down God's blessings from heaven and to protect her from evil."

The priest started to dispute the king's words, but Eanflæd laid a gentle hand on his arm. "I would not have you leave me, Romanus. Not now."

At her words, the priest bowed his head. "Then I needs must stay."

"But not I." Acca stepped forward. "If this old fool gets his wish to put himself into the wolf's lair, then I will go with him, lest on the way there he sets off chasing after some phantom of wyrd and ends, not in Mercia, but looking down a badger sett in Dal Riada. Besides, lord, on such an errand there will be need for someone with the gift of honeyed words and right speech." Acca pointed at the slight figure of the old priest, with his raven-feather cloak drawn tightly around his thin shoulders. "Should Penda give him leave to speak, his croaking might as well come from the beak of the bird that sits upon his back. Whereas if I speak, then the king of the Mercians shall hear a voice that has told the tales of our people into being, that has sung the song of the kings and brought the gods down from high heaven and set them before men in hall. Such a voice might even persuade Penda to lay aside his purpose and seek renewed friendship with you, lord. After all, if Penda's son can marry your daughter, then surely peace is possible between Bernicia and Mercia?"

"I fear," said Oswiu, "that marrying Ahlflæd to the Red Hand may have stirred Penda to this new wrath. Besides, he has reason enough to hate me already. After all, I took his eye."

At that, Coifi croaked, making the sound of a raven. Oswiu looked to him.

"Very well, Bran took the eye. But not having the raven to work his revenge upon, Penda must seek another. I have long awaited it." He looked around his counsellors. "Now the time has come. He seeks to destroy me. But I will not wait for him, like some hare caught in a snare." The king took the hands of Coifi and Acca. "You will go, together, into the hands of my enemy. I will give you my blessing, as king and as friend: may you be wise and subtle as the serpent, that you sow doubt among our enemies and bring time for your lord." With that, Oswiu breathed upon their hands and upon their brows, and kissed them both.

Stepping back, he looked at priest and scop.

"You must go quickly. I will gather all the gold I may in such time as remains, that you have enough to earn a hearing from Penda and the kings of the land. But above all, go fast."

Chapter 6

"I don't think the king meant this fast." Coifi, bobbing up and down on the horse, flung his arms around its neck in a final attempt to stop himself being thrown from the animal. But Acca urged his own mount on and, reaching over, grabbed the halter of the old priest's horse and pulled it along.

Feeling himself beginning to slip down the side of his animal's neck, Coifi cried out, "I'm going to fall."

Glancing round, Acca reached over and grabbed a handful of raven's feathers, with some of the old priest's thin shoulder beneath, and hauled him back upright.

"No, you're not," he said. Nevertheless, Acca slowed his animal down. His old friend had never been a good horseman. Back in the days, many years past now, when he had been chief priest to Edwin, Coifi had been forbidden from riding a stallion. This had been little loss for the priest, who was only comfortable sitting on the calmest of animals. As for the horses, they regarded Coifi with the same suspicion as he looked at them. But on this hard ride south, Coifi had, of necessity, to sit astride stronger and faster animals; it was only through some chance of fate, Acca thought, that he had made it so far without breaking leg or arm or neck. The small troop of warriors that accompanied them – for it was not safe for two ageing men to venture abroad carrying the treasure they brought with them – had learned to ride at a distance behind Coifi, ready to stop immediately should the old priest fall, again, from his horse.

But now, Acca saw, the need for haste was over.

He held up his hand. "Stop."

He was leading. The old road, the road of the emperors, had been rising, slowly but steadily, for the past mile, climbing the climbing land, but now Acca crested the ridge and he saw the road falling just as gradually into the vale below, where the straight road of the emperors met one of the hollow ways of the men of old, the ones who had first walked this land and scored paths by the passage of their feet and the hooves of their animals. Past the junction, scattered on either side of the road, he saw the largest camp of men and animals he had ever seen. Scanning over the tents and shelters, and round the makeshift paddocks holding horses and oxen, Acca started counting the banners and flags flying outside the larger tents and pavilions. As he was doing so, Coifi's horse crept up level with him.

"Penda?"

"Yes," said Acca. "But more than just Penda, many more. I can see twenty... twenty-five banners. They are too far for me to read from here, but most, I think, are the banners of kings or great thegns." The scop shook his head. "I have never seen an army so great."

"Well, let us be grateful," said Coifi. "An army this great is hard to hide and we have found it with little difficulty."

"With an army this great, Penda has no need to hide," said Acca.

Coifi squinted. The distance of the world had been disappearing into a blur, as if a fog that never lifted had fallen upon everything. Men's sight failed as they aged, but he had not known it would fall upon him in such a way. By squinting, he sought to clear some of that fog and, in the bright sun of the summer, he could see further. The scop spoke truly. In truth, Coifi had never seen so many men gathered together either. Even the great army Penda had brought to lay siege to Bamburgh was but a part of the array of men spread before them.

While Coifi continued to look at the army laid out before them, Acca set to ordering the warriors who had accompanied them.

"Ride back along the road. Two miles back, do you remember the ash by the side of the road, split in two as if by Thunor's hammer? There is a wood lying near the road at that point. Go there, and take cover in the wood, but keep watch upon the road. Should Penda accept the king's offer, we will return to find you and deliver the treasure to the king of the Mercians. But if we do not return in two days, or you see others searching for you, then take the treasure back to the king. You understand?"

The leader of the warriors, a fine, experienced man named Goda, nodded his understanding. "I would not send you alone into Penda's camp," he said to Acca.

"You see it," said Acca. "Even if you all came, could you guard us against so many?"

"No," said Goda, "but Penda would buy your lives dearly," he added with a grin.

"I would prefer that my life not be put up for sale," said Acca. "Besides, the king charged you with the care of the gold and silver he gave over to us. Keep it safe until we have need of it, Goda."

Goda made the courtesy, then wheeled his horse, and with the other men started back along the road to the split ash tree.

Acca watched them go, then turned his horse round.

"With so many men, it's strange that Penda has set no sentry here," said Coifi. "Such a post could see anyone approaching."

Acca pointed down the road. "It seems the king of the Mercians agrees with you."

Galloping towards them was a party of warriors, spear tips glinting in the summer sun.

*

"So, your king sends a scop and a priest as messengers."

Penda sat on the judgement seat that had been set beside his tent. Around him were the kings who rode under his banner: the king of the East Angles, the king of the East Saxons, the king of Lindsey, the kings of Gwynedd and Powys.

It was a still day and the banners hung limply from their poles, only stirring when a heat breeze sprang up, rustling the dry grass and bending the stiff arms of the teasels that lined the road of the emperors. As Penda's men had brought them towards the camp, Acca had expected to be blindfolded. But when they dismounted, the scouts had merely led them, none too gently but with nothing masking their eyes, through the camp. It was as if Penda did not care what they saw of his preparations.

In among the tents and shelters, it was much easier to see a banner

whenever the stuttering breeze spread it out. One flag, flicking out
as the wind pulled it, caught Acca's attention more than any other.

"Did you see that?" he asked, pointing.

Coifi looked to see, but the wind died away as soon as it had
risen.

"Keep watching," said Acca. "By that tent. Tell me, please, that
my eyes fail me and I saw that banner wrongly."

But then the wind had flicked the cloth into the air once more
and Coifi gasped his sight of it. "Deira," he said.

Among the dragons and wolves and bears and ravens that
fluttered above the army Penda had gathered around him was the
boar of Deira.

Now, standing before Penda, Acca looked at the assembled kings
for sight of Œthelwald. But there was no sign of him among the
other kings. Only the glimpse of the banner told the tale.

"Would a king that honours me send a scop and an old priest as
his messengers?"

Acca took one final, measured glance around. This was an
audience such as even he had never known before. Should it be his
final performance, it would be one to be remembered the length and
breadth of this land.

"*Hwæt!*"

At the old, familiar call to attention the conversations and
whisperings and movements all around the gathered kings came to
a stop. Never before had a messenger called such a group of kings to
attend to him.

"My lord, King Oswiu, Iding, ruler of Bernicia, master of the
lands north of the Humber, sends greetings to the kings here gathered
upon the borders of his land, and bids them a peaceful welcome. For
it has ever been my lord's desire to live at peace with the other kings
of this land, for he desires not war, if it may be avoided, but only
that which is his by right and by blood." Acca looked around the
assembled kings, engaging each by eye. "For his part, my lord has no
quarrel with any of you. Should you have quarrel with him, he has
given me leave to treat with you, to seek understanding of whatever

offence he may have committed against your majesty, that he might make recompense. For he has ever sought to treat with honour those who sit upon the thrones of this land and in particular those who share in the new life with him." Acca sought out, by sight, the kings of the East Saxons and the East Angles, the king of Gwynedd and the king of Strathclyde. The Britons, ancient foes of the Idings, met his gaze levelly and without shame, for in standing with Penda they followed in the long alliances of their peoples. But the kings of the East Saxons and the East Angles shifted under Acca's glance. "Such is my king's grace that he will treat with those who have taken thrones once held by men whom he accounted friends, until they were most cruelly slain. But then even the highest king might come to his throne by a treacherous slaying."

At this, the assembly as a whole seemed to gasp, for all there had heard the rumour that Penda had murdered Cearl, the previous king of Mercia, when he was Cearl's warmaster. Eyes flicked to where Penda sat, silent and hooded, upon the judgement seat, his black eye glittering as it looked upon the scop.

Penda held his hand up.

Under that upraised hand, even Acca, though he would have spoken further, fell silent.

"If this new life your king proclaims is so secure, why then does he send, beside you, the priest of the gods of our fathers?"

Acca made to answer, but still Penda held his hand up for silence, and beneath it the scop found he could not speak.

Standing behind the judgement seat, looking with satisfaction at them, Acca saw Penda's own priest, Wihtrun. Despite the summer heat, he still wore his wolf cloak over his shoulders, the head of the animal peering over his own, its teeth bared upon Wihtrun's forehead.

"Besides, I have not the patience to listen to the witterings of scops." Penda glanced around at the assembled kings. "If any here doubt where to lay their banner, thinking perhaps of the loyalty they once owed to Oswald, then there is one new come among us whom I would introduce to the rest of you."

Penda did not look round, but merely beckoned. "Come forth."

The flap of his tent was lifted aside and a man emerged, blinking at the light and the scrutiny.

"Œthelwald, Oswald son, king of Deira, marches with us against his faithless uncle," said Penda. As he spoke, Penda watched the two messengers standing in front of him. Though Acca tried, he could not stop some part of the shock he felt appearing on his face. But Coifi, hearing the sudden scraping of a grasshopper's legs and the whirr of its music, smiled.

Penda waited while the whispers of surprise at Œthelwald's presence died away.

"If you have an offer for me from your lord, then tell it. Else leave our presence, for we have many tasks to accomplish."

At last, Penda lowered his hand and Acca, released of its weight, could speak again.

"My lord, generous even to those who wrong him, offers great treasures of gold and silver to you, lord, and to all here present; for he has no wish for war."

"Great treasure? What does this great treasure consist of?"

"Gold, cunningly worked and inlaid with garnet, and silver, of coin and plate and bowl."

"How much?" asked Penda.

Hearing the question, Acca remembered the rumour that attended the king of the Mercians – that he was of peasant stock, of a family more used to dragging iron through the ground than wielding it in battle, and of giving render to the king rather than fighting beside him. Before, Acca had always thought the rumours of Penda's mean birth simply the chatter of enemies, but now, hearing the way in which Penda asked how much Oswiu was willing to pay for peace, Acca knew the rumours for truth: Penda must once have scrabbled among the tares and the scrapings to make good the weight of food to render to the king. Only such an upbringing could produce that tone – that particular tone which combined the certainty that the weights were fixed with the sudden, greedy hope that maybe they were faulty in your favour.

"One pound of gold and four pounds of silver," said Acca.

One or two gasps went up from the assembled kings. Such was treasure indeed.

But Penda held up his hand for silence.

"Words have no more weight than the wind. If you would have me hear your offer, then lay this pound of gold and four pounds of silver before me."

Acca spread his arms wide.

"Would I speak of that which I do not have? Would I cast myself into the wolf's lair on the back of a lie?" He looked around the kings, catching as many by the eye as he could. "Do I look like a man who wants to die?"

Cheers and calls went up at Acca's words, but Penda did not take his gaze from the men in front of him.

"You look like a man who tells stories to kings," Penda said. "But I would have the truth of this. One of you will go, and return with the gold and treasure whereof you speak, against the life of the other." The king of the Mercians pointed at Acca. "You will go. I would have some peace while you are away." Penda signalled to his guards. "Take the other and hold him. Put him in my tent."

Coifi, who had become lost in the spark of light upon the garnets on the buckle that held Penda's cloak, blinked back into awareness when the guards laid hold of him.

"What's happening?" he asked, as they dragged him, unresisting, away.

"It's all right," Acca called after him. "I'll be back to get you."

"If you are not back by nightfall, then he will not be alive when you do return," said Penda.

"But…" began Acca.

Penda shook his head.

"But…" Acca tried again.

Penda held his finger to his lips.

"But…" Acca tried a third time.

"Hasten," said Penda. And he glanced towards the west, where the sun was but two hands' breadth from setting.

Acca turned and ran from the assembly, accompanied by the laughter of kings, and the guards rushing after him.

But Penda raised his hand for quiet.

"He is not – quite – as stupid as he seems. It is clear from this that Oswiu seeks to gain time, for that is what I should do were I in his place." Penda looked around the watching kings. "I have often given thought to what my enemy might do." Sitting, hooded, upon the judgement seat, the king of the Mercians seemed to the eyes of the men watching less like a man than he had ever seemed before. His single, black eye glittered beneath his hood.

"Yes," said Penda. "I have given thought to what my enemy will do and, in sending these men, he does it. He will seek time." Penda looked around the assembled kings. "For you were late in assembling, and the season for war draws near its end. Least that is what Oswiu believes. He will seek to delay us, to sow confusion and doubt... and greed. But in doing this, he does what I wish him to. Let him offer gold and silver. We will take it. By what he offers we will know what he still has to give. By the time we march into his lands, the harvest will be in, and we shall burn it. Let all those who placed their trust in this Iding come to know that their trust was vain and their hope false."

Penda slowly stood from the judgement seat.

"I shall set the ways of ours fathers and our fathers' fathers against Oswiu's new life. Then all shall see, and see truly, which way men should take."

*

"Do you truly think the scop will return for you?"

Coifi looked up. In Penda's tent, the air was thick and stifling. Under his raven-feather cloak, trails of sweat trickled down between his shoulder blades. When he had first been put into its gloom, his hands tied together and the rope looped around one of the supports, he had thought of trying to pull the support down. But then the tent would simply have sagged down on top of him, and the guards forced to repitch it would have treated him even less kindly than they had when first tying him to it. Besides, there was no escaping from such a place. Even as he had stood beside Acca, Coifi had seen the unease that Penda had come to evoke in those that followed him. His tent stood alone, set in space where, in the rest of the camp, almost no space existed. None, not even other kings, would willingly set their tents alongside the king of the Mercians.

He wondered if it was ever thus.

No. For he had travelled with Penda through part of his kingdom when they went in disguise. Then, people sought him out, sought his company and his protection. Now, for sure, men sought his protection, but it was as much for fear of Penda as for assurance against others. Even the men of his own household now held back from their king.

They all feared Penda now.

Coifi was thinking on this when the tent flap opened, letting light into the gloom. Wihtrun slipped inside and came over to where Coifi squatted upon his heels.

"One pound of gold and four of silver. That is a lot to put before a man."

Coifi glanced up at the priest. "He will come back," he said.

Wihtrun rubbed a hand across his forehead. "It is hot in here," he said. He squatted down next to Coifi. "I can take you out of here, get you a drink."

Coifi made no answer, but stared at the man beside him. Then, despite himself, his gaze darted away after the shifting of a shadow.

"Here, pull the rope tight."

Wihtrun drew his seax from his belt and, setting blade to rope, cut Coifi free. The old priest, no longer held up, fell backwards.

Wihtrun took his wrist. "Up," he said, and hauled the older man to his feet. "It's cooler outside, and I will get you something to drink." Leading Coifi by the hand, Wihtrun took him from the tent. Emerging, blinking, into the light, Coifi saw that the sun was hanging low in the west. Half a hand's breadth held it from the horizon. Despite himself, Coifi could not help looking to see if Acca was coming. But what he could see of the old road of the emperors was empty, this late in the day. Any travellers would have sought shelter and safety for the night by now.

Coifi looked at Wihtrun. "Do you have wine? If this be my last drink, I would that it was something other than small beer."

"Yes, I have wine. Come." Still holding his arm, Wihtrun took Coifi through the camp to where large cooking fires burned and most of the wagons were circled. Never letting go of the old priest, Wihtrun elbowed his way through a hubbub of men to one of the wagons – manned by particularly heavily armed men – and, after a short but loud argument, one of the guards disappeared onto the wagon, to return a minute later with a flask, which he handed to Wihtrun amid further warnings as to the risks he was running in doing so. Listening, Coifi realized that the food and drink upon this wagon were for the king's use. It was only by claiming that the king himself wished the wine given to him, and by threatening to return, with Penda, to prove the claim, that Wihtrun had managed to extract a flask from its keeper.

"Come, it is good wine," said Wihtrun. "If your friend does not return, it will be with the taste of good wine in your mouth that you die – that, and his betrayal."

"He will not betray me," said Coifi. "But I am thirsty, and would drink."

Wihtrun leaned closer to him. "I would drink too," he whispered. "But if I am seen – and there are some in this camp who wander it, looking to spin lies against others – then I would have to explain my drinking of the king's wine with others. But you are our guest – and our prisoner. So, let us go where there are fewer eyes to see and no ears to hear, and there let us drink."

Wihtrun led Coifi through and out of the camp.

"Where are we going?" Coifi asked.

Wihtrun pointed ahead. "Where the ways cross," he said. "We will rest and drink there. The hollow way is shaded, and cool."

Reaching the place where the ways crossed, Coifi saw a post driven into the summer-hardened ground. From it, the skull of an animal glared blankly at the two men. Coifi saw a fly crawl from the eye socket and scrape its legs over its shining eyes.

It was strange, Coifi thought, how, though a mist had descended over his sight when looking at things far away, yet he could see that which was near more clearly than ever. Once, he would not have been able to make out the fly's eyes, but now he could see them. The fly, for its part, paid Coifi no heed, but continued with its business.

"The wine."

Coifi looked round to see Wihtrun holding the flask out to him. From the stain on the priest's lips, Coifi could tell that he had already made a start on slaking summer thirst. Taking the flask, Coifi drank. It was good wine.

The old priest drank again, wiping the back of his wrist over his mouth when he was finished. As he handed the flask back to Wihtrun, he said, "Now I understand why Acca says he must drink wine to keep his voice sweet."

"I hope he will return," said Wihtrun.

Coifi saw that, while he held the flask, he did not drink from it, but rather passed it distractedly from one hand to the other.

"If you have drunk enough, then I will have more," said Coifi. "The tent was stuffier than a compost heap in a shed."

"Here, drink." Wihtrun handed the flask back to Coifi. "I have drunk my fill." The priest looked at the older man as he raised the flask and drank, his throat bobbing as the wine went down. "It would be a great shame should your scop not return, for there are fewer of us now than there were, and though you serve my king's enemy, yet the greater service is to those whom we both serve."

Coifi stopped drinking, but still holding the flask to his lips, he looked with one eye past it to Wihtrun.

"The gods," said Wihtrun, seeing the question without it being spoken. "We are both priests to the gods."

Coifi resumed his drinking, but he shook his head as he did so. Wiping his mouth, he looked at Wihtrun. "I am a priest no more," he said.

But now Wihtrun shook his head. "Do not tell me that. Once you have walked the spirit ways and seen the play of wyrd in blood and light and water, then you will ever be a priest. Say to me that is not true, and I will speak no further."

But Coifi held silence. For once, his eyes did not wander, but were locked upon those of the man standing in front of him upon the crossing of the ways.

Wihtrun nodded. "What we have seen is not so easily forgotten, nor the pledges we made so easily abjured."

Coifi felt the wine, potent and warm, spreading from his belly, sending life and heat down into his legs and arms, and rising up to his head. He swayed slightly.

"While we can drink this wine here undisturbed, there was another reason I brought you to this crossroad." Wihtrun put his hand to the pole. The skull – Coifi thought it now the bone of a cat – looked at the two men standing before it. "I planted this here," said Wihtrun. "In the days of our fathers, every crossing of the ways was made holy by sacrifice, but now, men forget the customs of before. Men forget the gods." Wihtrun looked at Coifi, and anger sparked in his eyes. "You were the first to forsake them. I have heard how you desecrated the grove sacred to the gods at Goodmanham." The priest's hand strayed to his belt, where his seax lay sheathed. "I ought to kill you for what you did." Wihtrun drew the knife. The metal hissed as it slid from the sheath. The sun, low in the sky, painted the seax red.

Coifi made no move. He did not look at the knife approaching in Wihtrun's hand, but only the man. Tears had sprung in Wihtrun's eyes. They flowed down his cheeks. And he came closer, holding the knife.

"The tree of the world groans at the axe blows. I feel it, I hear it. The gods are forgotten and forsaken, and turn their eyes from us, their forgetters. Men follow after this new god, and none hearken after the cries of our forefathers." Wihtrun stopped in front of Coifi. He traced the tip of the seax down the side of Coifi's face, from eye to cheek, to the corner of his mouth. "I should kill you." The knife followed the line of Coifi's jaw down onto his throat. "A sacrifice to the gods you forsook." The tip slid down, over his chest, to rest above Coifi's heart.

Coifi stared into the eyes of the man who was going to kill him. Wihtrun wept.

Coifi raised his hand. He saw, laid out upon the man's cheek, the web of fate playing out in the tracks of tears. He wiped his finger over Wihtrun's cheek and wiped away the tears.

"Tell me," said Coifi, "what may I do to bring the gods back among men?"

And as the tears were wiped away, a great light of hope filled Wihtrun's face.

"You will help me?" he said. "For I see you perceive the workings of wyrd in a way that few others have, and none today."

"I would have men worship truly," said Coifi.

Wihtrun sheathed his knife and took hold of Coifi's thin shoulders. "Then it may be. For Woden walks among men again. He has not forsaken his people."

"Where have you seen the Hooded One?" asked Coifi. "For I have oft looked for him, but when I most thought to have seen him, it ever seemed to me afterwards that I was deceived."

"The Lord of Battles has come among men to feast upon the slain. For the High King has taken the mantle of the Father of Men. He has cast down those kings who had forsaken the ways of their fathers and accepted this new god; he has put in their place kings who cleave to the old ways and make sacrifice to the gods of our fathers -- and who honour those who can see the workings of wyrd." Wihtrun tightened his grasp on Coifi's shoulders. "It can be again as it was in the days of our fathers. Tell only where the High King may find the king of the Bernicians, and then it will be over. For with the great army that we bring, even such a stronghold as Bamburgh will fall. Then, when all men see that the Lord of Battles has triumphed, they will turn their faces from this new god and return to the ways of our fathers. A man may pledge to a lord, but the pledges made to the gods are greater, for they hold this middle-earth firm beneath the high heavens."

"Until the serpent rises," said Coifi.

"Until that day," agreed Wihtrun. "But so long as men stand fast beside their gods, that day may long be postponed. Help us stand firm, Coifi. Tell where we may find your lord – for without him, and his protection, this new way will quickly wither and die."

"I – I…" Coifi's eyes darted into the west, to where the sun was setting. And though the mist of unseeing veiled the distance, he saw the red that stained the sky and knew that it was blood.

"I will show where you may find him," said Coifi. "But is that all your king requires? Does he wish no other knowledge?"

"He would know where the other members of the king's family may be found. For it is the High King's wish to destroy the Idings, to wipe their blood from this middle-earth, that the old ways may return."

"Would the High King destroy women too? And children?"

"That their blood line fail: yes."

Coifi shook his head. "That is not the true way of kings."

But Wihtrun held up his hand. "That which a man may not do, a god may."

Coifi looked into his memory. "It is true some men name Woden the Slayer. But I had not thought the killing included children."

"Men also name Woden the Revenge Taker. By the actions of the Idings, the Lord of Battles has been displaced in men's hearts; the sweet sacrifices that filled this land with their smoke, reaching to high heaven, have been quenched. Now, the High King shall take vengeance on the father of the faithless." Wihtrun grasped Coifi's hand. "Help us root out this viper's nest."

"What would you have of me?"

"We know where Oswiu's sister lives, in her house upon the rocky head north of Bamburgh. But what of the rest of his blood line? Where are they?"

"There are few left, save those that remain with the king. His daughter, you know, has wed the Red Hand. Would the High King slay the wife of his son?"

"The son who ever delays to join his father, with one excuse after another? Penda has other sons, and worthier. Once the king of Bernicia is put down, the Red Hand may find his hand wiped clean."

"The king's nephew marches with you. His mother died some years ago. His sons fight alongside him. Who else would you know of?"

"There is also the mother of the woman who married the Red Hand. The High King has heard tell that she lives in the house established by the king's sister. Is this true?"

Coifi stared at the priest of the old gods in front of him. The setting sun cast its blood light upon his face. "Yes. She lives there," he said.

Wihtrun smiled. "Thank you," he said.

"Surely the king's nephew has already told you?"

"There are some things that are better asked twice."

"The holy house where they live is far from here. It would be no easy march to reach."

"Mayhap far by land. But not so far by river and sea."

Coifi nodded, his face blank. "That is clever. They look not to the sea for threat, but only to news of what happens elsewhere in this land – sea travellers are always welcomed."

"The High King has already sent his men forth. The king of Bernicia shall soon know this is a war like none he has ever faced before."

"What will happen to the king's nephew – when this is all over?"

"The High King is faithful to those who serve him well." Wihtrun looked hard at Coifi. "When there is a new king upon the throne in Bernicia, there will be need of a priest there, to re-establish the ways of our fathers among the people. It were better it was a man known to them already, one whom they trust."

Coifi nodded. He said no word but pointed back towards the camp. "Although my eyes grow weak, my ears still retain their sharpness. My friend has not forgotten me. He has returned."

*

Acca lay the chest on the ground in front of the assembled kings and thegns. He looked around, and saw all of them, the gold lust lighting their eyes, staring at the chest by his feet. But then he looked to the judgement seat and saw Penda, his black eye looking not at the chest but at the man who had brought it.

As he had carried the chest into the camp, Acca had planned

how he was going to tease the greed of the kings, how he would describe the richly worked gold, the cunning of the silversmiths. But now, seeing the black eye glitter from the shadows, the words he had thought of dried in his mouth and would not come. Instead, Acca simply bent down and opened the chest.

Many of the kings, and most of the thegns, gasped. But Penda did not even look down.

"The gift of my lord, King Oswiu!" Acca let the gold light, bathing his face and body, speak its spell into the hearts of the watching men. And it did.

One of the men, Æthelhere, king of the East Angles, stepped forward.

"This is a mighty gift, lord," he said. "I have not seen its like before." He glanced around and saw, in slight nods and the blinking of eyes, confirmation of what he spoke in the faces of those who listened. Emboldened, he continued. "With so much given to us, mayhap it were best to take what is given – for to make war is ever to risk everything upon a man falling in the shieldwall." This time, the nods were supported by some murmurs. "It is, as I said, a mighty gift, lord."

"You are right."

At Penda's words, whispers ran around the watching, listening men.

"It is indeed a mighty gift." Penda looked to Acca. "Tell me, scop, how many days did the Iding take to gather this great gift? Three? Four?"

Acca shifted upon his feet, unsure of what to say.

Penda looked to the kings waiting upon his words. "Think well on this. If the Iding could gather so much in so short a time, how much more may he gather if he be given longer? And what might we find when we enter his kingdom? I have seen the splendour of the palace of the Idings at Ad Gefrin; I have seen the height of the walls at Bamburgh. More gold and more silver than any king dreamed of might be hidden behind those walls, or beneath the palace." Penda rose from the judgement seat and started towards Acca. "If the Iding would buy peace with me, let him pay the price." He put his foot against the chest and kicked it over, spilling the gold and silver out upon the earth. "This is but the start. If the Iding will buy peace, tell him that it will cost him everything: all that he has. Tell the Iding that, scop. Ask him if he is willing to pay so much to save his throne – and his life."

Acca made to answer, but Penda held up his hand.

"There is no more to say. Return to the Iding with my message. If he would answer, tell him to make it soon. We march into his kingdom with the new day." The king started to turn away, then stopped. "Oh, and tell the Iding one more thing: his priest is staying with me."

Acca stared at Penda. "Bishop Finan? He is here?"

"No. The priest of the gods of our fathers."

"Coifi?" Acca looked around wildly, searching for sight of the old priest. "But we came as messengers, under the flag of truce."

"You think I am forcing him to stay? No – ask him. He stays by his own will." Penda looked round himself, searching among the gathered men for a face. "Wihtrun. Fetch the Iding's priest, that he may tell the truth of this to the scop. But see that the scop leaves before the night has fallen. I would not have him here on the morrow."

Penda turned to go.

"But what about the gold?" asked Æthelhere, king of the East Angles. "What will you do with that?"

Penda did not even look round. "Share it among yourselves," he said.

Later, as he hurried back to King Oswiu, Acca remembered well what he saw then: the kings of the land fighting over spilled gold and silver as if they were boys tussling in a field. Only the stricture that Penda insisted upon, that no one bear sword in his presence, prevented the brawl ending with several of the thrones of the land vacant.

But even such a sight did little to distract Acca from what Penda had told him. He looked, through the heaving scrum of men, for some sight of Wihtrun. But the priest found him first, pulling his arm and turning him so that he faced Coifi. The old priest was twitching and his eyes were rolling, as they did before a seizure took him and his spirit went wandering.

"Here, ask him if he stays by his own will," said Wihtrun.

"Is it true?" Acca took hold of Coifi's thin shoulders. "Is it true?" Under his hands, he could feel the old man's bones shaking. Coifi's eyes began to roll upwards. "No! Stop! Tell me, is it true?"

But Coifi's eyes rolled white. His trembling muscles suddenly went still, and he slumped, as limp as cloth, in Acca's hands. So sudden was the cutting of the cords that held his muscles that Acca, holding him, was pulled off balance and, as Coifi fell, he fell on top of him. So bony was the old priest that his body made no cushion beneath him, but rather it seemed that he fell upon a bag of sticks and stones.

Upon the floor, the muscles began to shake once more as the old man's back arched. But as his back arched, his arms flexed, tightening around the scop, pulling him back as he tried to get up, pulling his head close to Coifi's drooling mouth.

"Penda sends a boat to Æbbe's house."

The message was drool covered, flecked into Acca's ear as he struggled to get free, but he heard it. Through the shouts of the brawl and the noise of the camp, and Coifi's own grunts and squeals, he heard it and knew what to do.

Chapter 7

Oswiu drove his horse into the rain. The summer had broken into storm and he rode into it, the rain stinging his face, the thunder ringing about his ears. Lightning flashes, so frequent as to almost make a new sun under the overpowering gloom of the storm clouds, lit the roiling darkness above him. Wiping the rain from his eyes, he glanced back. They were still following. Oswiu rode at the head of a small group of men, galloping as fast as their horses and the storm allowed, across the farms and marshes that ran east of the hills and west of the sea, to his sister's holy house at Coldingham.

It was hard to tell in this storm light how much of the day was left, but it could not be long before the sun set behind the walls of cloud. Then the night would come and, if the lightning abated, it would be dark indeed. But he could not wait, even were the ground in front of his horse invisible.

Acca had arrived at the royal estate at Wooler as one dead and lashed to his animal. The horse was worse; when the gate warden lifted Acca from its back the beast fell dead.

"The king, the king."

The king was brought to him, and Acca told Oswiu that Penda had sent men by boat to the holy house at Coldingham, to take from there Æbbe and Rhieienmelth. He told how Penda held Coifi from returning home, but how the priest, feigning seizure, gave Acca the news of the raid Penda sent against the king's kin. He told how the treasure had bought them no time.

Acca fell back upon the bed, unable for once to speak further.

"You have done well, Acca," said the king. He took the scop's hand. "Know this: Penda thinks wrongly if he believes he may take my sister Æbbe from the holy house, for she has gone to visit the house at Ebchester. It is a wild and lonely place and they will not find her there. Now rest."

"But what of Rhieienmelth? Is she not there?" asked Acca.

"Yes," said Oswiu, "she is there. Where I sent her." He leaned down and kissed Acca on the brow. "Take the rest you may, friend. I have some hard riding to do."

Ahlfrith had wanted to go. "She is my mother!" he had said. "I must go to her."

But Oswiu, already arming himself, shook his head. "I need you to gather all you may and take them, by secret quiet ways, up into the hills. If the tale Acca tells be anywhere near the truth, if we had ten times the number of men, we might not stand before the army Penda has assembled." Oswiu drove his knuckles into his forehead. "It seems that everything I try goes amiss: the kings I brought to the new life Penda has killed; he has burst the net I spun around him."

"Then spin a new net, Father. Let me go to Mother."

But Oswiu shook his head. "Your mother is there because I listened to a man's lies. Now I, who threw her away before, must go to her, to save her if I may."

"Then let us both go," said Ahlfrith.

"No. You know one must stay and lead the people." Oswiu took his son's arm. "I will not fail her again."

Ahlfrith stared at his father's face, then slowly nodded. "Very well."

"Thank you." Oswiu let Ahlfrith go and continued arming himself, belting his mail about the waist. "Send messengers to every thegn you can: warn them of the storm and tell them to fly before it. We may outlast it; we cannot outfight it."

Ahlfrith had turned to go, then stopped. With his back still turned, he asked, "Do you want me to tell the queen where you go?"

Oswiu shook his head. "No. I will tell her."

He had found Eanflæd with her women. She was weaving, making a cloth, white and pure, for the baby that was swelling her belly. Hearing him enter, she had looked up from her work, her mouth still pursed in concentration, and a smile had begun to form upon her lips. Hanging on to his horse as he drove through the storm, Oswiu remembered that well. She had smiled when she looked up to see him.

But then, seeing the expression upon the king's face, the smile became grave. Eanflæd looked round her women.

"Leave us," she said. She glanced back to her husband. "The king wishes speech with me."

Oswiu stood aside as the women filed from the building. In this place, Eanflæd preferred to do her weaving, and the other tasks appointed to women, in a house set to the side of the great hall, but sited so that it caught the best of the sun while avoiding the worst of the wind – the hall here managed the opposite feat, being frequently draughty and always gloomy. It was not one of the estates the king favoured, but it was necessary to stop here, as elsewhere in his kingdom, to render judgement in disputes, to remind outlaws and those others who would prey on the men and women who laboured that there was a king in this land who would wreak vengeance on behalf of those who were ill used, and to collect and eat the food renders due to the king and his warriors from the people of the area.

When the women were out of the room – and after he had checked that they had moved far enough away that they could not hear what was being said – Oswiu turned to the queen.

"Rhieienmelth is in danger. Penda sends men, by boat, to take her. If I go quickly, I may save her."

Eanflæd nodded, looked down at the hands folded in her lap. They rested now upon the curve of her belly, where the child neared term.

"Might not Ahlfrith go in your place?" she asked.

"He wished to."

"Then let him."

"I may not." Oswiu stared at his wife, but she did not raise her eyes to him. He saw her smooth her hands over her belly, as women did, without knowing, when they neared term. "Is it long?" he asked.

"No," said Eanflæd, "not long."

"If it were anyone else, I would send Ahlfrith. But I put her there after I listened to a man's lies. I will not send another to make good my mistake."

Now Eanflæd looked up at her husband. "Wish you that she was still your wife?"

"No!" said Oswiu. He raised his hand, touched a finger to Eanflæd's cheek. "Not now."

Eanflæd took his hand and, turning her face, pressed it to her lips. "Go," she said. She looked up at him. "But do not die!"

Oswiu smiled. "Not if my will prevails."

Eanflæd pushed him away from her. "Hurry, before my will fails."

But as Oswiu went from the door, she called after him: "Be quick."

He had been. He had driven them all day, without rest or ease, riding north and east, taking the old trackways that ran north of the Great Wall of the emperors. As they had ridden, the storm had built behind them, the dark banks of cloud outpacing them despite the efforts of horse and man. First, the day had darkened, as if the sun was setting, then night itself seemed to fall, so thick was the darkness under the cloud. The very hair on the backs of Oswiu's arms had stood, such was the tension in the waiting air. Then the storm broke, as if the world ended. But though it seemed the great wolf had broken its chain and eaten the sun, and the serpent had risen from the sea, yet they rode on, the horses too exhausted by their efforts to summon the energy to panic at the storm.

Wiping the rain from his eyes, Oswiu looked ahead. He thought he heard the sound of dogs baying, as they did upon the hunt. But who would hunt in such a storm?

The stories of the Horned Hunter came to his mind. Pity the poor man whom that hunter's hounds scented: they would run him down, though he fled to the world's ending. If that hunt were abroad this day, then he must indeed hurry. Oswiu urged his horse on, but the beast, though willing, was all but spent. It managed no extra speed at his urging, but continued on, rolling up the ground under its hooves.

The sound came again. A wild baying. And it came from ahead.

It seemed as if the storm was slackening. The lightning had retreated to the clouds above, lighting them from within, but no longer striking down to the ground. Even the rain had slackened, so his eyes no longer filled with water when he looked ahead.

There, where the land rose up to a great hump. That was the dragon's head where the holy house lay, surely? Then he saw, rising over the dragon's head, the silhouette of buildings against the momentary glow of the lightning-filled clouds.

For a moment, Oswiu thought of slowing their approach, but the sound of hounds baying again reached him through the storm and, rising in the saddle, he waved his riders on as the horses, with one final surge, galloped up onto the rise of land that jutted into the sea, and along its ridge to the holy house, its whitewashed walls now clear before them.

The sound of dogs barking grew louder as they galloped closer. From the vantage point of his horse, Oswiu could see, despite the storm, figures milling around the huddle of buildings that together made the holy house. That they should be without in such weather filled him with foreboding, but he drove the horse on without stopping. Nearing the holy house, he began to see that the sisters of the place were gathered together outside the church, but they were all looking away from him, towards the end of the promontory. Then the curtain of rain drew back further, and as he and his riders swept around the outbuildings of the holy house, he saw three men, armed with spear and sword, standing before the sisters, holding them back.

The men saw him at the same moment Oswiu saw them. Two turned to face him, the third began to back away and then, turning, began to run. Without pausing, Oswiu swept past the first two, leaving his riders to deal with them, for he saw where the third was running and he heard where the sound of hounds baying was coming from.

At the tip of the promontory, where the land fell into the sea, five men stood in line across the spit of land. Facing them, with her back to the fall, was Rhieienmelth, and milling at her feet, barking furiously at the men before them, were her hunting dogs. That was the sound he had heard as they neared the holy house: Rhieienmelth, at bay with her hounds. Some of the dogs lay dead or wounded around her, but the rest maintained their defiance, teeth bared and snarling, as the line of men, swords held in front to protect them from the dogs, slowly advanced. They were pushing Rhieienmelth backwards, until she should either fall or be taken.

But such was the noise of the dogs that the advancing men did not hear the shouts of their companion, running back to them. Nor did he have long to cry out, for Oswiu, riding up behind, cut him down. He looked up from the kill and saw Rhieienmelth. And she saw him.

As Oswiu drove his horse on towards the line of men, angling the animal so he might ride past two or three of them on one pass, Rhieienmelth set her dogs on the advancing men. As the hounds leapt for them, the men struck out with sword, but did not think to guard behind. Two were cut down before the others knew aught of what was happening. The third, seeing the man next to him fall, turned in time to parry Oswiu's sword slash. Hauling back his horse with all his strength, Oswiu all but forced its hindquarters down to the ground, but the sodden earth slid beneath its hooves and the cliff edge fell away beneath it. Twisting, Oswiu swung his leg free and jumped from the saddle as the horse, crying protest, slipped over the cliff's edge. Sword in hand, hair dripping storm, Oswiu turned to face the man he had missed. But such was the fear of his onset that the man stood staring at Oswiu with slack jaw, for in truth it seemed that the Hunter himself had descended upon them. Oswiu advanced, sword low, storm behind, and the man, seeing him, turned and tried to run. The other two, seeing what was happening, made to flee as well.

But a man, running with his back to the pursuing teeth, is no match for a pack of hounds.

"Take them!" Rhieienmelth called, and they sprang after the running men.

They did not get far.

Oswiu left the task of finishing the men to his own warriors.

"Rhieienmelth."

She stood, her back against the furious sea. The waves surged behind her, sounding upon the rocks far below and sending white spume up into the air. The woman who had once been his queen, who had given birth to his children, stared past him, at the dogs worrying the dead men, and the others that lay whining and wounded, or dead, upon the ground.

"They saved me," she said softly. Then Rhieienmelth looked to the man approaching her. "You saved me," she said. She looked him in the face. "I did not think you would come."

"You are here because I listened to lies about you. I had to come."

Rhieienmelth stared at the face of the man who had fathered her children, and saw there now the shadow of another.

"We both loved him," she said.

"I know," said Oswiu. He put his hand out and touched her face. "And I you."

"I know," said Rhieienmelth.

Oswiu let his hand fall.

Rhieienmelth pointed at the dead men. "Penda?"

"Yes."

She looked back to the king. "I have done wrong," she said.

*

While Oswiu dried himself in front of the fire, Rhieienmelth told him of Œthelwald's meeting with Penda upon the island in the Humber. She told him how she had advised Œthelwald to march with Penda against his uncle. She told him why.

Oswiu listened and did not speak, for in her words he saw his actions laid bare. When she had finished, and they were silent, he looked into his memory hoard and knew what he found there.

"My brother would not have done as I did."

"There are few men like Oswald," said Rhieienmelth.

"And I least of all, though I ever had his example before me."

Oswiu began to put his clothes back on – still damp but no longer dripping. "We must go."

"Where?"

"To my people. Ahlfrith is leading them into the hills. Let Penda's army flow like water around them. When the flood has receded, we will return and reclaim our own."

But Rhieienmelth shook her head. "By coming here, by saving me, you paid the ransom for your fault. But I have fault of my own that I must pay, and that cannot be paid by returning with you."

"Where would you go then?"

"To right my wrong; to give good counsel after bad; to pull our kin from the treachery of my heart."

"You would go to Œthelwald? I have not ridden seven leagues to save you from Penda only for you to give yourself into his hands."

"I will not give myself into his hands. If his army be the size you tell me, then there will be women with it. Amid such a throng it is easy to stay hidden. And who would expect me to go there? Not Penda. No – even though men say Woden sends his ravens to whisper in his ear each night."

"Who says this?"

"I have heard the tale whispered around the fire by travellers finding shelter against the night."

Oswiu shook his head. "I know the raven that whispers in his ear and in his dreams, and it is not Woden that sends it."

"But can you not feel it? Your old gods crowd back around us. They walk in the shadows, beyond the reach of the light, and seek entry into men's hearts. They have entered Penda's heart. Where before there was only the desire for glory and for power, something new rules there now and even he knows it not. But I know it. I saw it when I faced him on the island, but I did not know that I saw it then. Only when I returned here, to the holy house, did I see in memory what I had failed to see in sight. Penda fears you now. He fears the Idings with all the fear of dying gods. So earn what time you can against him, but know this: in the end, you must face him."

Oswiu nodded. "This I think as well. But I would not lose such counsel again, not when I have found it once more."

But Rhieienmelth shook her head. "One wife under one roof is more than enough." She smiled and there was in that smile something of the woman Oswiu had known before the shadow had grown between them. "Although you might enjoy it, I doubt the queen would. Particularly a queen with child."

"I think you speak truly. But still, I would not have saved you only for you to throw your life away again."

Rhieienmelth laughed. "It was my dogs that saved me. Although you did help. But I promise I will not throw my life away. Not now."

"Good." Dressed, Oswiu stood. "Where will you go?"

"South." Rhieienmelth stood up after him. "I will make my own way."

"I will send some men with you."

"Then you will lose them. From what you say, Penda's army is too great to fight. But so great an army offers another way in. But for that I will need a man, someone who is skilled at adopting other faces and other voices. Do you have one such that you will give me?"

Oswiu thought. "Acca?"

Rhieienmelth smiled. "Yes, of course. He will be perfect."

"But Penda knows him."

"We will not be going to those parts of the camp where the kings set their tents."

"But it will take time for me to send for Acca to come here and it is not safe for you to remain in this holy house."

"I will meet him upon the way. Tell Acca that he will find me at the Stone Sisters – but tell him to be quick."

"I would not have you go alone when armies march through my kingdom: in such times, outlaws and other, darker, creatures emerge from the meres and the shadows to prey upon men – and women."

"Do not worry. My dogs will look after me." Rhieienmelth reached down and patted the head of one of the hounds that, seeing his mistress rise, had sat up from where he lay. "They have until now."

Chapter 8

"He's burning my land." Oswiu stood with his sons, Ahlfrith and Ecgfrith, on the flanks of one of the many fort-crowned hills that ran up the spine of the kingdom. From its height, they could see the columns of smoke, rising into the still, sultry air. For the storm that had broken over Oswiu on his ride to Coldingham had presaged not a change to cooler weather, but only a break in the summer's heat. The day after, the steam of the sun's rising had covered the land, making it seem as if they rode through a grey sea. But the sun had sucked the water from the land in two or three days and now, three weeks later, as summer edged towards autumn, the land lay brown and dry once more beneath the sapping sun.

Oswiu glanced up into the sky. After so many days of heat, the sky was no longer blue, but bronze. Dust hung in the air, and smoke – from the fires Penda's army set as they marched north, spreading out on either side of their approach to burn whatever they could not take. From where they stood, Oswiu and his sons could see the army's baggage train snaking back towards the south, riders scuttling to and from it as ants do when they march. Indeed, from their height, the men might as well have been ants.

"If rain would come, they could not burn so much," said Ahlfrith.

"Look," said Ecgfrith, pointing with excitement. "They're coming this way."

A troop of riders had peeled off from the main army and was making its way towards the line of hills. This had been the pattern through the summer: Penda's army making its slow, incendiary way through the low, rich lands of the kingdom, taking what they could and burning everything else, while Oswiu, with his men, kept to the hills, watching but doing nothing more. Many of the men chafed at this, but the older and wiser heads bade them be patient:

in the face of such numbers, it was better to wait. Those of his household who could not move fast and far, Oswiu had sent back to their homes and villages, if these lay far enough away from Penda's line of march. But the army sent men far to gather the food and supplies it needed; halls and hamlets fifteen and twenty miles from the invaders had been raided and burned. So many chose to remain with Oswiu, struggling along after those who could go faster. In this, they were helped by the queen. Her belly was fast swelling and she could no longer ride. In the hills, wagons could make barely a mile a day, so the men carried her upon a hurdle, taking turns from which none were spared: even the king took his place between the poles.

The long way behind White Law, Black Law and Gains Law, where the land levelled and the going was easier for a while, had given Oswiu time and chance to talk to his queen for a while. And she to him.

"You say Rhieienmelth seeks a way into Penda's camp, that she might persuade Œthelwald to turn back from his treachery?"

Oswiu, sweating between the poles, did not turn round but walked steadily on over the dry ground. Normally, his feet would be squelching through thick moss here, sinking into its wet grasp. But the summer had dried even the moss to a brown dead skin upon cracked mud. It made the walking easier, but it was harder on the feet – particularly when carrying a pregnant queen.

"Yes," said Oswiu. "That is what she told me. Although with Rhieienmelth, there is never any telling what she might do."

"It is as well you did not bring her back with you."

"That is what she said."

"She did?"

"'One wife under one roof is more than enough.' That is what she said."

"Then why do men not speak of Rhieienmelth the Deep Minded as they do of Eanflæd the Wise?"

"I suppose because her mind is not what men first remark on when they see Rhieienmelth."

"Oh." The queen fell silent for a while as Oswiu laboured on. The man holding the rear set of hurdles, ears agog, listened for further news that he might spread around the camp when they stopped for the night.

"Do you think she will try to speak with Œthelwald?" Eanflæd asked after they had marched in silence for some while.

Oswiu stopped and put down the hurdle.

"Yes, I think she will," he said. He gestured to the nearest men. "Your turn."

Now, as he stood upon the flank of the hill, looking down at the army burning its way through his kingdom, he wondered if Rhieienmelth was there, among them. Coifi, he knew, was with Penda's army, although the old priest had not managed to send any word to them so far. But there was little he could tell that they could not see. Penda's strategy was plain to see. To burn him into battle. But he had no intention of doing what his enemy wanted.

"Daddy," said Ecgfrith. He pointed at the smoke that hung, in place of clouds, over the kingdom. "If Penda keeps burning, will there be anything left when we come down from the hills?"

"Yes, yes of course there will be. He can't burn everything."

"Can't he?" Ahlfrith turned to his father. "He seems to be trying."

"That is what we did, when we raided Deira. It is the way of war. Some burning, some pillaging, and then a return to your hall with boasts and stories and no lives lost."

"I think Penda fights a different sort of war, Father."

"Daddy, look." Ecgfrith pointed once more.

Even from this distance, they could see that the troop of riders approaching the hill had unfurled a flag of truce.

Penda wanted to talk.

*

"The High King wishes no more destruction to be visited upon this land."

The messenger stood before Oswiu.

Seeing the riders approaching under the flag of truce, Oswiu had sent some of his own riders to meet them, with orders to bring back the messenger, and the messenger alone, blindfolded and hooded, that he might not learn where he was being taken.

Now, Oswiu met with him in his tent. It was stifling within, but only when the flap was pulled down did he allow the man's hood to be lifted and give him leave to speak.

"Then tell the king of the Mercians to return to his own land. And let the wolf call the foxes back to their lairs too."

"The wolf does not return to his den until he has made his kill."

"Then he will wait long, and far from home."

"The High King proposes another way."

Oswiu felt sweat trickling down the side of his face. "Is that what you have come to tell?"

"In asking peace, you gave already one pound of gold and four of silver. If you would have peace, then the High King will look with favour on your plea – if it comes weighted with gold."

Oswiu flicked the sweat away. "How much?"

"All of it."

"All?"

"All." The messenger made the courtesy. "If you would have an end to the burning, then send word. You will know where we are to be found."

"I can smell you."

The messenger made the courtesy again. "Gold shall end the fires."

When he had gone, blindfolded and taken from the camp, Oswiu called Ahlfrith to him and went in search of the queen. They found her, resting in the shade of a hawthorn that grew bent over, as a man bent with age, although it was wind that bent the tree's back.

The king squatted down beside her.

"It is too hot," said Eanflæd.

Oswiu lay his hand upon her belly. "I can feel him," he said.

"Her," said Eanflæd. "I think this one is a girl. She sits differently to Ecgfrith; lower."

"Oh. A girl."

"Do you want another son?" Eanflæd smiled tiredly at her husband. "If this be a girl, I will try again to give you a son."

Ahlfrith coughed. Oswiu looked up and laughed. "Sorry," he said. "But if this one is a girl then it will be the easier for you. Two sons are easier to provide for than three."

"Father, we are here to speak on Penda's offer."

"Yes." Oswiu gestured. "Sit down. There is shade here." He looked over to where his household and those others who had followed him lay sprawled out in whatever shade they could find, while the horses searched for grass that still held a little sap. "Would it be so bad, to put aside the throne? To live in these hills, far from men?"

Ahlfrith shook his head. "Father, you may wish to put aside the throne, but our people look to you for protection and hope. They see their homes burned, their crops pillaged and their children taken as slaves. And all we do is skulk in the hills and wait for the despoilers to slake their appetites. This is not the way of a king."

But before Oswiu could speak, Eanflæd answered. "I have passed the cup to many men, many brave warriors. I have heard them speak their deeds and boast of their battles. Yet I know that, for the most part, those battles were but the chance meeting of men, with victory going to the side that did not slip upon the bloody ground, or which fought with its back to the sun. In song and in hall, they say the way of kings is war. If we but endure against such an army, that is victory." Eanflæd put her hand upon her belly. "If we endure, then this child shall live."

Chapter 9

Not since the days of the emperors had such an army marched through this land. From where they watched, concealed within a tangled copse of trees, it seemed that the very earth seethed with men. The tents of the army spread far over the brown, parched earth. At its centre, visible despite the dust that hung in the bronze air, were the tents of the kings, each marked by a banner. But these banners all made a rough circle around the centre, where flew the wolf banner of the Iclingas.

The dog lying at Rhieienmelth's feet grumbled its impatience, but she quietened it with a gesture.

"Yes, I think it will work," she said, turning to Acca. "With such a throng, there will be many slavers."

Acca pointed to the west. "If we wait a little, there will be reason for us to seek shelter amid the tents." After so many days of clear skies, clouds were finally massing, building up in great towers upon the horizon.

"I for one will be glad to see the end of this parched summer," said Rhieienmelth. "As will my dogs. Won't you, boy?" She scratched round the ears of the dog nearest her feet, who licked her hand appreciatively. "It has been too hot for them."

"For men as well as dogs," said Acca. "But now the harvest month is upon us, surely the heat will ease?" He looked again to the west. "After sun, rain. And much of it, I should think."

Rhieienmelth nodded, but her attention was back with the camp. "You know what you have to do?"

"Yes. If you are sure?"

"Yes."

"Then I know." The scop pointed to the dogs. "What of them?"

"They will know their way home." Squatting down among the hounds, Rhieienmelth bade them farewell, then she stood up. "Come, let's go."

*

From within, the camp was even noisier and more chaotic than it appeared from afar. At its edges, women, and even children, were as numerous as men, but all appeared slatternly, slovenly creatures, who scattered whenever one of the great thegns came riding past, only to slowly flow back again.

"Make way, make way!" Acca cried, pushing some of the crush aside with one hand while holding the rope in his other. Rhieienmelth, hands bound together, eyes downcast, stumbled along behind him.

"Hey! What d'you want for that one?"

The shout was loud enough to rise through the general clamour, the squeal of animals being herded, terrified and unwilling, towards butchery, the screech of metal on metal as armourers ground swords and spears, and the calls of merchants selling wares and women selling themselves. Acca tried to ignore it, but the man who had shouted could not so easily be ignored when he heaved himself up from the stool in front of his tent and stood before them.

"Her," he said. "What d'you want for her?"

Acca looked the man up and down and shook his head. "She's not for the likes of you," he said.

The man put his finger on Acca's chest. "What d'you mean, the likes of me?"

For the camp followers, and not a few of the warriors, nothing filled the day so pleasurably as a fight. No sooner had the big man put his finger to Acca's chest than they started gathering.

Acca had an audience.

Behind him, eyes still cast down, Rhieienmelth looked slantwise for any sign of one of the kings or thegns who might know them by sight. But they were still far away from the centre of the camp, where the banners of the kings were beginning to flutter in the building breeze. Everybody could feel the change in the air, and this added to the rising excitement of the crowd.

Acca looked down at the thick finger on his chest. Then he slowly, languidly even, looked up at the man behind it. "Are all your parts so... thick?" he inquired.

Rhieienmelth heard the change in his voice, saw the way the scop had slightly pushed one hip forward. It was all she could do to keep a straight face. The watching crowd had no such constraints.

"No!" yelled one woman. "Everything else about him is small – and I should know!"

The man looked round, searching for the source of the jibe, but no sooner had he looked one way than someone else started up, until he was surrounded by laughing, pointing people.

"Tell you what," said Acca. "We'll swap. You take her and I'll take... you."

Seeing the big man's open-mouthed shock, the crowd laughed all the harder. Acca, apparently conscious of the audience for the first time, turned to them as if in surprise. "A big fellow like this would fetch a pretty price. You didn't think I meant..." Acca looked affectedly shocked. "Surely not!"

Various retorts suggested that was exactly what the crowd had thought.

Acca shook his head as if in disbelief. "Let's settle it, then. To demonstrate my manhood –" the scop turned towards the big man who still stood blocking his way – "I will wrestle you."

"What? No." The big man held up his hands. "No!"

"Oh, yes," said Acca. "Naked." He took a step towards him.

That was too much for the big man. He turned and ran, pushing his way through the laughing, cat-calling crowd.

The show over, the crowd began to disperse. Rhieienmelth, sidling closer, hissed at Acca, "Move on."

When they had left that part of the camp behind, Rhieienmelth said softly, "I don't think I've ever seen a slaver like you, Acca."

Acca did not look round, but his gait, already expansive, grew even wider. He was, Rhieienmelth saw, enjoying himself hugely.

In truth, Acca was far from being the only slaver hanging on the edges of the camp. Many had already collected three or four captives, hobbling them together and parading them around the camp looking for those who would buy. The people taken, Rhieienmelth saw, were mostly farmers and peasants, those who had not had time or speed enough to escape the advancing army, or who had thought that it would simply wash past, taking some sheep or a pig, but leaving everything else alone. That was the normal way of things, but this army was different. Most of the slaves Rhieienmelth had known at Oswald's court, and later at Oswiu's, were free slaves, men and women, sometimes whole families, who had given themselves into servitude at times of famine, that they might have food from the king's table, and live. Most would someday return to the village of their birth. But those people captured in war would be taken far away and few ever returned. The men and women and children, squatting hollow eyed and waiting, their legs tied together and their arms bound, knew this all too well.

The camp grew more crowded as they approached its centre. Some channels were kept open to allow men on horseback, messengers and the like, to ride quickly to the kings, but dogs and chickens and the occasional panicking sheep continually got in their way, as did the spreading tents. As Acca tripped over yet another rope, he cursed the way each tent, when left in place for more than a day, seemed to spread ever further outwards from its original pitch, taking over the space once left for people to make their way.

"Over there," Rhieienmelth said, pointing. Acca peered past the closely packed tents and pavilions, with their banners beginning to play out as the breeze stiffened, to where she indicated. There, the banner of the boar streamed out beside a pavilion.

"There will be men who know us there," whispered Rhieienmelth to Acca.

But the scop shook his head. "There are men there who know Acca the scop and Rhieienmelth the, er... Rhieienmelth the Fair. But even though they look upon us, they will not see us, for now I am Acca the slaver and you are that which I am selling." The scop saw Rhieienmelth looking at him as he spoke. "That is, they will not see us so long as you bow your head and shuffle as one without hope." He waited. "Yes, like that."

Taking up the rope once more, Acca started towards the pavilion of the king of Deira. Rhieienmelth struggled to keep her head bowed, even as bored men yelled after her, asking Acca for her price. But Acca just smiled and shook his head, calling out as he went that such a one was worthy of a king's bed.

Reaching a place where the tents, backing against each other, allowed somewhere to stop and talk without being seen, Acca tugged Rhieienmelth into the space.

"What now?" he whispered to her.

"Lead me to Œthelwald's tent," said Rhieienmelth. "If anyone asks where you are going, say you're taking the king a gift from Penda."

"Keep looking down," said Acca. "And try to walk more humbly... You walk like a queen."

Rhieienmelth looked at him.

Acca coloured. "I know you *are* a queen, but you would do well not to walk like one at the moment."

Rhieienmelth nodded. She took a breath, then set herself, head down, feet low. "Let us go," she said as dully as she could.

"That's it," said Acca.

"Go!"

Shaking his head, the scop pulled the rope. Emerging into the space that surrounded the king's tent Acca gave the rope a sharp tug so that Rhieienmelth stumbled and nearly fell.

"Hey! What's that?" The sentry, who had been looking west to the gathering clouds, turned to them at the sound of Rhieienmelth struggling to keep her feet.

"A present. For the king. From Penda."

The sentry looked Rhieienmelth up and down. "I wish Penda sent me presents like that," he said.

"Hands off," said Acca. "She's for the king only."

The sentry held up his hands. "Don't worry. You would not see me touching something the Hooded One gave. He'd know soon enough."

Acca looked curiously at the sentry. "Do you think so?"

The sentry leaned closer to him. "They say he's Woden, walking among us. That's why he knows everything: because he sends out his ravens to look into men's minds and hearts."

"Have you seen these ravens?" asked Acca.

"Course I have," said the sentry. He pointed into the sky, where dark flecks circled, riding the waves of the air.

"Seems to me that whenever I've seen an army on the move, I've seen ravens following it," said Acca.

"Not like these ravens," said the sentry. "These ones are his."

Acca nodded. "If you say so. Now, you'd better let me pass, or the Hooded One will want to know why you delay his gift to the king."

The sentry stood aside. "If there's some left over when the king's finished…"

Acca shook his head. "No. There will be nothing for you."

Pulling the rope, Acca led Rhieienmelth into the pavilion.

It was not as dim inside as he had expected. Panels had been lifted in the sides of the pavilion to let the light and the freshening breeze in. Œthelwald was sitting with two of his counsellors, men Acca vaguely recognized as among the most powerful thegns in Deira, but he looked up when Acca entered.

As their eyes met, Acca put off the cloak of a slaver he had been wearing and became again the scop Œthelwald had known when he was a boy.

"Acca! What are you doing here?"

"I have brought someone who wishes to see you, lord."

Acca stepped aside and Rhieienmelth entered.

Œthelwald stood up. "You have come to me," he said, smiling. But then he saw the rope tied around her wrists, and his eyes darkened. "Why has Acca bound you?" As he spoke, his hand went to the sword at his waist.

But Rhieienmelth shook her head. "I am bound at my own will – so that we might pass, unmarked, through this camp and come to you. For I must needs speak with you, son of my heart."

Œthelwald gestured to the thegns. "Go. I will call you when I would speak further on these matters."

While the men left the pavilion, Acca untied Rhieienmelth. Unbound, Rhieienmelth turned to the scop.

"Leave us to speak in peace, Acca."

Acca nodded. "When should I return?"

"Go not far. I will call you when I have finished."

Once the scop had left, Rhieienmelth turned to Œthelwald. "I have come, hurrying south, to tell you that the counsel I gave was false counsel. Penda sent men to take me. It was only the arrival of the king – the man I advised you against – that saved me. If you would hear me again, I counsel you to find some pretext to withdraw from Penda's service."

But Œthelwald shook his head. "Though I rejoice to see you, it is not so straightforward a matter to withdraw from the service of a king, and certainly not when he is yet waging war." Œthelwald looked searchingly at Rhieienmelth. "Are you certain the men he sent were meant to take you and not, rather, to bring you here, where you would be safe? As such, I rejoice that you have come to us anyway, for you will surely be better protected staying with me here than placing your trust in my uncle."

Rhieienmelth shook her head. "I am certain. The men Penda sent killed two of the monks and one sister of the holy house when they would not say where Æbbe was. They would have killed me if my dogs had not protected me."

"Ah, there you have the reason. I knew there must be one. Penda sought to take Æbbe. Such a hostage would be very valuable. You say my aunt was not at the holy house? Where was she then?"

"I thank all the saints that watch over us that she had gone to Ebchester…" Rhieienmelth stared at Œthelwald, for as she said the name a flicker of satisfaction passed over his face. "You – you would not tell Penda this, would you?"

"No, no. Of course not. But I am glad you have told me, for now I can ensure her protection."

Rhieienmelth stared at Œthelwald. "I thought that when I told you what Penda had done, what manner of king he is, you would surely know what to do."

"You do not understand what it is to be king. Sometimes I am not surprised that my uncle chose a new queen. I am sure Eanflæd, if she be as wise as men say, would understand why I must do what I am doing."

"Paint it as you will, it remains what it is: treachery."

"It is not treachery!" Œthelwald beat his fist into the palm of his hand. "Treachery is to betray your rightful lord and king. But I am the rightful king of Northumbria – not my uncle, nor any of his whelps, whether he sired them on you or his new queen. Only I am the son of Oswald. Only I should be king."

Rhieienmelth stared at Œthelwald. "You may be his son, but you are not his match."

"I shall overmatch him. Don't you see? When Penda casts my uncle down, he will need to find a new king for Bernicia, someone he can trust, someone the people there will follow. Who better than the son of Oswald? At a stroke, I will have become king of Northumbria, something that my uncle has not achieved – no, not though he murdered, most foully, the previous king of Deira."

"Do you truly think Penda will make you king in Oswiu's place?"

"He has already promised the throne to me."

"And you believe him?"

"More than I would believe my uncle!"

Rhieienmelth shook her head. "After your mother died bringing you to birth, your father asked me to care for you as one of my own. So I did." She looked round. "Acca! We are going." Turning back to Œthelwald she said, "I thank you. You have cleared the mist that clouded my eyes. Now I will return whence I came."

But Œthelwald stepped towards her. "No, dear mother of my heart. It would not be safe for you to return to the holy house, not through a land ravaged by war. You must stay here, with me."

Rhieienmelth, alarmed despite herself, stepped back. "Acca!" she called again. "Acca, where are you?"

"Here he is."

Acca was sent sprawling upon the floor of the tent. Standing behind him was Penda.

Chapter 10

"He has Rhieienmelth." Acca stood before Oswiu, Ahlfrith, Eanflæd and the king's other counsellors, head downcast.

Oswiu nodded. He forced his face to remain without expression. "Very well."

"Did you see aught of Coifi?" asked Eanflæd.

"No," said Acca. "But I was not kept long after they discovered us."

"Then why has it taken you so long to come to us?" asked Oswiu. "It is, by your own account, two weeks since you left Penda's camp."

"I could not find you," said Acca. "I looked where you had been, but you were not there." He pointed to the roof of the tent. Rain drummed upon it. Not the driving rain that had finally and completely broken the long summer of drought, but the persistent, soaking rain that had followed and had kept falling every day since. "The rain had washed away all tracks. It was no easy task to find you."

"Nor should it be," said Oswiu. "But why should Penda release you?"

"He had a message he wanted me to deliver to you." The scop put his hands behind his back and the slightly abstracted air of a messenger delivering a remembered message came over his face. "'The High King sends this message to the king of the Bernicians. Gold shall buy the return of the mother of your eldest son and daughter: all your gold.'" Acca's eyes came back into focus. "That is what he said."

Oswiu turned to his counsellors. Since the breaking of the drought, living upon the hills had become bleak and cold. Oswiu's people sloshed through channels of running water and the rain sheeted down the flanks of the animals. Though there was some dryness to be found within their tents, for they were thoroughly waxed, enough rain had fallen in the last few weeks for the ground to be sodden and the dampness to rise up into them, wherever they slept. Much of the food they carried with them had spoiled too, rendered inedible by the dampness that sprouted mould upon all but the most salted meat. As for the queen, her belly was swollen with the new life within it. The midwife said the baby must surely be born within the next week or two.

"It seems to me that we will not be able to endure a winter upon these hills. Not after the thirst of the summer and the wet of this autumn." Oswiu turned to Ahlfrith. "What word have you had back from our thegns?"

"They have sent what they will. In most cases, it was more than I thought. Taken together, there is maybe two pounds of gold and four of silver."

Oswiu nodded. "And the men have returned with the hoards we buried ourselves at the start of our long retreat?"

"Yes," said Ahlfrith. "Four pounds of gold and eight of silver."

"That is a good amount. It is enough to make some among the kings think it is all and to ask for their share before returning to their homes for the winter." He turned to Acca. "As you know where to find Penda, I will send you back to him. Tell him that we have gathered all our gold and that we are willing to give it to him, that there might be peace between us."

Acca looked hopefully at the king. "Will this be enough for peace?"

"Of course not," said Oswiu. "I know that, and Penda knows that I know that. But it will, I think, be enough to buy a winter's peace – time for the queen to bring our child to birth and for me to make new plans."

"There was another message I was to give you, if you agreed to give the gold Penda asked for."

Oswiu looked questioningly at the scop. "Would you not have told us this if we had not agreed to send the gold?"

"Yes, yes. I would have. I just had not the chance before."

Oswiu glanced at the queen and his warmaster. Neither gave, by their expressions, any sign of what they thought of this.

"Very well. We shall put that aside for now. What other message were you asked to deliver?"

"This." The scop's hands went behind his back. His eyes again took on the shine of memory. "'The High King sends this further message to the king of Bernicia. If he would buy peace, then he must do so in person. For a peace bonded by two kings, face to face, shall surely endure where a peace brokered by others shall just as surely fail.'"

Oswiu stared at Acca. "He expects me to come to speak with him? After what happened to Eanfrith?"

"The High King told that you would answer in such manner and he bade me say this further: 'The murder of Eanfrith under flag of truce was done by Cadwallon, king of Gwynedd, and he, the High King, had no part in it. The High King, as befits such a lord, is a man of his word and will respect any flag of truce that flies between you.'"

"Oh, stop calling him High King." Oswiu looked to his counsellors. "What say you?"

But before they could reply, Acca spoke again. "The Hi– the king of the Mercians said further. He said, if you would not come in person, then there would be no peace between you, not though you poured all the gold of all the kingdoms of all the world before him."

Hearing this, Oswiu sighed. He looked again to his counsellors, to his wife and to his son. "I suppose we have answer then. I will go, and I will take the gold, and I will buy us peace for a season."

"I will come with you," said Ahlfrith.

But Oswiu shook his head. "If this be a trap, better we not both enter it. Besides, if he takes me, someone must remain to take the queen to safety." Oswiu stood up from his stool. The rain, redoubling, drummed upon the tent and now it sounded like the throwing of thousands of stones. The rain was becoming hail. Winter would soon be coming to the mountains. The king turned to his son. "Give me pledge, Ahlfrith, in God's holy hearing, that you will look after the queen should I fall, and take her to her kinsmen in Kent. She will be safe there – as safe as anywhere in this land."

Ahlfrith stood up in front of the king. Looking at them, Eanflæd saw that Ahlfrith now stood taller than his father.

"I give pledge, I give it freely, before my father and my king, before God, that if you fall I shall see the queen safe to her own people."

"Thank you," said Oswiu. He turned back to Acca. "Take this message to Penda, king of the Mercians. Tell him I will meet him at the Wall. Tell him that I will give him, there, all the gold his heart, and the hearts of the kings that march with him, could desire. Tell him I will meet him one week hence, but that his army must be far to the south, yet visible from the Wall, that I may know I approach without treachery. In likewise, he shall see that I approach with only my own men about me. I shall come from the west, he from the east, and we shall meet ten miles west of my estate at the Wall, where we received his son, the Red Hand, into the new life. The place where we shall meet is marked by a single tree, an ash, that has rooted into the south side of the Wall and grows up from there. The point is half a mile to the east of a small fort. The Wall stretches straight, east and west, for a mile there, so that each shall see the other approaching atop the Wall. Let him come walking east along the wall alone, and I shall meet him in like wise. Then both shall know there is no treachery." Oswiu stopped. "Can you remember all that?"

"Yes," said Acca. "I remember the ancestors of all the kings of this land, I remember the tales of our people, I remember the dead in battle and the victories they won. I can remember a message."

"Very well. Tell Penda I shall see him, face to face, seven days hence."

Chapter 11

The rain had not stopped. Oswiu had led his household south, riding along the spines and ridges of the hills, and in that bitter march, the wind had not ceased and the rain had only paused when it turned to sleet and hail. The land ran with water, silver sheets flowing down the sides of the hills like hair. The riders who went before them, as scouts, reported through rain-washed eyes that Penda's army likewise struggled south. Although the way was easier on the farm lands east of the hills, and there were good paths and roads running south towards the Great Wall of the emperors, yet such were the number of feet and hooves and wheels rolling down them that the paths and roads became little more than mud rivers, holding the wheels of Penda's great army in their brown grasp. Such was the difficulty of moving the wagons that much of what the army had looted through the summer had been abandoned during the autumn, left to rot beside the road.

The scouts brought back the news of the difficulties the great army was having, but that hardly served to raise the spirits of Oswiu's household as they squelched south.

"Even the sheep look miserable."

Ecgfrith had noticed this as he trudged along, using some of the men as a wind break, and that became the refrain of the march, for he had added after his observation, "But I am not." So the men and women and the few children took to singing, to the tune of one of Acca's old songs, "Though the sheep are miserable, and the cows complain, while the wolves howl and the ravens moan, even if the hares hide and the foxes stay home, we sing and we chant because we are not."

When the men had first taken up this song, Ahlfrith had come to his father in some anger, saying that such noise would surely tell Penda's scouts where they were. But Oswiu bade him let them be.

"Any scout will have ears roaring with wind and his eyes stopped with the rain. Besides, even if Penda were to learn where to find us, he could hardly get much of his army up here – not with the paths and ways more rivers and streams than tracks. No, son, let them sing, for if they do not sing their hearts will falter."

So they sang as they marched, but the king did not sing. Riding at their head, his cloak drawn round his shoulders, his hood over his head, he stared into the rain mist, and there sought some way of defeating Penda. But as he stared into blankness, the thought came to his mind that Penda had defeated his brother; he had defeated Edwin, his uncle. Was he a better man, a better king, than they?

He knew the answer to that.

Then came the day when the curtain of rain drew aside enough for him to see the stone line the emperors had drawn across the land, from sea to sea. It snaked over hill and ridge, the towers upon it standing proud as the few remaining teeth of an old man poke from his gums, and the face it turned to the north was still, in many places, white. For Oswiu had heard tell that in the days of the emperors, the Great Wall was painted dazzling white, there as a sign to all that in passing beyond it they were entering the emperor's dominion – or leaving it.

Oswiu led his people over the trackways that ran down to the Wall from the hills to the north. Looking down upon the Wall from the last ridge, the land seemed to Oswiu's eye to be as much water as land, for the rain lay upon the sodden earth in great shallow pools, the tops of grasses poking spiked fingers from the rain-rippled surface to tell the depth was not great, but also that the land was so wet that it might accept no more rain for the moment.

The scouts having returned with report that there was no one to be seen to the south of the wall, or for many miles along its length to the west and, more particularly, to the east, Oswiu led his people down to the Wall. At this point there was, on the southern side, the ruins of a fort, still intact in its walls and, in some places, its ceilings. It would afford them some shelter from rain and wind.

Once he had settled his household there and seen, as much as was possible, to their wellbeing, Oswiu called all his counsellors together.

"Ahlfrith will have charge while I am gone." Oswiu stood amid his counsellors and the thegns who had followed him into the hills. He looked at the men about him. "If matters should go amiss and I not return, I charge you to follow him in all things, as you have me – and my brother before me. If I do not return, then the way east will be barred to you. Follow the paths west to Rheged. There may still be some welcome for you there, but do not linger: find a ship, and let it take you south, to the men of Kent. King Earconbert will surely accept into his service, for my sake and for the sake of his niece, Queen Eanflæd, so fine a group of men. If I have not returned by three days hence, you must go. Send no more men after me, but go." The king looked to Ahlfrith. "You understand this?"

"I understand," said Ahlfrith.

"Very well. Then give me your blessing, my son, my queen, my people, and pray for me to the lord of high heaven, and I will give you mine."

And one by one they came before him and laid their hands upon the king, and he laid his hands upon them. When, last of all, the queen came before him, Oswiu put his hands on head, and shoulders, and breathed upon her brow. Then he laid his hands upon her belly, where the child sat, and blessed it too.

"I… " the queen gasped. "I think you may have another child by the time you return."

"Then I must be swift," said Oswiu. And he kissed her too.

"Who will you take with you?" Ahlfrith asked. "For with such a treasure you surely may not ride alone."

"I have ridden this Wall many times. Few live near it, for many believe it wraith haunted. I will take but a few men, two or three, for speed is more important in this than strength of arms."

"Can I come, can I come?" Ecgfrith, hearing his half-brother speak with his father, had come to hear what kingly matters they spoke of.

Oswiu shook his head. "No, I am sorry," he said. "It would not be safe for you to come with me."

But as Ecgfrith's face fell, Ahlfrith took his father's arm and drew him aside. "Birth brings great peril to a woman, Father. Might it not be better, lest some mischance happen, that Ecgfrith be away from his mother as she labours?"

"What if this be but a trap? I would not have it catch my son as well as me."

"I do not say take him all the way. But if you take him part way, then set him with one or two trusted men to guard your line of retreat, he will have much to keep his mind upon while his mother labours in her own battle."

Oswiu nodded. "Ecgfrith," he called, "you are coming with me."

As the boy shouted his joy, Oswiu tried to calm him. "Not the whole way, mind." But Ecgfrith shouted all the louder. He was going with the king to face the enemy.

*

Riding east, Oswiu set riders to the north and south of the Wall. Those on the southern side had the easier ride, for the road of the emperors ran there. The riders on the north had to pick their way through rougher terrain, sometimes pulling away from the Wall to find a path. Oswiu kept Ecgfrith with him on the south side of the Wall. The boy was a fine horseman and even the continuing rain did not dampen his delight at the trust that had been placed in him.

A day's riding brought them to within sight of the fort that lay ten miles west of the king's estate at the Wall. The rain had settled into the fine mist that soaks and chills everything it touches.

Oswiu called his riders to a halt.

"Ecgfrith," he said. "You have the clear eyes of a… of youth. Can you see sign of aught amiss ahead? Any mark of man or rider?"

Ecgfrith straightened in the saddle, shielding his eyes against the rain. "I can see nothing at the fort, Father. And the way is clear beyond, all the way to where the tree grows from the Wall." The boy squinted into the rain. "It still has many leaves, but they are sure to fall soon, for most of them are brown, not green."

"Can you see aught beyond the tree? Any sign of a man upon the Wall, or riders beyond?"

Ecgfrith searched again. "No, Father. Not yet."

"Very well. You have done well, Ecgfrith – all that I asked you. So I give to you another task. You will have charge of the men I leave at the fort. Watch them, and watch over me, as I go to meet Penda. For I feel in my heart that he will surely come."

This last section of the Wall was all but intact. For the view it gave, Oswiu climbed up to its walkway, which was broken in only a few places, and walked the last stage towards the fort, with Ecgfrith beside him, and the men riding below. Walking on the Wall, there was no need for scouts upon the north side, for they could see better from atop the Wall than any man on horse might from its base.

"What shall we do if Penda is not here?" Ecgfrith asked his father as they approached the fort.

"This day is the day appointed to meet. If there is no sight of him, then we shall wait until the afternoon gives way towards evening. But if there is still no sign of Penda then, we shall withdraw, making as much speed as we can, for it would be too easy for him to fall upon us in the night at the fort. There is a cave, some miles back, that only a few men know of. We shall rest there the night if he does not come." Oswiu looked ahead, past the fort, along the straight line of the Wall towards the upraised hand of the tree. "But I think he will come."

*

"You have proven you have the best sight, Ecgfrith. You stand watch with Dunstan. Tell him if you see anything – anything at all. I will make sure all is well for the rest of us."

Leaving his son talking excitedly with Dunstan, Oswiu deployed his men around the ruined fort, ensuring that the best were put to watch over the approaches that might most easily conceal approaching warriors. That done, Oswiu looked to the south, searching for some sign, through the rain, of where the sun sat in the sky. As best he could judge, it was just past mid day. At this point in the season, at the mid mark of the autumn, the days were still nearly as long as the nights, so there were still a few hours before he would have to call a retreat to some more secret shelter. Until then, he set himself to watching too.

But it was Ecgfrith who saw first.

"Daddy, Daddy!" he called, forgetting in his excitement that he now called Oswiu Father rather than Daddy. "Over there. On the Wall. Past the tree. It's him."

And it did indeed seem to be him.

Shielding his eyes against the rain, Oswiu saw the figure of a man standing upon the Wall. He was hooded and he carried a staff in one hand, although the lie of his cloak told of a sword carried beneath it.

Oswiu called to his sentries, asking if any saw sign of other men. But there was no one else in view. Only the single, hooded figure.

"He's coming closer," said Ecgfrith, jumping up and down in his excitement. "It's him; it must be him."

"Yes," said Oswiu. "It's him. Penda."

He turned to Ecgfrith, but addressed the words as much to Dunstan. "I will go to him. If, as I approach, you see any sign of a trap, sound the horn, and I will return as fast as I may – be ready, then, and horsed, for we will not wait. But if you see no alarm, then wait on me. When I am ready I will signal for you to bring the gold forward. For that, one man will suffice. He will lead the horse along the road to me, with the gold and silver lashed over the animal's back. When he reaches the ash tree, he must tie the animal to the tree and return here, not waiting. Do you understand?"

"I understand, Daddy. I understand!"

"And you, Dunstan?"

Dunstan made the courtesy. "I understand, lord."

"Very well." Oswiu turned to the door that led out upon the Wall. The grey stone marched away eastward. In one or two places it had crumbled, but for the most part it stood level before him.

"Farewell."

Gathering his cloak about him, he stepped out upon the Wall.

The rain was cold upon his face, but he did not begrudge the cold, for it cleared the mind. He had felt a fog upon him these past weeks, as if he groped for landmarks in a place where he could see only as far as his hands could reach. But now, the rain had lifted the fog and he saw clearly.

Beyond the ash tree, the hooded figure raised his staff, as if in salute. In answer, Oswiu raised his arm. Then both men began to advance.

As he walked along the walkway, Oswiu watched for any sign of men hiding. But the emperors of old had built their Wall well. They had left no place near to it where a man might approach unseen: no gully or ditch, no copse or run of gorse. The land to either side was bare, with only the ash tree making a mark against the rock and grass.

Coming closer to the tree, Oswiu checked under his cloak that the hilt of his sword was not caught in some fold of material; nor his seax. The hooded figure approached steadily, changing neither his pace nor his attitude.

Twenty yards to the tree now.

Oswiu unclasped his cloak and pushed it back over his shoulders so that it would not get in his way should he need to draw sword. But the hooded figure simply walked on, neither unclasping cloak nor drawing back hood.

Oswiu stopped just shy of the tree. That way, he could be sure it would not block his men's sight of him.

The hooded figure continued to advance, until he stood under the tree. There, he stopped.

They were ten yards apart.

"Penda," said Oswiu. He strove to keep the question from his voice.

The hooded figure did not speak. In the shadow beneath the hood, Oswiu saw an eye glitter.

"I would have peace," said Oswiu.

Still the eye glittered, but no voice came from the depth of the shadow.

"I have the gold."

"If you would have peace, I would have the boy as well." The hooded figure pointed past Oswiu, and, feeling himself suddenly plunged into nightmare though he was yet waking, Oswiu turned, until he saw Ecgfrith, coming to him along the Wall. Beyond him, he saw Dunstan rushing after the boy, but Oswiu knew well how fast Ecgfrith could be and how elusive.

"Ecgfrith, Dunstan, go back!" he yelled at them, but the wind, backing to the north, ripped the words away from his mouth and threw the sound south, so it never reached the ears of his son. But Dunstan understood and, unsure, came to a shuffling halt.

Feeling a presence, Oswiu whipped back round.

Penda was there, standing but a few feet from sword thrust.

"I did not think you would bring your son," Penda said. He held his hand out towards Ecgfrith. "Are you brave, boy?" he called. "Will you bring peace between us?"

"I would rather kill you," said Ecgfrith, standing now beside his father. "But I know Daddy wants peace."

Slowly, Penda reached up and drew his hood back.

"Your brother lived with me when he was young, your half-brother. Are you as brave as he?"

"Braver!" said Ecgfrith.

"Then come with me. You will see such an army as you have never seen before. There will be peace between our kingdoms. And your daddy shall keep his throne."

Ecgfrith looked up uncertainly to his father. "Daddy?"

"You... you ask hostage?" Oswiu asked Penda.

Penda looked up from the boy to the man. "Yes, I ask hostage," he said.

"But you asked gold for peace, not a hostage."

"Now I will have both. But in return you will have a surer peace."

"If... if I agree, this shall be under the ancient custom? You pledge no harm to Ecgfrith so long as there is peace between us?"

"Of course. I would have the ancient customs restored – in this as in other things."

Oswiu squatted down next to his son. "Would you do this thing, Ecgfrith? I ask you of your own will, not mine. Would you do this?"

Ecgfrith stared into his father's face. "Do you think I'm brave, Daddy?"

"I know you are."

"I-I don't think I am, Daddy. Not really. But if I do this, then I'll know I'm brave. Like you."

Oswiu looked up again at Penda. "You swear this? You give oath?"

Penda put his hand to the trunk of the ash tree. "I give pledge upon this ash tree, the tree of the world that holds the high heavens and this middle-earth and the underworlds. I give pledge upon the fate weavers and the doom singers. I give pledge upon the Lord of Battles, the Master of the Slain. I give pledge in my name and in my hand and in the eye I gave and the eye I keep." Penda's black eye glittered. "Satisfied?"

*

Oswiu watched his son walk away. Penda walked beside him, his hood again covering his head. As they went further, receding behind the rain curtain, he saw Penda put his hand upon the boy's shoulder, as a father might do to his son.

The horse carrying the gold and silver followed them, pacing along beneath the Wall. One of Penda's men had come forward to claim it from where it was tethered to the ash tree. In all things save one, Penda had done what he had said. There had been no trap. He had kept his word.

But he had taken Oswiu's son.

Chapter 12

"If you are going to keep me prisoner, at least tell me what is happening," Rhieienmelth said to Œthelwald. She was riding upon a wagon. Or, rather, sitting upon it. The wagon itself was not going anywhere. Like most of the wagons that carried the supplies and the loot of the great army, it was stuck in mud. The despairing wagoners were attempting to cajole, kick and whip the oxen into motion, but the animals had given up, and were accepting the blows with the same resignation with which they accepted the rain. Seeing Œthelwald ride past, she had called to him and he had pulled his horse up so that he might speak. For Œthelwald saw fit to maintain the pretence that Rhieienmelth was there as his guest and of her own will.

Œthelwald gentled his horse. The unceasing rain had unsettled it, along with all the other animals, and left it prone to sudden frights and shies.

"We are going home. Back to our kingdoms. The High King has returned with a great treasure – greater than any of the kings have seen – and he has given it with open hands to all those faithful to him; and myself not least among them. He is faithful to those who serve him, Mother of my heart. Can you not see that?"

"I see that he brought a greater treasure than any gold back with him."

"Yes." Œthelwald shook his head. "You would have me trust a man who gives up his own son that he might buy a season longer upon his throne?"

Rhieienmelth shook her head. "Perhaps… perhaps you are right after all. I would see for myself that the boy is well. If that be the case, then I must needs agree that the High King keeps his pledge."

"I cannot take you now to see him," said Œthelwald, "for I am upon an errand the High King has set for me."

"For the sake of all the saints, can you not let me go and see on my own? Where do you think I might go in all this mud? We cannot even escape the road; think you I could escape the army?"

Œthelwald looked ahead, indecision filling his eyes.

"I would that you know the truth of this, Mother of my heart, so I will give you leave to go find the boy. The High King has given him into the care of his wife, Cynewisse. You will find him with her." Then Œthelwald turned his horse's head back to the front of the army – where some movement still happened – and urged it into motion.

Rhieienmelth turned to the wagon driver, who served also as her jailer. "You heard what he said?"

The man, not given to speaking, grunted.

"And farewell to you too."

Hitching her skirts up, Rhieienmelth climbed down from the wagon, searching for some firmer piece of ground that might take her weight. She did not find it. The mud sucked her foot down and she all but fell, just catching the wheel in time. The wagon driver looked down at her, but offered no help. She tried to pull her feet free, but the mud sucked her foot back.

"Here, take this."

Rhieienmelth almost fell as she twisted round to see who spoke, but she just managed to grab the out-thrust staff and save herself.

"Coifi!"

The old priest smiled at her over the length of ash. "If you hold, I will pull."

Digging his feet into the firmer ground beyond the track, Coifi pulled. With the staff to hold on to, Rhieienmelth managed to get first one foot then the other free.

"Coifi, I did not know you to be here." Then, at the words' meaning, Rhieienmelth stopped. "Why are you here?"

But Coifi took her hand. "Come with me," he said.

Exhausted wagoners lay everywhere beside the track, so they had to go some way across the sodden turf until they reached the small shelter of a hawthorn copse.

Having looked to see that no one else, fed up with the lack of progress, had taken shelter in the copse, Coifi told Rhieienmelth how he came to be with the great army. She would have told her story, but Coifi shook his head.

"I know how you come to be here," he said.

"How so?"

"Wihtrun told me. The High King's priest. He... has told me other things too." Coifi's head jerked round as something scuttled through the leaf mould behind them.

Rhieienmelth put her hand to Coifi's arm, calling him back to her.

"What things has this priest told you?"

"He wishes me to join him in renewing the old ways. He would have men worship the gods as they did in the days of our fathers, and not turn to the new god, the god of your fathers, Rhieienmelth. He thinks the gods have answered his prayers and accepted his sacrifice, for Penda has cast down Oswald and Edwin, Sigeberht and Anna. I thought that enough for him and I held my peace, for one thing I have learned in my years is that the fortunes of a king may change upon a single chance: the fortune that brought to Penda the kingship over other kings shall surely turn, as it turned for Æthelfrith and Edwin and Oswald before him. But I have learned that Wihtrun would do more to earn back the favour of the gods. For this is what he told me: 'If we would have the gods' favour return, then we must offer them sacrifice; true sacrifice. That which we value above all things. And what do we value above even gold? Life. To regain the gods' favour, we must offer them life in sacrifice.'" Coifi looked at Rhieienmelth. "Penda has in his hands the life Wihtrun would sacrifice."

"Ecgfrith?"

"Yes. The boy. And, I think, you as well, and mayhap Œthelwald too. But the boy is the important one. Ætheling. Iding. Of the blood of Oswald and Edwin."

"Will Penda agree to such a thing?"

"Once, I would have said no. But now?" Coifi's eyes darted after a falling drop of water. He slapped himself back to attention. "Fool.

Follow every raindrop in this season and you will only find more rain." He jerked his head back to Rhieienmelth. "Wihtrun has long whispered that the High King is Woden, the Lord of Battles, walking among us. But now I fear that Penda himself starts to believe it."

"How long before they do this?"

"I think he would not do such a deed in this kingdom, for the monks of the Holy Island have made it holy to the new god. A blood sacrifice on such ground would redound upon the one making it. But once they are back on home soil, where men still worship the old gods... I think Wihtrun will do it then." Coifi shook his head. "He has asked me to help."

"Surely you will not."

"No. But there is little time left. You must get word to Oswiu. Tell him. And tell him this also..." Coifi leaned closer to Rhieienmelth, and whispered. "The High King always goes among his army hooded, such that few ever see his face. A man dressed in like fashion might get far, for few would bar the High King's way, and fewer still would think another might pass himself off as Penda."

"You think someone might get to Ecgfrith in such fashion?"

"If fortune favours him greatly, yes. The boy is being kept by the king's wife and she is ever close to Penda. There is great danger there."

"But there is a chance."

"A chance, yes." Coifi looked out from the cover of the trees. It looked as if the great army was finally moving again. "But only if you can get word to Oswiu."

"How may I escape? It is true, Œthelwald gave me leave to seek after Ecgfrith and see that he is well, but I will not be able to wander alone for long."

"I will make a diversion for you," said Coifi. "This evening, when we stop, when you see great confusion near to the king's tent, that is the time to go."

"What will you do?" asked Rhieienmelth.

Coifi smiled. "Aidan told me what to do."

*

"Enough!"

Coifi, raven-feather cloak wrapped around his shoulders, bone rattle in his hand (although the bones in this rattle, to the watching eye, might have seemed strangely white and smooth, as if they had only lately been strung together), stood in the wide space that always seemed to open up around the king's tent when the army pitched camp for the night. While all the others, be they kings, thegns or common fighting men, crowded together, tent pitched close to tent and men sleeping side by side, a rough circle was always left around Penda's tent in which no other pavilion intruded – and certainly no one slept on the ground there. But now, Coifi stood in that broad though muddy space and, raising his hands up to the clouds, railed against the rain that continued to fall from them.

"Enough!" he cried again. As he shouted, tremors passed through his body in waves. "Thunor, god of thunder, I tell thee: enough! Rein in thy spite! Swallow thy pride!"

As Coifi continued to call against Thunor, men, then women and children, gathered slowly at first, but then more quickly as word spread, to see and hear what was going on outside the tent of the High King.

"Thunor, god of thunder, lord of the skies, we have seen enough of your face. You have washed this middle-earth with your tears, but cry no more, lest you wash the world away."

Coifi twitched, looking aside as rain traced wyrd, and the flap to the king's tent opened. The king, hooded and shadowed, stood in the shadows there but did not move or speak. His black eye glittered as he watched Coifi.

The fate weavings told Coifi a crowd had gathered. Time to make the diversion.

"Men, the All-Father has not abandoned this middle-earth!" Coifi turned from the clouds to the men gathered round. "He is here, walking among us!"

At these words, proclaimed so all might hear, a whisper passed through the watching, gathering crowd. Many had spoken quietly of such matters, but not until now had anyone said it openly before so many. And as the whispers passed through the crowd, many eyes turned to the opening of the tent, where the High King stood in shadows, watching and listening.

"Thunor, sky lord, if this be blessing upon us for the All-Father's presence, then we have been blessed enough!"

The trembles that had been passing through Coifi's body were growing more marked and intense. He was shaking, all of him was shaking, as he spoke.

"Thunor, Earth Shaker, if this be anger for taking the All-Father from you, know that he came to us; we did not call him."

Suddenly, Coifi fell upon his hands and knees and swung his head from left to right, looking now at the people close clustered around him.

"No, for we had forsaken the ways of our fathers and left the worship of the All-Father. Oath-sworn, we forsook our pledge, and turned our backs upon the Father of Men. But Woden is ever merciful to his children – he comes among us, as one of us, to win us back to our old ways, to turn our feet to the paths of our fathers."

Coifi squatted back upon his heels, heedless of the mud that squelched around his calves. He pointed, with bone rattle and hand, to the high heaven and then to the High King's tent, where Penda stood, hooded and listening.

"Thunor, sky god, hear me! Stay your blessing, take away your clouds, for I tell you, the All-Father has not abandoned you. He is here; he is the High King. He is Penda!"

And as Coifi spoke, a light shone from the sky and cast brightness upon him. The crowd gasped, and many pointed, for the clouds that had not lifted this past month had finally split, and through the gap the sun, low in the west, shone, and its light fell upon Coifi as he kneeled in the mud before the tent of the High King and proclaimed him Woden incarnate, walking among men.

A great cry went up from the crowd, and some men wept, while others began to chant the name of their king and some to sing the name of their god, so that the two became entwined and rose as one sound into the washed-clean air.

"Penda! Woden! Penda! Woden!" The names alternated, swelling and rising, as all the men of the army gathered around the king's tent, taking up the call and acclaiming him.

And the king, the High King, lord of the Mercians, master of the Magonsæte, made no sound, but came forth from his tent, and the sun shone upon him, although with his back to the west it did not raise the shadow beneath his hood, and he accepted, by his silence, the judgement of his people: in the flesh of their king, the All-Father walked among men.

Victory was certain. With the Lord of Battles as their lord, victory would always be certain.

*

"What's happening?"

The boy put his eye to the gap in the tent. He could hear the chanting and shouting outside; he had seen the crowd gather and the way Coifi had collapsed, spent and shaking, upon the muddy ground as the sun appeared; he had tried to see past the king, but he had been in the way, standing in the entrance to the tent, so he had pushed apart some of the stitching in a worn seam so that he might see out.

Now, he turned back to the woman and the other man, the only other people in the tent.

"What's happening?" he asked again. "Why are they all shouting outside? Is something wrong?"

But the woman shook her head. The man, for his part, barely heard the boy. He was gazing out at Penda with an expression of rapture.

"What's happening then?" the boy insisted.

"Don't worry, Ecgfrith," said Cynewisse. "The men are acclaiming the king, my husband, as Woden, walking among us."

"They're saying he's a god?" asked Ecgfrith.

"Yes, they are," said Cynewisse.

"Is he?" asked Ecgfrith. "Is he a god?"

Cynewisse looked past the boy, out of the tent, to the hooded figure of her husband. She had known him so long. But, it was true, there had been something different about him in these last few months, something deeper... something darker.

"I – I do not know," she said. "Mayhap."

But then the man, hearing her words, turned to the queen and the boy.

Wihtrun's eyes were shining. "He is a god," he said. "Make no mistake; he is a god indeed."

Chapter 13

She knew the screams as soon as she heard them. A woman in labour sounds like nothing else in this middle-earth – and she had screamed like that herself. Twice.

Oswiu and his household had come down from the hills.

As the great army had moved south, carrying the spoils of the summer's campaign and then, finally, the king's own son, the bedraggled, dispirited household of the king of the Bernicians had trailed down the steep paths from the hills. The queen, her belly straining with child, was carried down the hillsides, but despite the jolting, still the baby did not come.

Only when she came to some sort of rest, at one of the king's smaller estates in the shadow of the Simonside Hills, did her waters break. But the labour was long, and the midwife began to fear for the life of the queen and the child.

It had been a long, hard road to find the king. Rhieienmelth had made her escape when Coifi, in the sight of the whole army, proclaimed Penda to be Woden. She had slipped from the camp, leading a stolen horse, and then she had ridden north. But the rains of the past month had swollen all the rivers, making any crossing at the very least difficult and sometimes impossible. Moreover, she was a woman riding alone. Most of the time, Rhieienmelth chose to ride at night and lie up during the day in some lonely wood. Even so, she had only narrowly escaped the attentions of a pair of lordless men who had also seen the merits of hiding during the day in a tangled copse. On that occasion, her horse had saved her, leaping a stream the rains had turned to a small river where her pursuers' animals hesitated and refused. Pulling the panting beast's head round, so she could check that the men had given up the chase, Rhieienmelth gave silent thanks for all the hours she had spent hunting while living in Æbbe's holy house.

Then there had been the long search for the king, asking, where she dared, after his presence, until finally an old, almost wordless man standing ankle deep in his strip of field pointed to a distant ridge of land.

"Yon," he had said. "The king be there."

The tongue he spoke was close cousin to Rhieienmelth's own native language and he spoke no other. If not for that, she would have searched longer. As it was, riding to the hedge boundary of the king's estate, she saw the guards upon the gate and the purple and gold banner of the Idings flying beside the hall.

The guard had recognized her and rushed Rhieienmelth across the compound towards the great hall. It was as she was crossing the compound that she heard the screams. They came from a house, rapidly put together from timber and thatch, that stood aside from the hall: the renewed scream told the reason for its construction. It was a birthing house.

"The queen."

The guard shuddered as the scream trailed away, then he sketched a ragged cross from head to heart to shoulders. "It has been two days."

"She is strong if she still screams like that," said Rhieienmelth. She looked to the birthing house. "After two days, she will need to be."

The guard took Rhieienmelth to the hall and presented her to the door warden. When he looked askance at announcing a woman, the guard poked him with his hand. "Know you not that this is the mother of the king's son and daughter? Let her enter."

"The king has commanded I keep this door closed," said the door warden, "so he would not hear the cries of the queen."

As the warden said this, a new scream came from the birthing house, louder than any of those Rhieienmelth had heard before, but this one, in its falling, had a different tone to it: the sound of final, exhausted triumph.

She looked to the birthing house, head cocked, listening. And then it came. The thin wail of a new-born child, asking against its arrival in this middle-earth.

Rhieienmelth turned to the door warden. "You can open the door now," she said.

*

The king sat in silence upon the judgement seat. He stared into the distance, but saw nothing there, for there was no focus to his gaze.

"All my choices have gone amiss."

Oswiu looked to where Ahlfrith stood in the hall, speaking with his mother. They were, in looks, much alike.

Rhieienmelth had told that which she had travelled over many leagues and through much danger to tell: his son, given to buy peace, was going to die as sacrifice to buy back the favour of the old gods.

The king stood, and his face was as the ash of a fire that has long since died. He felt his legs tremble beneath him. He reached for the arm of the judgement seat, lest he fall.

Rhieienmelth it was who came to him then. She saw the look upon his face and remembered it of old; for it was how Oswiu looked when he most felt the loss of his brother, and the lack of him. She took his arm, making it seem to those watching not the support of a man failing in strength but the touch of one conveying news.

"There is one more matter I would tell you," she said. "Your mother asked my forgiveness when she lay on her death bed, but I would not give it. Now I would that I had. Go to Eanflæd, once husband – go to her and see your new child. She has crossed the dark valley to bring new life into this middle-earth; there is, in that, a sign. God has not forsaken you, Oswiu, nor his pledge with your people. Go to Eanflæd and see the truth of which I speak."

Taking his arm, she led him forth, and none stood in their way.

But when Rhieienmelth had brought the king to the birthing house, she stopped outside its door.

"It is not meet that I should enter here. Go in and bless your child."

The queen's women were waiting for him, and they opened the door. The air within the birthing house was thick with incense and the smell of blood and excrement. Faces, pale and exhausted but triumphant, turned towards him, but there was only one he sought.

The queen, Eanflæd, lay upon the rough bed. In her arms, nursing, was a baby.

A new life.

Sensing the watching silence, the queen looked up. Seeing the king, she smiled a weary smile.

Oswiu, king, went down upon one knee beside the bed. "Is it…" he began.

"A girl," finished Eanflæd.

"A girl." He nodded. "Good. That is good." Oswiu reached a hesitant hand towards the small head, then stopped without touching the baby.

"Go on," said Eanflæd. "Touch her."

Gently, as if it were an egg beneath his fingers, Oswiu laid his hand upon the baby's head.

"Child, I give you my blessing." He bent down and, breathing on the baby, kissed her.

The king stood up. "I will leave you now," he said, "for I have much to think on."

*

Night had come and Oswiu stood alone beneath the sky. His warriors, his thegns, had come to him, asking him to return to the light and warmth of the hall, but Oswiu remained without, under the stars. He drew his cloak around his shoulders. Autumn was passing. These were the first winter stars.

He heard footsteps, crunching frost-coated grass beneath them, and knew who came to him in the night.

"You were the one who loved the stars." He did not look round.

The footsteps stopped beside him.

Oswiu looked up at the long trailing light of the Milky Way. "You told me, when I was little, and scared, that we could always escape our enemies and climb those stairs. I would that you had not climbed them before me. Everything I have done has turned aside. All my plans have gone astray."

Oswiu raised his arm and pointed to the great hunter. "But that was your favourite. When the hunter rose in the winter time, you always told me it was a sign that one day we would return home. You were right. You were always right about such matters. But I am not the same as you. I do not have your trust."

But then Oswiu tilted his head, as if seeing the hunter for the first time. "Yet the hunter rises now as he did before. The ladder of stars still climbs the sky. And I have a daughter, a new life." Oswiu breathed out and he watched his breath mist before his face.

"We made no plan, did we, brother? When we returned from over the sea, we rode from the Holy Island with the men we had, to meet the king who had despoiled our land and killed our people. Since I took the throne, it seems to me all I have done is make plans and see them fail. All my wit – you might think that little enough, but for a while it seemed to me sufficient – has failed. There is naught else I can do. All my wriggling upon God's hook has not freed me – no, not though I gave my own son to keep my throne." Oswiu shook his head. "You would not have done as I have done. Will you tell me what I should do?"

The king tilted his head to hear, but no sound came to him. But then he gave a small laugh. "Is it so clear that it needs no words? I fear that is true, and yet I have not seen it before. I understand now. In truth, even if you had come before I would not have understood." Oswiu laughed again. "You did? See, I said I would not have understood – in that, at least, I was right." He breathed out again, the air misting before his face. "But now I see." He looked up at the ladder of stars ascending the sky, then bowed his head. "Will you give me your blessing?"

Then it seemed as if the cold fingers of a night wind were laid upon the king's head. And with his head bowed, Oswiu heard a sound he had not heard for many years: the wind rushing over stiff black feathers and then the coughing caw of the raven's call.

"You have sent Bran?"

The rush of air beaten down beneath wings cooled the back of Oswiu's neck.

Oswiu, king, remained with his head bowed as the steps he had heard approach went away again, the frost grass cracking beneath them.

*

Oswiu stood in the great hall. He looked out over the faces of the men who had remained faithful to him, who had followed him into the hills and thirsted there beneath the sun, who had slipped and squelched with him through the mud of autumn, and who now sat in the warmth of the hall as outside the first storm of winter lashed sleet and hail and rain against its wooden walls.

"I have failed you."

There was still enough pride in his heart for part of him to hope that some, perhaps many, would stand and cry "Nay!" to him. But no one did. Instead, they sat in watchful, listening silence. Oswiu glanced, once, beside him. His queen sat there, upon his right hand side, with the babe silent in her arms, looking up at him as he spoke, her face grave.

"I thought that I might buy peace with Penda – buy it with gold and with my son. I was wrong."

Some among the men nodded gravely at his words. Some, indeed, had wondered at the king's actions; fewer had spoken, but even those the king had ignored.

"Now, I go to make right what I did wrong. I go to claim back my son and regain our gold. If any would come with me, he will be welcome, even should there be ancient grudge between us. Let all be healed before I go, so that no man may bear me ill will should this matter go awry." Oswiu turned to Eanflæd. "Before all, I say what I said to you alone, my queen. Let this girl, the flesh of our flesh, be consecrated to God through all the days of her life. For Penda would make a sacrifice of blood, but I would make a sacrifice of life – a life lived in service of our Lord. And of my wealth, of the riches that remain when all else tarnishes and fails, I give twelve estates, that twelve holy houses be supported, henceforth and forever, to offer the sacrifice of prayer – the true sacrifice of men's hearts – to our Lord. For Penda, with his priest, would bring back the old gods. But we have forsaken them, for in them there is no life. The Lord of Life shall face the Lord of the Slain."

Oswiu looked slowly round the hall. "I go to war with Penda. I go to claim my son. Like enough I shall not return. Who here shall follow me?"

Chapter 14

"I cursed the rain all through the autumn, but now I see that it was a blessing."

Oswiu pointed through the screen of gorse and hawthorn that sheltered him and Ahlfrith from view.

They had crawled up the far side of the hill, leaving their horses tethered in its lea. The wind had backed to the east and it blew cold into their faces as they reached the crest, seeking always to find the patch of heather or the wind-blasted thorn that would break up their outline should anyone below glance westward, to the hills.

In pursuit of the great army, Oswiu had ridden south through Deira, taking the roads the army itself had travelled and trusting in the speed of their progress to outrun any message of pursuit. But why should Penda fear any pursuit? The great army, even somewhat reduced as men began to straggle away homewards, numbered more than a thousand. Some one hundred men rode with Oswiu. Others had pledged to follow, but the king would not wait for horses to be gathered or armour repaired.

"Ride now, or follow later – I go to war," he had cried as they swept south. And some, indeed, even answered his call in Deira; for the great army had fed while it made its way south through Deira, and all that Œthelwald might do had not stopped it. But even with those men, the army Oswiu had gathered was small before the host spread out below the king and his warmaster.

"See how the river has swollen," said Ahlfrith, pointing. "At other seasons, men and horses might ford there as easily as crossing the bridge. But now, after the rain of autumn, none might enter the Winwæd without drowning."

Oswiu looked to the west. The sun was but a hand's breadth from the ragged line of the mountains.

"They have not time to cross before dark," he said. "But what think you, Ahlfrith?" He pointed to the clouds massing beyond the mountains. "If I be not mistaken, there will be rain on the hills this night. With the river so swollen, the dawn might see Penda's army wake to find its feet wet."

But Ahlfrith shook his head. "There is no telling the weather this season. Even should the rain fall, the flood will like enough hinder us as much as Penda."

"Mayhap." Oswiu turned back to his spying upon Penda's camp. "But at least, with the day so late, they must wait until dawn to send the rest of the army across the bridge. And the vanguard on the far bank gives us fewer men to deal with."

"It gives me fewer men to deal with." Ahlfrith turned to his father. "Let me go. If I fail, then you may still prevail. But if you are caught, then we have no hope."

Oswiu shook his head. "This is what I have learned: even should we fail, and all be lost, there is still hope, for our hope is not confined to this life. But in this I trust our hope shall prevail in the sight of men too." He put his hand on his son's shoulder. "I thank you. But it must be me, for he is my son, and my fault put him in this peril. Surely you know this to be true?"

Slowly, Ahlfrith nodded.

"Very well. I will wait until full dark. Have the men ready; watch and listen for my sign." The king held up the hunting horn he had brought with him. "You know its voice. But if, as may be, there is too much noise for it to be heard, I will try to set flame to tent or pavilion: watch too for that."

"If you will not let me go in your place, then let me go with you, Father."

But again Oswiu shook his head, although he smiled. "Once before I went concealed and in disguise into my enemy's realm to claim that which was precious to me. Now I go again. I know what to do. Besides –" he pointed – "here, on the border of his own kingdom, Penda has barely bothered to set any sentries. He knows we have no army to match his." Oswiu smiled again, but this smile was grim. "He thinks himself a god among men. But we know, where he does not, that when a god takes flesh, he may die, as men die, and by the weapons that bring death to men and not in the jaws of the great wolf."

"I have heard many tales told of Penda. Are you sure there is no truth in them, Father?"

"I have stood face to face with Penda," said Oswiu. "He is no god – only a man. But the greater the fear his people have for him, the better goes it for me." He looked back west. The sun was falling behind the mountains. It would soon be dark. "Come, let us return. You must make the men ready and get them into position. For my part, I have my own preparations to make."

*

Ahlfrith was preparing the men, moving among them and telling each what he expected, when a cry went up from the edge of the camp. Men sprang to their feet, some making the sign against the evil eye, while others rasped blade from sheath or muttered prayers beneath their breath. Holding his hands up, Ahlfrith urged the men to silence, before turning to the object of their fear.

He had appeared, in silence, at the edge of the camp, shadow rimmed and fire edged: a hooded figure, eye glinting in the firelight.

Ahlfrith signalled to Acca to follow him and they went over to the hooded figure, looking it up and down.

The hooded one stood silent and still before them.

"Really quite good," said Acca. He put his head to one side. "You're very nearly the same size and build. In poor light, you should pass for him. Yes, not that bad for someone who has not been taught."

Ahlfrith looked sidelong at the scop, then back to the hooded figure. "Well, I think you look just like him," he said.

The hooded figure spoke, and the voice at least was unmistakably that of Oswiu. "But Acca has seen Penda more recently. What can I do to look more like him?"

"It's not so much the appearance; it's the way you carry yourself, the way you walk. You step out boldly, but Penda glides – with the cloak on and the hood up, he seems to float over the ground. Try to slide your feet over the ground." Acca cocked his head as the hooded figure began to move forwards. "Yes, that's better."

Then the hooded figure tripped and almost fell, stopping itself, but cursing. "I can't see where I'm stepping," Oswiu complained.

"Maybe it would be better if Father walked how he normally walks," said Ahlfrith.

Acca turned away. "He asked my thoughts; I gave them. It is not my fault if the king cannot glide without falling over."

"You try it with this hood on," said Oswiu. "But I'll remember what you said. In their camp, there will be more light, so I will be able to see better."

"Speaking of seeing," said Ahlfrith, "what have you done to cover your eye?"

"This." Oswiu reached up and drew the hood back from his head. He had wound a cloth round the side of the head where Penda's ruined eye had been. The king pushed the cloth up. "But I will need both eyes to make my way into Penda's camp."

He looked at the two men standing before him. "Acca, you have seen two kings fall under Penda's sword. Like enough, you will see a third. But you have been ever faithful to the kings of the Northumbrians. If I should fall, I charge you to make a song of my passing that will be remembered after I am gone." The king looked down at himself dressed in Penda's clothing. "I will at least make for a good riddle!"

Then he looked to his son, Ahlfrith. "You too have been ever faithful to me, my son." Oswiu took his hand and, raising it, turned to the watching, waiting men.

"I go before you," the king said. "Now, while I am gone, in all things take Ahlfrith's words as mine: follow him as you would me. And when I call, come quickly – or I will take all the gold for myself!"

At that, the men laughed, as Oswiu knew they would. Before a battle, even the weakest of jokes would raise mirth, for men's mirth at such time was laughter in the face of death.

As the men returned to their rituals – sharpening swords, cleaning armour, reciting prayer: the tasks they did to calm the mind and strengthen courage before the day of slaughter – Oswiu took Ahlfrith and led him to one side.

"If no sign should come from me, then think not to save me: I will be lost. Return to the queen, see to her safety, see that she is taken to her kin in Kent. After that, well…" Oswiu shrugged. "After that, you must judge. There will be little hope of defeating Penda then."

"But did you not tell me that our hope is not confined to this life?"

Oswiu laughed. "That is when you know the son has matched the father: when he gives the father his own advice. But I do not wish for you to throw your life after mine. And even if there is a sign, think well before attacking; see if Penda sets men waiting to trap you. Watch, in particular, for ropes strung low between tents, for those will trip a horse and send the rider flying. If you come, come fast and with fire. It is a strange thing, but amid all this water, fire will be our friend: use it well."

Ahlfrith nodded. "I will. I will set the men to binding torches, ready to put flames to the tents and wagons."

"Good. I will watch for you." Oswiu grasped his son's shoulders. "Listen for me; watch for me. Come quickly if I call. Go quickly if I do not."

"Give me your blessing, Father." Ahlfrith bowed his head.

Oswiu laid his hands on his son's head. "I give it; I give it right gladly. My blessing and the blessing of all the Idings." Then Oswiu lifted his son's head and looked into his face. "Think on this: if the day goes well, if God favours us and brings us victory, you will be a king tomorrow. For I will not suffer Œthelwald to rule further in Deira."

"Will you kill him? He is son to your brother."

"Though Œthelwald is blood to my blood, yet he is a traitor to us. Yes, I will kill him." Oswiu shook his head. "But I would not spend my leave-taking talking of him." The king embraced his son.

"God's blessing upon you. Now, I go, as David did, into the camp of my foe. Farewell."

"Farewell, Father."

Ahlfrith stood and watched as his father rode slowly from the camp and disappeared into the darkness.

*

Being a sentry meant being cold, wet and miserable, the young man decided. Mind, being in Penda's army during the last month had meant being cold, wet and miserable too. Not like the summer months, when it had not rained at all, and the only peril was catching too much sun and turning as red as cooked salmon. At least they were heading home now. That made the tedium and the cold of sentry duty easier to bear.

It was always the young men, the ones yet to prove themselves in the shieldwall, who were set to sentry duty. But how could he prove himself a warrior when the enemy did nothing but run before the High King's great army? They had run away all summer, leaving the land bare of defenders, ripe for the army's picking. And he'd done his own fair share of picking. The young man, Hutha, fingered his belt. He had sewn the jewels he had prised from the dead man's sword, blood-red garnets, into the belt itself, wrapping the material over the garnets and then sewing them tight. Hutha remembered the man's face: it was wide with surprise. Stupid that, he thought. All men knew they must die, so why had it come as a surprise? The greater surprise was that he'd found the body undespoiled. But then, the man had fallen in such a way that the hedge concealed him. Maybe he'd been defending his house. If so, it had been no great hall – although, in truth, it was a finer hall than Hutha's father's – but men died for all sorts of mean things. It occurred to Hutha that it was a better death to die defending your hall than for the sweating sickness to take you, or the sickness that consumed the body and left it but bones and skin before life finally left it. That was how his father had died. Hutha was determined not to die the same way.

Movement.

There, in the dark outside the camp. A shadow, moving, coming closer.

"Stop. Halt!"

Hutha held out his spear, its point catching the light from one of the many fires that sputtered on wet wood and even wetter ground behind him.

The shadow did not stop, but continued to approach.

"Stop!" Hutha said again.

The shadow came closer. It moved as a cloud of darkness.

"Stop! Now!"

But the shadow moved closer, coming into the faint firelight and, as it did so, it shrank from monstrous to human size – a man hooded and cloaked, walking towards Hutha.

"Lord! I am sorry." Hutha lifted the spear. "I did not know you had gone forth from the camp."

The hooded figure made no answer in words, but turned its head towards the guard. Beneath the hood, Hutha saw shadow and the glitter of a single eye. Hutha stood aside as the hooded figure entered the camp. He had heard tales of how the High King went abroad, walking unseen by day and by night, and now he knew these tales to be true, for he had seen the High King go into his tent but a short while ago, before he began his stint on guard, and had not thought the king would emerge again before light. As the High King passed, Hutha made the courtesy. It was, he thought, as well that he had not been asleep when the High King returned. He had been tired and sleepy; there had been no alarms for so long that it hardly seemed worth posting sentries, for surely there were no armies to match the High King's anywhere in this land, and Hutha had thought of propping his back against a tree and closing his eyes for a while, so that he would be sharper when he woke. Hutha turned to watch as the High King's hooded, silent figure passed into the camp. If he had been asleep when Penda returned, he would never have had chance to prove himself as a warrior.

Hutha turned back to his guard duties. Mind, now the High King had returned, he would likely not go forth again. Hutha propped his back against an alder tree and set his spear firmly, pushing the shaft into the soft earth. Maybe he might just close his eyes for a while. After all, there wouldn't be anyone else coming this way…

*

Oswiu pulled his cloak tighter and bowed his head. He had not thought of this, but now, on a night with no moon and clouds covering the stars, the only light came from below, from the fires sputtering all around the camp. But the light from ground-level fires rose and lit his face, where the light from sun or moon, being from above, would have served only to cast his face into deeper shadow. It was as well, then, that it was a cold night, with the wind backing north and east. No man would think it strange that the High King would pull his cloak tight and his hood down. But walking with his head bowed and his eyes low meant that he could not see clearly where he wished to go. Instead, he followed the lines of the rough paths set between the tents and wagons and sleeping men. Some, seeing him, made the courtesy, but he saw as many make the sign against the evil eye as he passed.

Penda's men feared him.

Oswiu called from his memory the image of the camp, laid out before him, that he had seen from the hill the evening before. It spread along the northern bank of the River Winwæd, making a rough half-circle. Penda's tent stood in the centre of the camp, apart from the other tents. Only the queen's tent was pitched close by, the two shelters adjoining each other. From what Acca had told him, Oswiu hoped to find Ecgfrith in the queen's tent.

But as Oswiu made his slow way through the camp, the sheer numbers of men he saw dismayed him. Even should he find and claim Ecgfrith, and Ahlfrith launch his attack, with so many men all around surely he would never be able to take Ecgfrith forth. Something much greater than a small diversion would be necessary to earn the time he needed to escape with his son.

Still, at least the fear and awe with which his men regarded Penda meant that Oswiu could make his way through the camp without having to speak to anyone. If he had been walking among his own men, he would have had to stop and speak to every second or third man. He would have been asked his opinion in some dispute over precedence, called over to tell again the tale of how he and Oswald took the kingdom from Cadwallon, or regaled with some story of how one of the men tupped a good wife by pretending to be her husband. But here, in Penda's camp, men shrank away from him.

Walking between the tents and round and past the forms of men lying upon the ground, Oswiu saw the signs of a weary army. They had been in the field for many months now. He saw armour left lying on damp ground next to its exhausted wearer; the iron would rust if left in such conditions, but the wearer no doubt thought that he would have chance to polish the rust from it when he returned to his own home. The plunder of his kingdom that would not fit upon the high-packed wagons lay in untidy piles all about the camp, each curled about by the men who had taken it, lying in heaps, snoring and open mouthed.

And behind the sounds of a sleeping camp there was the rush of water. As he made his way onwards, towards the centre of the camp, gaps would open between the clustered tents and he could see the dark rushing flow, pulling at the sedge and rush lining the banks of the river.

Sometimes a sentry, seeing him approach, called him to halt, but whenever they saw the hood and cloak of the High King emerging from the shadows, they stood aside and let him pass without word.

Coming upon one of the gaps that always form wherever men make camp, Oswiu paused. He was far from any camp fire and there was no one nearby, so he raised his lowered head and looked around. In the camp, amid the tents and wagons and men, it was far harder to keep his way, but he thought he saw the shifting shapes of the banners of kings ahead. From the vantage point earlier, he had seen that the kings who marched with Penda made camp near to him, forming a rough circle around a centre that was Penda's tent.

Oswiu took a breath. The air was cold, and bit his teeth and throat. There was a change in the air. He glanced up. The wind had torn the cloud into tatters and was pulling it over the sky. Through the gaps, the first stars of the night glittered. He was glad. If he was to die tonight, he would see the stars. Perhaps, if the wind freshened further, he might see the Milky Way. Surely that was how the soul climbed to God's high heaven. Though there were other, darker, paths for the spirit after death. The shudder and shake of it fell upon him then; the memory of the men he had killed, the memory of the man he had murdered. The Godfriend. Would God take vengeance for the murder of Oswine? Oswiu looked about, searching for some sign or sound: if he heard the sound of wind over feathers, or the cough of a raven, he would know that the bird was with him, and surely if Bran was with him then God's favour lay upon him too. But the night was still, save for the wind, and there was no dark shape in it.

Oswald was the one who had known. He was the one who always knew what God wanted him to do. Oswiu shook his head. For him, there was ever doubt.

But he did know that his son was captive. He knew it was his task to try to free him. That he did not doubt.

Oswiu marked the path to where the banners flew thickest. That was the way. Drawing the cloak about his shoulders and pulling the hood down, he set off towards where the High King waited.

*

Was it the cold that kept him from sleeping? Œthelwald had known cold nights before and slept through them. But here, by the River Winwæd, it seemed as though the wet of the river rose through the ground and into his bones, so that he shifted and turned and could not sleep. At length, giving up on that which would not come, Œthelwald rose. Wrapping a cloak around his shoulders, he stepped from his tent. As was his custom, he first glanced to the sky. The cloud of the early night had gone, he saw; torn into shreds by the wind. It was cold, and despite his cloak, the cold lay its fingers into his flesh. Œthelwald shivered. Winter was coming. The harvest had been poor, very poor, for the summer's heat had scorched the crops and then, when the longed-for rain finally came, it came not as saviour but as destroyer, ruining by flood what the sun had not finished through drought. There would be people starving by winter's end, and those who could still walk would come to him, bonding themselves into slavery for food to fill their belly. He made memory to check, when he returned finally to his own halls, what stores were laid in against the winter's dearth. They would have need of them all.

His own halls? He was already calling them that, although he had but lately come into their kingship. Œthelwald smiled to himself. He was getting used to being king. His smile broadened. In truth, he was enjoying it well. Yes, it had been a shock when Rhieienmelth had come to him, asking him to abjure his pledge to the High King, but then his heart mother had taken advantage of the uproar caused by Coifi declaring Penda to be Woden to make a quiet departure. He had made little effort to find her. After all, what could she do? A woman, alone, making her way where an army had recently passed. She would do well to survive long enough to make it back to Æbbe's holy house.

As for what Coifi had declared, Œthelwald knew the old priest had simply said what most of the army believed. Never had he known a king held in such awe. Normally, a king must work, through word and deed, to hold men to him. But Penda had no such need. He passed in silence among his men and yet they followed him; they would follow him across the grey sea. They would follow him, Œthelwald thought, through the gates of death itself, for they feared death less than they feared their king.

For himself, though, he knew well Penda was no god. He had seen the glitter in that black eye as he looked upon Coifi abasing himself in the mud, and he had seen the spark of amusement in it. Men did not become gods – not even High Kings. If they did, his own father would still live.

The thought of his father chilled him. He felt Oswald's shadow upon him and he sought to push the thought away, but it would not go. Rather than wait upon the shadow's leaving, Œthelwald began to walk, head down, searching for clear ground among the tent ropes and sleeping men.

That was why he did not see that he was not alone in moving through the sleeping camp. Œthelwald all but walked into the High King.

For his part, the High King was as surprised. He rapidly stepped back, but in doing so tripped upon a rope. And in that fall, his hood flew back and Œthelwald looked into the face of the High King and saw his uncle.

He froze.

Oswiu looked up at him.

Neither spoke. Neither moved.

Slowly, Œthelwald crept his fingers towards the hilt of his sword.

Oswiu, seeing the fingers move, made no like motion. Instead, he stared up into Œthelwald's face.

"You have the look of your father," he said. Oswiu spoke softly, so that no others might hear, but in the silence of the camp Œthelwald heard him clearly.

Fingers resting upon the hilt of his sword, Œthelwald made no other move. He waited.

Slowly, Oswiu pushed himself back onto his feet. He pulled the hood back over his head, but he raised his face so that he might look at Œthelwald and Œthelwald look at him.

"I have come for my son," Oswiu said. "Will you stop me?"

Œthelwald's mouth worked. A single cry would bring the camp down upon them.

In the firelight, Oswiu searched the face before him for some trace of the brother he had lost. He shook his head.

"It is as well my brother died and did not see this, for you are no son to him."

Œthelwald began to open his mouth.

Oswiu shook his head. "If you would do this thing, then be quick."

Œthelwald's hand trembled upon his sword. He stared at Oswiu, his jaw working. Abruptly, he turned away. "Fetch your son, if you are able. For my part, I will not betray you."

Oswiu stared at the young man in front of him. He nodded, then drew the hood down. Like a wraith, he turned and moved away through the camp.

For a moment, Œthelwald watched where he went, then he too turned away. He felt the wind cold upon his face. It had turned in the night, he remembered.

Then, as if from the air above, he heard a call, the caw of the bird of slaughter. There were many tales told of Bran, the raven that had followed his father. He looked up, searching the night. There, against the stars, he thought he saw a darker shadow moving through the sky. Œthelwald shivered and drew his cloak around his shoulders.

Making his way back to his tent, he bent down and roused his warmaster. "Wake the men quietly and have them ready." He glanced to the horizon. The first hint of light glimmered there. "It will be a red dawn."

*

The black wolf streamed in the wind. In the dim light cast by the embers of the night's fires, Penda's banner flared over the king's tent.

Standing at the edge of the gap that separated the tents of the kings from the tent of the High King, Oswiu saw the wolf hunting the air, its jaws snapping in the wind. There were more guards here, but still they stepped back when they saw him approach. He walked quickly, for he could not know if the alarm cry would soon go up. For the moment, blood held Œthelwald silent, but he did not think it would hold him long.

He looked to the king's tent. There was a guard outside it. A man who would know that his king slept within. But Ecgfrith was with the queen. Her tent, he saw, adjoined the king's, but the guard had less clear sight of it. Keeping to the shadows, Oswiu moved round so that he might see the tent entrance more clearly. There was a guard there too. But standing where he stood, he would have no sight of the entrance to the king's tent. He would not know whether the king slept within, or had gone forth into the night.

Besides, surely the guard to the tent of the queen would stand aside that the king might visit her in the night.

Oswiu was about to step forward when he suddenly thought on this: suppose the king had already gone in to be with his wife, and the guard waited without for him to finish?

There was no knowing.

Oswiu looked up, but amid the banked fires that glowed around the tents of the kings there was too much light to see the stair of stars in the sky. Under the cover of his cloak, he marked the cross over his heart, scratching it into his flesh with his thumbnail.

Then he started across the open ground.

The guard outside the queen's tent jolted from his reverie and lowered his spear, but then seeing the shape resolve into a familiar hooded figure he stood back.

"Lord."

Oswiu walked past the guard and, pulling aside the flap of the tent, went within.

And stopped.

It was dark, even darker than without, and he waited, without moving, for his eyes to see.

But first he listened.

Breathing. The slow breath of people sleeping.

One, two, three... He turned his head, listening. Maybe six.

As he waited, the darkness resolved into shapes. Humps, lying upon the ground: the queen's women, taking rest where they might, sleeping upon cut rushes or other foliage.

There. In the centre of the tent.

A bed.

Beside it, another, smaller.

With a small shape lying upon it.

Ecgfrith?

He waited, barely breathing, but in the darkness of the tent his eyes could see no more.

The small shape shifted, turned.

It moaned, muttered, spoke. "Mummy."

Ecgfrith.

Oswiu stepped forward, leaned down and put one hand over his son's mouth while the other held him down.

The boy's eyes snapped open. He tried to call out, but the hand held the cry back. He looked up, saw the hooded figure standing over him, and began to struggle.

Oswiu pushed his head down alongside the boy and whispered into his ear. "It's me."

Ecgfrith stopped struggling.

Under his hand, Oswiu felt the boy's lips moving, making a word. He felt the sound.

"Daddy?"

"Yes."

Oswiu pulled his head back enough so that the boy could see his face. Keeping one hand over Ecgfrith's mouth, he put his finger to his lips.

The boy nodded. He understood.

"Ecgfrith?" The voice was sleepy, a woman's voice. The queen's.

Oswiu turned to her. Cynewisse was sitting up, resting her weight upon her elbow.

"Lord." She glanced at the boy. "Is it time?"

Oswiu nodded.

"I thought it would be later."

Oswiu shook his head. In the darkness she could not see his face, not under his hood.

"I will come." The queen began to sit up.

Oswiu held his hand up. He shook his head.

"You are merciful, lord, to spare me this."

Oswiu stood up. He was holding the boy's hand. Ecgfrith scrambled up out of bed and stood beside him.

"I – I would not see it done, lord."

Oswiu, holding the boy's hand, turned to the entrance of the tent.

"Cynewisse."

Oswiu stopped. He knew that voice of old.

Slowly, he turned round.

Penda stood at the back of the tent, holding aside the flap that sealed and joined his tent to that of his queen.

Penda stared at the hooded figure standing before him.

"Woden," he whispered.

*

The dream began as it always did.

He lay among the dead, their bodies piled upon him, holding him immobile with their weight. Only his eye moved, ranging over the field of slaughter.

There were bodies everywhere, stretching further than his eye might see. But these men, for the most part, lay in the attitude of one taken from water: their faces were pale, their skin slack and no wounds marred their bodies. Water leaked from eyes that stared upwards; hair, lank and wet, dripped on armour and shield.

Nothing moved, save only the water dripping from the dead.

Then he heard it.

The cry of a raven.

The bird landed among the corpses and dipped its head, uttering its cry once more.

He tried not to follow it as it moved, lest it see the movement of his eye. The bird dipped its head again, and cawed.

It was calling.

That which it called came.

He was a man, hooded, carrying a staff. He walked over the dead, and their bones cracked beneath his feet, but he did not stumble or fall.

The raven called and he came.

His eye turned from one to the other.

The hooded figure held out his hand.

The raven took wing in a creak of feathers and landed upon the hooded figure's arm. It walked, stiff legged, up the man's arm to his shoulder. There, it dipped its head to his ear.

From where he lay among the dead, he watched the bird speak to its lord.

The hooded figure nodded.

The bird took wing, gliding low over the pale bodies and alighting by the great mound of the dead where he lay. It began to climb, its talons digging into dead flesh.

The hooded figure turned after the bird and, seeing where it went, followed, its feet grinding over the dead.

He tried to close his eye, but it would not close. He saw the raven slowly climbing over the dead, but even the fear of its butcher's beak could not drag his gaze away from the hooded figure. The staff ground into the faces of those it walked over, gouging pale holes in flesh and cracking bone.

The figure approached until it stood before the mound of bodies that bound him in their prison of flesh. The raven bent low and peered at him, its black eyes glittering. It dipped its head and cawed.

The hooded figure slowly nodded.

He had seen where he lay among the dead.

To the Lord of the Slain, the dead were no disguise.

Slowly, the hooded figure reached for him.

*

That was what woke him. Panting, sweating.

Penda sat up, staring blind into the dark. "Cynewisse."

She wasn't there. Where was she?

Then he remembered. The bed he lay upon was in no hall, but under the roof of a tent. Cynewisse was close. He had but to call her.

"Cynewisse."

But his voice stuck in his throat for the dryness of it.

He stood up, feeling the ground shift beneath him, the blood rush in his head. Then, steadying himself, Penda felt his way to the back of his tent and pulled the flap aside.

"Cynewisse."

Then he saw him: the Lord of the Slain. Men had acclaimed him the All-Father and he had played with that knowledge and used it, but in his heart Penda had known it not to be true.

Now the Lord of the Slain had come to him.

"Woden," Penda whispered.

The hooded one turned to face him. In the shadows beneath the hood, Penda could see no face. Just darkness.

Whispers, cries, sobs. The women were waking.

"Lord, what is it? What happens?"

Cynewisse looked from one to the other, from the hooded figure she had thought to be her husband to the man, unhooded, who clearly was.

"Get out," Penda hissed, not looking at her – not looking at anything save the figure before him. "Everyone out."

Cynewisse scrambled from the bed and pulled the flailing, screeching women after her.

Outside, the guard, seeing the women spill out, made to rush into the tent, but Cynewisse barred his way, grabbing his arms.

"No!" she said. "Woden is within. It is sacred ground; we may not enter. Run! Fetch the priest. Only he can help the High King."

The cries of the women began to echo round the camp, eerie in their pitch of dread. Men woke and came running, and the whispers spread among them: the king, the High King, faced the high king of heaven within. None might enter.

The kings of the East Angles and the East Saxons, of Gwynedd and Powys, spilled from their tents, asking what had happened, but the High King's guards held them back.

Œthelwald pulled his warmaster aside. "Get the men out of here," he said. "We're leaving."

Together, they ran towards where the men of Deira were camped, calling them from their tents and to their horses.

In the east, the sky was no longer dark but the grey of approaching dawn.

In the camp the shouts grew louder.

From where he watched, Ahlfrith heard the cries and wondered if this was the sign he waited on. But there had been no horn sounded, nor fire lit. He looked to the horizon. It would be dawn soon. He turned back to the camp: watching, waiting, listening.

Coifi twitched, woke.

He had been dreaming. Aidan had been speaking to him. It had been a good dream.

A face loomed over him, anxious, hands pulling him upwards.

"Quick, quick," said Wihtrun, tugging him to his feet. "The king needs us. He faces the Lord of the Slain alone." Wihtrun pulled at Coifi. "Come on! Only a priest may enter now. We must go to him."

Wihtrun dragged Coifi on. Trying to find the quickest way to the centre of the camp, Wihtrun pulled Coifi down towards the river, for no one had pitched tent on the bank. But the river had risen in the night. Wherever there was a gap in rush and sedge, water flowed outwards, cold and dark. The Winwæd was breaking its banks.

"We must help the king," Wihtrun shouted to Coifi as he pulled him along, splashing through the floodwater. Those men who had not gone rushing to the centre of the camp were waking to find water about them, pulling with its cold fingers at the plunder they had accumulated through long months of campaigning. Cries went up as men woke to find their belongings drifting away. Horses and oxen, tethered for the night, began to pull and panic as the water rose about their hooves.

"Come on," said Wihtrun. But Coifi had stopped. Wihtrun turned back to him. "Quick," he said. "Only we can help the king."

"Which one?" asked Coifi. There. In the river. The first glimmer of light. It had caught the dawn. He smiled. He saw the working of wyrd.

"What do you mean, which one?" asked Wihtrun.

"You're right," Coifi said. "There is only one."

"Come on!" Wihtrun reached for the old priest, but rather than holding back, Coifi stepped forward and wrapped his thin arms around Wihtrun.

"Wh-what are you doing?" asked Wihtrun.

"This," said Coifi. And he pushed sideways.

They fell into the river. And the water, in spate, pulled them into itself.

*

"Woden." Penda whispered the name.

The Lord of the Slain made no move.

"Would you slay me, Lord of Battles?" Penda looked into the darkness under the hood, but there was only shadow. He pointed at the boy who stood, rigid with fear it seemed, beside the hooded man. "He was for you. You did not have to take him."

Still the Master of Words gave no answer.

Penda felt sweat prick his skin. He could smell it. He knew well the smell, for he had smelled it oft enough on others. He smelled his fear.

Slowly, the hooded figure moved. In the darkness, Penda could barely see what it was doing, and then the answer came in steel. A sword cold glowed in the darkness. Patterns swam down its length.

The sword sang for blood.

The Lord of the Slain was going to kill him.

Slowly, Penda drew his own sword.

"They say a wolf will kill you, All-Father. I am Penda. I fight under the banner of the wolf. I am the wolf that will kill you."

The swords edged towards each other, points questing, as though smelling for blood. Penda searched in the darkness under the hood, but he could see nothing there, no sign of where the Lord of the Slain looked. Neither, in the darkness, could he see how his enemy stood, for his limbs were concealed beneath his cloak.

The swords met, sparked, flew apart.

The raven coughed.

Though he resisted, every dream that had woken him, screaming, from sleep pulled his eye to the sound.

Penda glanced.

In the dark, darker than the darkness, he saw the slaughter bird. He saw its butcher's bill and its black eye.

And in that instant, when Penda looked away into the darkness for no reason that he could see, Oswiu struck. He felt the slightest resistance as the sword pierced skin and muscle, then the greater friction as he pushed it deeper and deeper.

Penda looked down.

He saw the steel sliding out. He looked up, slack jawed. The sword dropped from his fingers and he clutched his hands to his chest.

The Lord of the Slain reached up and lowered his hood.

"It is a new god that slays you, king of the Mercians."

Oswiu reversed his grip, and cut downwards through air and dark and flesh and bone.

Penda fell.

Oswiu stood over the king of the Mercians, panting, breathless.

Ecgfrith ran to him and Oswiu put his arm round the boy's trembling shoulders.

"Quiet!"

He listened. Outside, he could hear cries and shouts and calls, but nothing that yet said Ahlfrith had launched his attack.

Penda was dead.

But there was still a camp of enemies between them and safety.

And, sooner or later, someone would come to see what was happening in the tent of the king.

"Ecgfrith." Oswiu leaned down to his son, whispering to him. "Take my steel. Set fire to the king's tent, then come back here. Can you do this?"

Ecgfrith drew himself up. "Yes. Yes, I can."

Oswiu felt the boy setting his strength against the trembling that threatened to disable him. "Go then."

While Ecgfrith hastened into Penda's tent, Oswiu knelt down to do what he had to do.

He smelled the fire spark, glanced back and saw the first glow of it.

"Come," he called to Ecgfrith, and the boy returned. "Stay behind me." He stood up, his hand holding what he had cut, and made his way towards the entrance to the tent. Through it, he could see the faces assembled around the tent turned towards it. With the silence, they were coming closer, creeping, creeping, to see what happened within.

Oswiu drew his hood back over his head. He stepped out of the tent. He held up what was in his hand.

For the last time, Penda's black eye glittered as it looked upon his men.

Cynewisse, the queen, stared upon the head of her husband and made no sound but fell to her knees and tore her nails down her cheeks, tracking them with blood. About her, her women wailed, and screamed the judgement the All-Father had brought down upon their king.

"The Lord of the Slain has killed the king!"

Behind Oswiu, the king's tent flared, framing the hooded figure that held the head of the High King aloft.

"The king is dead! The king is dead!" The cry went up, spreading, leaping from man to man as a fire will leap from roof to roof.

Panic spread in the wake of the cry, sending men running to tent and pack and horse, to gather whatever they might of their plunder before turning to flight. The gathered kings scattered, calling warmasters and thegns to them, crying the retreat.

At the centre of the camp, the hooded figure, with the boy yet standing beside him, reached beneath his cloak, pulled forth a horn and sounded it.

Cynewisse looked up from her grief. Her women yet remained around her, but all the men were running, scattering back to tent and horse and hoard.

Slowly, she got to her feet. Blood tracks ran down her face. She drew her seax from its sheath.

"There is no man left to avenge my lord," she said, "so I will avenge him." And, screaming, she ran at Oswiu, the knife raised above her head.

"Daddy!" Ecgfrith pulled his father round, for Oswiu was looking for sign of an answer to his signal as the dawn spread. The king saw the woman running towards him, death in her eyes. His hand went to his sword, then stopped. He would not begin this new life with a woman's blood on his hands.

"Catch." He threw Penda's head to her, then pointed to the tent. "The rest of him is within."

Already the flood water was reaching towards it.

"Gather him to you while you may." Oswiu stepped aside so that Cynewisse would not have to go near him to enter the tent.

Penda's wife stared at him. "We gave no such honour to your brother," she said.

Oswiu nodded. "I know." He pointed past Cynewisse, to her women. "You will need them to carry him forth."

As Cynewisse was about to enter the tent, Oswiu called after her: "Bury him well."

Cynewisse made to enter the tent, then stopped and looked back to Oswiu. "H-how did he die?"

"Fighting god."

Cynewisse nodded, then looked up at the rich fabric of the tent. "Then let this be his pyre – and mine." She reached for one of the brands that stood beside the tent and put it to the fabric. Wax soaked, the material caught at once, flaring up in the dim dawn light. Holding Penda's head, Cynewisse looked one final time at Oswiu.

"Your god won," she said. Then, turning, she went within and the flames closed around her.

"Daddy, Daddy!" Ecgfrith pulled his father round and pointed. More fires were flaring at the edge of the camp furthest from the river, spouting up amid cries and screams and the distant sight of men on horseback. Horns sounded, swords flashed in the first light of morning, and the terror-struck remnants of Penda's army realized that they had another enemy to contend with as well as the flooding river.

Ahlfrith had come.

The rumour of his coming spread quickly, carried by the sounds of panic and the flight of men and riderless horses.

With the river in spate, the only escape was the bridge. Men on horses laid about them with whips, and some with swords, clearing a path through the crowd that gathered around the bridge. Wagoners, hitching horse or oxen to their wagons, screamed their beasts into the crush. But the bridge was already close packed with the first to leave: the swiftest of the camp followers, running with whatever they could carry. In such a crush, the weakest were soon pushed to the edge of the bridge and began to fall. Caught amid the screaming, shouting people, first one horse and then another began to panic, rearing up then plunging forward. Riders tumbled into the black water, pulling people, heavy laden with plunder, in with them. The first wagon forced its way onto the bridge, but catching there, it blocked the path until the surging crowd pushed it out of the way. One wheel spun over the surging water and then, pushed further, the wagon slowly toppled into the river, pulling its team with it. Laden with plunder, the wagon caught on the bridge's arch. The flood pushed at it, but the wagon jammed tighter into the arch, and the water, blocked, surged upwards, breaking the banks on either side of the bridge and sweeping away many of the people who were fighting to get to safety.

Oswiu, seeing the fresh surge of floodwater, grabbed Ecgfrith's hand and began to make his way towards where he could see Ahlfrith and his men, torches burning, sweeping through the ragged defence of the guards and into the camp. Holding his sword ready in one hand, while the other held his son, Oswiu made a cautious way onwards. Men and women, and some children, streamed past him clutching the hastily grabbed remnants of the season's plunder. He saw, as if caught by the freeze flash of lightning, bags bumping against a warrior's knees as he dropped his sword rather than leave what he carried; a bucket, held to a woman's breast as tightly as a baby but filled with wool for weaving; brooches and buckles and rings festooning a man's arms so that no flesh showed through. Some of those fleeing carried treasure enough to buy a throne; others, clutching their trove just as firmly, had not enough to buy a chicken: it seemed not to matter what they carried, only that they took something with them from the rout.

But the more they carried, the heavier they were. Oswiu saw one man fall into a flood channel, but rather than let go of the sack he was carrying he attempted to find purchase and climb out: the water carried him away, still clutching the sack as if it were more dear to him than life.

The floodwaters were rising and Oswiu felt them pulling at his legs as he splashed between tents, looking for higher ground and heading towards where he could see the purple and gold banner of the Idings.

Purple and gold. He could see colours. Oswiu looked east. The sun was rising over a world of water.

As Oswiu neared the banner, he saw that his men had put aside their torches and were wielding swords and spears now, driving what defenders there were before them or passing them by to ride in among the rout.

"To me, to me!" he yelled, waving his sword above his head to attract attention.

"Ahlfrith! Brother!" Ecgfrith added his own, highpitched yell to his father's.

And they saw and they heard.

A hand pointed to them. The banner bearer, and the men beside him, rode towards where Oswiu waited, with his son by his side, amid the ruin of Penda's camp.

Ahlfrith pulled his horse up in front of them. He pointed at the rout, at the men laden with plunder attempting to swim the river in their panic and being swept away, at the banners of kings that floated in the black water.

"You said you'd give a signal, Father, but I didn't know you meant this. What did you do to them?"

Oswiu looked at his son. "I killed their god," he said.

Chapter 15

Acca picked his way between the bodies. Men, women and some children lay scattered over the streaked and muddy ground left behind by the flood, their skin as pale as the sky. Others moved between the corpses, but they had come to rob the dead of anything left to them by the flood, while Acca sought only to find one man among the fallen: Coifi.

The flood had receded near as quickly as it had risen, but by the time it had withdrawn, well nigh all the great army Penda had led north was destroyed. Most had died while trying to swim the river, washed away by the flood or pulled down by the plunder they tried to carry across with them, but many had been killed in the crush around the bridge, trampled underfoot in the panic to get away. Acca had seen armies disintegrate before, but never had he seen anything to compare with this. A gut fear had seized all Penda's army so that experienced warriors threw aside their swords and, while still weighed down by their armour, had flung themselves into the Winwæd in their desperation to get away. In the river, they drowned, their bodies floating downstream and then, as the river overflowed, carried with the outrush over the water meadows and pastures only to be left there, twisted and pale, when the flood withdrew. Among all the armies that had followed Penda, Acca had seen only one unaffected by the panic: as Ahlfrith's riders swept through the outer reaches of the camp, he had seen a force of men draw away to a hillock some half a mile distant and remain there, watching and unmoving, as the slaughter unfolded before them. As the sun rose, Acca saw the boar banner of Deira flying above those men. Œthelwald had stood aside from the battle. He stood aside still, the boar banner dipped in acknowledgment of the victor, while Oswiu and his men scoured the field of slaughter searching for their wounded and despoiling the dead of their weapons.

Acca knew the king would have to deal with his nephew, but for the moment, that was no concern to him. As the last stragglers fled or, throwing down their weapons, sued for mercy, he was already off his horse, searching through the captives and the dead for Coifi.

"Do you know aught of the priest Coifi?" Acca asked one of the captives, a young man, sitting in the mud with his head bowed as his captors threw dice for his spear and his shield and his brooch. The man did not look up.

"Coifi." Acca seized the captive's hair and pulled his head back. "The priest. Have you seen him?"

The young man – Acca saw he was barely more than a boy – shook his head. "I – I do not know the name."

"You will know him by sight if not name – he always wore a raven-feather cloak although, in these last years, there was more cloak than feather to it."

"Oh, oh yes. Him." The young man nodded. "I know him." His head dipped again. "I ran away," he muttered.

Acca pulled the boy's head back again. "Do you know what happened to him?"

The boy stared up blankly. "To who?"

"To Coifi. The priest." The boy still looked blank. "Raven-feather cloak."

"Him. Oh yes. He fell in the river. He pulled the other priest with him."

"Other priest. What other priest?"

"Wihtrun, the king's priest. Queen Cynewisse called them to come. I was sent to get Wihtrun, but he wanted to bring the raven-feather priest too. I told Wihtrun to hurry, but he said he must get the raven-feather…"

"Coifi," said Acca. "His name is Coifi."

"Yes, get Coifi, so he woke him up, but I saw them fall in the river."

"What happened?"

"I don't know. It was dark, maybe I didn't see right, but it was as if Coifi grabbed Wihtrun and pulled him into the river. I ran to try to save them, but the river had already taken them – and then I saw the fires start and the shouts that the king was dead. I – I don't know what happened to me then. I – I just started running. The next thing I know, something hit me on the head."

"Show me where you saw Coifi fall in the river."

The young man pointed at his feet. They were tied together.

Acca looked round for the guards. "I'm taking this one," he said, as he drew his seax and began cutting through the rope.

"Hang on," said the guard. "He'll fetch good silver, he will. I don't reckon the king'll be much pleased if you go off with his plunder just like that."

Acca drew himself up – although that still left him half a head below the guard. "Do you know who I am?" he said.

The guard sighed. "The king's scop. You don't happen not to know my name, do you?"

"I know you. I know you well," said Acca, "and if you don't want your name sung with the cravens and the stand backs, then you'll let me take this boy."

"Right, right," said the guard. "Just mind you bring him back. They'll expect the same number as they left me with."

Acca pulled the boy after him. "Come," he said. "Show me where you saw Coifi fall."

The guard watched them head towards the river. Puzzlement slowly spread across his face. "Hey, you never said my name," he called after them.

"That's because I don't know it," Acca called back, "and I hope I never will." He pulled the boy on and pointed. "Now, where was it?"

The river churned again within its banks. The boy looked up and down it, searching his memory against what he saw. Then he turned, helplessly, to Acca.

"It all looks different now," he said.

"If there is one thing I know, it is how to remember," said Acca. "Now… what is your name?"

"Hutha," said the boy.

"Now, Hutha, clear your mind of what you see now. Close your eyes. Think where you had come from, how many steps and what you passed. Then remember again what you saw when Coifi went into the river. There must have been a gap in the sedge there for him to pull Wihtrun in. How big a gap? You ran to the bank. What did you see on the far bank? Now, open your eyes and look again."

Hutha opened his eyes. He looked upriver and downriver, searching.

"There," he said, pointing downriver. "I think it was there."

They ran to where he pointed.

"Yes, yes, it was here," said Hutha.

But there was no sign of the priest.

"He'd have been washed downstream," said Hutha. "The river was flowing fast."

"Help me search for him," said Acca.

They made their way downstream, moving between the debris of the camp and washed-up bodies. Many of the bodies were naked, their clothes stripped from them first by the flood and then by the human scavengers who had descended upon the battlefield even while men were still fighting. When they came to such a corpse, if it was lying face down, Hutha would turn it over so that Acca might see the face. But they were all unknown to him, and soon they came to the ends of the camp.

Acca stopped and looked ahead. The river ran on eastwards, sullen and brown, but there was no sign of flooding here, away from the bridge.

"He must have been carried downriver," Acca said. "He'll be riding the whale road back to the lands of our fathers."

But Hutha pointed ahead. "See those willows and alders? I think one has fallen into the river. Anything floating downriver would like as not have been caught by it."

"The flood was too great; it would have carried him away," said Acca.

"It is only a few steps, master. It would be a shame not to look."

"Oh, very well." Acca had an abstracted air. He was already composing his lament for Coifi in his mind. "Lead on."

Hutha made his way through the slippery rushes and sedge towards the bank of willow and alder. The last straggly leaves of the year clung to the trees. Trailing branches hung down into the river, screening the bank from view. One alder, its roots undercut by the current, had half fallen into the river, only to jam into the river bed and hold fast. Hutha scrambled over the trunk, slick and slimy with mud, and stopped.

"Master," he called. "Master, I think you should see this."

"Have you found something?" Acca called. Faced with slipping and sliding over flood-soaked deadfall, he had let Hutha go ahead. Besides, he was halfway through composing his lament.

"Master, come and see," called Hutha.

"Oh, all right," said Acca. Holding the song in memory, he clambered over the trunk and pushed his way through the screen of willow branches. "What is... oh."

There, squatting beside the river, was a thin, pale figure. For a moment Acca could not tell who it was, then the figure moved, its head snapping one way then another. The movement told him who it was.

"Coifi."

The old priest did not look round. There, in the trail of willow in water...

Acca sagged. Relief vied with a fleeting, but intense, disappointment that he would not be able to sing the lament he had composed.

"You're all right," he said. "I – I didn't recognize you at first without your cloak."

At that, Coifi looked down at himself – at his naked, scrawny chest – and shivered.

"The river took it," he said. "Weregild for my life."

Acca sighed. "I should have saved myself the worry. I might have known you'd be somewhere, looking for the working of wyrd."

"I have a new name for wyrd now," said Coifi. "One Aidan told me: providence."

Chapter 16

"Before you render judgement, uncle, think on this: I did not betray you to Penda when I might have, nor did I take part in the battle, but took my men away and awaited the outcome here."

Œthelwald, king of Deira, stood beneath the boar banner of his throne, facing his uncle.

Oswiu, with Ahlfrith and their bodyguards, had ridden across the mud-streaked water meadows, their horses' hooves splashing through the remains of the flood, to where his nephew waited. Œthelwald had been flying the flag of truce all morning, but Oswiu had dispatched a messenger, telling him to wait, while he and Ahlfrith saw to their wounded – precious few – and gathered the spoils of victory. They had set the wagoners who had survived to dragging together what remained of Penda's plunder, while the prisoners were set to work digging graves for the dead.

Only when that was all in hand did Oswiu, with his eldest son, ride to where his nephew waited on him.

"You call me uncle now," said Oswiu, "but before, you were willing to drag me from my throne and despoil my land. Think me not rude if I call thee not nephew, but traitor." The king stood beneath the purple and gold banner of Bernicia, the colours flying in the breeze.

Œthelwald shook his head. "I was ever a voice for you in Penda's camp, uncle, arguing before the High King that we should withdraw even before you made payment."

Oswiu shook his head. "You have the look of your father about you: seeing you, I see him again. But you have not the sound of him." Oswiu sighed. "If you had but kept silence, then I would have thought better of you, for it would be as if Oswald stood before me again. But no, you chose to speak. Even in speech you might have won mercy, for it is true you kept peace when you might have betrayed me, and withdrew when you might have fought. If you had only told me what I know to be true: that you marched with Penda because you believed he must prevail and you would hold your throne, then I would have looked more kindly on you. But no, you lie, as you have ever lied to me." Oswiu stared at the man in front of him, so like his brother. "Oswald did not lie." He looked to his men. "Take him."

"No, no wait!" cried Œthelwald as the men laid hold of him. "Don't. Don't do it, uncle."

Oswiu held his hand up, staying his men.

"What do you think I'm going to do to you, Œthelwald?"

Œthelwald looked round wildly. His own men were backing off and showing no sign of coming to his aid. Œthelwald sagged in the grasp of the men holding him. He looked at his uncle.

"Put me to death," he said. "It's what I would do."

"Then it is as well you have not long been king, for in truth you are not worthy of a throne. I am not going to kill you, nephew. My brother's blood is in you and I will not shed it. No, I will find your blood its true home." Oswiu smiled. "My brother always wished to lay aside the sword and be a monk. Now you will do it for him." He looked to his men. "Take him to the holy house at Kirkdale. Tell the abbot he has a new monk and to mind this monk well."

Oswiu watched his men drag Œthelwald to the horses.

"You know," he said, watching the party of men leaving, "I'm going to have to find a new king for Deira. Someone loyal, someone who has remained faithful to me through everything. Someone I can trust." He looked to Ahlfrith. "Do you know anyone?"

Chapter 17

"They're coming! They're coming!"

Eanflæd looked up from her weaving. Æbbe was rushing towards her and, in her hurry, she'd hitched her robe to her knees so that it would not trip her. Eanflæd got up. The weaving fell to the ground in front of her.

"They're coming!"

Æbbe stopped in front of the queen, her face shining.

"You're sure?" asked Eanflæd, taking hold of her shoulders.

"Yes, yes," said Æbbe. "They ride behind the banner."

"I – I must make myself ready," said Eanflæd, suddenly nervous.

"Oh, don't be silly," said Æbbe, taking her hand. "Come on."

Pulling the queen along, Æbbe brought her to the church. "We'll wait here," she said, cocking her head to listen. "It won't be long."

It wasn't.

The troop of riders appeared on the track, riding behind the purple and gold banner of the Idings, and swept into the holy house at Coldingham, passing between the sisters, who waved and cheered as they came.

Eanflæd peered at the approaching riders, trying to see past the banner bearer to those who rode behind him, but they were hidden. It was only when the banner bearer came to a halt, pulling his horse to one side, that she saw those she had been looking for.

"Mummy!"

The boy jumped from his horse and came running towards her, but just as he was about to leap upon her, Ecgfrith pulled himself to a halt and, looking up at the queen, made the courtesy.

"Oh, come here!" cried Eanflæd, and she swept the boy into her arms.

"Let go, Mummy! Let go," said Ecgfrith. "The men will all

see." But in truth he did not struggle too hard to free himself from Eanflæd's embrace.

"He was very brave."

Eanflæd lifted her face from her son to see her husband looking upon her, smiling.

Ecgfrith pushed himself free.

"You should have seen it, Mummy – he killed Penda, straight through, like this!" And the boy, drawing his own sword, mimicked the fatal thrust.

Oswiu ruffled the boy's hair. "Go and tell your aunt all about it," he said. "She's eager to know. I want to speak to your mother."

Ecgfrith ran to Æbbe, waving his sword wildly as he demonstrated, with some embellishments, what had happened.

Eanflæd, seeing him, laughed. "I hope Æbbe will be careful. Ecgfrith might take out her eye, the way he's swinging that sword."

"She grew up with brothers swinging swords," said Oswiu. "She will be fine." He turned to his wife. "It is good to see you again, my queen."

"And to see you, my husband."

Oswiu pulled her towards him, and spoke so that no other might hear. "I would rather that you had not decided to wait on me here, at my sister's holy house. It is true that Rhieienmelth greatly aided me these past months, but I would rather that I did not see her."

Eanflæd then did something her husband had never heard her do before. She giggled.

Oswiu looked at her. "You laugh?"

"Oh, husband, do you think I would have waited here if Rhieienmelth were here too? She is brave and headstrong and beautiful and I would not have her within five leagues of you. Rhieienmelth is not here. She has gone."

"Gone? Gone where?"

"To Rome. On pilgrimage. She sent to me, asking if she might go, telling how she fretted at the confines of this place. I did not need to ask your sister what she would say, so I gave her leave. She rode forth two weeks past."

"Rome?" Oswiu shook his head in wonder. "But she did not set out alone, did she? It is a long road, and there are many dangers along the way."

"No, I did not send her alone. A young thegn, Benedict Biscop, came to me, saying he wished to travel to see the house of the holy apostles, Peter and Paul, so Rhieienmelth travels with him."

"Rome." Oswiu breathed the name of wonder. He looked at his son, still demonstrating to his sister how he had single-handedly defeated Penda and his army. He looked to his wife, her face turned to him in joy.

"I told Aidan this dream once, and now I tell you. I see myself, old, my hair frost touched, lying upon a bed. You are beside me, and Ecgfrith, a grown man, and I am dying. I am dying in my bed, not coughing my life away on a field of slaughter, drowning in my own blood." Oswiu looked to Eanflæd the Wise. "Is this a true dream?"

"Yes," she said. "It is."

Historical Note

Although scholars nowadays bridle at calling the time when the events of this book are set the Dark Ages (it's the Early Medieval in today's academic literature), there is a reason for the name, but it's not the one most people think. Yes, the Dark Ages were often brutal, and life expectancy was short, but it was by no means an era of unrelieved ignorance. No, where the name remains appropriate is in the lack of historical sources for the centuries after the legions sailed home, in AD 410, leaving the peoples of Britain to fend for themselves against the Saxon raiders that plagued their shores. For the three hundred years between the Romans leaving and Bede, the father of English history, we have precisely two contemporary documents dealing, albeit as a sideline to their main purposes, with the events after the end of empire: *De Excidio et Conquestu Britanniae* (*On the Ruin and Conquest of Britain*) by the monk Gildas, and Patrick's *Confessio*. Not much to show for three hundred years.

What happened?

The short answer is: the English – although they weren't English yet, but Saxons, Angles, Jutes and probably some other tribes from the flat countries of north-western Europe. These Germanic peoples had been raiding Britain since the end of the third century and, in response, the Romans built a series of forts around the coasts of Britain and north-western France. But when the legions withdrew, later authors tell us, the kings of the petty kingdoms that had formed in Britain after the withdrawal made a fateful decision: to employ some of these Saxons as mercenaries in their own internal wars. The Saxons – led by the brothers Hengist and Horsa – seeing a rich land ripe for the taking, set about taking it, revolting against their employers and setting up as kings in their own right.

Seeing the suspicious parallels with another pair of legendary founders (Romulus and Remus), scholars question the story, but the underlying narrative remains true: bands of pagan, Germanic warriors began expanding their rule, pushing the native Britons, who considered themselves the heirs to Roman civilization, westwards. This was the time of Arthur, if he existed: the champion of the Britons who for a time pushed back the Saxon advance. But although the newcomers continued to advance, it was a slow-motion conquest, spread over hundreds of years. It was Oswiu's father, Æthelfrith (d. 616), who decisively shifted the balance of power from the Britons to the Angles and the Saxons. After Æthelfrith, the key battles would be those fought between the contending kings of the Anglo-Saxon kingdoms.

And so we come to Oswiu. *Oswiu: King of Kings* is, as much as I could make it, a true story. Most of the people in it were real, living, breathing people (the *dramatis personae* at the front indicates which are historical and which are invented characters). Most of the historical information we have for Oswiu and his reign comes from Bede's *Ecclesiastical History of the English People*. Bede finished it around 731 – that is, some sixty years after Oswiu's death. Bede himself was a Northumbrian – he never moved much from the twin monasteries at Jarrow and Monkwearmouth – and he had access to eyewitnesses and records of Oswiu's life. Being Northumbrian, Bede was partisan towards his home kingdom, but this partiality did not extend to his portrayal of Oswiu. While Bede treats Oswald, Oswiu's elder brother and predecessor, as a saintly king he is much sterner towards Oswiu. It is from Bede that we learn of the civil strife with Oswine, king of Deira. I have taken the incident, where Oswine remonstrates with Aidan for giving away the horse he had presented to him and then, in turn rebuked, kneels before the priest, from Bede: it is one of the vivid anecdotes that pepper his text, bringing this distant people into the imagination of the reader with all the immediacy of a great novelist. And it is from Bede that we learn of how Oswine, faced with Oswiu's superior forces, disbanded his own army, but was then betrayed by Hunwald and killed. No propagandist for the Northumbrian monarchy, Bede made clear how strongly he disapproved of Oswine's murder.

One of the great virtues the reader of historical fiction shares with a child is the question that comes from both when presented with a vivid story: is it true?

So, is it true?

In answer, I have tried to keep to the historical record as much as possible. The task was complicated by the record being, frankly, pretty confusing in places. So here's what we do know.

Oswiu was born sometime around 612 and, when his father was killed in 616, went into exile with his mother, Acha, his elder brother, Oswald, and his sister, Æbbe. They sought refuge in the sea-spanning kingdom of Dal Riada, which took in roughly modern-day Argyll in Scotland and Antrim in Northern Ireland. St Columba – or Colm Cille to give him his Irish name – had founded a monastery on the island of Iona in 563 and Oswiu and his family converted to Christianity sometime during their exile. Although Oswiu, unlike his brother, seems to have struggled with some of the stricter elements of Christian morality (he fathered a child by an Irish princess while still in exile), his conversion was sincere and he remained an unswerving proponent of the new religion. While in exile, Oswiu and his brother Oswald fought alongside the warrior bands of the kings of Dal Riada and probably other kings too (hence the pregnancy of Fín, a princess of the Uí Néill dynasty).

When King Edwin was killed in battle by an alliance between Cadwallon of Gwynedd and Penda of Mercia, the throne of Northumbria was up for whoever could claim it. Eanfrith, half-brother to Oswiu and Oswald, made the first attempt, reigning over Bernicia for a year, until he was killed by Cadwallon.

Then it was the turn of the brothers. Oswald, presumably with Oswiu alongside him, although this is not explicitly stated in our sources, defeated Cadwallon in 634, and claimed control of both Bernicia and Deira. The events of Oswald's reign are covered in the Historical Note at the end of *Oswald: Return of the King*.

Once Oswiu comes to the throne, things become, at the same time, clearer and more obscure. Clearer, because we have more information about the events of Oswiu's reign than we do about

Oswald. More obscure, because it's sometimes difficult to make sense of these events.

Working forward from the start of *Oswiu: King of Kings*, we begin with the raid into Mercia, when Oswiu reclaims the relics of his brother. Bede tells us that a year after Oswald's death, Oswiu went with a great army and retrieved Oswald's head and arms. This seems most unlikely. Many, if not most, of the available warriors had been killed alongside Oswald when Penda defeated him at the Battle of Maserfield. Furthermore, reaching Oswestry would have meant marching through Mercia – and Penda would hardly have taken kindly to an enemy army marching through his kingdom. So, it seems much more likely that Oswiu recovered his brother's remains by leading a swift raid into Mercia, aiming to outride the news of his presence and escape before Penda could catch up with him. But, for the purposes of this story, I decided to investigate a different option: an undercover operation.

By their very nature, such operations often escape notice in the historical record, but we do know that Anglo-Saxon kings used subterfuge and even assassins in their dealings with each other; so I made Oswiu's raid into Mercia an undercover expedition. In all honesty, it probably did not happen like this, but the historical description seems even more unsatisfactory.

Moving on to Oswiu's marriages. Bede omits all mention of Rhieienmelth, although it is clear that the children of this marriage were too old to have been born to Eanflæd. But we do know that, within two years of becoming king of Bernicia, Oswiu married Eanflæd, the daughter of King Edwin. This was clearly done to strengthen his claim to the throne of Deira, although in the end the marriage does not seem to have helped Oswiu's claim. However, what happened to Rhieienmelth in the meantime? Of course, the simplest explanation, at a time when death could be caused by an infected finger, is that Rhieienmelth died, by disease or childbirth. Bede's slightly uncomfortable silence on the matter suggests something else though. If Rhieienmelth was put aside in favour of a more politically advantageous marriage, she would have needed somewhere to go.

The monasteries and convents of the new religion offered a safe and secure retirement for widowed or unwanted queens, so I think it likely Rhieienmelth went to one of these houses. It's my writer's fancy that places her in Coldingham, for Bede notes that the monastery later burned down – a result, he thought, of the conduct of monks and nuns given over to "eating, drinking, gossip, or other amusements": Rhieienmelth's influence continued long after her departure!

It seems clear that Oswiu married Eanflæd for the political weight she might provide him. As the daughter of King Edwin, whose power base lay in Deira, Oswiu and his advisers hoped that marriage to her would allow them to win the support of the witan of Deira and install Oswiu as king. Despite the marriage, the witan of Deira refused to support Oswiu, instead continuing to follow Oswine as king.

Although there is nothing in the record to support this, I find it plausible that, when Eanflæd journeyed north to meet her new husband, her mother, Æthelburh, would have gone with her. After all, Æthelburh had given birth to all her children in Northumbria. On such a trip, a stop at York would not be out of place.

As for Æthelburh, once she had seen her daughter married, she returned to Kent. The *Kentish Royal Legend* has her founding the twin monastery at Lyminge. In one of those unexpected survivals of the seventh century into the twenty-first, Lyminge has proved to be one of the richest Anglo-Saxon archaeological sites in the country, with the team led by Dr Gabor Thomas finding not only evidence for the monastic site but also the traces of a royal hall. The work is continuing; if you get a chance to visit, it is well worth doing so.

There is one area where I have diverted from the historical record: in the confused, and confusing, relations between the royal houses of Oswiu and Penda. In the long struggle between the two kings, Bede records that Penda's son, Peada, did indeed marry Oswiu's daughter, Ahlflæd; but he also tells us that Oswiu's son, Ahlfrith, married Penda's daughter. In an already crowded narrative, I decided that this was one dynastic marriage too many, and chose to ignore it for the purposes of this story.

Speaking of Peada, I fear that my portrayal of him does not do him justice. Bede speaks well of him and, after the death of Penda, he became king of Mercia. But his reign did not last long. At Easter the following year he died – poisoned by his wife, it is said. As for Ahlflæd, we do not know what happened to her after Peada's death, but the most likely outcome is that she too retired to one of the royal monasteries.

And what happened to Ahlflæd's brother, Ahlfrith, after the events of this book? He became king of Deira, reigning there while acknowledging his father as overlord. As king, Ahlfrith became a supporter of a young priest, Wilfrid. Wilfrid was very different from the priests who had come over from Iona with Ahlfrith's father; he had travelled widely through Europe – Wilfrid came from a wealthy and noble family – and he was determined to bring the church in Britain into line with the church in the wider world. Cut off from the rest of the church by the Anglo-Saxon invasions of the previous centuries, the church in Ireland had developed a number of distinctive practices and structures. Growing in a land never conquered by Rome – and one without cities – it was based on monasteries rather than on bishoprics. Irish monks tonsured their hair in a distinctive way, shaving the front of the head and allowing their hair to grow long at the back (I fear it might have looked like a rather severe mullet). Greatly influenced by the Desert Fathers, Irish monks sought in vain for a patch of desert in their own, well-watered land. But while Ireland lacked deserts, it was certainly not short of bogs and wild, wet and lonely islands. So that was where they went, sometimes trusting themselves so completely to God that they would set off in a boat with neither sail nor oar, letting God take them where he would.

But the most divisive difference was over Easter. The dating of Easter is a complex matter and I won't go into it here, but the result, in Northumbria, was that sometimes Easter was celebrated at different times, depending on whether you followed the Irish or Roman method of dating it. A problem, particularly when the king's household was still fasting while the queen's was feasting –

for Eanflæd's household followed the Roman method of calculating Easter that was used in Kent.

Under Wilfrid's influence, Ahlfrith also switched to celebrating Easter according to the Roman calendar and he began to agitate for the wholesale adoption of the continental religious practices.

Such disunity in the royal household was dangerous. To resolve matters, Oswiu called a meeting, the Synod of Whitby, in 664. At the synod, Wilfrid spoke for the Roman position while Colman, bishop of Lindisfarne after Finan, spoke for the Irish method of calculation. Presiding over the synod, Oswiu famously asked at its conclusion if it was true that Peter had been given the keys to the kingdom of heaven. When both Wilfrid and Colman agreed, Oswiu said, "Peter is guardian of the gates of heaven, and I shall not contradict him. I shall obey his commands in everything to the best of my knowledge and ability otherwise, when I come to the gates of heaven, there may be no one to open them, because he who holds the key has turned away."

So Ahlfrith's party had won the argument. By this time, in fact, most of Ireland had already adopted the Roman method of calculating Easter, although Iona held to its own ways a while longer. Colman returned to Iona with those monks who would not accept the new ways. But what of Ahlfrith? Although vindicated, he all but disappears from the historical record. Bede records some sort of conflict with his father, but whether this was over the matters resolved at Whitby or some other dispute, we do not know. The last mention we have of him is in stone, on the Bewcastle Cross in Cumbria, one of the two great, free-standing carved crosses (the other is the Ruthwell Cross) that are the highpoints of stonework at this time. The inscription on the west face of the cross may read (it is badly worn): "This Victory Cross set up by Hwætred, Wothgær, Olwfwolthu in the memory of Alcfrith a king and son of Oswiu. Pray for his soul." Did Ahlfrith win a victory near Bewcastle at the cost of his life? We don't know.

As for Oswiu himself, his dream came true. First of all the kings of Northumbria, he did not die in battle but in his bed, passing away in 670 at the age of fifty-eight. Ecgfrith, his son by Eanflæd, became king after him, and he seems to have been as belligerent a king as I have made him as a boy, until a catastrophic defeat while campaigning against the Picts at the Battle of Nechtansmere (20 May 685) saw Ecgfrith killed and an end to the northern expansion of Northumbria. In fact, the battle ranks as one of the most important in British history, for it served to ensure that England and Scotland would remain separate kingdoms through the following centuries.

Eanflæd outlived her husband and her son. After Oswiu's death, she went to live in the abbey at Whitby, where her daughter had become abbess after the death of Hild. While living in the monastery, Eanflæd oversaw the translation of the remains of her father, Edwin, to the abbey. Eanflæd died sometime after 685.

Outside the royal families, James the Deacon continued his lonely ministry around Catterick, living long enough to learn the outcome of the Synod of Whitby. Although Acca is an invented character, the song he sings at the wedding of Oswiu and Eanflæd is part of *The Dream of the Rood*, one of the most sublime of Old-English poems. Acca's partner in adventure, Coifi, is a historical character, but our sources only record him as Edwin's priest; it has been my decision to feature him in *Oswald: Return of the King* and *Oswiu: King of Kings*. But, with respect to Coifi, I do like to think of a small house that the great archaeologist Brian Hope-Taylor excavated during his work at Ad Gefrin: a modest little dwelling, Hope-Taylor speculated that it might have been Coifi's retirement home. I like to think of the old priest sitting outside the house as the sun set, watching the movement of the cloud shadows over the green flanks of Yeavering Bell.

The great palace at Ad Gefrin is a field now, and quiet. Stand on it, the grass whispering around your feet, and listen to the past. It is all around you. It is all around us.

If you love EDOARDO ALBERT's writing,
don't miss out on his non-fiction…

LONDON:
A SPIRITUAL HISTORY

Edoardo Albert is a born Londoner, son of migrants – and the city
has served as backdrop and participant to his religious pilgrimage,
as it has for countless others before him.

In these pages, Edoardo takes us down the backstreets of the
city, tracing a myriad of spiritual journeys, from the early days
of paganism, through the dominance of Christianity to the
multicultural worship scene of today.

Woven throughout is Edoardo's own quest for spiritual truth.
Written with an enticing mixture of ease, humour, and detail, this
is an enthralling read for all who are beguiled by this great city.

ISBN: 978 0 7459 5696 1 | e-ISBN: 978 0 7459 5697 8

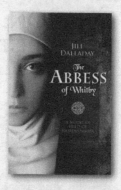

"This is skilful and accomplished writing."

– **Peter Tremayne, author of *The Sister Fidelma Mysteries***

SHE WILL FORGE A NEW BRITAIN

Hild is caught between two worlds. Handmaid to the goddess Eostre, she finds herself tossed from one power to another – the indifferent goddess, the callous King, her crass husband – before meeting the Christian priests of Iona and finding a home for her bruised spirit.

Then the young convert catches the eye of Aidan, a charismatic leader. Inspired and guided by him, she builds communities, creates trust, leads men. Even her old enemy, King Oswy, entrusts his child to her, and seeks her help to heal his divided kingdom.

A woman of power and wisdom, subtle and brilliant, she will change the history of her nation.

ISBN: 978 1 78264 154 4 | e-ISBN: 978 1 78264 155 1